SIX PLAYS FROM THE BEST OF THE MODERN BRITISH THEATER

Joe Orton's **WHAT THE BUTLER SAW** is a farcical peepshow about sexuality and power among the elite.

THE CHANGING ROOM by David Storey, which takes place in the locker room of a Yorkshire rugby team, challenges the audience's conventional notions of theater with its daring use of male nudity and its concern with images and ideas rather than narrative.

David Hare's satirical, often bitter play, **PLENTY,** deals with spiritual disillusionment during England's postwar years of "peace and plenty."

Harold Pinter's **BETRAYAL** uses reverse chronology to chart the effects of a single incident of infidelity.

In Hugh Whitemore's spy story with a twist **PACK OF LIES,** a loyal citizen's resolve and humanity are tested when she is asked to cooperate with British intelligence in their surveillance of a neighbor.

THE LIFE AND ADVENTURES OF NICHOLAS NICKLEBY, adapted by David Edgar from the novel by Charles Dickens, was one of the great theatrical events of the early '80s, employing a cast of 40 actors playing more than 140 roles over eight-and-a-half hours.

𝒞

Outstanding Contemporary Plays in SIGNET CLASSIC and SIGNET Editions

PLAYS FROM THE CONTEMPORARY BRITISH THEATER

Edited and
with an Introduction

by

Brooks McNamara

A MENTOR BOOK

MENTOR
Published by the Penguin Group
Penguin Books USA Inc., 375 Hudson Street,
New York, New York 10014, U.S.A.
Penguin Books Ltd, 27 Wrights Lane, London W8 5TZ, England
Penguin Books Australia Ltd, Ringwood,
Victoria, Australia
Penguin Books Canada Ltd, 10 Alcorn Avenue,
Toronto, Ontario, Canada M4V 3B2
Penguin Books (N.Z.) Ltd, 182–190 Wairau Road,
Auckland 10, New Zealand

Penguin Books Ltd, Registered Offices:
Harmondsworth, Middlesex, England

Published by Mentor, an imprint of New American Library,
a division of Penguin Books USA Inc.

First Printing, October, 1992
10 9 8 7 6 5 4 3 2 1

 REGISTERED TRADEMARK—MARCA REGISTRADA

Library of Congress Cataloging Card Number: 92–080223

(The following page constitutes an extension of this copyright page.)

Once again, to Nan

ACKNOWLEDGMENTS

With special thanks to four friends whose generosity and support helped to make this anthology possible: Diane Cleaver, Liz Hess, Cynthia Jenner, and Andrea Stulman Dennett.

CONTENTS

INTRODUCTION

The late sixties proved to be a watershed for the theatre of Europe and America. It was the beginning of a period marked by bold experiments in playwriting, by the development of extraordinary avant-garde production styles, and by important new connections between politics, social activism and performance. The result in the 1970s and 1980s was a theatre that accepted as commonplace many stage conventions and social attitudes that would have seemed unthinkable a few years before. The first volume in this series, *Plays From the Contemporary American Theater* (Mentor), presented a collection of American plays from the seventies and eighties. This companion volume offers six British plays from the same era: Joe Orton's *What the Butler Saw*, David Storey's *The Changing Room*, David Hare's *Plenty*, Harold Pinter's *Betrayal*, Hugh Whitemore's *Pack of Lies*, and David Edgar's adaptation of the Charles Dickens novel, *The Life and Adventures of Nicholas Nickleby*.

The beginnings of this remarkable period in British playwriting are often traced to John Osborne's 1956 work, *Look Back in Anger*, produced by the then newly formed English Stage Company, led by George Devine, at London's Royal Court Theatre. *Look Back in Anger* addresses explosive issues related to the English class system. With its clearcut anti-Establishment point of view, the play became a rallying point for Britain's Angry Young Men of the late fifties and a key document in the revolution that would soon overtake British playwriting. In a review of a recent book on the Royal Court, Amlin Gray wrote that *Look Back in Anger* "electrified the English theatre, both artists and audiences. George Devine saw at once that the Royal Court should not . . . be a European-style art theatre but a forum for new English writing. Following Osborne's triumph, artists from social and regional backgrounds rarely represented in other theatres flooded to the Court. Devine proclaimed that these new artists, the writers in particular, 'would dictate the character of the new theatre.' " During the fifties the English Stage Company, one of the most progressive British theatres of its day, went on to produce a number of thoughtful and controversial plays by new writers, among them John Arden's *Sergeant Musgrave's Dance* (1959) and Arnold Wesker's *Chicken Soup With Barley* (1958).

During the same years, Joan Littlewood's Theatre Workshop attempted to bring popular theatre with a radical social vision to working-class London audiences through the presentation of such plays as Brendan Behan's *The Quare Fellow* (1956), Shelagh Delaney's *A Taste of Honey* (1958), and the early communal creation, *Oh, What a Lovely War* (1963). But the center of the British theatre still lay in more conventional directions, both politically and artistically.

Beginning in the sixties, however, two important and widely praised new companies, the Royal Shakespeare and the National Theatre, also began to promote the work of less conventional playwrights. The National Theatre, which began operating in 1963, under the direction of Laurence Olivier with Kenneth Tynan as literary adviser, was primarily devoted to the production of classic plays, although it did offer a number of significant new British works. The Royal Shakespeare Company, chartered in 1961 and headed by Peter Hall, was particularly sympathetic to experimental work. Its commitment to experimentation was exemplified especially in the work of Peter Brook, whom Hall hired as a director in 1962. By the mid-sixties the RSC had become identified not only as the home of fine Shakespearean productions, but of innovative new foreign and British plays, and of production techniques that reflected the growing influence of the international avant-garde. During the sixties, the two companies produced such plays as Peter Shaffer's *The Royal Hunt of the Sun* (1964), Harold Pinter's *The Homecoming* (1965), Tom Stoppard's *Rosencrantz and Guildenstern are Dead* (1967), and Peter Nichols' *A Day in the Death of Joe Egg* (1967). Nevertheless, by the end of the decade, the government-supported RSC and National Theatre began to come under fire from anti-Establishment groups for their purported lavish subsidies and outrageous expenses in Britain's worsening economic climate. In addition, some theatre people suggested the attacks were partly due to the theatres' choice of less and less challenging work.

The radical tone of the sixties helped contribute to a growing protest against government censorship of the theatre. In response to censorship laws, William Gaskill, who had replaced Devine as the director of the English Stage Company, formed a "theatre club" at the Royal Court, a private membership organization designed to skirt government licensing of plays. In 1965, the Royal Court produced two highly controversial plays which had been denied licenses, Edward Bond's *Saved*, in which the murder of a baby takes place on stage, and John Osborne's *A Patriot for Me*, which graphically depicts homosexual acts. The result was an unsuccessful lawsuit brought by the government—and the repeal in 1968 of England's more than two-hundred-year-old censorship laws.

With the abolition of the theatrical censorship laws, the way opened for alternative or Fringe theatre, and for what has been called the "second wave" of new English playwrights. The Fringe was a product of many of the same social and artistic movements that were reshaping European and American performance in the late sixties and early seventies.The result throughout Europe and the United States was radical theatre practitioners' rejection of traditional values and conventional approaches to playwriting, acting and design.

The American off-off Broadway theater had an especially strong impact on the Fringe and its writers. Among its influences were the work of two theatre groups from New York City, Ellen Stewart's Cafe La Mama and Joseph Chaikin's Open Theatre, as well as the activities of a number of Americans in London. Among them were Nancy Meckler, founder of Freehold, Ed Berman of Interaction, and James Haynes of London's Arts Lab. Charles Marowitz, an American director and critic who had worked with Brook on the RSC's controversial Theatre of Cruelty season of 1963–64, promoted new experimental work at his London theatre, the Open Space.

The Fringe took different forms, but much of it was characterized by innovative approaches to physical production and unorthodox treatments of sexual, political, class and gender issues. Among the Fringe groups were the improvisation-based People Show; Welfare State, which developed an environmental approach to performance—touring English towns where the company presented plays based on local history and folklore; the Traverse Theatre Workshop, which developed plays through collective creation; the Pip Simmons Group, which drew on American avant-garde techniques; and the Portable Theatre and the Joint Stock Company, both of which presented the work of important second-wave writers. Gaskill opened an experimental theatre at the Royal Court, the Theatre Upstairs, and in 1969 launched the first Fringe festival, "Come Together." By the early seventies, women's theatre groups were beginning to emerge as a force in the British theatre, among them Monstrous Regiment and the Women's Theatre Group.

All in all, the Fringe rewrote many of the traditional rules of British theatre. As *New York Times* critic Mel Gussow noted recently, "during the heyday of . . . politically inclined theatrical organizations, English playwrights like Caryl Churchill, David Hare and Howard Brenton often reacted immediately to public issues. Faced with urgent political questions, the writers reached for their quill cudgels." The response from the established theatre to such work—and the generally leftist politics behind it—was not always enthusiastic. In the wake of "Come Together," one editorial writer charged that the Fringe had applied "a hatchet to traditional verbal theatre and its conventional actor/audience relationship," and that it was feeding "a growing polarisation between the left and the right, between the young and the old." Whether this was the case or not, the die was cast. British theatre had been radicalized and would never again be quite the same.

By the early seventies, the British Arts Council had come to accept the importance, or at least the inevitability, of the Fringe, and routinely granted government subsidies to alternative groups. As the seventies progressed, however, a worsening economic situation led to harder times for all of the subsidized venues. By the eighties, Britain's subsidized theatres were increasingly forced to raise ticket prices and to seek out private sponsorship in order to make ends meet. Along with the economic troubles of the eighties came a lessening of British playwrights' attention to social issues, and an accompanying decline of aggressive political performance—perhaps, as Gussow has suggested, "because theatres were worried about losing financial support." As Britain enters the nineties, the direction of its theatre—and the theatre's future vitality—are open questions.

There is no question, however, that the British theatre has enjoyed a remarkably creative quarter of a century, and that it has produced a long list of major playwrights. In addition to the writers whose work is found in this volume, and those already mentioned, some of the major contributors to the theatre during the seventies and eighties who deserve mention are Michael Frayn, Alan Ayckbourn, Christopher Hampton, Timerlake Wertenbaker, Sharman Macdonald, Brian Friel, Louise Page, Snoo Wilson, Howard Brenton, Sarah Daniels, Trevor Griffiths, Pam Gems, Ann Jelicoe, Stephen Lowe, Stephen Poliakoff, Peter Barnes, Nicholas Wright and Howard Barker. The impact of their work has been worldwide, and the United States, in particular, was a major beneficiary of this extraordinary period in British playwriting.

The six plays in this anthology possess a kind of dual citizenship. Although all of them are written by British authors and were first produced in England, each one has also made a considerable impact on the American stage. The importance of British plays across the Atlantic is obviously not new; since the eighteenth century, the work of English and Irish playwrights has been a vital part of American theatre. By the seventies and eighties, however, some critics, both in England and the United States, were complaining that the contemporary theatre in the United States—especially Broadway—had come to depend too heavily on Britain as a source of new work. British critic Martin Esslin, for example, suggested that he found it ironic that so many of "the more highbrow British imports (Stoppard, Simon Gray, Pinter) on Broadway" came from the subsidized companies of Britain. "In that sense," he commented, "the British taxpayer is subsidising the commercial magnates of Broadway. For [the subsidised theatres] have taken the initial risks, they have tested the product by getting excellent reviews from leading critics not only in London but in New York as well (since the New York papers follow the London scene), so that once a play like *Otherwise Engaged* or *No Man's Land* reaches Broadway it is practically immune against the main hazard, a bad review, and comes with all the accumulated snob-appeal of a world success."

Many American theatre people would claim that it is not all so clear-cut. The theatrical balance of trade between Britain and America has always been and continues to be complex at every level. However, one point is clear: there was a substantial decline of interest in writing for the professional theatre in the United States during the seventies and eighties, and a corresponding rise in the number of new British plays and musicals that appeared in America. The six plays in this collection were among those that helped to form a critical mass at the center of the American theatre.

Joe Orton's *What the Butler Saw* borrows its title from the traditional "penny-in-the-slot" peepshow which featured a butler peering through a keyhole at the racy goings-on among his upper-class employers. These peepshows were once common at British amusement arcades and seaside piers. Orton's play is a peepshow about sexuality and power—but a peepshow with a kind of built-in distorting mirror. As critic Charles Marowitz said about Orton's theme in *What the Butler Saw*, "in a world of madmen, the sane person doesn't stand a chance."

Orton, who was born in 1933, had a brief career in the theatre. His first full-length play, *Entertaining Mr. Sloane*, appeared in 1964, followed by *Loot* in 1966, and then several short works, and three television plays. *What the Butler Saw* was first produced in 1969, two years after Orton was murdered by his lover, Kenneth Halliwell, who then committed suicide. The small body of work Orton produced is generally considered today to contain some of the most brilliant and outrageous comedy to come out of modern England. John Lahr, who has written extensively about Orton, believes that the playwright "will be recognized as the major farceur of this century, combining Feydeau's gift for inventive plotting with a corrosive vision of social madness out-shining even Oscar Wilde in the pain and persistence of his wit."

What the Butler Saw virtually defies summary. As Edith Oliver of *The New Yorker* pointed out in her review, its elements include "untimely entrances and exits, mistaken identity, see-through disguises, multiple accusations and multiple deceptions, and sight gags galore, and one soon realizes, in the midst of the pandemonium, that nothing sacred—religious or secular—has gone unpinked." Much of its humor, Oliver added, "turns upon homosexuality, nyphomania, transvestism, and incest, among other sexual pranks." *What the Butler Saw* clearly exemplifies a play that could never have been produced in Britain before the repeal of the censorship laws.

The posthumous productions of Orton's play turned out to be controversial, to say the least. The play was first presented in London at The Queen's Theatre in 1969, and a year later at The McAlpin Roof Theatre in New York. There is reason to believe that it suffered from poor editing and ill-conceived productions in both cities. (Lahr details the complex situation in his 1978 study of Orton, *Prick Up Your Ears*.) In any case, *What the Butler Saw* opened to wildly mixed reviews; both in London and New York, critics asserted, with equal vehemence, that the play was either a total flop or a genuine masterpiece. Some reviewers disliked the two productions and crucified the script because of them. Orton's unorthodox vision of sexuality obviously put off others. In New York a few critics appeared to have no idea what Orton was talking about—several didn't understand the play's title and wondered why no butler ever appeared. The play's champions, on the other hand, made clear from the start that the script transcended its London and New York productions. In his review, George Oppenheimer concluded that Orton's *What the Butler Saw* was "by all odds his best play, and, unhappily, his last."

If *What the Butler Saw* is so crammed with plot that it almost defies synopsis, David Storey's *The Changing Room* seems, at first glance, to have no plot at all. The play, which takes place entirely in the locker room of a Yorkshire rugby team, simply presents the mundane events that occur there from before a game until sometime after its conclusion. There are twenty-two characters, none of them more central to the play than any of the others, and nothing extraordinary happens. The players, who make up the majority of the characters, work with a trainer, change into their uniforms, go out to play, return, shower, change into their street clothes, and leave for the day. They joke with one another, talk about homes and families, and nurse injuries. That is all.

Storey, the son of a Yorkshire coal miner, has been both a rugby player and an artist, as well as associate artistic director of the Royal Court, a distinguished novelist, playwright, and a television- and screenwriter. His work for the theatre includes *The Contractor* (London, 1969; New York, 1973) and *Home* (London and New York, 1970), two elusive, well-received plays about aspects of alienation. *London Times* critic Harold Hobson has called Storey "perhaps the most poetic in spirit of contemporary British dramatists."

The Changing Room was first presented at the Royal Court in London in 1971, and subsequently at the Long Wharf in New Haven in 1972 and the Morosco Theatre on Broadway in the following year. At one level, *The Changing Room* might appear as nothing more than pure documentary. However, as Helen Dawson wrote in *The Observer* about the 1971 London production, "the strength of the play lies not in its realism but in its artistry, its craftsmanlike devotion to form, detail and color." It is difficult to say, Dawson continues, "which is the most important influence on [Storey's] latest work—his first-hand knowledge of the game or his patiently observant, painterly eye."

The play is not always an easy one for Americans to follow; the combination of rugby terms and Yorkshire dialect render it somewhat inaccessible. But the American response to the play, like that in Britain, proved to be welcoming and enthusiastic, perhaps due to the perennial American interest in the lives of ordinary people, or perhaps because *The Changing Room* transcends language and plot to provide a universal experience. Emily Genauer, an art critic who reviewed the play in the *New York Post*, made its unique values clear. "Storey's approach," she wrote, "is primarily painterly and concerned with images, conditions and ideas, not narrative. . . . He's commenting on a social state, doing it with figures who move beautifully, rhythmically, mindlessly, helplessly . . . in the void into which time, circumstance and moral climate have locked them."

As with Storey, David Hare, the author of *Plenty*, is a multitalented man of the theatre; a director, manager, literary adviser, stage and television writer, and a prolific and respected playwright. The son of a ship's purser, Hare found his way to Cambridge, which he claims to have disliked intensely. With a Cambridge friend, Tony Bicat, he founded the Portable Theatre in 1968. He acted as literary manager and resident playwright at the Royal Court from 1969 to 1971, and later served as a director of the Joint Stock Theatre, one of the most important Fringe groups of the seventies. Hare became an associate director of the National Theatre in 1984.

Hare, who is very much a product of the aggressive anti-Establishment posture associated with the early years of the Fringe, is widely produced in England, and a number of his plays have also been seen in the United States. Among them are *Slag* (London, 1970; New York, 1971); *Knuckle* (London, 1974; New York, 1975); and *The Secret Rapture* (London, 1988; New York, 1989). *Plenty*, produced at the National Theatre in London in 1978, also played in Washington, D.C., in 1980 and in New York in 1982, where it was presented first at Joseph Papp's Public Theatre and after at the Plymouth Theatre on Broadway. It was made into a 1985 film starring Meryl Streep.

Plenty is perhaps Hare's most ambitious and most controversial play; in it he tackles large political and social issues which he finds at the heart of modern English life. As Hare once commented in an interview, "England breaks my heart. I find it almost impossible to live here. . . . How could people become so apathetic, so resigned to whatever Mrs. Thatcher and her government fling at them? It's a state of humiliation we never dreamed of, and it's very hard to know where change is going to come from." In *Plenty*, David Hare records what he sees as the erosion of English quality of life in the years following World War II. The play examines a young woman named Susan, played by Kate Nelligan in both London and New York, who served as a courier in Occupied France. Her response to England's dull, oppressive postwar years takes the form of violent disillusion and eventual madness. Susan is a somewhat enigmatic figure, and Nelligan, whose interpretation of the role was universally praised, saw her essentially as a victim of "her own inability to compromise." That does not mean, Nelligan explained, that "it wasn't a pretty shabby time, but you're not meant to think it's all right to destroy other people's lives because you feel your standards have been betrayed."

Finally, though, the play centers not so much on Susan as on the times in which she finds herself. Hare constantly moves us from her anguish directly to the exploration of greater societal problems. *Plenty* forms one link of a chain of important contemporary plays, from *Look Back in Anger* through *What the Butler Saw*, and on to *Nicholas Nickleby*, that explore the dark side of the English character. As critic Leo Sauvage pointed out, Hare was "chiefly interested in voicing a social and political comment on England's era 'of peace and plenty,' and his leading female is important to him solely as an instrument for lifting the lid on the nation's corrupton and hypocrisy. His style is satirical, offering bitter and sometimes forceful observations on politicians, diplomats, and the rest of the British gentlemen who kept a stiff upper lip and pretended to hold traditional values."

Harold Pinter's *Betrayal* explores Britain's upper-middle class in a style almost diametrically opposed to that of *Plenty*. Pinter's theatrical journey takes us inward, to the center of his characters' lives, with few, if any, references to a world beyond their own. Pinter, an actor, director, screenwriter, and playwright since the late fifties, is the author of some of the modern theatre's most distinguished plays, including *The Birthday Party* (London, 1958; New York, 1967), *The Caretaker* (London, 1960; New York, 1967), *The Homecoming* (London, 1965; New York, 1967), and *No Man's Land* (London, 1975; New York, 1976).

In a 1979 interview, at the time that *Betrayal* appeared in New York, Pinter remarked to critic Mel Gussow that "I've been writing for quite a long time, and in England over the last few years, there has been a very, very strong *young* wave of political playwrights." As a result, he said, some critics had come to feel that his own work was "slightly out of kilter with the needs of the time." In fact, Pinter's concerns are quite different from those of many of the younger writers who grew up in the highly politicized alternative theatre, but his approaches to language and structure are, in their way, as radical as almost anything found in contemporary British playwriting.

Betrayal, presented at the National Theatre in 1978, where Pinter held the position of associate artistic director, and at the Trafalgar in New York in 1980, was made into a film in 1983. The play explores the effects of a long-term adulterous relationship on a husband and wife and the wife's lover. The meticulously honed language in *Betrayal* represents characteristic Pinter—achingly spare, comic, and filled with the precisely articulated pauses central to all of his work. In fact, Pinter has said that the sum of the changes he made in *Betrayal* during the London rehearsals for the play consisted of deleting one word and one pause and adding another pause which to him "made all the damn difference."

As in *Plenty, Betrayal* moves back in time after its first scene. In Pinter's play, however, the subsequent scenes occur in reverse chronology. Only in the play's final minutes do we at last reach the incident that set the entire pattern of betrayal in motion. The rest of the play essentially comprises a revelation of what Robert Brustein called in his review, "the enactment, suppression, and exposure of adultery." Pinter's structural device proved to be a controversial one, both in England and America. A few critics found it glib. Stanley Kauffman, for instance, remarked that the reversal "doesn't in itself much magnify what is only an adroit little comedy. But it does permit a good production to enlist the poignancy of passing time that underlies every human action."

Benedict Nightingale in the *New Statesman*, however, saw the reverse structure as adding a unique perspective to the audience's view of what he called the "mechanics of cheating, the politics of betrayal." The "anti-clockwise" approach to plot, he noted, "substitutes the question 'how?' for the cruder 'what next?' in the minds of the audience." And in Nightingale's view, that approach "deepens and darkens our perception of the play, infecting the most innocent encounters with irony, dread and a sense of doom"—the elements that are so central to Pinter's theatre.

In *Pack of Lies* Hugh Whitemore presents a very different view of the politics of betrayal. Whitemore is the author of several plays, including the highly successful *Breaking the Code* (London, 1986; New York, 1987). He is best known, however, as a writer for films and, especially, television, and *Pack of Lies* originated from his *Act of Betrayal*, a television documentary drama that appeared on the BBC in 1971. Both the television drama and the play are based on an actual spy case, generally known as the Portsmouth Naval Secrets Case, and both trade on Britain's seeming fascination with spies and spying.

An American couple, Morris and Lona Cohen, disappeared from New York at the time that the F.B.I. arrested Julius and Ethel Rosenberg for spying. In 1954, the Cohens, dedicated Communists, were living in Ruislip, a middle-class London suburb, with new identities. Known as Peter and Helen Kroger, and claiming to be Canadians, their job was to transmit information gathered by another Soviet agent to Russia. M.1.5., the British Intelligence service, arrested the "Krogers" in 1961 and exchanged them for a British agent eight years later. At the time that *Pack of Lies* appeared, the "Krogers" were living in Poland.

Whitemore's television docu-drama stuck fairly close to the facts of the case. His *Pack of Lies*, produced in London at the Lyric Theatre in 1983, and in New York at the Royale in 1985, moves farther from the original events, although it depends upon the kind of detailed close-up dramaturgy that one associates with television writing. *Pack of Lies* focuses on the devastating effect of M.1.5's investigation on the Jackson family, friends and neighbors of the Krogers, whose house intelligence agents use as an observation point. In a way, *Pack of Lies* forms almost the antithesis of the conventional spy story; there is little suspense, and the characters in the play are relentlessly ordinary.

The emphasis lies elsewhere. Critic Gerald Weales defined it as follows: "The emotional line of the play is the disintegration of Barbara Jackson. She loses control of herself as she sees her family's presumably open and direct life disappearing under the pressure of a house invaded. She comes to believe that there is no difference between her betrayal of Helen and what the Krogers have done. . . ." For Whitemore this betrayal leads to a larger social and political issue which he discusses in his foreword to the play. "Is it ever possible," Whitemore asks, "for the average, relatively powerless man or woman to make anything more than a token stand against officialdom? Is it not potentially risky to allow the state (albeit for well-argued reasons) greater moral license than the individual? Or is it, perhaps, naïve to expect more than an approximate degree of truthfulness from governments and their spokesmen?"

Pack of Lies and David Edgar's stage adaptation of Charles Dickens's *The Life and Adventures of Nicholas Nickleby* stand at opposite poles in terms of scale, dramaturgy, and point of view about morality. *Nicholas Nickleby* appeared at the RSC in 1980 and at the Royale in New York the next year, a coproduction of the two Broadway giants, the Shubert Organization and the Nederlander Organization. The play results from a conscious decision on the part of Edgar and two directors from the RSC, Trevor Nunn and John Caird, to stage a Dickens novel in its entirety. As Caird explained, their intent was not "to put on a play with scenes from Dickens in it, or—like the films do—do the funny bits or the character bits and give the audience a nostalgia trip, reminding them of what the book was like when they read it. Our brief was to stage an entire Dickens novel without the omission of a single plot." Nunn originally conceived the idea of adapting a major novel for the theatre. Following a trip to Russia, where Dickens is frequently staged, Nunn contacted Edgar and asked him to work with the RSC company on an adaptation of a Dickens novel. Eventually they selected the 1839 work, *The Life and Adventures of Nicholas Nickleby*.

Edgar, who began as a journalist, has written for radio, television and films. Since 1984 he has acted as literary adviser to the RSC. Edgar's considerable body of work for the stage, including *The Jail Diary of Albie Sachs*, which was seen here in 1979 at the Manhattan Theatre Club, is frankly left-wing. Collective creation and a fascination with agit-prop structure had influenced much of Edgar's work. In short, Edgar was a logical choice to adapt a novel originally conceived on an epic scale, one that is a document of social conscience, written in part to expose the wretchedly bad proprietary schools found in nineteenth-century Yorkshire. (In view of the play's message about social justice, some critics found a certain irony in the high price of Broadway tickets to *Nickleby*, which put the show out of the reach of many people.)

Producing the play did not simply involve the RSC asking Edgar to sit down and adapt the novel for the stage. Instead, they began work on the script with the actors who would eventually perform in the play giving improvisations and readings from the novel. Then, armed with this initial collective work, together with strong input from directors and designers, Edgar created his adaptation. The eventual result was an eight-and-a-half-hour production, in 81 scenes, divided into two parts, featuring some 40 actors playing more than 140 roles.

Nicholas Nickleby ended up very much a collaboration between Edgar and the play's directors, designers and actors. Perhaps as a result, more than any other play in this collection it reflects the influence of recent avant-garde performance techniques in its script, and moves through time and space in a highly unorthodox way. The play's roots, are, however, quite varied. Of course, influences from the RSC's own stagings of Shakespeare appear here, as well as influences from the "story theatre" ideas of American director Paul Sills, Brecht, the 1930s agit-prop plays that interest Edgar, and from contemporary film editing. The play's style, Benedict Nightingale noted in *The New York Times*, is "fluent, free-ranging and humanly very precise."

The result of all these influences is a work about which *London Times*' critic Bernard Levin remarked: "Not for many years has London's theatre seen anything so richly joyous, so immoderately rife with pleasure, drama, color, and entertainment." The reception on our side of the Atlantic was no less enthusiastic. It is a great pleasure to me that the final selection in this anthology is *Nicholas*

Nickleby—not simply because it is a remarkable play, but because it also represents a remarkable event in the history of contemporary British—and American—theatre.

Brooks McNamara
New York University

What the Butler Saw

A PLAY IN TWO ACTS

by Joe Orton

What the Butler Saw was performed at the Queens Theatre, London, on March 5, 1969, under the direction of Robert Chetwyn. It was produced by Lewenstein-Delfont Productions Ltd. and H. M. Tennent Ltd, and had the following cast:

DR. PRENTICE .... *Stanley Baxter*
GERALDINE BARCLAY .... *Julia Foster*
MRS. PRENTICE .... *Coral Browne*
DR. RANCE .... *Ralph Richardson*
NICHOLAS BECKETT .... *Hayward Morse*
SGT. MATCH .... *Peter Bayliss*
Set by Hutchinson Scott; lighting by Joe Davis.

What the Butler Saw opened on Monday, May 4, 1970, at the McAlpin Rooftop Theater, McAlpin Hotel, New York City, under the direction of Joseph Hardy and was produced by Charles Woodward and Michael Kasdan.

DR. PRENTICE .... *Laurence Luckinbill*
GERALDINE BARCLAY .... *Diana Davila*
MRS. PRENTICE .... *Jan Farrand*
NICHOLAS BECKETT .... *Charles Murphy*
DR. RANCE .... *Lucian Scott*
SERGEANT MATCH .... *Tom Rosqui*
Production designed by William Ritman; costumes by Ann Roth.

The text that follows represents the official acting edition of this play for productions in the United States and Canada. The script, blocking moves and physical production notes have been prepared exactly from the New York production of the play.

This text is being printed with the permission of the Estate of Joe Orton and is not to be confused with a "reading" text of the play which is also available in the United States.

ACT I

The consulting room of an exclusive, private psychiatric clinic. A spring day. Doors lead to main hall U. R., the wards and dispensary D. R. Double doors U. L. lead to a hall and the garden off stage. Open closet with hangers and hooks D. L. above proscenium and just off stage. Desk, chairs, consulting couch upstage with curtains.

DR. PRENTICE *enters briskly from the hall.* GERALDINE BARCLAY *follows him.*

PRENTICE. Take a seat. Is this your first job?

GERALDINE. Yes, Doctor.

PRENTICE. (*Puts on a pair of spectacles, stares at her. He opens a drawer in the desk, takes out a notebook. Picking up a pencil.*) I'm going to ask you a few questions. (*He hands her a notebook and pencil.*) Write them down. In English, please. (*He returns to his desk, sits, smiles.*) Who was your father? Put that at the head of the page. (GERALDINE *crosses her legs, rests the notebook upon her knee and makes a note.*) And now the reply immediately underneath for quick reference.

GERALDINE. I've no idea who my father was.

PRENTICE. (*Is perturbed by her reply although he gives no evidence of this. He gives her a kindly smile.*) I'd better be frank, Miss Barclay. I can't employ you if you're in any way miraculous. It would be contrary to established practice. You did have a father?

GERALDINE. Oh, I'm sure I did. My mother was frugal in her habits, but she'd never economize unwisely.

PRENTICE. If you had a father why can't you produce him?

GERALDINE. He deserted my mother. Many years ago. She was the victim of an unpleasant attack.

PRENTICE. (*Shrewdly.*) She was a nun?

GERALDINE. No. She was a chambermaid at the Station Hotel.

PRENTICE. (*Frowns, takes off his spectacles and pinches*

5

the bridge of his nose.) Pass that large, leather-bound volume, will you? I must check your story. To safeguard my interests, you understand? (GERALDINE *lifts the book from the bookcase and takes it to* DR. PRENTICE. *Consulting the index.*) The Station Hotel? (*Opening the book, running his finger down the page.*) Ah, here we are! It's a building of small architectural merit built for some unknown purpose at the turn of the century. It was converted into a hotel by public subscription. (*Nods, wisely.*) I stayed there once myself as a young man. It has a reputation for luxury which baffles the most undemanding guest. (*Closes the book with a bang and pushes it to one side.*) Your story appears, in the main, to be correct. This admirable volume, of course, omits most of the details. But that is only to be expected in a publication of wide general usage. (*Puts on his spectacles.*) Make a note to the effect that your father is missing. Say nothing of the circumstances. It might influence my final decision. (GERALDINE *makes a jotting in her notebook.* DR. PRENTICE *takes the leather-bound volume to the bookcase.*) Is your mother alive? Or has she too unaccountably vanished? That is a trick question. Be careful—you could lose marks on your final scoring.

GERALDINE. I haven't seen my mother for many years. I was brought up by a Mrs. Barclay. She died recently.

PRENTICE. I'm so sorry. From what cause?

GERALDINE. An explosion, due to a faulty gas-main, killed her outright and took the roof off the house.

PRENTICE. Have you applied for compensation?

GERALDINE. Just for the roof.

PRENTICE. Were there no other victims of the disaster?

GERALDINE. Yes. A recently erected statue of Sir Winston Churchill was so badly injured that the special medal has been talked of. Parts of the great man were actually found embedded in my stepmother.

PRENTICE. Which parts?

GERALDINE. I'm afraid I can't help you there. I was too upset to supervise the funeral arrangements. Or, indeed, to identify the body.

PRENTICE. Surely the Churchill family did that?

GERALDINE. Yes. They were most kind.

PRENTICE. You've had a unique experience. It's not everyone who has their stepmother assassinated by a public utility. (*Shakes his head, sharing the poor girl's sorrow.*) Can I get you an aspirin?

GERALDINE. No, thank you, sir. I don't want to start taking drugs.

PRENTICE. Your caution does you credit, my dear. (*Smiles in a kindly fashion.*) Now, I have to ask a question which may cause you embarrassment. Please remember that I'm a doctor. (*Pause.*) What is your shorthand speed?

GERALDINE. I can manage twenty words a minute with ease, sir.

PRENTICE. And your typing speed?

GERALDINE. I haven't mastered the keyboard. My money ran out, you see.

PRENTICE. (*Takes the notebook and puts it aside.*) Perhaps you have other qualities which aren't immediately apparent. (*Pulls aside the curtains on the couch.*) Kindly remove your stockings. I wish to see what effect your stepmother's death had upon your legs.

GERALDINE. Isn't this rather unusual, Doctor?

PRENTICE. Have no fear, Miss Barclay. What I see before me isn't a lovely and desirable girl. It's a sick mind in need of psychiatric treatment. The body is of no interest to a medical man. A woman once threw herself at me. I needn't tell you that this is spoken in confidence. She was stark naked. She wished me to misbehave myself. And, d'you know, all I was conscious of was that she had a malformed navel? That's how much notice I take of women's bodies.

GERALDINE. Please forgive me, Doctor. I wasn't meaning to suggest that your attentions were in any way improper. (*Takes off her shoes and stockings.* DR. PRENTICE *runs a hand along her legs and nods, sagely.*)

PRENTICE. As I thought. You've a febrile condition of the calves. You're quite wise to have a check-up. (*Straightens and takes off his spectacles.*) Undress. (*Turns to the desk and takes off his coat.*)

GERALDINE. I've never undressed in front of a man before.

PRENTICE. I shall take account of your inexperience in these matters. (*Puts his spectacles on the desk and rolls back his cuffs.*)

GERALDINE. I couldn't allow a man to touch me while I was unclothed.

PRENTICE. I shall wear rubber gloves, Miss Barclay.

GERALDINE. (*Is worried and makes no attempt to conceal her growing doubts.*) How long would I have to remain undressed?

PRENTICE. If your reactions are normal you'll be back on your feet in next to no time.

GERALDINE. I'd like another woman present. Is your wife available?

PRENTICE. Mrs. Prentice is attending a more than usually lengthy meeting of her coven. She won't be back until this evening.

GERALDINE. I could wait until then.

PRENTICE. I haven't the patience, my dear. I've a natural tendency to rush things . . . something my wife has never understood. But I won't trouble you with the details of my private life till you're dressed. Put your clothes on this. Lie on that couch.

(GERALDINE *unzips and removes her dress and shoes.* DR. PRENTICE *puts dress on hanger and hangs it in D. L. closet. Puts shoes on closet floor.*)

GERALDINE. What is Mrs. Prentice like, Doctor? I've heard so many stories about her. (*Stands in her panties and bra.*)

PRENTICE. My wife is a nymphomaniac. Consequently, like the Holy Grail, she's ardently sought after by young men. I married her for her money, and, upon discovering her to be penniless, I attempted to throttle her . . . a mental aberration for which I've never forgiven myself. Needless to say, our relationship has been delicate ever since.

GERALDINE. (*With a sigh.*) Poor Dr. Prentice. How trying it must be for you. (*Climbing on to the couch.*) I wish there were something I could do to cheer you up. (*Closes the curtains.*)

PRENTICE. (*Puts on a white surgical coat.*) Well, my dear, if it'll give you any pleasure you can test my new contraceptive device.

GERALDINE. (*Looks through the curtain and smiles*

sweetly.) I'll be delighted to help you in any way I can, Doctor.

PRENTICE. (*With an indulgent, superior smile.*) Lie on the couch with your hands behind your head and think of the closing chapters of your favorite work of fiction. The rest may be left to me.

(GERALDINE *disappears behind the curtain.* DR. PRENTICE *goes to the drawer in his desk. Starts to unzip his trousers.* MRS. PRENTICE *enters from the hall. She is wearing a coat.*)

MRS. PRENTICE. Who are you talking to?

PRENTICE. (*Is surprised and angry at his wife's unexpected appearance. Flushing, guilty.*) I must ask you not to enter my consulting room without warning. You're interrupting my studies.

MRS. PRENTICE. (*Stares about the room.*) Well, who were you talking to? There's no one here. Have you taken up talking to yourself?

PRENTICE. I was dictating a memo to the head nurse. She's worried about her inability to control her bladder.

MRS. PRENTICE. Can urine be controlled by thinking of one's favorite work of fiction? Hers is *Tess of the d'Urbervilles*, you know?

PRENTICE. Whose?

MRS. PRENTICE. The head nurse.

PRENTICE. My theory is still in the planning stages. I'd rather not discuss it. Why have you returned so soon?

(DR. PRENTICE *turns his back and zips up his trousers.*)

MRS. PRENTICE. I arrived at my meeting to find the hall in an uproar. Helen Duncanon had declared herself to be in love with a man. And, as you know, the coven is primarily for lesbians. I myself am exempt from the rule because you count as a woman. We expelled Helen and by that time it was so late that I spent the night at the Station Hotel. It's so difficult being a woman.

PRENTICE. Well, I'm sure you're the best judge of that. (*A BUZZER sounds from the wards.*) It's an emergency in Ward B. They need me in Ward B. I trust you'll have left by the time I return. (*He goes.*)

MRS. PRENTICE. You can come in now. (NICHOLAS BECKETT *enters. He is a hotel page and wears a page boy's uniform.*) I'm not asking for my handbag back, or for the money you've stolen, but unless my dress is returned I shall file a complaint with your employer. You have until lunchtime.

NICK. I've already sold the dress for a lump sum. I could get it back at a price. I've also found someone to take an option on the photographs.

MRS. PRENTICE. (*Stares.*) What photographs?

NICK. I had a camera concealed in the room.

MRS. PRENTICE. When I gave myself to you the contract didn't include cinematic rights.

NICK. I'd like a hundred for the negatives. You've got until lunchtime.

MRS. PRENTICE. I shall complain to the manager.

NICK. It will do you no good. He took the photographs.

MRS. PRENTICE. Oh, this is scandalous! I'm a married woman.

NICK. You didn't behave like a married woman last night.

MRS. PRENTICE. I was upset. A lesbian friend of mine had just announced her engagement to a Member of Parliament.

NICK. You must be more careful in your choice of friends. Look, I could reconsider. I'd like to get out of the indecent photograph racket. It's so wearing on the nerves. Can you find me a worthwhile job? I had a hard boyhood.

MRS. PRENTICE. What kind of job do you want?

NICK. I'm an expert typist. I was taught by a man in the printing trade.

MRS. PRENTICE. (*Firmly.*) I'm willing to pay for the photographs, but I can't possibly recommend your typing.

NICK. I want a hundred for the negatives and the job of secretary to your husband!

MRS. PRENTICE. You put me in an impossible position.

NICK. No position is impossible when you're young and healthy.

PRENTICE. (*Enters.*) Who is he?

MRS. PRENTICE. I neglected to mention that having lost my handbag at the Station Hotel this young man was kind enough to drive me home on his motor bike.

PRENTICE. I see. Drinking so early? You'll be sodden before lunch.

NICK. Have you a family, sir?

PRENTICE. No. My wife said breast-feeding would spoil her shape. Though, from what I remember, it would've been improved by a little nibbling. She's an example of in-breeding among the lobelia-growing classes. A failure in eugenics, combined with a taste for alcohol and sexual intercourse, makes it most undesirable for her to become a mother.

MRS. PRENTICE. (*Quietly.*) I hardly ever have sexual intercourse.

PRENTICE. You were born with your legs apart. They'll send you to the grave in a Y-shaped coffin.

MRS. PRENTICE. (*With a brittle laugh.*) My trouble stems from your inadequacy as a lover! That's the reason for my never having an orgasm.

PRENTICE. How dare you say that! Your book on the climax in the female is largely autobiographical. (*Pause. He stares.*) Or have you been masquerading as a sexually responsive woman?

MRS. PRENTICE. My uterine contractions have been bogus for some time! (*She exits into hall.* NICK *follows her out.*)

PRENTICE. (*Looking after her.*) What a discovery! Married to a mistress of the fraudulent climax. It's no good. . . . It's no good lying there, Miss Barclay. My wife has returned.

GERALDINE. Will she be able to help with your examination?

PRENTICE. The examination is canceled until further notice. Get dressed!

MRS. PRENTICE. (*Re-entering.*) Has your new secretary arrived?

PRENTICE. (*Holds the underwear behind his back.* GERALDINE *is concealed by the curtain.*) Yes. I've got her particulars somewhere. (*Unable to conceal the underclothes behind his back, he drops them into a wastepaper basket.*)

MRS. PRENTICE. Have you ever given thought to a male secretary?

PRENTICE. A man could never get used to the work.

MRS. PRENTICE. My father had a male secretary. My mother said he was much better than a woman.

PRENTICE. I couldn't ask a young fellow to do overtime and then palm him off with a lipstick or a bottle of Yardley's. It'd be silk suits and Alfa Romeos if I so much as breathed on him.

MRS. PRENTICE. Try a boy for a change. You're a rich man. You can afford the luxuries of life.

PRENTICE. I can't possibly. I've already given Miss Barclay a preliminary interview. (*Takes* GERALDINE'S *dress from the closet and tries to sneak it over the top of the curtains.*)

MRS. PRENTICE. (*Turns and sees him with the dress.*) You must explain . . . (*In a surprised tone.*) What are you doing with that dress?

PRENTICE. (*Pause.*) It's an old one of yours.

MRS. PRENTICE. Have you taken up transvestism? I'd no idea our marriage teetered on the edge of fashion.

PRENTICE. Our marriage is like the peace of God—it passeth all understanding.

MRS. PRENTICE. Give me the dress. I need it.

PRENTICE. (*Reluctant.*) May I have the one you're wearing in exchange?

MRS. PRENTICE. I'm not wearing a dress. (*Slips off her coat. Under it she is dressed only in a slip.*)

PRENTICE. (*Cannot conceal his surprise.*) Why aren't you wearing a dress?

MRS. PRENTICE. (*Putting on* GERALDINE'S *dress.*) I'll tell you frankly and with complete candor. Please listen carefully and save your comments for later. (*Zips up the dress.*) My room at the hotel was small, airless and uncomfortable. A model of its kind. When I turned down the bed I noticed that the sheets were none too clean. I went to the linen closet, which I knew to be on the second floor, hoping to find a chambermaid. Instead I found a page boy, the one in fact who was just here. He enticed me into the closet and then made an indecent suggestion. When I repulsed him he attempted to rape me. I fought him off but not before he'd stolen my handbag and dress.

PRENTICE. It doesn't sound like the kind of behavior one expects at a four-star hotel.

MRS. PRENTICE. The boy has promised to return my

dress. He's sold it to a friend who probably intends using it at sex orgies.

PRENTICE. Do you realize what would happen if your adventures became public? I'd be ruined. The doors of society would be slammed in my face. Did you inform the authorities of this escapade?

MRS. PRENTICE. No.

PRENTICE. Why not?

MRS. PRENTICE. I saw in the boy a natural goodness that had all but been destroyed by the pressures of society. I promised to find him employment.

PRENTICE. What qualifications has he got?

MRS. PRENTICE. He can type.

PRENTICE. There aren't many jobs for male typists.

MRS. PRENTICE. Exactly. He's been depressed by his failure in business. That's why he took to rape.

PRENTICE. How do you hope to employ him? Is there a market for illegal entrance?

MRS. PRENTICE. I don't propose to lead him into a dead-end job. I want you to hire him as your secretary. He'll be back soon. You can check his credentials at your leisure. Where is Miss Barclay?

PRENTICE. She's upstairs.

MRS. PRENTICE. I shall inform her that the position is no longer vacant.

PRENTICE. Could I borrow one of your dresses for a while, my dear?

MRS. PRENTICE. I find your sudden craving for women's clothing a dull and, on the whole, a rather distasteful subject. (*Exits into the garden.*)

PRENTICE. Miss Barclay—the situation is fraught—my wife is under the impression that your dress belongs to her.

GERALDINE. (*Looks through the curtain.*) Can't we explain, as tactfully as possible, that she has made a mistake?

PRENTICE. I'm afraid that is impossible. You must be patient for a little longer.

GERALDINE. Doctor—I'm naked! You do realize that, don't you?

PRENTICE. Indeed I do, Miss Barclay. I'm sure it must cause you acute embarrassment. I'll set about finding you suitable clothing.

He turns to the wastepaper basket, and is about to re-move the underclothing when DR. RANCE *enters from the hall.* DR. PRENTICE *drops the clothing into the basket and puts the basket down.* GERALDINE *ducks behind the curtain out of sight.)*

RANCE. Good morning. Are you Dr. Prentice?

PRENTICE. Yes. Do you have an appointment?

RANCE. No. I never make appointments. I represent our government, your immediate superiors in madness.

PRENTICE. Which branch?

RANCE. The mental branch.

PRENTICE. Do you cover asylums proper or just houses of tentative madness?

RANCE. My authority is unlimited. I have the power to close your clinic on a moment's notice should I find it necessary. I'd even have sway over a rabbit hutch if the inmates were mentally disturbed.

PRENTICE. You're obviously a force to be reckoned with.

RANCE. Indeed I am, but I hope our relationship will be a pleasant one. I'd like to be given full details of your clinic. It's run, I understand, with the full knowledge and permission of the local hospital authorities. (*He looks behind the curtains.*) You specialize in the complete breakdown and its by-products?

PRENTICE. Yes, but it's highly confidential. My files are never open to strangers.

RANCE. You may speak freely in front of me, Prentice. Remember I represent the government. Now, is this your consulting room?

PRENTICE. Yes.

RANCE. What's down this corridor?

PRENTICE. The first door on the right is the dispensary and the doors at the end of the hall lead to the wards.

RANCE. Is your couch regulation size? It looks big enough for two.

PRENTICE. I do double consultations. Toddlers are often terrified of a doctor. So I've taken to examining their mothers at the same time.

RANCE. Has the theory received much publicity?

PRENTICE. I don't approve of scientists who publicize their theories.

RANCE. I must say I agree with you. I wish more scientists would keep their ideas to themselves. (*A piece of paper flutters from under the curtain. Picking up the paper.*) Is this something to do with you?

PRENTICE. It's a prescription, sir.

RANCE. (*Reading.*) "Keep your head down and don't make a sound?" (*Pause.*) Do you find your patients react favorably to such treatment?

PRENTICE. I can claim to have had some success with it.

RANCE. Your ideas, I think, are in advance of the times. Why is there a naked woman behind there?

PRENTICE. She's a patient, sir. I'd just managed to calm her down when you arrived.

RANCE. You were attacked by a naked woman?

PRENTICE. Yes.

RANCE. Well, Prentice, I don't know whether to applaud your daring or envy you your luck. I'd like to question her.

PRENTICE. (*Goes to the curtains.*) Miss Barclay, a gentleman wishes to speak to you.

GERALDINE. (*Looking through the curtain.*) I can't meet anyone without my clothes on, Doctor.

PRENTICE. (*Coolly, to* DR. RANCE.) Notice the obstinacy with which she clings to her suburban upbringing.

RANCE. Have you tried shock treatment?

PRENTICE. No.

RANCE. How long has she been a patient?

PRENTICE. The committal order hasn't yet been signed.

RANCE. Fill it out. I'll sign it.

PRENTICE. That's not my usual procedure, sir, to certify someone before examining them.

RANCE. The government requires certification before examination. Young woman, why did you take your clothes off? Did it never occur to you that your psychiatrist might be embarrassed by your behavior?

GERALDINE. I'm not a patient. I'm from the Friendly Faces Employment Bureau.

RANCE. (*Over his shoulder to* DR. PRENTICE.) When did these delusions first manifest themselves?

PRENTICE. (*Returning with a document.*) I've been aware of them for some time, sir.

RANCE. (*To* GERALDINE.) Do you imagine that any businessman would tolerate a naked typist in his office?

GERALDINE. (*Smiles and, in a reasonable manner, attempts to explain.*) Dr. Prentice asked me to undress in order that he might discover my fitness for the tasks ahead. There was no suggestion of my working permanently without clothing.

RANCE. (*To* DR. PRENTICE.) I shall take charge of this case. It appears to have all the bizarre qualities that make for a fascinating thesis. (*Signs the document.*) Make the necessary entry in your register and alert your staff of my requirements. (DR. PRENTICE *tears the document in half as he exits to the dispensary.* DR. RANCE *turns to* GERALDINE.) Young lady, is there a history of mental illness in your family?

GERALDINE. (*Primly.*) I find your questions irrelevant. I refuse to answer them.

RANCE. I've just certified you insane. You know that, don't you?

GERALDINE. What right have you to take such high-handed action?

RANCE. Every right. You've had a nervous breakdown.

GERALDINE. I'm quite sane!

RANCE. Pull yourself together. Why have you been certified if you're sane? Even for a madwoman she's unusually dense. (DR. PRENTICE *enters from the dispensary, wheeling a hospital trolley. On it are a rubber mattress, a pillow and a sheet. Over his arm,* DR. PRENTICE *carries a white hospital nightgown.* DR. RANCE *takes this from him. He throws it over the curtain to* GERALDINE.) Put that on!

GERALDINE. (*To* DR. RANCE.) Oh, thank you. It will be a great relief to be clothed again.

RANCE. (*Draws* DR. PRENTICE *aside.* GERALDINE *puts on the nightgown.*) What is the background of this case? Has the patient any family?

PRENTICE. No, sir. Her stepmother died recently after a remarkably intimate involvement with Sir Winston Churchill.

RANCE. What of the father?

PRENTICE. He appears to have been an unpleasant fellow. He made her mother pregnant at her place of employment.

RANCE. Was there any reason for such conduct?

PRENTICE. The patient is reticent on the subject.

RANCE. I find that strange. And very revealing. Prepare a sedative.

GERALDINE. Please call a taxi, sir. I wish to return home. I haven't the qualities required for this job.

RANCE. Lie on that trolley. You're slowing down your recovery rate, Miss Barclay.

(DR. PRENTICE *forces* GERALDINE *to take a pill and he lifts her onto the trolley. He covers her with the sheet. She gasps and bursts into tears.*)

GERALDINE. This is intolerable! You're a disgrace to your profession! I shall ring the medical association after lunch.

RANCE. Accept your condition without tears and without abusing those placed in authority.

GERALDINE. Am I mad, Doctor?

PRENTICE. No.

GERALDINE. Are you mad?

PRENTICE. No.

GERALDINE. Is this "Candid Camera"?

PRENTICE. There is a perfectly rational explanation for what has taken place. Keep calm. All will be well.

(MRS. PRENTICE *enters from the garden.*)

MRS. PRENTICE. (*Anxious.*) Miss Barclay is nowhere to be found.

RANCE. She's under strong sedation and on no account to be disturbed.

PRENTICE. (*Nervous, gives a fleeting smile in* DR. RANCE'S *direction.*) My wife is talking of my secretary, sir. She's been missing since this morning.

GERALDINE. I'm Geraldine Barclay. Looking for part-time secretarial work. I've been certified insane.

RANCE. (*To* MRS. PRENTICE.) Ignore these random reflections, Mrs. Prentice. They're an essential factor in the patient's condition. (*To* DR. PRENTICE.) Does she have the same name as your secretary?

PRENTICE. She's taken my secretary's name as her "nom-de-folie." Although morally reprehensible, there's little we can do legally, I'm afraid.

RANCE. (*Drying his hands.*) It seems a trifle capricious, but the insane are famous for their wild ways.

MRS. PRENTICE. I shall contact the employment agency. Miss Barclay can't have vanished into thin air. (*Goes into the hall.*)

PRENTICE. My wife is unfamiliar with the habits of young women, sir. I've known many who could vanish into thin air. And some who took a delight in doing so.

RANCE. In my experience young women vanish only at midnight and after a heavy meal. Were your relations with your secretary normal?

PRENTICE. Yes.

RANCE. Well, Prentice, your private life is your own affair. I find it shocking nonetheless. Did the patient know of your liaison with Miss Barclay?

PRENTICE. She may have.

RANCE. I see. A definite pattern is beginning to emerge. (*Returns to the trolley and stands looking down at* GERALDINE. *Takes a white coat from* DR. PRENTICE.) Under the influence of the drug you've just—oh, thank you—administered to Miss Barclay, she will be relaxed and unafraid. I'm going to ask you some questions which I want answered in a clear non-technical style. (*To* DR. PRENTICE.) She'll take that as an invitation to use bad language. (*To* GERALDINE.) Who was the first man in your life?

GERALDINE. My father.

RANCE. Did he assault you?

GERALDINE. No!

RANCE. (*To* DR. PRENTICE.) She may mean "Yes" when she says "No." It's elementary feminine psychology. (*To* GERALDINE.) Was your mother aware of your love for your father?

GERALDINE. I lived in a normal family. I had no love for my father.

RANCE. (*To* DR. PRENTICE.) I'd take a bet that she was the victim of an incestuous attack. She clearly associates violence and the sexual act. Her attempt, when naked, to provoke you to erotic response may have

deeper significance. (*To* GERALDINE.) Did your father
have any religious beliefs?

GERALDINE. I'm sure he did.

RANCE. (*To* DR. PRENTICE.) Yet she claims to have
lived in a normal family. The depth of her condition can
be measured from such a statement. (*To* GERALDINE.)
Did your father's church sanction rape? (*To* DR. PREN-
TICE.) Some religions will turn a blind eye to anything
as long as it's kept within the family circle. (*To* GERAL-
DINE.) Was there a church service before you were
assaulted?

GERALDINE. I can't answer these questions, sir. They
seem pointless and disgusting.

RANCE. I'm interested in rape, Miss Barclay, not the
aesthetics of cross-examination. Answer me, please!
Were you molested by your father?

GERALDINE. (*With a scream of horror.*) No, no, no!

RANCE. The vehemence of her denials is proof positive
of guilt. It's a textbook case!

PRENTICE. It's fascinating, sir, and the questions are
cleverly put together. Do they tie in with known facts?

RANCE. That need not cause us undue anxiety. Civili-
zations have been founded and maintained on theories
which refused to obey facts. As far as I'm concerned this
child was unnaturally assaulted by her own father. I shall
base my future actions upon that assumption.

PRENTICE. Perhaps there's a simpler explanation for
the apparent complexities of the case, sir.

RANCE. Simple explanations are for simple minds. I've
no use for either. I shall supervise the cutting of the
patient's hair. (*Wheels* GERALDINE *into the wards.*)

(DR. PRENTICE'S *glance falls on to the wastepaper basket. He shakes out* GERALDINE'S *underclothes, takes her
shoes from the closet.* MRS. PRENTICE *enters from the hall.*
DR. PRENTICE *swings round, turns his back on her and
walks away, bent double in an effort to conceal the clothing and shoes.*)

MRS. PRENTICE. The young man is here.

PRENTICE. Ohhhh.

MRS. PRENTICE. (*Alarmed by his strange conduct.*)
What's the matter? (*She approaches.*) Are you in pain?

PRENTICE. (*His back to her, strangled.*) Yes. Get me a glass of water.

(MRS. PRENTICE *hurries into the dispensary.* DR. PRENTICE *stares about him in desperation. He sees a tall vase of roses. He removes the roses and stuffs the under-clothing and one shoe into the vase. The second shoe won't go in. He pauses, perplexed. He is about to replace the roses when* MRS. PRENTICE *enters carrying a glass of water.* DR. PRENTICE *conceals the shoe under his coat.* MRS. PRENTICE *stares. He is holding the roses. He gives a feeble smile and presents them to her with a flourish.* MRS. PRENTICE *is surprised and angry.*)

MRS. PRENTICE. Here you are. Put them back at once!
PRENTICE. Ohhhh. (*The shoe slips and* DR. PRENTICE, *in an effort to retain it, doubles up.*)
MRS. PRENTICE. Should I call a doctor?
PRENTICE. No. I'll be all right.
MRS. PRENTICE. (*Offering him the glass.*) Here. Drink this.
PRENTICE. (*Backs away, still holding the roses and the shoe.*) I wonder if you'd get another glass? That one is quite the wrong shape.
MRS. PRENTICE. (*Puzzled.*) The wrong shape?
PRENTICE. Yes, the wrong shape.

(MRS. PRENTICE *stares hard at him, then goes into the dispensary.* DR. PRENTICE *tries to replace the roses in the vase. They won't go in. He picks up a pair of scissors from his desk and cuts the stalks down to within an inch or so of the heads. He puts the roses into the vase. He looks for somewhere to conceal the second shoe. He shoves it between the space on top of the books on the lower shelf of the bookcase. He sees the stalks on the floor and kneels down to clean them up.* MRS. PRENTICE *enters carrying another glass. She stops and stares.*)

MRS. PRENTICE. What are you doing now?
PRENTICE. (*Lifting his hands.*) Praying.
MRS. PRENTICE. This puerile behavior ill accords with your high academic standards. Here, drink this. The

young man I wish you to engage as your secretary has arrived.

PRENTICE. Perhaps he'd call back later. I'm not up to seeing anyone just now.

MRS. PRENTICE. I'll see what he says. He's an impatient young man.

PRENTICE. Is that why he took to rape?

(*She hurries away into the hall.* DR. RANCE *enters from the ward.*)

RANCE. You'll have no trouble recognizing the patient, Prentice. I've clipped her hair within an inch of the scalp.

PRENTICE (*Shocked.*) Was it quite wise to do that, sir? Is it in accord with the present enlightened approach to the mentally sick?

RANCE. Perfectly in accord. As a matter of fact I've published a monograph on the subject. I wrote it while studying at the psychic institute. My tutor advised it. A remarkable man. Having failed to achieve madness himself, he took to teaching it to others.

PRENTICE. And you were his prize pupil?

RANCE. There were some more able than I.

PRENTICE. Where are they now?

RANCE. In mental institutions.

PRENTICE. Running them?

RANCE. For the most part.

(MRS. PRENTICE *enters from the hall.*)

MRS. PRENTICE. (*To* DR. PRENTICE.) The young man insists upon punctuality. He'll give you five minutes.

PRENTICE. A prospective employee, sir. I'm afraid you must excuse me. He'll give me five minutes.

RANCE. Very well.

PRENTICE. It's useless to claim that Socialism has had no effect.

RANCE. Mrs. Prentice, is there no news of Miss Barclay?

MRS. PRENTICE. None. She's still missing. I've checked with the Employment Bureau. Their clients have strict instructions to call them immediately after an interview. Miss Barclay has failed to do so.

RANCE. A search party must be organized. (*To* DR. PRENTICE.) What have you in the way of dogs?

MRS. PRENTICE. A spaniel and a miniature poodle.

RANCE. Let them be unleashed! Geraldine Barclay must be found or the authorities informed.

MRS. PRENTICE. I'll contact the warden. He has charge of the gate and will know whether she left the building. (*Turns to go.*)

PRENTICE. No—don't do that. Miss Barclay is quite safe. I've just remembered. She's in the therapy workshop.

RANCE. (*Pause, surprised.*) Why did you keep the fact from us?

PRENTICE. It'd slipped my memory.

RANCE. Have you suffered from lapses of memory before?

PRENTICE. I can't remember.

RANCE. Your memory plays you false even on the subject of its own inadequacy?

PRENTICE. I may have had a blackout. I don't recall having one on any other occasion.

RANCE. You might have forgotten. You admit your memory isn't reliable.

PRENTICE. I can only state what I know, sir. I can't be expected to remember things I've forgotten.

MRS. PRENTICE. What's Miss Barclay doing in the therapy workshop?

PRENTICE. She's making white tarbabies for sale in color-prejudice trouble-spots.

(DR. RANCE *and* MRS. PRENTICE *exchange startled looks.*)

RANCE. You claim, Prentice, that you forgot your secretary was manufacturing these monstrosities?

PRENTICE. Yes.

RANCE. I can hardly credit it. Once seen, a white tarbaby is not easily forgotten. What was the object in creating these nightmare creatures?

PRENTICE. I hoped it might promote racial harmony.

RANCE. These hellish white mutations must be put out of their misery. I order you to destroy them before their baleful influence can make itself felt.

PRENTICE. (*Wearily.*) I'll get Miss Barclay to carry out your orders, sir. (*He goes out to the wards.*)

RANCE. The man's a second Frankenstein.

MRS. PRENTICE. I don't believe we've been introduced.

RANCE. I represent our government. The mental branch. I'm here to investigate your husband's clinic and I find his behavior gives me cause for grave disquiet. Are you convinced that his methods can result in the lessening of tension between the sane and the insane?

MRS. PRENTICE. The purpose of my husband's clinic isn't to cure, but to liberate and exploit madness.

RANCE. In this he appears to succeed only too well. Never have I seen matters conducted as they are in this house. Read that.

MRS. PRENTICE. (*Reading.*) "Keep your head down and don't make a sound"? (*Handing it back.*) What does it mean?

RANCE. It's a prescription of your husband's. He's using dangerously unorthodox methods in his treatment of the insane.

MRS. PRENTICE. I must confess that only this morning my husband prescribed the reading of Thomas Hardy to cure a disorder of the bladder.

RANCE. Now, you see what I mean. Have there been other schemes besides this tarbaby scandal?

MRS. PRENTICE. Endless ones. His letters to the newspapers are legion. From his first letter at the age of 12 speculating on the nature and extent of Nazi propaganda, to his latest published a month ago, in which he calls gentlemen's lavatories the last stronghold of male privilege. What do you think, Doctor? Is he a genius or just a highly strung fool?

RANCE. As a psychiatrist your husband seems not only ineffective but also undesirable.

MRS. PRENTICE. (*Discovers* GERALDINE'S *shoe and looks at it in amazement.*) Oh!

RANCE. (*Pause.*) What is it?

MRS. PRENTICE. A shoe.

RANCE. Is it yours?

MRS. PRENTICE. No.

RANCE. Let me see it. (*She hands him the shoe. He turns it over in his hand. Looking up, after a pause.*) I must ask you to be honest with me, Mrs. Prentice. Has Dr. Prentice at any time given you cause to doubt his own sanity?

MRS. PRENTICE. (*Gives a quick gasp of fear, rising to her feet.*) He's a respected member of his profession. His work in all fields has been praised by numerous colleagues.

RANCE. Let me remind you, Mrs. Prentice, that radical thought comes easily to the lunatic.

MRS. PRENTICE. (*Pause.*) You're quite right. I've known for some time that all was not well. I've tried to convince myself that my fears were groundless. All the while I knew I was deceiving myself.

RANCE. (*Quietly.*) What first aroused your suspicions?

MRS. PRENTICE. His boorish attitude towards my mother. He used to call her up on the telephone and suggest painful ways of committing suicide. Worn out at last by his pestering, she took his advice.

RANCE. And more recently, say from this morning, has there been an increase in his condition?

MRS. PRENTICE. Oh, yes. Quite definitely, Doctor. He had no sympathy for me when I complained of being assaulted by a page boy at the Station Hotel.

RANCE. What was the object of the assault?

MRS. PRENTICE. The boy wanted to rape me.

RANCE. Did he succeed?

MRS. PRENTICE. No.

RANCE. (*Shaking his head.*) The service in these hotels is dreadful.

MRS. PRENTICE. And now he has developed a craving for women's clothes.

RANCE. (*Picking up* GERALDINE'S *shoe.*) This confirms your story. I can't doubt that what you've told me has great significance. We must also take into account his admitted lapse of memory, and the attempts to create alien forms of life. Say nothing of our suspicions. Fancies grow like weeds in the unhealthy soil of a sick brain. (DR. PRENTICE *enters. Turning to him.*) Have you carried out my instructions?

PRENTICE. Yes.

RANCE. You guilty scientists will destroy the world with your shameful secrets. (*Takes* GERALDINE'S *shoe.*) Does this belong to your secretary?

PRENTICE. No. (*Pause.*) It's mine.

RANCE. *(Heavily, with irony.)* Are you in the habit of wearing women's footwear?

PRENTICE. *(Quickly, desperate.)* My private life is my own. Society must not be too harsh in its judgments. *(Tries to grab shoe from RANCE. RANCE won't let it go.)*

RANCE. Where is this secretary of yours? I've a few questions I'd like to put to her.

PRENTICE. I can't allow you to disturb her. She has work to do.

RANCE. I don't think you quite appreciate your position, Prentice. The powers vested in me by the government give the right to interview any member of your staff should occasion demand. (RANCE *dislodges shoe from* PRENTICE. *Thrusts it into his case.*) Where is Geraldine Barclay?

PRENTICE. She's in the garden.

RANCE. Ask her to step this way.

PRENTICE. She's making a funeral pyre for the tarbabies. It would be wrong to disturb her.

RANCE. Very well. I shall seek her out myself. You may be sure, Prentice, your conduct won't go unreported! *(Goes to the garden.)*

PRENTICE. *(Turns on his wife.)* What've you told him?

MRS. PRENTICE. Nothing but the truth.

PRENTICE. You've been spreading it around that I'm a transvestite, haven't you?

MRS. PRENTICE. There was a woman's shoe hidden in the bookcase. What was it doing there?

PRENTICE. Why were you rooting among my books?

MRS. PRENTICE. I was looking for the clippings file. I showed it to Dr. Rance.

PRENTICE. You'd no right to do that.

MRS. PRENTICE. Are you ashamed of the fact that you write to strange men?

PRENTICE. There's nothing suspect about my relationship with the editor of *The Times*.

MRS. PRENTICE. Dr. Rance and I are trying to help you. We're not satisfied with your condition.

PRENTICE. Neither am I. It's impossible and you're to blame.

MRS. PRENTICE. *(Turns on* DR. PRENTICE *resentfully.)* Whose fault is it if our marriage is on the rocks? You're selfish and inconsiderate.

PRENTICE. (*He backs her against the desk and begins to unzip her dress.*) Your irresponsible behavior causes me untold anxiety. Your nymphomania knows no bounds.

MRS. PRENTICE. You've no psychological understanding of the difficulties I face.

PRENTICE. (*Her dress is off her shoulders.*) Unless you're very careful you'll find yourself in a suitcase awaiting collection!

MRS. PRENTICE. These veiled threats confirm the doubts I already have of your sanity.

(NICK *enters from the hall, carrying a dress on a hanger.*)

NICK. I'm tired of waiting, madam. I believe this is yours. Do you want it?

MRS. PRENTICE. (*With delight.*) My dress!

PRENTICE. A dress? I'll take that. (*Grabs the dress and hanger from* NICK.)

MRS. PRENTICE. I shall inform Dr. Rance of your theft of one of my dresses.

PRENTICE. Don't raise your voice.

NICK. If you'll hand over the money, madam, I'll let you have the photos. However, some guarantee of employment must be given before I part with the negatives.

PRENTICE. What's he talking about?

MRS. PRENTICE. He has in his possession a series of pornographic studies of me. He took them last night without my knowledge.

PRENTICE. I suppose I shall have to turn pederast to get you out of this mess. Take a biscuit from the barrel and retire to your room. (*He chases her out the hall door.*)

NICK. I'm sorry if my behavior last night caused your wife undue anxiety, but I've a burning desire to sleep with every woman I meet.

PRENTICE. That's a filthy habit and, in my opinion, very injurious to the health.

NICK. It is, sir. My health's never been the same since I went off stamp collecting.

PRENTICE. We have an overall moral policy in this clinic from which even I am not exempt. While you're with us as my secretary I shall expect you to show an interest in no one's sexual organs but your own.

NICK. I would miss a lot of fun that way.
PRENTICE. That is the purpose of the exercise.

(DR. RANCE *enters from the garden.*)

RANCE. I can find no trace of your secretary. I might add, Prentice, that my patience is all but exhausted. Unless I discover her whereabouts within the next few minutes you'll find yourself in serious trouble. (*Exits to the wards.*)

MRS. PRENTICE. (*Enters from the hall.*) They've called from the front desk. A policeman is in the hall. He wishes to speak to some member of the household.

PRENTICE. Ask him to wait. Tell him I'll see him in a moment.

(MRS. PRENTICE *goes into the hall.* NICK *stands and appeals to* DR. PRENTICE, *emotional.*)

NICK. Oh, sir! They've come to arrest me!

PRENTICE. This paranoia is uncalled for. The officer has probably called to ask me for the hand of my cook in marriage.

NICK. You're wrong, sir! They'll give me five years if I'm caught.

PRENTICE. Why are you in danger of arrest?

NICK. Well, sir, as your wife has already told you, I attempted last night to misbehave myself with her. I didn't succeed.

PRENTICE. I'm sure you didn't. Despite all appearances to the contrary, Mrs. Prentice is harder to get into than the reading room of the British Museum.

NICK. Undeterred I took the elevator to the third floor of the hotel where a party of schoolgirls were staying. Oh, sir, what lonely and aimless lives they lead! I did what I could to bring them some happiness.

PRENTICE. (*With a frown.*) Was there no mistress in attendance?

NICK. She occupied a room across the corridor.

PRENTICE. Did you disturb her?

NICK. No. And she'll never forgive me for it. It was she who reported the incident to the police. Oh, sir! Don't turn me over to the law.

(DR. RANCE *enters from the dispensary*.)

RANCE. I warn you, Prentice, unless you're prepared to cooperate in finding Miss Barclay I shall call upon you to account for her disappearance. If you're unable to do so the police must be informed. (*Goes into the garden*.)

PRENTICE. (*Turns to* NICK, *an idea dawning. Abruptly*.) Take your clothes off.

NICK. (*Pause*.) Are you going to fool around with me, sir?

PRENTICE. Certainly not! Is that what usually happens when men ask you to take your clothes off?

NICK. Yes. They usually give me money.

PRENTICE. How much? Oh, never mind. Strip! I want you to impersonate my secretary, Geraldine Barclay. It will solve both our problems. (*Gives* NICK *the dress*.) It's of particular importance to convince that man that you're my secretary. You should encounter no real difficulties there. He's an elderly man. I don't suppose he's checked with the original lately. That done, plead illness and leave the house. I'll be waiting with your own clothes. The operation completed, you'll be given a sum of money and a ticket for any destination you choose. If you run into trouble I shall deny all knowledge of you. Put this on. (*Hands* NICK *the dress*.)

(MRS. PRENTICE *enters from the hall. She stops in horror, seeing* NICK *only in his shorts*.)

MRS. PRENTICE. The policeman is still waiting. What devilry are you up to now?

PRENTICE. I'm carrying out a medical examination.

MRS. PRENTICE. But you're a psychiatrist. Why do you need the child undressed?

PRENTICE. (*Smiling, with enormous patience*.) My investigations upon his clothed body would be strictly "unscientific" and, inevitably, superficial. In order to assure myself that he's going to be of use to me I must examine him fully. And skin-wise.

MRS. PRENTICE. You ogre! Never, in my whole life, have I heard anything so lame and stupid. This folly will get you struck off the Medical Register. (*Picking up*

NICK'S *uniform.*) Come with me, dear. (*Takes the uniform into the garden.*)

NICK. What do we do now, sir? If that policeman comes in I can't even make a run for it.

PRENTICE. Dress in there. (*Shoves him toward the dispensary. Then goes to the hall and calls in friendly tones.*) Would you like to step this way, officer? I'm sorry to have kept you waiting.

NICK. Shoes, sir!

(DR. PRENTICE *swings round in alarm.*)

PRENTICE. Shoes! (*Takes* GERALDINE'S *shoe from* DR. RANCE'S *brief case and throws it to* NICK. *He goes to the vase and lifts the roses quickly. He puts a hand into the vase, searching for the other shoe.* SERGEANT MATCH *enters from the hall.* NICK *darts back into the dispensary.* DR. PRENTICE *holds the roses. In cold tones:*) Would you mind not entering my consulting room without permission?

MATCH. (*A little put out.*) You asked me to come in, sir.

PRENTICE. I don't believe I did. Wait outside.

SERGEANT MATCH *leaves the room.* DR. PRENTICE *takes the roses and shakes* GERALDINE'S *shoe from the vase.* MRS. PRENTICE *enters from the garden.* PRENTICE, *caught with the flowers, hides the shoe behind his back and offers the roses to her. She steps back in amazement.*)

MRS. PRENTICE. What have you done with that boy? Why do you keep giving me flowers?

PRENTICE. It's because I'm very fond of you, my dear.

MRS. PRENTICE. Your actions grow wilder with every passing moment. Why were you rude to the policeman?

PRENTICE. He barged in without so much as a by-your-leave.

MRS. PRENTICE. But he said you asked him to come in. Had you forgotten?

PRENTICE. Yes. (*Pause.*) My memory isn't what it was. Tell him I'll see him now.

(MRS. PRENTICE *goes into the hall.*)

GERALDINE. Dr. Prentice. (*Enters from the dispensary. Her hair has been cut short. She is wearing the hospital nightdress.* NICK *enters just behind her; takes the shoe from* PRENTICE *and darts back into the dispensary.*)
PRENTICE. Miss Barclay! What are you doing here?

(SERGEANT MATCH *enters from the hall,* PRENTICE *shields* GERALDINE *from* MATCH *with his body.*)

MATCH. Sorry for the misunderstanding, sir.
PRENTICE. (*Turning, abrupt.*) Please remain outside. I think I made myself plain.
MATCH. (*Pause.*) You don't wish to see me?
PRENTICE. No. (SERGEANT MATCH *goes into the hall.*)
GERALDINE. Nothing would induce me to remain on your staff a moment longer, Doctor. I wish to give notice.
PRENTICE. Your disclosures could ruin me. Give me a chance to get us out of this mess.
GERALDINE. You must put matters right by telling the truth.
PRENTICE. (*Pulls curtains round couch.*) Hide behind here. Nothing unpleasant will happen. You have my word as a gentleman.
GERALDINE. We must tell the truth!
PRENTICE. That's a thoroughly defeatist attitude. (*Bundles her behind the curtain.*)
GERALDINE. (*Looking through the curtain.*) At least give me back my clothes. I feel naked without them.

(DR. PRENTICE *offers the vase with the underwear in it.* GERALDINE *takes out underclothes and retreats behind curtains. As* PRENTICE *stands with roses in his hands and the vase,* MRS. PRENTICE *and* SERGEANT MATCH *enter from the hall.* MRS. PRENTICE *clutches* MATCH'S *arm.*)

MRS. PRENTICE. Oh, if he presents me with those flowers again I shall faint! (*They watch in silence as* DR. PRENTICE *replaces the roses with an air of confidence. Without* GERALDINE'S *clothes under them the stalks are*

too short. The flowers vanish into the vase. MRS. PREN-
TICE *cries out in surprise.*) Oh, he's cut the stalks off! His
lunacy is beyond belief.

PRENTICE. Excuse my wife's hysteria. A man tried to
molest her last night. Her recovery is far from complete.

MATCH. I understand that Mrs. Prentice introduced
the young man to you, sir?

PRENTICE. Yes, but we won't prefer charges.

MATCH. I believe your wife to be ill-advised in not
repeating her experiences before a judge and jury. However, as it happens, I'm not concerned with this case. I'm
interested in the youth's movements between midnight
and seven A.M. During that period he is alleged to have
misconducted himself with a party of schoolchildren.

MRS. PRENTICE. How vile and disgraceful!

MATCH. Yes, ma'am. After carrying out a medical examination our lady doctor is up in arms. She can't wait
to meet this fellow face to face.

PRENTICE. Well, Sergeant, he isn't on the premises. If
he turns up you'll be informed.

MRS. PRENTICE. (*Shocked.*) How dare you give mis-
leading information to the police? (*To* SERGEANT
MATCH.) He was here. I have his clothes upstairs.

MATCH. Very wise of you to confiscate his clothing,
ma'am. If more women did the same the number of cases
of rape would be halved.

PRENTICE. (*At the desk.*) Or doubled.

MRS. PRENTICE. Disregard anything my husband says.
I'll get the clothing. (*Goes into the garden.*)

MATCH. (*Turns to* DR. PRENTICE.) I'm also anxious,
sir, to trace the whereabouts of a young woman called
Barclay. (DR. PRENTICE *coughs.*) Can you help in my
inquiries?

PRENTICE. Why do you wish to see Miss Barclay?

MATCH. It's a matter of national importance. Miss
Barclay's—

PRENTICE. Shh! I must ask you to lower your voice. I
specialize in patients who are allergic to sound. . . .
They've been known to become violent at the merest
whisper.

MATCH. Miss Barclay's stepmother, a woman of otherwise unblemished character, died recently. Shortly before
her death her name had been linked in a most unpleasant

way with that of Sir Winston Churchill. Mrs. Barclay's association with the great man gave offense in some circles. However, the local council, composed by and large of no-nonsense men and women in their sixties, decided in view of his war record to overlook Sir Winston's moral lapse. Under expert guidance he was to be reintegrated into society. The task accomplished, it became clear that the great man was incomplete. The council decided to sue the heirs of Mrs. Barclay for those parts of Sir Winston which an army-type medical had proved to be missing. The council's lawyers obtained an exhumation order. Early this morning Mrs. Barclay's coffin was opened in the presence of the Lord Mayor and Lady Mayoress of this borough. Fainting women were held back as the official in charge searched high and low for council property. His efforts were not crowned with success. Mrs. Barclay had taken nothing with her to the grave except those things which she ought to have done. That is when the matter came to the attention of the police.

PRENTICE. You suspect my secretary of having stolen certain parts of Sir Winston Churchill?

MATCH. Yes.

(MRS. PRENTICE enters, with NICK'S uniform, from the garden.)

MRS. PRENTICE. Sergeant, here is proof that the young man was in this room.

MATCH. He can't get far without clothing.

PRENTICE. His progress without clothing last night was enviable.

MATCH. (To DR. PRENTICE.) You still claim, sir, that you have no knowledge of the youth's whereabouts?

PRENTICE. Yes.

MATCH. And what has become of Miss Barclay?

PRENTICE. I've no idea.

MRS. PRENTICE. You told Dr. Rance she was burning the tarbabies. (SERGEANT MATCH looks from one to the other in amazement.) Was that a lie?

PRENTICE. It may have been. I can't remember.

MRS. PRENTICE. (Gives an impatient toss of her head.) You must talk to Dr. Rance, Sergeant. He's from the government. He may be able to account for my husband's unusual behavior pattern. Please tell him that his specialized knowledge is urgently required.

MATCH. Where would the doctor be?

MRS. PRENTICE. In the garden. (SERGEANT MATCH *goes into the garden.*) Now, darling, try to remember why you damaged the flowers in this vase. It may have a direct bearing on the case. (*Exits to the garden with the vase.*)

GERALDINE. (*Pokes her head through the curtain.*) Tell the truth, sir. All your troubles spring from a lack of candor.

PRENTICE. My troubles spring from a misguided attempt to seduce you.

GERALDINE. (*With a gasp.*) You never told me you were seducing me. You said you were interested in my mind.

(SERGEANT MATCH *appears from the garden.* GERALDINE *ducks behind the curtain.*)

MATCH. Are you sure that Dr. Rance is out here, sir?

PRENTICE. Yes.

MATCH. Where would he be then?

PRENTICE. In the shrubbery. We've a naked elf on a birdbath. We often have trouble with Peeping Toms.

MATCH. I'd like you to accompany me, sir.

(DR. PRENTICE *shrugs and follows* SERGEANT MATCH *into the garden.* GERALDINE *steps down from the couch. She is wearing her panties and bra. She carries the nightgown. She picks up* NICK'S *uniform. She hurries to the dispensary. She retreats at once dropping the nightgown. She scurries to the hall, checks herself and scuttles back to the couch. She climbs behind the curtains. As* NICK *enters from the dispensary, dressed in women's clothing,* MRS. PRENTICE *enters from the garden with the roses in a small vase.*)

MRS. PRENTICE. Are you Geraldine Barclay?

NICK. Yes.

MRS. PRENTICE. Where have you been?

NICK. (*Primly.*) I've been attending to the thousand

and one duties that occupy the average secretary during her working hours.

MRS. PRENTICE. It doesn't take the whole morning to file your nails, surely?

NICK. I had to lie down. I was sick.

MRS. PRENTICE. Are you pregnant?

NICK. I can't discuss my employer's business with you.

MRS. PRENTICE. What was your last job?

NICK. I was a hostess at the "One, Two, Three" Club.

MRS. PRENTICE. (*Purses her lips in disapproval.*) It's obvious that you're unsuited to the work here. I shan't recommend you for employment. (DR. PRENTICE *and* SERGEANT MATCH *enter from the garden. To* SERGEANT MATCH.) Ah, Sergeant. This is Geraldine Barclay. She'll be happy to help you in your inquiries.

MATCH. (*To* NICK.) Miss Barclay, I must ask you to produce, or cause to be produced, the missing parts of Sir Winston Churchill.

NICK. What do they look like?

MATCH. You're claiming ignorance of the shape and structure of the objects sought?

NICK. I'm in the dark.

MATCH. You handled them only at night? We shall draw our own conclusions.

NICK. I'm not the sort of girl to be mixed up in that kind of thing. I'm an ex-member of the Brownies.

MATCH. Are you concealing unlawful property about your person?

NICK. No.

MATCH. I'll have to call medical evidence to prove your story, miss. You must be thoroughly looked into.

PRENTICE. I'm a qualified doctor.

MATCH. Only women are permitted to examine female suspects.

PRENTICE. Doesn't that breed discontent in the force?

MATCH. Among the single men there's a certain amount of bitterness. Married men who are familiar with the country are glad to be let off extra map-reading.

MRS. PRENTICE. Sergeant, I'll examine Miss Barclay. That will solve all our problems. Come along, Miss Barclay.

MATCH. Thank you, ma'am. I accept your kind offer.

(MRS. PRENTICE *leads* NICK *into the garden. A siren sounds from the wards; then a buzzer.* DR. RANCE *enters from the wards.*)

RANCE. Prentice! The patient has escaped. I've sounded the alarm.

MATCH. How long has the patient been gone, sir?

RANCE. Only a few minutes. This is her gown. She must be naked then.

MATCH. Any steps you feel may be necessary to recover your patient may be taken, sir. (DR. RANCE *crosses, hurries into the hall.*) She must've come through this room. You and I were in the garden. Mrs. Prentice was upstairs. Escape would be out of the question. She must still be in this room. (*Turns to* DR. PRENTICE *in triumph.*) Only one hiding place is possible. (*Pulls the curtain on the couch aside.* GERALDINE *is revealed. She is wearing* NICK'S *uniform, his hat. Taking in the picture at a glance.*) Are you from the Station Hotel?

GERALDINE. (*Answers in a scared voice.*) Yes.

MATCH. I want a word with you, my lad. (*Takes out his notebook. The siren and buzzer wail.*)

(*Blackout.*)

CURTAIN

ACT II

Continuous. The siren and buzzer. They stop. EVERY-
ONE *is as they were at the end of ACT I.*

MATCH. Are you from the Station Hotel?
GERALDINE. Yes.
MATCH. I want a word with you, my lad. You're under
arrest.
GERALDINE. (*To* SERGEANT MATCH.) You've no idea
how glad I am to be arrested.
MATCH. Why?
GERALDINE. I'm in great danger.
MATCH. Who from?
GERALDINE. Dr. Prentice. His conduct is scandalous.
Take me to the police station. I shall prefer charges.
MATCH. (*To* DR. PRENTICE.) Have you anything to
say, sir?
PRENTICE. Yes. What this young woman claims is a
tissue of lies.
MATCH. (*Pause.*) This is a boy, sir. Not a girl. If you're
baffled by the difference it might be as well to approach
both with caution. (*To* GERALDINE.) Let's hear what
you've got to say for yourself.
GERALDINE. I came here for a job. On some pretext
the doctor got me to remove my clothes. Afterwards he
behaved in a strange manner.
MATCH. (*Glances at* DR. PRENTICE *in disapproval.*
MATCH *turns to* GERALDINE. *Quietly.*) Did he, at any
time, attempt to interfere with you?
PRENTICE. You'll be disappointed, Sergeant, if you
imagine that that boy has lost his virginity.
MATCH. I hope he'll be considerably more experienced
before he loses that, sir. What reason had you for taking
off his clothes?
PRENTICE. I wished to assure myself of his unquestion-
ing obedience. I give a prize each year.
MATCH. Have you been in trouble of this kind before?
PRENTICE. I'm not in trouble.

36

MATCH. You must realize this boy is bringing a serious charge against you?

PRENTICE. Yes. It's ridiculous. I'm a married man.

MATCH. Marriage excuses no one the freak's roll-call.

PRENTICE. I'm a respected member of my profession. Your accusations are absurd.

MATCH. It's not for me to bring accusations in a matter I don't fully understand.

PRENTICE. The boy has an unsavory reputation. Last night requires explaining before this morning.

GERALDINE. I had nothing to do with the disgraceful happenings at the Station Hotel.

MATCH. You deny that on the night of Thursday last you did behave in an obscene manner with a section of the Priory Road School for Girls?

GERALDINE. Yes.

MATCH. Nicholas Beckett, I warn you that anything you say will be taken down and may be used in evidence against you.

GERALDINE. My name is not Nicholas Beckett.

MATCH. (*Pause, with a frown.*) Then why d'you suppose I'd wish to arrest you?

GERALDINE. To safeguard my interests?

PRENTICE. You imagine you'll be safe from acts of indecency in a police station?

GERALDINE. Of course.

PRENTICE. I wish I shared your optimism.

RANCE. (*Enters from the hall.*) Full security arrangements are in force. No one is to leave the clinic without written permission. Prentice, get your secretary to issue warrants to every member of the staff.

PRENTICE. I'll do that, sir, as soon as she's ready to resume her normal duties.

MATCH. Are you Dr. Rance?

RANCE. Yes.

MATCH. (*To* DR. RANCE.) Would you help us clear up a spot of trouble, Doctor? It's a matter of some urgency. Last night this young man assaulted a number of female schoolchildren. This morning he was assaulted in his turn.

RANCE. (*With a shrug.*) What can I say? It's a case of "be done by as you did."

MATCH. The boy has made a serious charge against

Dr. Prentice. He claims he was forced to strip and lie on a couch.

RANCE. (*To* DR. PRENTICE.) A complete list of your indiscretions would make a best seller. Have you behaved in an unseemly manner?

PRENTICE. No! It's just that my nerves are on edge.

RANCE. You should consult a qualified psychiatrist.

PRENTICE. I am a qualified psychiatrist.

RANCE. You're a fool. That isn't quite the same thing. Though, in your case, the two may have much in common. (*To* SERGEANT MATCH.) Has the boy come to your notice before?

MATCH. Not on a case of this kind. That's why we have to be careful. As the doctor rightly says, he has an unsavory reputation. It may be that he bears Dr. Prentice a grudge.

RANCE. (*To* DR. PRENTICE.) Perhaps this accusation springs from disappointment. It might have been wiser if you hadn't rejected the young fellow's blandishments.

PRENTICE. Unnatural vice can ruin a man.

RANCE. Ruin follows the accusation, not the vice. Had you committed the act you wouldn't now be facing the charge.

PRENTICE. I couldn't commit the act. I'm a heterosexual.

RANCE. I wish you wouldn't use these Chaucerian words. It's most confusing. (*To* SERGEANT MATCH.) How do you propose to get to the bottom of this affair?

MATCH. A reputable person must examine the lad.

GERALDINE. I refuse to be examined!

MATCH. You can't refuse. You're under arrest.

GERALDINE. I'm not Nicholas Beckett. I want to be taken to prison.

MATCH. If you aren't Nicholas Beckett you can't go to prison. You're not under arrest.

GERALDINE. (*Pause, biting her lip.*) I am Nicholas Beckett.

MATCH. Then you're under arrest. You'll submit to a medical examination.

RANCE. And I shall conduct it. The mind of the victim of this kind of assault must be considered equally with the body.

GERALDINE. I haven't been assaulted.

RANCE. Then why make such a foul accusation?

GERALDINE. I didn't accuse anyone. The sergeant made the accusation.

RANCE. (*To* SERGEANT MATCH.) Has Dr. Prentice assaulted you too? (*To* DR. PRENTICE.) Is it policemen or young boys you're after? At your age it's high time you came to a decision. (*To* SERGEANT MATCH.) Wait outside. I shall examine the boy and make my report. Afterwards I'll take a look at you, too.

MATCH. (*Stunned.*) At me?

RANCE. Yes. We can't be too careful.

MATCH. It seems a bit unusual, sir.

RANCE. You're in a madhouse. Unusual behavior is the order of the day.

MATCH. Only for patients.

RANCE. We've no privileged class here. We practice democratic lunacy. (SERGEANT MATCH *goes into the hall.*) Take your clothes off, sonny. Lie on the couch.

GERALDINE. I shouldn't've behaved as I did, sir. I wasn't harmed.

RANCE. You enjoyed the experience? Would you enjoy normal intercourse?

GERALDINE. No. I might get pregnant— (*Realizes her mistake and attempts to cover up.*) —or be the cause of pregnancy in others.

RANCE. (*Quick to notice the error, turns to* DR. PRENTICE.) He's just given away a vital piece of information. (*Advances on* GERALDINE.) Do you think of yourself as a girl?

GERALDINE. No.

RANCE. Why not?

GERALDINE. I'm a boy.

RANCE. (*Kindly.*) Do you have the evidence about you?

GERALDINE. (*Her eyes flashing an appeal to* DR. PRENTICE.) I must be a boy. I like girls.

RANCE. (*Stops and wrinkles his brow, puzzled. Aside, to* DR. PRENTICE.) I can't quite follow the reasoning there.

PRENTICE. Many men imagine that a preference for women is, ipso facto, a proof of virility.

RANCE. (*Nodding, sagely.*) Someone should really write a book on these folk myths. (*To* GERALDINE.)

Take your trousers down. I'll tell you which sex you belong to.

GERALDINE. (*Backing away.*) I'd rather not know!

RANCE. You wish to remain in ignorance?

GERALDINE. Yes.

RANCE. I can't encourage you in such a self-indulgent attitude. You must face facts like the rest of us. (*Forces* GERALDINE *back to the couch.*)

PRENTICE. You're forcing the boy to undergo a repetition of a traumatic experience, sir. He might go insane.

RANCE. This is a mental home. He couldn't choose a more appropriate place. (*To* GERALDINE.) Undress. My time is valuable.

GERALDINE. (*Unable to stand the ordeal any longer, cries out to* DR. PRENTICE *in anguish.*) I can't go on, Doctor! I must tell the truth. (*To* DR. RANCE.) I'm not a boy! I'm a girl!

RANCE. (*To* DR. PRENTICE.) Excellent. A confession at last. He wishes to believe he's a girl in order to minimize the feelings of guilt after homosexual intercourse.

GERALDINE. (*Wide-eye, desperate.*) I pretended to be a boy. I did it to help Dr. Prentice.

RANCE. How does it help a man if a girl pretends to be a boy?

GERALDINE. Wives are angry if they find their husbands have undressed and seduced a girl.

RANCE. But boys are fair game? I doubt whether your very personal view of society would go unchallenged.

(*Provoked beyond endurance,* GERALDINE *flings herself into* DR. RANCE'S *arms and cries hysterically.*)

GERALDINE. Undress me then, Doctor! Do whatever you like, only prove that I'm a girl.

RANCE. (*Pushes away and turns, frigidly, to* DR. PRENTICE.) If he's going to carry on like this he'll have to be strapped down.

(MRS. PRENTICE *enters from the garden.*)

MRS. PRENTICE. (*To* DR. RANCE.) Dr. Rance, would you take a look at Miss Barclay? She refuses to undress in front of a woman.

RANCE. How about in front of a man?

MRS. PRENTICE. I haven't sounded her on the subject.

RANCE. I wonder if I could tempt her. I'll give it a try. She may be a nymphomaniac. (*To* DR. PRENTICE.) If this boy becomes foul-mouthed keep him on the boil till I return. (*Goes to the garden, followed by* MRS. PRENTICE. GERALDINE *pulls herself together.*)

GERALDINE. I'll go through the garden, Doctor. I can get a taxi home.

PRENTICE. That isn't possible. Dr. Rance has arranged for strict security precautions to be in force until the patient is recaptured.

GERALDINE. When the patient is recaptured can I go?

PRENTICE. No.

GERALDINE. Why not?

PRENTICE. You *are* the patient.

(GERALDINE *gives a little cry of distress.* DR. RANCE *re-enters.*)

RANCE. Prentice, your secretary is standing on a table fighting off any attempt to undress her. She seems incapable of conducting herself in a proper manner.

PRENTICE. She's given me no cause for complaint.

RANCE. But you expect a secretary to misbehave herself. It's a condition of employment. (*Faces* DR. PRENTICE, *candidly.*) Do you realize the woman uses a razor?

PRENTICE. I see nothing remarkable in that. Mrs. Prentice has occasion sometimes to remove unwanted hair.

RANCE. From her chin? There are two sexes. The unpalatable truth must be faced. Your attempts at a merger can end in heartbreak.

(MRS. PRENTICE *enters from the garden, a syringe in her hand, leading a chastened* NICK *by the hand.*)

MRS. PRENTICE. Miss Barclay is calmer now, Doctor. I've given her a sedative.

RANCE. (*Turning to* NICK, *shaking his head.*) What an absorbing picture of the mind in decay. Why won't you allow Mrs. Prentice to undress you?

MRS. PRENTICE. Her objections appear to be religious. She claims to be at one with God.

RANCE. Come here, sonny. Were you present when Dr. Prentice used this youth unnaturally?

NICK. What is unnatural?

RANCE. (*To* MRS. PRENTICE.) How disturbing the questions of the mad can be.

MRS. PRENTICE. (*Nodding to* GERALDINE.) Has my husband misbehaved with that boy?

RANCE. It's impossible to say with any degree of accuracy. He refuses to cooperate with a medical examination.

MRS. PRENTICE. (*To* DR. PRENTICE.) What happened to the other boy?

RANCE. Which boy?

MRS. PRENTICE. The one my husband undressed.

RANCE. This is the boy he undressed.

MRS. PRENTICE. No. He undressed the boy who made a nuisance of himself to me.

RANCE. (*Pause.*) Isn't this the same one?

MRS. PRENTICE. No.

RANCE. (*Staring, perplexed.*) There's another boy?

MRS. PRENTICE. He was being interviewed for a secretarial post. My husband made him undress.

RANCE. (*Coldly, to* DR. PRENTICE.) How long have you been a pervert?

PRENTICE. I'm not a pervert!

RANCE. How would you describe a man who mauls young boys, importunes policemen and lives on terms of intimacy with a woman who shaves twice a day?

PRENTICE. I'd say the man was a pervert.

RANCE. I'm glad you're beginning to face the realities of the situation. (*To* GERALDINE.) Who are you if you're not Nicholas Beckett?

(GERALDINE *looks to* DR. PRENTICE *and bites her lip.*)

PRENTICE. His name is Gerald Barclay.

RANCE. (*Indicating* NICK.) Is he this young woman's brother?

PRENTICE. No.

RANCE. What happened then to Nicholas Beckett?

PRENTICE. He left an hour ago to resume his duties at the Station Hotel.

MRS. PRENTICE. He can't have! I took his uniform. He'd be naked.

PRENTICE. From what one hears of the Station Hotel the uniform is optional.

RANCE. (*Shaking his head, worried.*) I hope we haven't lost another one. We'll be alone with our miracle drugs if many more go. (*To* MRS. PRENTICE.) Find out whether the boy has returned to the hotel.

MRS. PRENTICE. I'll call immediately. (*Goes into the hall.*)

RANCE. (*Turns to* DR. PRENTICE.) Prepare the necessary papers. I'm certifying these two.

(*Cries of alarm come from* NICK *and* GERALDINE.)

NICK. Can't you do something about him, sir? He's off his head.

RANCE. (*Sternly.*) I am a representative of order, you of chaos. Unless that fact is faced, I can never hope to cure you. (*To* DR. PRENTICE.) Make out the committal orders for me to sign.

PRENTICE. (*Upset and angry.*) I can't agree to such drastic action. We've no evidence of insanity. These children are no more ill than I am.

RANCE. But your condition is worse than hers.

PRENTICE. I can't accept that.

RANCE. No madman ever accepts madness. Only the sane do that. I'm relieving you of your post as head of the clinic. You'll do as I say from now on.

PRENTICE. I resent your handling of this affair, sir. I shall make my views known to the commissioners.

RANCE. I doubt whether the views of a madman will carry much weight with the commissioners.

PRENTICE. I'm not mad. It only looks that way.

RANCE. Your actions today could get the Archbishop of Canterbury declared non-compos.

PRENTICE. I'm not the Archbishop of Canterbury.

RANCE. That will come at a later stage of your illness.

PRENTICE. Your interpretation of my behavior is misplaced and erroneous. If anyone borders on lunacy it's you yourself!

RANCE. Bearing in mind your abnormality, that is a normal reaction. The sane appear as strange to the mad as the mad to the sane. Take two of these. (*Takes red pillbox from pocket.*)

PRENTICE. (*Looking at the pillbox.*) What are they?

RANCE. Dangerous drugs intended to relieve your pathologically elevated mood. Be careful not to exceed the stated dose. I shall return shortly. All of you remain here. (*Exits to the wards.*)

NICK. Why is he wearing my uniform?

GERALDINE. Why is she wearing my shoes?

PRENTICE. He isn't a boy. He's a girl. She isn't a girl. She's a boy. And we'll all be sharing the same cell at this rate.

NICK. If we changed clothes, sir, we could get things back to normal.

PRENTICE. We'd then have to account for the disappearance of my secretary and the page boy.

GERALDINE. But they don't exist!

PRENTICE. When people who don't exist disappear the account of their departure must be convincing.

NICK. (*Pause.*) Is the policeman corruptible?

PRENTICE. Why?

NICK. I must have his uniform.

PRENTICE. For what reason?

NICK. To arrest Nicholas Beckett.

PRENTICE. But you're Nicholas Beckett.

NICK. Once I've arrested myself you can write me off.

GERALDINE. Aren't you multiplying our problems instead of dividing them?

NICK. (*To* DR. PRENTICE.) Some glib pretext will get her out of the way. Then she and I can change clothes.

(DR. RANCE *enters from the wards.*)

RANCE. I'm putting this youth into a padded cell. Rampant hermaphroditism must be discouraged.

PRENTICE. Quite right.

GERALDINE. (*With a sob.*) Twice declared insane in one day! And they said I'd be working for a cheerful, well-spoken crowd. Oh, I'm glad my parents are dead. This would've killed them. (DR. RANCE *takes her to the wards.*)

PRENTICE. (*To* NICK.) I'll get the sergeant to undress so you can have his uniform. I'm suspected of the offense, I might as well commit it. We'll need something to calm him down. A mild tranquilizer wouldn't harm him, I suppose. You'll find a box of anti-depressants in the top right-hand drawer of my desk. (NICK *goes to the desk and takes a square, white pillbox from the drawer.* DR. PRENTICE *opens the hall door. Calling, friendly.*) Would you step this way, Sergeant? (*To* NICK.) Hide in there.

(NICK *hands* DR. PRENTICE *the white pillbox and hides in the closet.* SERGEANT MATCH *enters from the hall.*)

MATCH. You wish to speak to me, Doctor?

PRENTICE. Yes. Dr. Rance has asked me to examine you. I'd like you to undress and lie on that couch.

MATCH. (*Pause.*) I haven't been interfered with.

PRENTICE. Never mind about that. Strip down to your underwear.

MATCH. (*Sitting on couch, unlacing boots.*) If you make any attempt to arouse me, Doctor, I shall call for help.

PRENTICE. It's easy to see why you've never been interfered with. You place too many obstacles in the way. Come along. Come along. Speed is essential.

(SERGEANT MATCH *takes off his boots.* NICK *appears from the closet.* DR. PRENTICE *hands him the boots.* SERGEANT MATCH *takes off his tunic and hands it to* DR. PRENTICE. DR. PRENTICE *throws tunic to* NICK *who retreats.* SERGEANT MATCH *drops his trousers.* MRS. PRENTICE *enters from the hall. Seeing the* SERGEANT *without his trousers, she screams loudly. Shocked and embarrassed,* SERGEANT MATCH *pulls up his trousers.*)

MRS. PRENTICE. (*Icily.*) What were you doing with your trousers down, officer?

MATCH. The doctor is going to examine me.

MRS. PRENTICE. Why?

MATCH. There's reason to suppose that I had a nasty experience a short time ago.

MRS. PRENTICE. What kind of experience?

PRENTICE. He was meddled with.

MRS. PRENTICE. By whom?

PRENTICE. Me.

MRS. PRENTICE. And why are you examining him?

PRENTICE. To find out whether his story is true.

MRS. PRENTICE. Don't you know?

PRENTICE. No. I didn't feel a thing.

MRS. PRENTICE. (*With a toss of her head.*) Where is Dr. Rance?

PRENTICE. He's just certified the hotel page. He's putting him in a padded cell.

MRS. PRENTICE. I must speak to him. Things are getting out of control. (*Hurries into the ward.*)

PRENTICE. (*Turns to* SERGEANT MATCH.) Remove your trousers, Sergeant, and we'll continue. (SERGEANT MATCH *takes off his trousers and hands them to* DR. PRENTICE. *He is naked except for his underpants and socks. With a flourish* DR. PRENTICE *takes the red pillbox from his pocket and hands it to the* SERGEANT. *Smiling.*) Swallow these. Take as many as you like. They're quite harmless. (*The* SERGEANT *accepts the box.*) Now I want you to lie on this couch and concentrate on the closing chapters of your favorite work of fiction. (SERGEANT MATCH *lies on the couch.* DR. PRENTICE *pulls the curtain around him and hurries to the closet with the trousers. He meets* NICK *in the doorway.* NICK *carries the* SERGEANT'S *uniform.* DR. PRENTICE *hands him the trousers. To* NICK.) In the garden you'll find a little summerhouse. You won't be disturbed in there. (NICK *goes into the garden with the clothes.* DR. PRENTICE *goes to the desk.* NICK *reappears, without the uniform.*)

NICK. The helmet, sir!

PRENTICE. (*Hurries to the couch.*) The helmet, Sergeant!

MATCH. (*From behind the curtain.*) In the hall, sir.

PRENTICE. (*To* NICK.) Miss Barclay's clothes are in the closet.

(NICK *hurries into the hall with the uniform to get the helmet.* MRS. PRENTICE *enters from the ward.* NICK *re-enters from the hall, wearing only underpants and the helmet. Upon seeing him,* MRS. PRENTICE *shrieks and follows* NICK *into the garden.* DR. PRENTICE *ducks under the desk and runs into the hall with the dress [the one* NICK *has just changed out of] and* GERALDINE'S *shoes [which* NICK *has also just left there].*)

MRS. PRENTICE. (*Re-enters alone.*) This place is like a madhouse!

RANCE. (*Enters from the wards.*) Where is Dr. Prentice?

MRS. PRENTICE. I don't know. When I returned from telephoning the Station Hotel he was undressing the sergeant.

RANCE. How would you describe his relations with the sergeant?

MRS. PRENTICE. Strange and, in many ways, puzzling. He's called him into this room on several occasions and then abruptly dismissed him.

RANCE. Playing the coquette, eh? Well, well, it adds spice to a love affair. What news of the missing patient?

MRS. PRENTICE. None.

RANCE. And what's the report from the Station Hotel?

MRS. PRENTICE. They state that they have no page called Gerald Barclay on their register. The youth you've certified insane must be an impostor.

RANCE. And what of Nicholas Beckett—the real page boy?

MRS. PRENTICE. He hasn't returned to the hotel. And when he disappeared his uniform was in my possession.

RANCE. (*Greatly concerned.*) Two young people—one mad and one sexually insatiable—both naked—are roaming this house. At all costs we must prevent a collision. Oh, this is incredible. When I publish it, I'll make my fortune. My "documentary type" novelette will go into twelve record-breaking reprints. I'll be able to leave the service of the government and bask in the attentions of those who, like myself, find other people's iniquity puts money in their purse. (DR. RANCE *picks up red pillbox from floor in front of couch.*) What's this? The pills I gave your husband? It's empty. He's taken an overdose! We have here terrible evidence of conflict. His tormented mind, seeking release, has led him to attempt to destroy himself.

MRS. PRENTICE. (*Gasps with shock and amazement.*) Suicide? This is so unexpected.

RANCE. Just when one least expects it, the unexpected always happens. We must find him before it's too late.

(*They both exit into the hall.* DR. PRENTICE *and* NICK *enter simultaneously from the dispensary and the garden.* DR. PRENTICE *carries the shoes and dress.* NICK *is wearing the* SERGEANT'S *uniform.*)

PRENTICE. Miss Barclay has escaped from the padded cell! (*A sound from behind the curtains. They part the curtains of the couch and* SERGEANT MATCH *tumbles forward drugged into insensibility.* DR. PRENTICE *and* NICK *react to the* SERGEANT'S *condition and catch him. They place him in a sitting position in a chair.* DR. PRENTICE *feels in his pocket and pulls out the square white pillbox. His eyes widen. He clutches his throat.*) My God! I've poisoned him! (DR. PRENTICE *puts the dress down and attempts to drag* SERGEANT MATCH *to his feet. The* SERGEANT *moans, stares about him in a stupor and shivers uncontrollably.*)

NICK. (*Holding the* SERGEANT'S *pulse.*) He's frozen, sir.

PRENTICE. The effect of the drug. We find the same process at work in corpses. He'll be all right if we get him in the open air so he can sleep it off.

NICK. Get some clothes on him and dump him outside. (*He picks up the dress.*)

PRENTICE. (*Wringing his hands.*) How will I explain the presence in my garden of the drugged police sergeant?

NICK. (*Putting the dress onto* SERGEANT MATCH.) You're guilty. You don't have to explain. Only the innocent do that.

PRENTICE. (*Puts* GERALDINE'S *shoes in his pants pockets. He and* NICK *carry* SERGEANT MATCH *to the garden in the chair.*) Oh, if this ever gets out I'll be reduced to casting horoscopes.

(MRS. PRENTICE *enters from the hall, followed immediately by* DR. RANCE. *They look at each other for an instant. She exits to the garden,* RANCE *to the wards. They both re-enter immediately.*)

MRS. PRENTICE. Dr. Rance, I've just seen my husband carrying a woman into the shrubbery.

RANCE. Was she struggling?

MRS. PRENTICE. No.

RANCE. Then a new and frightening possibility presents itself. The drugs in this box— (*He lifts up the bright red pillbox.*) —may not have been used for suicide, but for murder. Your husband has made away with his secretary!

MRS. PRENTICE. Isn't that a little melodramatic, Doctor?

RANCE. Lunatics *are* melodramatic. The subtleties of drama are wasted on them. Everything is now clear. The final chapters of my book are knitting together: incest, buggery, outrageous women and strange love-cults catering to depraved appetites. All the fashionable bric-a-brac. (*To* MRS. PRENTICE.) My "unbiased account" of the case of the infamous sex-killer Prentice will undoubtedly add a great deal to our understanding of such creatures. Society must be made aware of the growing menace of pornography. The whole treacherous avant-garde movement will be exposed for what it is—an instrument for inciting decent citizens to commit bizarre crimes against humanity and the state! (*He pauses, a little overcome, and wipes his brow.*) You have, under your roof, my dear, one of the most remarkable lunatics of all time. We must institute a search for the corpse. As a transvestite, fetishist, bisexual murderer. Dr. Prentice displays considerable deviation overlap. We may get necrophilia too. As a sort of bonus. (DR. PRENTICE *enters from the garden with an empty chair; replaces it by the desk. He still has the shoes in his pockets. Turning, and giving a disdainful stare:*) Would you confirm, Prentice, that your wife saw you carrying a body into the shrubbery?

PRENTICE. Yes. I have an explanation for my conduct.

RANCE. I'm not interested in your explanations. I can provide my own. Where is your secretary?

PRENTICE. I've given her the sack. (*Puts shoes on the desk.*)

RANCE. (*Aside to* MRS. PRENTICE.) He killed her and wrapped her body in a sack. The word association is very clear.

PRENTICE. I haven't killed anyone!

RANCE. Your answer is in accord with the complex structure of your neurosis.

PRENTICE. The person my wife saw wasn't dead. They were asleep.

RANCE. (*To* MRS. PRENTICE.) He hopes for a resurrection. We've a link here with primitive religion. (*To* DR. PRENTICE.) Why have you turned your back on the God of your fathers?

PRENTICE. I'm a rationalist.

RANCE. You can't be a rationalist in an irrational world. It isn't rational. (*Pointing to the shoes.*) Was it your intention to wear these shoes for auto-erotic excitement?

PRENTICE. No, I'm a perfectly normal man.

RANCE. (*To* MRS. PRENTICE.) His belief in normality is quite abnormal. (*To* DR. PRENTICE.) Was the girl killed before or after you took her clothes off?

PRENTICE. He wasn't a girl. He was a man.

MRS. PRENTICE. He was wearing a dress.

PRENTICE. He was a man for all that.

RANCE. Women wear dresses, Prentice, not men. I won't be a party to the wanton destruction of a fine old tradition. Did you change clothes with your victim before it died?

PRENTICE. Nobody died! The person you saw me with was a policeman who'd taken an overdose of narcotics.

MRS. PRENTICE. Why was he dressed as a woman?

PRENTICE. He was naked when I found him. The dress was readily to hand.

MRS. PRENTICE. Where were his own clothes?

PRENTICE. A boy had stolen them. (DR. RANCE *draws* MRS. PRENTICE *aside, his face a mask of disapproval.*)

RANCE. Mrs. Prentice, the time has come to call a halt to this Graeco-Roman hallucination. Is there a strait jacket in the house?

MRS. PRENTICE. Modern methods of treatment have rendered the strait jacket obsolete.

RANCE. I'm well aware of that. We still use them nonetheless. Have you one here?

MRS. PRENTICE. The porter has a few.

RANCE. We can take no chances with your husband in his present condition. Keep him occupied until I return. (*He goes.*)

PRENTICE. Is this another of your plots to undermine my reputation for sound judgment, you treacherous harpy?

MRS. PRENTICE. (*Gently.*) Dr. Rance believes that you've caused a poor girl's death, darling. You may be called upon to accept a period of restraint.

PRENTICE. Miss Barclay isn't dead!

MRS. PRENTICE. Produce her then and your difficulties will be over.

PRENTICE. I can't.

MRS. PRENTICE. Why not?

PRENTICE. You're wearing her dress. (*With a shrug of resignation.*) You surprised me this morning when I was attempting to seduce her.

MRS. PRENTICE. (*Smiles a smile of disbelief.*) If we're to save our marriage, my dear, you must admit that you prefer boys to women.

PRENTICE. (*Is stunned by her suggestion. He rounds on her in a fury.*) I won't have you making scandalous allegations about a matter of which you know nothing.

MRS. PRENTICE. (*Tossing her head.*) The page at the hotel accused you of behaving in an indecent manner.

PRENTICE. That wasn't a boy. It was a girl.

MRS. PRENTICE. Admit that you prefer your sex to mine. I've no hesitation in saying that I do.

PRENTICE. You filthy degenerate! Take your clothes off! (*He unzips her dress.*)

MRS. PRENTICE. (*Eagerly.*) Are you going to beat me? Do if you wish. Your psychotic experiences are immensely valuable to you and should be encouraged rather than thwarted or repressed. (*Gasping as he slaps her.*) Oh, my darling! This is the way to sexual adjustment in marriage. (RANCE *enters from the hall with two strait jackets, a witness to the final moment.* PRENTICE *picks up the dress, throws it over his arm; and with the shoes he exits proudly into the garden.*)

RANCE. What are you doing?

MRS. PRENTICE. Oh, Doctor, during your absence my husband became violent and struck me.

RANCE. Did you enjoy it?

MRS. PRENTICE. At first. But the pleasures of the senses quickly pall.

RANCE. We must lose no time in putting Dr. Prentice

under restraint. We'll need help in the enterprise. Have you no brawny youth upon whom you can call in time of stress?

MRS. PRENTICE. I'm a married woman, Doctor! Your suggestion is in the worst of taste.

(NICK *enters from the garden dressed in the* SERGEANT'S *uniform.*)

NICK. Doctor, I'd like a word with you about my brother, Nicholas Beckett. I've just arrested him.

RANCE. Why?

NICK. He'd broken the law.

RANCE. And because of that he's to be treated as a common criminal? What's happened to the Anglo-Saxon love of fair play? Did you see Dr. Prentice in the garden?

NICK. No.

RANCE. We must find him. We have reason to believe he has killed his secretary.

NICK. (*Horrified.*) He can't have. He's got the Order of the Garter.

RANCE. These cabalistic signs are of no more use in warding off evil than the moons and stars on a sorcerer's hat. We shall need your help in tracking down that mindless killer.

NICK. (*With a groan.*) Oh, Doctor, I'm sick of all this. I have to make a confession.

RANCE. You must call for an appointment. I can't listen to confessions off the cuff.

NICK. I am Nicholas Beckett. (*Takes off his helmet.*) I dressed as Geraldine Barclay at the doctor's request, never imagining that I was unwittingly assisting a psychopath. (*To* MRS. PRENTICE.) That's why I objected to being undressed. It would've embarrassed me.

RANCE. Have you aided other men in their perverted follies?

NICK. During my last term at school I was the slave of a corporal in the Army.

RANCE. Were you never warned of the dangers inherent in such relationships?

NICK. When he was sent overseas he left me a copy of "The Way to Healthy Manhood."

RANCE. (*Drily, to* MRS. PRENTICE.) A case of opening

the barn door after the horse is in. (*To* NICK. *He picks up the strait jacket.*) This is a strait jacket. I require your help in persuading Dr. Prentice to put it on. There may be violence. His body has a mind of its own. (*To* MRS. PRENTICE.) Have you any guns?

MRS. PRENTICE. Guns?

RANCE. (*Opens a drawer in the desk and takes out two guns.*) Oh, here. There are two. Take one.

MRS. PRENTICE. You will make sure before you fire that my husband isn't waving an olive branch?

RANCE. An olive branch can be used as an offensive weapon. I'm loath to certify a fellow psychiatrist. It causes such bad feelings within the profession. (*Goes into the garden.*)

MRS. PRENTICE. (*To* NICK.) Take no chances. Call for help the minute you see Dr. Prentice. (*Goes to the hall door, waving the gun. She goes into the hall.*)

(NICK *opens the strait jacket.* DR. PRENTICE *enters from the garden, carrying the dress taken from* MRS. PRENTICE.)

PRENTICE. Oh, there you are. Miss Barclay is nowhere to be found. Have you seen her? I want you to cooperate with me in getting things back to normal in this house.

MATCH. (*Enters from the garden swaying unsteadily.*) I'm ready to be examined when you are, Doctor. (*He stumbles into the wards. As he crosses,* PRENTICE *slaps his helmet on his head.*)

GERALDINE. (*Wearing* NICK'S *uniform, staggers in from the garden.*) They're combing the grounds for us, Doctor! They've got guns. What shall we do?

PRENTICE. It would help me considerably if you'd take your clothes off. You must lose no time in getting undressed. Both of you.

NICK. (*Pause.*) If I do that, sir, will you put this on? (*He holds up the jacket.*)

PRENTICE. (*Angry, losing patience.*) Of course not! That's a strait jacket. I won't be a party to kinky capers. You've lived too long at the Station Hotel to know how decent people behave. Now do as I say and undress!

GERALDINE. (*Tearful, beating him away.*) You're behaving like a maniac!

NICK. He is a maniac. He's murdered a woman and hidden her body somewhere.

PRENTICE. Who is responsible for these vile stories?

NICK. Dr. Rance is having you certified. (*Waving the jacket.*) I've got to get you into this! (*He leaps upon* DR. PRENTICE *and attempts to put him into the strait jacket.*)

MATCH. (*Enters from the wards—retreats immediately.*) I'm ready when you are, Doctor!

PRENTICE. (*To* NICK.) Put that down. Take your clothes off. Don't you know the penalty for impersonating a sergeant? Put on your own clothing. Give this youth that tunic and put on this dress and all our problems will be solved.

(NICK *takes off his uniform.* GERALDINE *pulls down her trousers.* NICK *is now naked except for his underpants.* GERALDINE *exits into wards.* MRS. PRENTICE *enters from the hall in her underwear, waving a gun. She advances on* DR. PRENTICE.)

MRS. PRENTICE. (*Waving gun at him.*) Come with me and lie down!

PRENTICE. The woman is insatiable.

MRS. PRENTICE. Unless you make love to me I shall shoot you.

PRENTICE. No husband can be expected to give his best at gun point. (*He backs away and exits into the garden. She shoots at him.*)

(*Hearing the shot,* NICK, *who has crouched behind the desk to hide from* MRS. PRENTICE, *runs into the hall. A SECOND SHOT.* GERALDINE *enters from the wards, sees* MRS. PRENTICE *and retreats back into the wards. THIRD SHOT.* MATCH *enters from wards, sees* MRS. PRENTICE *and exits running into the garden. FOURTH SHOT.* NICK *enters from the hall and exits running into the garden.* MRS. PRENTICE *follows after him, then re-enters immediately as* DR. RANCE *enters from the hall.*)

MRS. PRENTICE. Doctor Rance! Doctor Rance! The world is full of naked men running in all directions!

RANCE. When did these delusions start?

MRS. PRENTICE. Just now.

RANCE. It's not difficult to guess what's on your mind, my dear. Are you having marital troubles?

MRS. PRENTICE. Well, yes. My husband refuses to prescribe anything.

RANCE. A man shouldn't have to drug his wife to achieve a happy union.

MRS. PRENTICE. I don't want drugs. I want account taken of my sexual nature.

RANCE. Where do you keep your tranquilizers? (GERALDINE *runs out from the wards. She has taken off the uniform and wears her own panties and bra.*) At last we've caught the patient! Get the strait jacket! (*Takes one from the chair.*)

GERALDINE. I'm not a patient. I'm telling the truth!

RANCE. It's much too late to tell the truth. (*Ties* GERALDINE *down.*) These final harrowing scenes will be lavishly illustrated with graphs showing the effect of her downfall upon her poor tortured mind. Meanwhile, in his temple of love, the hideous Dr. Prentice and his acolyte are praying to their false gods, unaware that the forces of reason have got their measure. (MRS. PRENTICE *steps back.*) Fetch a syringe. (MRS. PRENTICE *goes into the wards.*)

GERALDINE. (*Trussed up, unable to move.*) What have I done to deserve this? I've always led such a respectable life.

RANCE. Where is the body?

GERALDINE. I don't know.

RANCE. Are you under the seal of the confessional? What black rites were you initiated into by that foul priest of the Unknown? (GERALDINE *sobs, unable to speak.* DR. RANCE *abruptly throws himself on to her and holds her in his arms.*) Let me cure your neurosis! It's the only thing I want out of life.

(MRS. PRENTICE *enters from the dispensary, carrying a hypodermic syringe and bowl.*)

MRS. PRENTICE. What is the meaning of this exhibition?

RANCE. (*Breaking away from* GERALDINE.) It's a new and hitherto untried type of therapy. I think it's viable under the circumstances.

MRS. PRENTICE. Your treatment seems designed to

plunge the patient deeper into lunacy rather than achieve any lasting cure.

RANCE. Someone whose unconscious is as quirky as your own could hardly be expected to understand my methods.

MRS. PRENTICE. What do you mean by that?

RANCE. I'm referring to those naked men you encounter with an increasing degree of frequency.

MRS. PRENTICE. You've seen them too.

RANCE. What does that prove? Merely that you've given me your wretched disease. Give me that! (*He takes the hypodermic from her.*)

MRS. PRENTICE. Shouldn't I swab the patient's arm?

RANCE. You don't imagine I'm wasting this stuff on her, do you? (*He rolls back his sleeve.*) For what it costs an ounce, it would be criminal. (*He gives himself an injection.*) Go and call the police. (*Puts the hypodermic aside.*)

MRS. PRENTICE. There's a policeman outside, naked in the center of the garden.

RANCE. If he is, indeed, naked, how do you dare to presume he is a policeman?

MRS. PRENTICE. He's wearing his helmet.

RANCE. The bounds of decency have long been overstepped in this house. Your subconscious cannot be encouraged in its skulduggery. Remain where you are. I'll call the police. (RANCE *exits to wards.*)

(NICK *appears from the garden.*)

MRS. PRENTICE. Oh, I'm losing my mind!

GERALDINE. (*Calls to* NICK.) Help me!

NICK. Why are you tied up?

GERALDINE. Dr. Rance did it. He says I'm mad.

NICK. He's a psychiatrist, he must know. He wouldn't put you in a strait jacket if you were sane. He'd have to be mad.

GERALDINE. He is mad!

NICK. (*To* GERALDINE.) Is she mad?

GERALDINE. She thinks she is. She imagines you're a figment of her imagination.

NICK. (*To* MRS. PRENTICE, *nodding to* GERALDINE.)

Mrs. Prentice, she can see me. Doesn't that prove I'm real?

MRS. PRENTICE. No. She's mad.

NICK. If you think I'm a phantom of your subconscious you must be mad. Why were you chasing me with a gun? Do you think I'm mad?

MRS. PRENTICE. (*With a hysterical giggle.*) I am mad! (DR. RANCE *enters.* NICK *grabs her gun.*)

PRENTICE. (*Entering from the garden as* DR. RANCE *is putting* MRS. PRENTICE *into a strait jacket.*) Are you all mad? Stop! A husband must be allowed to put his own wife into a strait jacket. It's one of the few pleasures left in modern marriage. (*Grabs gun from* NICK.) Stand away! Doctor Rance! Your conduct today has been a model of official irresponsibility and I'm going to certify you.

RANCE. (*Quietly, with dignity.*) No. I am going to certify you.

PRENTICE. I have the weapon. You have the choice. What is it to be? Madness or death, neither of which would enable you to continue to be employed by the Government.

RANCE. That isn't true. The higher reaches of the civil service are recruited entirely from corpses or madmen. Your deterrent is useless. Put it down. (DR. RANCE *takes out his own gun and points it at the astonished* DR. PRENTICE. *Holding* DR. PRENTICE *at bay with the gun.*) I'll have you in a jacket within the hour.

PRENTICE. Is that a record for you?

RANCE. By no means. I once put a whole family into a communal strait jacket.

PRENTICE. How proud your mother must've been.

RANCE. She wasn't, I'm afraid. It was my own family, you see. I've a snapshot of the scene at home. My foot placed squarely upon my father's head. I sent it to Sigmund Freud and had a charming postcard in reply.

(SERGEANT MATCH *enters from the garden.*)

MATCH. (*To* RANCE.) I'm still ready to be examined, Doctor.

RANCE. (*To* PRENTICE, *in a firm voice.*) What have you done with Geraldine Barclay?

GERALDINE. (*Feebly.*) I'm here.

MATCH. (*To* GERALDINE, *with all the dignity he can muster.*) Will you kindly produce, or cause to be produced, the missing part of Sir Winston Churchill?

PRENTICE. Stop! All of you! (*Grabs gun from* RANCE.) We are now approaching what our racier novelists term the climax. Release my wife and the young woman, too. The story you're about to hear is concerned solely with the heart: the mind and its mysteries could not have been further from my thoughts when, early this morning, in what must be the most ill-timed attempt at seduction ever, I persuaded that young woman to take her clothes off.

GERALDINE. (*To* DR. RANCE.) Mrs. Prentice mistook my dress for her own and, by an oversight, you mistook me for a patient. Dr. Prentice asked me to keep quiet in order to protect his good name. What could I do? I was terrified of exposure.

MRS. PRENTICE. You were naked at the time?

GERALDINE. Yes. Under duress I agreed to help the doctor. I've never ceased reproaching myself. The whole day has been spent fighting to retain my self-respect.

PRENTICE. Oh, if I live to be ninety, I'll never again attempt sexual intercourse.

RANCE. I'd be willing to stake my professional reputation upon the fact that this girl has been the victim of an incestuous attack. I won't go back upon my diagnosis. My publishers will sue me for loss of royalties.

GERALDINE. (*Stepping from the couch.*) I'm sure my shorthand speed has been affected by what I've suffered today. (*Tearful, to* DR. PRENTICE.) And I wish to report the loss of my lucky elephant charm.

RANCE. (*Takes a brooch from his pocket.*) Is this the piece of jewelry to which you refer? I removed it from your neck when I cut your hair.

GERALDINE. Yes. It has great sentimental value. (DR. RANCE *passes brooch to* MRS. PRENTICE *who gives it to* GERALDINE.)

NICK. Look. I've got one like that. (*Shows* GERALDINE *a brooch.*)

MRS. PRENTICE. A single brooch can be made of these two fragments. Oh, my heart is beating like a wild thing!

(DR. RANCE *examines the brooch.*)

NICK and GERALDINE. It's true!

MATCH. Two elephants carrying a richly engraved howdah in which is seated a young and beautiful woman—perhaps a princess of the royal line—magnificent example of oriental craftsmanship. (*To* MRS. PRENTICE.) How did you know this was a single piece?

MRS. PRENTICE. It belonged to me once. Many years ago, when I was a young woman, I was raped in a linen closet on the second floor of the Station Hotel. As the man left me he pressed that brooch into my hands in part payment.

MATCH. How did these children come to be in possession of the separate halves?

MRS. PRENTICE. I paid for my misdemeanor by conceiving twins. It was impossible for me to keep them—I was by then engaged to be married to a promising young psychiatrist. I decided to abandon them to their fate. I broke the brooch in half and pinned a separate piece to each babe. I then placed them at either end of the small country town in which I was resident. Some kind people must've brought the children up as their own. (*Hugging* NICK *and* GERALDINE.) Oh, children! I am your mother! Can you ever forgive me for what I did?

NICK. What kind of mother must you have been to stay alone at the Station Hotel?

MRS. PRENTICE. I was employed as a chambermaid. I did it for a joke shortly after the war. The effect of a Labour Government on the middle classes had to be seen to be believed.

GERALDINE. Was our father also employed by the Station Hotel?

MRS. PRENTICE. I never saw your father. The incident occurred during a power failure. I became pregnant as I waited for normal services to be resumed.

PRENTICE. You'll find an inscription on the back of the brooch, sir—"To Lillian from Avis. Christmas 1939." I found that brooch many years ago. It was on the pavement outside a large department store.

RANCE. Who were Lillian and Avis?

PRENTICE. I've no idea. It fell from the collar of a Pekinese. Lillian and Avis may have been the creature's owners. (*He stares about him in shame.*) I haven't seen it since I pressed it into the hand of a chambermaid whom I debauched shortly before my marriage.

MRS. PRENTICE. (*With a cry of recognition.*) I understand now why you suggested that we spend our wedding night in a linen closet!

PRENTICE. I wished to recreate a moment that was very precious to me. My darling, we have been instrumental in uncovering a number of remarkable peccadilloes today.

RANCE. (*To* PRENTICE, *with wild delight.*) If you are this child's father my book can be written in good faith—she *is* the victim of an incestuous attack!

MRS. PRENTICE. And so am I, Doctor! My son has a collection of photographs which prove beyond doubt that he attempted to seduce me in the same hotel—indeed in the same linen closet where his conception took place.

RANCE. Double incest is even more likely to produce a best-seller than murder—and this is as it should be for love must bring greater joy than violence.

DR. PRENTICE. Come, let us put on our clothes and face the world. (*They all turn to the audience and bow crisply and formally.*)

(*Blackout.*)

CURTAIN

The Changing Room

A PLAY

by David Storey

The Changing Room was performed at the Royal Court Theatre, London, on November 9, 1971, under the direction of Lindsay Anderson, with the following cast:

SPENCER	*Alun Armstrong*
HARRY	*John Barrett*
FENCHURCH	*Peter Childs*
KENDAL	*Warren Clarke*
FIELDING	*David Daker*
THORNTON	*Paul Dawkins*
TREVOR	*Michael Elphick*
SANDFORD	*Brian Glover*
CLEGG	*Matthew Guiness*
STRINGER	*David Hall*
COPLEY	*Geoffrey Hinsliff*
WALSH	*Edward Judd*
CROSBY	*Barry Keegan*
TALLON	*Brian Lawson*
JAGGER	*Mark McManus*
LUKE	*Don McKillop*
OWENS	*Frank Mills*
PATSY	*Jim Norton*
MORLEY	*Edward Peel*
MOORE	*John Price*
MACKENDRICK	*John Rae*
ATKINSON	*Peter Schofield*

Scenery and costumes by Jocelyn Herbert.

The Changing Room was performed at the Morosco Theatre, New York, on March 6, 1973, under the direction of Michael Rudman, with the following cast:

HARRY RILEY, the Cleaner	*Louis Beachner*
PATRICK "PATSY" WALTER TURNER, No. 2, Wing	*Doug Stender*

FIELDING, No. 10, Forward ....*Rex Robbins*

"MIC" MORLEY, No. 13, Forward ....*Jack Schultz*

"KENNY" KENDAL, No. 12, Forward ......*John Lithgow*

LUKE, the Masseur .... *Jake Dengel*

"FENNY" GORDON FENCHURCH, ...*William Rhys*
  No. 5, Wing

COLIN JAGGER, No. 3, Centre ....*John Tillinger*

TREVOR, No. 1, Full-back ....*George Hearn*

WALSH, No. 8, Forward ....*Tom Atkins*

"SANDY" SANDFORD, ...*John Braden*
  The Assistant Trainer

BARRY COPLEY, No. 7, Scrum-half........*James Sutorius*

JACK STRINGER, No. 3, Centre .... *Richard D. Masur*

BRYAN ATKINSON, No. 11, Forward ....*James Hummert*

BILLY SPENCER, No. 15, Reserve ....*Mark Winkworth*

JOHN CLEGG, No. 9, Hooker....................*Ron Siebert*

FRANK MOORE, No. 14, Reserve............. *Alan Castner*

CLIFFORD OWENS, ...*Robert Murch*
  No. 6, Team Captain

DANNY CROSBY, the Trainer ....*George Ede*

TALLON, the Referee ....*Peter DeMaio*

SIR FREDERICK THORNTON,...............*William Swetland*
  the Club Owner

MACKENDRICK, the Club Secretary............. *Ian Martin*

MATCH ANNOUNCER.......................................*Emery Battis*

Produced by Charles Bowden, Lee Reynolds, Isobel Robins; set by David Jenkins; costumes by Whitney Blausen; lighting by Ronald Wallace, and the production coordinator was Diana Shumlin.

The play is set in the changing room of a Rugby League Team in the North of England. The play is in three acts, with two intermissions.

SOME BACKGROUND INFORMATION

1. A "try" is a score equivalent in importance to a touchdown.
2. "Laking" means playing, so these men "lake football."
3. The "pitch" is the playing field.
4. The football they lake is Rugby League, a very tough, professional, tackling, running and kicking

game played mainly in Yorkshire and Lancashire in which they wear little or no padding.

5. The teams are generally owned by a wealthy man. The salaries are about $40 a week and in most cases are, for the players, a supplement to their regular wage in another job. They usually work during the week in the mines or textile mills, though a few are teachers.

6. The conditions of their play are roughly analagous to what used to be called "semi-pro" baseball and football in the United States. There are some teams now in the States called "minor league" football teams who play under similar conditions.

7. Another apt comparison is professional boxing in that the men who play are, for the most part, trying to elevate themselves both socially and economically from the edges of poverty.

8. Unlike Rugby Union, an amateur sport, this is a working class game played for a dwindling working class audience.

9. The forwards (Fielding, Walsh, Morley, Clegg, Atkinson, Kendal) take the most punishment and generally are large and sometimes older men.

10. The backs (Fenchurch, Patsy, Jagger, Copley, Trevor, and Owens) are smaller, faster men, give and take less punishment, and though there are few stars in this game, tend to take most of the credit.

11. The Captain, Owens, because it is a free-flowing game with very little stopping, has a greater responsibility for command than his American counterpart and in many cases is more respected by the players than the coach (or "trainer") Crosby.

12. It is a very rough game, full of fouling and physical exhaustion.

13. A "scrum" is a kind of cross between what happens on the line of scrimmage in American football and toss-up in basketball.

ACT I

A changing room; afternoon. The light comes from glazed panels high in the wall and from an electric light. Across the back of the stage is the main changing bench, set up against the wall and running its entire length. A set of hooks, one for each player, is fastened at head-height to the wall, with the name of a player above each hook. Underneath the bench, below each hook, is a locker, also labelled. A jersey and a pair of shorts have been set out beneath one of the hooks. A rubbing-down table with an adjustable head-rest stands in front of the bench. S. R. a glazed door opens to an entrance porch; downstage L. is a stove, with a bucket of coal, overhung by a mirror advertising ale. Upstage L. is the open entry to the bath and showers; buckets, stool, hose and tap, etc. Downstage R. is a wooden door, closed, leading to the offices. A second table stands against the wall. There's a pair of metal scales with individual metal weights on a metal arm. By the rubbing-down table stands a large wicker-work basket. A wooden chair with a rounded back is set against the wall, S. L. Tanoy music is being played, light, militaristic. HARRY enters from the bath. He's a broken-down man, small, stooped, in shirt-sleeves, rolled, and a sleeveless pullover. He's smoking and carries a sweeping brush, on the look-out for anything he might have missed. He sweeps: looks round the floor: sweeps, finally lifts corner of the boxed-in rubbing-down table and sweeps the debris underneath. Takes out his cigarette, looks round, finds nowhere to drop it, then crosses to the fire, drops it in, sets the brush against the wall, puts coal from the bucket on the fire, warms his hands, shivers. PATSY enters from the porch. He's a smart, lightly-built man, very well groomed, hair greased, collar of an expensive overcoat turned up; brisk, businesslike, narcissistic, no evident sense of humour.

PATSY. Harry . . .
HARRY. Patsy . . .

PATSY. Cold.

HARRY. Bloody freezing, lad. (*Rubs his hands, reaches to the fire again.* PATSY, *evidently familiar with his routine, goes to his locker, gets out his boots, unfolds his jersey and shorts already lying on the bench.*)

PATSY. No towel.

HARRY. No. No. Just fetching those ... (HARRY *takes his brush and exits through bath entrance.* PATSY, *having checked his jersey, examined its number (2), collar, etc.— no marks—does the same with his boots—laces, studs, lining. He then crosses to the fire, takes out a comb from an inside pocket and smoothes his hair down in the mirror. He's doing this as* HARRY *re-enters carrying several neatly-folded towels. He puts one on the bench by* PATSY'S *peg, then goes to the wicker-work basket, lifts the lid and gets out several more towels. Having checked them, counting soundlessly to himself, he puts them all in the basket, save three which he begins to arrange on the massage table.* PATSY, *having combed his hair and admired himself in the mirror, clears his nose and spits in the fire.* HARRY, *laying out towels.*) Thought it'd be snowed off.

PATSY. Snow?

HARRY. Bloody forecast.

PATSY. Not cancel ought in this dump, I can tell you .. Shoulder ... I've no skin on from here to here. There's not a blade o' grass on that bloody pitch ... sithee ... look at that ... (*Pulls up his sleeve:* HARRY *looks across with no evident interest.*)

HARRY. Aye.

PATSY. Watered t'bloody pitch we 'ad last week. Froze over ten minutes after. Took a run at t'bloody ball ... took off ... must have travelled twenty bloody yards without having lift a finger.

HARRY. Aye.

PATSY. Ice. (HARRY *is laying out the rest of the jerseys now, and shorts.*) Be better off with a pair of skates. (*Glances behind him, into the mirror: smoothes hair.*) If there's a young woman comes asking for me afterwards, will you tell her to wait up in the office? Be frozen to death out there.

HARRY. Aye ...

PATSY. By Christ ... (*Rubs his hands, standing with his back to the fire.*)

HARRY. Comes from Russia.

PATSY. What?

HARRY. Cold . . . Comes fro' Russia . . .

PATSY. Oh . . . (*Nods.*)

HARRY. Read a book . . . they had a special machine . . . blew these winds o'er, you see . . . specially freezing . . . mixed it with a chemical . . . frozen ought . . . Froze the entire country . . . Then Ireland . . . Then crossed over to America and froze it out . . . Then, when everything wa' frozen, they came o'er in special boots and took over . . . Here . . . America . . . Nobody twigged it. Nobody cottoned on, you see.

PATSY. Oh . . . (*Glances at himself in mirror again.*) You think that's what's happening now, then?

HARRY. Cold enough . . . Get no warning . . . Afore you know what's happening . . . Ruskies here.

PATSY. Couldn't be worse than this lot.

HARRY. What?

PATSY. Stopped ten quid i' bloody tax last week . . . I tell you . . . I'm paying t'government to keep me i' bloody work . . madhouse . . . If I had my time o'er again I'd emigrate . . . America . . . Australia . . .

HARRY. Wherever you go they'll find you out.

PATSY. What?

HARRY. Ruskies . . . Keep your name down in a bloody book . . . (*Looks across.*) Won't make any difference if you've voted socialist. Have you down there . . . up against a wall . . .

PATSY. Thy wants to read one or two bloody facts, old lad.

HARRY. Facts? What facts? . . . I read in one paper that in twenty-five years not one country on earth'll not be communist . . . (PATSY *crosses back to his peg and starts taking off his overcoat.*) Don't worry. There'll be no lakin' bloody football then.

PATSY. They play football i' Russia as much as they play it here.

HARRY. Aye . . . (*Waits, threatening:* PATSY *doesn't answer, preoccupied with his overcoat.*) You: football . . . You: coalmine . . . You: factory . . . You: airforce . . . You: . . . *Siberia.*

PATSY. Haven't you got a bloody coat-hanger? Damn-well ask for one each week.

HARRY. Aye. Don't worry . . . (*Starts to go.*) Not bloody listen until they find it's bloody well too late. (*Goes off to the bath-entrance, disgruntled.* FIELDING *enters, a large, well-built man, slow, easy-going, 35-6. He's dressed in an overcoat and muffler; he has a strip of plaster above his left eye.*)

FIELDING. Patsy.

PATSY. Fieldy . . .

FIELDING. Freeze your knuckles off today. (*Blows in hands, goes over to the fire, stoops, warms hands.*) By Christ . . . (PATSY *is holding up his coat in one hand, dusting it down lightly, paying no attention to* FIELDING'S *entrance.* HARRY *comes back in with wooden coathanger.*)

HARRY. Have no bloody servants theer, you know.

PATSY. What's that? (*Examining coat.*)

HARRY. No servants. Do your own bloody carrying theer. (*Gives* PATSY *the hanger and goes back to laying out the playing kit.*)

FIELDING. What's that, Harry? (*Winks to* PATSY.)

PATSY. Bloody Russians. Going to be invaded.

HARRY. Don't you worry. It can happen any time, you know.

PATSY. Going to freeze us, with a special liquid . . . Then come over . . . (*To* HARRY.) What wa're it? . . . i' special boots.

HARRY. It all goes back, you know.

PATSY. Back?

HARRY. To bloody Moscow . . . Ought you say here's reported back . . . Keep all thy names in a special book.

FIELDING. Keep thy name in a special bloody book . . . Riley . . . first name, Harry . . . special qualifications, can talk out of the back of his bloody head.

HARRY. Don't you worry.

FIELDING. Nay, I'm not worried. They can come here any day of the bloody week for me. Sup of ale . . .

PATSY. Ten fags . . .

FIELDING. That's all I need. (FIELDING *sneezes hugely: shakes his head, gets out his handkerchief, blows his nose, lengthily and noisily. After gazing at* FIELDING, *threatening,* HARRY *turns off the tanoy.*) I thought o' ringing up this morning . . . Looked out o' the bloody winder. Frost . . . (*Crosses over to* PATSY.) Got this house, now, just

outside the town . . . wife's idea, not mine . . . bloody
fields . . . hardly a bloody sign of human life . . cows
. . . half a dozen sheep . . . goats . . . (*Starts peeling
the plaster from above his eye:* PATSY *pays no attention,
arranging his coat on the hanger and picking off one or
two bits.*) Middle of bloody nowhere . . . if I can't see a
wall outside on t'window I don't feel as though I'm living
in a house . . . How's it look?

PATSY. (*Glances up, briefly.*) All right.

FIELDING. Bloody fist. Lose forra'd . . . Copped him
one afore the end. Had a leg like a bloody melon . . .
Get Lukey to put on a bit of grease . . . (*Feeling the
cut.*) Should be all right. How's your shoulder?

PATSY. All right. (*Eases it.*) Came in early. Get it
strapped.

FIELDING. Where we lived afore, you know, everything you could bloody want; pit, boozer, bloody dogs.
As for now . . . trees, hedges, miles o' bloody grass . . .
where's the jock-straps, Harry? (*Inspecting his kit which
HARRY has now hung up.*) I thought of ringing up and
backing out. Flu . . . Some such like. (*Sneezes.*) By God
. . . He'll have me lakin' here, will Harry, wi' me bloody
cobblers hanging out. (MORLEY *has now entered from the
porch; thick-set, squat figure, dark-haired. Wears a jacket,
unbuttoned, with a sweater underneath; hard, rough, un-
complicated figure.*) Nah, Morley, lad, then, how's thy
keeping?

MORLEY. Shan't be a second . . . Just 'od on. (*Goes
straight over to the bath-entrance, unbuttoning his flies.
He's followed in by* KENDAL; *a tall, rather well-built man,
late twenties, wearing an old overcoat with a scarf and
carrying a paper parcel; a worn, somewhat faded man.
HARRY has gone to the basket and is now getting out a
pile of jockstraps which he lays on the table.*)

KENDAL. (*To* HARRY.) Here . . . see about my boots?
Bloody stud missing last Thursday . . . (*To* FIELDING.)
Suppose to check them every bloody week. Come up to
training and nearly bust me bloody ankle. God Christ,
they don't give a sod about bloody ought up here . . .
Patsy . . .

PATSY. Kenny . . . (*Having hung up his coat starts taking off his jacket.*)

KENDAL (*To* FIELDING.) Bought one of these electric tool-sets . . .

FIELDING. (*To* PATSY.) Tool-sets . . . (PATSY *nods.*) Got all the tools that I need, Kenny.

KENDAL. Bloody saw . . . drill, bloody polisher. Just look.

FIELDING. What do you do with that? (*Picks out a tool.*)

KENDAL. Dunno.

PATSY. Take stones out of hosses' hoofs, more like. (*They laugh.* MORLEY *comes back in.*)

FIELDING. Dirty bugger. Pisses i' the bloody bath.

MORLEY. Been in that bog, then have you? (*To* HARRY.) You want to clean it out.

HARRY. That lavatory was new this season . . . (*Indicating* FIELDING.) He'll tell you; one we had afore I wouldn't have used. (MORLEY *goes straight to the business of getting changed; coat off, sweater, then shoes and socks; then starts examining his ankle.*)

FIELDING. Harry doesn't use a lavatory, do you?

MORLEY. Piles it up behind the bloody posts.

FIELDING. Dirty bugger.

HARRY. Don't worry. It all goes down.

MORLEY. Goes down? (*They laugh.*) Goes down where, then, lad?

PATSY. He's reporting it back, tha' knows, to Moscow.

MORLEY. Moscow? Moscow?

HARRY. Somebody does, don't you bloody worry. Everything they hear.

FIELDING. Nay, Harry, lad. Thy should have warned us. (*Puts his arm round* HARRY'S *shoulder.*)

HARRY. Don't worry. You carry on. (*Breaks away from* FIELDING'S *embrace.*) You'll be laughing t'other side of your bloody face. (*Exits.*)

FIELDING. (*Holding jersey up.*) Given me number three, an' all. I'll be all right jumping up and down i' middle o' yon bloody backs.

KENDAL. By God. (*Rubbing his hands at the fire.*) I wouldn't mind being on the bloody bench today. (*Pause.* LUKE *comes in: wearing a track-suit and baseball shoes and carrying a large hold-all, plus a large tin of vaseline; sets them down by the massage-table. A small, middle-aged man, perky, brisk, grey-haired.*)

FIELDING. Nah, Lukey, lad. Got a drop o' rum in theer, then, have you?

LUKE. Aye. Could do with it today.

MORLEY. Lukey . . .

KENDAL. Lukey . . .

LUKE. Who's first on, then? (*Indicating the table.*) By Christ . . . (*Rubs his hands.*)

PATSY. My bloody shoulder . . .

LUKE. Aye. Right, then. Let's have a look. (*Rummaging in his bag, gets out crepe bandage.* PATSY *is stripped to his shirt by now; takes it off, hangs it and comes over in his vest and trousers; sits on the edge of the table for* LUKE *to strap it up.*)

MORLEY. Bloody ankle, Lukey . . .

LUKE. Aye. All right.

FIELDING. (*Examining* PATSY'S *shoulder.*) By God, there's nowt theer, lad. Which shoulder wa're it?

MORLEY. Sprained it.

FIELDING. Sprained it.

MORLEY. Twisted it i' bed. (*They laugh.* PATSY *pays no attention; holds his elbow as if one shoulder gives him great pain.* HARRY *comes back in with remaining jerseys.*)

LUKE. Right, then, lad. Let's have it off. (*Having got out all his equipment, helps* PATSY *off with his vest.*)

KENDAL (*To* MORLEY.) Look at that, then, eh? (*Shows him his tool-kit.*) Sand-paper . . . polisher . . . circular saw . . .

FIELDING. (*Stripping.*) What're you going to mek with that, then, Kenny?

KENDAL. Dunno . . . shelves.

MORLEY. What for?

KENDAL. Books.

FIELDING. (*Laughs.*) Thy's never read a bleeding book.

KENDAL. The wife reads . . . (MORLEY *laughs.*) Got three or four at home. Cupboards . . . Any amount o' things . . . Pantry door. Fitments . . .

FIELDING. Fitments. (*They laugh; look over at* KENDAL; *he re-examines the tools inside the parcel.*)

MORLEY. T'only bloody fitment thy needs, Kenny . . . Nay, lad, they weern't find wrapped up inside that box. (*They laugh;* FIELDING *sneezes.* KENDAL *begins to pack up his parcel.* HARRY *has gone out, having set the re-*

maining jerseys. The door from the porch opens; FEN-
CHURCH, JAGGER *and* TREVOR *come in.* FENCHURCH *is
a neatly groomed man, small, almost dainty; wears a suit
beneath a belted raincoat. He carries a small holdall in
which he keeps his boots; self-contained, perhaps even at
times a vicious man.* JAGGER *is of medium height, but
sturdy. He wears an overcoat, with an upturned collar,
and carries a newspaper; perky, rather officious, cocky.*
TREVOR *is a studious-looking man; wears glasses, is fairly
sturdily built; quiet, level-headed; a schoolmaster.*)

FIELDING. Fenny.

MORLEY. Fenchurch.

FENCHURCH. Na' lad.

MORLEY. Jagger.

JAGGER. Come up in old Fenny's bleeding car . . . (*To*
LUKE.) By God; nearly needed thee there, Lukey . . .
Blind as a bloody bat is yon . . Old feller crossing the
bleedin' road; tips him up the arse with his bloody
bumper.

FENCHURCH. He started coming backwards. In't that
right, then, Trevor?

TREVOR. Aye. He seemed to.

LUKE. Did he get your name?

JAGGER. Old Fenny gets out of the bleedin' car . . .
how much did you give him?

FENCHURCH. A bloody fiver.

TREVOR. A ten bob note.

JAGGER. The bloody miser . . .

TREVOR. Bends down, tha knows . . .

JAGGER. He picks him up . . .

TREVOR. Dusts down his coat . . .

JAGGER. Asks him how he was . . . Is that right?
That's all you gave him?

FENCHURCH. Gone to his bloody head if I'd have given
him any more. (*They laugh.*)

TREVOR. You told him who you were, though, Fen.
(*Instructional.*)

JAGGER. Offers him his bloody autograph. (*They
laugh.*)

MORLEY. I went up to Fenny's one bloody night . . .
He said, 'I won't give you my address . . . just mention
my name to anyone you see . . .' Stopped a bobby at the
end of his bloody road; 'Could you tell me where Gordon

Fenchurch lives? Plays on the wing for the bloody City?'
'*Who?*' 'Fenchurch.' 'Fenchurch? Never heard of him.'
(*They laugh.* FENCHURCH, *taking no notice of this, has
merely got out his boots and begun to examine them.*
HARRY *has come in with boots.*)

JAGGER. Ay up, ay up. Ay up. He's here. Look what
the bloody ragman's brought. (WALSH *comes in; a large,
somewhat commanding figure. He wears a dark suit with
a large carnation in the button-hole. He enters from the
offices, pausing in the door. He's smoking a cigar. His
age, 35-40. Stout, fairly weather-beaten. There are cries
and mocking shouts at his appearance: 'Ay up, ay up,
Walshy,' 'What's this?'*)

WALSH. And er . . . who are all these bloody lay-
abouts in here?

FIELDING. The bloody workers, lad. Don't you worry.

WALSH. I hope the floor's been swept then, Harry . . .
Keep them bloody microbes off my chair . . . (*Comes
in.*) Toe-caps polished with *equal* brightness, Harry . . .
(*To* JAGGER.) I hate to find one toe-cap brighter than
the next.

JAGGER. White laces.

WALSH. White laces. (HARRY *has set the boots down;
goes out.*)

MORLEY. Where you been, then, Walshy?

WALSH. Been?

FIELDING. Been up in the bloody offices, have you?
(*Gestures overhead.*)

WALSH. . . . Popped up. Saw the managing director.
Enquired about the pitch . . . Asked him if they could
heat it up . . . thaw out one or two little bumps I noticed.
Sir Frederick's going round now with a box of matches
. . . applying a drop of heat in all the appropriate places
. . . Should be nice and soft by the time you run out
there.

FIELDING. Thy's not coming with us, then?

WALSH. Nay, not for bloody me to tell . . .

MORLEY. It's up to more important folk than Walsh . . .

WALSH. Not more important . . . more influential . . .
(*Watching* TREVOR.) Saw you last week with one of
your classes, Trev . . . where wa're it, now, then. Let
me think . . .

TREVOR. Don't know.

WALSH. Quite close to the Municipal Park . . . (*Winks to* JAGGER.) By God, some of the girls in that bloody school . . . how old are they, Trev?

TREVOR. Fourteen.

WALSH. Fourteen. Could have fooled me, old lad. Could have bloody well fooled me entirely. Old Trevor: guides them over the road, you know . . . *by hand*.

FENCHURCH. Where have you been, then, Walshy?

WALSH. (*Conscious of his carnation quite suddenly, then cigar.*) Wedding.

JAGGER. A wedding.

WALSH. Not mine . . . Sister-in-law's as a matter of fact.

TREVOR. Sister-in-law?

WALSH. Married to me brother. Just got married a second time. Poor lass . . . Had to come away. Just got going . . . T'other bloody team's arrived . . .

JAGGER. Seen the bus? (*Gestures size, etc.*)

WALSH. Ran over me bloody foot as near as not . . . 'Be thy bloody head next, Walsh' . . . Said it from the bloody window! . . . Said, 'Bloody well get out theer and tell me then' . . . gesturing at the field behind. (*They laugh.*) Load o' bloody pansies. Tell it a glance . . . Off back there, as a matter of fact. Going to give a dance . . . Thy's invited, Jagger, lad. Kitted out . . . Anybody else fancy a dance tonight? Champagne . . . (*Belches; holds stomach.*) I'll be bloody ill if I drink owt else . . .

LUKE. Thy doesn't want to let old Sandford hear you.

WALSH. Sandford. Sandford . . . Drop me from this team, old lad . . . I'd gi'e him half o' what I earned.

LUKE. One week's dropped wages and he's round here in a bloody flash.

WALSH. There was some skirt at that bloody wedding, Jagger . . . (*To* TREVOR.) Steam thy bloody glasses up, old lad.

JAGGER. You're forgetting now . . . Trevor here's already married.

WALSH. She coming to watch, then, Trev, old lad?

TREVOR. Don't think so. No.

WALSH. Never comes to watch. His wife . . . A university degree . . . what wa're it in?

TREVOR. Economics.

WALSH. Economics . . . (*To* FENCHURCH.) How do

you fancy being wed to that, Fenchurch? (FENCHURCH *goes off through bath-entrance.*)

JAGGER. Wouldn't mind being married to bloody ought, wouldn't Fenny.

FIELDING. Tarts; should see the bloody ones he has. (WALSH *has warmed his hands, rubbing.*)

WALSH. Kenny; how's thy wife keeping, then, old lad?

KENDAL. All right.

WALSH. (*Looking in the parcel.*) Bought her a do-it-yourself kit, have you?

KENDAL. Bought it for meself.

MORLEY. Going to put up one or two shelves and cupboards . . . and what was that, now?

FIELDING. Fitments.

MORLEY. Fitments.

WALSH. By Christ; you want to be careful theer, old lad . . . Ask old Jagger. He's very keen on fitments.

LUKE. Come on, Walsh. You'll be bloody well still talking there when it's time to be going out . . . Morley: let's have a bloody look, old lad. (HARRY *has come in with last boots.* LUKE *has strapped up* PATSY'S *shoulder.* PATSY *goes back to finish changing, easing his shoulder.* MORLEY *comes over to the bench; sits down on it, half-lying, his legs stretched out.* LUKE *examines his ankle; massages with oil; starts to strap it.* WALSH *boxes with* JAGGER *then goes over to his peg.*)

WALSH. How's thy fitments, Jagger? Sithee, Harry; I hope thy's warmed up Patsy's jersey.

MORLEY. Don't want him catching any colds outside . . . (*They laugh.* PATSY *has taken his jersey over to the fire to warm, holding it in front of him.*)

FENCHURCH. (*Returning.*) Seen that bloody bog?

JAGGER. Won't catch sir Frederick, now, in theer.

FENCHURCH. Thy wants to get it seen to, Harry.

HARRY. Has been seen to . . .

WALSH. Alus go afore I come. Drop off at the bloody peek-a-boo . . . now what's it called?

JAGGER. Nude-arama.

WALSH. Best pair o' bogs this side o' town . . . Lukey, gi'e us a rub, will you, when I'm ready? (*Slaps* LUKE'S *shoulder then backs up to the fire, elbowing* PATSY *aside.* LUKE *is strapping* MORLEY'S *ankle.*)

MORLEY. Good Christ . . . go bloody steady. (*Winces.*)

LUKE. Does it hurt?

MORLEY. Too tight.

TREVOR. (*Watching.*) Don't worry. It'll ease up. (HARRY *goes off.*)

FIELDING. (*Calling.*) What've you got on this afternoon, then, Jagger?

JAGGER. (*Looking at his paper.*) A fiver.

FIELDING. What's that, then?

JAGGER. Two-thirty.

WALSH. I've got bloody 'Albatross.'

JAGGER. You what?

WALSH. Seven to one.

JAGGER. You've never.

WALSH. What you got, then?

JAGGER. 'Little Nell.' (HARRY *has come in with shoulder-pads and tie-ups.*)

WALSH. 'Little Nell.' Tripped over its bloody nose-bag . . . now, when wa're it . . .

JAGGER. See thy hosses home, old lad.

WALSH. About ten hours after the bloody start. (*They laugh.* HARRY *is taking shoulder-pads to* JAGGER, PATSY, FENCHURCH, *dropping the tie-ups for the stockings on the floor, then giving the last of the shoulder-pads to* JAGGER. SANDFORD *has come in through the office door. He's a man of about 40, medium build; he wears an overcoat, which is now open, and carries a programme with one or two papers clipped to a pen. Stands for a moment in the door, sniffing: the others notice him but make no comment, almost as if he wasn't there.*)

SANDFORD. I can smell cigar smoke . . . (*Looks round.*) Has somebody been smoking bloody cigars? (WALSH, *back to the fire, is holding his behind him.*)

JAGGER. It's Harry, Mr. Sandford. He's got one here.

WALSH. That's not a bloody cigar he's got, old lad.

HARRY. I don't smoke. It's not me. Don't worry. (*They laugh.*)

MORLEY. Come on, now, Harry. What's thy bloody got? (HARRY *avoids them as* JAGGER *sets at him, goes.*)

SANDFORD. (*To* WALSH.) Is it you, Ken?

WALSH. Me?

FIELDING. Come on, now, bloody Walsh. Own up.

WALSH. Wheer would I get a bloody cigar? (*Puts the cigar in his mouth; approaches* SANDFORD.) I was bloody

well stopped five quid this week. Thy never telled me
. . . What's it for, then, Sandy?

SANDFORD. Bloody language.

WALSH. Language?

SANDFORD. Referee's report . . . Thy wants to take
that out.

WALSH. Out? (*Puffs.* SANDFORD *removes it; carefully
stubs it out.*)

SANDFORD. You can have it back when you're bloody
well dressed and ready to go home . . . If you want the
report you can read it in the office.

WALSH. Trevor: exert thy bloody authority, lad. Players' representative. Get up in that office . . . (*To* SAND-
FORD.) If there's any been bloody well smoked I shall
bloody well charge thee; don't thee bloody worry . . .
Here, now: let's have it bloody back. (*Takes it out of*
SANDFORD'S *pocket; takes* SANDFORD'S *pencil; marks the
cigar. They laugh.*) Warned you. Comes bloody expensive, lad, does that. (*Puts cigar back; goes over to bench
to change.*)

SANDFORD. (*To* MORLEY.) How's thy ankle?

MORLEY. All right. Bit stiff.

LUKE. (*To* SANDFORD.) It'll ease up. Don't worry.

SANDFORD. Patsy: how's thy shoulder?

PATSY. All right. (*Eases it: winces.*) Strapped it up.
(*He's now put on a pair of shoulder pads and is getting
ready to pull on his jersey. The others are now in the early
stages of getting changed, though* WALSH *has made no
progress, and doesn't intend to, and* FENCHURCH *and*
JAGGER *are reading the racing page of the paper, still
dressed.* HARRY *has come in; puts down more tie-ups;
wanders round picking up pieces from the floor, trying to
keep the room tidy. The door from the porch opens and*
COPLEY *comes in, limping, barging against the door; he's
followed in by* STRINGER. COPLEY *is a stocky, muscular
man, simple, good-humoured, straight-forward.* STRINGER
*is tall and slim; aloof, with little interest in any of the
others. He goes straight to his peg and checks his kit; nods
briefly to the others as he crosses.* COPLEY *staggers to the
fire.*)

COPLEY. God . . . It's like a bloody ice-ring out theer
. . . Christ . . . (*Pulls up his trouser leg.*)

SANDFORD. Are you all right . . .

COPLEY. Just look at that.

WALSH. Blood. Mr. Sandford . . . Mr. Sandford. Blood.

COPLEY. You want to get some salt down, Harry . . . (*To* SANDFORD.) Thy'll have a bloody accident out theer afore tonight. (LUKE *crosses over to have a look as well; he and* SANDFORD *gaze down at* COPLEY'S *knee.*)

JAGGER. You all right, then, Stringer?

STRINGER. Aye.

JAGGER. No cuts and bruises.

STRINGER. No.

MORLEY. Get nowt out of Stringer. In't that right, then, Jack? (STRINGER *doesn't answer.*)

LUKE. Well, I can't see a mark.

COPLEY. Could'a sworn it wa' bloody cut.

WALSH. Want to cry off there, Mr. Sandford. (*To* COPLEY.) Seen the bloody pitch thy has.

COPLEY. Piss off. (*They laugh.*)

SANDFORD. (*To* STRINGER.) Jack, then. You all right?

STRINGER. Aye.

SANDFORD. Who else is there?

JAGGER. There's Captain bloody Owens; saw him walking up.

FENCHURCH. Stopped to give him a bloody lift.

JAGGER. Said he was warming up.

WALSH. Warming up! (*Blows raspberry. They laugh.*)

JAGGER. Silly prick.

SANDFORD. (*To* TREVOR.) You all right?

TREVOR. Thanks.

SANDFORD. Saw your wife the other night.

TREVOR. So she said.

WALSH. Ay, ay. Ay, ay . . .

FENCHURCH. Heard that.

WALSH. Bloody Sandford . . .

JAGGER. Thy should coach old Trevor, Sandy, not his wife.

SANDFORD. It was a meeting in the Town Hall, as a matter of fact.

WALSH. Sithee— Harry; pricked up his bloody ears at that.

FIELDING. What was the meeting about, then, Mr. Sandford?

SANDFORD. Just a meeting.

FENCHURCH. Town Hall, now; that's a draughty bloody place, is that. (*They laugh.* HARRY *goes out.*)

WALSH. Come on, now, Trevor. What's it all about?

TREVOR. Better ask Mr. Sandford.

WALSH. He'll have no idea. Can't spell his name for a bloody start. (*They laugh. The door opens.* ATKINSON *comes in, followed by* SPENCER, CLEGG *and* MOORE.)

ATKINSON. Jesus! Jesus! Lads! Look out! (*Crosses, rubbing hands, to fire.*)

CLEGG. How do. How do. (*Follows him over to the fire, rubbing hands.*) By God, but it's bloody freezing. (ATKINSON *is a tall, big-boned man, erect, easy-going; he wears a ³/₄ length jacket and flat cap.* CLEGG *is a square, stocky, fairly small man, bare-headed, in an overcoat and scarf.*)

MORLEY. Here you are, then, Cleggy. I've gotten the spot just here, if you want to warm your hands. (*They laugh.* SPENCER *and* MOORE *are much younger men; they come in, nervous, hands in pockets.*) How's young Billy keeping, then?

SPENCER. All right.

WALSH. Been looking after him, have you, Frank?

MOORE. Be keeping a bloody eye on thee, then, Walsh.

FIELDING. Babes in the bloody wood, are yon.

ATKINSON. Here, then. I hear that the bloody game's been cancelled.

FENCHURCH. Cancelled?

COPLEY. Cancelled?

FENCHURCH. Cancelled?

MORLEY. Here, then, Bryan; who told you that?

ATKINSON. A little bird . . .

CLEGG. We were coming up . . .

JAGGER. Give over . . .

FENCHURCH. Piss off.

COPLEY. Rotten bloody luck. (ATKINSON *and* SPENCER *laugh.*) Sit on their bloody backsides up yonder.

MORLEY. Give ought, now, to have me hands in Sir Frederick's bloody pockets . . .

WALSH. Dirty bloody sod . . .

MORLEY. Warming. Warming . . .

WALSH. Come on, now, Sandy. Let it out. (*To* ATKIN-

SON *and* CLEGG.) He's been having it off here, now, with Trevor's wife.

TREVOR. All right, Walsh.

LUKE. We've had enough of that.

SANDFORD. The meeting . . . was about . . . a municipal centre.

JAGGER. A municipal what?

FENCHURCH. Centre.

CLEGG. A municipal centre.

SANDFORD. There you are. I could have telled you.

WALSH. Sir Frederick bloody Thornton.

ATKINSON. (*Echoes.*) Sir Frederick bloody Thornton.

JAGGER. What?

WALSH. Going to build it . . .

SANDFORD. That's right.

WALSH. Votes for it on the bloody council . . .

JAGGER. Puts in his tender . . .

ATKINSON. (*Echoes.*) Puts in his tender . . .

SANDFORD. He's not even on the council.

CLEGG. All his bloody mates are, though.

SANDFORD. He asked me to attend, as a matter of fact. There are more important things in life than bloody football.

CLEGG. Not today there isn't.

SANDFORD. Not today there, John, you're right . . . Now, then, Frank; are you all right?

MOORE. Aye.

SANDFORD. Billy?

SPENCER. Aye. I'm fine.

SANDFORD. Right. Let's have you bloody well stripped off . . . None of you seen Clifford Owens, have you?

MOORE. No.

SPENCER. No . . .

SANDFORD. (*Looking at watch.*) By God; he's cutting it bloody fine. (*With varying speeds, they've all started stripping off.* HARRY *has distributed all the kit and checked it.* LUKE, *after strapping* MORLEY'S *ankle, has started strapping* STRINGER'S *body, wrapping it round and round with tape,* STRINGER *standing by the table, arms held out.*)

WALSH. (*To* SANDFORD.) Here, then . . . Get a bit of stuff on . . . Let's see you do some bloody work. (WALSH *lies down on the table.* LUKE *has put his various medicine bottles from his bag by the table.* SANDFORD *opens one, pours oil onto the palm of his hand and starts to rub* WALSH *down.*)

KENDAL. Is there anywhere I can keep this, Lukey?

COPLEY. What you got in there, Kenny?

MORLEY. He's bought an electric tool-kit, Luke.

KENDAL. Aye.

FIELDING. Show him it, Kenny. Let him have a look.

KENDAL. Drill . . . electric polisher . . . sandpaper . . . electric saw . . . Do owt with that. (*Shows it to* COPLEY; FENCHURCH *and* JAGGER *look at it as well.*)

COPLEY. We better tek it with us yonder, Kenny. Bloody well mek use o' that today. (*They laugh.*)

STRINGER. I've got one of those at home.

KENDAL. Oh?

STRINGER. Aye.

JAGGER. (*Winking at the others.*) Is that right, then Jack?

STRINGER. Get through a lot o' work wi' that.

JAGGER. Such as?

KENDAL. Book-cases.

JAGGER. Book-cases?

STRINGER. I've made one or two toys, an' all.

KENDAL. Any amount of things.

STRINGER. That's right.

FENCHURCH. Who did you give the toys to, Jack?

STRINGER. What?

JAGGER. Toys.

STRINGER. Neighbour's lad . . .

FENCHURCH. Your mother fancies you, then, with one of those?

STRINGER. She doesn't mind.

COPLEY. You ought to get together here with Ken.

ATKINSON. Bloody main-stand could do with a few repairs. (*They laugh.*)

WALSH. Take no bloody notice, Jackie . . . If thy's got an electric tool-kit, keep it to thysen . . . Here, then, Sandy . . . lower . . . lower! (*They laugh.*) By God, I could do that better, I think, mesen.

LUKE. Kenny; leave it with me, old lad. I'll keep an eye on it . . . Anybody else now? Fieldy, how's thy eye?

FIELDING. Be all right. A spot of bloody grease.

LUKE. (*To* COPLEY.) Barry. Let's have your bloody

back, old lad. (*Gets out more bandage.* STRINGER *and* FENCHURCH *have put on shoulder-pads;* PATSY, *changed and ready, crosses to the mirror to comb his hair, examine himself, gets out piece of gum, adjusts socks, etc. The tin of grease stands on the second table by the wall; after the* PLAYERS *have stripped, got on their shorts, they dip in the tin and grease up; legs, arms, shoulders, neck, ears. The stockings they fasten with the tie-ups* HARRY *has dropped on the floor; a slight air of expectation has begun to filter through the room; players rubbing limbs, rubbing hands together, shaking fingers, flexing, tense. At this point* CROSBY *comes in; he's dressed in a track-suit and enters from the office; a stocky, gnarled figure, late forties or fifties.*)

CROSBY. Come on . . . come on . . . half-ready . . . The other team are changed already . . . (*Calls of 'Ah, give over.' 'Get lost.' 'Silly sods,' etc.*)

SANDFORD. Clifford hasn't come yet, Danny.

CROSBY. He's upstairs.

WALSH. Upstairs.

CROSBY. (*Looking round at the others, on tip-toe, checking those present.*) Bill? Billy?

SPENCER. Aye . . . I'm here. (*Coming out.*)

CROSBY. Frank?

MOORE. Aye . . . I'm here.

CROSBY. On the bench today, then, lads. (SANDFORD *slaps* WALSH *who gets up to finish changing.* CLEGG *lies down to be massaged.* LUKE *is strapping* COPLEY'S *body with crepe bandage and strips of plaster.*)

WALSH. What's old Owens doing upstairs?

CROSBY. Minding his own bloody business, lad.

CLEGG. Having a word with His Highness is he?

CROSBY. Patsy. How's your shoulder, lad?

PATSY. All right . . . stiff . . . (*Eases it up and down in illustration.*)

CROSBY. Fieldy. How's thy eye?

FIELDING. All right.

CROSBY. (*Suddenly sniffing.*) Bloody cigars. Who the hell's been smoking?

LUKE. What?

CROSBY. Not ten minutes afore a bloody match. Come on.

SANDFORD. Oh . . . aye . . . here . . .

CROSBY. You know the bloody rule in here, then, Sandy?

SANDFORD. Yes. Aye. Sorry. Put it out.

LUKE. Is Clifford changed, then, Danny?

CROSBY. (*Distracted.*) What?

LUKE. Need a rub, or strapping up, or ought?

CROSBY. Changed . . . He's gotten changed already.

WALSH. Bloody well up theer? By God, then. Bridal bloody suite is that.

CROSBY. Jack? All right, then, are you?

STRINGER. Fine. Aye . . . Fine. All right.

CROSBY. Trevor?

TREVOR. All right.

CROSBY. Bloody well hard out theer. When you put 'em down . . . knock 'em bleeding hard.

WALSH. And what's Owen's bloody well been up to? Arranging a bloody transfer, is he? Or asking for a rise? (*They laugh.*)

CROSBY. Patsy. (*Reading from a list.*) Harrison's on the wing this afternoon. Alus goes off his left foot, lad.

PATSY. Aye. Right. (*Rubs arms, legs, etc. He and* CLEGG *laugh.*)

CROSBY. Barry, scrum-half: new. When you catch him knock him bloody hard . . Morley?

MORLEY. Aye!

CROSBY. Same with you. Get round. Let him know you're theer . . . Same goes for you, Bryan.

ATKINSON. Aye.

CROSBY. Kenny . . . Let's see you bloody well go right across.

MORLEY. He's brought something to show you here, Mr. Crosby.

CROSBY. What?

MORLEY. Kenny . . . Show him your bloody outfit, Ken.

KENDAL. (*After a certain hesitation.*) Piss off! (*They laugh.*)

WALSH. You tell him, Kenny, lad. That's right.

JAGGER. (*To* KENDAL.) Anybody gets in thy road . . . (*Smacks his fist against his hand.*)

CLEGG. Ne'er know which is bloody harder. Ground out yon or Kenny's loaf. (*They laugh.*)

CROSBY. Jack . . . Jagger . . .

STRINGER. Aye.

JAGGER. Aye . . .

CROSBY. Remember what we said. Keep together . . . don't be waiting theer for Trev . . . If Jack goes right, then you go with him . . . Trevor; have you heard that, lad?

TREVOR. Aye.

CROSBY. Use your bloody eyes . . . John?

CLEGG. Aye?

CROSBY. Let's have a bit of bloody service, lad.

CLEGG. Cliff been complaining, has he?

CROSBY. Complained about bloody nowt. It's me who's been complaining . . . Michaelmas bloody Morley . . . when you get that bloody ball . . . remember . . . don't toss it o'er your bloody head.

WALSH. Who's refereeing then, old lad?

CROSBY. Tallon. (*Groans and cries.*)

JAGGER. Brought his bloody white stick, then, has he?

FENCHURCH. Got his bloody guide-dog, then?

CROSBY. Barry. (*Undisturbed: to* COPLEY.) Watch your putting in near your own line . . . No fists. No bloody feet. Remember . . . But when you hit them. Hit them bleeding hard. (*Looks at his watch.*) There's some gum. Walshy; how's thy back?

WALSH. She told me, Danny, she'd never seen ought like it. (*They laugh.* CROSBY *drops the packets of chewing-gum on the table; goes over to talk to the players separately, helping them with jerseys, boots, etc.* CLEGG *gets up from the table;* JAGGER *comes to have his leg massaged by* SANDFORD. *Faint military MUSIC can be heard from outside and the low murmur of a crowd.* FIELDING *comes over to have his eye examined by* LUKE; *he greases it over.* FIELDING *goes back.*)

CROSBY. Any valuables: let me have 'em . . . Any watches, ear-rings, anklets, cigarettes . . . (*Laughter; jeers:*) 'Might as well chuck 'em out o'bloody winder,' 'Give over.' (FIELDING, LUKE *and* SANDFORD *take valuables and put them in their pockets.* OWENS *comes in through the office door; dressed in a track-suit; bright red with CITY on the back; underneath he's already changed. Medium-build, unassuming, bright, about 30-32 years old, he's rubbing his hands together, cheerful; a shy man, perhaps, but now a little perky.*)

OWENS. All right, then. Are we ready?

JAGGER. Sod off.

FENCHURCH. Give over.

FIELDING. Where you been? (*Cries and shouts.* HARRY *has come in with track-suits; gives them to* MOORE *to give out; goes out.*)

OWENS. Told me upstairs you were fit and ready. 'Just need you, Cliff,' they said, 'to lead them out.'

WALSH. And how's Sir Frederick keeping, then?

OWENS. Asked me to come up a little early.

ALL. Ay, ay. Ay, ay. What's that? Give over.

OWENS. Fill him in on the tactics we intend to use today.

SANDFORD. That's right.

JAGGER. What tactics are those, then, Clifford?

OWENS. Told him one or two hand signals he might look out for, Jag. (*They laugh. The players are picking up gum, tense, flexing; occasionally one or other goes out through the bath-entrance, returning a few moments later.* HARRY *has come in with buckets and bottles of water.*) Freeze the eye-balls off a copper monkey, boy, today. By God . . . (*Goes over to the fire.*) Could do with a bit more coal on, Harry.

LUKE. Get cramp if you stand in front of that.

WALSH. Got cramp in one place, Luke, already. (*They laugh.*)

OWENS. Just watch the ball today, boy. Come floating over like a bloody bird.

WALSH. If you listened to half he said afore a bloody match you'd never get out on that bloody field . . . Does it all, you know, inside his bloody head . . . How many points do you give us, then, today?

OWENS. Sod all. You'll have to bloody earn 'em, lad.

SANDFORD. That's the bloody way to talk.

CROSBY. Harry . . . where's the bloody resin board, old lad?

JAGGER. Let's have a bloody ball, an' all. (*Roar off of the crowd.* HARRY *goes off through bath-entrance.*)

MORLEY. What bonus are we on today, then, Danny?

CROSBY. All bonus thy'll get, lad, you'll find on t'end o' my bloody boot . . . Now come on, come on, then, lads. Get busy . . . (CROSBY *is moving amongst the players; now all of them are almost ready: moving over to the mirror, combing hair, straightening collars, tightening boots, chewing, greasing ears, emptying coat pockets of wallets, etc., handing them to* CROSBY, SANDFORD *or* LUKE. TALLON *comes in; a soldierly man of about 40, dressed in a black referee's shorts and shirt.*)

TALLON. You all ready, then, in here?

SANDFORD. Aye. Come in, Mr. Tallon. We're all ready, then. All set.

TALLON. Good day for it.

CROSBY. Aye. Take away a bit o' frost.

TALLON. Right. I'll have a look. Make sure that nobody's harbouring any weapons. (*A couple of players laugh.* TALLON *goes round to each player, examines his hands for rings, his boots for protruding studs; feels their bodies for any belts, buckles or protruding pads; he does it quickly; each player nods in greeting; one or two remain aloof. As* TALLON *goes round* HARRY *comes back with the resin board and two rugby balls; sets the board on the table against the wall. The players take the balls, feel them, pass them round, lightly, casual.* HARRY *moves off, to the bath-entrance. He takes the coal-bucket with him.* OWENS *takes off his track-suit to several whistles; exchanges greetings, formally, with* TALLON. *After each player's been examined he goes over to the resin board, rubs his hands in the resin; tries the ball.* SPENCER *and* MOORE *have pulled on red track-suits over their playing gear.*)

WALSH. By God; I could do with wekening up . . . Lukey; where's thy bloody phials?

OWENS. Off out tonight, then, Walshy, lad?

WALSH. I am. Two arms, two legs, one head; if you pass the bloody ball mek sure I'm bloody looking. (*They laugh.*)

OWENS. Ton o'rock there, Walshy, lad.

WALSH. Second bloody half . . . where wa're it? . . . 'Walshy! Walshy! Walshy!' . . . . Passes . . . Fastening me bloody boot, what else.

JAGGER. Never looks.

WALSH. Came down like a ton o' bloody lead. (*They laugh.* LUKE *has got out a tin of ammonia phials. The players take them, sniff, coughing, flinging back their heads; pass them on to the others. Several of the 'backs don't bother.* WALSH *takes his; breathes deeply up either nostril; no effect.*)

JAGGER. Shove a can o' coal-gas up theer; wouldn't make much bloody difference.

WALSH. Mr. Tallon! Mr. Tallon! You haven't inspected me, Mr. Tallon! (*They laugh;* TALLON *comes over, finishing off.*)

TALLON. All right, then, Walshy. Let's have a look. (WALSH, *arms upraised, submits ponderously to* TALLON'S *inspection. Then:*)

WALSH. Count 'em! Count 'em! Don't just bloody look. (*The players laugh.* TALLON *finishes; goes over to the door.*)

TALLON. (*To the room.*) Remember . . . keep it clean . . . play fair. Have a good game, lads. Play to the whistle.

ALL. Aye. All right.

TALLON. All right, then, lads. I'll see you. May the best team win. Good luck. (*An electric bell rings as* TALLON *goes out.*)

CROSBY. Okay. Five minutes . . . Forr'ads. Let's have you . . . Billy? Frank? You ready?

MOORE. Aye.

SPENCER. Aye . . .

CROSBY. Over here, then. O'd these up. (CLEGG *raises his arms;* WALSH *and* FIELDING *lock in on either side, casual, not much effort.* ATKINSON *and* KENDAL *bind together and put their heads in between the three in front.*)

FIELDING. Ger off. Ger off!

WALSH. A bit lower there, then, Kenny . . . Lovely. Beautiful.

CLEGG. Just right. (*They laugh.*)

CROSBY. (*Holding the forwards with* SPENCER *and* MOORE.) All right. All right. (MORLEY *leans on* ATKINSON *and* KENDAL, *then, at* CROSBY'S *signal, puts his head between them as they scrum down.* SPENCER, MOORE *and* CROSBY *are linked together.*) Let's have a ball . . . Cliff . . . Barry . . . Number four; first clear scrum we get; either side . . . (*Takes the ball* SANDFORD'S *brought him.*) Our possession, theirs . . . Clifford . . . Jagger . . . Jack . . . that's right. (*The rest of the players take up positions behind;* COPLEY *immediately behind, then* OWENS, *then* STRINGER, JAGGER, PATSY *on one side,* FENCHURCH *on the other;* TREVOR *stands at the back.*) Right, then? Our ball, then . . . (CROSBY *puts the ball in at* CLEGG'S *feet;*

it's knocked back through the scrum to COPLEY, *then it's passed, hand to hand, slowly, almost formally, out to* PATSY; *as each player passes it he falls back; the scrum breaks up, falls back to make a line going back diagonally and ending with* FENCHURCH.)

WALSH. From me. To you . . . (*Laughter.*)

CROSBY. All right. All right. (*When the ball reaches* PATSY *he passes it back; to* JAGGER, *to* STRINGER, *to* OWENS, *to* COPLEY, *then to each forward in turn, each calling the Christian name of the one who hands it on, until it reaches* FENCHURCH.)

WALSH. Run, Fenny! Run!

JAGGER. Go on. Go on! It'll be t'on'y bloody chance thy has. (*They laugh.*)

WALSH. I never know whether it's bloody speed or fear with Fenny . . . The sound of a pair of bloody feet behind. (WALSH *catches his backside; they laugh.*)

CROSBY. All right. All right . . . Trev; number six.

SANDFORD. Come up on your positions, lads; remember that. (*They get down as before, though this time* MORLEY *stands out and takes* COPLEY'S *place.* COPLEY *falls back:* OWENS *falls back behind him;* JAGGER *and* PATSY *stand on one side of him,* STRINGER *and* FENCHURCH *on the other.* TREVOR *stands immediately behind him.*)

CROSBY. Remember: first time up . . . Cliff'll give his signal . . . our head; their put in . . . doesn't matter . . . (CROSBY *puts the ball in the scrum as before: the forwards play it back between their feet.* MORLEY *takes it, turns, passes it back to* COPLEY; COPLEY *passes it back to* OWENS, OWENS *to* TREVOR, *who runs and mimes a drop kick.*)

JAGGER. Pow! (HARRY *has come in with coal-bucket.*)

WALSH. Now thy's sure thy won't want thy glasses, Trev? (*One or two laugh.*)

TREVOR. Just about.

WALSH. If you can't see the posts just give a shout. (*They laugh.*)

JAGGER. Walshy here'll move 'em up. (*Laughter.*)

CROSBY. All right. All right. I'll say nowt else . . . (*The door from the office has already opened.* THORNTON *comes in, tall, dressed in a fur-collared overcoat; a well-preserved man of about 50. He's accompanied by* MACK-

ENDRICK, *a flushed-face man of about 60; he wears an overcoat, a scarf and a dark hat.*)

THORNTON. Hope I'm not intruding, Danny.

CROSBY. No, no. Not at all.

THORNTON. Thought I'd have a word.

SANDFORD. That's right. (SANDFORD *gestures at the players; they move round in a half-circle as* THORNTON *crosses to the centre.*)

THORNTON. Chilly in here. That fire could do with a spot of stoking . . .

MACKENDRICK. Harry . . . spot o' coal on that.

HARRY. Aye . . . Right . . . (HARRY *mends the fire.*)

THORNTON. Just to wish you good luck, lads.

PLAYERS. Thanks . . .

THORNTON. Fair play, tha knows, has always had its just rewards.

SANDFORD. Aye . . .

THORNTON. Go out . . . play like I know you can . . . there'll not be one man disappointed . . . Now, then. Any grunts and groans? Any complaints? No suggestions? (*Looks round.*)

JAGGER. No . . .

FENCHURCH. No, Sir Frederick . . .

CROSBY. No.

SANDFORD. No, Sir Frederick . . .

THORNTON. Right, then . . . Mr. Mackendrick here'll be in his-office, afterwards . . . if there's anything you want, just let him know . . . Good luck. Play fair. May the best team win . . . Cliff. Good luck.

OWENS. Thanks. (*Shakes his hand.*)

MACKENDRICK. Good-luck, Cliff . . . Good-luck, lads . . .

PLAYERS. Aye . . . Thanks.

THORNTON. Danny.

CROSBY. Aye. Right . . . Thanks.

THORNTON. Good-luck, lads. See you later.

MACKENDRICK. Danny . . . (*Waves, cheerily, and followed by* THORNTON, *goes. Silence. Broken finally by* HARRY, *stoking fire. Crowd roars off: fanfare MUSIC: the opposing team runs on. A bell rings in the room.*)

CROSBY. Right, then, lads . . . Cliff? Ought you'd like to add.

OWENS. No. (*Shakes his head.*) Play well, lads . . .

PLAYERS. Aye . . . (*The players, tense, nervous, start to line up prior to going out.* OWENS *takes the ball; he heads the column. Crowd roars again; loudspeaker, indecipherable, announcing names.*)

WALSH. Harry, make sure that bloody bath is hot. (HARRY *looks across, he nods his head.*) Towel out, tha knows . . . me bloody undies ready . . .

CROSBY. Bloody Walsh . . . come on. Line up . . . (*Groans, moans: the players line up behind* OWENS [6]. TREVOR [1], PATSY [2], JAGGER [3], STRINGER [4], FENCHURCH [5], COPLEY [7], WALSH [8], CLEGG [9], FIELDING [10], ATKINSON [11], KENDAL [12], MORLEY [13]. SPENCER [15] *and* MOORE [14], *in red track-suits, with CITY on the back, are helping* LUKE *and* SANDFORD *collect the various pieces of equipment; spare kit, track-suits, sponges, medical bag, spare ball, bucket.* CROSBY *holds the door.*)

OWENS. Right, then?

ALL. Right. Ready. Let's get off. (*Belches, groans.*)

CROSBY. Good-luck, Trev . . . good-luck, lad . . . good-luck . . . Good-luck, Mic . . . (*He pats each player's back as they move out; moments after* OWENS *has gone there's a great roar outside.* CROSBY *sees the team out, then* SPENCER *and* MOORE *in track-suits, then* LUKE *and* SANDFORD; *he looks round, then he goes, closing the door. The roar grows louder: MUSIC.* HARRY *comes in; wanders round; looks at the floor for anything that's been dropped; picks up odd tapes, phials. Goes to the fire; puts on another piece, stands by it, still. The crowd roar grows louder. Then, slowly; LIGHTS and SOUND FADE.*)

CURTAIN

ACT II

The same. About thirty-five minutes later. The dressing-room is empty, the light switched off; there's a faint glow from the fire. The roar off of the crowd; rising to a crescendo, fading. The door from the porch opens. THORNTON *enters, rubbing his hands, followed by* MACKENDRICK.

THORNTON. By God . . . (*Gasps, shudders, stumbling round.*) Where's the light switch?

MACKENDRICK. Here . . . (*Light switched on.*)

THORNTON. How much longer?

MACKENDRICK. (*Looks at his watch.*) Twelve . . . fifteen minutes.

THORNTON. Could do with some heating in that bloody box . . . either that or we watch it from the office. (*Crosses to the fire and warms his hands.*) Anybody in here, is there?

MACKENDRICK. (*Looks into the bath-entrance.*) Don't think so.

THORNTON. Got your flask?

MACKENDRICK. Empty. (*Shows him.*)

THORNTON. (*Rubbing his hands.*) Send up to the office.

MACKENDRICK. (*Calls through the bath-entrance.*) Harry! (MACKENDRICK *listens; no answer. Goes to office entrance.*)

THORNTON. You go, Mac . . . He'll be up in the bloody canteen, that lad. (THORNTON *has settled himself in the chair in front of the fire. The crowd roars off.*)

MACKENDRICK. Shan't be a second.

THORNTON. Second cabinet on the right; my office.

MACKENDRICK. Right. (*Hesitates; goes off through office door.* THORNTON *settles himself in front of the fire; crowd roars off, raises his head, listens. The roar dies; he leans forward, puts piece of coal on the fire. Door bangs off, stamping of feet; coughs, growls, clearing of throat,*

92

sighs. HARRY *comes in from the bath-entrance, muffled up; balaclava, scarf, cap, ex-army overcoat, gloves.*)

HARRY. Oh . . . Oh . . . (*About to hurry to the fire sees* THORNTON *and stops, about to go back.*)

THORNTON. That's all right. Come in, Harry . . . Taking a breather.

HARRY. I just nipped up to the er . . .

THORNTON. That's all right, lad.

HARRY. Cup o' tea.

THORNTON. Pull up a chair, lad. (*Moves his own over fractionally;* HARRY *looks round. There's no other chair. He remains standing where he is.*) Nowt like a coal fire. Hardly get it anywhere now, you know . . . Synthetic bloody fuel. Like these plastic bloody chickens. Get nought that's bloody real no more.

HARRY. Aye . . . (*Sways from one foot to the other.*)

THORNTON. Water's hot, then, is it?

HARRY. What?

THORNTON. For the bath.

HARRY. Oh. Aye . . . (*Pause.*) I've just stoked up.

THORNTON. I'd have given you a hand myself if I'd have known.

HARRY. Aye.

THORNTON. By God: that box . . . like ice . . . (*Takes hands out of his gloves.*) Can't feel a thing.

HARRY. It comes fro' Russia.

THORNTON. What?

HARRY. The cold.

THORNTON. Oh . . .

HARRY. East wind . . . Blows from the Russian steppes.

THORNTON. (*Looks up.*) More North-West today, I think.

HARRY. Over the Baltic . . . Norway . . . (THORNTON *has raised his hand; the crowd's roar rises; he listens.* HARRY *waits. The roar dies down.*)

THORNTON. Them, I think . . . Score today, our lads; they'll raise the bloody roof.

HARRY. I've read it in a book.

THORNTON. What?

HARRY. The Russians . . . when the wind blows to the west—spray it with a special gas.

THORNTON. Good God.

HARRY. Without anybody knowing . . . Breathe it . . . Take it in . . . (*Breathes in.*) Slows down your mind . . . (*Illustrates with limp arms and hands.*) Stops everybody thinking.

THORNTON. I think our lads've had a drop of that today. By God, I've never seen so many bloody knock-ons . . . dropped passes . . .

HARRY. I've been a workman all my life.

THORNTON. Oh . . . Aye.

HARRY. I used to work in a brick-yard afore I came up here.

THORNTON. It's a pity you're not back theer, Harry lad. Bloody bricks we get. Come to pieces in your bloody hand . . . Had a house fall down the other day. Know what it was . . . ? Bricks . . . crumbled up . . . Seen nothing like it . . . . Still . . .

HARRY. Knew your place before. Now, there's everybody doing summat . . . And nobody doing owt.

THORNTON. Still. Go with it, Harry.

HARRY. What . . .

THORNTON. Can't go against your times . . . (*Twists round.*) Sent Mac up for a bloody snifter . . . Had time to mek the bloody stuff by now. (*Crowd roar rises, reaches crescendo, dies, booing.*) Don't know why they do that job, you know. Refereeing. Must have a stunted mentality, in my view. To go on with a thing like that.

HARRY. Be all communist afore long.

THORNTON. Aye. (*Pokes fire.*) If the Chinese don't get here afore.

HARRY. It's happening all the time. In the mind . . . Come one day, they'll just walk in. Take over . . . There'll be nobody strong enough to stop them. They'll have all been brainwashed . . . You can see it happening . . .

THORNTON. *Mac!* (*Calls.*) Takes that man a fortnight to brew a cup of tea. Accountant . . . He'll be up there now, counting the bloody gate receipts. I don't think he's at all interested in bloody football . . . He's never slow, you know, to tell us when we've made a bloody loss. (*Banging outside,* MACKENDRICK *comes in with the bottle.*) Thought you'd been swigging the bloody bottle.

MACKENDRICK. It wasn't in the cabinet . . . I had to get it from the bar . . . Got to sign about four receipts

. . . Anybody gets a drink in this place they bloody well deserve it, lad.

THORNTON. No glasses?

MACKENDRICK. Here. (*Takes two from his pocket.*)

THORNTON. Was that a score?

MACKENDRICK. Penalty. Missed.

THORNTON. Them? Or us.

MACKENDRICK. Seven, two. Them. It'll take some pulling back . . . Harry. (*Nods.*)

HARRY. Mr. Mackendrick.

MACKENDRICK. Wrapped up for the weather, Harry.

HARRY. Aye.

THORNTON. Been telling me, comes from Russia.

MACKENDRICK. Russia.

THORNTON. Weather.

MACKENDRICK. Weather!

THORNTON. Might have bloody guessed . . . (*To* HARRY.) Got a cup, then, have you? Try a drop o' this.

HARRY. Don't drink. Thanks all the same, Sir Frederick.

THORNTON. Nay, no bloody titles here, old lad. Freddy six days o' the week. (*To* MACKENDRICK.) Sir Frederick to the wife on Sundays. (*He and* MACKENDRICK *laugh.* THORNTON *drinks.*) By God; brings back a drop of life, does that.

MACKENDRICK. (*Drinks, gasps.*) Grand . . . Lovely. (*Roar of the crowd; huge, prolonged. They listen.*)

THORNTON. Have a look. Go on. Quick. You've missed it . . . (MACKENDRICK *goes to the porch; disappears outside.*) How do you think they compare to the old days, Harry?

HARRY. Players? . . . Couldn't hold a bloody candle . . . In them days they'd do a sixteen hour shift *then* come up and lake . . . Nowadays: it's all machines . . . and they're *still* bloody puffed when they come up o' Sat'days. Run round yon field a couple of time: finished. I've seen 'em laking afore with broken arms, legs broke . . . shoulders . . . Get a scratch today and they're in here, flat on their bloody backs, iodine, linament, injections . . . If they ever played a real team today they wouldn't last fifteen bloody seconds. That's my view. That's what I think of them today. Everywheer. There's not one of them could hold a candle to the past. (*Roar and cheering from the crowd.* THORNTON *twists round and listens*.) They'll wek up one morning and find it's all too late . . . (MACKENDRICK *comes back in*.)

MACKENDRICK. Scored.

THORNTON. (*Pleased*.) Try?

MACKENDRICK. Converted.

THORNTON. Who wa're it?

MACKENDRICK. Morley.

THORNTON. By God. Bloody genius that lad. (MACKENDRICK *pours a drink*.)

MACKENDRICK. Harry . . . ?

HARRY. No thanks, Mr. Mackendrick.

THORNTON. Harry here's been enlightening me about the past . . . Nothing like the old days, Mac.

HARRY. Aye!

MACKENDRICK. Bloody bunkum.

THORNTON. What's that? (*Laughs, pleased*.)

MACKENDRICK. God Christ . . . If this place was like it was twenty years ago—and that's not *too* far back— you wouldn't find me here for a bloody start . . . As for fifty years ago. Primeval . . . Surprised at thee, then, Harry lad.

HARRY. Aye . . . (*He turns away*.)

MACKENDRICK. Have another snifter.

THORNTON. Thanks. (MACKENDRICK *pours it in*.)

MACKENDRICK. (*To* HARRY.) I'd have thought thy'd see the difference, lad. (HARRY *doesn't answer, turns away*.) Washed i' bloody buckets, then . . . e't dripping instead o' bloody meat . . . urinated by an hedge . . . God Christ, bloody houses were nobbut size o'this, seven kiddies, no bloody bath, no bed . . . fa'ther out o'work as much as not.

HARRY. There's many as living like that right now!

MACKENDRICK. Aye. And there's a damn sight more as not.

THORNTON. I never knew you had strong feelings, Mac.

MACKENDRICK. About one or two bloody things I have. (*He pours himself another drink. A faint roar from the crowd*.) I suppose you're more on his side, then?

THORNTON. Nay. I'm on nobody's bloody side, old lad . . . I had a dream the other night . . . I was telling Cliff afore the match . . . I came up here to watch a match . . . looked over at the tunnel . . . know what I saw run out? (*Laughs.*) Bloody robots on artificial grass. (*Laughs again.*) And up in the bloody box were a couple of fellers, just like Danny, flicking bloody switches . . . twisting knobs. (*Laughs.*) I laugh now. I wo'k up in a bloody sweat, I tell you. (*Roar from the crowd, applause. Noises off, boots, shouting.*) Ay up. Ay up . . . (*Springs up.*)

HARRY. You'll wake up one day . . . I've telled you . . . You'll wek up one day . . . You'll find it's bloody well too late. (*Goes off through bath-entrance.*)

MACKENDRICK. Aren't you staying to see them in?

THORNTON. I'll pop in in a couple of jiffies, lad . . . You stay and give 'em a bloody cheer . . . (*Slaps his shoulder.*) Shan't be long . . . (*Calls through to bath-entrance.*) Harry . . . I'll pursue that argument another time. (*Nods, winks at MACKENDRICK then goes out smartly via the office door. MACKENDRICK moves the chair from in front of the fire just as the players start to come in. FENCHURCH comes in first, shaking his hand violently; he's followed by LUKE carrying his bag.*)

FENCHURCH. Jesus! Jesus! Bloody hell.

LUKE. Here . . . Let's have a look. Come on.

JAGGER. (*Following him in.*) It's nothing . . . bloody nothing . . .

FENCHURCH. Bloody studs, you see . . . Just look! (*He holds it up, wincing, as LUKE takes it. He groans, cries out as LUKE examines it. The others are beginning to flood in: stained jerseys, gasping, bruised, exhausted. HARRY brings in two bottles of water which the players take swigs from and spit out into LUKE's bucket which MOORE has carried in.*)

LUKE. Nothing broken. It'll be all right.

SANDFORD. Do you want me to bind it for you, then?

FENCHURCH. No, no. No . . . No.

JAGGER. Can't hold the ball with a bandage on.

COPLEY. Don't worry Fenny lad, match o'er have you off to hospital. Operation. Have it off. Not going to have you troubled, lad, by that.

FENCHURCH. Sod off. (*They laugh. WALSH, groaning, collapses on the bench.*)

WALSH. I'm done. I'm finished. I shall never walk again. Sandy . . . Bring us a cup o' tea, old lad.

SANDFORD. You'll have a cup o' bloody nothing. Have a swab at that. (*Splashes a cold sponge in his face and round his neck. Splutters, groans, finally wipes his face and neck.* CROSBY *has come in with the remainder of the players.*)

CROSBY. Well done. Well done. Start putting on the pressure in the second half.

JAGGER. Pressure?

FENCHURCH. Pressure . . .

JAGGER. That *was* the bloody pressure. Anything from now on is strictly left-overs, Danny lad . . . I'm knackered. Look at that. Use hammers on that bloody pitch out theer . . .

MACKENDRICK. Well done, then, lads. Well done.

FIELDING. You watching in here, then, Mr. Mackendrick, are you?

MACKENDRICK. Out there, old lad. I wouldn't miss it.

CLEGG. See that last try . . . ?

MACKENDRICK. . . . Go down in the bloody book will that.

SANDFORD. Keep moving. Don't sit still.

CROSBY. That's right. Keep moving . . . Walshy. Get up off your arse. (WALSH *takes no notice, drinks from bottle.*) Bryan? How's your ankle?

ATKINSON. All right. I think. It'll be all right.

FIELDING. Just look at that. Can't move me bloody finger.

CROSBY. Keep away from that bloody fire . . . Sandy, keep 'em moving round, old lad. (LUKE *and* SANDFORD *are examining individual players:* MOORE *and* SPENCER *helping out with laces, tightening boots, handing round the bottles.*) Any new jerseys? Any new shorts? (*A couple of players call: 'No . . . No thanks.'*)

COPLEY. Over here, lads . . . I'll have one . . .

CROSBY. Trevor? How's your hands?

TREVOR. All right. (*Holds them up, freezing.*)

CROSBY. Keep moving, lad. Keep shifting.

TREVOR. Be all right. (TREVOR *is quite cold: hands and arms together, then rubbing himself, trying to get warm.*)

CROSBY. Barry?

COPLEY. No. No. All right.

STRINGER. Bloody cold out theer. I read it i' the paper last night. Seven degrees of frost.

SANDFORD. Bloody well move faster, lad.

STRINGER. I am moving faster. It bloody catches up with you.

KENDAL. Ears, look. Can't bloody feel 'em.

JAGGER. Still on, then, Kenny, are they?

KENDAL. Aye. Think so. Better have a look. (*Crosses to mirror. They're gradually getting over their first shock of entering the warmer room, sucking sponges, rinsing their mouths from the bottle, rubbing on more grease, adjusting boot fastenings and socks. Those on the move move quite slowly, tired, panting.*)

FENCHURCH. What's the bloody score, then, lads?

FIELDING. Never notices on the bloody wing.

COPLEY. Picking his bloody nose.

FIELDING. Talking to the crowd.

MOORE. Seven-seven, Fenny, lad.

CLEGG. (*To* MOORE *and* SPENCER.) Bloody cold, you lads, out theer.

SPENCER. Freezing.

MOORE. Fro'zen.

WALSH. Mr. Crosby, sir.

CROSBY. What's that?

WALSH. Isn't it time we had a substitute out theer. These lads are dying to get on and lake.

CROSBY. They'll get on in *my* bloody time, not yours. Now get up. Come on. Get moving. I've told thee, Walsh, before. (PATSY *is sitting down, having his leg 'stretched' by* SANDFORD—PATSY'S *leg stretched out before him*, SANDFORD *pressing back the toe of his boot. To* PATSY.) You all right?

PATSY. Bloody cramp. God . . (*Groans, winces.*)

WALSH. Another bloody fairy . . .

CLEGG. Go on. Give him summat, Sandy . . .

WALSH. Here. Let's have a bloody hold.

PATSY. S'all right. S'all right. S'all right. (PATSY *springs up, flexes leg.*)

WALSH. S'all in the bloody mind, tha knows . . . Here. Have a look at my bloody back, then, will you? (SANDFORD *lifts his jersey at the back.*)

SANDFORD. Got a cut.

WALSH. How many stitches?

SANDFORD. Twenty or thi'ty. Can't be sure.

WALSH. Go on. Go on. Get shut . . . (*Players laugh.*) Fieldy: have a bloody look, old lad. (FIELDING *lifts*

WALSH'S *shirt and looks: slaps his back.* WALSH *goes over to the bucket, gets sponge, squeezes it down his back.*)

LUKE. (*Calling, with linament, etc.*) Any more for any more?

JAGGER. Any bruises, cuts, concussions, fractures . . .

COPLEY. One down here you could have a look at, Lukey. (*Opens shorts, players laugh.* THORNTON *has come in from the porch entrance.*)

THORNTON. Well played, lads. Well done . . . Morley: bloody fine try was that, young man.

MORLEY. Thank you, sir.

THORNTON. (*To* CROSBY.) Not often we see a run like that . . .

CROSBY. No. That's right.

THORNTON. Good kick, Clifford. Good kick was that.

OWENS. Aye. (*During this period has been out, through the bath-entrance, to wash his face and hands, almost like an office worker, set for home. Has come in now, drying face and hands.*)

THORNTON. Trevor: dropped goal: a bloody picture.

TREVOR. Thanks.

THORNTON. How're your hands?

TREVOR. Frozen.

THORNTON. Saw you catch that ball: didn't know you'd got it. (*Laughs.*)

TREVOR. Numb . . . (*Laughs, rubs his hands.*)

THORNTON. Kenny. (KENDAL *nods.*)

WALSH. Sir Frederick: how d'you think I managed, then?

THORNTON. Like a dream, Walshy. Like a dream.

JAGGER. Bloody nightmare, I should think, more likely. (*The players laugh.*)

CROSBY. He could bloody well do wi' wekening up . . . There's half on you asleep out yon . . . Fieldy . . . Bryan . . . *move across. Go with it* . . . It's no good waiting till they come . . . Bloody hell . . . Trevor theer, he's covering all that side . . . Colin, *bloody interceptions:* It's no good going in, lad, every time . . . they'll be bloody well waiting for it soon . . . three times that *I* saw Jack here had to take your man . . .

WALSH. Billy?

SPENCER. Aye?

WALSH. Go eavesdrop at their door, old lad.

SPENCER. Aye! (*Laughs.*)

WALSH. Find out all their plans. (*They laugh.*)

CROSBY. As for bloody Walsh. A boot up the backside wouldn't go astray. I'll swear at times thy's running bloody backwards, lad.

WALSH. I am. I bloody am . . . Too bloody cold today for running forr'ad. (*They laugh; claps his cold hands either side of* SANDFORD'S *face.* SANDFORD, *saying, 'Gerrof,' steps back.* CROSBY *goes into private, whispered conversation with individual players.*)

MACKENDRICK. How're you feeling, Trevor, lad?

TREVOR. All right.

MACKENDRICK. Cut your ear there, lad . . . Not bad . . . (*Examines it.*) Sandy? . . . Put a spot o' grease on that. (SANDFORD *comes across;* TREVOR *winces.*) Take care of the professional men, you know. These lot— (*Gestures round.*) Bloody ten a penny. (*Jeers;* MACKENDRICK *takes no notice.*) Have you ever tried playing i' mittens, then?

TREVOR. No.

MACKENDRICK. Some players do, you know. Particularly in your position . . . In the amateur game, you know . . . Still. No need to tell you that, I'm sure.

TREVOR. Aye . . . I'll just pop off in theer. Shan't be a minute.

MACKENDRICK. Aye . . . aye! (*Slaps his back.* TREVOR *goes off through bath-entrance. Electric bell rings.*)

CROSBY. All right. All right. I'm saying no more. Quick score at the beginning, be all right . . . Cliff. At the fourth tackle, Cliff, try number five. (*To the rest.*) Have you got that?

PLAYERS. Aye.

CROSBY. Have you got that?

PLAYERS. Aye!!

CROSBY. Be bloody ready . . . Patsy?

PATSY. Aye.

CROSBY. Fenny?

FENCHURCH. Aye. All right.

CROSBY. Get *up* there! Bloody well stuck in.

FENCHURCH. Aye.

CROSBY. Bryan . . .

ATKINSON. Aye.

CROSBY. Harder. *Harder* . . . Kenny?

KENDAL. Aye?

CROSBY. *Bang 'em!* You're not tucking the buggers up in bed.

KENDAL. Aye.

CROSBY. Let's bloody well see it, then . . . I want to *hear* those sods go down . . . I want to feel that bloody stand start shaking . . . Johnny: have you got that, lad?

CLEGG. Aye.

CROSBY. Good possession . . . If their hooker causes any trouble let *Walshy* bang his head.

WALSH. I already have done, lad. Don't worry. (*They laugh.*)

CROSBY. Cliff? Ought you want to add?

OWENS. No. No. Mark your man. Don't wait for somebody else to take him. (*Roar of the crowd off. They look to* THORNTON; *he's been going round to individual players, nodding formally, advising, giving praise.* TREVOR *comes back in.*)

THORNTON. Good luck, lads. Keep at it. Don't let the pressure drop. Remember, it's thy advantage second half. Away from home, for them, it always tells.

CROSBY. Aye . . .

THORNTON. Good luck.

PLAYERS. (*Uninterested.*) Aye . . . thanks . . .

THORNTON. Go up and shake them lads out o' the bloody boardroom, Mac . . . They'll watch the match from up theer if they get half a chance . . .

MACKENDRICK. Aye . . . Good luck, lads. Don't let up.

PLAYERS. No . . . Aye . . .

MACKENDRICK. See you after. Keep it up. Well done . . . (*On his way out.*) Well done . . . Well done, Trev. (*Slaps* TREVOR'S *back as he goes.* THORNTON *smiles round, nods at* CROSBY, *then follows* MACKENDRICK *out.*)

CROSBY. Watch Tallon near your line.

PLAYERS. (*Moving off.*) Aye . . . aye.

OWENS. All right, then, lads. We're off . . .

CROSBY. Barry . . .

COPLEY. Aye. (*On move out, hands clenched.*)

CROSBY. Are you listening . . .

COPLEY. Aye. Aye. Don't worry.

CROSBY. Right, then . . . Fieldy, how's thy eye?

FIELDING. All right.

CROSBY. It's bloody well opened. Look. (*To* LUKE.)

FIELDING. Aye. Aye. It'll be all right. (*Dismisses it, goes.*)

CROSBY. Billy, Frank . . .

PLAYERS. Aye . . . aye . . . All right. (*Filing out. They go.* CROSBY *nodding to each one at the door, advising, slapping backs.* LUKE *and* SANDFORD *start collecting the kit to take out.* MOORE *and* SPENCER, *still in their track-suits, pick up a bucket and a bag between them, waiting to follow* CROSBY *out after the players have gone. Roar of the crowd off as the players go out.* HARRY *has come in to collect the towels, tapes, bottles, etc., left lying around.*)

LUKE. See you out there, Danny . . . (*Packing his bag.*)

CROSBY. Patsy. Fenny!

SPENCER. Aye.

CROSBY. Right . . . (*They go.* SANDFORD, LUKE *and* HARRY *are left.*)

LUKE. Well, then, Harry . . . How's t'a barn?

HARRY. All right.

LUKE. Been warming up, in here, then, have you?

HARRY. I bloody haven't.

SANDFORD. I'm not so sure I wouldn't prefer it here meself. (*Warming hands at fire. Crowd roar off.*) Ay up. Ay up. That's it. We're off. (*He zips up his track-suit top, pulls his scarf round his neck.*)

LUKE. Be with you in a sec, old lad.

SANDFORD. All right. (*Goes.* LUKE *and* HARRY *work in silence for a moment. Then:*)

LUKE. Do you ever back on matches, Harry?

HARRY. What?

LUKE. Bookies.

HARRY. I don't.

LUKE. Nor 'osses?

HARRY. Nowt.

LUKE. What do you do in your spare time, then?

HARRY. I don't have any spare time.

LUKE. What do you do when you're not up here, then?

HARRY. I'm alus up here.

LUKE. Sleep up here, then, do you? (*Roar off.* LUKE *raises head, listens, packs his bag.*)

HARRY. I sleep at home.

LUKE. Where's home?

HARRY. Home's in our house. That's where home is.

LUKE. A damn good place to have it, lad.

HARRY. Bloody keep it theer, an' all.

LUKE. Thornton here, then, was he, first half?

HARRY. Aye.

LUKE. Crafty . . . He'll never put himself out, you know, unduly.

HARRY. And Mackendrick.

LUKE. Where one goes his shadder follows.

HARRY. It's his place . . . He can do what he likes . . . He can sit in here the whole afternoon if he bloody likes.

LUKE. I suppose he can. (*Roar off.*) F'un him up here, you know, one night.

HARRY. What's that?

LUKE. Sir Frederick . . . Came back one night . . . Left me tackle . . . Saw a light up in the stand . . . Saw him sitting theer. Alone. Crouched up. Like that.

HARRY. His stand. Can sit theer when he likes.

LUKE. Ten o'clock at night.

HARRY. Ten o'clock i' the bloody morning. Any time he likes. (LUKE *fastens his bag.*)

LUKE. Is it true, then, what they say?

HARRY. What's that?

LUKE. Thy's never watched a match.

HARRY. Never.

LUKE. Why's that?

HARRY. My job's in here. Thy job's out yonder.

LUKE. They ought to set thee on a pair o' bloody rails. (*Goes over to the door.*)

HARRY. Most jobs you get: they're bloody nowt . . . (LUKE *pauses at the door.*) Don't know what they work for . . .

LUKE. What?

HARRY. Not anymore. Not like it was . . .

LUKE. Well, thy works for the bloody club.

HARRY. I work for Sir Frederick, lad; for nob'dy else. (LUKE *looks across at him.*) I mu'n run the bloody bath. (*He goes.* LUKE *watches from the door, then looks round*

for anything he's forgotten. Comes back in, gets scissors.
Sound, off, from the bath-entrance, of running water. He
crosses to the door and goes. HARRY *comes back a mo-*
ment later. He gets towels from the basket and lays them
out on the bench, by each peg. At one point there's a roar
and booing from the crowd, trumpets, rattles. It dies away
to a fainter moan. He turns on the TANOY.)

TANOY. (*Accompanied by roaring of the crowd.*) '. . .
Copley . . . Clegg . . . Morley . . . Fenchurch . . . inside
. . . passes . . . Jagger . . . Stringer . . . Tackled. Fourth
tackle. Scrum down. Walsh . . . Fielding . . . Walsh having words with his opposite number! Getting down. The
scrum is just inside United's half . . . almost ten yards in
from the opposite touch . . . put in . . . some rough play
inside that scrum . . . Referee Tallon's blown up . . .
free kick . . . no . . . scrum down . . . not satisfied with
the tunnel . . . ball in . . . Walsh's head is up . . .
(*Laughter.*) There's some rough business inside that
scrum . . . my goodness! . . . ball comes out . . . Morley
. . . Copley . . . Owens . . . Owens to Trevor . . . *Trevor*
is going to drop a goal . . . too late . . . He's left it far
too late . . . They've tried that once before . . . Kendal
. . .' (*He switches the* TANOY *off. Great roar outside.*
HARRY *has crossed to the fire; more coal; pokes it, goes*
off to the bath-entrance. A moment later the door from
the porch opens: SANDFORD *comes in.*)

SANDFORD. (*Calling.*) Luke? . . . Luke?

HARRY. (*Re-emerging.*) He's just gone . . .

SANDFORD. Oh, Christ . . .

HARRY. Anything up?

SANDFORD. Gone through the bloody tunnel . . .
Missed him. (*Roar increasing off.* SANDFORD *hurries out.*
HARRY *stands in the centre of the room, waiting. Baying*
of the crowd. A few moments later voices off, 'Hold the
bloody door.' 'This side.' 'This side.' 'Take his shoulder.'
'I'm all right. I'm all right. Don't worry.' *The door opens:*
KENDAL *comes in, supported by* CROSBY *and* MOORE.)

KENDAL. It's all right . . . It's bloody nowt . . . Where
is it? Where's he put it?

CROSBY. Get him down . . . no over here. Over here.
On this. (*They take him to the massage table.*)

KENDAL. Now, don't worry. Don't worry . . . Don't
worry. I'll be all right . . .

MOORE. S'all right, Kenny, lad. All right.

CROSBY. Doesn't know where he is . . . Now, come on. Lie down, Kenny, lad. Lie down.

KENDAL. S'all right. S'all right.

CROSBY. Where's bloody Lukey . . . Frank, get us a bloody sponge. Harry: 'od him down. (CROSBY *tries to hold* KENDAL *down: having been laid on the table he keeps trying to sit up.* HARRY *comes over to the table. He watches, but doesn't help.*)

HARRY. (*To* MOORE.) Over theer . . . that bucket. (MOORE *goes off to the bath-entrance.*)

CROSBY. Come on, Kenny. Come on . . . Lie down, lad.

KENDAL. S'all right . . . S'all right . . . I'll go back on.

CROSBY. You'll go nowhere, lad . . . Come on . . . Come on, then, Kenny, lad. Lie still. I want to bloody look . . . Come on . . . (*The door opens.* SANDFORD *comes in, followed by* LUKE, *with his bag.*)

LUKE. How is he? . . . Don't move him . . . Let's have a look.

CROSBY. Where's thy been? . . . On thy bloody holidays, ha'st tha?

LUKE. Let's have a look . . . I was coming up . . .

CROSBY. Nose . . . (*Steps back:* SANDFORD *takes hold.* CROSBY *gets a towel, wipes his hands.*)

KENDAL. Nose . . . It's me nose, Lukey . . .

LUKE. Lie still, lad, now. Lie still.

KENDAL. I can't bloody see, Lukey . . .

LUKE. Now just lie still . . . That's it . . . That's right . . . (MOORE *has brought the sponge.*) Get some clean water, lad. That's no good . . .

SANDFORD. Here . . . here . . . I'll get it. (*To* MOORE.) Come round here. Get 'od o' this. (MOORE *takes* SANDFORD'S *place,* SANDFORD *goes off to bath-entrance.* LUKE *has looked at* KENDAL'S *wound. His face is covered in blood. Sponges round* KENDAL'S *cheeks and mouth, then stoops down to his bag, gets out cotton wool.* KENDAL *is still trying to get up.*)

MOORE. It's all right, Kenny, lad. All right.

KENDAL. Can't see . . .

LUKE. Now just keep your eyes closed, lad . . . Harry, can you get a towel?

MOORE. I don't think Ken wa' even looking . . . His

bloody head came down . . . bloody boot came up . . . (HARRY *has passed over a towel.* MOORE *takes it.*)

LUKE. Shove it underneath his head . . . Kenny? Keep your head still, lad. (SANDFORD *has brought in a bowl of water.* LUKE *wipes away the blood with cotton wool, examines the damage.* SANDFORD *pours a drop of disinfectant from the bottle into the bowl of water.* LUKE *dips in the cotton wool, wipes* KENDAL'S *nose.* CROSBY, *not really interested, having wiped the blood from his hands and his track-suit, looks on impatiently over* LUKE'S *back.*)

KENDAL. A bit o' plaster, I'll go back on.

LUKE. Nay, lad. The game's over for you today.

KENDAL. I'll be all right . . . I'll get back on . . .

CROSBY. He's off, then, is he?

LUKE. Aye . . .

SANDFORD. Aye . . . (*Gestures up.*) I'll take him up.

CROSBY. Right . . . Frank. Come on. Not have you hanging about down here.

SANDFORD. Who you sending on?

CROSBY. (*Looks round. To* FRANK.) Do you think you can manage then, out theer?

MOORE. Aye!

CROSBY. Come on, then. Let's have you up. (MOORE, *quickly, jubilantly, strips off his track-suit.*)

CROSBY. Lukey . . .

LUKE. Aye.

CROSBY. As soon as you've done. Let's have you up . . . Kenny, do you hear that, lad?

KENDAL. (*Half-rising.*) Aye . . .

CROSBY. Well done, lad . . . Just do as Lukey says . . .

KENDAL. Aye . . .

CROSBY. (*To* MOORE.) Come on. Come on. Not ready yet . . . (*Has gone to the door,* MOORE *scrambles out of the suit.* CROSBY *goes.* MOORE, *flexing his legs, pulling down his jersey, etc., follows him. He goes.*)

LUKE. Theer, then, Kenny . . . (*Has finished washing the wound and has dressed it with a plaster. He now helps* KENDAL *up with* SANDFORD'S *assistance.*) If there's ought you want, just give a shout.

KENDAL. There's me electric tool-kit, Luke . . .

LUKE. I've got it here, old lad . . . Thy'll be all right . . .

KENDAL. Fifteen quid that cost . . . just o'er . . .

SANDFORD. Here, then. Come on . . . Let's have you in the bath. Come on. Come on, now . . . It wouldn't do you much good if you dropped it in . . . (KENDAL *has got up from the table.* SANDFORD *helps him over to the bath-entrance.* LUKE *finishes packing his bag. The porch door opens,* MACKENDRICK *comes in.*)

MACKENDRICK. How is he?

LUKE. He'll be all right.

MACKENDRICK. Too bloody slow, you know. If I've said it once I've said it . . .

LUKE. Aye.

MACKENDRICK. (*Calls through.*) How're you feeling, Kenny, lad?

KENDAL. (*Off.*) All right.

MACKENDRICK. All right, Sandy?

SANDFORD. (*Off.*) Aye. I'll have him in the bath.

MACKENDRICK. Taking him up . . . ? (*Gestures up.*)

SANDFORD. (*Off.*) Aye.

MACKENDRICK. I'll see about a car.

SANDFORD. (*Off.*) Shan't be long.

MACKENDRICK. (*To* LUKE.) I'll go up to the office.

LUKE. Tool-kit. (*Shows him.* MACKENDRICK *looks in.*) Bloody shelves . . .

MACKENDRICK. Poor old Kenny . . .

LUKE. Bloody wife.

MACKENDRICK. Like that, then, is it?

LUKE. Been round half the teams i' the bloody league . . . one time or another. (*Packs his bag and goes over to the bath-entrance.*) I'll get on up, then, Sandy, lad.

SANDFORD. (*Off.*) Aye.

LUKE. Be all right, then, Kenny, lad?

KENDAL. (*Off.*) Aye . . . (LUKE *collects his bag.*)

LUKE. You'll see about a taxi, then?

MACKENDRICK. Aye. (*Roar off. They lift their heads.*)

LUKE. Another score.

MACKENDRICK. (*Gestures at bath-entrance.*) I'll get up and tell Sir Freddy, then. (MACKENDRICK *goes out by the office entrance,* LUKE *by the porch.* HARRY *is left alone. He's cleared up the bits of cotton wool and lint; he collects the used towels.* SANDFORD *brings in* KENDAL'S *used kit, drops it on the floor, gets a towel.*)

SANDFORD. Take care of that, then, Harry . . .

HARRY. Aye.

SANDFORD. Them his clothes?

HARRY. Aye. (SANDFORD *gets them down. He goes to the bath-entrance with the towel.*)

SANDFORD. (*Off.*) Come on, then, Kenny . . . Let's have you out. (HARRY *re-tidies the massage-table, resetting the head-rest which, for* KENDAL'S *sake, has been lowered. A moment later* KENDAL'S *led in with a towel round him.*) Can you see ought?

KENDAL. Bloody dots . . .

SANDFORD. No, this way, lad, then. Over here.

KENDAL. Is the game over, Sandy . . . ?

SANDFORD. Just about. Sit theer. I'll get you dried . . . (KENDAL *sits on the bench.* SANDFORD *dries his legs and feet, then he dries his head.* HARRY *looks on.*) Pass his shirt, then, will you? (HARRY *passes* KENDAL'S *shirt and vest over. There's a roaring of the crowd, off.*)

KENDAL. Are we winning?

SANDFORD. Come on, then . . . Get your head in this.

KENDAL. Can't remember . . . (HARRY *pulls his vest and shirt round his head.* KENDAL *dazedly pushes in his arms.*)

HARRY. What's he done?

SANDFORD. Nose.

HARRY. Bro'k it, has he?

SANDFORD. Aye.

KENDAL. Remember shopping.

SANDFORD. We've got it here, old lad. Don't worry.

KENDAL. Bloody fifteen quid . . .

HARRY. F'ust one this year.

SANDFORD. Come on, then, lad . . . Let's have you up. (SANDFORD *helps* KENDAL *to his feet.* HARRY *watches, hands in pockets.* KENDAL *leans on* SANDFORD, SANDFORD *pulls on his trousers.*)

HARRY. Three collar-bones we had one week . . . Two o' theirs . . . the last un ours . . . Ankle . . . Bloody thigh-bone, once . . . Red hair.

SANDFORD. (*To* KENDAL.) Come on, come on, then, lad . . . 'od up.

HARRY. He never played again.

KENDAL. Steam boilers, lad . . . Bang 'em in . . . Seen nothing like it. Row o' rivets . . . Christ . . . Can hardly see ought . . . Sandy?

SANDFORD. Here, old lad. Now just hold tight . . .

Come on. Come on, now. Let's have you out of here
. . . (*To* HARRY.) Will you see if Mr. Mackendrick's got
that car? . . . (*As* HARRY *goes.*) Harry, can you find me
coat as well? (HARRY *goes, stiffly, leaves by office entry.
Roar off, rises to peak, applause, bugles, rattles.* KENDAL
turns to sound as if to go.) Nay, lad, can't go with nothing
on your feet. (*Sits him down, puts on his socks and
shoes.*)

KENDAL. (*Dazed.*) Started lakin' here when I wa' fifteen, tha knows . . . Intermediates . . . Then I went out,
on loan, to one of these bloody colliery teams . . . bring
'em up at the bloody week-end in bloody buckets . . .
play a game o' bloody football . . . booze all Sunday . . .
back down at the coal-face, Monday . . . Seen nothing
like it. Better ring my wife.

SANDFORD. What?

KENDAL. She won't know.

SANDFORD. She's not here today, then?

KENDAL. No . . .

SANDFORD. I'll see about it, lad. Don't worry.

KENDAL. If I'm bloody kept in, or ought . . .

SANDFORD. Aye. It'll be all right.

KENDAL. The woman next door has got a phone.

SANDFORD. Aye. I'll see about it, lad. All right. (*Gets
up.*) Let's have your coat on. (KENDAL *stands*, SAND-
FORD *helps him into his raincoat.*)

KENDAL. I wa' going to get a new un . . .

SANDFORD. I won't bother with your tie.

KENDAL. . . . until I bought this drill . . .

SANDFORD. Aye! (*Laughs.*)

KENDAL. Start saving up again . . .

SANDFORD. That's right. (HARRY *comes in through the
office door. He brings in* SANDFORD'S *overcoat.*)

HARRY. There's a taxi outside already.

SANDFORD. Good.

HARRY. (*Watches* SANDFORD'S *efforts.*) Alus one or
two out theer.

SANDFORD. Yeh.

HARRY. Sat'days.

SANDFORD. Could alus use Sir Frederick's car, then.

HARRY. Aye . . .

SANDFORD. How're you feeling, lad?

KENDAL. All right.

SANDFORD. Come on, then, lad . . . Just fasten this
. . . (KENDAL *holds his head up so* SANDFORD *can fasten
on the dressing* LUKE *has left; it covers his nose and is
fastened with plaster to his cheeks.*)

KENDAL. Is it broke?

SANDFORD. There's a bit of a gash, old lad.

KENDAL. Had it broken once before . . .

SANDFORD. Can you manage to the car? (*Collects his
coat.*)

KENDAL. Wheer is it, then? (*Turns either way.*)

SANDFORD. Here it is, old lad . . . (*Hands him his
parcel.*)

KENDAL. Have to get some glasses . . . hardly see . . .

SANDFORD. (*To* HARRY.) Looks like Bloody Genghis
Khan . . . Come on, then, Kenny . . . Lean on me. (*To*
HARRY.) Still got me bloody boots on . . . I'll get them
in the office . . . See you, lad. (HARRY *watches them go.
He waits, then he picks up the used towel, takes it off to
dump inside the bath-entrance. He comes back, looks
round, switches on the* TANOY, *crowd roar.*)

TANOY. '. . . to Walsh . . . reaches the twenty-five . . .
goes down . . . plays back . . . (*Roar.*) Comes to Clegg
to Atkinson . . . Atkinson to the substitute Moore . . .
Moore in now, crashes his way through . . . goes down
. . . Walsh comes up . . . out to Owens . . . Owens
through . . . dummies . . . beautiful move . . . to Stringer,
Stringer out to Patsy . . . Patsy out to Trevor who's come
up on the wing . . . kicks . . . Copley . . . Fenchurch . . .
Fielding . . . *Morley* . . . (*Roar.*) Ball bounces into touch
. . . scrum . . . (*Pause, dull roar.*) Growing dark now
. . . ball goes in, comes out, Tallon blows . . . free kick
. . . scrum infringement . . . one or two tired figures
there . . . can see the steam, now, rising from the backs
. . . Trevor's running up and down, blowing in his hands
. . . Kick . . . good kick . . . (*Crowd roar.*) Finds touch
beyond the twenty-five . . . (*Crowd roar.* HARRY *sits,
listening. Fade, sound and light.*)

CURTAIN

ACT III

The same. Noise, shouting, singing, screeching, cries off. The TANOY *is playing music. Song from bath.* PATSY, *a towel round his waist, is drying himself with a second towel, standing by his clothes. He does it with the same care with which he prepared himself for the match.* HARRY *is picking up the mess of discarded shorts, jerseys, jockstraps, putting them on the basket. A pile of towels stands on the rubbing-down table.* SPENCER *is half-dressed in trousers and shirt, combing his wet hair in the mirror.* CROSBY *is going round checking boots, putting pairs together by the massage table to be collected up.*

CROSBY. (*To* SPENCER.) Up there waiting for you, is she, Billy?

SPENCER. Aye. All being well. (*Combing in mirror.*) Bloody expecting me to play today, an' all.

CROSBY. Ne'er mind. Next week: might be in luck.

SPENCER. Bloody away next week!

CROSBY. Maybe she'll have to bloody travel.

SPENCER. Not the travelling kind, you know.

CROSBY. Can't win 'em all, old lad. Don't worry . . . (*Calls.*) Come on. Let's have you out o' there . . . (*Switches off TANOY, moves on. To* PATSY.) How're you feeling, then old lad?

PATSY. All right. (*Winces, eases arm.*)

CROSBY. How's thy shoulder?

PATSY. All right. Bit stiff.

CROSBY. Bloody lovely try. Worth any amount o' bloody knocks is that.

PATSY. Aye.

CROSBY. Couple more next week . . . should be all right.

PATSY. Aye. (*Doesn't respond, drying himself, turns to check his clothes.* JAGGER *comes bursting in from the bath.*)

JAGGER. Dirty bugger . . . dirty sod . . . Danny, go bloody stop him. (*Snatches towel, rubs his hair vigor-*

112

ously.) Walshy—pittling in the bloody bath. (*Song from bath*.)

SPENCER. (*Calling through*.) Thy'll have to disinfect that bloody water . . . (*Laughing*.)

WALSH. (*Off*.) This *is* disinfectant, lad.

CROSBY. Come on, Walshy: let's have you out . . . (CROSBY *takes a towel and dries* JAGGER'S *back*.)

JAGGER. Dirty bugger, dirty sod!

WALSH. (*Off*.) Come on, Jagger. You could do with a bloody wash.

JAGGER. Not in that, you dirty sod . . . Set bloody Patsy onto you, if you don't watch out. (*Water comes in from the bath*.) Dirty! Dirty! . . . (*Dances out of the way: laughter and shouting off*.)

CROSBY. Come on, Trevor. Teach 'em one or two manners, then . . . Bloody college-man . . . going to go away disgusted with all you bloody working lads. (*Another jet of water*. CROSBY *lurches out of the way*.) Bloody well be in there if you don't watch out. (*Jeers, cries*.)

COPLEY. (*Off*.) Too bloody old!

CLEGG. (*Off*.) Come on, Danny. Show us what you've got.

CROSBY. Got summat here that'll bloody well surprise you, lad . . . (*Laughter, cries*.) And you! (*Laughter off*.) Sithee . . . Billy. Go in and quieten 'em down.

SPENCER. Nay . . . gotten out in one bloody piece. Not likely. Send Harry in. He'll shift 'em out. (HARRY *looks up, they laugh. He doesn't respond. Singing starts off, then all join in from the bath*. LUKE *comes in*.)

CROSBY. Got through, then, did you?

LUKE. He'll be all right . . .

JAGGER. Kenny?

LUKE. Broken nose.

JAGGER. Keeping him in, then, are they?

LUKE. Aye.

JAGGER. Give his missus chance to bloody roam.

LUKE. (*Goes over to* PATSY.) How's it feel, old lad?

PATSY. All right. (*Eases his shoulder, stiffly*.)

LUKE. Come in tomorrow: I'll give you a bloody rub.

PATSY. Right.

LUKE. Need a drop of stuff on theer. (*Goes to his bag*. TREVOR *has come in, wiping himself down with a towel*.)

TREVOR. Just look . . . just beginning to get up circulation . . . (*Flexes his fingers.*)

JAGGER. Circulate a bit lower down for me. (CROSBY *has a towel and now dries* TREVOR'S *back.*)

TREVOR. Bloody shaking, still. Just look. (*Holds out his hands, trembling.*)

CROSBY. Don't worry. This time to-morrow . . . (*Flicks towel to* SPENCER, *who finishes rubbing* TREVOR'S *back.*)

SPENCER. What's thy teach, then, Trev?

TREVOR. Mathematics.

SPENCER. Maths . . .

TREVOR. One of your subjects, is it?

SPENCER. One . . . (*Laughs.*)

LUKE. T'other's bloody lasses, Trev.

SPENCER. Nay, I gi'e time o'er to one or two other things, an' all. (*They laugh.*)

JAGGER. Here . . . Got the two-thirty, Lukey, have you?

LUKE. Somewheer . . . (*Tosses the paper over from his pocket.*)

SPENCER. (*To* TREVOR.) That kind o' mathematics, Trev. (*Slaps his back, finished drying.*)

TREVOR. Shoulda known. (*Turns away to get dressed.*)

JAGGER. Let me see . . . (*Examines stop-press.*) One-thirty . . . (*To* SPENCER.) Quite a bit fastened up on that . . . Two o'clock . . . (*Reading.*) two-thirty . . . No . . .

CROSBY. What's that, Jagger, lad? (JAGGER *tosses paper down, goes to his clothes.*)

SPENCER. Let's have a look.

JAGGER. (*To* LUKE.) Don't say a word to bloody Walsh.

LUKE. Shan't say a word. (*Laughs.*) Not a sausage. (LUKE *has dabbed an orange staining antiseptic on* PATSY'S *arm; now he crosses to* TREVOR; *as* TREVOR *starts to dress he moves round him, dabbing on antiseptic with cotton wool.*) Hold still. Hold still. (CLEGG *comes in, drying.*)

CLEGG. Bit lower down there, Lukey.

LUKE. Aye. (*Laughs.*)

SPENCER. (*Reading.*) Bloody 'Albatross.' Seven to one.

JAGGER. What d'you back, Billy, lad?

SPENCER. Same as you, Jag. 'Little Nell.' (*To* LUKE.) Tipped the bloody 'oss himself.

JAGGER. Bloody Walsh . . . Never hear the end.

CLEGG. What's that? (JAGGER, *dry, has started to dress.* SPENCER *has taken the towel from* CLEGG *and is drying his back.*)

JAGGER. 'Albatross,' come up . . . (*Gestures off.*)

CLEGG. (*To* SPENCER.) What's that?

SPENCER. Sithee, I'm saying nowt. (*Flicks the towel to him, picks up another.* COPLEY *has come in, followed by* FENCHURCH. SPENCER *goes to dry* COPLEY'S *back;* CROSBY *to dry* FENCHURCH'S.)

COPLEY. Sithee, there ought to be a special bloody bath for those dirty bloody buggers, I'm muckier now than when I bloody well went in.

WALSH. (*Off, siren-call.*) Barry! Barry! *We can't do without you, Barry!*

COPLEY. (*Calling.*) Sod off.

MORLEY. (*Siren, off.*) *Barry . . . y!*

WALSH. (*Siren, off.*) Barry . . . y . . .

MORLEY. (*Off.*) Barr . . . y! We're *waiting*, Barry!

COPLEY. (*Calling.*) Piss off! (*Song from bath.*)

CROSBY. Come on, Fieldy . . . Keep those ignorant sods in line.

FIELDING. (*Off.*) I'm in the bloody shower. I'm not in with those mucky bloody sods.

JAGGER. How're you feeling, Fenny, lad?

FENCHURCH. All right . . . Results in theer, then, are they? (*Indicating paper.*)

CLEGG. Aye. (CLEGG *has picked it up to read. Reads.*) 'Latest score, twelve-seven.' Patsy: they didn't get thy try . . . Sithee, pricked up his bloody ears at that. (*They laugh.* PATSY, *having turned, goes back to dressing.*)

FENCHURCH. Fifteen-seven . . .

JAGGER. Fifteen-seven.

FENCHURCH. Put a good word in with Sir Frederick, then.

CROSBY. Good word about bloody what, then, lad?

FENCHURCH. Me and Jagger, Danny boy . . . Made old Patsy's bloody try . . . In't that right, then Jagger lad?

PATSY. Made me own bloody try. Ask Jack . . .

(STRINGER *has come in, shaking off water.* CROSBY *goes to him with a towel, dries his back.*)

MORLEY. (*Off.*) Any more for any more? (*Laughter off.*)

WALSH. (*Off.*) Barry . . . y! *We're waiting, Barry!*

FENCHURCH. Take no notice. Silly sod.

STRINGER. Where's Cliff, then?

JAGGER. Up in the directors' bath, old lad.

STRINGER. Is that right, then?

CROSBY. Captain's privilege, lad.

STRINGER. Bloody hell . . . (*Snatches towel, goes over to the bench to dry himself.* LUKE *is still going round, dabbing on antiseptic.*)

LUKE. Any cuts, bruises, ought that needs fastening up?

JAGGER. I've a couple of things here that need a bit of bloody attention, Lukey . . .

LUKE. What's that? (*Goes over:* JAGGER *shows him. They laugh.* PATSY *has crossed to the mirror to comb his hair.*)

PATSY. Did you see a young woman waiting for me up there Danny? (*Groans and jeers from the players.*)

CLEGG. How do you do it, Patsy? I can never make that out.

FENCHURCH. Nay, his girl-friend's a bloody school-teacher. Isn't that right, then, Patsy? (PATSY *doesn't answer, combs his hair, straightens his tie*).

JAGGER. School-teacher?

FENCHURCH. Teaches in Trevor's bloody school . . . Isn't that right, then, Trev? (TREVOR *nods, doesn't look up; gets on with his dressing.*)

JAGGER. What do you talk about, then, Patsy? (*They laugh.* PATSY *is crossing to his coat. With some care he pulls it on.*)

CLEGG. (*Having gone to him.*) The moon in *June* . . . Is coming out quite *soon!*

WALSH. (*Off.*) Barr . . . y! *Where are you, Barr . . . y!*

COPLEY. Piss off, you ignorant sod.

MORLEY. (*Off.*) Barry . . . y! *We're waiting*, Barr . . . y! (*Laughter off.*)

LUKE. Sithee . . . clean forgot. Can you sign these autograph books, there's a half a dozen lads outside . . . (*Takes them from his pocket, puts them on the table.*)

JAGGER. By God, just look at that! (PATSY *has already crossed to the table.*) Pen out in a bloody flash . . . (PATSY *takes out a pen clipped to his top pocket, writes.* JAGGER *stoops over his shoulder to watch.*) He can write, an' all . . . 'Patrick Walter Turner.' Beautiful. Bloody beautiful is that.

PATSY. Piss off.

JAGGER. Here, now. Bloody language, Trev! . . . Hears that, she'll never speak to you again.

FENCHURCH. Put you down in her bloody book . . .

JAGGER. Black mark.

FENCHURCH. One thousand lines . . .

JAGGER. 'I must not bloody swear, you cunt!' (*They laugh.* FIELDING *comes in, picks up a towel,* SPENCER *goes over to dry his back.*)

FIELDING. They're going to be in theer a bloody fo't-night . . . Harry—go in and pull that bloody plug.

HARRY. (*Doesn't look up.*) Aye. (*Burst of laughter, shouts off,* "Give over! Give over! You rotten bloody sod!")

STRINGER. They could do with putting in separate bloody showers in theer.

CROSBY. What's that, Jack?

STRINGER. Separate showers. It's not hygienic, getting bathed together.

CLEGG. It's not. He's right. That's quite correct.

FENCHURCH. Put a bit o' color in your cheeks, old lad.

STRINGER. I've got all the color theer I need.

JAGGER. Played a grand game today, though, Jack. (*Winks at the others.*)

STRINGER. (*Mollified.*) Aye.

JAGGER. Marvellous. Bloody fine example, that.

STRINGER. Aye. Well . . . I did my best.

JAGGER. Them bloody forwards, see them clear a way. (*They laugh,* STRINGER *dries his hair, rubbing fiercely.* ATKINSON *comes in from the bath, limping.* CROSBY *gets a towel, dries his back.*)

LUKE. Let's have you on here, Bryan. Let's have a look. (LUKE *waits by the table while* ATKINSON *gets dry.*)

MORLEY. (*Off.*) Barry! *Where are you, Barry!*

WALSH. (*Off.*) Barry! *We're waiting,* Barry . . . (COP-LEY *looks round, sees one of the buckets, takes it to the bath-entrance, flings the cold water in. Cries and shouts off. The players laugh.*)

CROSBY. Go on. Here . . . Here's a bloody 'nother. (COPLEY *takes it, flings the water in. Cries, shouts off. The players laugh, looking over at the bath-entrance.* AT-KINSON *is dry now and, a towel round him, he lies down on the massage table.* LUKE *examines his leg.* PATSY, *having got on his coat, has returned to the mirror: final adjustments, collar, tie, hair . . .* STRINGER *continues getting dressed.* TREVOR *joins* PATSY *at the mirror.* FEN-CHURCH, JAGGER, CLEGG *are almost dressed,* FIELDING *just beginning.*)

JAGGER. Go on, Barry! Ought else you've bloody got! (COPLEY *looks round, sees nothing.*)

CROSBY. Here . . . Come on . . . Turn on that bloody hose. (*He picks up the end of the hose by the bath-entrance; turns the tap. They spray the water into the bath-entrance. Cries and shouts from the bath. The players call out: "More! More! Go on! All over!" Cries and shouts off. A moment later* MOORE *and* MORLEY *come running in, shaking off water, the players scattering.*)

MOORE. Give over! Give over! Ger off! (*They grab towels, start rubbing down.*)

WALSH. (*Off.*) More! More! Lovely! Lovely! . . . That's it, now, lads . . . No. No. Right . . . Lovely. Lovely . . . Bit lower, Barry . . . Lovely! Grand! (*The players laugh.*)

CROSBY. (*To* COPLEY.) All right . . .

LUKE. That's enough . . .

CROSBY. Nowt'll get through that bloody skin, I can tell you. (*Calls through.*) We're putting the lights out in ten minutes, lad . . . You can stay there all night if tha bloody wants. (COPLEY *turns off the tap. The players go back to getting dressed.*)

STRINGER. All over me bloody clothes. Just look.

FIELDING. Here . . . here, old lad. I'll mop it up . . . Grand game today, then, Jack.

STRINGER. Aye . . . All right. (CROSBY *dries* MOORE'S *back,* SPENCER *dries* MORLEY'S.)

CROSBY. What's it feel like, Frank?

MOORE. Grand . . . Just got started.

FIELDING. Knows how to bloody lake, does Frank . . . ten minutes . . .

MOORE. Nearer thi'ty.

FIELDING. Just time to get his jersey mucky . . .

CROSBY. He'll bloody show you lads next week . . .

FIELDING. Can't bloody wait to see, old lad.

WALSH. (*Off.*) Barry . . . *I'm waiting*, Barry! (*The players laugh.*)

COPLEY. Well, I'm bloody well not waiting here for thee! (*They laugh. The door from the office has opened.* THORNTON, *followed by* MACKENDRICK, *comes in.*)

THORNTON. Well done, lads . . . Bloody champion . . . well done . . . They'll not come here again in a bloody hurry . . . not feel half so bloody pleased . . . How's thy feeling, Patsy, lad?

PATSY. All right, sir.

THORNTON. Lovely try . . . Bloody text-book, lad . . . Hope they got that down on bloody film . . . Frank? How's it feel, young man?

MOORE. Pretty good. All right.

CROSBY. Just got started . . .

FIELDING. Just got into his stride, Sir Frederick.

THORNTON. Another ten minutes . . . he'd have had a bloody try. (*They laugh.*) Set'em a bloody fine example, lad, don't worry. Well played there, lad. Well done.

MACKENDRICK. Well done, lad.

THORNTON. How's your leg, then, Bryan?

ATKINSON. Be all right. (ATKINSON *is still on the table.* LUKE *is massaging the leg with oil.*)

THORNTON. Nasty bloody knock was that.

ATKINSON. Went one way . . . Me leg went t'other.

THORNTON. (*To* TREVOR.) How's your hands now, then, lad?

TREVOR. All right. Fine, thanks. (TREVOR *has pulled on his club blazer; looks up from dusting it down.*)

THORNTON. (*To* FIELDING.) I hope you're going to get your eye seen to there, old lad.

FIELDING. Aye.

THORNTON. Bad news about old Kenny.

PLAYERS. Aye . . .

WALSH. (*Off.*) Barr . . . y . . . I am *waiting*, Barry!

THORNTON. Who's that, then? Bloody Walsh?

CROSBY. Aye.

THORNTON. (*Going to the bath-entrance.*) And who's thy waiting for, then, Walshy?

WALSH. (*Pause. Off.*) Oh, good evening, Sir Frederick . . .

THORNTON. I'll give you Sir bloody Frederick . . . I'll be inside that bath in a bloody minute.

WALSH. (*Off.*) Any time, Sir Frederick, any time is good enough for me. (*The players laugh.* MACKENDRICK *has moved off amongst the players, going first to* PATSY, *then to* TREVOR, *slapping backs, 'Well done. Good match.'* THORNTON *turns back to the players.*)

THORNTON. I think we ought to charge Walsh bloody rent, spends more time here than he does at home.

CROSBY. Thy had five quid off him here last week, swearing to the referee.

MACKENDRICK. That's right. We did! (*They laugh.*)

THORNTON. No luck this week, then, I fancy?

CROSBY. Shouldn't think so. Tallon's not above bloody answering back.

THORNTON. Shifty bugger is old Walshy . . . Grand try in the first half, Mic. Good game.

MORLEY. Thanks. (MORLEY, *his back dried by* SPENCER, *is now getting dressed.*)

THORNTON. Bloody well stuck to you in the second half, I noticed.

MORLEY. Aye . . . Hardly room to move about.

THORNTON. Was Kenny's an accident, then . . . Or someb'dy catch him?

MORLEY. A bit slow, I think, today.

ATKINSON. Too cold . . .

FIELDING. Too cold.

MORLEY. It went right through you.

THORNTON. There's a bloody frost out theer already . . . Shouldn't be surprised if it snows tonight . . . Jagger, grand game, lad. Well done.

JAGGER. Thanks, Sir Frederick.

THORNTON. Shook their centre a time or two, I saw.

JAGGER. Always goes off the bloody left foot.

THORNTON. So I noticed . . . (*To* STRINGER.) Well done there, Jack. Well played.

STRINGER. Aye.

THORNTON. One of your best games for a long time, lad . . . Not that the others haven't been so bad. (*Laughs.*) Liked your tackling. Stick to it . . . Low, low!

STRINGER. Aye! That's right!

THORNTON. Any knocks, bruises?

STRINGER. No. No. Be all right.

THORNTON. Come up tomorrow if you're feeling stiff. Lukey here'll be doing his stuff.

LUKE. Aye . . . That's right. (*He slaps* ATKINSON *who gets up and starts to dress.*) Gi'e us a couple o' hours i' bed . . . mek it ten o'clock, old lad. (*After wiping his hands* LUKE *starts to check his bottles, cotton-wool, etc., packing them in his bag.*)

THORNTON. Bloody gossip shop is this on a Sunday morning . . . Isn't that right, then, Mac?

MACKENDRICK. Aye. It is.

PATSY. I'll . . . er . . . get off, then, Sir Frederick . . . See you next week, then, all being well.

THORNTON. Your young lady waiting, is she?

PATSY. Aye . . . I think so.

THORNTON. Grand game. Well done.

PATSY. Thanks, Sir Frederick . . . See you next week, Mr. Mackendrick.

MACKENDRICK. Aye. Aye. Well done, young man.

PATSY. Bye, lads!

PLAYERS. (*Without much interest.*) Aye . . . bye . . . cheerio.

MORLEY. Gi'e her a big kiss, then, Patsy, lad. (*Chorus of laughter.*)

JAGGER. Gi'e her one for me, an' all.

FENCHURCH. And me.

COPLEY. And me.

FIELDING. And me.

ATKINSON. And me.

CLEGG. And me.

MOORE. And me.

SPENCER. And me, an' all. (*They laugh.* PATSY *goes, leaves through the porch entrance.*)

MACKENDRICK. Bloody good example there is Pat . . . Saves his bloody money . . . Not like some.

CLEGG. Saves it for bloody what, though, Mac?

MACKENDRICK. He's got some bloody brains has Pat . . . puts it i' the bank, for one . . .

FIELDING. Big-headed sod.

CROSBY. What's that?

LUKE. He's got some good qualities has Pat.

FIELDING. I don't know where he keeps them then. (*They laugh.*)

THORNTON. (*To* MACKENDRICK.) Nay, don't look at me, old lad. (THORNTON *laughs, has gone over to the fire to warm his hands.*)

JAGGER. (*Calling.*) Sing us a song, then, Jack, old love.

STRINGER. Sing a bloody song thysen. (*They laugh.* OWENS *has come in from the office: dressed in a smart suit, a neat, cheerful, professional man.*)

OWENS. Look at this. Bloody opening-time. Not even dressed.

MORLEY. Where's thy been, then, Cliff?

JAGGER. Up in Sir Frederick's private shower room, have you?

OWENS. I thought it might be crowded, lads, today. What with that and the bloody cold . . . (*Winks, crosses to the massage table. Loudly.*) Got a bit o' plaster, have you Lukey?

PLAYERS. Give over! Give over! Get off!

OWENS. Got a little cut here . . .

PLAYERS. Give over! Give over! Get off! (OWENS, *winking, goes over to the fire to warm his hands.*)

JAGGER. Give him a bloody kiss, Sir Frederick . . . that's all he bloody wants. (*They laugh.* WALSH *appears at the bath-entrance, a towel around his middle. He stands in the bath-entrance, nodding, looking in.*)

WALSH. I thought I could hear him . . . (*To* OWENS.) Come to see the workers, have you? How long're you going to give us, lad?

OWENS. I'll give thee all the time thy wants, old love. (*The others laugh.*)

WALSH. I've been waiting for you, Barry . . . (*Gestures back. The others laugh.*)

FENCHURCH. What's thy want him for, then, Walsh?

CROSBY. What's he after, Barry? What's he want?

WALSH. He knows what I've been waiting for. (*They laugh.*)

LUKE. We're bloody well closing shop in a couple o' minutes, Walsh. You want to hurry up. You'll be turned out without thy bloody clothes.

ATKINSON. T'only bloody bath he gets is here. (*They laugh. He still stands there, gazing in, confronted.*)

COPLEY. Come on, then, Walshy. Show us what you've got.

WALSH. I'll show thee bloody nowt, old lad. (*Moves over towards his clothes.*) Keeping me bloody waiting . . . sat in theer. (*They laugh.*) I was *waiting* for you, Barry . . . (*They laugh.*)

CLEGG. Come on, then, Walshy, lad . . .

FENCHURCH. Gi' us a bloody shock.

MORLEY. Mr. Mackendrick, here: he's been hanging on for hours. (*They laugh.*)

MACKENDRICK. Nay, don't bring me into it, old lad. I've seen all of Walshy that I bloody want. (WALSH, *with great circumspection, the towel still around him, has started to put on his clothes, vest and shirt.*)

WALSH. Tell my bloody wife about you, Jagger . . . Dirty bloody sod . . .

CROSBY. (*To all of them.*) Come on, come on, then. Let's have you out . . .

HARRY. Have you all finished, then, in theer? (*Most of the players now are dressed. One or two have started to smoke.* OWENS *and* THORNTON *stand with their backs to the fire, looking on.* HARRY *has collected up the jerseys, stockings, shorts and towels. He's worked anonymously, overlooked, almost as if, for the players, he wasn't there.*)

WALSH. What?

HARRY. Have you finished with that bath?

WALSH. What do you want me to bloody do? Sup the bloody stuff, old lad? (*They laugh.*)

HARRY. I'll go and empty it, then.

FENCHURCH. Mind how you touch that water, lad.

FIELDING. Bloody poisonous, is that. (HARRY, *without any response, goes to the hose, takes it in to the bath, reappears, turns the tap, goes off to the bath.* TALLON *has put his head in from the office entrance; he's dressed in an overcoat and scarf, and carries a small hold-all.*)

TALLON. Just say good night, then, lads.

PLAYERS. Aye . . . aye . . . Good night . . . Good night . . .

TALLON. A good game, lads.

CROSBY. Aye.

TALLON. Both sides played very well. And in very difficult conditions, too.

CROSBY. Aye. Aye. That's right.

TALLON. Sorry about Kendal . . . I hear they've taken him off.

LUKE. Aye . . . He'll be all right.

TALLON. Keeping him in, then, are they?

MACKENDRICK. Aye. That's right.

TALLON. Say goodnight, then, Mr. Mackendrick . . . See you soon. (*Crosses; shakes hands with* MACKEN-DRICK.)

MACKENDRICK. I don't think you've met Sir Frederick.

TALLON. No. No. I haven't.

THORNTON. Admired your refereeing very much.

TALLON. Thank you. Thank you very much, sir.

THORNTON. See you up here again, then, soon, I hope.

TALLON. Aye. Aye. Our job, though, you never know.

THORNTON. If you bring the same result with you, you can come up every bloody week, tha knows. (*They laugh.*) Going upstairs, then, are you? (*Mimes drink.*)

TALLON. No. No. I've to catch me train. Otherwise I would. This weather. You can never chance your luck . . . Well, goodbye. It's been a pleasure. (*Nods to* OWENS, *ducks his head to the others, goes.*)

WALSH. Anybody heard the bloody two-thirty?

JAGGER. No.

FENCHURCH. No.

SPENCER. No.

LUKE. No.

FIELDING. No.

MOORE. No.

WALSH. (*Back to them, getting dressed.*) By God, sunk me bloody week's wages theer . . . You haven't got a paper, Mac?

MACKENDRICK. No. No. Haven't had a chance.

COPLEY. Let's see. Now here's one . . . What wa're it, now?

WALSH. (*Dressing.*) Two-thirty.

COPLEY. (*Reading.*) 'One o'clock . . . one-thirty . . . two o'clock . . . two-fifteen . . .'

WALSH. Come on, come on, come on . . . (JAGGER *points it out.*)

COPLEY. Two-thirty! . . . Let's see now. What d'thy bet?

WALSH. Just tell us the bloody winner. Come on. Come on.

COPLEY. What's this, now? . . . Can't see without me glasses . . . Little . . . what is it?

WALSH. Oh, God.

COPLEY. Nell.

WALSH. Hell fire . . . Can't bloody well go home tonight.

COPLEY. (*Still reading.*) Worth having something on, was that.

WALSH. Tell bloody Jagger: don't tell me.

JAGGER. And Fenny. (*Winking.*)

WALSH. And Fenny . . . Here. Let's have a look. (*They wait, watching, suppressing their laughter as* WALSH, *eyes screwed up, short-sighted, reads.*) Here! . . . Here! . . . What's this . . . (*Eyes screwed, still reads. They burst out laughing.*) Just look at that. Bloody 'Albatross'! *Seven to one!* (*Shows it to* ATKINSON *to be confirmed.*)

ATKINSON. That's right.

WALSH. I've won, I've won. (*Embraces* STRINGER *who's standing near him, fastening his coat.*)

STRINGER. Go on. Go on. Ger'off. (*The players laugh.*)

WALSH. By God, that's made my bloody day, has that.

MACKENDRICK. More interested in that than he is in bloody football.

WALSH. I am. I am, old lad . . . More bloody brass in this for a bloody start. (*Laughs, finishes his dressing.*) By God, then, see old Barry now . . . Wish thy'd washed my bloody back, then, don't you?

COPLEY. I think I bloody do. That's right. (*They laugh.*)

FIELDING. Well, then, lads. I'm off . . .

PLAYERS. See you, Fieldy . . . Bye.

LUKE. Watch that bloody eye.

FIELDING. Aye. Aye. It'll be all right.

THORNTON. Bye, Fieldy. Well done, lad.

FIELDING. Aye . . . (*Goes.*)

JAGGER. Fenny . . . Ar't'a barn, then? . . . Trev?

FENCHURCH. Aye . . . (*Packing his bag.*)

TREVOR. Aye.

WALSH. Lukey, where's my bloody cigar, old lad? (*They laugh.* LUKE *gets out the cigar.* JAGGER *and*

Trevor *have gone to the door, joined by* Fenchurch *carrying his bag.*)

Jagger. See you, lads, then.

All. Aye.

Trevor. Bye.

All. Bye . . . See you.

Mackendrick. Well done, Trevor, lad.

Trevor. Aye . . . (*They go.* Walsh *is lighting up.*)

Thornton. (*Going.*) Mind you don't choke on that, then, Walshy.

Walsh. Don't bloody worry . . . From now on . . . Trouble free! (*Blows out a cloud of smoke for his amusement.*)

Thornton. Bye, lads . . . Clifford?

Owens. Aye. Shan't be a minute.

Thornton. Time for a snifter, lads, tha knows . . . (*Gestures up.*)

All. Aye . . .

Copley. Bye, Sir Frederick. (Thornton *goes through the office entrance.* Mackendrick, *nodding, follows.* Crosby, *picking up a couple of remaining boots, goes off through the bath-entrance.*)

Stringer. Well, I've got everything, I think. I'm off.

Copley. Enjoyed yourself today, then, Jack?

Stringer. Aye. All right.

Clegg. They tell me your mother was here this afternoon, then, Jack.

Stringer. As likely.

Copley. T'only bloody fan he's got.

Stringer. I've got one or two more, an' all. (*They laugh.*)

Atkinson. Give you a lift into town, Jack, if you like.

Stringer. No . . . no . . . I like to walk. (*He goes. They laugh.*)

Walsh. Here . . . Here you are, then, Cliff. (Walsh, *having finished dressing, adjusted his button-hole and combed his hair in the mirror, gets out another cigar. The others watch in amazement.*)

Owens. Thanks, Walshy . . . Thanks very much . . . Won't smoke it now. (*Smells it appreciatively.*)

Walsh. Save it.

Owens. Appreciate it later.

Walsh. Not like these ignorant bloody sods . . .

COPLEY. Well, bloody hell . . .

WALSH. Come today, tha knows . . . gone tomorrer.

CLEGG. Bloody hell.

COPLEY. The stingy bugger . . . (WALSH *laughs: a last look round, coat.* CROSBY *comes back in through bath-entrance.*)

CROSBY. Come on. Come on. Let's have you out. (*Claps his hands.*)

CLEGG. A bloody fistful . . .

WALSH. Just one. Just one. (*Puffs at his own.*) Just the odd one, old son.

COPLEY. Greasing round the bloody captain, Danny.

WALSH. Keep in wi' me bloody captain. Never know when you might need a bloody favour. Isn't that right, then, Cliff?

OWENS. That's right. (*They laugh, going.*)

ATKINSON. Well, then, Walshy . . . Gonna buy us one? (*Gestures up.*)

WALSH. I might . . . (*They've moved over to the office door, except for* OWENS, CROSBY *and* LUKE.) Barry here, o' course, will have to do without . . . (*To* CROSBY.) Never came when I bloody called . . . As for the rest . . . I might stand a round . . . Might afford it . . . And one for thee, old lad. All right?

SPENCER. All right.

WALSH. (*Looking back.*) What was Jagger's horse, now?

LUKE. Little Nell.

WALSH. Little Nell! (*He laughs.*)

CLEGG. Are you coming, Frank?

MOORE. Aye. Aye. I will.

WALSH. (*To* MOORE.) Thy's kept bloody quiet, old lad . . .

MOORE. Aye . . .

WALSH. Don't let these bloody lads upset you.

MOORE. No. No. (*Laughs.*)

WALSH. (*Puts his arm round* MOORE'S *shoulder, going.*) Sithee, Barry . . . first flush o' bloody success is that.

COPLEY. Mic? (*Leaving.*)

MORLEY. Aye. Just about. (*They go, laughing; burst of laughter and shouts outside. Silence.* LUKE *has packed his bag, he zips it up.* CROSBY *is picking up the rest of the equipment, odd socks, shirts.* OWENS *gets out a ciga-*

rette, offers one to CROSBY, *who takes one, then offers one to* LUKE *who shakes his head. There's a sound of* HARRY *singing off, hymn.* OWENS *flicks a lighter, lights* CROSBY'S *cigarette, then his own.*)

PLAYERS. (*Off.*) We waited for you, Barry.

CROSBY. Not two bloody thoughts to rub together . . . (*Gestures off.*) Walshy.

OWENS. No. (*Laughs.*)

CROSBY. Years ago . . . ran into a bloody post . . . out yonder . . . split the head of any other man . . . Gets up, looks round, says, 'By God,' then . . . 'Have they teken him off?' (*They laugh.* LUKE *swings down his bag.*)

LUKE. I'm off.

CROSBY. See you, Lukey.

LUKE. Cliff . . .

OWENS. Thanks, Lukey.

LUKE. (*Calls.*) Bye, Harry . . . (*They wait, hymn continues.*)

CROSBY. Wandered off . . . (*Indicating* HARRY *off.*)

LUKE. Aye . . . See you, lads. (*Collects autograph books.*)

OWENS. Bye, Lukey. (LUKE *goes with his bag through the porch entrance.* CROSBY *picks up the last pieces.*)

CROSBY. How're you feeling?

OWENS. Stiff.

CROSBY. Bloody past it, lad, tha knows.

OWENS. Aye. One more season, I think, I'm finished. (CROSBY *laughs.*) Been here, tha knows, a bit too long.

CROSBY. Nay, there's nob'dy else, old lad . . .

OWENS. Aye . . . (*Laughs.*)

CROSBY. Need thee a bit longer to keep these lads in line.

OWENS. Aye. (*Laughs.*)

CROSBY. Did well today.

OWENS. They did. That's right.

CROSBY. Bloody leadership, tha see, that counts.

OWENS. (*Laughs.*) Aye . . .

CROSBY. (*Calls through to bath.*) Have you finished, then, in theer . . . (*No answer. To* OWENS.) Ger'up yonder . . .

OWENS. Have a snifter . . .

CROSBY. Another bloody season yet. (*Puts out the light.*) Poor old Fieldy.

OWENS. Aye.

CROSBY. Ah, well . . . this time tomorrer . . .

OWENS. Have no more bloody worries then. (*They laugh.* CROSBY *puts his arm round* OWENS. *They go. Singing from the bath has paused.* HARRY *comes in, looks round. He carries a sweeping brush. Starts sweeping. Picks up one or two bits of tape, etc. Turns on the tanoy,* LIGHT MUSIC. *Sweeps. The remaining LIGHT and the sound of the tanoy slowly FADE.*)

Plenty

A DRAMA

by David Hare

Plenty was first performed at the Lyttelton Theatre on April 7, 1978, under the direction of the author. The cast was as follows:

SUSAN TRAHERNE	*Kate Nelligan*
ALICE PARK	*Julie Covington*
RAYMOND BROCK	*Stephen Moore*
CODENAME LAZAR	*Paul Freeman*
A FRENCHMAN	*Robert Ralph*
SIR LEONARD DARWIN	*Basil Henson*
MICK	*David Schofield*
LOUISE	*Gil Brailey*
M AUNG	*Kristopher Kum*
MME AUNG	*Me Me Lai*
DORCAS FREY	*Lindsay Duncan*
JOHN BEGLEY	*Tom Durham*
SIR ANDREW CHARLESON	*Frederick Treves*
ANOTHER FRENCHMAN	*Timothy Davies*

Settings by Hayden Griffin; costumes by Deirdre Clancy; music by Nick Bicât.

Plenty was produced by Joseph Papp at the Plymouth Theatre, New York, on January 6, 1983, under the direction of Mr. Hare, with the following cast:

ALICE PARK	*Ellen Parker*
SUSAN TRAHERNE	*Kate Nelligan*
RAYMOND BROCK	*Edward Herrmann*
CODENAME LAZAR	*Ben Masters*
FRENCHMAN #1	*Ken Meseroll*
LEONARD DARWIN	*George N. Martin*
MICK	*Daniel Gerroll*
LOUIS	*Johann Carlo*

M. AUNG..Conrad Yama
MME. AUNG..Ginny Yang
DORCAS FREY..Madeleine Potter
JOHN BEGLEY..Jeff Allin
SIR ANDREW CHARLESON................................Bill Moor
FRENCHMAN #2....................................Pierre Epstein

Sets by John Gunter; costumes by Jane Greenwood;
lighting by Arden Fingerhut; music by Nick Bicât.

SCENE 1

Knightsbridge. Easter 1962

A wooden floor. At the back of the stage high windows give the impression of a room which has been stripped bare. Around the floor are packing cases full of fine objects. At the front lies a single mattress, on which a naked man is sleeping face downwards. SUSAN *sits on one of the packing cases. In her middle thirties, she is thin and well-presented. She wastes no energy. She now rolls an Old Holborn and lights it.* ALICE *comes in from the street, a blanket over her head. She carries a small tinfoil parcel. She is small-featured, slightly younger and busier than* SUSAN. *She wears jeans. She drops the blanket and shakes the rain off herself.*

ALICE. I don't know why anybody lives in this country. No wonder everyone has colds all the time. Even what they call passion, it still comes at you down a blocked nose. (SUSAN *smokes quietly.* ALICE *is distracted by some stray object which she tosses into a packing case. The man stirs and turns over. He is middle aged, running to fat and covered in dried blood.* SUSAN *cues* ALICE.)

SUSAN. And the food.

ALICE. Yeah. The wet. The cold. The flu. The food. The loveless English. How is he?

SUSAN. Fine. (ALICE *kneels down beside him.*)

ALICE. The blood is spectacular.

SUSAN. The blood is from his thumb. (ALICE *takes his penis between her thumb and forefinger.*)

ALICE. Turkey neck and turkey gristle, isn't that what they say? (*A pause.* SUSAN *smokes.*) Are you sure he's O.K.?

SUSAN. He had a couple of Nembutal and twelve fingers of Scotch. It's nothing else, don't worry.

ALICE. And a fight.

SUSAN. A short fight. (ALICE *takes the tinfoil parcel and opens it. Steam rises.*)

ALICE. Chinese takeaway. Want some?

SUSAN. It's six o'clock in the morning.

ALICE. Sweet and sour prawn.

SUSAN. No thanks.

ALICE. You should. You worked as hard as I did.

135

When we started last night, I didn't think it could be done. (ALICE *gestures round the empty room. Then eats.* SUSAN *watches, then gets up and stands behind her with a key.*)

SUSAN. It's a Yale. There's a mortise as well but I've lost the key. There's a cleaning lady next door, should you want one, her work's good but don't try talking about the blacks. You have a share in that garden in the centre of the square, you know all those trees and flowers they keep locked up. The milkman calls daily, again he's nice, but don't touch the yoghurt, it's green, we call it Venusian sperm. (*Pause.*) Good luck with your girls. (SUSAN *turns to go.* ALICE *gets up.*)

ALICE. Are you sure you can't stay? I think you'd like them.

SUSAN. Unmarried mothers, I don't think I'd get on.

ALICE. I'm going to ring round at nine o'clock. If you just stayed on for a couple of hours . . .

SUSAN. You don't really want that. Nobody would. (*Pause.*) You must tell my husband . . .

ALICE. You've given me the house, and you went on your way.

SUSAN. Tell him I left with nothing that was his. I just walked out on him. Everything to go. (SUSAN *smiles again and goes out. There is a pause. The man stirs again at the front of the stage.* ALICE *stands still holding the sweet and sour prawn.*)

BROCK. Darling. (BROCK *is still asleep. His eyes don't open as he turns over.* ALICE *watches very beadily. There is a long pause. Then he murmurs:*) What's for breakfast?

ALICE. Fish.

SCENE 2

St. Benoît. November 1943
Darkness. From the dark the sound of the wireless. From offstage, a beam of light flashes irregularly, cutting up through the night. Then back to dark.

ANNOUNCER: Ici Londres. Les voix de la liberté. Ensuite quelques messages personnels. Mon Oncle Albert a Perdu son Chien. Mon—Oncle—Albert—A—Perdu—Son—Chien.

(*A heavy thump in the darkness. Then the sound of someone running towards the noise. A small amount of light shows us the scene. LAZAR is trying to disentangle himself from his parachute. He has landed at the edge of the wood. At the back SUSAN runs on from a great distance, wrapped in a greatcoat against the cold. She has a scarf round her face so that only her eyes can be seen. She is extremely nervous and vulnerable, and her uncertainty makes her rude and abrupt.*)

SUSAN. Eh, qu'est-ce que vous faites ici?

LAZAR. Ah rien. Laisse-moi un moment, je peux tout expliquer. (SUSAN *takes a revolver from her pocket and moves towards him. She stoops down, feels the edge of* LAZAR's *parachute.*)

SUSAN. Donnez-moi votre sac. (LAZAR *throws across the satchel which has been tied to his waist.* SUSAN *looks through it, then puts the gun back in her pocket.*) And your French is not good. (SUSAN *moves quickly away to listen for sounds in the night.* LAZAR *watches then speaks quietly to her back.* LAZAR *is a codename, he is of course English.*)

LAZAR. Where am I?

SUSAN. Please be quiet. I can't hear when you speak. (*Pause.*) There's a road. Through the wood. Gestapo patrol.

LAZAR. I see.

SUSAN. I thought I heard something.

LAZAR. Are you waiting for supplies?

SUSAN. On the hour. There's meant to be a drop. I thought it was early, that's why I flashed.

LAZAR. I'm sorry. We had to take advantage of your light. We were losing fuel. I'm afraid I'm meant to be eighty miles on. Can you . . . could you tell me where I am?

SUSAN. You've landed near a village called St. Benoît. It's close to a town called Poitiers, all right?

LAZAR. Yes. I think. I have heard of it you know. (*Pause. She half turns but still does not look at him.*)

SUSAN. Hadn't you better take that thing off?

LAZAR. We are in the same racket, I suppose?

SUSAN. Well we're pretty well dished if we aren't. Did you spot any movement as you came down?

LAZAR. None at all. We just picked out your light.

SUSAN. If you didn't see anything I'd like to hold on. We need the drop badly—explosives and guns.

LAZAR. Have you come out on your own? (*A pause. He has taken off his jump-suit. Underneath he is dressed as a French peasant. Now he puts a beret on.*) You'd better tell me, how does this look?

SUSAN. I'd rather not look at you. It's an element of risk which we really don't need to take. In my experience it is best, it really is best if you always obey the rules.

LAZAR. But you'd like me to hold on and help you I think? (*Pause.*) Listen I'm happy I might be of some use. My own undertaking is somewhat up the spout. Whatever happens I'm several days late. If I could hold on and be of any help . . . I'm sure I'd never have to look you in the face.

SUSAN. All right, if you could just . . .

LAZAR. Look the opposite . . . yes. I will. I'm delighted. (*He does so.*) All right?

SUSAN. If you could hold on, I'm sure I could find you a bike.

LAZAR. Would you like a cigarette?

SUSAN. Thank you very much. (*Pause.*) Cafés are bad meeting places, much less safe than they seem. Don't go near Bourges, it's very bad for us. Don't carry anything in toothpaste tubes, it's become the first place they look. Don't laugh too much. An Englishman's laugh, it just doesn't sound the same. Are they still teaching you to broadcast from the lavatory?

LAZAR. Yes.

SUSAN. Well don't. And don't hide your receiver in the cistern, the whole dodge is badly out of date. The Gestapo have been crashing into lavatories for a full two months. Never take the valley road beyond Poitiers, I'll show you a side road. (*Pause.*) And that's it really. The rest you know, or will learn.

LAZAR. How long have you been here?

SUSAN. Perhaps a year. Off and on. How's everyone at home?

LAZAR. They're fine.

SUSAN. The boss?

LAZAR. Fine. Gave me some cufflinks at the aerodrome. Told me my chances.

SUSAN. Fifty-fifty?

LAZAR. Yes.

SUSAN. He's getting out of touch. (*Pause.*)

LAZAR. How has it been?

SUSAN. Well . . . the Germans are still here. We keep them here, keep them occupied. Blow up their bridges, devastate the roads, so they have to waste their manpower chasing after us. Divert them from the front. It's the worst thing about the job, the more successful you are, the longer it goes on.

LAZAR. Until we win.

SUSAN. Yes. (*Pause.*) A friend . . . a friend who was here used to say, never kill a German, always shoot him in the leg. That way he goes to hospital where he has to be looked after, where he'll use up enemy resources. But a dead soldier is forgotten and replaced. (*Pause.*)

LAZAR. Do you have dark hair?

SUSAN. What?

LAZAR. One strand across your face. Very young. Sitting one day next to the mahogany door. At the recruitment place. And on the shelf above your shoulder the Encyclopaedia Britannica. (SUSAN *turns.*)

SUSAN. You know who I am. (*The sound of an aeroplane.* SUSAN *moves back and begins to flash her torch up into the night.* LAZAR *crosses.*)

LAZAR. That's it over there.

SUSAN. Wait.

LAZAR. Isn't that it?

SUSAN. Don't move across. Just wait.

LAZAR. That's the drop. (*The light stops. And the sound of the plane dies.* SUSAN *moves back silently and stands behind* LAZAR *looking out into the field.*)

SUSAN. It's all right, leave it. It's safer to wait a moment or two.

LAZAR. Oh my God.

SUSAN. What?

LAZAR. Out across the field. Look . . .

SUSAN. Get down. (*They both lie down.*)

LAZAR. He's picking it up. Let's get away from here.

SUSAN. No.

LAZAR. Come on for God's sake . . .

SUSAN. No.

LAZAR. If it's the Gestapo . . .

SUSAN. Gestapo nothing, it's the bloody French. (*From where they have been looking comes a dark figure running like mad with an enormous parcel wrapped in a parachute.* SUSAN *tries to intercept him. A furious row breaks out in heavy whispers.*) Posez ça par terre, ce n'est pas à vous.

FRENCHMAN. Si, c'est à nous. Je ne vous connais pas.

SUSAN. Non, l'avion était anglais. C'est à nous.

FRENCHMAN. Non, c'est désigné pour la résistance.

LAZAR. Oh God. (*He stands watching as* SUSAN *handling the* FRENCHMAN *very badly begins to lose her temper. They stand shouting in the night.*)

SUSAN. Vous savez bien que c'est nous qui devons diriger le mouvement de tous les armements. Pour les Français c'est tout à fait impossible . . .

FRENCHMAN. Va te faire foutre.

SUSAN. Si vous ne me le donnez pas . . .

FRENCHMAN. Les Anglais n'ont jamais compris la France. Il faut absolument que ce soit les Français qui déterminent notre avenir.

SUSAN. Posez ça . . .

FRENCHMAN. C'est pour la France. (*The* FRENCHMAN *begins to go.* LAZAR *has walked quietly across to behind* SUSAN *and now takes the gun from her pocket. The* FRENCHMAN *sees it.*)

FRENCHMAN. Arr yew raven mad?

LAZAR. Please put it down. (*Pause.*) Please. (*The* FRENCHMAN *lowers the package to the ground. Then stands up.*) Please tell your friends we're sorry. We do want to help. Mais parfois ce sont les Français mêmes qui le rendent difficile.

FRENCHMAN. Nobody ask you. Nobody ask you to come. Vous n'êtes pas les bienvenus ici. (SUSAN *about to reply but* LAZAR *holds up his hand at once.*)

LAZAR. Compris.

FRENCHMAN. Espèce de con. (*There is a pause. Then the* FRENCHMAN *turns and walks out.* LAZAR *keeps him covered, then turns to start picking the stuff up.* SUSAN *moves well away.*)

LAZAR. Bloody Gaullists. (*Pause.*) I mean what do they have for brains?

SUSAN. I don't know.

LAZAR. I mean really.

Susan. They just expect the English to die. They sit and watch us spitting blood in the streets. (Lazar *looks up at* Susan, *catching her tone. Then moves towards her as calmly as he can.*)

Lazar. Here's your gun. (Lazar *slips the gun into* Susan's *pocket, but as he does she takes his hand into hers.*) We must be off.

Susan. I'm sorry, I'm so frightened.

Lazar. I must bury the silk.

Susan. I'm not an agent, I'm just a courier. I carry messages between certain circuits . . .

Lazar. Please . . .

Susan. I came tonight, it's my first drop, there is literally nobody else, I can't tell you the mess in Poitiers . . .

Lazar. Please.

Susan. My friend, the man I mentioned, he's been taken to Buchenwald. He was the wireless operator, please let me tell you, his name was Tony . . .

Lazar. I can't help.

Susan. I have to talk . . .

Lazar. No.

Susan. What's the point, what's the point of following the rules if . . .

Lazar. You mustn't . . .

Susan. I don't want to die. I don't want to die like that. (*Suddenly* Susan *embraces* Lazar, *putting her head on his shoulder and crying uncontrollably. He puts his hand through her hair. Then after a long time, she turns and walks some paces away, in silence. They stand for some time.*)

Lazar. Did you know . . . did you know sound waves never die? So every noise we make goes into the sky. And there is a place somewhere in the corner of the universe where all the babble of the world is kept. (*Pause. Then* Lazar *starts gathering the equipment together.*) Come on, let's clear this lot up. We must be off. I don't know how I'm going to manage on French cigarettes. Is there somewhere I can buy bicycle clips? I was thinking about it all the way down. Oh yes and something else. A mackerel sky. What is the phrase for that?

Susan. Un ciel pommelé.

Lazar. Un ciel pommelé. Marvellous. I must find a place to slip it in. Now. Where will I find this bike?

(LAZAR *has collected everything and gone out.* SUSAN *follows him.*)

SUSAN. I don't know your name.

SCENE 3

Brussels. June 1947
From the dark the sound of a small string orchestra gives way to the voice of an ANNOUNCER.

ANNOUNCER. Ici Radio Belgique INR. Et maintenant notre soirée continue avec la musique de Victor Sylvester et son orchestre. Victor Sylvester est parmi les musiciens anglais les plus aimés à cause de ses maintes émissions à la radio anglaise pendant la guerre.

(*Evening. A gilt room. A fine desk. Good leather chairs. A portrait of the King. Behind the desk* SIR LEONARD DARWIN *is working, silver-haired, immaculate, well into his late forties. A knock at the door and* RAYMOND BROCK *comes in. An ingenuous figure, not yet thirty, with a small moustache and a natural energy he finds hard to contain in the proper manner. He refers constantly to his superior and this makes him uneasy.*)

BROCK. Sir Leonard . . .
DARWIN. Come in.
BROCK. A few moments of your time. If I could possibly . . .
DARWIN. You have my ear.
BROCK. The case of a British national who's died. It's just been landed in my lap. A tourist named Radley's dropped dead in his hotel. It was a coronary, seems fairly clear. The Belgian police took the matter in hand, but naturally the widow has come along to us. It should be quite easy, she's taking it well. (DARWIN *nods.* BROCK *goes to the door.*)
BROCK. Mrs. Radley. The ambassador. (SUSAN *has come in. She is simply and soberly dressed. She looks extremely attractive.*)
DARWIN. If you'd like to sit down. (*She sits opposite him at the desk.* BROCK *stands respectfully at the other side of the room.*) Please accept my condolences. The

Third Secretary has told me a little of your plight. Natu
rally we'll help in any way we can.

BROCK. I've already taken certain practical steps. I've
been to the mortuary.

SUSAN. That's very kind.

BROCK. Belgian undertakers.

DARWIN. One need not say more. Your husband had
a heart attack, is that right?

SUSAN. Yes. In the foyer of our hotel.

DARWIN. Painless . . .

SUSAN. I would hope. He was packing the car. We
were planning to move on this morning, we only have
two weeks. We were hoping to make Innsbruck, at least
if our travel allowance would last. It was our first holiday
since the war.

DARWIN. Brock, a handkerchief.

SUSAN. No. (*Pause.*)

BROCK. I was persuaded to opt for an embalming I'm
afraid. It may involve you in some small extra cost.

SUSAN. Excuse me but you'll have to explain the point.

BROCK. Sorry?

SUSAN. Of the embalming I mean. (BROCK *looks to
his superior, but decides to persist.*)

BROCK. Well particularly in the summer it avoids the
possibility of the body exploding at a bad moment. I
mean any moment would be bad, it goes without saying,
but on the aeroplane say.

SUSAN. I see.

BROCK. You see normally you find the body's simply
washed . . . I don't know how much detail you want me
to provide . . .

DARWIN. I would think it better if . . .

SUSAN. No. I would like to know. Tony was a doctor,
he would want me to know. (BROCK *pauses, then speaks
with genuine interest.*)

BROCK. To be honest I was surprised at how little
there is to do. There's a small bottle of spirit, colourless,
and they simply give the body a wash. The only other
thing is the stomach, if there's been a meal, a recent
meal . . .

SUSAN. Tony had . . .

BROCK. Yes, he had breakfast I think. You insert a
pipe into the corpse's stomach to let the gases out. They

insert it and there's a strange sort of sigh. (DARWIN *shifts*.)

DARWIN. If er . . .

BROCK. It leaves almost no mark. Apparently so they told me, the morgue attendants when they're bored, sometimes set light to the gas for a joke. Makes one hell of a bang.

DARWIN. Shall we all have a drink? (DARWIN *gets up*. BROCK *tries to backtrack*.)

BROCK. But of course I'm sure it didn't happen in this particular case.

DARWIN. No. There is gin. There is tonic. Yes?

SUSAN. Thank you. (DARWIN *mixes drinks and hands them round*.)

BROCK. I'm afraid we shall need to discuss the practical arrangements. I know the whole subject is very distressing but there is the question . . . you do want the body flown back?

SUSAN. Well I can hardly stash it in the boot of the car. (*A pause*. DARWIN *lost*.)

DARWIN. What the Third Secretary is saying . . . not buried on foreign soil.

SUSAN. No.

BROCK. Quite. You see for the moment we take care of it, freight charges, and his majesty's government picks up the bill. But perhaps later we will have to charge it to the estate, if there is an estate, I'm sorry, I don't mean to interfere . . .

SUSAN. I'm sure there'll be enough to pay for it all. Tony made a very reasonable living. (DARWIN *gets up*.)

DARWIN. Well I think we now understand your needs. I shall go downstairs and set the matter in train.

BROCK. Would you prefer it if I did that sir?

DARWIN. No, no. You stay and talk to Mrs. Radley. I'll have a word with the travel people, make a booking on tomorrow morning's flight, if that suits?

SUSAN. Yes of course.

DARWIN. You will be going with the body I assume?

SUSAN. Yes.

DARWIN. Are there other dependents? Children?

SUSAN. No. (DARWIN *goes out. A pause*.)

BROCK. If . . .

SUSAN. He doesn't like you.

BROCK. Sorry.

SUSAN. The ambassador.

BROCK. Oh. Well no. (*Pause.*) I don't think he's over the moon about you.

SUSAN. I shouldn't have said that.

BROCK. No, it's just . . . Darwin thinks disasters are examinations in etiquette. Which fork to use in an earthquake.

SUSAN. Darwin, is that his name?

BROCK. Yes, the mission all thinks it's God's joke. God getting his own back by dashing off a modern Darwin who is in every aspect less advanced than the last. (*He smiles alone.*) I'm sorry. We sit about in the evenings and polish our jokes. Brussels is rather a debilitating town.

SUSAN. Is this a bad posting for you?

BROCK. I'd been hoping for something more positive. Fresher air. The flag still flies over a quarter of the human race and I would like to have seen it really. Whereas here . . . we're left with the problems of the war . . . (*He smiles again.*) Have you met any prison wardens?

SUSAN. No.

BROCK. It's just they talk exactly like us. I was hoping for Brixton but I got the Scrubs. Just the same.

SUSAN. Does nobody like it here?

BROCK. The misery is contagious, I suppose. You spend the day driving between bombsites, watching the hungry, the homeless, the bereaved. We think there are thirty million people loose in Europe, who've had to flee across borders, have had to start again. And it is very odd to watch it all from here. (*He gestures round the room.*) Had you been married long?

SUSAN. We met during the war.

BROCK. I did notice some marks on the body.

SUSAN. Tony was a wireless operator with S.O.E. Our job was harassment behind the lines. Very successful in Holland, Denmark. Less so in France. Tony was in a circuit the Gestapo destroyed. Then scattered. Ravensbruk, Buchenwald, Saarbrucken, Dachau. Some were tortured, executed.

BROCK. What did you do?

SUSAN. I was a courier. I was never caught. (*She looks straight at* BROCK.) I wasn't his wife.

BROCK. No.

SUSAN. Had you realized that?

BROCK. I'd thought it possible. (*Pause.*)

SUSAN. What about Darwin, did he realize?

BROCK. Lord no, it would never occur to him.

SUSAN. Motoring together it was easier to say we were man and wife. In fact I was barely even his mistress. He simply rang me a few weeks ago and asked if I'd like a holiday abroad. I was amazed. People in our organization really didn't know each other all that well. You made it your business to know as little as possible, it was a point of principle. Even now you don't know who most of your colleagues were. Perhaps you were in it. Perhaps I met you. I don't know. (*Pause.*) Tony I knew a bit better, not much, but I was glad when he rang. Those of us who went through this kind of war, I think we do have something in common. It's a kind of impatience, we're rather intolerant, we don't suffer fools. And so we get rather restless back in England, the people who stayed behind seem childish and a little silly. I think that's why Tony needed to get away. If you haven't suffered . . . well. And so driving through Europe with Tony I knew that at least I'd be able to act as I pleased for a while. That's all. (*Pause.*) It's kind of you not to have told the ambassador.

BROCK. Perhaps I will. (*He smiles.*) May I ask a question?

SUSAN. Yes.

BROCK. If you're not his wife, did he have one?

SUSAN. Yes.

BROCK. I see.

SUSAN. And three children. I had to lie about those, I couldn't claim them somehow. She lives in Crediton in Devon. She believes that Tony was travelling alone. He'd told her he needed two weeks by himself. That's what I was hoping you could do for me.

BROCK. Ah.

SUSAN. Phone her. I've written the number down. I'm afraid I did it before I came. (SUSAN *opens her handbag and hands across a card.* BROCK *takes it.*)

BROCK. And lie?

SUSAN. Yes. I'd prefer it if you lied. But it's up to you. (*She looks at* BROCK. *He makes a nervous half-laugh.*) All right doesn't matter . . .

BROCK. That's not what I said.

SUSAN. Please, it doesn't matter. (*Pause.*)

BROCK. When did you choose me?

SUSAN. What?

BROCK. For the job. You didn't choose Darwin.

SUSAN. I might have done. (*Pause.*)

BROCK. You don't think you wear your suffering a little heavily? This smart club of people you belong to who had a very bad war . . .

SUSAN. All right.

BROCK. I mean I know it must have put you on a different level from the rest of us . . .

SUSAN. You won't shame me you know. There's no point. (*Pause.*) It was an innocent relationship. That doesn't mean unphysical. Unphysical isn't innocent. Unphysical in my view is repressed. It just means there was no guilt. I wasn't particularly fond of Tony, he was rather slow-moving and egg-stained if you know what I mean, but we'd known some sorrow together and I came with him. And so it seemed a shocking injustice when he fell in the lobby, unjust for him of course, but also unjust for me, alone, a long way from home, and worst of all for his wife, bitterly unfair if she had to have the news from me. Unfair for life. And so I approached the embassy. (*Pause.*) Obviously I shouldn't even have mentioned the war. Tony used to say don't talk about it. He had a dread of being trapped in small rooms with Jewish women, I know exactly what he meant. I should have just come here this evening and sat with my legs apart, pretended to be a scarlet woman, then at least you would have been able to place me. It makes no difference. Lie or don't lie. It's a matter of indifference. (BROCK *gets up and moves uncertainly around the room.* SUSAN *stays where she is.*)

BROCK. Would you . . . perhaps I could ask you to dinner? Just so we could talk . . .

SUSAN. No. I refuse to tell you anything now. If I told you anything about myself you would just think I was pleading, that I was trying to get round you. So I tell you nothing. I just say look at me—don't creep round the furniture—look at me and make a judgement.

BROCK. Well. (DARWIN *reappears. He picks up his drink and sits at his desk as if to clear up. There is in fact nothing to clear up, so mostly he just moves his watch round. He talks the while.*)

DARWIN. That's done. First flight tomorrow without a hitch. (BROCK *stands as if unaware* DARWIN *has come back.*)

SUSAN. Thank you very much.

DARWIN. If there's anything else. There is a small chapel in the embassy if you'd like to use it before you go.

SUSAN. Thank you. (BROCK *turns and walks abruptly out of the room.* SUSAN *smiles a moment.* DARWIN *puts on his watch.*) Have you been posted here long?

DARWIN. No, not at all. Just a few months. Before that, Djakarta. We were hoping for something sunny but Brussels came along. Not that we're complaining. They've certainly got something going here.

SUSAN. Really?

DARWIN. Oh yes. New Europe. Yes yes. (*Pause.*) Reconstruction. Massive. Massive work of reconstruction. Jobs. Ideals. Marvellous. Marvellous time to be alive in Europe. No end of it. Roads to be built. People to be educated. Land to be tilled. Lots to get on with. (*Pause.*) Have another gin.

SUSAN. No thanks.

DARWIN. The diplomat's eye is the clearest in the world. Seen from Djakarta this continent looks so old, so beautiful. We don't realize what we have in our hands.

SUSAN. No. (BROCK *reappears at the door.*)

BROCK. Your wife is asking if you're ready for dinner sir.

DARWIN. Right.

BROCK. And she wants your advice on her face. (DARWIN *gets up.*) I'll lock up after you sir.

DARWIN. You'll see Mrs. Radley to her hotel?

BROCK. Of course.

DARWIN. Good-bye Mrs. Radley. I'm sorry it hasn't been a happier day. (DARWIN *goes out.* BROCK *closes the door. He looks at* SUSAN.)

BROCK. I've put in a call to England. There's an hour's

delay. (*Pause.*) I've decided to lie. (BROCK *and* SUSAN *stare at each other. Silence.*) Will you be going back with the body?

SUSAN. No. (BROCK *goes to the door and listens. Then turns back and removes the buttonhole. He looks for where to put it. He finds his undrunk gin and tonic and puts it in there. Then he takes his jacket off and drops it somewhat deliberately on the floor. He takes a couple of paces towards* SUSAN.)

BROCK. Will you remind me to cancel your seat?

SCENE 4

Pimlico. September 1947
From the dark the sound of a string quartet. It comes to an end. Then a voice.

ANNOUNCER. This is the BBC Third Programme. Vorichef wrote *Les Ossifiés* in the year of the Paris Commune, but his struggle with Parkinson's disease during the writing of the score has hitherto made it a peculiarly difficult manuscript for musicologists to interpret. However the leader of the Bremen ensemble has recently done a magnificent work of reclamation. Vorichef died in an extreme state of senile dementia in 1878. This performance of his last work will be followed by a short talk in our series 'Musicians and Disease'.

(*A bed-sitter with some wooden chairs, a bed and a canvas bed with a suitcase set beside it. A small room, well maintained but cheerless.* ALICE *sits on the floor in a chalk-striped men's suit and white tie. She smokes a hookah.* SUSAN *is on the edge of the bed drinking cocoa. She is wearing a blue striped shirt. Her revolver lies beside her.* BROCK *is laid out fast asleep across two chairs in his pinstripes. Next to him is a large pink parcel, an odd item of luxury in the dismal surroundings. By the way they talk you know it's late.*)

SUSAN. I want to move on. I do desperately want to feel I'm moving on.
ALICE. With him?

SUSAN. Well that's the problem isn't it? (*Pause*. ALICE *smiles*.)

ALICE. You are strange.

SUSAN. Well what would you do?

ALICE. I'd trade him in.

SUSAN. Would you?

ALICE. I'd choose someone else off the street.

SUSAN. And what chance would you have tonight, within a mile, say, within a mile of here?

ALICE. Let me think. Does that take in Victoria Station? (*They smile. The hookah smokes*.)

SUSAN. That thing is disgusting.

ALICE. I know. It was better when the dung was fresh.

SUSAN. I don't know why you bother . . .

ALICE. The writer must experience everything, every kind of degradation. Nothing is closed to him. It's really the degradation that attracted me to the job.

SUSAN. I thought you were going to work tonight . . .

ALICE. I can't write all the time. You have to live it before you can write it. What other way is there? Besides nicking it.

SUSAN. Is that done?

ALICE. Apparently. Once you start looking it seems most books are copied out of other books. Only it's called tribute. Tribute to Hemingway. Means it's nicked. Mine's going to be tribute to Scott Fitzgerald. Have you read him?

SUSAN. No.

ALICE. *Last Tycoon*. Mine's going to be like that. (BROCK *grunts*.) He snores.

SUSAN. You should get a job . . .

ALICE. I've had a job, I know what jobs are like. Had a job in your office.

SUSAN. For three days.

ALICE. It was enough.

SUSAN. How are you going to live?

ALICE. Off you mostly. (*She smiles*.)

SUSAN. I want to move on. I do desperately want to feel I'm moving on. (*Pause*.) I work so hard I have no time to think. The office is worse. Those brown invoices go back and forth, import, export . . .

ALICE. I remember.

SUSAN. They get heavier and heavier as the day goes

on, I can barely stagger across the room for the weight
of a single piece of paper, by the end of the day if you
dropped one on the floor, you'd smash your foot. The
silence is worse. Dust gathering. Water lapping beyond
the wall. It seems unreal. You can't believe that because
of the work you do ships pass and sail across the world.
(*She stares a moment.*) Mr. Medlicott has moved into my
office.

ALICE. Frightful Mr. Medlicott?

SUSAN. Yes.

ALICE. The boss.

SUSAN. He has moved in. Or rather, more sinister still
he has removed the frosted glass between our two offices.

ALICE. Really?

SUSAN. I came in one morning and found the partition
had gone. I interpret it as the first step in a mating dance.
I believe Medlicott stayed behind one night, set his ledger aside, ripped off his tweed suit, took up an axe,
swung it at the partition, dropped to the floor, rolled
over in the broken glass till he bled, till his whole body
streamed blood, then he cleared up, slipped home, came
back next morning and waited to see if anything would
be said. But I have said nothing. And neither has he.
He puts his head down and does not lift it till lunch. I
have to look across at his few strands of hair, like sea-
weed across his skull. And I am frightened of what the
next step will be.

ALICE. I can imagine.

SUSAN. The sexual pressure is becoming intolerable.
(*They smile.*) One day there was a condom in his trouser
cuff. I tried to laugh it off to myself, pretended he'd been
off with some whore in Limehouse and not bothered to
take his trousers off, so that after the event the condom
had just absent-mindedly fallen from its place and lodged
alongside all the bus tickets and the tobacco and the rai-
sins and the paper-clips and all the rest of it. But I know
the truth. It was step two. And the dance has barely
begun. (*Pause.*) Alice. I must get out.

ALICE. Then do. Just go. Have you never done that?
I do it all the time.

SUSAN. They do need me in that place . . .

ALICE. So much the better, gives it much more point.
That's always the disappointment when I leave, I always

go before people even notice I've come. But you . . .
you could really make a splash. (BROCK *stirs*.) He stirs.

SUSAN. I'd like to change everything but I don't know
how. (*She leans under her bed, pulls out a shoebox, starts
to oil and clean her gun*.)

ALICE. Are you really fond of him?

SUSAN. You don't see him at his best. We had a week
in Brussels which we both enjoyed. Now he comes over
for the weekend whenever he can. But he tends to be
rather sick on the boat.

ALICE. You should meet someone younger.

SUSAN. That's not what I mean. And I don't really
like young men. You're through and out the other side
in no time at all.

ALICE. I can introduce you . . .

SUSAN. I'm sure. I've only known you three weeks,
but I've got the idea. Your flair for agonized young men.
I think you get them in bulk from tuberculosis wards . . .

ALICE. I'm just catching up, that's all.

SUSAN. Of course . . .

ALICE. I was a late starter.

SUSAN. Oh yes, what are you, eighteen?

ALICE. I started late. Out of guilt. I had a protected
childhood. Till I ran away. And very bad guilt. I was
frightened to masturbate more than once a week, I
thought it was like a torch battery, you know use it too
much and it runs out. (BROCK *wakes*.) He wakes. (*They
watch as he comes round*.)

BROCK. What time is it?

ALICE. Raymond, can you give us your view? I was
just comparing the efficiency of a well-known household
object with . . .

SUSAN. Alice leave him alone.

ALICE. It's getting on for five.

BROCK. I feel terrible.

SUSAN. (*Kissing his head*.) I'll get you something to
eat. Omelette all right? It's only powder I'm afraid . . .

BROCK. Well . . .

SUSAN. Two spoons or three? And I'll sprinkle it with
Milk of Magnesia . . . (*She goes out into the kitchen*.)

BROCK. It seems a bit pointless. It's only twelve hours
till I'm back on the boat. (*He picks up the gun*.) Did I
miss something?

ALICE. No. She's just fondling it.

BROCK. Ah. (*He looks round.* ALICE *is watching him all the time.*) I can't remember what . . .

ALICE. Music. On the wireless. You had us listening to some music.

BROCK. Ah that's right.

ALICE. Some composer who shook.

BROCK. I thought you'd have gone. Don't you have a flat?

ALICE. I did. But it had bad associations. I was disappointed in love.

BROCK. I see.

ALICE. And Susan said I could sleep here.

BROCK. (*Absently admiring her suit.*) I must say I do think your clothes are very smart.

ALICE. Well I tell you he looks very good in mine. (*She nods at the parcel.*) Do you always bring her one of those?

BROCK. I certainly try to bring a gift if I can.

ALICE. You must have lots of money.

BROCK. Well, I suppose. I find it immoderately easy to acquire. I seem to have a sort of mathematical gift. The stock exchange. Money sticks to my fingers I find. I triple my income. What can I do?

ALICE. It must be very tiresome.

BROCK. Oh . . . I'm acclimatizing you know. (*Smiles.*) I think everyone's going to be rich very soon. Once we've got over the effects of the war. It's going to be coming out of everyone's ears.

ALICE. Is that what you think?

BROCK. I'm absolutely sure. (*Pause.*) I do enjoy these weekends you know. Susan leads such an interesting life. Books. Conversation. People like you. The Foreign Office can make you feel pretty isolated, also to be honest make you feel pretty small, as if you're living on sufferance, you can imagine . . .

ALICE. Yes.

BROCK. Till I met Susan. The very day I met her, she showed me you must always do what you want. If you want something you must get it. I think that's a wonderful way to live don't you?

ALICE. I do. (*Pause. She smiles.*) Shall I tell you how my book begins?

BROCK. Well . . .

ALICE. There's a woman in a rape trial. And the story is true. The book begins at the moment where she has to tell the court what the accused has said to her on the night of the rape. And she finds she can't bring herself to say the words out loud. And so the judge suggests she writes them down on a piece of paper and it be handed round the court. Which she does. And it says, 'I want to have you. I must have you now.' (*She smiles again.*) So they pass it round the jury who all read it and pass it on. At the end of the second row there's a woman jurist who's fallen asleep at the boredom of the trial. So the man next to her has to nudge her awake and hand her the slip of paper. She wakes up, looks at it, then at him, smiles and puts it in her handbag. (*She laughs.*) That woman is my heroine.

BROCK. Well yes. (SUSAN *returns, sets food on* BROCK'S *knee. Then returns to cleaning her gun.* ALICE *tries to re-light her hookah.*)

SUSAN. Cheese omelette. What were you talking about?

ALICE. The rape trial.

SUSAN. Did you tell Raymond who the woman was?

BROCK. What? (ALICE *and* SUSAN *laugh.*)

ALICE. Oh sod this stuff.

SUSAN. I said it was dung.

ALICE. I was promised visions.

BROCK. Well . . .

ALICE. It's because I'm the only bohemian in London. People exploit me. Because there are no standards, you see. In Paris or New York, there are plenty of bohemians, so the hashish is rich and sweet and plentiful but here . . . You'd be better off to lick the gum from your ration card.

SUSAN. Perhaps Raymond will be posted to Morocco, bring some back in his bag . . .

BROCK. I don't think that's really on.

SUSAN. Nobody would notice, from what you say. Nobody would notice if you smoked it yourself.

ALICE. Are they not very sharp?

SUSAN. Not according to Raymond. The ones I've met are buffoons . . .

BROCK. Susan please . . .

SUSAN. Well it's you who call them buffoons . . .

BROCK. It's not quite what I say.

SUSAN. It's you who tells the stories. That man Darwin . . .

BROCK. Please . . .

SUSAN. How he needs three young men from public schools to strap him into his surgical support . . .

BROCK. I told you that in confidence.

SUSAN. In gloves.

ALICE. Really?

BROCK. Darwin is not a buffoon.

SUSAN. From your own lips . . .

BROCK. He just has slight problems of adjustment to the modern age.

SUSAN. You are laughing.

BROCK. I am not laughing.

SUSAN. There is a slight smile at the corner of your mouth . . .

BROCK. There is not. There is absolutely no smile.

SUSAN. Alice, I will paraphrase, let me paraphrase Raymond's view of his boss, I don't misrepresent you dear, it is, in paraphrase, in sum, that he would not trust him to stick his prick into a bucket of lard. (BROCK *puts his omelette to one side, uneaten.*) Well is he a joke or is he not?

BROCK. Certainly he's a joke.

SUSAN. Thank you.

BROCK. He's a joke between us. He is not a joke to the entire world. (*A pause.* BROCK *looks at* ALICE. *Then he gets up.*) I think I'd better be pushing off home. (BROCK *goes and gets his coat. Puts it on.* SUSAN *at last speaks, very quietly.*)

SUSAN. And I wish you wouldn't use those words.

BROCK. What?

SUSAN. Words like 'push off home.' You're always saying it. 'Bit of a tight corner', 'one hell of a spot.' They don't belong.

BROCK. What do you mean?

SUSAN. They are not your words. (*Pause.*)

BROCK. Well I'm none too keen on your words either.

SUSAN. Oh yes which?

BROCK. The words you've been using this evening.

SUSAN. Such as?

BROCK. You know perfectly well.

SUSAN. Such as, come on tell me, what words have I used?

BROCK. Words like . . . (*Pause.*) Bucket of lard. (*Pause.*)

SUSAN. Alice there is only the bath or the kitchen.

ALICE. I know. (ALICE *goes out.* SUSAN *automatically picks up the omelette and starts to eat it.*)

BROCK. Are you going to let her live with you?

SUSAN. I like her. She makes me laugh. (*Pause.*)

BROCK. I'm sorry, I was awful, I apologize. But the work I do is not entirely contemptible. Of course our people are dull, they're stuffy, they're death. But what other world do I have? (*Pause.*)

SUSAN. I think of France more than I tell you. I was seventeen and I was thrown into the war. I often think of it.

BROCK. I'm sure.

SUSAN. The most unlikely people. People I met only for an hour or two. Astonishing kindnesses. Bravery. The fact you could meet someone for an hour or two and see the very best of them and then move on. Can you understand? (*Pause.* BROCK *does not move.*) For instance there was a man in France. His codename was Lazar. I'd been there a year I suppose and one night I had to see him on his way. He just dropped out of the sky. An agent. He was lost. I was trying to be blasé, trying to be tough, all the usual stuff—and then suddenly I began to cry. Onto the shoulder of a man I'd never met before. But not a day goes by without my wondering where he is. (BROCK *moves towards her.*)

BROCK. Susan.

SUSAN. I think we should try a winter apart. I really do. I think it's all a bit easy this way. These weekends. Nothing is tested. I think a test would be good. And what better test than a winter apart?

BROCK. A winter together. (*Pause. They smile.*)

SUSAN. I would love to come to Brussels, you know that. I would love to come if it weren't for my job. But the shipping office is very important to me. I do find it fulfilling. And I just couldn't let Mr. Medlicott down. (*Pause.*) You must say what you think. (BROCK *looks at*

SUSAN *hard, then shrugs and smiles.*) I know you've been dreading the winter crossings, high seas . . .

BROCK. Don't patronize me, Susan.

SUSAN. Anyway, perhaps in the spring, it would be really nice to meet . . .

BROCK. Please don't insult my intelligence. I know you better than you think. I recognize the signs. When you talk longingly about the war . . . some deception usually follows. (BROCK *kisses* SUSAN.) Good-bye.

(BROCK *goes out.* SUSAN *left standing for a few moments. Then she picks up the plate and goes quickly to the kitchen.* ALICE *comes out of the bathroom at once in a dressing-gown: She has a notebook in her hand which she tosses the length of the room, so it lands on a chair. She settles on her back in the camp bed.* SUSAN *reappears at the door.*)

SUSAN. Did you hear that?

ALICE. Certainly. I was writing it down. (SUSAN *looks across at her, but* ALICE *is putting pennies on her eyes.*) My death-mask.

SUSAN. Don't.

ALICE. I dream better. (*Pause.*)

SUSAN. Do you know what you're doing tomorrow?

ALICE. Not really. There's a new jazz band at the one-o-one. And Ken wants to take me to Eel Pie Island in his horrid little car. I say I'll go if I get to meet Alistair. I really do want to meet Alistair. Everyone says he's got hair on his shoulder-blades and apparently he can crack walnuts in his armpits.

SUSAN. Oh well, he'll never be short of friends.

ALICE. Quite. (SUSAN *turns out light. Dim light only. She looks at the parcel.*)

SUSAN. What should I be doing with this?

ALICE. If we can't eat it, let's throw it away. (SUSAN *turns out the other light. Darkness. The sound of* SUSAN *getting into bed.*) Your friend Brock says we're all going to be rich.

SUSAN. Oh really? (*Pause.*)

ALICE. Peace and plenty.

SCENE 5

Temple. May 1951
Music, a cello leading. The Embankment, *beside a lamp overlooking the river.* Night. SUSAN *stands, thickly wrapped. For the first time, she is expensively dressed. She is eating hot chestnuts.* MICK *appears at the back. His is from the East End. He looks twenty, smart and personable. He speaks before she knows he's there.*

MICK. Five hundred cheese-graters.

SUSAN. Oh no.

MICK. I got five hundred cheese-graters parked round the side. Are you interested?

SUSAN. I'm afraid you're too late. We took a consignment weeks ago. (SUSAN *laughs.* MICK *moves down beside her.*)

MICK. Where we looking?

SUSAN. Across the river. Over there.

MICK. Where?

SUSAN. South Bank. That's where the fireworks are going to be. And there's my barrage balloon.

MICK. Oh yeah. What does it say?

SUSAN. Don't say that, that's the worst thing you can say.

MICK. It's dark.

SUSAN. It says Bovril.

MICK. Oh Bovril.

SUSAN. Yes. It's meant to blaze out over London.

MICK. Surprised it hasn't got your name on.

SUSAN. What do you mean?

MICK. Everywhere I go. (*Pause. They look at each other.* SUSAN *smiles and removes a napkin from her coat pocket, and unfolds its bundle.*)

SUSAN. I managed to steal some supper from the Festival Hall. There's a reception for its opening night. They're using your cutlery, I'm happy to say.

MICK. I wish I could see it.

SUSAN. Yes, yes, I wish you could too. (*She smiles.*) I've actually decided to leave the Festival now. Having worked so hard to get the wretched thing on. I'm thinking of going into advertising.

MICK. Ah very good.

SUSAN. I met some people on the Bovril side. It's . . . well I doubt if it'll stretch me, but it would be a way of having some fun. (*Pause*.) Would you like a canapé?

MICK. How's Alice?

SUSAN. She's very well.

MICK. Haven't seen her lately.

SUSAN. No.

MICK. She went mainstream you see. I stayed revivalist. Different religion. For me it all dies with Dixie. (*He takes a canapé.*) So how can I help?

SUSAN. I'm looking for a father. I want to have a child. (*Pause*.) Look it really is much easier than it sounds. I mean marriage is not involved. Or even looking after it. You don't even have to see the pregnancy through. I mean conception will be the end of the job. (MICK *smiles.*)

MICK. Ah.

SUSAN. You don't want to?

MICK. No, no I'm delighted, I'm lucky to be asked . . .

SUSAN. Not at all.

MICK. But it's just . . . your own people. I mean friends, you must have friends . . .

SUSAN. It's . . .

MICK. I mean . . .

SUSAN. Sorry.

MICK. No, go on, say.

SUSAN. The men I know at work, at the Festival, or even friends I've known for years, they just aren't the kind of people I would want to marry.

MICK. Ah.

SUSAN. I'm afraid I'm rather strongminded as you know, and so with them I usually feel I'm holding myself in for fear of literally blowing them out the room. They are kind, they are able, but I don't see . . . why I should have to compromise, why I should have to make some sad and decorous marriage just to have a child. I don't see why any woman should have to do that.

MICK. But you don't have to marry . . .

SUSAN. Ah well . . .

MICK. Just go off with them.

SUSAN. No that's really the problem you see. These same men, these kind and likeable men, they do have another side to their nature and that is they are very limited in their ideas, they are frightened of the unknown, they want a quiet life where sex is either sport or duty but absolutely nothing in between, and they simply wouldn't agree to sleep with me if they knew it was a child I was after.

MICK. But you wouldn't have to tell them . . .

SUSAN. I did think that. And then I thought it would be dishonest. And so I had the idea of asking a person whom I barely knew. (*Pause.*)

MICK. What about the kid?

SUSAN. What?

MICK. Doesn't sound a very good deal. Never to see his dad . . .

SUSAN. It's not . . .

MICK. I take it that is what you mean.

SUSAN. I think it's what I mean.

MICK. Well?

SUSAN. The child will manage.

MICK. How do you know?

SUSAN. Being a bastard won't always be so bad . . .

MICK. I wouldn't bet on it.

SUSAN. England can't be like this for ever. (MICK *looks at her.*)

MICK. I would like to know . . .

SUSAN. Yes?

MICK. I would like to know. Why you chose me. I mean, how often have you met me?

SUSAN. Yes, but that's the whole point . . .

MICK. With Alice a few times . . .

SUSAN. And you sold me some spoons.

MICK. They were good spoons.

SUSAN. I'm not denying it. (MICK *smiles.*)

MICK. And Alice says what? That I'm clean and obedient and don't have any cretins in the family . . .

SUSAN. It's not as calculated as that.

MICK. Not calculated? Several hundred of us, was there, all got notes . . .

SUSAN. No.

MICK. Saying come and watch the Festival fireworks, tell no one, bring no friends. All the secrecy, I thought you must at least be after nylons . . .

SUSAN. I'll buy nylons. If that's what you want. (*They stare at each other.*)

MICK. So why me?

SUSAN. I like you.

MICK. And?

SUSAN. 'I love you'? (*Pause.*) I chose you because . . .
I don't see you very much. I barely ever see you. We
live at opposite ends of town. Different worlds.

MICK. Different class.

SUSAN. That comes into it. (*There is a pause.* MICK
looks at her. Then moves away. Turns back. Smiles.)

MICK. Oh dear.

SUSAN. Then laugh. (*Pause.*) I never met the man who
I wanted to marry. (*They smile.*)

MICK. It can't be what you want. Not deep down.

SUSAN. No.

MICK. I didn't think so.

SUSAN. Deep down I'd do the whole damn thing by
myself. But there we are. You're second best. (*They
smile again.*)

MICK. Five hundred cheese graters.

SUSAN. How much?

MICK. Something over the odds. A bit over the odds.
Not much.

SUSAN. Done. (*Pause.*) Don't worry. The Festival will
pay. (SUSAN *moves across to* MICK. *They kiss. They look
at each other. He smiles. Then they turn and look at the
night. He is barely audible.*)

MICK. Fireworks. If you . . .

SUSAN. What?

MICK. Stay for the fireworks.

SUSAN. If you like. (*Pause.*)

MICK. Great sky.

SUSAN. Yes.

MICK. The light. Those dots.

SUSAN. A mackerel sky.

MICK. What?

SUSAN. That's what they call it. A mackerel sky.

SCENE 6

Pimlico. December 1952
From the dark the sound of Charlie Parker *and his
saxophone. Night. The bed-sitting room transformed. The
beds have gone and the room is much more comforting.
Three people.* SUSAN *is working at her desk which is cov-*

ered with papers and drawings. ALICE *is standing over a table which has been cleared so that she may paint the naked body of* LOUISE *who lies stretched across its top. She is in her late teens, from Liverpool.* ALICE *is a good way on with the job. The record ends.*

SUSAN. This is hell.

ALICE. No doubt.

SUSAN. I am living in hell. (SUSAN *sits back and stares at her desk.* ALICE *goes to the record player.*)

ALICE. Shall we hear it again?

SUSAN. You're only allowed it once. Hear it too much and you get out of hand.

ALICE. It's true. (*She turns it off and returns to painting.*) I'd give that up if I were you. We have to go pretty soon . . .

SUSAN. Why do I lie?

ALICE. We have to get there by midnight.

SUSAN. What do I do it for?

ALICE. It's your profession.

SUSAN. That's what's wrong. In France . . .

ALICE. Ah France.

SUSAN. I told such glittering lies. But where's the fun in lying for a living?

ALICE. What's today's?

SUSAN. Some leaking footwear. Some rotten shoe I have to advertise. What is the point? Why do I exist?

ALICE. Sold out.

SUSAN. Sold out. Is that the phrase? (*Pause.* ALICE *paints.* SUSAN *stares.*)

ALICE. Hang on. Let me have a look. (LOUISE *moves on to her stomach.*)

SUSAN. To produce what my masters call good copy, it is simply a question of pitching my intelligence low enough. Shutting my eyes and imagining what it's like to be very, very stupid. This is all the future holds for any of us. We will spend the next twenty years of our lives pretending to be thick. 'I'm sorry, Miss Traherne, we'd like to employ you, but unfortunately you are not stupid enough.' (SUSAN *tears up the work she is doing and sits back glaring.* ALICE *explains to* LOUISE.)

ALICE. You're all trunk up to here, OK?

LOUISE. Yeah right.

ALICE. The trunk is all one, so you just have to keep
your legs together. Then you break into leaf, just above
the bust . . .

LOUISE. Do I get conkers?

ALICE. No. If you were a chestnut, you'd get conkers.
But you're an oak.

LOUISE. What does an oak have?

ALICE. An oak has acorns.

LOUISE. Acorns?

ALICE. But you won't need them, I promise you. We
scorn gimmicks. We will win as we are.

SUSAN. (*To herself.*) The last night of the year . . .

ALICE. And I will sell a great many paintings . . .
(*Pause.* ALICE *paints.*) Louise is staying with Emma and
Willy . . .

SUSAN. Oh yes?

LOUISE. I met them in the street, I'd just left home,
come down the A6 . . .

SUSAN. Good for you.

LOUISE. I couldn't believe my luck.

ALICE. Willy's going as a kipper, I do know that. And
Emma's a prostitute though how we're meant to know
it's fancy dress I really can't think.

LOUISE. I've gathered that.

ALICE. Otherwise I expect the usual historical riffraff.
Henry VIII, that sort of thing. We ought to walk it with
a naked oak.

LOUISE. Will that friend of yours be there? (*A moment.* SUSAN *looks across at* ALICE *and* LOUISE.)

ALICE. No. He'll be tucked up with his syphilitic wife.

LOUISE. Why doesn't he . . .

SUSAN. Shut up Louise.

ALICE. It's all right. Ask what you want. (*Pause.*)

LOUISE. How do you know she's syphilitic?

ALICE. How do you think, she passed it down the line.

LOUISE. Oh God.

ALICE. Or somebody passed it and I've decided to
blame her. It seems right somehow. She's a very plausi-
ble incubator for a social disease. Back down. (LOUISE
turns again.)

LOUISE. Why doesn't he leave?

ALICE. Who?

LOUISE. Your friend.

ALICE. Ah well if they ever did leave their wives, perhaps the whole sport would die. For all of us.

SUSAN. Roll on 1953. (ALICE *smiles and resumes painting.*)

ALICE. Actually the clinic says it's non-specific urethritis which I find rather insulting. I did at least expect the doctor to come out and apologize and say I'm sorry not to be more specific about your urethritis, but no, they just leave you in the air. (*As she is talking* MICK *has appeared at the door.*)

MICK. I wonder, does anyone mind if I come in?

ALICE. Mick? (MICK *moves into the room.*)

MICK. Would you mind if I . . .

SUSAN. How did you get this address?

ALICE. Do you two know each other?

MICK. Happy New Year. (*Pause.*)

ALICE. Mick, may I introduce you to Louise.

LOUISE. Hello, Mick.

MICK. Hello, Louise.

ALICE. Louise is going to the Arts Ball, I'm painting her . . .

MICK. Ah.

ALICE. She's going as a tree.

SUSAN. Mick, I really don't want to talk to you.

ALICE. What's wrong?

MICK. Is she really going to walk down the street like that?

SUSAN. I thought we'd agreed. You promised me, Mick. You made a promise. Never to meet again. (*A pause.* MICK *looks down.*)

MICK. I just thought . . . well it's New Year's Eve and well . . . one or two weeks have gone by . . .

SUSAN. Have you been watching the house? Is that how you found me? Have you been following me home? (*She stares across at him.* LOUISE *has swung down from the table.*)

LOUISE. Does anyone mind if I put my clothes on? (*In the silence she picks up her clothes and goes into the kitchen.* ALICE *speaks quietly.*)

ALICE. She's not finished. She'll look good when it's done. (*Pause.*)

SUSAN. I asked Mick to father a child, that's what we're talking about . . .

MICK. Oh Christ.

SUSAN. Well we have tried for over eighteen months, that's right? And we have failed.

MICK. Right.

SUSAN. Which leaves us both feeling pretty stupid, pretty wretched I would guess, speaking for myself. And there is a point of decency at which the experiment should stop.

MICK. Susan . . .

SUSAN. We have nothing in common, never did, that was part of the idea . . .

MICK. It just feels bad . . .

SUSAN. The idea was fun, it was simple, it depended on two adults behaving like adults . . .

MICK. It feels very bad to be used.

SUSAN. I would have stopped it months ago, I would have stopped it in the second month . . .

MICK. You come out feeling dirty.

SUSAN. And how do I feel? What am I meant to feel? Crawling about in your tiny bedroom, paper-thin walls, your mother sitting downstairs . . .

MICK. Don't bring my mum into this.

SUSAN. Scrabbling about on bombsites, you think I enjoy all that?

MICK. Yeah. Very much. I think you do. (*Pause.* ALICE *looks away.* SUSAN *moves quietly away as if to give it up.* MICK *calms down.*) I just think . . .

SUSAN. I know what you think. You think I enjoy slumming. Then why have I not looked for another father? Because the whole exploit has broken my heart. (*Pause.*)

MICK. You think it's my fault . . .

SUSAN. Oh Lord is that all you're worried about?

MICK. You think it's something to do with me?

SUSAN. That was part of it, never to have to drag through this kind of idiot argument . . .

MICK. Well it is quite important.

SUSAN. You don't understand. You don't understand the figures in my mind. (*Pause.*) Look Mick there is gentlemen's footwear. It must be celebrated. I have to find words to convey the sensation of walking round London on two pieces of reconstituted cardboard stuck together with horseglue. And I have to find them tonight. (SUSAN

goes to her desk, takes out fresh paper. Starts work. LOU-
ISE *comes from the kitchen, plainly dressed.)*

LOUISE. I'll tell the others. You may be late. (ALICE
*stoops down and picks up a couple of papiermâché green
branches.)*

ALICE. There are some branches. You have to tie
them round your wrists.

LOUISE. Thanks all the same. I'll just go as myself.
(LOUISE *goes out. There is a silence, as* SUSAN *works at
her desk.* ALICE *sits with her hand over her eyes.* MICK
*sits miserably staring. This goes on for some time until
finally* SUSAN *speaks very quietly, without looking up
from her desk.)*

SUSAN. Mick will you go now please?

MICK. You people are cruel.

SUSAN. Please.

MICK. You are cruel and dangerous.

SUSAN. Mick.

MICK. You fuck people up. This little tart and her
string of married men, all fucked up, all fucking ruined
by this tart. And you . . . and you . . . (MICK *turns to*
SUSAN. SUSAN *gets up and walks quietly from the room.
A pause.* ALICE *is looking at him.)* Why doesn't she listen? (SUSAN *reappears with her revolver. She fires it just
over* MICK'S *head. It is deafeningly loud. He falls to the
ground. She fires three more times.)* Jesus Christ.

SCENE 7

Knightsbridge. October 1956
*From the dark, music, emphatic, triumphant. The room
we saw in Scene One. But now decorated with heavy velvet curtains, china objects and soft furniture. A diplomatic
home. Both men in dinner-jackets:* BROCK *smokes a cigar
and drinks brandy. Opposite him is an almost permanently smiling Burmese* M. AUNG, *short, dogmatic. The
music stops.*

AUNG. Two great nations, sir. The Americans and the
English. Like the Romans and the Greeks. Americans
are the Romans—power, armies, strength. The English
are the Greeks—ideas, civilization, intellect. Between
them they shall rule the world.

(DARWIN *appears putting his head round the door. He is also in a dinner-jacket. He appears exhausted*.)

DARWIN. Good Lord, I hope you haven't hung on for me.

BROCK. Leonard, come in, how kind of you to come.

DARWIN. Not at all. (BROCK *ushers him in*. AUNG *stands*.)

BROCK. Our little gathering. We'd scarcely dared hope . . .

DARWIN. There seemed nothing left to do.

BROCK. Leonard, you know M. Aung, of course?

AUNG. Mr. Darwin.

DARWIN. Rangoon . . .

BROCK. Now first secretary, Burmese embassy.

AUNG. An honour. A privilege. A moment in my career. I shake your hand. (*He does so*.)

DARWIN. Good, good. Well.

BROCK. Let me get you a drink.

DARWIN. That would be very kind.

BROCK. I'll just tell my wife you're here. (BROCK *goes out*. AUNG *smiles at* DARWIN.)

AUNG. Affairs of state?

DARWIN. Yes if you . . .

AUNG. Say no more. We have eaten. We did not wait. In Burma we say if you cannot be on time do not come at all.

DARWIN. Really?

AUNG. But of course the English it is different. At your command the lion makes its bed with the lamb . . .

DARWIN. Hardly.

AUNG. Don't worry. All will be well. Ah Darwin of Djakarta, to have met the man, to have been alone with him. I shall dine in on this for many years . . .

DARWIN. Dine out on this.

AUNG. Ah the English language, she is a demanding mistress, yes?

DARWIN. If you like.

AUNG. And no one controls her so well as you sir. You beat her and the bitch obeys. (*He laughs*.) The language of the world. Good, good. I have learnt the phrase from you. Out of your mouth. Good, good. I am behind you sir.

(SUSAN *appears in a superbly cut evening dress. She is dangerously cheerful.* BROCK *follows her.*)

SUSAN. Leonard, how good of you to make an appearance.

DARWIN. I'm only sorry I've been delayed. (SUSAN *and* DARWIN *kiss.*)

SUSAN. Brock says you're all ragged with fatigue. I hear you've been having the most frightful week . . .

DARWIN. It has been yes.

SUSAN. Well don't worry. Here at least you can relax. You've met Mr. Aung.

DARWIN. Indeed.

SUSAN. You can forget everything. The words 'Suez Canal' will not be spoken.

DARWIN. That will be an enormous relief.

SUSAN. They are banned, you will not hear them.

DARWIN. Thank you my dear.

SUSAN. Nasser, nobody will mention his name.

DARWIN. Quite.

SUSAN. Nobody will say blunder or folly or fiasco. Nobody will say 'international laughing stock'. You are among friends, Leonard. I will rustle up some food. (*She smiles at* AUNG.) Mr. Aung I think the gentlemen may wish to talk.

AUNG. Of course, in such company I am privileged to change sex. (AUNG *gets up to follow* SUSAN *out.*)

SUSAN. Nobody will say 'death-rattle of the ruling class'. We have stuck our lips together with marron glacé. I hope you understand. (SUSAN *and* AUNG *go out. Pause.*)

BROCK. Sorry I . . .

DARWIN. It's all right.

BROCK. I did ask her to calm down.

DARWIN. I'm getting used to it.

BROCK. She's been giving me hell. She knows how closely you've been involved . . .

DARWIN. Do you think we could leave the subject Brock? (*Pause.*) I'm eager for the drink.

BROCK. Of course.

DARWIN. At least she got rid of that appalling wog. I mean in honesty Raymond what are you trying to do to me . . .

BROCK. I'm sorry sir.

DARWIN. This week of all weeks. He had his tongue stuck so far up my fundamental all you could see of him were the soles of his feet. (BROCK *takes over a tray of drinks*.) Mental illness, is it? Your wife?

BROCK. No, no she just . . . feels very strongly. Well you know . . .

DARWIN. But there has been mental illness?

BROCK. Not really. A breakdown. Before we were married. Some years ago. She'd been living very foolishly, a loose set in Pimlico. And a series of jobs, pushing herself too hard. Not eating. We got engaged when she was still quite ill, and I have tried to help her back up.

DARWIN. That's very good.

BROCK. Well . . .

DARWIN. Second marriage of course. Often stabilizes.

BROCK. What?

DARWIN. The chap in Brussels. (*Pause.*) The stiff.

BROCK. Ah yes.

DARWIN. You don't have to be ashamed . . .

BROCK. No I'm not it's . . .

DARWIN. In the diplomatic service it isn't as if a mad wife is any kind of professional disadvantage. On the contrary it almost guarantees promotion.

BROCK. Well . . .

DARWIN. Some of the senior men, their wives are absolutely barking. I take the word 'gouache' to be the giveaway. When they start drifting out of rooms saying, 'I think I'll just go and do my gouaches dear,' then you know you've lost them for good and all.

BROCK. But Susan isn't mad.

DARWIN. No, no. (*Pause.*) Is there a Madame Aung?

BROCK. In the other room.

DARWIN. I knew there had to be. Somehow. And no doubt culturally inclined. Traditional dance, she'll tell us about, in the highlands of Burma. Or the plot of *Lohengrin*.

BROCK. Leonard . . .

DARWIN. I'm sorry. I think I've had it Brock. One more Aung and I throw in the can. (*Pause.*) Do you mind if I have a cherry?

BROCK. What?

DARWIN. The maraschinos. I'm so hungry, it's all those bloody drugs we have to take.

BROCK. Let me . . .

DARWIN. Stay. (*Pause.*) We have been betrayed. (DARWIN *reaches into the cocktail cherries with his fingers, but then just rolls them slowly in his palm.*) We claim to be intervening as a neutral party in a dispute between Israel and Egypt. Last Monday the Israelis launched their attack. On Tuesday we issued our ultimatum saying both sides must withdraw to either side of the canal. But Raymond, the Israelis, the aggressors, they were nowhere near the canal. They'd have had to advance a hundred miles to make the retreat.

BROCK. Who told you that?

DARWIN. Last week the Foreign Secretary went abroad. I was not briefed. We believe he met with the French and the Israelis, urged the Israelis to attack. I believe our ultimatum was written in France last week, hence the mistake in the wording. The Israelis had reckoned to reach the canal, but met with unexpectedly heavy resistance. I think the entire war is a fraud cooked up by the British as an excuse for seizing the canal. And we, we who have to execute this policy, even we were not told. (*Pause.*)

BROCK. Well . . . what difference does it make?

DARWIN. My dear boy.

BROCK. I mean it . . .

DARWIN. Raymond.

BROCK. It makes no difference.

DARWIN. I was lied to.

BROCK. Yes but you were against it from the start.

DARWIN. I . . .

BROCK. Oh come on, we all were, the Foreign Office hated the operation from the very first mention so what difference does it make now . . .

DARWIN. All the difference in the world.

BROCK. None at all.

DARWIN. The government lied to me.

BROCK. If the policy was wrong, if it was wrong to begin with . . .

DARWIN. They are not in good faith.

BROCK. I see, I see, so what you're saying is, the British may do anything, doesn't matter how murderous, doesn't matter how silly, just so long as we do it in good faith.

DARWIN. Yes. I would have defended it, I wouldn't have minded how damn stupid it was. I would have defended it had it been honestly done. But this time we are cowboys and when the English are the cowboys, then in truth I fear for the future of the globe. (*A pause.* DARWIN *walks to the curtained window and stares out.* BROCK *left sitting doesn't turn as he speaks.*)

BROCK. Eden is weak. For years he has been weak. For years people have taunted him, why aren't you strong? Like Churchill? He goes round, he begins to think I must find somebody to be strong on. He finds Nasser. Now he'll show them. He does it to impress. He does it badly. No one is impressed. (DARWIN *turns to look at* BROCK.) Mostly what we do is what we think people expect of us. Mostly it's wrong. (*Pause.*) Are you going to resign?

(*The sound of laughter as* SUSAN, MME. AUNG, M. AUNG *and* ALICE *stream into the room.* MME. AUNG *is small, tidy and bright.* ALICE *is spectacularly dressed.*)

SUSAN. Mme Aung has been enthralling us with the story of the new Bergman film at the Everyman.

DARWIN. Ah.

BROCK. Ah yes.

SUSAN. Apparently it's about depression, isn't that so, Mme Aung?

MME AUNG. I do feel the Norwegians are very good at that sort of thing.

SUSAN. Is anything wrong? (SUSAN *stands and looks at* BROCK *and* DARWIN.) Please do sit down everyone. I'm sorry I think we may have interrupted the men.

BROCK. It's all right.

SUSAN. They were probably drafting a telegram . . .

BROCK. We weren't.

SUSAN. That's what they do before they drop a bomb. They send their targets notice in a telegram. Bombs tonight, evacuate the area. Now what does that indicate to you, M Aung?

BROCK. Susan, please.

SUSAN. I'll tell you what it indicates to me. Bad conscience. They don't even have the guts to make a war any more. (*Pause.*)

DARWIN. Perhaps Mme Aung will tell us the story of the film. This is something I'd be very keen to hear.

MME AUNG. I feel the ladies have already . . .

ALICE. We don't mind.

SUSAN. It's all right. Go ahead. We like the bit in the mental ward.

MME AUNG. Ah yes.

SUSAN. Raymond will like it. You got me out of the bin didn't you dear?

BROCK. Yes, yes.

SUSAN. That's where he proposed to me. A moment of weakness. Of mine, I mean.

BROCK. Please darling . . .

SUSAN. I married him because he reminded me of my father.

MME AUNG. Really?

SUSAN. At that point of course I didn't realize just what a shit my father was. (*Pause.*)

ALICE. I'm sorry. She has a sort of psychiatric cabaret. (SUSAN *laughs.*)

SUSAN. That's very good Alice. And there's something about Suez which . . .

BROCK. Will you please be quiet? (*Pause.*) The story of the film. (MME. AUNG *is embarrassed. It takes her considerable effort to start.*)

MME AUNG. There's a woman . . . who despises her husband . . . (*Pause.*)

SUSAN. Is it getting a little bit chilly in here? October nights. Those poor parachutists. I do know how they feel. Even now. Cities. Fields. Trees. Farms. Dark spaces. Lights. The parachute opens. We descend. (*Pause.*) Of course we were comparatively welcome, not always ecstatic, not the Gaullists of course, but by and large we did make it our business to land in countries where we were welcome. Certainly the men were. I mean, some of the relationships, I can't tell you. I remember a colleague of mine telling me of the heat, of the smell of a particular young girl, the hot wet smell he said. Nothing since. Nothing since then. I don't think the Egyptian girls somehow . . . no. Not in Egypt now. I mean there were broken hearts when we left. I mean, there are girls today who mourn the dead Englishmen who died in Dachau, who died naked in Dachau, men with whom they had spent a single night. (*Pause. The tears are pouring down* SUSAN's *face, she can barely speak.*) But then . . . even for myself I do like to make a point of sleeping with men I don't know. I do find once you get to know them you usually don't want to sleep with them any more . . . (BROCK *gets up and shouts at the top of his voice across the room.*)

BROCK. Please can you stop, can you stop fucking talking for five fucking minutes on end?

SUSAN. I would stop, I would stop, I would stop fucking talking if I ever heard anyone else say anything worth fucking stopping talking for. (*Pause. Then* DARWIN *moves.*)

DARWIN. I'm sorry. I apologize. I really must go. (*He crosses the room.*) M Aung. Farewell.

AUNG. We are behind you sir. There is wisdom in your expedition.

DARWIN. Thank you.

AUNG. May I say sir, these gyps need whipping and you are the man to do it?

DARWIN. Thank you very much. Mme Aung.

MME AUNG. We never really met.

DARWIN. No. No. We never met, that is true. But perhaps before I go, I may nevertheless set you right on a point of fact. Ingmar Bergman is not a bloody Norwegian, he is a bloody Swede. (*He nods slightly.*) Good night everyone. (DARWIN *goes out.* BROCK *gets up and goes to the door, then turns.*)

BROCK. Leonard. He's going to resign. (*Pause.*)

SUSAN. Isn't this an exciting week? Don't you think? Isn't this thrilling? Don't you think? Everything is up for grabs. At last. We will see some changes. Thank the Lord. Now, there was dinner. I made some more dinner for Leonard. A little ham. And chicken. And some pickles and tomato. And lettuce. And there are a couple of pheasants in the fridge. And I can get twelve bottles of claret from the cellar. Why not? There is plenty. Shall we eat again?

INTERVAL

SCENE 8

Knightsbridge. July 1961
From the dark the voice of a PRIEST.

PRIEST. Man that is born of woman hath but a short time to live and is full of misery. He cometh up and is cut down like a flower. He fleeth and never continueth in one stay. In the midst of life we are in death. Of whom may we seek for succour but of thee O Lord, who for our sins art justly displeased?

(*The room is dark. All the chairs, all the furniture, all the mirrors are covered in white dust-sheets. There is a strong flood of light from the hall which silhouettes the group of three as they enter, all dressed in black. First* BROCK, *then* DORCAS, *a tall heavily-built, seventeen-year-old blonde and then* ALICE *who, like the others, does not remove her coat.* ALICE'S *manner has darkened and sharpened somewhat.* BROCK *goes to take the sheets off two chairs.*)

BROCK. I must say I'd forgotten just how grim it can be.
ALICE. All that mumbling.
BROCK. I know. And those bloody hymns. They really do you no good at all. (*He wraps a sheet over his arm.*) Would you like to sit down in here? I'm afraid the whole house is horribly unused. (*The women sit.* BROCK *holds his hand out to* DORCAS.) You and I haven't had a proper chance to meet.
ALICE. I hope you didn't mind . . .
BROCK. Not at all.
ALICE. My bringing Dorcas along.
BROCK. She swelled the numbers.
DORCAS. I had the afternoon off school.
BROCK. I'm not sure I'd have chosen a funeral . . .
DORCAS. It was fine.
BROCK. Oh good.
DORCAS. Alice told me she was a very good friend of yours.
BROCK. Well she is.

DORCAS. Who she hadn't seen for a very long time and she was sure you wouldn't mind me . . . you know . . .

BROCK. Gatecrashing?

DORCAS. Yes.

BROCK. At the grave.

DORCAS. It sounds awful.

BROCK. You were welcome as far as I was concerned.

DORCAS. The only thing was . . . I never heard his name.

BROCK. His name was Darwin.

DORCAS. Ah.

(SUSAN *stands unremarked in the doorway. She has taken her coat off and is plainly dressed in black, with some books under her arm. Her manner is quieter than before, and yet more elegant.*)

SUSAN. Please nobody get up for me. (SUSAN *moves down to the front where there are two cases filled with books on the floor.*)

BROCK. Ah Susan . . .

SUSAN. I was just looking out some more books to take back.

BROCK. Are you all right?

SUSAN. Yes, fine.

ALICE. Susan, this is Dorcas I told you about.

SUSAN. How do you do?

DORCAS. How do you do? (SUSAN *tucks the books away.*)

ALICE. I teach Dorcas history.

BROCK. Good Lord, how long have you done that?

ALICE. Oh . . . I've been at it some time.

DORCAS. Alice is a very good teacher you know.

BROCK. I'm sure.

ALICE. Thank you Dorcas.

DORCAS. We had a poll and Alice came top. (*They smile at each other.*)

BROCK. Where do you teach?

ALICE. It's called the Kensington Academy.

BROCK. I see.

ALICE. It's in Shepherd's Bush.

DORCAS. It's a crammer.

ALICE. For the daughters of the rich and the congenitally stupid. Dorcas to a T.

DORCAS. It's true.

ALICE. There's almost nothing that a teacher can do.

DORCAS. Alice says we're all the prisoners of our genes.

ALICE. When you actually try to engage their attention, you know that all they can really hear inside their heads is the great thump-thump of their ancestors fucking too freely among themselves.

DORCAS. Nothing wrong with that.

ALICE. No?

DORCAS. Stupid people are happier.

ALICE. Is that what you think? (*They smile again.* BROCK *watches.*)

BROCK. Well . . .

SUSAN. Raymond, could you manage to make us some tea?

BROCK. Certainly if there's time . . .

SUSAN. I'm sure everyone's in need of it. (BROCK *smiles and goes out.*) Alice rang me this morning. She said she was very keen we should meet.

ALICE. I didn't realize you were going back so soon.

SUSAN. It's a problem I'm afraid. My husband is a diplomat, we're posted in Iran, I haven't been to London for over three years. Then when I heard of Leonard's death I felt . . . I just felt very strongly I wanted to attend.

DORCAS. Alice was saying he'd lost a lot of his friends. (SUSAN *looks across at* ALICE.)

SUSAN. Yes, that's true.

DORCAS. I didn't understand what . . .

SUSAN. He spoke his mind over Suez. In public. He didn't hide his disgust. A lot of people never forgave him for that.

DORCAS. Oh I see. (*Pause.*) What's . . .

ALICE. It's a historical incident four years ago, caused a minor kind of stir at the time. It's also the name of a waterway in Egypt. Egypt is the big brown country up the top righthand corner of Africa. Africa is a continent . . .

DORCAS. Yes thank you.

ALICE. And that's why nobody was there today. (ALICE *looks up at* SUSAN *but she has turned away.*) I got that panic, you know, you get at funerals. I was thinking, I really don't want to think about death . . .

SUSAN. Yes.

ALICE. Anything, count the bricks, count the trees, but don't think about death . . . (*She smiles.*) So I tried to imagine Leonard was still alive, I mean locked in his coffin but still alive. And I was laughing at how he would have dealt with the situation, I mean just exactly what the protocol would be.

SUSAN. He would know it.

ALICE. Of course. Official procedure in the case of being buried alive. He many times one may tap on the lid. How to rise from the grave without drawing unnecessary attention to yourself.

SUSAN. Poor Leonard.

ALICE. I know. But he did make me laugh. (SUSAN *looks at her catching the old phrase. Then turns at once to* DORCAS.)

SUSAN. Alice said I might help you in some way.

DORCAS. Well yes.

SUSAN. Of course. If there's anything at all. (*She smiles.*)

DORCAS. Did she tell you what the problem was?

ALICE. There isn't any problem. You need money, that's all.

DORCAS. Alice said you'd once been a great friend of hers, part of her sort of crowd . . .

SUSAN. Are they still going then?

ALICE. They certainly are.

DORCAS. And that you might be sympathetic as you'd . . . well . . . as you'd known some troubles yourself . . .

ALICE. Dorcas needs cash from an impeccable source. (*Pause.*)

SUSAN. I see.

DORCAS. I'd pay it back.

SUSAN. Well I'm sure.

DORCAS. I mean it's only two hundred pounds. In theory I could still get it for myself, perhaps I'll have to but Alice felt . . .

ALICE. Never mind.

DORCAS. No I think I should, I mean, I think I should say Alice did feel as she'd introduced me to this man . . . (*Pause.* ALICE *looks away.*) Just because he was one of her friends . . . which I just think is silly, I mean for God's sake I'm old enough to live my own life . . .

SUSAN. Yes.

DORCAS. I mean I am seventeen. And I knew what I was doing. So why the hell should Alice feel responsible?

SUSAN. I don't know.

DORCAS. Anyway the man was a doctor, one of Alice's famous bent doctors, you know, I just wanted to get hold of some drugs, but he wouldn't hand over unless I agreed to fool around, so I just . . . I didn't think anything of it.

SUSAN. No.

DORCAS. It just seemed like part of the price. At the time. Of course I never guessed it would be three months later and wham the knitting needles.

SUSAN. Yes. (*Pause.*)

DORCAS. I mean to be honest I could still go to Daddy and tell him. Just absolutely outright tell him. Just say Daddy I'm sorry but . . .

ALICE. Wham the knitting needles.

DORCAS. Yes. (SUSAN *looks across at* ALICE. *The two women stare steadily at each other as* DORCAS *talks.*) But of course one would need a great deal of guts. (*Pause.*) I mean I can't tell you how awful I feel. I mean, coming straight from a funeral . . . (SUSAN *suddenly gets up and walks to the door, speaking very quietly.*)

SUSAN. Well I'm sure it needn't delay us for too long . . .

DORCAS. Do you mean . . .

SUSAN. Kill a child. That's easy. No problem at all. (SUSAN *opens the door. She has heard* BROCK *with the tea-tray outside.*) Ah Raymond, the tea.

BROCK. I have to tell you the car has arrived.

SUSAN. Oh good.

BROCK. The driver is saying we must get away at once. (SUSAN *has gone out into the hall.* BROCK *sets the tray down near* DORCAS *and* ALICE *and begins to pour.*) It must be two years since I made my own tea. Persian labour is disgustingly cheap.

DORCAS. I thought you said they . . .

ALICE. It's another name for Iran.

DORCAS. Oh I see. (SUSAN *has re-appeared with her handbag and now goes to the writing desk. She folds the sheet back and lowers the lid.*)

BROCK. Susan I do hope you're preparing to go.

SUSAN. I will do, I just need a minute or two . . .

BROCK. I don't think we have time to do anything but
. . . (SUSAN *walks over to him.*)

SUSAN. I do need some tea. Just to wash down my
pill. (*A pause.* BROCK *smiles.*)

BROCK. Yes of course. (SUSAN *takes the cup from his
hand. Then goes back to the desk where she gets out a
cheque book and begins to write.*)

ALICE. So Raymond you must tell us about life in Iran.

BROCK. I would say we'd been very happy out there.
Wouldn't you Susan?

SUSAN. Uh-huh.

BROCK. I think the peace has done us both a great
deal of good. We were getting rather frenzied in our last
few months here. (*He smiles.*)

ALICE. And the people?

BROCK. The people are fine. In so far as one's seen
them you know. It's only occasionally that you manage
to get out. But the trips are startling, no doubt about
that. There you are. (BROCK *hands* ALICE *tea.*)

ALICE. Thank you.

BROCK. The sky. The desert. And of course the poverty. Living among people who have to struggle so hard.
It can make you see life very differently.

SUSAN. Do I make it to cash?

ALICE. If you could. (BROCK *hands* DORCAS *tea.*)

DORCAS. Thanks.

BROCK. I do remember Leonard, that Leonard always
said, the pleasure of diplomacy is perspective, you see.
Looking across distances. For instance we see England
very clearly from there. And it does look just a trifle
decadent. (*He smiles again and drinks his tea.*)

SUSAN. I'm lending Dorcas some money.

BROCK. Oh really, is that wise?

ALICE. She needs an operation.

BROCK. What?

ALICE. The tendons of her hands. If she's ever to play
in a concert hall again.

BROCK. Do you actually play a . . . (SUSAN *gets up
from her desk.*)

SUSAN. Raymond could you take a look at that case?
One of those locks is refusing to turn.

BROCK. Ah yes. (BROCK *goes to shut the case.* ALICE *watches smiling as* SUSAN *walks across to* DORCAS *to hand her the cheque.*)

SUSAN. Here you are.

DORCAS. Thank you.

SUSAN. Don't thank us. We're rotten with cash. (BROCK *closes the case.* SUSAN *gathers the cups on to the tray and places it by the door.*)

BROCK. If that's it then I reckon we're ready to go. I'm sorry to turn you out of the house . . .

ALICE. That's all right.

BROCK. Alice, you must come and see us . . .

ALICE. I shall.

BROCK. My tour has been extended another two years. Dorcas I'm happy to have met. I hope your studies proceed, under Alice's tutelage. In the meanwhile perhaps you might lend me a hand . . . (*He gestures at the cases.*) Susan's lifeline. Her case full of books. (DORCAS *goes to carry out the smaller case.*) Susan, you're ready?

SUSAN. Yes I am.

BROCK. You'll follow me down? (SUSAN *nods but doesn't move.*) Well . . . I shall be waiting in the car. (BROCK *goes out with the large case.* DORCAS *follows.*)

DORCAS. Alice, we won't be long will we?

ALICE. No.

DORCAS. It's just it's biology tonight and that's my favourite. (*Off.*) Do I put them in the boot?

BROCK. (*Off.*) If you could. (SUSAN *and* ALICE *left alone do not move. A pause.*)

SUSAN. I knew if I came over I would never return. (*She pulls the sheet off the desk. It slinks on to the floor. Then she moves round the room, pulling away all the sheets from the furniture, letting them all fall. Then takes them from the mirrors. Then she lights the standard-lamps, the table-lamps. The room warms and brightens.* ALICE *sits perfectly still, her legs outstretched. Then* SUSAN *turns to look at* ALICE.) I've missed you. (BROCK *appears at the open door.*)

BROCK. Susan. Darling. Are we ready to go?

SCENE 9

Whitehall. January 1962
From the dark the sound of a radio interview. The IN-
TERVIEWER is male, serious, a little guarded.

VOICE. During the war, you were one of the few
women to be flown into France?
SUSAN. Yes.
VOICE. And you were also one of the youngest?
SUSAN. Yes.
VOICE. Did you always have complete confidence in
the organization that sent you?
SUSAN. Yes of course.
VOICE. Since the war it's often been alleged that SOE
was amateurish, its recruitment methods were haphaz-
ard, some of its behavior was rather cavalier. Did you
feel that at the time?
SUSAN. Not at all.
VOICE. The suggestion is that it was careless of human
life. Did you ever feel that any of your colleagues died
needlessly?
SUSAN. I can't say.
VOICE. But if you . . .
SUSAN. Sorry, if I could . . .
VOICE. Yes, of course.
SUSAN. You believed in the organization. You had to.
If you didn't you would die.
VOICE. But surely you must have had an opinion . . .
SUSAN. No. I had no opinion. I have an opinion now.
VOICE. And that is?
SUSAN. That it was one part of the war from which
the British emerge with the greatest possible valour and
distinction. (*A slight pause.*)
VOICE. Do you ever get together with former col-
leagues and talk about the war?
SUSAN. Never. We aren't clubbable.

(*The Foreign Office. A large room in Scott's Palazzo.
A mighty painting above a large fireplace in an otherwise
barish waiting room. It shows Britannia Colonorum
Mater in pseudo-classical style. Otherwise the room is un-
cheering. A functional desk, some unremarkable wooden*

chairs, a green radiator. An air of functional disuse. Two people. SUSAN *is standing at one side smartly dressed again with coat and handbag;* BEGLEY *stands opposite by an inner door. He is a thin young man with impeccable manners. He is twenty-two.*)

BEGLEY. Mrs. Brock, Sir Andrew will see you now. He only has a few minutes I'm afraid. (*At once through the inner door comes* SIR ANDREW CHARLESON *in a double-breasted blue suit. He is in his early fifties, dark-haired, thickening, almost indolent. He cuts less of a figure than* DARWIN *but he has far more edge.*)

CHARLESON. Ah Mrs. Brock.

SUSAN. Sir Andrew.

CHARLESON. How do you do? (SUSAN *and* CHARLESON *shake hands.*)

CHARLESON. We have met.

SUSAN. That's right.

CHARLESON. The Queen's Garden Party. And I've heard you on the wireless only recently. Talking about the war. How extraordinary it must have been. (*Pause.*)

SUSAN. This must seem a very strange request.

CHARLESON. Not in the slightest. We're delighted to see you here. (BEGLEY *takes two chairs out from the wall and places them down opposite each other.*) Perhaps I might offer you a drink.

SUSAN. If you are having one.

CHARLESON. Unfortunately not. I'm somewhat liverish.

SUSAN. I'm sorry.

CHARLESON. No, no, it's a hazard of the job. Half the diplomats I know have bad offal I'm afraid. (*He turns to* BEGLEY.) If you could leave us Begley . . .

BEGLEY. Sir.

CHARLESON. Just shuffle some papers for a while. (BEGLEY *goes through the inner door.* CHARLESON *gestures* SUSAN *to sit.*) You mustn't be nervous you know, Mrs. Brock. I have to encounter many diplomatic wives, many even more distinguished than yourself, with very similar intent. It is much commoner than you suppose.

SUSAN. Sir Andrew, as you know I take very little part in my husband's professional life . . .

CHARLESON. Indeed.

SUSAN. Normally I spend a great deal of time on my

own . . . with one or two friends . . . of my own . . . mostly I like reading, I like reading alone . . . I do think to be merely your husband's wife is demeaning for a woman of any integrity at all . . . (CHARLESON *smiles*.)

CHARLESON. I understand.

SUSAN. But I find for the first time in my husband's career I am beginning to feel some need to intervene.

CHARLESON. I had a message, yes.

SUSAN. I hope you appreciate my loyalty . . .

CHARLESON. Oh yes.

SUSAN. Coming here at all. Brock is a man who has seen me through some very difficult times . . .

CHARLESON. I am told.

SUSAN. But this is a matter on which I need to go behind his back. (CHARLESON *gestures reassurance*.) My impression is that since our recall from Iran he is in some way being penalized. (CHARLESON *makes no reaction*.) As I understand it, you're Head of Personnel . . .

CHARLESON. I'm the Chief Clerk, yes . . .

SUSAN. I've come to ask exactly what my husband's prospects are. (*Pause*.) I do understand the foreign service now. I know that my husband could never ask himself. Your business is conducted in a code, which it's considered unethical to break. Signs and indications are all you are given. Your stock is rising, your stock is falling . . .

CHARLESON. Yes.

SUSAN. Brock has been allocated a fairly lowly job, backing up the common market.

CHARLESON. He's part of the push into Europe, yes . . .

SUSAN. The foreign posts he's since been offered have not been glittering.

CHARLESON. We offered him Monrovia.

SUSAN. Monrovia. Yes. He took that to be an insult. Was he wrong? (CHARLESON *smiles*.)

CHARLESON. Monrovia is not an insult.

SUSAN. But?

CHARLESON. Monrovia is more in the nature of a test. A test of nerve, it's true. If a man is stupid enough to accept Monrovia, then he probably deserves Monrovia. That is how we think.

SUSAN. But you . . .

CHARLESON. And Brock refused. (*He shrugs*.) Had we

wanted to insult him there are far worse jobs. In this building too. In my view town-twinning is the *coup de grâce*. I'd far rather be a martyr to the tsetse fly than have to twin Huddersfield with Bergen-op-Zoom.

SUSAN. You are evading me. (*Pause.* CHARLESON *smiles again.*)

CHARLESON. I'm sorry. It's a habit as you say. (*He pauses to re-think. Then with confidence.*) Your husband has never been a flyer Mrs. Brock . . .

SUSAN. I see.

CHARLESON. Everyone is streamed, a slow stream, a fast stream . . .

SUSAN. My husband is slow?

CHARLESON. Slow-ish.

SUSAN. That means . . .

CHARLESON. What is he? First Secretary struggling towards Counsellor. At forty-one it's not remarkable you know.

SUSAN. But it's got worse.

CHARLESON. You think?

SUSAN. The last six months. He's never felt excluded from his work before.

CHARLESON. Does he feel that?

SUSAN. I think you know he does. (*Pause.*)

CHARLESON. Well I'm sure the intention was not to punish him. We have had some trouble in placing him it's true. The rather startling decision to desert his post . . .

SUSAN. That was not his fault.

CHARLESON. We were told. We were sympathetic. Psychiatric reasons?

SUSAN. I was daunted at the prospect of returning to Iran.

CHARLESON. Of course. Persian psychiatry. I shudder at the thought. A heavy-handed people at the best of times. We understood. Family problems. Our sympathy goes out . . .

SUSAN. But you are blocking his advance. (CHARLESON *thinks, then changes tack again.*)

CHARLESON. I think you should understand the basis of our talk. The basis on which I agreed to talk. You asked for information. The information is this: that Brock is making haste slowly. That is all I can say.

SUSAN. I'm very keen he should not suffer on my account. (SUSAN's *voice is low.* CHARLESON *looks at his hands.*)

CHARLESON. Mrs. Brock, believe me I recognize your tone. Women have come in here and used it before . . . I also have read the stories in your file, so nothing in your manner is likely to amaze. I do know exactly the kind of person you are. When you have chosen a particular course . . . (*He pauses.*) When there is something which you very badly want . . . (*He pauses again.*) But in this matter I must tell you Mrs. Brock it is more than likely you have met your match. (*The two of them stare straight at each other.*) We are talking of achievement at the highest level. Brock cannot expect to be cosseted through. It's not enough to be clever, everyone here is clever, everyone is gifted, everyone is diligent. These are simply the minimum skills. Far more important is an attitude of mind. Along the corridor I boast a colleague who in 1945 drafted a memorandum to the government advising them not to accept the Volkswagen works as war reparation, because the Volkswagen plainly had no commercial future. I must tell you, unlikely as it may seem, that man has risen to the very, very top. All sorts of diplomatic virtues he displays. He has forebearance. He is gracious. He is sociable. Perhaps you begin to understand . . .

SUSAN. You are saying . . .

CHARLESON. I am saying that certain qualities are valued here above a simple gift of being right or wrong. Qualities sometimes hard to define . . .

SUSAN. What you are saying is that nobody may speak, nobody may question . . .

CHARLESON. Certainly tact is valued very high. (*Pause.* SUSAN *very low.*)

SUSAN. Tell me Sir Andrew, do you never find it in yourself to despise a job in which nobody may speak his mind?

CHARLESON. That is the nature of the service, Mrs. Brock. It is called diplomacy. And in its practice the English lead the world. (*He smiles.*) The irony is this: we had an empire to administer, there were six hundred of us in this place. Now it's to be dismantled and there are six thousand. As our power declines, the fight among us for access to that power becomes a little more urgent, a little uglier perhaps. As our influence wanes, as our empire collapses, there is little to believe in. Behaviour is all. (*Pause.*) This is a lesson which you both must learn. (*A moment, then* SUSAN *picks up her handbag to go.*)

SUSAN. I must thank you for your frankness, Sir Andrew . . .

CHARLESON. Not at all.

SUSAN. I must however warn you of my plan. If Brock is not promoted in the next six days, I am intending to shoot myself. (SUSAN *gets up from her seat.* CHARLESON *follows quickly.*) Now thank you and I shan't stay for the drink . . .

CHARLESON. (*Calls.*) Begley . . .

SUSAN. I'm due at a reception for Australia Day. (CHARLESON *moves quickly to the inner door.* SUSAN *begins talking very fast as she moves to go.*)

CHARLESON. Begley.

SUSAN. I always like to see just how rude I can be. Not that the Australians ever notice of course. So it does become a sort of Zen sport, don't you think? (BEGLEY *appears.*)

CHARLESON. John I wonder could you give me a hand?

BEGLEY. Sir. (SUSAN *stops near the door, starts talking yet more rapidly.*)

SUSAN. Ah the side-kick, the placid young man, now where have I seen that character before?

CHARLESON. If we could take Mrs. Brock down to the surgery . . .

SUSAN. I assure you Sir Andrew I'm perfectly all right.

CHARLESON. Perhaps alert her husband . . .

BEGLEY. If you're not feeling well . . .

SUSAN. Look, people will be waiting at Australia House. I can't let them down. It will be packed with angry people all searching for me, saying where is she, what a let-down. I only came here to be insulted and now there's no chance . . . CHARLESON *looks at* BEGLEY *as if to co-ordinate a move. They advance slightly.*)

CHARLESON. I think it would be better if you . . . (SUSAN *starts to shout.*)

SUSAN. Please. Please leave me alone. (CHARLESON *and* BEGLEY *stop.* SUSAN *is hysterical. She waits a mo-*

ment.) I can't . . . always manage with people. (*Pause.*)
I think you have destroyed my husband you see.

SCENE 10

Knightsbridge. Easter 1962
*From the dark the sound of some stately orchestral
chords: Mahler, melodic, solemn. It is evening. The room
has been restored to its former rather old-fashioned splendour. The curtains are drawn. At a mahogany table sits
ALICE. She is putting a large pile of leaflets into brown
envelopes. Very little disturbs the rhythm of her work. She
is dressed exactly as for Scene One. BROCK is sitting at
another table at the front of the stage. He has an abacus
in front of him and a pile of ledgers and cheque stubs.
He is dressed in cavalry twills with a check shirt open at
the neck. The music stops. The stereo machine switches
itself off.*

BROCK. Well I suppose it isn't too bad. Perhaps we'll
keep going another couple of years. A regime of mineral
water and lightly browned toast. (*He smiles and stretches.
Then turns to look at ALICE. There is a bottle of mineral
water on the table in front of her.*) I assume she's still in
there.

ALICE. She paces around. (BROCK *gets up and pours
some out.*)

BROCK. I told her this morning . . . we'll have to sell
the house. I'm sure we can cope in a smaller sort of flat.
Especially now we don't have to entertain. (*He takes a
sip.*) I can't help feeling it will be better, I'm sure. Too
much money. I think that's what went wrong. Something
about it corrupts the will to live. Too many years spent
sploshing around. (*He suddenly listens.*) What?

ALICE. Nothing. She's just moving about. (*He turns to
ALICE.*)

BROCK. Perhaps you'd enjoy to take the evening off.
I'm happy to do duty for an hour or two.

ALICE. I enjoy it. I get to do my work. A good long
slog for my charity appeal. And I've rather fallen out
with all those people I knew. And most of them go off
on the march to ban the bomb.

BROCK. Really? Of course. Easter Weekend. (*He*

*picks his way through the remains of an Indian takeaway
meal which is on* ALICE'S *table, searching for good
scraps.*)

ALICE. Except for Alistair and I've no intention of
spending an evening with him, or her as he's taken to
calling himself.

BROCK. How come?

ALICE. Apparently he's just had his penis removed.

BROCK. Voluntarily? It's what he intended I mean?

ALICE. I believe. In Morocco. And replaced with a
sort of pink plastic envelope, I haven't seen it, he says
he keeps the shopping list in there, tucks five pound
notes away so he says.

BROCK. I thought that strange young girl of yours
would ring. (ALICE *looks up for a moment from her
work.*)

ALICE. No, no. She decided to move on. There's some
appalling politician I'm told. On the paedophiliac wing
of the Tory party. She's going to spend the summer swab-
bing the deck on his yacht. Pleasuring his enormous un-
derside. It's what she always wanted. The fat. The inane.
(*She looks up again.*) If you've nothing to do you could
give a hand with these. (BROCK *takes no notice, casts
aside the scraps.*)

BROCK. Looking back, I seem to have been eating all
the time. My years in the Foreign Service I mean. I don't
think I missed a single canapé. Not one. The silver tray
flashed and bang, I was there.

ALICE. Do you miss it?

BROCK. Almost all the time. There's not much glam-
our in insurance you know. (*He smiles.*) Something in
the Foreign Office suited my style. Whatever horrible
things people say. At least they were hypocrites, I do
value that now. Hypocrisy does keep things pleasant for
at least part of the time. Whereas down in the City they
don't even try.

ALICE. You chose it.

BROCK. That's right. That isn't so strange. The strange
bit is always . . . why I remain. (*He stands staring a moment.*) Still, it gives her something new to despise. The
sad thing is this time . . . I despise it as well. (ALICE
*reaches for a typed list of names, pushes aside the pile of
envelopes.*)

ALICE. Eight hundred addresses, eight hundred names
. . . BROCK *turns and looks at her.*)

BROCK. You were never attracted? A regular job?

ALICE. I never had time. Too busy relating to various
young men. Falling in and out of love, turns out to be
like any other career. (*She looks up.*) I had an idea that
lust . . . that lust was very good. And could be made
simple. And cheering. And light. Perhaps I was simply
out of my time.

BROCK. You speak as if it's over. (*Pause.*) How long
since anyone took a look next door?

ALICE. That's why I think it may be time to do good.
(SUSAN *opens the door, standing dressed as for Scene
One. She is a little dusty.*)

SUSAN. I need to ask you to move out of here. I am
in temporary need of this room. You can go wherever
you like. And pretty soon also . . . you're welcome to
return. (*She goes off at once to the desk where she picks
items off the surface and throws them quietly into cubby-
holes.* ALICE *is looking at* BROCK.)

BROCK. You'd better tell me, Susan, what you've done
to your hands.

SUSAN. I've just been taking some paper from the wall.

BROCK. There's blood.

SUSAN. A fingernail. (*Pause.*)

BROCK. Susan, what have you actually done? (BROCK
gets up and goes to the door, looks down the corridor.
SUSAN *stands facing the desk, speaks quietly.*)

SUSAN. I thought as we were going to get rid of the
house . . . and I couldn't stand any of the things that
were there . . . (*He turns back into the room. She turns
and looks at him.*) Now what's best to be doing in here?
(BROCK *looks at her, speaks as quietly.*)

BROCK. Could you look in the drawer please, Alice,
there's some Nembutal . . .

ALICE. I'm not sure we should . . .

BROCK. I shan't ask you again. (ALICE *slides open the
drawer, puts a small bottle of pills on the table.* BROCK
moves a pace towards SUSAN.) Listen, if we're going to
have to sell this house . . .

SUSAN. You yourself said it, I've often heard you say,
it's money that did it, it's money that rots. That we've
all lived like camels off the fat in our humps. Well, then,

isn't the best thing to do . . . to turn round simply and give the house away? (*She smiles.*) Alice, would this place suit your needs? Somewhere to set down all your unmarried mothers. If we lay out mattresses, mattresses on the floor . . .

ALICE. Well, I . . .

SUSAN. (*Without warning she raises her arms above her head.*) By our own hands. (*Pause.*) Of our own free will. An Iranian vase. A small wooden Buddha. Twelve marble birds copied from an Ottoman king. (*Pause.*) What possible use can they be? Look out the bedroom window, I've thrown them away. (*She opens the door and goes at once into the corridor. At once* BROCK *crosses the room to the desk to look for his address book.* ALICE *starts clearing up the leaflets and envelopes on the table in front of her.*)

BROCK. I suppose you conspired.

ALICE. Not at all.

BROCK. Well, really?

ALICE. That was the first that I've heard.

BROCK. In that case, please, you might give me some help. Find out what else she's been doing out there. (SUSAN *reappears dragging in two packing cases, already half full. She then starts gathering objects from around the room.*)

SUSAN. Cutlery, crockery, lampshades and books, books, books. Encyclopaedias. Clutter. Meaningless. A universe of things. (*She starts to throw them one by one into the crates.*) Mosquito nets, golf clubs, photographs. China. Marble. Glass. Mementoes in stone. What is this shit? What are these godforsaken bloody awful things? (BROCK *turns, still speaking quietly.*)

BROCK. Which is the braver? To live as I do? Or never, ever to face life like you? (*He holds up the small card he has found.*) This is the doctor's number, my dear. With my permission he can put you inside. I am quite capable of doing it tonight. So why don't you start to put all those things back? (*A pause.* SUSAN *looks at him, then to* ALICE.)

SUSAN. Alice, would your women value my clothes?

ALICE. Well, I . . .

SUSAN. It sounds fairly silly, I have thirteen evening dresses though.

BROCK. Susan.

SUSAN. Obviously not much use as they are. But possibly they could be re-cut. Re-sewn? (*She reaches out and with one hand picks up an ornament from the mantelpiece which she throws with a crash into the crate. A pause.*)

BROCK. Your life is selfish, self-interested gain. That's the most charitable interpretation to hand. You claim to be protecting some personal ideal, always at a cost of almost infinite pain to everyone around you. You are selfish, you are brutish, you are unkind. You are jealous of other people's happiness as well, determined to destroy other ways of happiness they find. I've spent fifteen years of my life trying to help you, simply trying to be kind, and my great comfort has been that I am waiting for some indication from you . . . some sign that you have valued this kindness of mine. Some love perhaps. Insane. (*He smiles.*) And yet . . . I shan't ever really give in, I won't surrender till you're well again. And that to me would mean your admitting one thing: that in the life you have led you have utterly failed, failed in the very, very heart of your life. Admit that. Then perhaps you might really move on. (*Pause.*) Now I'm going to go and give our doctor a ring. I plan at last to beat you at your own kind of game. I am going to play as dirtily and ruthlessly as you. And this time I am certainly not giving in. (BROCK *goes out. A pause.*)

SUSAN. Well. (*Pause.*) Well, goodness. What's best to do? (*Pause.*) What's the best way to start stripping this room? (SUSAN *doesn't move.* ALICE *stands watching.*)

ALICE. Susan, I think you should get out of this house. I'll help you. Any way I can.

SUSAN. Well, that's very kind.

ALICE. Please.

SUSAN. I'll be going just as soon as this job is done. (*Pause.*)

ALICE. Listen, if Raymond really means what he says . . . (SUSAN *turns and looks straight at* ALICE.) You haven't asked me, Susan, you see. You haven't asked me what I think of the idea. (SUSAN *frowns.*)

SUSAN. Really, Alice, I shouldn't need to ask. It's a very sad day when one can't help the poor. (ALICE *suddenly starts to laugh.* SUSAN *sets off across the room, resuming a completely normal social manner.*)

ALICE. For God's sake, Susan, he'll put you in the bin.

SUSAN. Don't be silly, Alice, it's Easter weekend. It must have occurred to you . . . the doctor's away. (BROCK *reappears at the open door, the address book in his hand.* SUSAN *turns to him.*) All right, Raymond? Anything I can do? I've managed to rout out some whiskey over here. (*She sets the bottle down on the table, next to the Nembutal.*) Alice was just saying she might slip out for a moment or two. Give us a chance to sort our problems out. I'm sure if we had a really serious talk . . . I could keep going till morning. Couldn't you? (SUSAN *turns to* ALICE.) All right, Alice?

ALICE. Yes. Yes, of course. I'm going, I'm just on my way. (*She picks up her coat and heads for the door.*) All right if I get back in an hour or two? I don't like to feel I'm intruding. (*She smiles at* SUSAN. *Then closes the door.* SUSAN *at once goes back to the table.* BROCK *stands watching her.*)

SUSAN. Now, Raymond. Good. Let's look at this thing. (SUSAN *pours out a spectacularly large scotch, filling the glass to the very rim. Then she pushes it a few inches across the table to* BROCK.) Where would be the best place to begin?

SCENE 11

Blackpool. June 1962
From the dark music. Then silence. Two voices in the dark.

LAZAR. Susan. Susan. Feel who I am.

SUSAN. I know. I know who you are. How could you be anyone else but Lazar?

(*And a small bedside light comes on.* LAZAR *and* SUSAN *are lying sideways across a double bed, facing opposite ways. They are in a sparsely furnished and decaying room.* LAZAR *is in his coat, facing away from us as he reaches for the nightlight.* SUSAN *is also fully dressed, in a big black man's overcoat, her hair wild, her dress crumpled around her thighs. The bedside light barely illuminates them at all.*)

SUSAN. Jesus, Jesus. To be happy again. (*At once* SUSAN *gets up and goes into what must be the bathroom. A shaft of yellow light from the doorway falls across the bed.*)

LAZAR. Don't take your clothes off whatever you do. That would spoil it hopelessly for me.

SUSAN. (*Off.*) I'm getting my cigarettes. I roll my own . . .

LAZAR. My goodness.

SUSAN. Tell you, there are no fucking flies on me. (*She has reappeared with her holdall which is crumpled and stained. She sits cross-legged on the end of the bed. She starts to roll two cigarettes.*)

LAZAR. This place is filthy.

SUSAN. It's a cheap hotel.

LAZAR. They seem to serve you dust on almost everything.

SUSAN. You should be grateful for dust, did you know? If it weren't for all the dust in the atmosphere, human beings would be killed by the heat from the sun.

LAZAR. In Blackpool?

SUSAN. Well.

LAZAR. Are you kidding me? (SUSAN *reaches into the overcoat pocket.*)

SUSAN. I was given some grass, shall I roll it in?

LAZAR. Just the simple cigarette for me. (SUSAN *nods.*) I hope you don't mind my choosing Blackpool. It's just that I work near . . .

SUSAN. Don't tell me any more.

LAZAR. Do you know how I found you? Through the BBC. I happened to hear that programme a few months ago. I rang them. They said you were married. You were living in London. So they gave me an address. I went round.

SUSAN. I left it weeks ago.

LAZAR. Yes. Well I gathered. At least I met a man. I assume he must have been your husband. He seemed rather evasive I'm afraid. He said there'd been trouble. He'd only just managed to get back into his house . . .

SUSAN. Oh, Lord.

LAZAR. There'd been trouble with the police. And violence, it seems.

SUSAN. Was he angry?

LAZAR. Angry? No. We talked for a bit. He just

seemed very sorry not to be with you. Anyway he said you'd left him. He gave me an address. (*Pause.*)

SUSAN. Listen I have to tell you I've not always been well. I have a weakness. I like to lose control. I've been letting it happen, well, a number of times.

LAZAR. Is it . . .

SUSAN. I did shoot someone about ten years ago.

LAZAR. Did you hurt him?

SUSAN. Fortunately no. At least that's what we kept telling him. Raymond went and gave him money in notes. He slapped them like hot poultices all over his wounds. I think it did finally convince him on the whole. It was after Raymond's kindness I felt I had to get engaged.

LAZAR. Why do people . . .

SUSAN. Marry? I don't know. Are you . . . (*Pause.*)

LAZAR. What? Ask me anything at all.

SUSAN. No. It's nothing. I don't want to know. (*She smiles again.*)

LAZAR. Do you ever see him?

SUSAN. Good gracious no. I've stripped away everything, everything I've known. There's only one kind of dignity that's in living alone. The clothes you stand up in, the world you can see . . .

LAZAR. Susan . . . let me tell you . . .

SUSAN. No please. I don't want to know. (*Pause.* SUSAN *is suddenly still.*) I want to believe in you. Please tell me nothing. That's best. (*Pause.* SUSAN *does not turn around.* LAZAR *suddenly gets up, and goes to get his coat and gloves from his suitcase.* SUSAN *looks down at the unmade cigarette in her hands. Then she starts to make the roll-up again.*)

SUSAN. How long till dawn? Do you think we should go? If we wait till morning we'll have to pay the bill. I can't believe that can be the right thing to do. (*She smiles.*) Is there an early train do you know? Though just where I'm going I'm not really sure. (*Pause.*) I hope you'll forgive me. The grass has gone in. (*She licks along the edge of the joint, then lights it.* LAZAR *stands still, his suitcase beside him.*)

LAZAR. I don't know what I'd expected.

SUSAN. Mmm?

LAZAR. What I'd hoped for, at the time I returned.

Some sort of edge to the life that I lead. Some sort of feeling their death was worthwhile. (*Pause.*) Some day I must tell you. I don't feel I've done well. I gave in. Always. All along the line. Suburb. Wife. Hell. I work in a corporate bureaucracy as well . . . (SUSAN *has begun to giggle.*)

SUSAN. Lazar, I'm sorry, I'm just about to go.

LAZAR. What?

SUSAN. I've eaten nothing. So I just go . . . (*She waves vaguely with her hand. Then smiles. A pause.*)

LAZAR. I hate, I hate this life that we lead . . .

SUSAN. Oh God here I go. (*Pause.*) Kiss me. Kiss me now as I go. (LAZAR *moves towards* SUSAN *and tries to take her in his arms. But as he tries to kiss her, she falls back on to the bed, flopping down where she stays.* LAZAR *removes the roach from her hand. Puts it out. Goes over and closes his case. Then picks it up. Goes to the bathroom and turns the light off. Now only the nightlight is on.* LAZAR *goes to the door.*)

LAZAR. A fine undercover agent will move so that nobody can ever tell he was there. (LAZAR *turns the nightlight off. Darkness.*)

SUSAN. Tell me your name. (*Pause.*)

LAZAR. Codename. (*Pause.*) Codename. (*Pause.*) Codename Lazar. (LAZAR *opens the door of the room. At once music plays. Where you would expect a corridor you see the fields of France shining brilliantly in a fierce green square. The room scatters.*)

SCENE 12

St. Benoît. August 1944

The darkened areas of the room disappear and we see a French hillside in high summer. The stage picture forms piece by piece. Green, yellow, brown. Trees. The fields stretch away. A high sun. A brilliant August day. . . . ANOTHER FRENCHMAN *stands looking down into the valley. He carries a spade, is in wellingtons and corduroys. He is about forty, fattish with an unnaturally gloomy air. Then* SUSAN *appears climbing the hill. She is nineteen. She is dressed like a young French girl, her pullover over her shoulder. She looks radiantly well.*

FRENCHMAN. Bonjour ma'moiselle.

SUSAN. Bonjour.

FRENCHMAN. Vous regardez le village?

SUSAN. Oui, je suis montée la colline pour mieux voir. C'est merveilleux.

FRENCHMAN. Oui. Indeed the day is fine. (*Pause.* SUSAN *looks across at the* FRENCHMAN.)

FRENCHMAN. We understand. We know. The war is over now.

SUSAN. 'I climbed the hill to get a better view.' (*She smiles.*) I've only spoken French for months on end.

FRENCHMAN. You are English? (SUSAN *nods.*) Tower Bridge.

SUSAN. Just so. (*The* FRENCHMAN *smiles and walks over to join* SUSAN. *Together they look away down the hill.*)

FRENCHMAN. You join the party in the village?

SUSAN. Soon. I'm hoping, yes, I'm very keen to go.

FRENCHMAN. Myself I work. A farmer. Like any other day. The Frenchman works or starves. He is the piss. The shit. The lowest of the low. (SUSAN *moves forward a little, staring down the hill.*)

SUSAN. Look. They're lighting fires in the square. And children . . . coming out with burning sticks. (*Pause.*) Have you seen anything as beautiful as this? (SUSAN *stands looking out. The* FRENCHMAN *mumbles ill-humouredly.*)

FRENCHMAN. The harvest is not good again this year.

SUSAN. I'm sorry. (*The* FRENCHMAN *shrugs.*)

FRENCHMAN. As I expect. The land is very poor. I have to work each moment of the day.

SUSAN. But you'll be glad I think. You're glad as well? (SUSAN *turns, so the* FRENCHMAN *cannot avoid the question. He reluctantly concedes.*)

FRENCHMAN. I'm glad. Is something good, is true. (*He looks puzzled.*) The English . . . have no feelings, yes? Are stiff.

SUSAN. They hide them, they hide them from the world.

FRENCHMAN. Is stupid.

SUSAN. Yes, yes, it's stupid. It may be . . . (*Pause.*)

FRENCHMAN. Huh?

SUSAN. That things will quickly change. We have

grown up. We will improve our world. (*The* FRENCHMAN
stares at SUSAN. *Then offers gravely:*)

FRENCHMAN. Perhaps . . . perhaps you like some
soup. My wife.

SUSAN. All right. (SUSAN *smiles. They look at each
other, about to go.*)

FRENCHMAN. The walk is down the hill. Comrade.

SUSAN. My friend. (*Pause.*) There will be days and
days and days like this.

Betrayal

by Harold Pinter

Betrayal was first presented by the National Theatre, London, on November 15, 1978, with the following cast:

EMMA.. *Penelope Wilton*
JERRY.. *Michael Gambon*
ROBERT .... *Daniel Massey*

Designed by John Bury
Directed by Peter Hall

Betrayal was presented by Roger L. Stevens, Robert Whitehead and James M. Nederlander at the Trafalgar Theatre, in New York City, on January 5, 1980. It was directed by Peter Hall, and designed by John Bury. The cast was as follows:

JERRY.. *Raul Julia*
EMMA... *Blythe Danner*
ROBERT .... *Roy Scheider*

The Barman and Waiter were played by Ian Thomson and Ernesto Gasco, respectively.

Betrayal can be performed without an interval, or with an interval after Scene 4.

to Simon Gray

ACT I

SCENE 1

Pub. 1977. Spring. Noon. EMMA *is sitting at a corner table.* JERRY *approaches with drinks, a pint of bitter for him, a glass of wine for her. He sits. They smile, toast each other silently, drink. He sits back and looks at her.*

JERRY. Well . . .

EMMA. How are you?

JERRY. All right.

EMMA. You look well.

JERRY. Well, I'm not all that well, really.

EMMA. Why? What's the matter?

JERRY. Hangover. (*He raises his glass.*) Cheers. (*He drinks.*) How are you?

EMMA. I'm fine. (*She looks round the bar, back at him.*) Just like old times.

JERRY. Mmn. It's been a long time.

EMMA. Yes. (*Pause.*) I thought of you the other day.

JERRY. Good God. Why? (*She laughs.*) Why?

EMMA. Well, it's nice, sometimes, to think back. Isn't it?

JERRY. Absolutely. (*Pause.*) How's everything?

EMMA. Oh, not too bad. (*Pause.*) Do you know how long it is since we met?

JERRY. Well I came to that exhibition, when was it—?

EMMA. No, I don't mean that.

JERRY. Oh you mean alone?

EMMA. Yes.

JERRY. Uuh . . .

EMMA. Two years.

JERRY. Yes, I thought it must be. Mmnn. (*Pause.*)

EMMA. Long time.

JERRY. Yes. It is. (*Pause.*) How's it going? The Gallery?

202

EMMA. How do you think it's going?

JERRY. Well. Very well, I would say.

EMMA. I'm glad you think so. Well, it is, actually. I enjoy it.

JERRY. Funny lot, painters, aren't they?

EMMA. They're not at all funny.

JERRY. Aren't they? What a pity. (*Pause.*) How's Robert?

EMMA. When did you last see him?

JERRY. I haven't seen him for months. Don't know why. Why?

EMMA. Why what?

JERRY. Why did you ask when I last saw him?

EMMA. I just wondered. How's Sam?

JERRY. You mean Judith.

EMMA. Do I?

JERRY. You remember the form. I ask about your husband, you ask about my wife.

EMMA. Yes, of course. How is your wife?

JERRY. All right. (*Pause.*)

EMMA. Sam must be . . . tall.

JERRY. He is tall. Quite tall. Does a lot of running. He's a long distance runner. He wants to be a zoologist.

EMMA. No, really? Good. And Sarah?

JERRY. She's ten.

EMMA. God. I suppose she must be.

JERRY. Yes, she must be. (*Pause.*) Ned's five, isn't he?

EMMA. You remember.

JERRY. Well, I would remember that. (*Pause.*)

EMMA. Yes. (*Pause.*) You're all right, though?

JERRY. Oh . . . yes, sure. (*Pause.*)

EMMA. Ever think of me?

JERRY. I don't need to think of you.

EMMA. Oh?

JERRY. I don't need to *think* of you. (*Pause.*) Anyway I'm all right. How are you?

EMMA. Fine, really. All right.

JERRY. You're looking very pretty.

EMMA. Really? Thank you. I'm glad to see you.

JERRY. So am I. I mean to see you.

EMMA. You think of me sometimes?

JERRY. I think of you sometimes. (*Pause.*) I saw Charlotte the other day.

EMMA. No? Where? She didn't mention it.

JERRY. She didn't see me. In the street.

EMMA. But you haven't seen her for years.

JERRY. I recognised her.

EMMA. How could you? How could you know?

JERRY. I did.

EMMA. What did she look like?

JERRY. You.

EMMA. No, what did you think of her, really?

JERRY. I thought she was lovely.

EMMA. Yes. She's very . . . She's smashing. She's thirteen. (*Pause.*) Do you remember that time . . . oh God
it was . . . when you picked her up and threw her up
and caught her?

JERRY. She was very light.

EMMA. She remembers that, you know.

JERRY. Really?

EMMA. Mmnn. Being thrown up.

JERRY. What a memory. (*Pause.*) She doesn't know
. . . about us, does she?

EMMA. Of course not. She just remembers you, as an
old friend.

JERRY. That's right. (*Pause.*) Yes, everyone was there
that day, standing around, your husband, my wife, all
the kids, I remember.

EMMA. What day?

JERRY. When I threw her up. It was in your kitchen.

EMMA. It was in your kitchen. (*Silence.*)

JERRY. Darling.

EMMA. Don't say that. (*Pause.*) It all . . .

JERRY. Seems such a long time ago.

EMMA. Does it?

JERRY. Same again? (*He takes the glasses, goes to the
bar. She sits still. He returns, with the drinks, sits.*)

EMMA. I thought of you the other day. (*Pause.*) I was
driving through Kilburn. Suddenly I saw where I was. I
just stopped, and then I turned down Kinsale Drive and
drove into Wessex Grove. I drove past the house and
then stopped about fifty yards further on, like we used
to do, do you remember?

JERRY. Yes.

EMMA. People were coming out of the house. They
walked up the road.

JERRY. What sort of people?

EMMA. Oh . . . young people. Then I got out of the car and went up the steps. I looked at the bells, you know, the names on the bells. I looked for our name. (*Pause.*)

JERRY. Green. (*Pause.*) Couldn't see it, eh?

EMMA. No.

JERRY. That's because we're not there any more. We haven't been there for years.

EMMA. No we haven't. (*Pause.*)

JERRY. I hear you're seeing a bit of Casey.

EMMA. What?

JERRY. Casey. I just heard you were . . . seeing a bit of him.

EMMA. Where did you hear that?

JERRY. Oh . . . people . . . talking.

EMMA. Christ.

JERRY. The funny thing was that the only thing I really felt was irritation. I mean irritation that nobody gossiped about us like that, in the old days. I nearly said, now look, she may be having the occasional drink with Casey, who cares, but she and I had an affair for seven years and none of you bastards had the faintest idea it was happening. (*Pause.*)

EMMA. I wonder. I wonder if everyone knew, all the time.

JERRY. Don't be silly. We were brilliant. Nobody knew. Who ever went to Kilburn in those days? Just you and me. (*Pause.*) Anyway, what's all this about you and Casey?

EMMA. What do you mean?

JERRY. What's going on?

EMMA. We have the occasional drink.

JERRY. I thought you didn't admire his work.

EMMA. I've changed. Or his work has changed. Are you jealous?

JERRY. Of what? (*Pause.*) I couldn't be jealous of Casey. I'm his agent. I advised him about his divorce. I read all his first drafts. I persuaded your husband to publish his first novel. I escort him to Oxford to speak at the Union. He's my . . . he's my boy. I discovered him when he was a poet, and that's a bloody long time ago now. (*Pause.*) He's even taken me down to Southampton

to meet his Mum and Dad. I couldn't be jealous of
Casey. Anyway it's not as if we're having an affair now,
is it? We haven't seen each other for years. Really, I'm
very happy if you're happy. (*Pause.*) What about Robert? (*Pause.*)

EMMA. Well . . . I think we're going to separate.

JERRY. Oh?

EMMA. We had a long talk . . . last night.

JERRY. Last night?

EMMA. You know what I found out . . . last night?
He's betrayed me for years. He's had . . . other women
for years.

JERRY. No. Good Lord. (*Pause.*) But we betrayed him
for years.

EMMA. And he betrayed me for years.

JERRY. Well I never knew that.

EMMA. Nor did I. (*Pause.*)

JERRY. Does Casey know about this?

EMMA. I wish you wouldn't keep calling him Casey.
His name is Roger.

JERRY. Yes. Roger.

EMMA. I phoned *you*. I don't know why.

JERRY. What a funny thing. We were such close
friends, weren't we? Robert and me, even though I
haven't seen him for a few months, but through all those
years, all the drinks, all the lunches . . . we had together,
I never even gleaned . . . I never suspected . . . that
there was anyone else . . . in his life but you. Never.
For example, when you're with a fellow in a pub, or a
restaurant, for example, from time to time he pops out
for a piss, you see, who doesn't, but what I mean is, if
he's making a crafty telephone call, you can sort of sense
it, you see, you can sense the pip pip pips. Well, I never
did that with Robert. He never made any pip pip telephone calls in any pub I was ever with him in. The funny
thing is that it was me who made the pip pip calls—to
you, when I left him boozing at the bar. That's the funny
thing. (*Pause.*) When did he tell you all this?

EMMA. Last night. I think we were up all night.
(*Pause.*)

JERRY. You talked all night?

EMMA. Yes. Oh yes. (*Pause.*)

JERRY. I didn't come into it, did I?

EMMA. What?

JERRY. I just—

EMMA. I just phoned you this morning, you know, that's all, because I . . . because we're old friends . . . I've been up all night . . . the whole thing's finished . . . I suddenly felt I wanted to see you.

JERRY. Well, look, I'm happy to see you. I am. I'm sorry . . . about . . .

EMMA. Do you remember? I mean, you do remember?

JERRY. I remember. (*Pause.*)

EMMA. You couldn't really afford Wessex Grove when we took it, could you?

JERRY. Oh, love finds a way.

EMMA. I bought the curtains.

JERRY. You found a way.

EMMA. Listen, I didn't want to see you for nostalgia, I mean what's the point? I just wanted to see how you were. Truly. How are you?

JERRY. Oh what does it matter? (*Pause.*) You didn't tell Robert about me last night, did you?

EMMA. I had to. (*Pause.*) He told me everything. I told him everything. We were up . . . all night. At one point Ned came down. I had to take him up to bed, had to put him back to bed. Then I went down again. I think it was the voices woke him up. You know . . .

JERRY. You told him everything?

EMMA. I had to.

JERRY. You told him everything . . . about us?

EMMA. I had to. (*Pause.*)

JERRY. But he's my oldest friend. I mean, I picked his own daughter up in my own arms and threw her up and caught her, in my kitchen. He watched me do it.

EMMA. It doesn't matter. It's all gone.

JERRY. Is it? What has?

EMMA. It's all all over. (*She drinks.*)

See 226

SCENE 2

Later, Jerry's House. Study. 1977. Spring. JERRY *sitting.* ROBERT *standing, with glass.*

JERRY. It's good of you to come.

ROBERT. Not at all.

JERRY. Yes, yes, I know it was difficult . . . I know
. . . the kids . . .

ROBERT. It's all right. It sounded urgent.

JERRY. Well . . . You found someone, did you?

ROBERT. What?

JERRY. For the kids.

ROBERT. Yes, yes. Honestly. Everything's in order.
Anyway, Charlotte's not a baby.

JERRY. No. (*Pause.*) Are you going to sit down?

ROBERT. Well, I might, yes, in a minute. (*Pause.*)

JERRY. Judith's at the hospital . . . on night duty. The
kids are . . . here . . . upstairs.

ROBERT. Uh—huh.

JERRY. I must speak to you. It's important.

ROBERT. Speak.

JERRY. Yes. (*Pause.*)

ROBERT. You look quite rough. (*Pause.*) What's the
trouble? (*Pause.*) It's not about you and Emma, is it?
(*Pause.*) I know all about that.

JERRY. Yes. So I've . . . been told.

ROBERT. Ah. (*Pause.*) Well, it's not very important,
is it? Been over for years, hasn't it?

JERRY. It is important.

ROBERT. Really? Why? (JERRY *stands, walks about.*)

JERRY. I thought I was going to go mad.

ROBERT. When?

JERRY. This evening. Just now. Wondering whether to
phone you. I had to phone you. It took me . . . two
hours to phone you. And then you were with the kids
. . . I thought I wasn't going to be able to see you . . .
I thought I'd go mad. I'm very grateful to you . . . for
coming.

ROBERT. Oh for God's sake! Look, what exactly do
you want to say? (*Pause.* JERRY *sits.*)

JERRY. I don't know why she told you. I don't know
how she could tell you. I just don't understand. Listen,
I know you've got . . . look, I saw her today . . . we had
a drink . . . I haven't seen her for . . . she told me, you
know, that you're in trouble, both of you . . . and so on.
I know that. I mean I'm sorry.

ROBERT. Don't be sorry.

JERRY. Why not? (*Pause.*) The fact is I can't understand . . . why she thought it necessary . . . after all these years . . . to tell you . . . so suddenly . . . last night . . .

ROBERT. Last night?

JERRY. Without consulting me. Without even warning me. After all, you and me . . .

ROBERT. She didn't tell me last night.

JERRY. What do you mean? (*Pause.*) I know about last night. She told me about it. You were up all night, weren't you?

ROBERT. That's correct.

JERRY. And she told you . . . last night . . . about her and me. Did she not?

ROBERT. No, she didn't. She didn't tell me about you and her last night. She told me about you and her four years ago. (*Pause.*) So she didn't have to tell me again last night. Because I knew. And she knew I knew because she told me herself four years ago. (*Silence.*)

JERRY. What?

ROBERT. I think I will sit down. (*He sits.*) I thought you knew.

JERRY. Knew what?

ROBERT. That I knew. That I've known for years. I thought you knew that.

JERRY. You thought I knew?

ROBERT. She said you didn't. But I didn't believe that. (*Pause.*) Anyway I think I thought you knew. But you say you didn't?

JERRY. She told you . . . when?

ROBERT. Well, I found out. That's what happened. I told her I'd found out and then she . . . confirmed . . . the facts.

JERRY. When?

ROBERT. Oh, a long time ago, Jerry. (*Pause.*)

JERRY. But we've seen each other . . . a great deal . . . over the last four years. We've had lunch.

ROBERT. Never played squash though.

JERRY. I was your best friend.

ROBERT. Well, yes, sure. (JERRY *stares at him and then holds his head in his hands.*) Oh, don't get upset. There's no point. (*Silence.* JERRY *sits up.*)

JERRY. Why didn't she tell me?

ROBERT. Well, I'm not her, old boy.

JERRY. Why didn't you tell me? (*Pause.*)

ROBERT. I thought you might know.

JERRY. But you didn't know for *certain*, did you? You didn't *know!*

ROBERT. No.

JERRY. Then why didn't you tell me? (*Pause.*)

ROBERT. Tell you what?

JERRY. That you knew. You bastard.

ROBERT. Oh, don't call me a bastard, Jerry. (*Pause.*)

JERRY. What are we going to do?

ROBERT. You and I are not going to do anything. My marriage is finished. I've just got to make proper arrangements, that's all. About the children. (*Pause.*)

JERRY. You hadn't thought of telling Judith?

ROBERT. Telling Judith what? Oh, about you and Emma. You mean she never knew? Are you quite sure? (*Pause.*) No, I hadn't thought of telling Judith, actually. You don't seem to understand. You don't seem to understand that I don't give a shit about any of this. It's true I've hit Emma once or twice. But that wasn't to defend a principle. I wasn't inspired to do it from any kind of moral standpoint. I just felt like giving her a good bashing. The old itch . . . you understand. (*Pause.*)

JERRY. But you betrayed her for years, didn't you?

ROBERT. Oh yes.

JERRY. And she never knew about it. Did she?

ROBERT. Didn't she? (*Pause.*)

JERRY. I didn't.

ROBERT. No, you didn't know very much about anything, really, did you? (*Pause.*)

JERRY. No.

ROBERT. Yes you did.

JERRY. Yes I did. I lived with her.

ROBERT. Yes. In the afternoons.

JERRY. Sometimes very long ones. For seven years.

ROBERT. Yes, you certainly knew all there was to know about that. About the seven years of afternoons. I don't know anything about that. (*Pause.*) I hope she looked after you all right. (*Silence.*)

JERRY. We used to like each other.

ROBERT. We still do. (*Pause.*) I bumped into old Casey the other day. I believe he's having an affair with my wife. We haven't played squash for years, Casey and me. We used to have a damn good game.

JERRY. He's put on weight.

ROBERT. Yes, I thought that.

JERRY. He's over the hill.

ROBERT. Is he?

JERRY. Don't you think so?

ROBERT. In what respect?

JERRY. His work. His books.

ROBERT. Oh his books. His art. Yes his art does seem
to be falling away, doesn't it?

JERRY. Still sells.

ROBERT. Oh, sells very well. Sells very well indeed.
Very good for us. For you and me.

JERRY. Yes.

ROBERT. Someone was telling me—who was it—must
have been someone in the publicity department—the
other day—that when Casey went up to York to sign his
latest book, in a bookshop, you know, with Barbara
Spring, you know, the populace queued for hours to get
his signature on his book, while one old lady and a dog
queued to get Barbara Spring's signature, on her book.
I happen to think that Barbara Spring . . . is good, don't
you?

JERRY. Yes. (*Pause.*)

ROBERT. Still, we both do very well out of Casey,
don't we?

JERRY. Very well. (*Pause.*)

ROBERT. Have you read any good books lately?

JERRY. I've been reading Yeats. *Significance of this memory!*

ROBERT. Ah. Yeats. Yes. (*Pause.*)

JERRY. You read Yeats on Torcello once. *See 229*

ROBERT. On Torcello?

JERRY. Don't you remember? Years ago. You went
over to Torcello in the dawn, alone. And read Yeats.

ROBERT. So I did. I told you that, yes. (*Pause.*) Yes.
(*Pause.*) Where are you going this summer, you and the
family?

JERRY. The Lake District.

SCENE 3

Flat. 1975. Winter. JERRY *and* EMMA. *They are sitting.
Silence.*

JERRY. What do you want to do then? (*Pause.*)

EMMA. I don't quite know what we're doing, any more, that's all.

JERRY. Mmnn. (*Pause.*)

EMMA. I mean, this flat . . .

JERRY. Yes.

EMMA. Can you actually remember when we were last here?

JERRY. In the summer, was it?

EMMA. Well, was it?

JERRY. I know it seems—

EMMA. It was the beginning of September.

JERRY. Well, that's summer, isn't it?

EMMA. It was actually extremely cold. It was early autumn.

JERRY. It's pretty cold now.

EMMA. We were going to get another electric fire.

JERRY. Yes, I never got that.

EMMA. Not much point in getting it if we're never here.

JERRY. We're here now.

EMMA. Not really. (*Silence.*)

JERRY. Well, things have changed. You've been so busy, your job, and everything.

EMMA. Well, I know. But I mean, I like it. I want to do it.

JERRY. No, it's great. It's marvellous for you. But you're not—

EMMA. If you're running a gallery you've got to run it, you've got to be there.

JERRY. But you're not free in the afternoons. Are you?

EMMA. No.

JERRY. So how can we meet?

EMMA. But look at the times you're out of the country. You're never here.

JERRY. But when I am here you're not free in the afternoons. So we can never meet.

EMMA. We can meet for lunch.

JERRY. We can meet for lunch but we can't come all the way out here for a quick lunch. I'm too old for that.

EMMA. I didn't suggest that. (*Pause.*) You see, in the past . . . we were inventive, we were determined, it was

. . . it seemed impossible to meet . . . impossible . . . and yet we did. We met here, we took this flat and we met in this flat because we wanted to.

JERRY. It would not matter how much we wanted to if you're not free in the afternoons and I'm in America. (*Silence.*) Nights have always been out of the question and you know it. I have a family.

EMMA. I have a family too.

JERRY. I know that perfectly well. I might remind you that your husband is my oldest friend.

EMMA. What do you mean by that?

JERRY. I don't *mean* anything by it.

EMMA. But what are you trying to say by saying that?

JERRY. Jesus. I'm not *trying* to say anything. I've said precisely what I wanted to say.

EMMA. I see. (*Pause.*) The fact is that in the old days we used our imagination and we'd take a night and make an arrangement and go to an hotel.

JERRY. Yes. We did. (*Pause.*) But that was . . . in the main . . . before we got this flat.

EMMA. We haven't spent many nights . . . in this flat.

JERRY. No. (*Pause.*) Not many nights anywhere, really. (*Silence.*)

EMMA. Can you afford . . . to keep it going, month after month?

JERRY. Oh . . .

EMMA. It's a waste. Nobody comes here. I just can't bear to think about it, actually. Just . . . empty. All day and night. Day after day and night after night. I mean the crockery and the curtains and the bedspread and everything. And the tablecloth I brought from Venice. (*Laughs.*) It's ridiculous. (*Pause.*) It's just . . . an empty home.

JERRY. It's not a home. (*Pause.*) I know . . . I know what you wanted . . . but it could never . . . actually be a home. You have a home. I have a home. With curtains, etcetera. And children. Two children in two homes. There are no children here, so it's not the same kind of home.

EMMA. It was never intended to be the same kind of home. Was it? (*Pause.*) You didn't ever see it as a home, in any sense, did you?

JERRY. No, I saw it as a flat . . . you know.

EMMA. For fucking.

JERRY. No, for loving.

EMMA. Well, there's not much of that left, is there? (*Silence.*)

JERRY. I don't think we don't love each other. (*Pause.*)

EMMA. Ah well. (*Pause.*) What will you do about all the . . . furniture?

JERRY. What?

EMMA. The contents. (*Silence.*)

JERRY. You know we can do something very simple, if we want to do it.

EMMA. You mean sell it to Mrs Banks for a small sum and . . . and she can let it as a furnished flat?

JERRY. That's right. Wasn't the bed here?

EMMA. What?

JERRY. Wasn't it?

EMMA. We bought the bed. We bought everything. We bought the bed together.

JERRY. Ah. Yes. (EMMA *stands.*)

EMMA. You'll make all the arrangements, then? With Mrs Banks? (*Pause.*) I don't want anything. Nowhere I can put it, you see. I have a home, with tablecloths and all the rest of it.

JERRY. I'll go into it, with Mrs Banks. There'll be a few quid, you know, so . . .

EMMA. No, I don't want any *cash*, thank you very much. (*Silence. She puts coat on.*) I'm going now. (*He turns, looks at her.*) Oh here's my key. (*Takes out keyring, tries to take key from ring.*) Oh Christ. (*Struggles to take key from ring. Throws him the ring.*) You take it off. (*He catches it, looks at her.*) Can you just do it please? I'm picking up Charlotte from school. I'm taking her shopping. (*He takes key off.*) Do you realise this is an afternoon? It's the Gallery's afternoon off. That's why I'm here. We close every Thursday afternoon. Can I have my keyring? (*He gives it to her.*) Thanks. Listen. I think we've made absolutely the right decision. (*She goes. He stands.*)

SCENE 4

Robert and Emma's House. Living room. 1974. Au-

tumn. ROBERT *pouring a drink for* JERRY. *He goes to the door.*

ROBERT. Emma! Jerry's here!

EMMA. (*Off.*) Who?

ROBERT. Jerry.

EMMA. I'll be down. (ROBERT *gives the drink to* JERRY.)

JERRY. Cheers.

ROBERT. Cheers. She's just putting Ned to bed. I should think he'll be off in a minute.

JERRY. Off where?

ROBERT. Dreamland.

JERRY. Ah. Yes, how is your sleep these days?

ROBERT. What?

JERRY. Do you still have bad nights? With Ned, I mean?

ROBERT. Oh, I see. Well, no. No, it's getting better. But you know what they say?

JERRY. What?

ROBERT. They say boys are worse than girls.

JERRY. Worse?

ROBERT. Babies. They say boy babies cry more than girl babies.

JERRY. Do they?

ROBERT. You didn't find that to be the case?

JERRY. Uh . . . yes, I think we did. Did you?

ROBERT. Yes. What do you make of it? Why do you think that is?

JERRY. Well, I suppose . . . boys are more anxious.

ROBERT. Boy babies?

JERRY. Yes.

ROBERT. What the hell are they anxious about . . . at their age? Do you think?

JERRY. Well . . . facing the world, I suppose, leaving the womb, all that.

ROBERT. But what about girl babies? They leave the womb too.

JERRY. That's true. It's also true that nobody talks much about girl babies leaving the womb. Do they?

ROBERT. I am prepared to do so.

JERRY. I see. Well, what have you got to say?

ROBERT. I was asking you a question.

JERRY. What was it?

ROBERT. Why do you assert that boy babies find leaving the womb more of a problem than girl babies?

JERRY. Have I made such an assertion?

ROBERT. You went on to make a further assertion, to the effect that boy babies are more anxious about facing the world than girl babies.

JERRY. Do you yourself believe that to be the case?

ROBERT. I do, yes. (*Pause.*)

JERRY. Why do you think it is?

ROBERT. I have no answer. (*Pause.*)

JERRY. Do you think it might have something to do with the difference between the sexes? (*Pause.*)

ROBERT. Good God, you're right. That must be it. (EMMA *comes in.*)

EMMA. Hullo. Surprise.

JERRY. I was having tea with Casey.

EMMA. Where?

JERRY. Just around the corner.

EMMA. I thought he lived in . . . Hampstead or somewhere.

ROBERT. You're out of date.

EMMA. Am I?

JERRY. He's left Susannah. He's living alone round the corner.

EMMA. Oh.

ROBERT. Writing a novel about a man who leaves his wife and three children and goes to live alone on the other side of London to write a novel about a man who leaves his wife and three children—

EMMA. I hope it's better than the last one.

ROBERT. The last one? Ah, the last one. Wasn't that the one about the man who lived in a big house in Hampstead with his wife and three children and is writing a novel about—?

JERRY. (*To* EMMA.) Why didn't you like it?

EMMA. I've told you actually.

JERRY. I think it's the best thing he's written.

EMMA. It may be the best thing he's *written* but it's still bloody dishonest.

JERRY. Dishonest? In what way dishonest?

EMMA. I've told you, actually.

JERRY. Have you?

ROBERT. Yes, she has. Once when we were all having
dinner, I remember, you, me, Emma and Judith, where
was it, Emma gave a dissertation over the pudding about
dishonesty in Casey with reference to his last novel. 'Drying Out.' It was most stimulating. Judith had to leave
unfortunately in the middle of it for her night shift at the
hospital. How is Judith, by the way?

JERRY. Very well. (*Pause.*)

ROBERT. When are we going to play squash?

JERRY. You're too good.

ROBERT. Not at all. I'm not good at all. I'm just fitter
than you.

JERRY. But why? Why are you fitter than me?

ROBERT. Because I play squash.

JERRY. Oh, you're playing? Regularly?

ROBERT. Mmnn.

JERRY. With whom?

ROBERT. Casey, actually.

JERRY. Casey? Good Lord. What's he like?

ROBERT. He's a brutally honest squash player. No,
really, we haven't played for years. We must play. You
were rather good.

JERRY. Yes, I was quite good. All right. I'll give you
a ring.

ROBERT. Why don't you?

JERRY. We'll make a date.

ROBERT. Right.

JERRY. Yes. We must do that.

ROBERT. And then I'll take you to lunch.

JERRY. No, no. I'll take you to lunch.

ROBERT. The man who wins buys the lunch.

EMMA. Can I watch? (*Pause.*)

ROBERT. What?

EMMA. Why can't I watch and then take you both to
lunch?

ROBERT. Well, to be brutally honest, we wouldn't actually want a woman around, would we, Jerry? I mean
a game of squash isn't simply a game of squash, it's
rather more than that. You see, first there's the game.
And then there's the shower. And then there's the pint.
And then there's lunch. After all, you've been at it.
You've had your battle. What you want is your pint and
your lunch. You really don't want a woman buying you

lunch. You don't actually want a woman within a mile of the place, any of the places, really. You don't want her in the squash court, you don't want her in the shower, or the pub, or the restaurant. You see, at lunch you want to talk about squash, or cricket, or books, or even women, with your friend, and be able to warm to your theme without fear of improper interruption. That's what it's all about. What do you think, Jerry?

JERRY. I haven't played squash for years. (*Pause.*)

ROBERT. Well, let's play next week.

JERRY. I can't next week. I'm in New York.

EMMA. Are you?

JERRY. I'm going over with one of my more celebrated writers, actually.

EMMA. Who?

JERRY. Casey. Someone wants to film that novel of his you didn't like. We're going over to discuss it. It was a question of them coming over here or us going over there. Casey thought he deserved the trip.

EMMA. What about you?

JERRY. What?

EMMA. Do you deserve the trip?

ROBERT. Judith going?

JERRY. No. He can't go alone. We'll have that game of squash when I get back. A week, or at the most ten days.

ROBERT. Lovely.

JERRY. (*To* EMMA.) Bye. Thanks for the drink.

EMMA. Bye. (ROBERT *and* JERRY *leave. She remains still.* ROBERT *returns. He kisses her. She responds. She breaks away, puts her head on his shoulder, cries quietly. He holds her.*)

ACT II

SCENE 5

Hotel Room. Venice. 1973. Summer. EMMA *on bed reading.* ROBERT *at window looking out. She looks up at him, then back at the book.*

EMMA. It's Torcello tomorrow, isn't it?
ROBERT. What?
EMMA. We're going to Torcello tomorrow, aren't we?
ROBERT. Yes. That's right.
EMMA. That'll be lovely.
ROBERT. Mmn.
EMMA. I can't wait. (*Pause.*)
ROBERT. Book good?
EMMA. Mmn. Yes.
ROBERT. What is it?
EMMA. This new book. This man Spinks.
ROBERT. Oh that. Jerry was telling me about it.
EMMA. Jerry? Was he?
ROBERT. He was telling me about it at lunch last week.
EMMA. Really? Does he like it?
ROBERT. Spinks is his boy. He discovered him.
EMMA. Oh. I didn't know that.
ROBERT. Unsolicited manuscript. (*Pause.*) You think it's good, do you?
EMMA. Yes, I do. I'm enjoying it.
ROBERT. Jerry thinks it's good too. You should have lunch with us one day and chat about it.
EMMA. Is that absolutely necessary? (*Pause.*) It's not as good as all that.
ROBERT. You mean it's not good enough for you to have lunch with Jerry and me and chat about it?
EMMA. What the hell are you talking about?
ROBERT. I must read it again myself, now it's in hard covers.
EMMA. Again?
ROBERT. Jerry wanted us to publish it.

219

EMMA. Oh, really?

ROBERT. Well, naturally. Anyway, I turned it down.

EMMA. Why?

ROBERT. Oh . . . not much more to say on that subject, really, is there?

EMMA. What do you consider the subject to be?

ROBERT. Betrayal.

EMMA. No, it isn't.

ROBERT. Isn't it? What is it then?

EMMA. I haven't finished it yet. I'll let you know.

ROBERT. Well, do let me know. (*Pause.*) Of course, I could be thinking of the wrong book. (*Silence.*) By the way, I went into American Express yesterday. (*She looks up.*)

EMMA. Oh?

ROBERT. Yes. I went to cash some travellers cheques. You get a much better rate there, you see, than you do in an hotel.

EMMA. Oh, do you?

ROBERT. Oh yes. Anyway, there was a letter there for you. They asked me if you were any relation and I said yes. So they asked me if I wanted to take it. I mean, they gave it to me. But I said no, I would leave it. Did you get it?

EMMA. Yes.

ROBERT. I suppose you popped in when you were out shopping yesterday evening?

EMMA. That's right.

ROBERT. Oh well, I'm glad you got it. (*Pause.*) To be honest, I was amazed that they suggested I take it. It could never happen in England. But these Italians . . . so free and easy. I mean, just because my name is Downs and your name is Downs doesn't mean that we're the Mr and Mrs Downs that they, in their laughing Mediterranean way, assume we are. We could be, and in fact are vastly more likely to be, total strangers. So let's say I, whom they laughingly assume to be your husband, had taken the letter, having declared myself to be your husband but in truth being a total stranger, and opened it, and read it, out of nothing more than idle curiosity, and then thrown it in a canal, you would never have received it and would have been deprived of your legal right to open your own mail, and all this because of Venetian je m'en foutisme. I've a good mind to write to the Doge of Venice about it. (*Pause.*) That's what stopped me taking it, by the way, and bringing it to you, the thought that I could very easily be a total stranger. (*Pause.*) What they of course did not know, and had no way of knowing, was that I am your husband.

EMMA. Pretty inefficient bunch.

ROBERT. Only in a laughing Mediterranean way. (*Pause.*)

EMMA. It was from Jerry.

ROBERT. Yes, I recognised the handwriting. (*Pause.*) How is he?

EMMA. Okay.

ROBERT. Good. And Judith?

EMMA. Fine. (*Pause.*)

ROBERT. What about the kids?

EMMA. I don't think he mentioned them.

ROBERT. They're probably all right, then. If they were ill or something he'd have probably mentioned it. (*Pause.*) Any other news?

EMMA. No. (*Silence.*)

ROBERT. Are you looking forward to Torcello? (*Pause.*) How many times have we been to Torcello? Twice. I remember how you loved it, the first time I took you there. You fell in love with it. That was about ten years ago, wasn't it? About . . . six months after we were married. Yes. Do you remember? I wonder if you'll like it as much tomorrow. (*Pause.*) What do you think of Jerry as a letter writer? (*She laughs shortly.*) You're trembling. Are you cold?

EMMA. No.

ROBERT. He used to write me at one time. Long letters about Ford Madox Ford. I used to write to him too, come to think of it. Long letters about . . . oh, W. B. Yeats, I suppose. That was the time when we were both editors of poetry magazines. Him at Cambridge, me at Oxford. Did you know that? We were bright young men. And close friends. Well, we still are close friends. All that was long before I met you. Long before he met you. I've been trying to remember when I introduced him to you. I simply can't remember. I take it I *did* introduce him to you? Yes. But when? Can you remember?

EMMA. No.

ROBERT. You can't?

EMMA. No.

ROBERT. How odd. (*Pause.*) He wasn't best man at our wedding, was he?

EMMA. You know he was.

ROBERT. Ah yes. Well, that's probably when I introduced him to you. (*Pause.*) Was there any message for me, in his letter? (*Pause.*) I mean in the line of business, to do with the world of publishing. Has he discovered any new and original talent? He's quite talented at uncovering talent, old Jerry.

EMMA. No message.

ROBERT. No message. Not even his love? (*Silence.*)

EMMA. We're lovers.

ROBERT. Ah. Yes. I thought it might be something like that, something along those lines.

EMMA. When?

ROBERT. What?

EMMA. When did you think?

ROBERT. Yesterday. Only yesterday. When I saw his handwriting on the letter. Before yesterday I was quite ignorant.

EMMA. Ah. (*Pause.*) I'm sorry.

ROBERT. *Sorry?* (*Silence.*) Where does it . . . take place? Must be a bit awkward. I mean we've got two kids, he's got two kids, not to mention a wife . . .

EMMA. We have a flat.

ROBERT. Ah. I see. (*Pause.*) Nice? (*Pause.*) A flat. It's quite well established then, your . . . uh . . . affair?

EMMA. Yes.

ROBERT. How long?

EMMA. Some time.

ROBERT. Yes, but how long exactly?

EMMA. Five years.

ROBERT. *Five years?* (*Pause.*) Ned is one year old. (*Pause.*) Did you hear what I said?

EMMA. Yes. He's your son. Jerry was in America. For two months. (*Silence.*)

ROBERT. Did he write to you from America?

EMMA. Of course. And I wrote to him.

ROBERT. Did you tell him that Ned had been conceived?

EMMA. Not by letter.

ROBERT. But when you did tell him, was he happy to

= ~~Kate~~ Anna before Dooley (OT-68-69)

know I was to be a father? (*Pause.*) I've always liked
Jerry. To be honest, I've always liked him rather more
than I've liked you. Maybe I should have had an affair
with him myself. (*Silence.*) Tell me, are you looking forward to our trip to Torcello?

SCENE 6

Later. Flat. 1973. Summer. EMMA *and* JERRY *standing,
kissing. She is holding a basket and a parcel.*

EMMA. Darling.

JERRY. Darling. (*He continues to hold her. She laughs.*)

EMMA. I must put this down. (*She puts basket on
table.*)

JERRY. What's in it?

EMMA. Lunch.

JERRY. What?

EMMA. Things you like. (*He pours wine.*) How do I
look?

JERRY. Beautiful.

EMMA. Do I look well?

JERRY. You do. (*He gives her wine.*)

EMMA. (*Sipping.*) Mmmnn.

JERRY. How was it?

EMMA. It was lovely.

JERRY. Did you go to Torcello?

EMMA. No.

JERRY. Why not?

EMMA. Oh, I don't know. The speedboats were on
strike, or something.

JERRY. On strike? *See 228-29*

EMMA. Yes. On the day we were going.

JERRY. Ah. What about the gondolas?

EMMA. You can't take a gondola to Torcello.

JERRY. Well, they used to in the old days, didn't they?
Before they had speedboats. How do you think they got
over there?

EMMA. It would take hours.

JERRY. Yes, I suppose so. (*Pause.*) I got your letter.

EMMA. Good.

JERRY. Get mine?

EMMA. Of course. Miss me?

JERRY. Yes. Actually, I haven't been well.

EMMA. What?

JERRY. Oh nothing. A bug. (*She kisses him.*)

EMMA. I missed you. (*She turns away, looks about.*) You haven't been here . . . at all?

JERRY. No.

EMMA. Needs Hoovering.

JERRY. Later. (*Pause.*) I spoke to Robert this morning.

EMMA. Oh?

JERRY. I'm taking him to lunch on Thursday.

EMMA. Thursday? Why?

JERRY. Well, it's my turn.

EMMA. No, I meant why are you taking him to lunch?

JERRY. Because it's my turn. Last time he took me to lunch.

EMMA. You know what I mean.

JERRY. No. What?

EMMA. What is the subject or point of your lunch?

JERRY. No subject or point. We've just been doing it for years. His turn, followed by my turn.

EMMA. You've misunderstood me.

JERRY. Have I? How?

EMMA. Well, quite simply, you often do meet, or have lunch, to discuss a particular writer or a particular book, don't you? So to those meetings, or lunches, there is a point or a subject.

JERRY. Well, there isn't to this one. (*Pause.*)

EMMA. You haven't discovered any new writers, while I've been away?

JERRY. No. Sam fell off his bike.

EMMA. No.

JERRY. He was knocked out. He was out for about a minute.

EMMA. Were you with him?

JERRY. No. Judith. He's all right. And then I got this bug.

EMMA. Oh dear.

JERRY. So I've had time for nothing.

EMMA. Everything will be better, now I'm back.

JERRY. Yes.

EMMA. Oh, I read that Spinks, the book you gave me.

JERRY. What do you think?

EMMA. Excellent.

JERRY. Robert hated it. He wouldn't publish it.

EMMA. What's he like?

JERRY. Who?

EMMA. Spinks.

JERRY. Spinks? He's a very thin bloke. About fifty. Wears dark glasses day and night. He lives alone, in a furnished room. Quite like this one, actually. He's . . . unfussed.

EMMA. Furnished rooms suit him?

JERRY. Yes.

EMMA. They suit me too. And you? Do you still like it? Our home?

JERRY. It's marvellous not to have a telephone.

EMMA. And marvellous to have me?

JERRY. You're all right.

EMMA. I cook and slave for you.

JERRY. You do.

EMMA. I bought something in Venice—for the house. (*She opens the parcel, takes out a tablecloth. Puts it on the table.*) Do you like it?

JERRY. It's lovely. (*Pause.*)

EMMA. Do you think we'll ever go to Venice together? (*Pause.*) No. Probably not. (*Pause.*)

JERRY. You don't think I should see Robert for lunch on Thursday, or on Friday, for that matter?

EMMA. Why do you say that?

JERRY. You don't think I should see him at all?

EMMA. I didn't say that. How can you not see him? Don't be silly (*Pause.*)

JERRY. I had a terrible panic when you were away. I was sorting out a contract, in my office, with some lawyers. I suddenly couldn't remember what I'd done with your letter. I couldn't remember putting it in the safe. I said I had to look for something in the safe. I opened the safe. It wasn't there. I had to go on with the damn contract . . . I kept seeing it lying somewhere in the house, being picked up . . .

EMMA. Did you find it?

JERRY. It was in the pocket of a jacket—in my wardrobe—at home.

EMMA. God.

JERRY. Something else happened a few months ago— I didn't tell you. We had a drink one evening. Well, we had our drink, and I got home about eight, walked in the door, Judith said, hello, you're a bit late. Sorry, I said, I was having a drink with Spinks. Spinks? she said, how odd, he's just phoned, five minutes ago, wanted to speak to you, he didn't mention he'd just seen you. You know old Spinks, I said, not exactly forthcoming, is he? He'd probably remembered something he'd meant to say but hadn't. I'll ring him later. I went up to see the kids and then we all had dinner. (*Pause.*) Listen. Do you remember, when was it, a few years ago, we were all in your kitchen, must have been Christmas or something, do you remember, all the kids were running about and suddenly I picked Charlotte up and lifted her high up, high up, and then down and up, down and up. Do you remember how she laughed?

EMMA. Everyone laughed.

JERRY. She was so light. And there was your husband and my wife and all the kids, all standing and laughing in your kitchen. I can't get rid of it.

EMMA. It was your kitchen, actually. (*He takes her hand. They stand. They go to the bed and lie down.*) Why shouldn't you throw her up? (*She caresses him. They embrace.*) See 207

SCENE 7

Later. Restaurant. 1973. Summer. ROBERT *at table drinking white wine. The waiter brings* JERRY *to the table.* JERRY *sits.*

JERRY. Hullo, Robert.
ROBERT. Hullo.
JERRY. (*To the waiter.*) I'd like a Scotch on the rocks.
WAITER. With water?
JERRY. What?
WAITER. You want it with water?
JERRY. No. No water. Just on the rocks.
WAITER. Certainly signore.
ROBERT. Scotch? You don't usually drink Scotch at lunchtime.
JERRY. I've had a bug, actually.
ROBERT. Ah.
JERRY. And the only thing to get rid of this bug was

Scotch—at lunchtime as well as at night. So I'm still
drinking Scotch at lunchtime in case it comes back.

ROBERT. Like an apple a day.

JERRY. Precisely. (*Waiter brings Scotch on rocks.*)
Cheers.

ROBERT. Cheers.

WAITER. The menus, signori. (*He passes the menus,
goes.*)

ROBERT. How are you? Apart from the bug?

JERRY. Fine.

ROBERT. Ready for some squash?

JERRY. When I've got rid of the bug, yes.

ROBERT. I thought you had got rid of it.

JERRY. Why do you think I'm still drinking Scotch at
lunchtime?

ROBERT. Oh yes. We really must play. We haven't
played for years.

JERRY. How old are you now, then?

ROBERT. Thirty-six.

JERRY. That means I'm thirty-six as well.

ROBERT. If you're a day.

JERRY. Bit violent, squash.

ROBERT. Ring me. We'll have a game.

JERRY. How was Venice?

WAITER. Ready to order, signori?

ROBERT. What'll you have? (JERRY *looks at him,
briefly, then back to the menu.*)

JERRY. I'll have melone. And Piccata al limone with
a green salad.

WAITER. Insalata verde. Prosciutto e melone?

JERRY. No. Just melone. On the rocks.

ROBERT. I'll have prosciutto and melone. Fried
scampi. And spinach.

WAITER. E spinaci. Grazie, signore.

ROBERT. And a bottle of Corvo Bianco straight away.

WAITER. Si, signore. Molte grazie. (*He goes.*)

JERRY. Is he the one who's always been here or is it
his son?

ROBERT. You mean has his son always been here?

JERRY. No, is *he* his son? I mean, is he the son of the
one who's always been here?

ROBERT. No, he's his father.

JERRY. Ah. Is he?

ROBERT. He's the one who speaks wonderful Italian.

JERRY. Yes. Your Italian's pretty good, isn't it?

ROBERT. No. Not at all.

JERRY. Yes it is.

ROBERT. No, it's Emma's Italian which is very good. Emma's Italian is very good.

JERRY. Is it? I didn't know that. (*Waiter with bottle.*)

WAITER. Corvo Bianco, signore.

ROBERT. Thank you.

JERRY. How was it, anyway? Venice.

WAITER. Venice, signore? Beautiful. A most beautiful place of Italy. You see that painting on the wall? Is Venice.

ROBERT. So it is.

WAITER. You know what is none of in Venice?

JERRY. What?

WAITER. Traffico. (*He goes, smiling.*)

ROBERT. Cheers.

JERRY. Cheers.

ROBERT. When were you last there?

JERRY. Oh, years.

ROBERT. How's Judith?

JERRY. What? Oh, you know, okay. Busy.

ROBERT. And the kids?

JERRY. All right. Sam fell off—

ROBERT. What?

JERRY. No, no, nothing. So how was it?

ROBERT. You used to go there with Judith, didn't you?

JERRY. Yes, but we haven't been there for years. (*Pause.*) How about Charlotte? Did she enjoy it?

ROBERT. I think she did. (*Pause.*) I did.

JERRY. Good.

ROBERT. I went for a trip to Torcello.

JERRY. Oh, really? Lovely place.

ROBERT. Incredible day. I got up very early and— whoomp—right across the lagoon—to Torcello. Not a soul stirring.

JERRY. What's the 'whoomp'?

ROBERT. Speedboat.

JERRY. Ah. I thought—

ROBERT. What?

JERRY. It's so long ago. I'm obviously wrong. I thought one went to Torcello by gondola.

See 223

ROBERT. It would take hours. No, no,—whoomp—across the lagoon in the dawn.

JERRY. Sounds good.

ROBERT. I was quite alone.

JERRY. Where was Emma?

ROBERT. I think asleep.

JERRY. Ah.

See 223

ROBERT. I was alone for hours, as a matter of fact, on the island. Highpoint, actually, of the whole trip.

JERRY. Was it? Well, it sounds marvellous.

ROBERT. Yes. I sat on the grass and read Yeats.

JERRY. Yeats on Torcello?

See 211

ROBERT. They went well together. (*Waiter with food.*)

WAITER. One melone. One prosciutto e melone.

ROBERT. Prosciutto for me.

WAITER. Buon appetito.

ROBERT. Emma read that novel of that chum of yours—what's his name?

JERRY. I don't know. What?

ROBERT. Spinks.

JERRY. Oh Spinks. Yes. The one you didn't like.

ROBERT. The one I wouldn't publish.

JERRY. I remember. Did Emma like it?

ROBERT. She seemed to be madly in love with it.

JERRY. Good.

ROBERT. You like it yourself, do you?

JERRY. I do.

ROBERT. And it's very successful?

JERRY. It is.

ROBERT. Tell me, do you think that makes me a publisher of unique critical judgement or a foolish publisher?

JERRY. A foolish publisher.

ROBERT. I agree with you. I am a very foolish publisher.

JERRY. No you're not. What are you talking about? You're a good publisher. What are you talking about?

ROBERT. I'm a bad publisher because I hate books. Or to be more precise, prose. Or to be even more precise, modern prose, I mean modern novels, first novels and second novels, all that promise and sensibility it falls upon me to judge, to put the firm's money on, and then to push for the third novel, see it done, see the dust jacket done, see the dinner for the national literary edi-

tors done, see the signing in Hatchards done, see the
lucky author cook himself to death, all in the name of
literature. You know what you and Emma have in common? You love literature. I mean you love modern prose
literature. I mean you love the new novel by the new
Casey or Spinks. It gives you both a thrill.

JERRY. You must be pissed.

ROBERT. Really? You mean you don't think it gives
Emma a thrill?

JERRY. How do I know? She's your wife. (*Pause.*)

ROBERT. Yes. Yes. You're quite right. I shouldn't have
to consult you. I shouldn't have to consult anyone.

JERRY. I'd like some more wine.

ROBERT. Yes, yes. Waiter! Another bottle of Corvo
Bianco. And where's our lunch? This place is going to
pot. Mind you, it's worse in Venice. They really don't
give a fuck there. I'm not drunk. You can't get drunk
on Corvo Bianco. Mind you . . . last night . . . I was up
late . . . I hate brandy . . . it stinks of modern literature.
No, look, I'm sorry . . . (*Waiter with bottle.*)

WAITER. Corvo Bianco.

ROBERT. Same glass. Where's our lunch?

WAITER. It comes.

ROBERT. I'll pour. (*Waiter goes, with melon plates.*)
No, look, I'm sorry, have another drink. I'll tell you what
it is, it's just that I can't bear being back in London. I
was happy, such a rare thing, not in Venice, I don't mean
that, I mean on Torcello, when I walked about Torcello
in the early morning, alone, I was happy, I wanted to
stay there forever.

JERRY. We all . . .

ROBERT. Yes, we all . . . feel that sometimes. Oh you
do yourself, do you? (*Pause.*) I mean there's nothing
really wrong, you see. I've got the family. Emma and I
are very good together. I think the world of her. And I
actually consider Casey to be a first rate writer.

JERRY. Do you really?

ROBERT. First rate. I'm proud to publish him and you
discovered him and that was very clever of you.

JERRY. Thanks.

ROBERT. You've got a good nose and you care and I
respect that in you. So does Emma. We often talk about
it.

JERRY. How is Emma?
ROBERT. Very well. You must come and have a drink sometime. She'd love to see you.

SCENE 8

Flat. 1971. Summer. Flat empty. Kitchen door open. Table set; crockery, glasses, bottle of wine. JERRY comes in through front door, with keys.

JERRY. Hullo. (EMMA'S *voice from kitchen.*)

EMMA. Hullo. (EMMA *comes out of kitchen. She is wearing an apron.*) I've only just got here. I meant to be here ages ago. I'm making this stew. It'll be hours. (*He kisses her.*) Are you starving?

JERRY. Yes. (*He kisses her.*)

EMMA. No really. I'll never do it. You sit down. I'll get it on.

JERRY. What a lovely apron.

EMMA. Good. (*She kisses him, goes into kitchen. She calls. He pours wine.*) What have you been doing?

JERRY. Just walked through the park.

EMMA. What was it like?

JERRY. Beautiful. Empty. A slight mist. (*Pause.*) I sat down for a bit, under a tree. It was very quiet. I just looked at the Serpentine. (*Pause.*)

EMMA. And then?

JERRY. Then I got a taxi to Wessex Grove. Number 31. And I climbed the steps and opened the front door and then climbed the stairs and opened this door and found you in a new apron cooking a stew. (EMMA *comes out of the kitchen.*)

EMMA. It's on.

JERRY. Which is now on. (EMMA *pours herself a vodka.*) Vodka? At lunchtime?

EMMA. Just feel like one. (*She drinks.*) I ran into Judith yesterday. Did she tell you?

JERRY. No, she didn't. (*Pause.*) Where?

EMMA. Lunch.

JERRY. Lunch?

EMMA. She didn't tell you?

JERRY. No.

EMMA. That's funny.

JERRY. What do you mean, lunch? Where?

EMMA. At Fortnum and Mason's.

JERRY. Fortnum and Mason's? What the hell was she doing at Fortnum and Mason's?

EMMA. She was lunching with a lady.

JERRY. A lady?

EMMA. Yes. (*Pause.*)

JERRY. Fortnum and Mason's is a long way from the hospital.

EMMA. Of course it isn't.

JERRY. Well . . . I suppose not. (*Pause.*) And you?

EMMA. Me?

JERRY. What were you doing at Fortnum and Mason's?

EMMA. Lunching with my sister.

JERRY. Ah. (*Pause.*)

EMMA. Judith . . . didn't tell you?

JERRY. I haven't really seen her. I was out late last night, with Casey. And she was out early this morning. (*Pause.*)

EMMA. Do you think she knows?

JERRY. Knows?

EMMA. Does she know? About us?

JERRY. No.

EMMA. Are you sure?

JERRY. She's too busy. At the hospital. And then the kids. She doesn't go in for . . . speculation.

EMMA. But what about clues? Isn't she interested . . . to follow clues?

JERRY. What clues?

EMMA. Well, there must be some . . . available to her . . . to pick up.

JERRY. There are none . . . available to her.

EMMA. Oh. Well . . . good. (*Pause.*)

JERRY. She has an admirer.

EMMA. Really?

JERRY. Another doctor. He takes her for drinks. It's . . . irritating. I mean, she says that's all there is to it. He likes her, she's fond of him, etcetera, etcetera . . . perhaps that's what I find irritating. I don't know exactly what's going on.

EMMA. Oh, why shouldn't she have an admirer? I have an admirer.

JERRY. Who?

EMMA. Uuh . . . you, I think.

JERRY. Ah. Yes. (*He takes her hand.*) I'm more than that. (*Pause.*)

EMMA. Tell me . . . have you ever thought . . . of changing your life?

JERRY. Changing?

EMMA. Mmnn. (*Pause.*)

JERRY. It's impossible. (*Pause.*)

EMMA. Do you think she's being unfaithful to you?

JERRY. No. I don't know.

EMMA. When you were in America, just now, for instance?

JERRY. No.

EMMA. Have you ever been unfaithful?

JERRY. To whom?

EMMA. To me, of course.

JERRY. No. (*Pause.*) Have you . . . to me?

EMMA. No. (*Pause.*) If she was, what would you do?

JERRY. She isn't. She's busy. She's got lots to do. She's a very good doctor. She likes her life. She loves the kids.

EMMA. Ah.

JERRY. She loves me. (*Pause.*)

EMMA. Ah. (*Silence.*)

JERRY. All that means something.

EMMA. It certainly does.

JERRY. But I adore you. (*Pause.*) I adore you. (EMMA *takes his hand.*)

EMMA. Yes. (*Pause.*) Listen. There's something I have to tell you.

JERRY. What?

EMMA. I'm pregnant. It was when you were in America. (*Pause.*) It wasn't anyone else. It was my husband. (*Pause.*)

JERRY. Yes. Yes, of course. (*Pause.*) I'm very happy for you.

SCENE 9

Robert and Emma's House. Bedroom. 1968. Winter. The room is dimly lit. JERRY *is sitting in the shadows. Faint music through the door. The door opens. Light. Music.* EMMA *comes in, closes the door. She goes towards the mirror, sees* JERRY.

EMMA. Good God.

JERRY. I've been waiting for you.

EMMA. What do you mean?

JERRY. I knew you'd come. (*He drinks.*)

EMMA. I've just come in to comb my hair. (*He stands.*)

JERRY. I knew you'd have to. I knew you'd have to comb your hair. I knew you'd have to get away from the party. (*She goes to the mirror, combs her hair. He watches her.*) You're a beautiful hostess.

EMMA. Aren't you enjoying the party?

JERRY. You're beautiful. (*He goes to her.*) Listen. I've been watching you all night. I must tell you, I want to tell you. I have to tell you—

EMMA. Please—

JERRY. You're incredible.

EMMA. You're drunk.

JERRY. Nevertheless. (*He holds her.*)

EMMA. Jerry.

JERRY. I was best man at your wedding. I saw you in white. I watched you glide by in white.

EMMA. I wasn't in white.

JERRY. You know what should have happened?

EMMA. What?

JERRY. I should have had you, in your white, before the wedding. I should have blackened you, in your white wedding dress, blackened you in your bridal dress, before ushering you into your wedding, as your best man.

EMMA. My husband's best man. Your best friend's best man.

JERRY. No. Your best man.

EMMA. I must get back.

JERRY. You're lovely. I'm crazy about you. All these words I'm using, don't you see, they've never been said before. Can't you see? I'm crazy about you. It's a whirlwind. Have you ever been to the Sahara Desert? Listen to me. It's true. Listen. You overwhelm me. You're so lovely.

EMMA. I'm not.

JERRY. You're so beautiful. Look at the way you look at me.

EMMA. I'm not . . . looking at you.

JERRY. Look at the way you're looking at me. I can't

wait for you. I'm bowled over, I'm totally knocked out, you dazzle me, you jewel, my jewel. I can't ever sleep again, no listen, it's the truth. I won't walk, I'll be a cripple, I'll descend, I'll diminish, into total paralysis, my life is in your hands, that's what you're banishing me to, a state of catatonia, do you know the state of catatonia? do you? do you? the state of . . . where the reigning prince is the prince of emptiness, the prince of absence, the prince of desolation. I love you.

EMMA. My husband is at the other side of that door.

JERRY. Everyone knows. The world knows. It knows. But they'll never know, they'll never know, they're in a different world. I adore you. I'm madly in love with you. I can't believe that what anyone is at this moment saying has ever happened has ever happened. Nothing has ever happened. Nothing. This is the only thing that has ever happened. Your eyes kill me. I'm lost. You're wonderful.

EMMA. No.

JERRY. Yes. (*He kisses her. She breaks away. He kisses her. Laughter off. She breaks away. Door opens.* ROBERT.)

EMMA. Your best friend is drunk.

JERRY. As you are my best and oldest friend and, in the present instance, my host, I decided to take this opportunity to tell your wife how beautiful she was.

ROBERT. Quite right.

JERRY. It is quite right, to . . . to face up to the facts . . . and to offer a token, without blush, a token of one's unalloyed appreciation, no holds barred.

ROBERT. Absolutely.

JERRY. And how wonderful for you that this is so, that this is the case, that her beauty is the case.

ROBERT. Quite right. (JERRY *moves to* ROBERT *and takes hold of his elbow.*)

JERRY. I speak as your oldest friend. Your best man.

ROBERT. You are, actually. (*He clasps* JERRY'S *shoulder, briefly, turns, leaves the room.* EMMA *moves towards the door.* JERRY *grasps her arm. She stops still. They stand still, looking at each other.*)

PACK OF LIES

by Hugh Whitemore

Pack of Lies was first presented by Michael Redington in association with Bernard Sandler and Eddie Kulukundis at the Theatre Royal, Brighton, on 11 October 1983, and subsequently at The Lyric Theatre, London, on 26 October 1983, under the direction of Clifford Williams, with the following cast:

BOB JACKSON	*Michael Williams*
BARBARA JACKSON	*Judi Dench*
JULIE JACKSON	*Eva Griffith*
HELEN KROGER	*Barbara Leigh-Hunt*
PETER KROGER	*Larry Hoodekoff*
STEWART	*Richard Vernon*
THELMA	*Elizabeth Bell*
SALLY	*Penny Ryder*

Designed by Ralph Koltai
Lighting by Robert Ornbo

Presented by Arthur Cantor and Bonnie Nelson Schwartz, by arrangements with Michael Redington in association with Bernard Sandler and Eddie Kulukundis, the play had its New York premiere on February 11, 1985, at the Royale Theatre, under the direction of Clifford Williams, with the following cast:

BOB JACKSON	*George N. Martin*
BARBARA JACKSON	*Rosemary Harris*
JULIE JACKSON	*Tracy Pollan*
HELEN KROGER	*Dana Ivey*
PETER KROGER	*Colin Fox*
STEWART	*Patrick McGoohan*
THELMA	*Kaiulani Lee*
SALLY	*June Ballinger*

Set and Costume Design by Ralph Koltai
Lighting Design by Natasha Katz

The play takes place in a suburb of London during the
autumn and winter of 1960–61. The main events of the
story are true.

FOREWORD

In 1961 Helen and Peter Kroger were found guilty of
spying for the Russians and were sentenced to twenty
years' imprisonment. In 1969 they were exchanged for a
Briton jailed in Moscow, and flew off to Poland amidst
a great hullabaloo in the press.

Shortly after the Krogers' release, Gay Search, a
young journalist, was having dinner with Cedric Messina,
who was then producing BBC's *Play of the Month* series.
Conversation touched on the Krogers, and Miss Search
said, "I know them. In fact, they were our neighbours."
She then told Messina the full story of her involvement
with the Krogers and how her family had played a key
part in their capture. Messina was amazed and excited
by the story. The following day he telephoned me to say
that he believed he had unearthed a good subject for a
television play. Miss Search and I met, discussed the
project with Messina, and I was subsequently commis-
sioned to write a play, which was entitled *Act of Betrayal.*
It was transmitted in January 1971 and was well received
by both the press and the public.

Long after the play's production, the subject and its
implications stayed in my mind. The television script had
adhered very closely to known facts and, as is always the
case with documentary drama, the scope for imaginative
development of characters and situations was limited. In
addition to the themes of loyalty and deception, I became increasingly preoccupied with the role of the ordinary citizen in our society. Is it ever possible for the
average, relatively powerless, man or woman to make
anything more than a token stand against officialdom? Is
it not potentially risky to allow the state (albeit for well-
argued reasons) greater moral licence than the individual? Or is it, perhaps, naive to expect more than an

approximate degree of truthfulness from governments and their spokesmen?

With these thoughts in mind, I decided to rework the basic story of *Act of Betrayal* in a longer, less restricted, more fictionalised form. *Pack of Lies* is the result.

Before starting work on the play, I wrote to the man who was in charge of MI5's day-by-day handling of the case (the character called Stewart is not, I hasten to add, a portrait of this man, but an entirely fictional creation). In my letter, I made it clear that all I wanted was an informal conversation and that I was not hoping for any startling or indiscreet disclosures. The gentleman replied most courteously, but regretted that he was unable to meet me. He said that his "former masters" had imposed "a total embargo on interviews of any sort." Although I detected traces of ironic humour in the tone of his letter, I couldn't help asking myself a few more questions: Who are these "former masters"? Who gave them their authority? How can we, the general public, be sure that they are acting wisely? And if not, how can we control them?

Gay Search and her father helped me most generously in the writing of this play; my thanks to them, and to Clifford Williams, Sarah Moorehead and Michael Redington, who, in addition to his many managerial duties, thought of the excellent title. My thanks also to Arthur Cantor.

Hugh Whitemore

For Judy

ACT I

Bob enters and addresses the audience. He is in his forties. He wears a grey suit.

BOB. I was out in the garden when I heard the door-bell. It was a Saturday afternoon. I was just pottering about, sweeping up leaves and so on. Barbara and Julie had gone shopping. When I opened the front door I found a man and a woman smiling at me. They were holding a Bible and some religious pamphlets. "We've come to bring you the key to great happiness," the man said. "Thanks very much," I said, "but I'm happy enough as it is"—and shut the door quickly before they had a chance to say another word. They walked away slowly, still smiling—I could see them through the window. I suppose they were used to having doors slammed in their faces. Later, when I was back in the garden, I thought to myself, "Well, it's true—I am happy—it's true." And for a moment I stood there, grinning from ear to ear, just because I felt happy for no particular reason. (*He grins.*) It was marvellous.

(Lights up. Day. A small semi-detached house near London, typical of the thousands of suburban homes that were built between the wars. Stage R. is the sitting-room: tiled fireplace, net curtains at the bay window, chintz-covered chairs and sofa, small tables, a sideboard, a radiogram, framed paintings of flowers on the walls. Stage L. is the kitchen, with a back door leading to the garden. US. is the entrance hall and front door, which has a stained-glass panel. A telephone stands on a table beside the stairs leading to the unseen bedrooms. BOB goes to the kitchen, where his wife, BARBARA, is preparing break-

242

fast. He sits at the table, picks up the newspaper, and pours himself some tea.)

BARBARA. What's Julie doing?

BOB. I don't know. Getting dressed.

BARBARA. It's almost eight o'clock.

BOB. Yes, I told her.

BARBARA. (*Calling.*) Julie? (*to* BOB.) I do wish we didn't have this awful rush every morning.

BOB. It doesn't matter, I'll give her a lift.

BARBARA. Why can't we have breakfast like civilised human beings for a change?

BOB. Well, never mind.

BARBARA. (*Irritated.*) Never mind . . . !

(JULIE *enters—a teenager wearing school uniform.*)

JULIE. Sorry.

BARBARA. About time.

JULIE. Sorry.

BARBARA. Every morning it's the same—why do you do it? Rush, rush, rush.

JULIE. I didn't hear the alarm.

BARBARA. That's because you went to bed so late.

JULIE. It wasn't that late.

BOB. When I was your age I was in bed by half-past nine and no arguing.

JULIE. That's just silly.

BOB. No, it's not, you need your rest.

JULIE. What's the point of going to bed if I can't sleep?

BARBARA. If you went to bed earlier you'd go to sleep earlier.

JULIE. No, I wouldn't.

BOB. You might.

JULIE. No, I wouldn't. I don't feel sleepy at night—only in the mornings.

BARBARA. Oh, Julie.

JULIE. It's not my fault—

BOB. No, nothing ever is.

JULIE. —it's biological.

BOB. What is?

BARBARA. Shall I make toast?

BOB. What's biological?

JULIE. Feeling tired. Has the postman been?

BARBARA. Julie . . .

JULIE. What?

BARBARA. Do you want some toast?

JULIE. No, thanks.

BARBARA. You must have something before you go to school.

JULIE. I'll have an apple.

BARBARA. That's not enough.

BOB. What's biological about feeling tired?

JULIE. It all depends when you reach your peak. You're either a day person or a night person. (*Biting into an apple.*) You're day people and I'm not.

BOB. Trust you to be different.

JULIE. It's true. These apples aren't very nice.

BARBARA. Have a glass of milk, then.

JULIE. Isn't there anything else?

BOB. Tea?

JULIE. Not at breakfast time.

BOB. What's wrong with tea?

JULIE. Couldn't we have coffee or fruit juice or something?

BARBARA. Fruit juice . . . ?

JULIE. People don't have tea with breakfast anymore. It's so old-fashioned.

BOB. What are you talking about?

JULIE. —and boring.

BOB. What is?

BARBARA. Have some cornflakes. You like cornflakes.

(*The front door bell rings.*)

JULIE. I'll go. (JULIE *goes to the front door.*)

BOB. What on earth is she talking about?

BARBARA. Try and get her to eat something.

BOB. She won't listen to me.

(JULIE *opens the front door.* HELEN *and* PETER *enter; they are carrying a large object [in fact, an artist's easel] wrapped in a tablecloth.* HELEN *is a tall, large-boned American in her forties; she invariably wears slacks and sweaters.* PETER, *her husband, is about fifty, also an American; he too prefers casual clothes.*)

HELEN. Hi, sweetheart.

JULIE. Hello, Auntie Helen—Uncle Peter.

BOB. (*to* BARBARA.) God, it's Helen, that's all we need.

BARBARA. Ssshhh.

HELEN. (*to* PETER.) Don't push, for Chrissake!

PETER. Sorry. (JULIE *is staring at the tablecloth-shrouded object.*)

JULIE. What's that?

HELEN. Surprise, surprise! (*to* PETER.) Back off! You're pushing it right into my goddam ribs.

PETER. Sorry, honey.

HELEN. (*to* JULIE.) My husband is physically maladjusted, do you know that?

PETER. (*Grinning.*) Maladjusted . . . ?

HELEN. I don't mean maladjusted. Will you open the door please, sweetheart? He malfunctions. What do you call it? No coordination—(BOB *pushes back his chair and stands up.*)

BOB. What's going on out there?

HELEN. Tell him to lift something—he goes right ahead and pushes it.

PETER. That's not true.

HELEN. Mind that table—Jesus! (*Entering the sitting room.*) Over there—put it over there. Hi, Bob, where is she?

BOB. She's in the kitchen getting the breakfast.

HELEN. Barbara, where are you? Barbara! (BARBARA *enters from the kitchen.*)

BARBARA. I'm here. (*With a flourish,* HELEN *gestures towards the easel.*)

HELEN. (*Singing.*) Happy birthday to you,

Happy birthday to you,

Happy birthday, dear Barbara . . .

Happy birthday—to—you!

(BARBARA *stares in amazement.* PETER *smiles.*)

PETER. We couldn't find any paper big enough—hence the tablecloth. (JULIE *and* BOB *are giggling.*)

HELEN. Go on—open it up.

BARBARA. (*Trying not to laugh.*) Oh, Helen . . .

HELEN. What's the matter?

BARBARA. It's not my birthday.

HELEN. Whaat?! (PETER *shouts with laughter.*)

BARBARA. It's next week. The twenty-ninth.

PETER. What did I say? What did I tell you?

HELEN. Don't give me that, you said no such thing.

PETER. "When's Barbara's birthday?" you said, and I said the twenty-ninth.

HELEN. You didn't.

PETER. I did.

HELEN. You didn't.

PETER. I did.

HELEN. (*Turning to* BARBARA.) The twenty-ninth . . . ?

BARBARA. That's right.

HELEN. (*To* PETER.) You said the nineteenth.

PETER. I didn't.

HELEN. You did.

PETER. I swear to you I did not.

HELEN. What are you trying to do to me? Jesus! It's like that goddam film—what's it called?—you know—Ingrid Bergman thinks she's going crazy, but it's her husband all the time—it's Cary Grant or James Mason or someone—

PETER. Charles Boyer.

HELEN. He keeps telling her the wrong things so she thinks she's going crazy—is that what you're trying to do? (*To* BOB.) He said the nineteenth. I know he said the nineteenth.

PETER. If I did, I'm sorry—my mistake, okay? (*To* BARBARA.) Come on, you'd better open it up.

BARBARA. Shall I?

HELEN. I'm sure as hell not taking it back home again.

JULIE. Yes, go on.

BARBARA. What is this, some terrible joke?

PETER. Let me give you a hand, it's a bit tricky. (PETER *unwraps the easel.*)

JULIE. Wow!

HELEN. Well—do you like it? (BARBARA *stands speechless for a moment, unable to find the words to express her delight.*)

PETER. It's an easel. For your paintings.

HELEN. She knows it's an easel, you dumdum. (*To* BARBARA.) Come on—don't keep us in suspense—do you like it or don't you?

BARBARA. I love it. It's wonderful. I don't know what to say.

PETER. Now that you're going to these art classes, we thought you ought to have all the regular . . . (*He completes the sentence with a gesture towards the easel.*)

BARBARA. You shouldn't have done this, it's much too extravagant.

HELEN. (*Overlapping.*) Now, don't give me any of that English phoney-baloney about "Oh, you shouldn't have," and all that horse-shit. You're my very good and dear friend, Barbara, and if I want to buy you a fancy birthday present, no one's going to stop me, okay? Okay?

BARBARA. (*Smiling.*) Okay.

HELEN. And if it ain't your birthday, who cares—what the hell—we'll call it a thanksgiving present.

JULIE. Thanksgiving for what?

HELEN. Thanksgiving for what . . . ? (*Improvising rapidly.*) Okay, I'll tell you for what. How many people are there living in London? Six million? Eight? Let's say six, okay? So that means it was something like three-million-to-one that we'd find ourselves living across the street from wonderful folk like and— and if that ain't the cause for some kind of thanksgiving, I don't know what is! (BARBARA *laughs and embraces* HELEN.)

BARBARA. Oh, Helen, dear Helen—you're priceless!

(*Lights fade.* BARBARA, HELEN, BOB, JULIE, *and* PETER *exit.* STEWART *enters and addresses the audience. He is in his forties, wearing a raincoat and a dark blue suit. He might be mistaken for an averagely successful provincial solicitor.*)

STEWART. Eventually our investigations led us to a street in Ruislip. It was autumn, 1960. Ruislip, I should explain, is a suburb of London. It lies to the northwest of the metropolis and is one of the places one drives through on the way to Oxford. That is how I remember it, at any rate: as somewhere glimpsed briefly through car windows, generally at dusk, generally in the rain— neat rows of semi-detached houses; small front gardens, each with its square of lawn and herbaceous border; bay windows; clipped hedges; and every so often, where the downstairs curtains have yet to be drawn, the blueish flickering light of a television set. And that, since all stories have to begin somewhere, is where this particular story began for me—or rather this particular chapter of this particular story, for the case as a whole had been occupying my attention for several months. It is, by the way, by and large—true.

(*Lights fade.* STEWART *exits. Lights up. Dusk.* BARBARA *and* HELEN *are coming downstairs.* BARBARA *is carrying a dress;* HELEN *is wearing an almost-completed dress [some of it is still only pinned together], and carrying the dress she arrived in.*)

HELEN. Where do you want me to go?

BARBARA. In the sitting-room.

HELEN. (*Going into the sitting-room.*) Jesus, it's cold in here. You ought to get central heating.

BARBARA. (*Switching on the electric fire.*) Well, one day. (HELEN *drapes her own dress over a chair and positions herself in the centre of the room.*)

HELEN. Okay, what do you want me to do?

BARBARA. Just stand still. I want to make sure that it fits all right.

HELEN. God, you're a fast worker.

BARBARA. I've got to get a move on if it's going to be ready for Christmas. Hold your arm up. Let me look at the sleeve.

HELEN. Like this? (HELEN *extends her right arm.*)

BARBARA. Yes, that's fine. (*Thus, for a moment,* BARBARA *and* HELEN *stand face-to-face, with their arms extended, almost like ballroom dancers.* HELEN, *realising this similarity, suddenly grabs* BARBARA *by the waist and whirls her across the room.*)

HELEN. Hey, come on—let's dance!

BARBARA. (*Protesting but laughing.*) Stop it, Helen, stop it.

HELEN. (*Singing.*) "Shall we dance, pom pom pom pom—Shall we dance deedle-eedle"—come on.

BARBARA. (*Laughing.*) Oh, Helen, you are a fool.

HELEN. Do you ever go dancing? I never go dancing. I used to love dancing when I was a girl.

BARBARA. Where could you dance round here?

HELEN. We could organise something. Why not? We

could have dances in the afternoon. What are they called? Tea dances. We could have tea dances in Cranley Drive.

BARBARA. Who'd come?

HELEN. Lots of people, I bet.

BARBARA. All the men are at work.

HELEN. Okay, so we could ask some of the boys from school.

BARBARA. They're a bit young.

HELEN. Who cares? They're a good-looking bunch.

BARBARA. Some of them.

HELEN. That guy Julie likes—he's really good-looking.

BARBARA. You mean Malcolm Granger?

HELEN. Don't you think he's good-looking?

BARBARA. He's completely irresponsible. Have you seen the way he races around on that motorbike of his? He'll get himself killed one of these days.

HELEN. If you're worried, tell her.

BARBARA. I can't.

HELEN. Why not?

BARBARA. She thinks I worry about everything.

HELEN. She's right, you do.

BARBARA. I try not to.

HELEN. It's your nature, you can't help it—she knows that, I know that, we all know that. (*She squeezes* BAR-BARA'S *hand comfortingly.*) Now, listen, here's what you do if you're worried: you tell her she's too young to go riding about on motorcycles.

BARBARA. I've told her that already.

HELEN. Then she won't. She's a good girl. She'll do what you say. (BARBARA *unconvinced, says nothing.* HELEN *grins.*) You know something? Malcolm Granger has a beautiful body. I saw him at the pool last summer. Beautiful! Maybe I should lure him round to the house when Peter goes to one of his antiquarian book sales. What do you think? Shall I introduce him to the more sophisticated charms of an older woman? (BARBARA *does not respond; she is preoccupied with her anxieties about* JULIE.)

BARBARA. I wish you'd say something to her.

HELEN. Say what?

BARBARA. About going on the motorbike. (HELEN *looks at* BARBARA.)

HELEN. You really are worried.

BARBARA. Yes, I am.

HELEN. What can I say?

BARBARA. She'd listen to you.

HELEN. What about Bob? Why doesn't he talk to her?

BARBARA. You know what Bob's like. She can't do a thing wrong as far as he's concerned. (*Brief pause.*) Please. There's no one else I can ask . . . Please. (HELEN *hesitates.*)

HELEN. Okay.

BARBARA. (*Relieved.*) Would you?

HELEN. Okay, if it'll make you any happier.

BARBARA. Well, it would.

HELEN. Okay.

BARBARA. Thanks. I hate asking.

HELEN. Don't be silly. (*Deliberately changing the mood.*) It's beautiful, this dress—really beautiful. You're such a clever girl, Barbara. You do so many things real good. You've got golden hands.

BARBARA. What a funny thing to say.

HELEN. Well, it's true.

(JULIE *opens the front door. She's wearing coat, scarf, and gloves over her school uniform. She carries a satchel.*)

JULIE. (*Calling.*) Mum!

BARBARA. (*Calling.*) In here, Julie. (*Whispering to* HELEN.) Don't tell her I asked you to say anything.

HELEN. Of course I won't. Don't worry. (JULIE *enters the sitting room and kisses* BARBARA.)

JULIE. Hello, Mum. Hello, Auntie Helen.

HELEN. Hi, Julie, sweetheart.

BARBARA. How was choir practice?

JULIE. Boring. Every year it's *The Messiah*. If only we could do something different. It's so boring doing the same old thing year after year.

BARBARA. Everything's boring as far as you're concerned.

JULIE. The dress looks smashing.

HELEN. Doesn't it? (HELEN *starts to change dresses.*)

BARBARA. It's quite an easy pattern.

HELEN. Don't be so modest. Be proud. If I could make a dress like this, I'd be really proud of myself.

BARBARA. You could if you tried.

HELEN. Honey, I couldn't and you know it. I've got five thumbs and no finesse.

BARBARA. (*Smiling.*) Oh, Helen.

HELEN. It's true. I remember, when I was a kid, one of the farm hands saying to me—I'd just done something stupid or clumsy or both—and he said, "God help the man you marry, Miss Helen, you may be okay with cattle, but you'll be a disaster in the home."

BARBARA. Oh, what nonsense.

HELEN. He was right.

BARBARA. (*To* JULIE.) Don't start making yourself comfortable, Julie. Remember: homework first.

JULIE. Can't I even have a cup of tea?

BARBARA. Do you know what the time is? Your father will be home in a minute.

HELEN. Come on, Barbara, give the poor girl a cup of tea.

BARBARA. You spoil her. (BARBARA *gets up and goes to the kitchen.*)

HELEN. Well, why not? (*To* JULIE.) Hey—I see the folk down the street are having a bonfire party tomorrow. Are you going?

JULIE. (*Dismissively.*) Oh no. (*She gets up, picks up her satchel, coat, scarf, and gloves, crosses into the hall and into the kitchen, putting her things down on the chair at the table.* HELEN *follows and sits at the table.*)

HELEN. Too old for fireworks, huh?

JULIE. I've got better things to do.

BARBARA. Yes, she's got better things to do—like homework. (*To* JULIE.) Cake or biscuits?

JULIE. (*Irritated.*) Oh, Mum . . . ! Neither, I *told* you.

BARBARA. (*To* HELEN.) Have you heard about this stupid diet?

JULIE. It's not stupid. Look at Sue Galleyford.

BARBARA. She's always been a big girl.

JULIE. Only because she eats so much.

BARBARA. Well, I think it's ridiculous—someone of your age . . .

(*The telephone rings.*)

JULIE. I'll go—it's probably Maureen.

BARBARA. Hang your coat up! How many more times?

JULIE. Sorry, sorry. (JULIE *picks up her raincoat and exits to the hall.*)

BARBARA. If it's that insurance man, tell him to ring back later.

JULIE. Okay. (JULIE *closes the kitchen door. She hangs her raincoat on a peg and then answers the telephone.*)

BARBARA. Would you like a cup of tea?

HELEN. No, thanks, I'd better not. (BARBARA *makes tea for* JULIE.) Say, whatever happened to the Pearsons?

BARBARA. The Pearsons . . . ?

HELEN. Brian and Betty, down at number twenty-three.

BARBARA. They're all right, as far as I know.

HELEN. I've been round there half a dozen times and there's never anyone at home. I just wondered if they're okay. (JULIE *returns.*)

JULIE. Who's that?

HELEN. The Pearsons.

JULIE. They've gone on holiday. (*To* BARBARA.) It's for you, Mum.

HELEN. (*To* JULIE.) At this time of the year?

JULIE. Only for a week. They're back tomorrow. (BARBARA *goes to the door.*)

BARBARA. (*To* JULIE.) Who is it?

JULIE. A man.

BARBARA. What man?

JULIE. He didn't say.

BARBARA. Oh, Julie . . . (BARBARA *exits, closing the door. She goes to the telephone.* JULIE *pours tea for herself.*)

JULIE. Do you want some?

HELEN. No, thanks. (JULIE *sips her tea;* HELEN *watches her.*) Well, now, young lady, and how are you today?

JULIE. Fine.

HELEN. Good.

JULIE. (*Mock American accent.*) Fine and dandy.

HELEN. Let's hope it stays that way.

JULIE. (*Glancing at* HELEN.) Why shouldn't it?

HELEN. You tell me. (JULIE *turns, frowning, to face* HELEN.)

JULIE. What's the matter, Auntie Helen?

HELEN. I thought you weren't supposed to go riding about on motorcycles.

JULIE. Oh.

HELEN. Yes—oh.

JULIE. When did you see me?

HELEN. The other afternoon, with young Mr. you-know-who.

JULIE. Malcolm.

HELEN. Yes, Malcolm. I thought all that was strictly verboten.

JULIE. He was only bringing me home from school—and he's very careful.

HELEN. Your momma doesn't think so.

JULIE. You know what she's like: she worries about everything.

HELEN. Only because she loves you.

JULIE. She keeps treating me like a little girl. She doesn't realise that I'm grown up. (HELEN *looks at* JULIE; *she smiles affectionately.*)

HELEN. No. No, and I don't suppose she ever will. (*She goes to* JULIE *and kisses her.*) Okay, I won't say a word. It'll be our secret. Don't do anything silly, do you hear me?

JULIE. (*She smiles.*) I won't. Thanks. (BARBARA *returns.*)

BARBARA. Come on, Julie, what about that homework?

JULIE. (*To* HELEN, *smiling.*) See what I mean?

BARBARA. See what?

JULIE. Nothing. (*She picks up her cup of tea and goes to the door.*) Who was that on the phone?

BARBARA. Someone for your father. (JULIE *slings her satchel over her shoulder.*)

JULIE. Bye, Auntie Helen.

HELEN. Bye, sweetheart—work hard.

JULIE. I will. (JULIE *exits and goes upstairs.*)

HELEN. She's a good girl. (BARBARA *finds* JULIE'S *gloves on a chair.*)

BARBARA. If only she wasn't so untidy. (HELEN *has now changed back into her own clothes.*)

HELEN. There are worse things in life than being untidy.

BARBARA. You ought to try living with her. It takes at least half an hour to clear up the mess after she's gone to school: books and clothes all over the place—not to mention all the washing and ironing and mending. She doesn't do a thing for herself, it's disgraceful, really.

HELEN. Say what you like—she's a good girl and I'm

very fond of her. (BARBARA *glances at* HELEN, *mildly surprised by her uncharacteristically serious tone of voice.*)

BARBARA. Yes—well, she's very fond of you.

HELEN. I hope so.

BARBARA. You know she is.

HELEN. I guess I do. (*She sighs.*) I'd give a lot to have a daughter like Julie. You don't know how lucky you are.

(BOB *opens the front door. He is wearing a raincoat and a dark grey suit.*)

BOB. (*Calling.*) Hello.

HELEN. Hey, there's your old man. I must go.

JULIE. (*Off.*) Hello, Daddy!

HELEN. The dress is truly beautiful.

BARBARA. (*With a smile.*) Thank you.

(HELEN *goes to the hall.* BOB *is taking off his raincoat, which he hangs on a peg by the front door.*)

BOB. Ah—Helen.

HELEN. Don't look so worried, I'm just going. Is it still raining?

BOB. It's raining, it's cold, and it's windy.

HELEN. Only one place to be on a night like tonight. Bed. Tucked up in bed, all cosy and warm, with the wind whistling outside. A little nooky, maybe. Poifeck, as my old Aunt Sophie used to say. (*Grinning at* BARBARA.) Hey. Maybe I'll call Malcolm Granger and see if he wants a few mind-broadening experiences. (*Calling upstairs; blowing a kiss to* BARBARA.) Bye, honey. Bye, Bob. Bye, sweetheart.

JULIE. Bye. (HELEN *exits, closing the front door as she goes.* BOB *turns, smiling, to* BARBARA, *who is standing by the kitchen door.*)

BOB. What's all that about Malcolm Granger?

BARBARA. Just a silly joke. (BARBARA *closes the kitchen door; she turns to face* BOB; *she is clearly anxious about something.*)

BOB. You all right?

BARBARA. Bob, listen—somebody's been ringing up for you—I think it's urgent.

BOB. What is? Who?

BARBARA. His name's Stewart.

BOB. Stewart what?

BARBARA. That's his surname—Mr. Stewart.

BOB. Who is he?

BARBARA. I don't know.

BOB. What does he want?

BARBARA. I don't know.

BOB. Didn't you ask him?

BARBARA. Of course I asked him! He said he wanted to talk to you. I told him you weren't here and could he ring back later, and he said no, he'd like to come and see us.

BOB. What about?

BARBARA. I don't know—he got all cagey and said he couldn't explain on the phone.

BOB. He's probably just a salesman.

BARBARA. No, he's something to do with the police.

BOB. The police . . . ?

BARBARA. He said if we were worried about him coming round here, we could ring Scotland Yard and speak to a Superintendent Smith. (BOB *stares at her, but says nothing.*) And he said it's confidential; we mustn't tell anyone. (*Momentarily at a loss for words,* BOB *walks aimlessly across the room.*)

BOB. When did he ring?

BARBARA. About five or ten minutes ago.

BOB. Right . . . (*He goes to the door.*) . . . right, I'll talk to this man Smith. Where's his number?

BARBARA. It's on the pad.

BOB. Right. (BOB *goes to the telephone and dials the number.* BARBARA *remains by the kitchen door, observing.*)

BARBARA. Ask him what it's all about.

BOB. Yes, right. (*On telephone.*) Hello? . . . Hello, yes—could I speak to Superintendent Smith, please? My name's Jackson. (*Pause.*) Hello? Is that Superintendent Smith? . . . Yes, good evening—um—I understand a man called Stewart rang my wife just now and, um . . . Oh, did he? . . . Yes . . . Yes . . . Well, yes, of course, if it's important . . . Yes . . . Yes—um—can you tell me what it's all about? . . . Oh, I see . . . Right . . . Yes, I will . . . Thank you, Superintendent. Goodbye.

BARBARA. Well? (BOB *replaces the receiver. He turns to face* BARBARA.)

BOB. Well, it's obviously pretty important.

BARBARA. What did he say?

BOB. That's what he said. He said it's pretty important, and he'd be grateful if we could spare the time to talk to this Mr. Stewart. (*A moment of silence.* BARBARA *looks at* BOB *as if she had expected him to make more of a stand.*) He was very polite . . . very—you know, friendly and pleasant. (*No response from* BARBARA.) What else could I say?

BARBARA. What time is he coming?

BOB. Eight o'clock.

BARBARA. I'd better get on with the supper, then.

BOB. Right.

(*Lights fade.* PETER *enters and addresses the audience.*)

PETER. I remember how shy they were when we first met. Helen and I went across and introduced ourselves: "Hi," we said, "we're your new neighbours." Well, Bob and Barbara stared at us as if we'd just stepped out of a flying saucer. They seemed a little reassured when we told them we were Canadians not American, but even so it took quite a time before they could accept us as regular human beings. A month or so later, they asked us to tea, and that's when we first met Julie. "Julie's short for Juliet," said Barbara, "Juliet as in *Romeo and Juliet.*" Then Bob said, "We saw the old film with Norma Shearer and Leslie Howard just after we got engaged, and we made up our minds there and then: If we ever had a girl she was going to be called Juliet." "And so she was," said Barbara. "And so she was," said Bob. I was touched by the way they would finish each other's stories. It wasn't interrupting, it was more of a mutual orchestration of shared memories; a shared enjoyment of their life together. A kind of celebration. I said this to Helen when we got back home. She pooh-poohed it and said I was being sentimental; but pretty soon after she admitted that she too was beginning to feel a certain affection for them—Julie especially.

(PETER *exits. Lights up. Evening.* BARBARA *and* BOB *are in the sitting-room, waiting anxiously for* MR. STEWART *to arrive. The curtains are drawn. A moment of silence.*)

BARBARA. What's the time?

BOB. Ten to. (*Brief pause.*)

BARBARA. I wish we knew what it was all about.

BOB. Well, I did ask, didn't I? I couldn't do more than that. (BARBARA *sighs. Pause.*)

BARBARA. I keep wondering if it's anything to do with Malcolm.

BOB. Why should it be?

BARBARA. He's been in trouble with the police.

BOB. What sort of trouble?

BARBARA. Something to do with his motorbike. Speeding, I think.

BOB. I thought Julie wasn't seeing him anymore.

BARBARA. She still likes him.

BOB. What's that supposed to mean?

BARBARA. What?

BOB. Is she still seeing him or isn't she?

BARBARA. Well, I don't know. I can't be sure.

BOB. Haven't you asked her?

BARBARA. Well, yes, but supposing she has seen him—and supposing—

(*The front doorbell rings.* BARBARA *and* BOB *rise to their feet; they stand facing each other.*)

BOB. He's here.

BARBARA. He's early. (BOB *turns to the door, but hesitates.*)

BARBARA. Quickly! We don't want Julie to answer the door.

(BOB *goes into the hall.* BARBARA *pats the cushions into shape.* BOB *opens the front door.* STEWART *enters. He is wearing a trilby hat, a raincoat, and a dark blue suit.*)

STEWART. Mr. Jackson?

BOB. Yes, that's right.

STEWART. Good evening, my name's Stewart. I spoke to your wife on the phone.

BOB. Yes, do come in, please.

STEWART. Thank you. (STEWART *walks into the hall.* BOB *closes the front door and goes to the sitting-room.*)

BOB. This way.

STEWART. Thank you. (BOB *and* STEWART *enter the sitting-room.*)

BOB. This is my wife. Mr. Stewart.

STEWART. How do you do, Mrs. Jackson?

BARBARA. How do you do? (*They shake hands.*)

BOB. Let me take your coat.

STEWART. Thank you. (STEWART *takes off his raincoat; he gives it and his trilby hat to* BOB.) Sorry I'm a bit early. I expected heavy traffic, but the roads were empty. It's all these gales, I suppose. People are staying at home.

BOB. Yes. Yes, I suppose they are. (BOB *takes* STEWART'S *raincoat and hat and hangs them in the hall.*)

STEWART. Dreadful floods in the south. Did you hear the news?

BARBARA. No, I . . .

STEWART. Quite dreadful.

(*A brief, rather awkward silence.* BOB *returns.*)

BARBARA. Please sit down, Mr. Stewart.

STEWART. Thank you. (*Brief pause.*)

BOB. Now, then—what can we do for you?

STEWART. Is your daughter at home?

BARBARA. Yes, she's upstairs—doing her homework.

STEWART. I wonder, would it be possible to disturb her for a few minutes?

BOB. Well, I . . . (*An anxious hesitation.*) . . . do you have to see her?

STEWART. I rather wanted to see you all, if that's possible—*en famille,* as it were.

BOB. She's not in any trouble, is she?

STEWART. Oh no, good Lord, no.

BARBARA. Well, that's a relief, anyway. (*She smiles.*) I'll go and get her.

STEWART. Thank you. (BARBARA *exits. Pause.*)

BOB. I spoke to Superintendent Smith.

STEWART. Yes, so he said. (*A smile.*) It's a bit melodramatic, I suppose, ringing Scotland Yard and all that, but—well, it's a good quick way of telling people that we're—you know—trustworthy, unlikely to run off with the family silver. (STEWART *grins.* BOB, *too tense for*

light-hearted pleasantries, merely nods. Brief pause.) I
gather you're with AirSpeed Research?

BOB. Yes.

STEWART. That must be jolly interesting. Don't you
find it interesting?

BOB. Yes, oh yes, I enjoy it.

STEWART. Travel about a bit, do you?

BOB. Well not much; up and down to Liverpool
mostly.

STEWART. Ah. (*He smiles.*) One tends to think of people in the aircraft industry as flying off all over the world
at the drop of a hat.

BOB. Not me, I'm afraid.

STEWART. Pity. (STEWART *smiles at* BOB; *there is another awkward silence before* BARBARA *returns with*
JULIE.)

BARBARA. This is our daughter, Julie, Mr. Stewart.

STEWART. How do you do, Miss Jackson?

JULIE. How do you do? (STEWART *and* JULIE *shake
hands. Everyone sits down.*)

BOB. May I offer you a drink, sir? Whisky, sherry?

STEWART. No, thanks, not for me, but please don't let
me stop you.

BOB. No . . . no, I'm not much of a drinker.

STEWART. Neither am I. Shockingly expensive these
days.

BOB. Yes, isn't it.

STEWART. Shocking. (*Brief pause; he smiles.*) Well,
now, let me apologise for barging in on you like this. It's
a bit alarming, I know, when a complete stranger rings
up out of the blue, and I'm most grateful for your, ah—
for your allowing me to come here—most grateful. The
trouble is, it's a bit difficult for me to explain—precisely—what all this is about, what I do, and so on, because so much of my work concerns confidential matters,
and I'm simply not allowed to discuss them in any detail.

BOB. Fair enough.

JULIE. Are you a policeman?

STEWART. Not really, no—although some of my duties—do tend to overlap with those of the police force.
In actual fact, I'm a civil servant—(*He grins.*) and that,
as we all know, can cover a multitude of sins. (*He laughs;
nobody responds to his joke; he rises to his feet.*) Do you

mind if I wander about? I find it so much easier to, um . . .

BARBARA, BOB. (*Giving their consent.*) No, please.

STEWART. Thank you. (*He paces slowly across the room.*) Now, then . . . the reason why I'm here. Well, we need your help, it's as simple as that. We've become very interested in one particular chap and we're anxious to find out what he does, where he goes, and so on. And the only way we can do that is by asking a lot of rather boring questions. In other words, it's just a straightforward, routine enquiry. There's nothing to be nervous about—it's just routine.

BOB. Who is this man? Do we know him?

BARBARA. Does he live round here?

STEWART. He comes here most weekends. We think he has friends in this part of the world.

(*The telephone rings.*)

BOB. Damn—sorry.

STEWART. Not to worry. (BOB *goes to answer the telephone.*)

BOB. (*On telephone.*) Hello? . . . Oh, Maureen—hang on a minute . . . (*To* JULIE.) It's Maureen.

JULIE. Tell her I'll ring back later.

BOB. (*On telephone.*) She says she'll ring back later . . . What? . . . Right . . . Yes, I'll tell her . . . Yes, all right—bye-bye. (BOB *replaces the receiver and returns to the sitting-room.*) She said she can't come round tomorrow evening.

JULIE. Why not?

BOB. I don't know. Ring her later. (*To* STEWART.) Sorry.

STEWART. Not to worry. Um . . . where was I?

JULIE. You were saying about this man coming here to see his friends.

STEWART. Ah yes. Now we don't know who they are or where exactly they live; we don't even know why he comes here so regularly. It might just be friendship, of course, but somehow I rather doubt it.

JULIE. Why?

STEWART. He's a busy man, Miss Jackson, and if he takes the trouble to come out here every weekend, then

I'm sure he does so for a very good reason. And that's why we think it's important to find out as much as we can about these weekly jaunts—and about these mysterious friends of his. Now—I've got a photograph of him some-where . . . (*He finds the photograph in his jacket pocket.*) . . . I'd like you all to take a look at it, if you will, and tell me if you think you've seen him before and if so, where. (*Murmurs of assent.*) Mrs. Jackson . . .

BARBARA. (*Looking at the photograph.*) No, I've never seen him.

STEWART. Mr. Jackson?

BOB. (*Looking at the photograph.*) No.

STEWART. Miss Jackson.

JULIE. (*Looking at the photograph.*) No, sorry.

STEWART. You're all quite sure?

BOB.		Yes.
BARBARA.	(*Together.*)	Quite sure.
JULIE.		Yes.

STEWART. Yes, I see. Thank you. (*He puts the photograph back into his pocket.*) Well, never mind, it was a long shot, anyway.

JULIE. What's he done, this man?

STEWART. I'm afraid I can't tell you that, Miss Jackson.

JULIE. How do you know he comes here at weekends? Has somebody actually seen him?

STEWART. Oh yes, we've been keeping an eye on him for some time.

JULIE. Do you mean following him?

STEWART. (*He smiles at her obvious excitement.*) Well, yes, I suppose I do. But it's not as easy as it looks on the films, you know, following people—especially in a place like this, with all these narrow roads and footpaths. That's why I hoped that one of you might have seen him. It would have saved my chaps a lot of time and trouble.

JULIE. Would you like us to keep a look-out for him?

STEWART. Yes, that would be splendid. (*Quickly adding a few words of restraint.*) But do remember—you must remember that this is all very confidential. Not a word to anyone.

BOB. Of course.

STEWART. You do understand that, don't you, Miss Jackson? No whispering secrets to your chums at school.

JULIE. Yes, all right. I promise.

STEWART. Good, excellent. Thank you.

JULIE. What happens next?

BARBARA. Ssshhh, Julie.

STEWART. (*Smiling.*) That's a damn good question; I only wish I knew the answer.

BOB. Well, if there's anything we can do . . .

STEWART. Thank you. (*He takes a notepad from his coat pocket.*) As a matter of fact, there are one or two things I'd like to ask you before I go—just a few details . . . (*Opening the notepad.*) You've lived here quite some time, I believe?

BOB. Yes, over twenty years.

STEWART. Really?

BOB. Since March 1939.

STEWART. My word. (*Taking a pen from his pocket.*) So you'd know most of the other people here in Cranley Drive?

BOB. My wife does, certainly.

STEWART. Yes . . . (*Turning to* BARBARA.) What about the Galleyfords at number thirty-eight? Do you know them?

BARBARA. Oh yes, they've been here almost as long as we have. Their daughter's the same age as Julie.

STEWART. And they're English, I take it?

BOB. Yes—well, British—Mrs. Galleyford comes from Cardiff.

STEWART. Right. (*He makes a note.*) Then there's the Duncans at number forty . . .

BARBARA. He's retired—they're both in their seventies—they don't go out much.

STEWART. (*Making another note.*) And across the road, at number forty-five—the Krogers.

BARBARA. Helen and Peter. They're our best friends, really. He's a bookseller.

BOB. Book-dealer. Antiquarian books, you know, first editions.

STEWART. Ah yes.

BOB. They're Canadian.

BARBARA. But they're very nice. They've been here about five years.

STEWART. Any family?

BARBARA, BOB. (*Together.*) No.

STEWART. (*Making another note.*) And next to them, at number forty-three . . . (*Peering at his notes.*) I can't read my own writing.

BARBARA. John and Sheila Henderson.

STEWART. (*Writing a correction.*) Henderson . . . yes.

BARBARA. They both go out to work, so I don't really know them. They moved in . . . (*To* BOB.) . . . when?

BOB. About a year ago.

BARBARA. A year ago, yes.

STEWART. Right, good. (*Closing the notepad.*) That's very useful. Thank you. (*He puts the notepad into his pocket and turns to* BOB.) Now, you said you might be willing to help, Mr. Jackson.

BOB. Yes, of course.

STEWART. Well, what we have to do is this: We have to station observers in various parts of the district and find out where this man goes, where he spends his Saturdays and Sundays. The problem is—how can our people observe without being observed? In Piccadilly at rush-hour, it couldn't be easier—but here, where everybody knows everybody else, it's really very difficult. The observer has to be concealed. There's no other way. (*A brief hesitation.*) So that's what we need. A room. Somewhere. That's how you can help. (*A moment of silence.*)

BOB. You mean a room *here* . . . ?

STEWART. It would only be for a couple of days: tomorrow and Sunday. (BARBARA *and* BOB *exchange anxious glances.*)

BOB. Well, I don't know about that . . .

BARBARA. You mean—one of your men—here, in the house?

STEWART. It would be a young lady. More natural, we thought. If any questions were asked, you can say she's a member of your art club. It is an art club you belong to, isn't it?

BARBARA. (*Amazed that he knows this.*) Well, yes. (STEWART *gestures to the paintings on the wall.*)

STEWART. Are these yours?

BARBARA. Yes.

STEWART. Very good. Very good indeed. (*He smiles at* BARBARA, *and then turns to* BOB.) Well, what do you think? It seems to me that the smaller window upstairs at the front would probably be the best.

JULIE. (*Excitedly.*) That's my room!

STEWART. (*He smiles.*) A good look-out post, eh, Miss Jackson?

JULIE. Oh yes—perfect.

BARBARA. I'm not too keen on having somebody actually inside the house.

JULIE. Why not?

BARBARA. Julie, please.

STEWART. It's your decision. You must decide.

BOB. Couldn't your people watch from a car—a parked car—couldn't they do that?

STEWART. They *could*, yes—but not here. The roads are far too empty. An unfamiliar vehicle parked for any length of time would be painfully conspicuous. Don't you agree?

BOB. (*Reluctantly.*) Well, yes . . .

BARBARA. Why don't you try Helen and Peter at number forty-five? They've got a much better view than we have.

STEWART. I'm afraid we can't go from house to house trying to find the best view. Apart from anything else, we have to make sure that the people we go to are people we can trust—and it takes quite a bit of time to do that.

BOB. To do what?

STEWART. To make the necessary enquiries.

BOB. You mean you've had us screened?

STEWART. We checked. (*A small smile.*) Better to be safe than sorry, after all. And since you're working on classified material at AirSpeed Research, we already knew something about you.

(*Brief pause,* BOB *is shaken to learn that he has been the subject of a security check; he looks at* BARBARA *and then back to* STEWART.)

BOB. I see. So it's really important, then . . . ?

STEWART. We think it might be, yes.

BOB. What about . . . I mean—would it be dangerous?

STEWART. Dangerous . . . ?

BOB. Well, presumably this man's committed a crime of some sort.

STEWART. He's not a thug, if that's what you mean. There's no danger of any physical violence.

BOB. But he is a criminal . . . ?

STEWART. Let's say we have every reason to believe that he's involved in some kind of illegal activity. (BOB *turns to* BARBARA.)

BOB. What do you think?

BARBARA. It's up to you. (BOB *hesitates for a moment; he then turns to* STEWART *and nods his approval.*)

BOB. All right, then. (*To* BARBARA.) All right?

BARBARA. (*With a nod.*) All right.

STEWART. (*He smiles delightedly.*) Thank you—thank you very much indeed. (*Turning to* BARBARA.) Would half-past nine tomorrow be convenient?

BARBARA. What for?

STEWART. For my girl to arrive.

BARBARA. Oh yes . . . yes, that'll be fine.

STEWART. I think it might be a good idea if she came in through the back garden, it's well hidden from the road and she could use the kitchen door, couldn't she? Would that be all right?

BARBARA. I suppose so.

STEWART. Her name's Thelma by the way, I think you'll like her.

(*They all exit. Lights fade.* THELMA *enters and addresses the audience: she is in her late twenties, a sturdily built ex-regular army girl; she wears a sweater and slacks.*)

THELMA. I noticed that everything had been tidied away; the furniture smelt of lavender polish and there was a vase of fresh flowers on the hall table; it was as if the house had been put on its best behaviour. I went upstairs, to the daughter's bedroom. There was a half-empty mug of coffee, still warm, on the bedside table. On the chest-of-drawers, a tin of Max Factor talcum powder stood beside a bottle of perfume, shaped like a cat. Holiday postcards from friends were stuck around the mirror. There was a portable gramophone and some records: Roy Orbison and the Everly Brothers. She was reading *Wuthering Heights*. I could hear the Jacksons moving and talking downstairs. They were talking quietly because there was a stranger in the house. (*Brief pause.*) The day passed uneventfully, and when I left, at half-past five, Mrs. Jackson asked me if I had been comfortable.

I couldn't help smiling. Surveillance jobs usually mean spending hours, if not days, in cold empty rooms—or, worse, crouched in the back of a van. "Yes, thanks," I said, "Very nice," I said, "very comfortable."

(THELMA *exits. Lights up. Evening.* BARBARA *and* BOB *are seated in armchairs in the sitting-room.* BARBARA *is sewing;* BOB *is reading a newspaper. The electric fire casts a cosy glow across the hearth. Pause.* BOB *yawns and turns a page of his newspaper.*)

BARBARA. I wonder where he is?

BOB. (*Without looking up.*) Who?

BARBARA. The man they're looking for. (*No response; brief pause.*) I wonder what he's doing tonight? (*Pause;* BARBARA *raises her head and looks at* BOB.) Perhaps he's married. Do you think he is?

BOB. Stop worrying.

BARBARA. I'm not worrying.

BOB. (*Lightly.*) You could've fooled me. (*Pause.*)

BARBARA. We don't know anything about him. Nothing. We don't even know what he's done.

BOB. We don't need to.

BARBARA. Because of us he might be arrested. Just think of that. We ought to know something. (BOB *lowers his newspaper.*)

BOB. Because of *us* . . . ?

BARBARA. Because we let them watch. (BOB *grins.*)

BOB. Trust you to say a thing like that.

BARBARA. Like what?

BOB. Trust you to find a way of blaming yourself. Doesn't matter what it is, does it? If there's a hole in my sock, if the car breaks down—it's always your fault. Well, this isn't. (BARBARA *looks at him, but says nothing.*) So stop worrying. (BARBARA *nods her head, but her expression remains troubled and anxious.*) Do you fancy a cup of tea?

BARBARA. Do you?

BOB. I don't mind.

BARBARA. A bit later, then.

BOB. Right. (BOB *stands up, stretches, strolls to the window, and draws the curtains. He glances across the road.*) It looks as if Helen and Peter are having an early night. Off for a bit of—what does she call it?—off for a bit of nooky. (BARBARA *smiles, but remains silent.* BOB *goes back to his chair.*) I just can't imagine it, can you?

BARBARA. What?

BOB. All these wild nights we hear so much about. I can't imagine them actually performing.

BARBARA. Oh, I don't know. Peter's quite attractive. (BOB *glances at* BARBARA, *mildly surprised.*)

BOB. Is he?

BARBARA. Well, not unattractive. (BOB *grins.*)

BOB. God, the idea of waking up alongside Dizzy Lizzie—the mind boggles! (BARBARA *smiles.* BOB *resumes reading his newspaper;* BARBARA *sews; a clock strikes the half hour;* BOB *turns a page of his newspaper.*)

BARBARA. Do you remember that time we saw a man being arrested outside the bus station?

BOB. What man?

BARBARA. Don't you remember?

BOB. Who . . . ?

BARBARA. We were going somewhere, the three of us—Julie was quite small—and we saw these policemen running into the bus station. Then they grabbed a man and took him away. Don't you remember? His clothes were all stained and dirty. I thought he was old at first, an old tramp or something, but when he walked past I could see he was young—younger than me. And he was crying. Don't you remember? I thought it was so sad. He wasn't just crying, he was sobbing. It was awful. (BOB *stares at* BARBARA; *there is a moment of silence before he speaks.*)

BOB. What am I supposed to say to that?

BARBARA. I don't know.

BOB. What?

BARBARA. (*She shrugs.*) Nothing.

BOB. He might have bashed some old lady over the head and pinched her handbag. Supposing he had. How would you feel about him then?

BARBARA. People don't stop being people just because they've done something wrong. They still have feelings.

BOB. (*Firmly.*) Look—it's nothing to do with us, none of it. Mr. Stewart says this man's mixed up with something criminal, something illegal—well, fine, that's all we need to know. Who he is and what he's done just doesn't matter. It's none of our business. (*No response.*) Well, is it?

BARBARA. I don't know.

BOB. Well, it isn't. Take it from me. (*Again he opens his newspaper;* BARBARA *sews; pause.*) Is it the same girl coming back tomorrow?

BARBARA. Yes.

BOB. Thelma.

BARBARA. Thelma, yes.

BOB. She seems quite nice. (*He turns a page of his newspaper.*) Must be a bit boring, sitting upstairs all day. (*He glances at* BARBARA.) Still, just think; this time tomorrow, it'll all be over. She'll have gone.

(*Lights fade.* BARBARA *walks DS, and addresses the audience.*)

BARBARA. Sunday—a really beautiful morning, almost summery, not a cloud in the sky. It must have been about eleven o'clock when Bob and Julie went out to wash the car—well, not quite eleven, the church bells were still ringing. I love the sound of church bells on Sunday mornings. I'd got a shoulder of lamb for lunch and I'd just finished doing the vegetables when Thelma came down for a cup of coffee. We went into the sitting room and stood there, by the window. I thought how friendly she was—not at all what I imagined a police girl would be like. Then Julie came in for some clean water and told us about her friend Maureen Chapman—apparently there's been some sort of domestic disaster: she'd let the bath overflow and the hall ceiling needed redecorating—Julie asked if she could go round after lunch and help, and of course I said yes. Thelma and I were both talking, laughing, saying what a mess it must have been, when Thelma suddenly looked out of the window. I looked out too, I don't know why, I just did. Helen's front door was open and somebody was coming out of the house. It was a man. I'd never seen him before. He didn't look round to say goodbye, he just hurried to the gate and went off along the road. He had disappeared before I realised who it was. Thelma turned to me and said, "Did you see what I saw?" I couldn't speak. I just nodded. It was the man in the photograph, the man Mr. Stewart was looking for. Thelma went to make a phone call. I just stood there, by the window. I could hear Julie laughing and talking as she cleaned the car. The church bells were still ringing. Although I didn't know what it meant, I felt sure something terrible had happened. Then Thelma came back. "Mr. Stewart's coming to see you this afternoon," she said, "it's very important. Don't tell Julie." (*Brief pause.*) Somehow I forced myself to eat some lunch. The meat kept turning and turning in my mouth. I couldn't swallow. When Julie went off to paint Maureen's ceiling, I told Bob what had happened. He gave me a hug. "Don't worry," he said, "there's nothing to worry about." But as he held me in his arms, I could feel his hands trembling.

(*Lights up. Afternoon.* BARBARA *walks directly into the sitting room, where* BOB *and* STEWART *are awaiting.*)

STEWART. You actually saw this man yourself, Mrs. Jackson?

BARBARA. Yes, I did.

STEWART. You saw him come out of number forty-five Cranley Drive and hurry away along this road?

BARBARA. Yes.

STEWART. And you're quite sure it was the same man—the man whose photograph I showed you?

BARBARA. Yes, oh yes.

STEWART. Yes, I see. (*He turns to* BOB.) Well, it seems you missed all the excitement, Mr. Jackson. You were cleaning your car, I believe?

BOB. Yes.

STEWART. Just here, in front of your house?

BOB. Yes.

STEWART. Yes, well . . . you can see how easy it is for him to come and go without being observed. Amazing, isn't it? (*No response;* STEWART *strolls across the room.*) He must have arrived in Ruislip yesterday lunchtime; that's when his car was seen, anyway. Saturday lunchtime to Sunday morning. Presumably he spent the night with these friends of yours. (*Brief pause;* STEWART *turns to* BOB.) Have you told your daughter about any of this?

BOB. No.

STEWART. Good, that's probably just as well. Don't tell her—for the time being, at any rate. Where is she?

BARBARA. Out with some friends.

STEWART. Oh good. (*He takes a cigarette pack from his jacket pocket.*) Do you mind if I . . . ?

BOB. No no, please do.

STEWART. Thank you. Well, what a surprise. It must have been quite a surprise for you, Mrs. Jackson; something of a bolt out of the blue, I should imagine. (*No response.*) He was on his way to fetch his car when you saw him. He always parks it in the same place: outside that block of flats—what's it called? That block of flats in the next street.

BARBARA. Ruislip Court.

STEWART. Yes, Ruislip Court. He always parks it there. It's an unusual car, you may have seen it: a white Studebaker Farina, licence number ULA 61. Does that ring any bells? (BARBARA *shakes her head.*)

BOB. No, sorry.

STEWART. No, well, never mind. (*A small smile.*) I can't imagine why he chose a flashy job like that; singularly inappropriate in his line of business.

BOB. What is that?

STEWART. What?

BOB. What is his line of business? (STEWART *hesitates.*) Can't you tell us what he's done?

STEWART. Well, we're not entirely sure. We think he may have entered the country illegally. (*Pause.*)

BARBARA. What does that mean?

STEWART. What?

BARBARA. I don't understand what you mean.

STEWART. We think he may have entered this country with a false passport and under an assumed name, Gordon Lonsdale. (*Brief pause;* BARBARA *and* BOB *are both looking at* STEWART, *clearly waiting for him to say more.*) It's difficult to be absolutely sure. We'll need to make a few more enquiries. It's early days yet.

BARBARA. Yes, but what's he actually done? Why won't you tell us? (STEWART *turns and looks directly at* BARBARA.)

STEWART. We think he may be working—covertly— for a foreign government.

BOB. Covertly . . . ?

STEWART. Secretly.

BOB. You mean he's a spy . . . ?

STEWART. Well, something of that sort—but I'd rather not jump to conclusions until we know a little more.

BOB. (*Almost laughing.*) But what would a spy be doing in Peter's house?

STEWART. Well, quite . . .

BOB. There must be some mistake.

BARBARA. Shouldn't we tell them? Shouldn't we warn them?

STEWART. All in good time, Mrs. Jackson.

BOB. Oh, come on, you're not suggesting that they're involved with this man, are you? (STEWART *responds with an ambiguous shrug.*)

BARBARA. Oh no—not Helen and Peter—they wouldn't do a thing like that.

STEWART. Maybe not.

BARBARA. But we've known them for years, Mr. Stewart—five years!

STEWART. Yes, so you said.

BARBARA. Oh, but look . . . how can you even think such a thing? He must be just a casual friend.

BOB. A business friend.

BARBARA. Yes, another bookseller—something like that.

STEWART. Well, possibly. (*Silence.* BOB *rises to his feet.*)

BOB. I think I'll have a drink. Barbara? Sir? (*She shakes her head.*)

STEWART. No, thank you. (BOB *pours a neat scotch for himself. Pause.*) So your friends have never spoken about this Mr. Lonsdale?

BOB. No, never.

BARBARA. Never.

STEWART. That's a bit strange, don't you think?

BOB. Why strange?

STEWART. A man who comes to see them almost every weekend . . . you'd have thought they would have mentioned his name at the very least. (*Brief pause.*) Wouldn't you have thought so, Mrs. Jackson?

BARBARA. I don't know . . .

STEWART. You may be right, of course, he may be just a casual friend, but he's not a bookseller—that's for sure. He's director of a firm called Allo Security Products Limited; they make anti-burglar devices for cars. A bit of a man-about-town, too—ritzy flat near Regent's Park, plenty of girlfriends—not at all the sort you'd expect to get pally with the Krogers. (BARBARA *stares at* STEWART; *vague suspicions are beginning to form in her mind.*)

BARBARA. You seem to know an awful lot about him.

STEWART. Not enough, alas.

BARBARA. Are you sure you didn't know where to find him?

STEWART. (*He glances sharply at* BARBARA.) How do you mean?

BARBARA. It seems very lucky choosing our house. Right opposite Helen and Peter's. I mean—that seems almost too good to be true.

STEWART. (*With an easy smile.*) These things do happen, Mrs. Jackson. We all deserve a little luck from time to time. (BARBARA *makes no response.* STEWART *strolls across the room and sits facing her.*) At the risk of sounding rather unfriendly, it's my duty to draw your attention to the Official Secrets Act. We're all bound by it, you know, as we're bound by any other law. I'd intended to bring the Declaration along for you both to sign—but what with one thing and another, I quite forgot. Not that it matters really. The signing of the Act is just a way, the customary way, of reminding you of its existence and its importance. (*A smile.*) Legal red tape. And we get plenty of that in my job, I can tell you. (*Brief pause.*) All we're asking for is discretion: sensible, reasonable discretion. All right? (BARBARA *and* BOB *nod their heads.* STEWART *grins and rises to his feet.*) Good! Well, now . . . tell me about the Krogers.

BOB. Tell you what?

STEWART. Anything. What sort of people are they?

BOB. They're damn good neighbours.

STEWART. Yes, but what do you know about them? Where did they live before they came here?

BOB. South London. Catford, I think.

STEWART. And you said they're Canadians . . . ?

BARBARA. Yes.

STEWART. Canadians—not Americans?

BARBARA. Oh no—Helen's most particular about that. I remember once somebody introduced them as an

American couple and Helen got really angry: "Canadian," she said, "not American—Canadian!" She almost shouted it.

STEWART. Whereabouts in Canada do they come from? Do you know?

BOB. No.

STEWART. No idea at all?

BOB. Helen was brought up in the country somewhere.

BARBARA. She's always telling Julie stories about her life on the farm.

STEWART. What sort of stories?

BOB. How she could climb trees better than any of the boys.

BARBARA. Chop wood.

BOB. Ride horses, that sort of thing, you know.

STEWART. (*He smiles.*) So she was a real tom-boy.

BARBARA. (*Also smiling.*) She still is. Mind you, I'm never quite sure how much of it to believe.

STEWART. Ah. (*The smile fades from* BARBARA'S *face as she realises the possible significance of her last remark.*)

BARBARA. Well . . . they're just stories she tells Julie. She probably exaggerates a bit.

STEWART. Yes. (*Brief pause.*) What about Peter Kroger? What sort of a person is he?

BOB. Very different from Helen.

BARBARA. Completely different.

BOB. A marriage of opposites, we always say.

BARBARA. He's very quiet. Bookish, you know.

BOB. Intellectual.

BARBARA. Yes, he's an intellectual.

STEWART. And where's his bookshop—in London?

BOB. He used to have a shop in the Strand, but now it's a mail-order business. He sends out lists and works from home.

STEWART. Uh-huh. And you'd say that they're happy—it's a happy marriage?

BOB. Oh, very.

BARBARA. Very happy.

STEWART. Yes, I see. (BARBARA *bows her head, fighting back tears.*)

BARBARA. I do hate talking about them like this.

STEWART. Yes, I'm sorry. It's a most unpleasant situation, I know. Rotten luck. (*Pause.* BOB *rests a comforting hand on* BARBARA'S *shoulder.*)

BOB. What happens now?

STEWART. Well, obviously it's in everybody's best interest to get to the bottom of, uh . . . well, whatever's going on. We have to find out what this fellow Lonsdale's up to. That's very important.

BOB. Yes.

STEWART. Crucially important.

BOB. Yes.

STEWART. Likewise your friends, the Krogers: Are they involved with him or are they not? (*Brief pause.*) All of which means, alas, that we'll have to trespass upon your hospitality for just a few more days.

BARBARA. (*Her head jerks up.*) What?

STEWART. The point is this: We think Lonsdale may be in a spot of trouble. He's had a few business problems just recently—money problems—and this could make him do something rash, reckless. If he does, we want to know about it. And that means keeping an eye on things. And that means keeping somebody here in this house— as from tomorrow, if that's possible.

BARBARA. (*Aghast.*) You mean—

BOB. (*Overlapping.*) Tomorrow? Why tomorrow? I thought he only came here at weekends.

STEWART. We can't be sure. Things might change.

BARBARA. You mean you want to keep somebody here every day?

STEWART. Just for a week or so.

BARBARA. (*Incredulous.*) Every day . . . ?

STEWART. Well, yes.

BARBARA. Oh, but you can't expect us to do that— it's out of the question.

STEWART. We'd disturb you as little as possible . . .

BARBARA. No, I'm sorry.

STEWART. . . . and I wouldn't ask if it wasn't really necessary.

BOB. Yes, but look—

BARBARA. What about Julie? What about her homework?

BOB. Yes.

STEWART. No problem there. It gets dark at—what?— four-thirty, five—no point us staying after that.

BARBARA. Yes, but think how she'll *feel*; she'll be so upset.

STEWART. Upset . . . ?

BARBARA. Because of Helen and Peter; she's very fond of them.

BOB. She loves them.

BARBARA. She does.

STEWART. Well, there's no need to worry her with any of this.

BOB. We'll have to tell her something.

STEWART. Say it's just a routine investigation—there's no need to go into details.

BARBARA. She won't believe that.

STEWART. Why not? Children accept things very easily.

BARBARA. She's not a child.

BOB. There must be an easier way of finding out.

STEWART. I only wish there were.

BOB. Why don't you just go across and ask them?

STEWART. You mean the Krogers?

BOB. Yes.

STEWART. Ask them what?

BOB. Ask them what they know about this man—what he was doing there this morning.

STEWART. Supposing they're involved with him in some way?

BARBARA. Oh, but they're not. I know they're not.

STEWART. Supposing they are . . .

BARBARA. They're not.

STEWART. Just suppose. We can't afford to take the risk. (*Brief pause.*) Well, can we?

BARBARA. You've obviously decided what you're going to do, so why bother to ask us?

STEWART. Try to look at it from my point of view, Mrs. Jackson. Lonsdale was seen coming out of their house. That's bound to create a certain amount of suspicion. It's bound to. We can't ignore it. We can't pretend it never happened. We have to act accordingly. We have to. (*Pause.*)

BOB. So what are you saying? What are you suggesting?

STEWART. Only that the present arrangement should continue . . . for a week or so. That's all. Nothing more.

BARBARA. I don't think you understand, Mr. Stewart.

Helen and Peter are our best friends. We see them every day.

STEWART. Yes, I know.

BARBARA. Helen, especially. She's always popping in.

STEWART. Yes, I know.

BARBARA. Well, you can't expect me to talk to her and have cups of tea with her when I know there's somebody spying on her from Julie's bedroom. I can't do that. I can't. Well, I won't. I'm sorry.

STEWART. Perhaps you could try . . . just for a day or two.

BARBARA. Why should I? (*Always the peacemaker,* BOB *recognises a bellicose tone in* BARBARA'S *voice; he turns pacifically to* STEWART.)

BOB. It's asking a hell of a lot, you know.

STEWART. (*Quietly.*) I'm afraid I must insist.

BOB. *Insist* . . . ?

STEWART. Earnestly implore.

BARBARA. Oh, it's just not fair, Mr. Stewart.

STEWART. It's not, I agree—but being fair has a pretty low priority at the moment. (*Pause.*) I really am very sorry. (*Pause.*)

BOB. Would it be the same girl?

STEWART. Well, yes, I thought so. There might have to be another one—just to give Thelma a bit of a rest. It can be quite tiring, you know, peering out of a window all day long. You'd be surprised. We'll have a separate telephone line installed upstairs. No bell, of course, just a little red light—so it shouldn't be too irksome for you. (BOB *takes a deep breath; he turns to* BARBARA.)

BOB. What do you think?

BARBARA. (*Tersely.*) You know what I think. (BOB *sighs. Brief pause.*)

BOB. Well, if it's only a week . . . (*He nods his head, giving reluctant consent.*)

STEWART. Thank you, Mr. Jackson. (*He turns to* BARBARA.) I find this part of my job very painful and unpleasant. Unfortunately—it has to be done.

BARBARA. You're wrong about Helen and Peter. It's nothing to do with them.

STEWART. Time alone will tell.

BARBARA. They've been such good friends, such close friends . . .

STEWART. And you think you'd have guessed?

BARBARA. We'd have guessed something—instinctively.

STEWART. Mrs. Jackson, people like Lonsdale and his colleagues spend their lives deceiving people like you. It's their job, their profession, and they do it with the utmost skill and conviction. If they didn't, they'd be finished.

(*The front door opens and* JULIE *enters. She is wearing a raincoat over her paint-spattered sweater and slacks.*)

JULIE. (*Calling as she enters.*) Mum!

BOB. In here, Julie. (JULIE *takes off her raincoat as she enters the sitting-room.*)

JULIE. Oh, hello, Mr. Stewart. (STEWART *rises to his feet.*)

BARBARA. (*Before* STEWART *has a chance to respond.*) You're covered in paint! *Covered!*

JULIE. I know, I know. I'm going to have a bath. (*To* STEWART.) I've been painting a ceiling and it kept dripping down. (*Turning to leave.*) Any sign of that man?

BOB. (*Hastily interposing.*) Julie, listen—there's been a change of plan. Thelma's not going after all.

JULIE. Oh, good.

STEWART. She'll only be here in the daytime, of course—so perhaps you wouldn't mind if she invaded your bedroom again?

JULIE. No, that's fine.

BOB. And you mustn't tell anyone.

JULIE. I know.

BOB. It's important, Julie—not anyone.

JULIE. I know! (*Smiling at* STEWART.) Don't worry, Mr. Stewart, I won't breathe a word.

STEWART. (*With a smile.*) No, I'm sure you won't.

JULIE. Bye, then. (JULIE *exits and goes upstairs. Pause.*)

STEWART. Well, there's nothing more to say, is there? (*Turning to* BOB.) If you have any problems, just telephone Superintendent Smith at Scotland Yard.

BOB. Right. (STEWART *turns to* BARBARA.)

STEWART. Thank you again, Mrs. Jackson. I'll do everything I can to make our presence here as unobtrusive as possible.

(STEWART *goes to the hall;* BOB *follows.* BARBARA *remains motionless for a moment; she then walks across the room and draws the curtains. She switches on the light.* BOB *and* STEWART *are shaking hands in the hall.* STEWART *goes out.* BOB *closes the front door and returns to the sitting-room;* BARBARA *turns and glares at him.*)

BOB. Don't blame me.

BARBARA. I don't want those people here. I don't want them in the house!

BOB. Be reasonable. There was nothing I could do.

BARBARA. You could have said no, couldn't you?

BOB. Well, hardly.

BARBARA. You're always the same with people like that.

BOB. Like what?

BARBARA. You know what I mean—like a schoolboy in front of the headmaster.

BOB. Look, there's no point in—

BARBARA. I just don't want to talk about it, Bob. I don't want anything to do with it! (BARBARA *turns from him and paces across the room.*) What about Julie?

BOB. What about her?

BARBARA. What are we going to say to her?

BOB. Well, nothing—I mean . . .

BARBARA. What?

BOB. Well . . .

BARBARA. Doesn't it worry you that we're deceiving her like this?

BOB. We're not deceiving her.

BARBARA. We're not telling her the truth. You heard him tell us just now, "Don't tell Julie." Doesn't that make you feel *sick*? (*Pause.* BARBARA *and* BOB *stand facing each other.*)

BOB. Look—there was nothing we could do.

BARBARA. Of course there was.

BOB. We couldn't say no.

BARBARA. Why not?

BOB. Well, suppose he's right . . .

BARBARA. Right about what?

BOB. Helen and Peter knowing this man.

BARBARA. Oh, for heaven's sake . . . !

BOB. It's possible—I mean it's possible.

BARBARA. Don't be ridiculous.

BOB. You just think about it.

BARBARA. Don't be ridiculous.

BOB. When have we ever seen them on a Saturday or Sunday? When? You just think about it.

BARBARA. Dozens of times.

BOB. Not once.

BARBARA. What about that trip to the zoo?

BOB. What trip?

BARBARA. When was it? Two or three months ago.

BOB. That was August Bank Holiday Monday. We never see them at weekends—never.

BARBARA. Of course we do.

BOB. Never.

BARBARA. Oh, that's just—

BOB. What?

BARBARA. Nonsense.

BOB. Is it?

BARBARA. You know it is.

(*The telephone rings.* BOB *turns from* BARBARA; *he goes to the hall and answers the telephone.*)

BOB. (*On telephone.*) Hello? . . . Oh, hello, Maureen—just a minute . . . (*He calls upstairs.*) Julie! It's for you!

JULIE. (*Off.*) Who is it?

BOB. Maureen.

JULIE. (*Off.*) I'm getting changed. I'll ring back later.

BOB. (*On telephone.*) Did you hear that? She'll ring later . . . Right . . . Right . . . Yes, all right—bye-bye. (BOB *replaces the receiver. He returns to the sitting-room.* BARBARA *has not moved. They stand facing each other. Pause.*) Shall I ring up and say we've changed our minds? I'll ring that man at Scotland Yard, shall I? Would you like me to do that? Shall I?

BARBARA. It's too late.

BOB. Why? Why, what do you mean?

BARBARA. You know what I mean.

(BARBARA *walks past him and exits to the kitchen. Lights fade.* BOB *exits.* BARBARA *exits through the back door. Lights up. Day. Music from the kitchen radio.* BAR-

BARA *enters from the garden, carrying some vegetables. She is wearing an apron. The front doorbell rings. BARBARA reacts with a degree of alarm. She puts the vegetables on the kitchen table and switches off the radio. The doorbell rings again. BARBARA goes quickly, almost on tip-toe, to the sitting-room. She peers round the edge of the curtains. She springs back. She stands tense and motionless by the window. The doorbell rings again. BARBARA can delay no longer; she walks to the hall and opens the front door. HELEN enters; she is wearing outdoor clothes and carries a shopping basket. PETER follows behind.)*

HELEN. Jesus, you were a long time.

BARBARA. Sorry, sorry.

HELEN. We thought you must be out.

BARBARA. No, I . . .

HELEN. Weren't in the john, were you?

BARBARA. No . . .

HELEN. (*As she walks to the sitting-room.*) If there's one thing I hate, it's being hauled out of the john in the middle of it. (BARBARA *closes the front door.*)

PETER. How are you, Barbara?

BARBARA. I'm just about to do some painting.

PETER. We're not staying, don't worry. We're just—

HELEN. (*Overlapping.*) We're going up to town. Is there anything you want? (*She catches sight of the easel.*) Hey—how's the easel?

BARBARA. What?

HELEN. The easel—is it okay?

BARBARA. Oh yes. Yes, it's fine.

HELEN. If it's not, you just say and I'll take it back.

BARBARA. No, it's fine, I love it.

HELEN. The guy in the store said he'd change it if you didn't like it.

PETER. (*To* HELEN.) She says it's fine, she loves it, what more can she say? (*Going to the door.*) Come on, let's leave the girl in peace.

HELEN. What's the hurry?

PETER. The whole idea was to get up to town before the crowds, remember?

HELEN. Okay, okay.

PETER. (*To* BARBARA.) We're making an early start

on the Christmas shopping. Helen's got a list a mile long.
(*To* HELEN.) Show her.

HELEN. Show her . . . ?

PETER. Show her the list.

HELEN. You've got it. I gave it to you.

PETER. You didn't.

HELEN. In the kitchen—you were putting your coat on.

PETER. You put it in your purse.

HELEN. I did what?

PETER. Didn't you?

HELEN. (*Suddenly remembering.*) I left it on the kitchen table—Jesus!

PETER. Are you sure?

HELEN. Sure I'm sure—it's on the goddam table.

PETER. (*He grins.*) Okay, I'll go get it. (*To* HELEN, *as he goes to the hall.*) And I want you outside, in the car, ready to go, in five minutes—okay?

HELEN. Okay.

PETER. (*To* BARBARA.) Take care of yourself, Barbara.

BARBARA. You too. (PETER *exits.*)

HELEN. Just imagine going up to town and forgetting your goddam shopping list! Jeeze, I must be going out of my mind. (BARBARA, *ill-at-ease, manages a small smile.* HELEN *watches as* BARBARA *prepares to start painting.*) So who's the mystery man, huh? And don't pretend you don't know what I'm talking about.

BARBARA. What?

HELEN. Yesterday afternoon—about four o'clock—I saw some guy walking across the street. It looked like he was coming from here.

BARBARA. Well, yes, he was.

HELEN. Aha! It's lucky I knew your old man was at home, otherwise I might have gotten very suspicious indeed. Who is he?

BARBARA. Oh—just a friend of Bob's.

HELEN. Yeah, I thought so. Didn't I see him at your wedding anniversary?

BARBARA. No, that was somebody else.

HELEN. Are you sure?

BARBARA. Quite sure.

HELEN. Gee, that's funny. I could have sworn he was the guy Bob introduced me to. What's his name?

BARBARA. Um . . . Stewart.

HELEN. Stewart?

BARBARA. He's never been here before, so you can't have met him.

HELEN. Okay, if you say so. (HELEN *strolls to the door*.) Now, look, about this Christmas shopping—what do you think Julie would like?

BARBARA. Oh, look, you mustn't bother . . .

HELEN. What do you mean—bother? It's no bother. I love buying her presents. It gives me pleasure. She's always so appreciative. I was wondering about a blouse. Do you think she'd like that? A silk blouse.

BARBARA. Well, yes, that would be lovely, but you mustn't be too extravagant.

HELEN. Why not, for heaven's sake? There's nothing I enjoy more than real sinful extravagance. (*She winks playfully*.) Born to be bad, that's me. (*She kisses* BARBARA *on the cheek*.) I'd better go, I'll see you later, honey. (*Going to the door*.) Do you want anything from the shops?

BARBARA. (*Suddenly, impulsively*.) Helen—(HELEN *pauses, looking back at* BARBARA.) We're thinking of having a few friends in for a drink on Saturday evening. Would you and Peter like to come?

HELEN. Oh, we can't this Saturday. What a shame.

BARBARA. Well, we'll change it. We'll make it next Saturday. Saturday a week.

HELEN. Saturday's always difficult for us. I'd better say no. Peter likes to do his accounts at the weekend. You know that. We told you. (*She smiles*.) Thanks for asking. Ciao! (HELEN *exits*. BARBARA *remains motionless*.)

END OF ACT I

ACT II

(Lights up. Day. The back door opens and THELMA *enters from the garden; she is wearing a crash helmet, goggles, a waterproof cape, and leggings.)*

THELMA. Mrs. Jackson? It's me. Sally?

*(*SALLY *walks down the stairs. She is about thirty; pleasant, but rather plain; middle-class. She wears a sweater, skirt and raincoat; she is carrying an umbrella. She goes to the kitchen.)*

SALLY. You're late.

THELMA. I know, sorry. There's been an accident on the Western Avenue and the traffic's murder. *(She takes off her motorcycling gear.)* What about that rain—did you see it? I really thought the end of the world had come.

SALLY. That motorbike of yours makes a hell of a noise. Are you sure Mr. Stewart said you could bring it?

THELMA. Of course—why not? There are dozens of motorbikes around here. You don't think the Krogers are going to notice one extra, do you? *(Looking around.)* Where's Mrs. Jackson?

SALLY. Out shopping.

THELMA. Poor thing. I hope she didn't get caught in that storm. *(She drapes her cape and leggings over a chair.)* God, I'm dying for a cup of tea. How about you?

SALLY. No, thanks. I've just had one. *(*THELMA *goes to the sink and fills the electric kettle.)*

THELMA. Look, don't worry—I always park the bike round the corner. I park it somewhere different every day—and never outside the house. *(Switching on the kettle.)* So what's been happening this morning?

SALLY. Nothing much—just routine comings and goings.

THELMA. As per usual. *(She yawns.)* It's going to be a long job, this one.

SALLY. Do you think so?

THELMA. Don't you?

SALLY. (*She shrugs.*) I don't know.

THELMA. Oh yes—this is a biggie. I can smell it. (*Spooning tea into the pot.*) Mr. Stewart went to the American Embassy yesterday—twice.

SALLY. How do you know?

THELMA. Sylvia told me. She went out with Bill last night. He was duty driver yesterday, and he told her. Twice in a day! That must mean it's a biggie. (THELMA *takes a bottle of milk from the fridge and puts it on the table.*)

SALLY. Don't leave the milk there. You'll have Mrs. Jackson tut-tutting you.

THELMA. (*Not understanding.*) Why?

SALLY. She always puts milk in a jug, haven't you noticed? She obviously thinks milk in bottles is common. (THELMA *makes no response; she takes a jug from a cupboard and pours the milk into it.* SALLY *watches.*) Can you imagine what her life must be like? Dusting and washing and ironing and polishing and cooking. God. No wonder she's as dull as she is.

THELMA. I like her. (SALLY *looks at her.*)

SALLY. Yes, you do, don't you? (*She buttons her raincoat.*) She thinks we're going at the end of the week.

THELMA. Did she say so?

SALLY. Sort of. She keeps dropping hints.

THELMA. Like what?

SALLY. "It'll seem strange without you next week," that sort of thing, you know.

THELMA. What did you say?

SALLY. Well, nothing. What could I say? (THELMA *sighs, but says nothing; she is standing by the window, waiting for the kettle to boil.*) Right, then—I'll be off.

THELMA. Right. (SALLY *goes to the back door.*)

THELMA. Clark Gable died.

SALLY. Yes, I heard it on the radio.

THELMA. I think it's really sad, don't you? No more Clark Gable. Gone forever. (*The front door opens.* SALLY *and* THELMA *swing round, suddenly alert.* BARBARA *enters; she is wearing a raincoat and carrying shopping bags.*) Mrs. Jackson?

BARBARA. (*Closing the front door.*) Hello.

SALLY. Let me give you a hand.

BARBARA. What a dreadful morning! Did you see that rain?

SALLY. Wasn't it awful?

THELMA. I thought the end of the world had come.

SALLY. At least you didn't get too wet.

BARBARA. No, I was lucky. (*To* THELMA, *who is making the tea.*) Pour me a cup, would you, Thelma? (*Putting the shopping bags on the table.*) Those bags weigh a ton.

SALLY. Is it raining now?

BARBARA. Not really—but there's more on the way, by the look of it.

SALLY. I'd better go. (*To* THELMA, *as she goes to the back door.*) I'll see you tomorrow.

THELMA. It's Pat tomorrow—I don't come back till Saturday.

SALLY. Okay, I'll see you then. Bye, Mrs. Jackson.

BARBARA. Bye, Sally.

THELMA. Bye. (SALLY *exits.*)

BARBARA. She's a nice girl.

THELMA. (*Pouring the tea.*) Milk and two sugars?

BARBARA. Yes, please. (*She starts to unload the shopping.*) I got some sausages for lunch. Do you like sausages?

THELMA. I love them—but you really must stop cooking all these meals for us.

BARBARA. I'd hardly call sausages a meal.

THELMA. Mr. Stewart would be furious if he knew.

BARBARA. Don't tell him, then.

THELMA. (*Grinning.*) Don't worry, I won't. (BARBARA *takes some tins of food to the store cupboard.*)

THELMA. (*Giving a cup of tea to* BARBARA.) Here . . .

BARBARA. Thanks. (BARBARA *and* THELMA *sip their tea. Pause.*)

THELMA. Clark Gable died, did you know?

BARBARA. Yes. What was it—a heart attack or something?

THELMA. Yes, I think so. Sad isn't it. (*Pause.*) Mind you, he wasn't as good as Gregory Peck. Or Richard Burton. I think he's wonderful. Did you see him on TV the other night?

BARBARA. No.

THELMA. He was wonderful. Those eyes. That voice.

(*The front doorbell rings. Silently, furtively,* THELMA *gathers together her motorcycling gear and hurries up-*

stairs. BARBARA *waits, tense, until the coast is clear. Then she goes to the front door and opens it.* HELEN *enters.*)

HELEN. Hi, honey, how are you?

BARBARA. Helen . . .

HELEN. I've brought this tin back. (*She displays the cake-tin she is carrying, and walks to the kitchen.*)

BARBARA. Oh yes . . . thanks. (BARBARA *closes the front door and follows* HELEN.)

HELEN. Those little cookies were deelicious, Barbara. So light and crisp—yummy! How do you do it?

BARBARA. Oh—just a knack.

HELEN. Some knack. (*She turns, smiling, to* BARBARA.) So how's life? Is everything okay?

BARBARA. Yes, fine.

HELEN. How's Julie? I haven't seen her for ages.

BARBARA. She's fine—um . . . working hard.

HELEN. Come to that, I haven't seen you either. You gave me those cookies on Monday, and here we are—it's Thursday. (*Mock-accusingly.*) Have you been avoiding me, Barbara?

BARBARA. (*A stab of alarm.*) Have I what?

HELEN. A joke, dear—I was joking.

BARBARA. Sorry, I didn't hear what you said.

HELEN. You're not mad at me, are you?

BARBARA. What?

HELEN. Well, are you?

BARBARA. No no, of course not. I've been a bit busy, that's all.

HELEN. Busy doing what?

BARBARA. Oh, nothing much.

HELEN. Busy doing nothing much . . . ?

BARBARA. Well, you know how it is.

HELEN. (*Lightly.*) No, I don't. I'm beginning to feel like a girl in the bad breath commercial. (*She smiles; no response from* BARBARA.) How's the dress coming along?

BARBARA. The dress . . . ?

HELEN. My party dress.

BARBARA. Almost finished. Ready next week.

HELEN. Terrific! (*Glancing at the empty mugs on the table.*) Hey, what's all this?

BARBARA. What's all what?

HELEN. Two mugs of tea on the kitchen table. Don't tell me you've got a lover hiding away upstairs.

BARBARA. Oh dear—fancy that. I haven't even washed up yet. (*Quickly plunging the mugs into the sink.*) Isn't that awful?

HELEN. (*She stares at* BARBARA.) Are you sure you're all right, honey? You look kinda pale.

BARBARA. No, it's nothing, just a headache.

HELEN. Take a pill.

BARBARA. I have.

HELEN. Take another pill.

BARBARA. Yes, all right.

HELEN. I'll go get you one, shall I?

BARBARA. No, please . . .

HELEN. You know me: Pills and potions keep me going. I'll run upstairs and see what you've got.

BARBARA. It's all right, Helen. Please don't fuss! (HELEN *frowns, startled by* BARBARA'S *irritability.*)

HELEN. Fuss . . . ?

BARBARA. I'm sorry, I'm sorry. I didn't mean to be rude.

HELEN. You be just as rude as you like, honey. I mean, jeeze, if you can't shout at friends, who can you shout at?

BARBARA. I didn't mean to shout. I'm sorry. (HELEN *goes to* BARBARA *and takes her by the hand.*)

HELEN. Look, I'll tell you what. Why don't you put your feet up, go to bed—read a book or something, huh?

BARBARA. Yes, perhaps I will.

HELEN. It'll only make things worse if you try to keep going.

BARBARA. Yes.

HELEN. How about some magazines . . . Would you like some magazines?

BARBARA. No, please—I don't feel like reading.

HELEN. Are you sure?

BARBARA. (*She nods.*) I think I'd rather just go to sleep.

HELEN. Okay, you know best. (*She goes to the front door;* BARBARA *follows.*) Now, look—if there's anything I can do—and I mean anything . . .

BARBARA. That's very kind of you, Helen.

HELEN. Well, for God's sake—what are friends for? (*She smiles at* BARBARA.) You take care of yourself.

BARBARA. You too.

HELEN. Go right upstairs and have a good long rest.

BARBARA. Yes, I will.

HELEN. Good girl. See you tomorrow. Ciao.

(HELEN *opens the front door and goes out.* BARBARA *closes the front door. She shuts her eyes and leans back against the wall. Suddenly, she feels the bile rising in her throat; she runs to the kitchen and vomits into the sink.* THELMA *walks down the stairs; she pauses halfway.*)

THELMA. Mrs. Jackson . . . ? (*No response.*) Are you all right, Mrs. Jackson?

BARBARA. Leave me alone—just leave me alone!

(*Lights fade.* THELMA *and* BARBARA *exit. Lights up. Evening.* BOB *and* STEWART *enter the sitting-room.* STEWART *removes his coat.*)

STEWART. I hope you don't think I've been neglecting you, Mr. Jackson.

BOB. No no.

STEWART. I've been meaning to come round, but the days just flash by, don't they? (STEWART *turns to face* BOB.) I gather from my girls that your wife is becoming increasingly unhappy with the, um . . . (*Pause.*) Is she?

BOB. Well, yes.

STEWART. You should have told me. (*Pause.*) There's not much I can do.

BOB. No.

STEWART. You do understand that, don't you? Well, of course you do, I know you do. You're a reasonable man, after all. (*Pause.*)

BOB. Can I get you a drink, sir?

STEWART. Thank you very much. Whisky and water, if that's all right. (BOB *goes to fetch a drink for* STEWART *and himself.* STEWART *glances at his wristwatch.*) What time does she get back from her art club?

BOB. Any minute now.

STEWART. Oh good. (*He takes his cigarette pack from his jacket pocket.*) May I?

BOB. Please.

STEWART. Would it help, do you think, if I tried to clarify the situation a little?

BOB. How do you mean?

STEWART. Perhaps she feels she's being kept in the dark. Does she? Is that the problem, do you think?

BOB. Something like that, yes.

STEWART. Well, in that case, it's a problem easily solved. (*He smiles; pause.*) By the way, I meant to ask: Somebody was saying that you and the Krogers have got the same sort of car—is that right?

BOB. Yes.

STEWART. You've both got black Ford Consuls?

BOB. Yes.

STEWART. How extraordinary. (*No response.*) Or perhaps it isn't. What do you think?

BOB. There are plenty of Consuls about—specially around here.

STEWART. Yes, true. (*Brief pause.*) Nevertheless—to find two black Ford Consuls owned by such close neighbours—I must say that strikes me as being rather . . . well, rather surprising. (*No response.*) How did it happen? Whose car came first?

BOB. Ours. Helen said how nice it was, how smart, and so on—and then Peter told me they were going to get one exactly the same.

STEWART. Uh-huh. (*Brief pause.*) Is he a car person? Is he interested in cars?

BOB. No, not particularly.

STEWART. He just took a fancy to yours . . .

BOB. Well, yes.

STEWART. (*He smiles.*) Well, why not? It's a very nice car. What are his interests? Does he have any hobbies?

BOB. Nothing special. I don't think, um . . . (*Pause.*) Books, of course. Apart from that . . . nothing much. (*Pause.*) He likes music. He listens to music a lot.

STEWART. On the radio?

BOB. And records. He's got quite a collection.

STEWART. Don't tell me he's one of these hi-fi fanatics.

BOB. Well, a bit, I suppose—stereo sound, FM radio, headphones, you know; rumble filters. All that sort of stuff.

STEWART. Headphones?

BOB. He likes classical music and she doesn't. She can't stand it. So he listens to his records through the headphones.

STEWART. Well, that's one way of avoiding domestic strife, I suppose. What about Mrs. Kroger? Does she have a hobby?

BOB. No, not really. She's too much of a Dizzy Lizzy to do anything properly. Poor old Helen. She makes us laugh.

STEWART. How often do you go to the Krogers' house?

BOB. Hardly ever. Barbara pops in for a cup of tea most weeks, but as far as I'm concerned—well, four or five times a year—birthdays, Christmas, that sort of thing, you know. (STEWART *nods; pause.*) Peter works at home—I think we told you. That makes it a bit difficult. We're always afraid of disturbing him.

STEWART. Yes, quite. Apart from you, does Mrs. Kroger have any particular friends?

BOB. She's friendly with everyone. She's a very friendly woman.

STEWART. In what way?

BOB. (*Not understanding the question.*) What?

STEWART. How does this friendliness manifest itself?

BOB. (*Irritated.*) She's just an ordinary friendly woman. She pops in for a chat, she worries if anything's wrong, she takes an interest in people, that's all.

STEWART. Takes an interest . . . ?

BOB. Well, you know.

STEWART. Perhaps you could give me an example.

BOB. (*Angrily.*) I don't often see her, Mr. Stewart, I'm at work when she comes round; Barbara's the one she talks to, not me. I don't know what she does or what she says. Anyway, there's nothing sinister about being friendly, is there?

STEWART. Nothing sinister, no. It just adds to the pattern.

BOB. Pattern?

STEWART. Well, if the Krogers are mixed up in this business—and I say if—if they are, then it would be essential for them to know what's going on. Any change of routine, any change of neighbour . . . it could be dangerous for them.

BOB. You can make anything look suspicious if you try hard enough.

STEWART. True.

BOB. I mean, all that stuff about the cars. Why shouldn't they buy a car like ours if they want to?

STEWART. No reason at all—on the other hand, it could be construed as an extremely clever thing to do.

BOB. Clever, why?

STEWART. Because it would certainly confuse anyone who might be watching them; I mean, if one of my chaps saw a black Ford Consul parked in Cranley Drive he couldn't be sure, at a glance, whether the Krogers were at home or whether you were. Might be useful, that. (BOB *stares at* STEWART; *he says nothing*.) It's not terribly important, I agree—it's just one of those little details that tend to arouse interest. And it's only when you start adding all these things together that a significant pattern begins to emerge.

(BOB *stares at* STEWART. *He opens his mouth to speak, but before he can say anything, the front door opens and* BARBARA *enters; she is wearing her tweed coat and carrying a shopping bag filled with oil-paints and brushes*.)

BARBARA. (*Calling.*) It's only me.

BOB. (*Calling.*) We're in here. (BARBARA *goes to the sitting-room. She stares at* STEWART.)

BARBARA. Mr. Stewart.

STEWART. Do forgive me for dropping in like this. I just wanted to make sure that everything is all right. (*Brief pause.*) Is everything all right? (BARBARA *puts down her shopping bag and unbuttons her coat. Pause.*)

BARBARA. I thought the girls would be going last weekend.

STEWART. Well—no, I'm terribly sorry.

BOB. Mr. Stewart says he'll explain.

BARBARA. First it was two days, then a week, then two weeks . . . how much longer? (STEWART *responds with a friendly smile.*)

STEWART. Let me put you in the picture, shall I? Let me tell you something about the background to this case.

It won't solve your problems, I know, but it may help you to live with them for just a little longer. (*Brief pause.* BARBARA *turns to* BOB.)

BARBARA. Have you offered Mr. Stewart a cup of tea?

BOB. Yes, I—

STEWART. Thank you, Mrs. Jackson. Your husband has been more hospitable. (BARBARA *goes to the door.*)

BARBARA. I'll just take my coat off. (BARBARA *goes to the hall and hangs her coat on a peg.* STEWART *turns to* BOB.)

STEWART. Julie's gone to the cinema, I believe?

BOB. Yes.

STEWART. Yes, I thought it would be a good idea to come when she was out. Fewer complications. (*A smile.*) And the fewer of them the better, eh? (*Pause.*) What has she gone to see?

BOB. Um . . . I'm not sure. (*To* BARBARA, *as she returns.*) What's Julie gone to see?

BARBARA. *The Millionairess.*

STEWART. Oh, that's frightfully good. We enjoyed it enormously. Peter Sellers is marvellous. First-class. (BAR-BARA *turns abruptly to* STEWART.)

BARBARA. Look, since you're here, there's something I must tell you.

STEWART. (*Friendly.*) What's that?

BARBARA. I don't know how much longer I can go on like this. (*Brief pause.*)

STEWART. Yes. Yes, I'm sorry.

BARBARA. Apart from anything else, I'm worried about Julie—she's got so much work to do for her exams, and all this is very unsettling for her.

STEWART. Yes, of course.

BARBARA. I know it's important, what you're doing here, but we have got our own lives to lead, after all. You must have known it would be more than a couple of days. You should have told us.

STEWART. It's always difficult to know how long these jobs will take.

BARBARA. It's getting worse—much worse.

STEWART. Yes, I'm sure.

BOB. Seeing Helen and Peter.

STEWART. Yes.

BARBARA. Every time I see her, every time she comes

round . . . it makes me feel quite ill. (*Brief pause.*) I can't sleep.

STEWART. Well, if it's any comfort to you, we still don't know how they fit into this, uh . . . into this particular puzzle. Obviously they must fit in somehow. I mean, as friends of Lonsdale's they must have a place somewhere. But how or where or why, we don't yet know. Maybe they met him in Canada—and since he's travelling on a Canadian passport, that's a distinct possibility. But, at the moment, all we can do is speculate. (*Brief pause.*) Sorry I can't be more . . . reassuring.

BOB. What about Lonsdale? Do you know anything more about him?

STEWART. Anything more . . . ?

BOB. You said he might be a spy of some sort. Is he? You weren't quite sure.

STEWART. Ah yes. (*He glances at* BOB, *surprised, perhaps, to realise how little information has been imparted.*) Well—well . . . Since the last war, submarines have become an increasingly important element in defence strategy—both for us and NATO and—most especially—the Russians. They have a vast fleet of submarines—at least seven hundred, probably more. But the effective value of this fleet has been drastically reduced by the various techniques of underwater detection that have been developed by our NATO chaps—ASDICs, sonar buoys, and so on. Needless to say, Moscow is most anxious to learn the secrets of these devices. And so spies were sent here to find out all they could. The man in charge of this operation is the man who visits your friends every weekend, the man calling himself Gordon Lonsdale.

BOB. Good God.

STEWART. Oh yes, he's an important chap, make no mistake about that—almost certainly a high-ranking officer in the KGB: Russian Intelligence. And so far, he's been remarkably successful. But the trouble with spying is that you can't always rely on fellow professionals: You often need the help of amateurs. Traitors. And such creatures can be notoriously unstable. Lonsdale needed inside help; and eventually he found a suitable collaborator, an Englishman called Harry. We became interested in Harry about a year ago. He's a naval man, works at the Underwater Weapons Establishment. Fiftyish, not much of a career, divorced. A bit of a boozer. In fact, he's been boozing rather a lot recently—spending a lot of money in local pubs, far more than he can reasonably afford. And always with the same girlfriend; so we decided to keep an eye on her and we discovered that she works in the same establishment—in the records section where all the secret material on underwater weapons is filed. They're always together—every evening: eating, drinking in plush restaurants. And there's never any shortage of cash. Where do they get it? (*Brief pause.*) They come to London about once a month. They meet Lonsdale; they give him the secrets so earnestly desired by the Russians; and he gives them the cash. (*Pause. BARBARA and BOB stare at each other, almost unable to believe their ears.*)

BARBARA. But . . . but if you think that . . . why haven't you arrested them?

STEWART. (*He smiles.*) Yes, that's what the Admiralty wants to know. We've had several sharp memos about it. But the point is, there are bound to be others involved—not just Harry and his girlfriend—not just Lonsdale—there are bound to be others, and we want to catch the whole lot. That's why we've got to keep watching Lonsdale for just a few more days. The kettle's already bubbling; we must wait for it to boil. (*Pause.*)

BARBARA. Do you mean watching Lonsdale, or do you mean watching Helen and Peter?

STEWART. I mean, watching everyone who's been in regular contact with him. Everyone. And anyone. (*Pause.*)

BOB. Are you quite sure there isn't any danger?

STEWART. To you? Absolutely none.

BOB. What about Barbara and Julie? They're on their own here most of the time—and I keep thinking—if this man Lonsdale gets frightened or suspicious—what then?

STEWART. There'll be no violence, I can assure you of that. The KGB don't employ hooligans for this sort of operation.

BARBARA. How can you be sure?

STEWART. Because I am.

BARBARA. How can you be?

STEWART. Because it's my job to be—and I'm very good at my job.

BOB. It's all very well for you, you're used to this sort

of thing. I mean, all this talk of the Russians and the KGB . . .

STEWART. Yes, it must seem very alarming.

BOB. Well, it is alarming.

STEWART. Not as far as you and I are concerned.

BARBARA. I wish I could believe that.

STEWART. There's absolutely no need to worry, I know what I'm talking about. I have spent most of my adult life studying the supposedly secret workings of Russian Intelligence. It's a fascinating task—rather like bird-watching. And just as a bird-watcher gets to know the most intimate habits of his favourite species, so I know how these fellows operate. I know their methods. And it's not just guesswork. You'd be amazed what you can find out when you try hard enough. For example . . . I know more about the KGB Chairman than I do about my next-door neighbour. His name's Shelepin—(*A small smile.*)—the KGB chap, not my next-door neighbour, Aleksandr Nikolaevich Shelepin. He's got a flat in Kutuzovsky Prospekt—very nice, too, palatial by Soviet standards; and it's furnished with all those little luxuries that only the chosen members of the Party elite are able to enjoy: TV, radiogram, piano, bottles of real scotch in the sideboard. He always has an early breakfast; eggs, ham, black Russian bread, tea, a nip of brandy, and then, at eight-fifteen, a chauffeur-driven car takes him to Moscow Centre, the KGB headquarters in Dzerzhinsky Square. It's quite a pleasant building: grey stone, looks more Flemish than Russian; it used to belong to an insurance company before the Revolution. A harmless-looking place. You wouldn't give it a second glance. But there's a courtyard tucked away behind and in that courtyard is the Lubyanka Prison, where hundreds of people have died. Thousands. (*Pause.*) Shelepin's office is on the third floor. It's got a high ceiling, polished parquet, a couple of old-fashioned sofas, wood-panelled walls. There are six telephones on his desk, one of which is a direct line to the Kremlin. He often works long hours, so there's a bedroom next door in case he's kept late by some particularly intransigent problem. (*Brief pause.*) Sometimes he strolls across the Persian carpet and looks down at the people hurrying along the Marx Prospekt. He controls those people and they know it. You could,

I suppose, say much the same about any senior civil servant looking down at the rush-hour crowds in Whitehall. But there's one big difference: Shelepin's control is absolute. (*Pause.*) He's youngish, too—not yet forty-three. He likes sports, particularly football, and he enjoys going to the theatre. What's more he's got a weakness for ice-cream, which is not surprising because Russian ice-cream is the best in the world. "*Morozhennoe pazhahlsta*" is a phrase that every tourist should memorize; it means "Ice-cream, please." Anyone who goes to Russia should make a point of trying the ice-cream. (*He smiles.*) And all I know about my next-door neighbour is that his name is Warrender and that he subscribes to the *National Geographic* magazine. (*Pause.*) So the answer to your question is no, there's no danger, absolutely not. The merest hint of any strong-arm behaviour would cause the most almighty diplomatic rumpus—and that's the one thing the Soviets want to avoid at all costs. So there's nothing to worry about. I guarantee it. (*Turning to* BARBARA.) Does that put your mind at rest, Mrs. Jackson? There's nothing to worry about. (*Pause.* BOB *and* STEWART *look at* BARBARA, *waiting for her response. She rises to her feet.*)

BARBARA. So the girls will be here for some time, then?

STEWART. Well, I hope not—for all our sakes. A few days, perhaps. That's the plan.

BARBARA. Yes, I see. (*She manages the ghost of a smile.*) Well, if you'll excuse me, I've got some jobs to do. (*She goes to the door.*) Is that all right? Do you mind if I go?

STEWART. No no, of course not. Thank you for being so patient.

BARBARA. I don't have much choice, do I? (BARBARA *goes to the kitchen, where she stands staring out of the window.* STEWART *turns to* BOB *and smiles.*)

STEWART. I'm not quite sure what I expected her to say, but I certainly expected more than that.

BOB. She never says much when she's upset.

STEWART. No, well . . . some people don't. (*Pause.*) It must be the most frightful strain. Appalling.

BOB. Yes.

STEWART. If you think it's getting too much for her,

you will let me know, won't you? Just telephone Superintendent Smith; I'll pop round any time.

BOB. Right.

STEWART. Good. Well—I'd better be going. (STEWART *picks up his overcoat.*)

STEWART. Don't forget—day or night—don't hesitate to ring. (STEWART *is putting on his overcoat.*) On the other hand, of course, some women can be remarkably tough. I've noticed it time and time again. Tough and resilient. Much more so than many men. Oh yes. (BOB *nods, but says nothing.* STEWART *goes to the kitchen.* BOB *follows.*) Good night, Mrs. Jackson.

BARBARA. Good night.

STEWART. How are my young ladies behaving themselves? No problems in that department, I trust?

BARBARA. Oh no, they're very quiet and considerate.

STEWART. Good. I'm glad to hear it. (*He turns to* BOB *and shakes him by the hand.*) I'm most grateful, Mr. Jackson. Thank you for being so cooperative. Good night.

BOB. Good night, Mr. Stewart. (BOB *opens the back door.* STEWART *exits.* BOB *closes the door. He looks at* BARBARA. *Aware of his gaze, she glances at him.*)

BARBARA. Tea or cocoa? Which would you like? Tea or cocoa? (BOB *goes to her.*)

BOB. Look, I know how you feel. But it was good of him to come round and explain all those things. I mean, he didn't have to. (BARBARA *busies herself at the sink.*)

BARBARA. I've made up my mind what I'm going to do: I'm not going to think about it. We've got to lead a normal life—for Julie's sake, if not our own. Let them do what they like. I'm not going to think about it. (BARBARA *fills the electric kettle with water.*) Tea or cocoa?

BOB. Tea, I think.

BARBARA. Right. Go and sit down, I'll bring it in.

(*Lights fade.* BOB *exits.* BARBARA *walks DS. and addresses the audience.*)

BARBARA. Bob's mother was such a frail little thing. I never knew his father; he died long before we met. He was a clerk with an insurance company. She lived alone, Bob's mother, she lived alone in a small draughty house in Canterbury. She used to visit us twice a year, but she always went home after a week. "I don't want to be any trouble," she'd say. It was the most important thing in all her life—not being any trouble. When her roof leaked, she refused to tell the landlord. "He's been very good to me," she said. "I don't want to make a fuss." When she was ill and dying, she wouldn't call the doctor after six o'clock in the evening. She'd lay alone in that miserable house, more worried about making a fuss than anything else. Her life was governed by fear, bless her heart. She was afraid of post office clerks, bus conductors, anyone in uniform. And, like a child, she thought if she kept very still and didn't say anything, nobody would take any notice of her. And she was right—they didn't.

(*Lights up. Late afternoon.* BARBARA *goes to the sitting room. She fetches a cardboard box, some tissue paper and the now-completed dress for* HELEN. *She starts to fold the dress.* THELMA *walks down the stairs; she is wearing a raincoat and headscarf. She knocks on the sitting-room door and enters.*)

BARBARA. Don't tell me it's half-past.

THELMA. Mr. Stewart said I could leave early. (*Glancing up,* BARBARA *sees that* THELMA *is not wearing her usual motorcycling gear.*)

BARBARA. No bike today?

THELMA. Trouble with the clutch. (*She looks at the dress.*) Who's that for?

BARBARA. (*Somewhat embarrassed.*) Actually—Helen. I promised it to her ages ago.

THELMA. It's lovely. Really professional.

BARBARA. Well, hardly.

THELMA. It is—really. You are lucky—having a talent like that.

BARBARA. I wouldn't call it much of a talent, Thelma.

THELMA. Well, I think it is. I was hopeless at needlework when I was at school. Hopeless at needlework, dreadful at art. Everything I did looked the same: trees, people, buildings—you couldn't tell one from the other. Cats, flowers, elephants—they all looked the same. (BARBARA *smiles;* THELMA *buttons her raincoat.*)

I wish I had a hobby like you, I wish there was something I could do really well.

BARBARA. Oh, I'm sure there is.

THELMA. (*Cheerfully.*) No, there's not. There never has been. I can do lots of things sort of half well—but nothing really tip-top. I don't stick at things long enough, that's my trouble. It's what Dad calls my grasshopper mind. (*She grins.*) Well, I'll see you tomorrow. Usual time.

BARBARA. Yes, right.

THELMA. I'm coming instead of Pat. She's got a filthy cold.

BARBARA. Right. (THELMA *goes to the door;* BARBARA *plucks up courage to summon her back.*) Thelma . . . (THELMA *pauses by the door.*) Is there any news?

THELMA. News . . . ?

BARBARA. Yes, news. Nobody tells us anything.

THELMA. Well, no. Not as far as I know. (BARBARA *looks directly at* THELMA.)

BARBARA. Mr. Stewart came to see us.

THELMA. Yes. Yes, I know that.

BARBARA. He told us about Harry and his girlfriend. And the Russians, what they're trying to do, what they're trying to find out.

THELMA. Yes.

BARBARA. Did you know he was coming?

THELMA. Well, yes.

BARBARA. You never said anything about it. (*No response.*) I suppose he told you not to. (*No response.*) Did he? (*No response.*) He didn't even mention Helen and Peter. I mean, he didn't tell us whether they're—you know—actually . . . (*The sentence drifts away in silence;* THELMA *says nothing.*) Well, of course they must be involved. It's obvious. Any fool can see that. (*Looking at* THELMA.) Why didn't he tell us?

THELMA. Well, I can't . . . (*Pause.*)

BARBARA. What?

THELMA. You know I can't tell you anything.

BARBARA. Why not?

THELMA. You know I can't.

BARBARA. (*Angry.*) So you think it's all right, do you, just to let things go on like this.

THELMA. Well, no, I mean—

BARBARA. (*Overlapping*.) You think that's all right, do you? Is that what you think?

THELMA. (*Firmly*.) If I could do anything, I would—but I can't. (*Silence.* BARBARA *sighs. Her head bows forward. She sits motionless.*)

BARBARA. To tell you the truth, Thelma, I don't really care. I don't care what they've done. Helen and Peter. It doesn't make any difference. Not now. (*Pause; she raises her head and looks at* THELMA.) Isn't that strange? I don't really care. I cared at first, of course. When I first thought, when I first realised . . . all the deceit and lies and . . . I was so angry, I was so hurt—I was so *hurt*, Thelma . . . and I wanted—well, I don't know what I wanted. I wanted them to be punished, I suppose; I wanted them to be taken away and punished. But those feelings don't last very long, do they? And I keep thinking how kind she's been—and she has been very kind. She's been very kind to Julie. (*Pause.*) I don't care what she's done, she's still my friend. (*Pause;* BARBARA *sits motionless.*) I'll tell you what chokes me, Thelma: it's that Mr. Stewart not telling us anything, not telling us about Helen and Peter, treating us like a couple of kids who can't be trusted. How dare he! (*Pause.*) Can you imagine what it's been like? Can you? (*No response.*) Last Friday, when I went shopping, I looked at the women all round me. And I thought, "I'm not like them. I'm not like the others. I may look like them, but I'm not." (*Pause.*) It hurts telling all these lies. It really hurts. It's like a dead weight on my stomach. It's like grief. You can't forget it. (*Pause.*) And he won't tell us. Why not? Does he think we can't be trusted. Does he think we're too stupid to understand? Or perhaps he thinks it doesn't matter. (*A shaft of bitterness.*) Well, that's it, of course—why should he bother about us? We're the sort of people who stand in queues and don't answer back. Why should he bother? We'll just do as we're told and not ask any questions. (*Pause—and then with a sudden passion.*) Well, I hate him! *I hate him!* I want to smack his smiling face and say, "How dare you! How dare you treat us like that! Who the hell do you think you are!" (*Pause; her passion subsides.*) I won't though, will I? Of course I won't. I can say all these things to you because you're just Thelma who likes Richard Burton and sausages for lunch. But I can't tell him and he knows it. That's how it works, of course. That's how he gets his own way. (*Pause; silence.*)

THELMA. Look, I'm sorry. (BARBARA *raises her head and looks at* THELMA.)

BARBARA. I bet he knew when he first came here, didn't he?

THELMA. Knew what?

BARBARA. About Helen and Peter.

THELMA. I don't know.

BARBARA. I thought it seemed incredible at the time; seeing Lonsdale that first Sunday.

THELMA. It could have been a coincidence.

BARBARA. Could it?

THELMA. Well, I don't know. Mr. Stewart doesn't tell me anything, either. I just do what I'm told.

BARBARA. I suppose that's what he'd say, isn't it?

THELMA. He might. (*Pause.*)

BARBARA. If only it hadn't been us. If only it hadn't been Helen and Peter. I lie awake every night thinking, "Why them . . . why us?" (*Pause.*) This time last year, everything was so perfect. (*Pause.* THELMA *takes* BARBARA *by the hand.*)

THELMA. I'll tell you what I think: It's a waste of time looking for reasons. That's what I think. Good things happen, bad things happen. One day you win the pools, the next you fall down stairs. Nobody's to blame. It's nobody's fault. These things just happen. Start looking for reasons and you'll go barmy. (*She grins.*) Honest. Trust me. Thelma knows. (THELMA *squeezes* BARBARA'S *hand.*) Can I get you something? How about a nice cup of tea? (BARBARA *smiles.*)

BARBARA. You're just like my husband. He thinks a cup of tea will cure anything. (THELMA *smiles.* BARBARA *rises to her feet.*) Off you go. The buses will be packed.

THELMA. Are you sure you're all right? (BARBARA *nods.*) I'll see you tomorrow, then. (BARBARA *nods.*) I'm sorry.

BARBARA. It's not your fault.

THELMA. It's nobody's fault. You just remember that.

(THELMA *goes to the sitting-room door. The front door opens and* JULIE *enters, returning from school.*)

JULIE. Hello, Thelma, how are you?

THELMA. Fine, thanks—how are you?

JULIE. Fine—where's Mum? (BARBARA *emerges from the sitting-room.*)

BARBARA. Here I am. (*She kisses* JULIE.) Had a good day?

JULIE. Pretty gruesome. (THELMA *goes towards the kitchen.*)

THELMA. Bye, then, see you tomorrow.

BARBARA. Bye, Thelma. I hope you get your bike back soon.

THELMA. Yes, so do I. (*To* JULIE, *as she opens the kitchen door.*) I'll have to ask your boyfriend to give me a lift. That's a smashing bike he's got. What is it, a Triumph?

(JULIE'S *mouth falls open in dismay.* BARBARA *stares at her, appalled.*)

BARBARA. Julie . . . !

JULIE. He was only giving me a ride home.

BARBARA. How many times have we told you?

JULIE. Yes, I know—

BARBARA. (*Overlapping.*) How many times?

JULIE. (*Overlapping.*) Yes, I'm sorry—

BARBARA. (*Overlapping.*) And you promised. You gave your word!

JULIE. I'm sorry, Mum. I'm sorry!

BARBARA. So that's the sort of daughter I've got— somebody who goes behind my back—

JULIE. (*Overlapping.*) I'm sorry!

BARBARA. (*Overlapping.*)—somebody who lies and cheats!

JULIE. I'm sorry, I'm sorry!

BARBARA. I'll never be able to trust you ever again— never again—never! (JULIE *bursts into tears and runs upstairs.*)

JULIE. I'm sorry, I'm sorry, I'm sorry, I'm sorry!

(JULIE *exits. A door slams. Silence.* BARBARA *stands, trembling and breathless, momentarily exhausted by her outburst.* THELMA *remains standing by the kitchen door.*

BARBARA *sobs. Lights fade.* BARBARA *and* THELMA *exit.* PETER *enters and addresses the audience.*)

PETER. In the winter of 1932, when the Depression was at its worst, a friend took me to a meeting—an informal and private meeting—in New York City. On our way there, we walked along Riverside Drive. Literally hundreds of unemployed and hungry men were camping there in tiny shacks and shanties. I saw in their faces a degree of hopelessness and despair I had never seen before. (*Brief pause.*) I remembered those brave words about "life, liberty, and the pursuit of happiness." And I felt a sudden surge of anger that such noble ideals should have been betrayed—forgotten. Why did it happen—how? (*Brief pause.*) When I got to the meeting, I found a small group of maybe seven or eight men and women, mostly young, mostly about my age. It was cold that night, and there was no heat in the apartment; we stood around wearing overcoats. An older man read to us from the works of Marx and Lenin. He had a soft voice; gentle; I've never forgotten it. He said, "The ruin of capitalism is imminent. Every attempt to establish a truly human society upon the old capitalist foundations is foredoomed to absolute failure. We are thus confronted by two alternatives, and two only. There must be either complete disintegration, further brutalization and disorder; absolute chaos, or else Communism." (*Brief pause.*) That evening, my whole life changed.

(*Lights up. Evening. A Christmas tree, decorated with coloured lights, stands in the sitting-room.* BARBARA, BOB, JULIE, *and* HELEN *are grouped around the tree singing a carol.* PETER *joins them.*)

ALL. With the Angelic host proclaim,
"Christ is born in Bethlehem."
Hark! the herald-angels sing
Glory to the new-born King!

(JULIE *and* HELEN *cheer.* HELEN *is slightly drunk.*)

HELEN. Hey—wasn't that something?
JULIE. Wonderful!

HELEN. Terrific! Come on, let's have a drink . . . (*Taking a bottle of sherry from the coffee table.*) . . . one more little drink . . .

PETER. (*Stepping forward anxiously.*) I think it's time to go home.

HELEN. Time to go home? Whaddya mean—time to go home? What are you talking about? I don't want to go home—I'm having fun! (*To* JULIE.) How about a drink for you, honey-chile?

JULIE. (*She glances at* BOB, *seeking his permission.*) Well, I . . .

BOB. There's some lemonade in the kitchen.

HELEN. Come on, Bob, a glass of sherry won't do her any harm. Let the girl live a little. Jeeze—when I was her age I was drinking bourbon like it was mother's milk! (HELEN *laughs raucously.*)

PETER. Helen, please . . .

HELEN. Get off my back, will you? Stop nagging! Don't be such a goddam spoil-sport.

PETER. (*Sharper.*) Helen. (HELEN *swings round to face him; her initial reaction seems to be one of anger; brief pause; her mood changes, and she becomes immediately contrite.*)

HELEN. Okay. Okay. Sorry. (*She grins.*) Loudmouth Helen does it again. "You never know when to stop. You always go too far." Jesus, how many times have I heard that! (*Smiling at* PETER.) Okay—just one more little drink, then home. Okay?

PETER. It's getting late.

HELEN. So what? It's Christmastime—I'm with my friends—and I'm happy. Come on; relax. (*Turning to* JULIE.) Hey—do you know what this reminds me of? Christmas at Aunt Sophie's. We always went to Aunt Sophie's when I was a kid—every Christmas. She had the most beautiful little house. Beautiful. And she loved brass—there was brass everywhere: kettles, spark guard, candlesticks, a great brass pot filled with indoor plants. A log fire and gleaming brass. And she'd do everything as it was when she was a kid. We always had roast goose and chocolate honey-cake. And there she'd sit, after dinner, my old Aunt Sophie, licking her fingers to pick up the crumbs of chocolate honey-cake—and all of a sudden she'd burst out crying. "What's the matter?" we'd say.

"Why are you crying, Aunt Sophie?" And she'd dry her eyes and blow her nose and lick her chocolatey fingers. "Nothing's the matter," she'd say. "I'm crying because everything's just poifeck." (*She smiles.*) Well, I reckon that's how I feel right now. (*Moved by this story,* JULIE *goes to* HELEN *and embraces her.* HELEN *kisses* JULIE *on the forehead. The telephone rings.*)

JULIE. That'll be Maureen. (JULIE *goes to the hall.* HELEN *looks at* BARBARA, BOB, *and* PETER—*three unsmiling faces.*)

HELEN. Oh, come on, you guys. It's party-time remember? Jesus, I've had more laughs at a funeral. Come on—let's goose it up a little! (JULIE *calls from the hall.*)

JULIE. It's for you, Dad. It's Mr. Stewart. (BOB *glances sharply at* BARBARA, *and hurries to the phone.*)

BOB. Right. (BARBARA, *unable to move or speak, just watches him go.* JULIE *returns to the sitting room.*)

HELEN. Stewart . . . Stewart . . . I've heard that name before . . . Stewart Granger . . . James Stewart . . . Hey, did you see James Stewart in *Vertigo*? He was terrific—terrific! (*Nobody responds.* HELEN *reaches for another drink.*) I think I'll have another drink. Don't look at me like that, Peter—it's just one for the road—one more for the road, okay? (BOB *comes back into the sitting-room.* BARBARA *scarcely dares speak to him. She rises to her feet.*)

BOB. Merry Christmas. That's all. He just said, "Merry Christmas." A bit late in the day. Still—nice of him.

(HELEN *begins to sing boisterously "We wish you a Merry Christmas."* JULIE, PETER, *and* BOB *join in. Eventually even* BARBARA *begins to sing with them.* BARBARA, BOB, PETER, *and* JULIE *exit; the Christmas tree is removed.* HELEN *addresses the audience.*)

HELEN. In 1950 we had an apartment on East 71st Street—nothing fancy, but I loved it. I've never been much of a home-maker—anyone will tell you that—but that place was special, it was the kind of place I always wanted. The sun streamed in through the kitchen window. It was all yellow and bright and cheery and warm. I even made curtains for that window. One evening, Peter came home early. "We've got to leave," he said. "The Rosenbergs have been arrested. We've got to leave." I looked at Peter. His mouth had gone dry; he moistened his lips with his tongue. "When?" I asked. "Tonight," he said. "We've got to get the hell out of here as fast as we can." And that's what we did. We left our clothes in the closet, books on the shelves, food in the refrigerator. We could've stayed, I suppose, and taken our chances—but we didn't. And from then on, there was no turning back.

(*Lights fade.* HELEN *exits. Lights up. Day.* BARBARA *and* BOB *are in the kitchen; they stand facing* STEWART, *who has just entered.*)

STEWART. I'm sorry to disturb your Saturday, but I thought you'd be glad to know that it'll soon be over.

BARBARA. Over . . . ?

STEWART. As far as you're concerned, anyway.

BARBARA. The girls will be going.

STEWART. They will indeed.

BOB. When?

STEWART. As from today. (BARBARA *and* BOB *stare at each other, amazed.*)

BOB. What do you mean?

BARBARA. What's happened? I mean—why today? Has anything happened?

STEWART. Not yet. But with any luck . . . (*He allows the sentence to drift away into an infuriatingly ambiguous silence.*)

BARBARA. (*Sharply.*) What? With any luck, what? (STEWART *responds to the anger in her voice; his reply is unusually direct and unveiled.*)

STEWART. Harry—the man I told you about—he's on his way to London with his girlfriend. We believe that they will have another meeting with Lonsdale. And if they do, we shall arrest them. (*A moment of silence.*)

BOB. What about Helen and Peter?

STEWART. (*Evenly.*) Yes, we'll pick them up this afternoon. If everything goes according to plan.

BARBARA. This afternoon . . . (*She sits suddenly, heavily, on the sofa.*)

BOB. What have they done?

STEWART. They're Lonsdale's transmitting station. He brings them information which they dispatch to KGB headquarters, either hidden in the books that Peter Kroger posts to fictitious clients in various parts of Europe, or presumably by radio. I'm sorry to tell you so bluntly, but there's no doubt about it: Your friends are both Communist agents with many years' experience behind them. And their name's not Kroger by the way, and they're American—not Canadian. I thought it better that you hear it from me rather than read about it in the newspapers. (BARBARA *and* BOB *remain motionless, stunned.*)

BARBARA. When I think of the hours she's spent in this house . . . in this room . . . (*She lapses into silence for a moment; she looks up at* STEWART.) Was it *all* a lie—I mean everything she's ever told us? (*Almost imploringly.*) Was it?

STEWART. Well, not everything, I suppose.

BARBARA. I mean, all those stories about her life on the farm—wasn't that the truth?

STEWART. Apparently not. Her parents emigrated from Poland. They lived in a place called Utica in New York State. Her father was fairly well-off; he made his money during Prohibition. He was a bootlegger. (*Brief pause.*) Peter Kroger was a schoolteacher. He became a Communist in the thirties and fought in the Spanish Civil War. (*Pause.*)

BARBARA. How could she do it? How *could* she? I've never had many friends, not close friends, not what you'd call close . . . never. (*Brief pause; she struggles to prevent herself from weeping.*) But I trusted Helen. I thought she was brash and noisy and sometimes a bit silly . . . but I trusted her. I loved her.

STEWART. (*Sympathetically.*) Well, I'm quite sure that her affection for you is perfectly genuine. There's no reason to doubt that.

BARBARA. (*Angrily.*) No reason . . . ? What do you mean, no reason? There's every reason to doubt everything she's ever said or done!

STEWART. Yes, well, you're bound to feel like that. And there's nothing anyone can do to soften the blow. I only wish there were. (*A moment of silence.*)

BARBARA. I tell you what I wish, Mr. Stewart. I wish you had never come here. (BOB, *startled by these words, swings round towards* BARBARA.)

STEWART. (*Gently.*) Yes, I'm sure . . .

BARBARA. I wish you'd never set foot inside this house!

BOB. Don't let's start blaming Mr. Stewart—it's not his fault.

BARBARA. (*To* STEWART, *ignoring* BOB.) Helen may have lied to us—but you've gone one better. You made us do the lying; we've even lied to our own daughter.

BOB. We haven't *lied* to her.

BARBARA. We haven't told her the truth, have we? What's she going to do when she finds out?

BOB. She'll understand.

BARBARA. Will she?

BOB. Of course she will.

STEWART. I'm sure she'll realise you were only trying to protect her.

BARBARA. Oh, do stop making excuses! Helen's lying and we're lying—we're all playing the same rotten game.

STEWART. Well, hardly.

BARBARA. Of course we are. What's the difference between one lie and another? (*Her anger rising.*) When I hear you making excuses for what we've done, I feel sick with fear—physically sick! People like you can find excuses for anything. (BOB *steps forward, anxious to make peace.*)

BOB. Look, there's no sense in upsetting yourself like this.

BARBARA. I'm not upsetting myself! I'm trying to explain how I feel—I'm trying to face up to the fact that I have betrayed Helen as much as she has betrayed me.

STEWART. That's just not so.

BARBARA. Isn't it?

BOB. Of course not.

(*Silence. Upstairs,* SALLY *is emerging from the bedroom, wearing outdoor clothes and carrying an unplugged telephone. She walks downstairs and taps on the kitchen door, opening it a fraction.*)

SALLY. Excuse me, sir, I'm going now.

STEWART. Yes, all right. (SALLY *exits.* STEWART *turns to* BOB.)

STEWART. I think I'd better come back tomorrow, don't you? When everything's over and done with. (*He turns to* BARBARA.) Try not to judge yourself too harshly, Mrs. Jackson. It won't do anybody any good—least of all yourself.

BARBARA. (*Quietly.*) What'll happen to them?

STEWART. The Krogers? They'll be sent for trial, I suppose. And then imprisoned. (BARBARA'S *head bows forward.*)

BARBARA. But they love each other. They're happy together and now they'll be separated. Maybe forever. (STEWART *gazes at* BARBARA; *he sighs.*)

STEWART. I'm sorry I've caused you so much pain. I only wish there was something I could do. (*A small smile.*) I keep saying the same old thing, don't I? But there's nothing else I can say; nothing I can do; nothing any of us can do.

BARBARA. You could have told us the truth. You knew all this ages ago. Why didn't you tell us? (STEWART *hesitates briefly before he replies.*)

STEWART. I had to be careful. You might have warned the Krogers.

BARBARA. What makes you think I won't now?

STEWART. (*Attempting a confident smile.*) Well.

BARBARA. If I was brave enough, I would. I would. Really, I would. (*Her eyes fill with tears.*) If I was brave enough, I'd go across the road—I'd bang on the door, and I'd say to them, "Get out—get out before they catch you—please, please, get out—please . . . !"

(*She runs to the sitting-room;* STEWART *and* BOB *follow. The front doorbell rings.* BARBARA *looks out of the window.*)

BARBARA. It's Helen! (*They all converse in hushed, urgent whispers.*)

BOB. It can't be!

BARBARA. Well, it is.

(*The doorbell rings again.*)

STEWART. (*To* BOB.) Answer the door. Answer the door, Mr. Jackson.

(BARBARA *flees to the kitchen.* BOB *goes to the hall.* STEWART *follows* BARBARA. BOB *opens the front door.* HELEN *enters.*)

HELEN. Hi, Bob—how's life?

BOB. Oh well, you know. Not so bad.

HELEN. Is Barbara home?

BOB. Well, yes—but she's feeling a bit off-colour.

HELEN. Off-colour . . . ?

BOB. Tired, you know. (HELEN *goes to the sitting-room;* BOB *follows.* BARBARA *struggles to recover her composure; she goes to the sitting-room.*)

HELEN. Why didn't you call me? I'd have come over and cooked lunch.

BOB. She's not ill—just tired.

(BARBARA *enters the sitting-room.*)

HELEN. Barbara, honey—what is it? What's the matter?

BARBARA. It's nothing—really.

BOB. She's got a rotten headache.

HELEN. Again? You ought to see a doctor, honey.

BARBARA. Yes, well . . .

HELEN. You make her go, Bob—she won't go unless you make her.

BOB. Yes, I will. (HELEN *goes to* BARBARA.)

HELEN. Gee, you're looking real pale. Are you sure it's just a headache?

BARBARA. Quite sure.

BOB. She's just tired.

HELEN. There's a lot of flu about. Maybe it's flu.

BARBARA. It's just another silly headache. (*Satisfied that the* JACKSONS *will not reveal any secrets,* STEWART *exits through the kitchen door.*)

HELEN. Headaches aren't silly. (*Glancing at* BARBARA.) Are you sure there's nothing wrong?

BARBARA. (*A little too sharply.*) Wrong?

BOB. (*Hastily.*) No no, she's all right.

HELEN. It's not like you, getting all these headaches. You've had three in a month.

BARBARA. I suppose I'm worried, that's all.

HELEN. What about?

BARBARA. Oh—this and that . . . things, you know.

HELEN. What things?

BARBARA. Well, nothing special, nothing in particular, nothing serious. (HELEN *sits beside* BARBARA.)

HELEN. Now, come on—don't be shy. You just tell your Auntie Helen all about it.

BARBARA. It's nothing.

HELEN. Make yourself scarce, Bob—let me talk to her alone.

BOB. It's Julie and her exams.

BARBARA. (*Gratefully following* BOB's *lead*.) Yes, it's Julie and her exams.

HELEN. Don't worry about Julie—she'll be okay.

BOB. They're very important, these exams.

HELEN. She'll be okay. You know she will. She'll do fine.

BARBARA. Well, I hope so.

HELEN. You must stop worrying, honey—otherwise you'll make yourself really ill.

BARBARA. Yes.

HELEN. I mean it.

BARBARA. Yes.

HELEN. So stop worrying, okay?

BARBARA. (*Managing a smile*.) I'll try.

HELEN. (*Squeezing* BARBARA'S *arm*.) That's my girl! (HELEN *rises to her feet*.) Where is Julie? Out with the boys?

BOB. She's gone to a hockey match.

HELEN. If I were you, honey, I'd go upstairs and have a proper rest.

BARBARA. Yes, all right.

HELEN. Go to bed and pamper yourself. Bob'll bring you a cup of tea, won't you, Bob?

BOB. Of course.

HELEN. Make a fuss of yourself. You deserve it. (*She pauses by the door*.) Hey, listen—before I go—there's something I ought to tell you.

BARBARA. What's that?

HELEN. Peter and I have been—well, we've been thinking about the future.

BOB. What about it?

HELEN. I've been feeling kinda low just recently—the January blues, I guess. Anyway, we both think it's time to move on.

BARBARA. Move on . . . ?

BOB. (*Together*.) Move where?

HELEN. Peter's got some friends in Australia. We're

thinking of packing our bags and going over there for six months or so. It's only an idea, of course, but Peter seems pretty keen. (BARBARA *and* BOB *exchange a brief glance.*)

BOB. Well, that's . . . that's quite a big idea.

HELEN. Sure is. (*She grins.*) Just think of it: all that sun—Bondi Beach—all those sexy young Aussies just waiting for Helen Kroger to put in an appearance. Sounds good, eh? Just poifeck.

BOB. Yes, it sounds marvellous.

BARBARA. (*Rising to her feet.*) Yes, it does—it sounds marvellous.

HELEN. You think so?

BARBARA. Yes, I do.

HELEN. (*She smiles.*) Trying to get rid of us, huh?

BARBARA. No, seriously—I think you should—it'd do you good, a change of scene—

HELEN. Well, maybe.

BARBARA. (*Urgently.*) No, really—I mean it—don't . . .

(HELEN *stares at* BARBARA. *The telephone rings.* BARBARA *goes to the hall.* BOB *rightly suspects that* HELEN *is puzzled by* BARBARA'S *uncharacteristically emotional behaviour; he tries to ease the atmosphere with a light-hearted explanation.*)

BOB. The phone never stops these days—and it's always for Julie.

BARBARA. (*On telephone.*) Hello? . . . Oh, hello, Maureen . . .

BOB. (*Grinning at* HELEN.) See what I mean?

BARBARA. (*On telephone.*) What? . . . No, she's not; she's gone down to the Sports Centre . . . When? This evening? . . . Yes, all right . . . Yes, I'll tell her—hang on a minute . . . (*Writing a note.*) 14 Hillcroft Road . . . Yes, I'll tell her . . . Bye-bye, Maureen, bye-bye. (BARBARA *replaces the receiver and returns to the sitting-room. She and* HELEN *stand facing each other.* HELEN'S *expression is grave and concerned.*)

HELEN. Are you sure there's nothing wrong? (BARBARA *nods.*)

BARBARA. Quite sure.

HELEN. Well, you just let me know if there's anything I can do, okay? (BARBARA *nods.*) Take good care of

her, Bob—she's a very special lady. Give my love to
Julie. Ciao.

(HELEN *goes out. Lights fade. Distant sound of church
bells. Lights up. Day.* STEWART, BOB, *and* BARBARA *are
in the sitting-room.*)

STEWART. Is Julie not here?

BOB. No, she's gone down to the shops. They forgot
to send us the Sunday paper.

STEWART. Ah. (*Brief pause.*) She doesn't know . . . ?
She didn't see anything?

BOB. No.

STEWART. No—Well, there wasn't much to see, really.
(*A moment of awkward, uneasy silence.*)

BOB. Everything went off all right, then?

STEWART. Oh yes. Absolutely according to plan.
Couldn't have been better.

BOB. What, um . . . (*He hesitates as if unwilling to
learn the truth.*) . . . what actually happened?

STEWART. We picked up Lonsdale and his two chums
outside the Old Vic, then we came here. It was about
half-past six—perhaps you saw the car?

BOB. We weren't looking.

STEWART. No, well . . . Superintendent Smith told the
Krogers that they were going to be arrested on suspicion
of offences against the Official Secrets Act. Mrs. Kroger
asked if she could go and stoke the boiler before they
left the house, but Mr. Smith was naturally suspicious.
He had a look in her handbag. He found a six-page letter
in Russian, apparently from Lonsdale to his wife—a glass
slide containing three microdots—and a typed sheet of
numbers, presumably some sort of a code. (*A small
smile.*) I'm not surprised she wanted to stoke the boiler.
(BARBARA *and* BOB *make no response. Brief pause.*)
And I was right about the radio transmitter. It was hidden under the kitchen floor.

BOB. Where are they now?

STEWART. Bow Street Police Station. (BARBARA *and*
BOB *remain silent.* STEWART *strolls across to the window.*) I'm afraid you'll have the Press poking around for
a week or so—it's a damn good story, you can't blame

them. But after that, all being well, you'll be left in peace.

BOB. Will we have to go to court?

STEWART. Oh no, there'll be no need for that. We'll see that your names aren't even mentioned.

(*The front door opens and* JULIE *enters; she is carrying a Sunday newspaper.*)

JULIE. Mum, what's going on?

BOB. In here, Julie. (JULIE *enters the sitting-room.*)

JULIE. Oh, hello, Mr. Stewart.

STEWART. Hello, Miss Jackson.

JULIE. (*To* BARBARA.) There's a whole crowd of people in Auntie Helen's house—what's going on?

BARBARA. Oh Julie . . .

STEWART. Yes, perhaps I should explain—

JULIE. (*Turning to* STEWART, *suddenly alarmed.*) Has something happened?

STEWART. Yes, I'm afraid so—in fact—well, the truth is, they've been arrested.

JULIE. *Arrested* . . . ?!

BARBARA. We couldn't tell you, Julie . . .

BOB. (*Overlapping.*) It was for your own good.

BARBARA. (*Overlapping.*) . . . we couldn't tell you it was them.

JULIE. But why—what's happened?

STEWART. They're the ones we've been watching. (JULIE *stares at* STEWART.)

JULIE. Auntie Helen and Uncle Peter . . . ?

STEWART. We had to find out, you see. We had to be sure—that's why we came here.

JULIE. Find out *what*?

STEWART. Evidence. We had to have proof that they were passing on secrets.

JULIE. (*Aghast.*) What do you mean?

STEWART. They're spies. They're working for the Russians. (*Silence.*)

JULIE. (*Barely audible.*) I don't believe it.

BARBARA. It's true, darling . . . really, it is. (JULIE *gasps; her hands fly to her face;* BARBARA *goes to her.*)

BARBARA. Oh, Julie, my Julie, I'm so sorry.

JULIE. (*Louder.*) I don't believe it.

BOB. Mum's right. It's true. (BARBARA *embraces*
JULIE; *they are both weeping*.)

BARBARA. We wanted to tell you, but we couldn't.
We didn't know what to do.

JULIE. How could she do it? How could she do it?
How could she do it?

BARBARA. Oh, Julie, don't—please don't—please!

JULIE. (*Her voice rising*.) How could she do it how
could she do it how could she do it how could she do it
how could she do it how could she do it how could she
. . . (JULIE *breaks away from* BARBARA *and runs upstairs*.)

BARBARA. (*With a terrible cry of anguish*.) Julie!

(*Lights fade*. BOB *steps forward to address the
audience*.)

BOB. Julie went up to her room. She collected together
all the things that Helen and Peter had ever given her—
the handkerchiefs, the necklace, the silk blouse; she took
them out into the garden and burnt them. (*Pause*.) A
few days later, Mr. Stewart called round with a present
for Barbara; a thank-you present, he said, for looking
after his girls for all those weeks. It was a box of six
fish knives and forks. Silver-plated. (*Pause*.) The Krogers
were sentenced to twenty years' imprisonment. Later, we
discovered that Helen was a colonel in the KGB.
(*Pause*.) Julie's bitterness did not last. Curious to see her
Auntie Helen again, she went to visit her in Holloway
Prison. Towards the end of their conversation, Helen
said, "I'll never forgive your mother—never." After
eight years, they were released from prison in exchange
for an Englishman who had been jailed by the Russians.
They flew to Poland to start a new life. A crowd of
journalists watched them go. "Let's all be friends," said
Helen. (*Pause*.) A few weeks after that, a Sunday afternoon it was, Barbara went into the kitchen, sat down on
a chair, and died. A heart attack. She was so young, still
in her fifties. I miss her more as time goes by. More—
not less. Is it always like that?

CURTAIN

PRONUNCIATION OF RUSSIAN WORDS

Aleksandr: AH-LĀK-'SAHN-DR
Nikolaevich: NEEKO-'LĪYEH-VEECH
Shelepin: SHEH-'LĀ-PEEN
Kutuzovsky: KOO-'TOO-ZOF-SKEE
Prospekt: PRO-'SPÅKT
Dzerzhinsky: DZAIR-'ZHEEN-SKEE
Lubyanka: LOOB-'YAHNK-AH
Morozhennoe: MOH-'ROH-ZHĀ-(or ə)-'NOH-YĀ
Pazhahlsta: PAH-'ZHAHLə-ZDAH

The Life and Adventures of Nicholas Nickleby

by Charles Dickens,
adapted for the stage by
David Edgar

The *Life and Adventures of Nicholas Nickleby* was performed by the Royal Shakespeare Company at the Aldwych Theatre, London, on June 5–6, 1980, under the direction of Trevor Nunn and John Caird, with the following cast:

THE NICKLEBY FAMILY

NICHOLAS NICKLEBY	*Roger Rees*
KATE NICKLEBY	*Susan Littler*
RALPH NICKLEBY	*John Woodvine*
MRS NICKLEBY	*Jane Downs*

LONDON

NEWMAN NOGGS	*Edward Petherbridge*
HANNAH	*Clare Travers-Deacon*
MISS LA CREEVY	*Rose Hill*
SIR MATTHEW PUPKER	*David Lloyd Meredith*
MR BONNEY	*Terence Harvey*
IRATE GENTLEMAN	*Patrick Godfrey*
FURIOUS GENTLEMAN	*Ben Kingsley*
FLUNKEY	*Timothy Kightley*
MUFFIN BOYS	*Andrew Hawkins Timothy Spall*
MR SNAWLEY	*William Maxwell*
SNAWLEY MAJOR	*Janet Dale*
SNAWLEY MINOR	*Clare Travers-Deacon*
BELLING	*Stephen Rashbrook*
WILLIAM	*John McEnery*
WAITRESSES	*Sharon Bower Juliet Hammond-Hill*
COACHMAN	*Clyde Pollitt*
MR MANTALINI	*John McEnery*
MADAME MANTALINI	*Thelma Whiteley*
FLUNKEY	*Griffith Jones*
MISS KNAG	*Janet Dale*
RICH LADIES	*Sharon Bower Shirley King*

MILLINERS .... *Suzanne Bertish, Sharon Bower,*
Juliet Hammond-Hill, Cathryn Harrison,
Ian East, William Maxwell, Julie Peasgood,
Stephen Rashbrook, Clare Travers-Deacon

YORKSHIRE
MR SQUEERS .... *Ben Kingsley*
MRS SQUEERS .... *Lila Kaye*
SMIKE .... *David Threlfall*
PHIB .... *Cathryn Harrison*
FANNY SQUEERS .... *Suzanne Bertish*
YOUNG WACKFORD SQUEERS .... *Timothy Spall*
JOHN BROWDIE .... *Bob Peck*
TILDA PRICE .... *Julie Peasgood*
Boys
TOMKINS .... *William Maxwell*
COATES .... *Andrew Hawkins*
GRAYMARSH .... *Alan Gill*
JENNINGS .... *Terence Harvey*
MOBBS .... *Christopher Ravenscroft*
BOLDER .... *Mark Tandy*
PITCHER .... *Sharon Bower*
JACKSON .... *Nicholas Gecks*
COBBEY .... *John Matshikiza*
PETERS .... *Teddy Kempner*
SPROUTER .... *Juliet Hammond-Hill*
ROBERTS .... *Ian East*
MCTAGGART .... *Neil Phillips*

LONDON AGAIN
MR KENWIGS .... *Patrick Godfrey*
MRS KENWIGS .... *Shirley King*
MORLEENA KENWIGS .... *Clare Travers-Deacon*
MR LILLYVICK .... *Timothy Kightley*
MISS PETOWKER .... *Cathryn Harrison*
MR CROWL .... *Ian East*
GEORGE .... *Alan Gill*
MR CUTLER .... *Jeffery Dench*
MRS CUTLER .... *Janet Dale*
MRS KENWIGS' SISTER .... *Sharon Bower*
STOUT LADY .... *Rose Hill*
MISS GREEN .... *Jane Downs*
BENJAMIN .... *Teddy Kempner*
PUGSTYLES .... *Roderick Horn*

OLD LORD ....*Griffith Jones*
YOUNG FIANCÉE ....*Juliet Hammond-Hill*
LANDLORD ....*Jeffery Dench*

PORTSMOUTH

MR VINCENT CRUMMLES .... *Graham Crowden*
MRS CRUMMLES ....*Lila Kaye*
THE INFANT PHENOMENON ....*Julie Peasgood*
MASTER PERCY CRUMMLES .... *Teddy Kempner*
MASTER CRUMMLES............................... *Mark Tandy*
MRS GRUDDEN ....*Rose Hill*
MISS SNEVELLICCI .... *Suzanne Bertish*
MR FOLAIR ....*Timothy Spall*
MR LENVILLE ....*Neil Phillips*
MISS LEDROOK ....*Juliet Hammond-Hill*
MISS BRAVASSA.. *Sharon Bower*
MR WAGSTAFF .... *Ben Kingsley*
MR BLIGHTEY..*Jeffery Dench*
MISS BELVAWNEY ....*Janet Dale*
MISS GAZINGI ....*Clare Travers-Deacon*
MR PAILEY.. *William Maxwell*
MR HETHERINGTON .... *Andrew Hawkins*
MR BANE ....*Stephen Rashbrook*
MR FLUGGERS ....*Griffith Jones*
MRS LENVILLE...*Shirley King*
MR CURDLE..*Hubert Rees*
MRS CURDLE .... *Susan Littler*
MR SNEVELLICCI ....*John McEnery*
MRS SNEVELLICCI................................... *Thelma Whiteley*

LONDON AGAIN

SCALEY ....*Clyde Pollitt*
TIX .... *Teddy Kempner*
SIR MULBERRY HAWK................................... *Bob Peck*
LORD FREDERICK VERISOPHT ....*Nicholas Gecks*
MR PLUCK .... *Teddy Kempner*
MR PYKE ....*John Matshikiza*
MR SNOBB .... *Christopher Ravenscroft*
COLONEL CHOWSER .... *Norman Tyrrell*
BROOKER..*Clyde Pollitt*
MR WITITTERLEY .... *Roderick Horn*
MRS WITITTERLEY ....*Janet Dale*
ALPHONSE .... *Stephen Rashbrook*

OPERA SINGERS.............*Sharon Bower Andrew Hawkins*
                             John Woodvine
CHARLES CHEERYBLE....................*David Lloyd Meredith*
NED CHEERYBLE...*Hubert Rees*
TIM LINKINWATER..*Griffith Jones*
THE MAN NEXT DOOR .... *Patrick Godfrey*
KEEPER..*Alan Gill*
FRANK CHEERYBLE...................... *Christopher Ravenscroft*
NURSE.. *Thelma Whiteley*
MADELINE BRAY..............................*Juliet Hammond-Hill*
ARTHUR GRIDE..*Jeffery Dench*
WALTER BRAY .... *Norman Tyrrell*
PEG SLIDERSKEW.....................................*Suzanne Bertish*
HAWK'S RIVAL .... *Edward Petherbridge*
CAPTAIN ADAMS .... *Andrew Hawkins*
WESTWOOD ....*Neil Phillips*
CROUPIER..*Timothy Spall*
CASINO PROPRIETOR............................. *Graham Crowden*
SURGEON .... *Timothy Kightley*
UMPIRE.. *Roderick Horn*
POLICEMEN.........................*Andrew Hawkins Mark Tandy*
MRS SNAWLEY..*Janet Dale*
YOUNG WOMAN ....*Clare Travers-Deacon*

Musicians

MIKE STEER...............................*Music Director/Keyboards*
CHRISTOPHER LACEY.. *Flute*
VICTOR SLAYMARK.. *Clarinet*
PETER WHITTAKER ....*Bassoon*
PETER CAMERON... *Trumpet*
RODERICK TEARLE .... *Trumpet*
DUNCAN HOLLOWOOD ....*Horn*
DAVID HISSEY .... *Trombone*
BRIDGET HURST/WILFRED GIBSON........................... *Violin*
ALISTAIR MCLACHLAN.. *Violin*
ALAN WALLEY ....*Bass*
GEORGE WEIGAND ....*Guitar/Banjo*
TONY MCVEY...*Percussion*

Wedding Anthem sung by Choristers from St Paul's Cathedral, Master of the Choir Barry Rose.

Sets by John Napier and Dermot Hayes; lighting by David Hersey; music and lyrics by Stephen Oliver; Assistant to designers John Thompson.

The Royal Shakespeare Company production of *The Life and Adventures of Nicholas Nickleby* was presented by James M. Nederlander, The Shubert Organization, Elizabeth I. McCann and Nelle Nugent at the Plymouth Theatre, in New York City, on October 4, 1981, under the direction of Trevor Nunn and John Caird (assisted by Leon Rubin), with the following cast:

THE NICKLEBY FAMILY

NICHOLAS NICKLEBY	*Roger Rees*
KATE NICKLEBY	*Emily Richard*
RALPH NICKLEBY	*John Woodvine*
MRS. NICKLEBY	*Priscilla Morgan*

LONDON

NEWMAN NOGGS	*Edward Petherbridge*
HANNAH	*Hilary Townley*
MISS LA CREEVY	*Rose Hill*
SIR MATTHEW PUPKER	*David Lloyd Meredith*
MR. BONNEY	*Andrew Hawkins*
IRATE GENTLEMAN	*Patrick Godfrey*
FLUNKEY	*Timothy Kightley*
MR. SNAWLEY	*William Maxwell*
SNAWLEY MAJOR	*Janet Dale*
SNAWLEY MINOR	*Hilary Townley*
BELLING	*Stephen Rashbrook*
WILLIAM	*John McEnery*
WAITRESSES	*Sharon Bower, Sally Nesbitt*
COACHMAN	*Clyde Pollitt*
MR. MANTALINI	*John McEnery*
MADAME MANTALINI	*Thelma Whiteley*
FLUNKEY	*Richard Simpson*
MISS KNAG	*Janet Dale*
RICH LADIES	*Sharon Bower, Shirley King*
MILLINERS	*Suzanne Bertish, Sharon Bower, Lucy Gutteridge, Cathryn Harrison, Ian East, William Maxwell, Sally Nesbitt, Stephen Rashbrook, Hilary Townley*

YORKSHIRE

MR. SQUEERS	*Alun Armstrong*
MRS. SQUEERS	*Lila Kaye*

SMIKE	*David Threlfall*
PHIB	*Sally Nesbitt*
FANNY SQUEERS	*Suzanne Bertish*
YOUNG WACKFORD SQUEERS	*Ian McNeice*
JOHN BROWDIE	*Bob Peck*
TILDA PRICE	*Cathryn Harrison*
Boys	
TOMKINS	*William Maxwell*
COATES	*Andrew Hawkins*
GRAYMARSH	*Alan Gill*
JENNINGS	*Patrick Godfrey*
MOBBS	*Christopher Ravenscroft*
BOLDER	*Mark Tandy*
PITCHER	*Sharon Bower*
JACKSON	*Nicholas Gecks*
COBBEY	*John McEnery*
PETERS	*Teddy Kempner*
SPROUTER	*Lucy Gutteridge*
ROBERTS	*Ian East*

LONDON AGAIN

MR. KENWIGS	*Patrick Godfrey*
MRS. KENWIGS	*Shirley King*
MORLEENA KENWIGS	*Hilary Townley*
MR. LILLYVICK	*Timothy Kightley*
MISS PETOWKER	*Cathryn Harrison*
MR. CROWL	*Ian East*
GEORGE	*Alan Gill*
MR. CUTLER	*Jeffery Dench*
MRS. CUTLER	*Janet Dale*
MRS. KENWIGS' SISTER	*Sharon Bower*
LADY FROM DOWNSTAIRS	*Rose Hill*
MISS GREEN	*Priscilla Morgan*
BENJAMIN	*Teddy Kempner*
PUGSTYLES	*Roderick Horn*
OLD LORD	*Richard Simpson*
YOUNG FIANCÉE	*Lucy Gutteridge*
LANDLORD	*Jeffery Dench*

PORTSMOUTH

MR. VINCENT CRUMMLES	*Christopher Benjamin*
MRS. CRUMMLES	*Lila Kaye*
THE INFANT PHENOMENON	*Hilary Townley*

MASTER PERCY CRUMMLES .... *Teddy Kempner*
MASTER CRUMMLES .... *Mark Tandy*
MRS. GRUDDEN .... *Rose Hill*
MISS SNEVELLICCI .... *Suzanne Bertish*
MR. FOLAIR .... *Clyde Pollitt*
MR. LENVILLE .... *Christopher Ravenscroft*
MISS LEDROOK .... *Lucy Gutteridge*
MISS BRAVASSA .... *Sharon Bower*
MR. WAGSTAFF .... *Alun Armstrong*
MR. BLIGHTEY .... *Jeffery Dench*
MISS BELVAWNEY .... *Janet Dale*
MISS GAZINGI .... *Sally Nesbitt*
MR. PAILEY .... *William Maxwell*
MR. HETHERINGTON .... *Andrew Hawkins*
MR. BANE .... *Stephen Rashbrook*
MR. FLUGGERS .... *Richard Simpson*
MRS. LENVILLE .... *Shirley King*
MR. CURDLE .... *Hubert Rees*
MRS. CURDLE .... *Emily Richard*
MR. SNEVELLICCI .... *John McEnery*
MRS. SNEVELLICCI .... *Thelma Whiteley*

LONDON AGAIN
SCALEY .... *Ian McNeice*
TIX .... *Teddy Kempner*
SIR MULBERRY HAWK .... *Bob Peck*
LORD FREDERICK VERISOPHT .... *Nicholas Gecks*
MR. PLUCK .... *Teddy Kempner*
MR. PYKE .... *Mark Tandy*
MR. SNOBB .... *Christopher Ravenscroft*
COLONEL CHOWSER .... *Timothy Kightley*
BROOKER .... *Clyde Pollitt*
MR. WITITTERLEY .... *Roderick Horn*
MRS. WITITTERLEY .... *Janet Dale*
ALPHONSE .... *Stephen Rashbrook*
OPERA SINGERS .... *Sharon Bower, Andrew Hawkins*
John Woodvine
CHARLES CHEERYBLE .... *David Lloyd Meredith*
NED CHEERYBLE .... *Hubert Rees*
TIM LINKINWATER .... *Richard Simpson*
THE MAN NEXT DOOR .... *Patrick Godfrey*
KEEPER .... *Alan Gill*
FRANK CHEERYBLE .... *Christopher Ravenscroft*

NURSE	*Thelma Whiteley*
ARTHUR GRIDE	*Jeffery Dench*
MADELINE BRAY	*Lucy Gutteridge*
WALTER BRAY	*Christopher Benjamin*
PEG SLIDERSKEW	*Suzanne Bertish*
HAWK'S RIVAL	*Edward Petherbridge*
CAPTAIN ADAMS	*Andrew Hawkins*
WESTWOOD	*Alan Gill*
CROUPIER	*Ian McNeice*
CASINO PROPRIETOR	*Patrick Godfrey*
SURGEON	*Timothy Kightley*
UMPIRE	*Roderick Horn*
POLICEMEN	*Andrew Hawkins, Mark Tandy*
MRS. SNAWLEY	*Janet Dale*
YOUNG WOMAN	*Hilary Townley*

Musicians

DONALD JOHNSTON	*Musical Conductor/Piano*
MEL RODNON	*Flute*
SEYMOUR PRESS	*Clarinet*
ETHAN BAUCH	*Bassoon*
LOWELL HERSHEY	*Trumpet*
ROBERT ZITTOLA	*Trumpet*
CHRISTINE SNYDER	*French Horn*
DANIEL REPOLE	*Trombone*
SANDRA BILLINGSLEA	*Violin*
KAREN RITSCHER	*Viola*
DOC SOLOMON	*Bass*
BRUCE YUCHITEL	*Banjo*
JACK JENNINGS	*Percussion*

Wedding Anthem sung by Choristers from St. Paul's Cathedral, Master of the Choir Barry Rose.

The designers were John Napier and Dermot Hayes; costumes were by John Napier; and the lighting was by David Hersey. The American production was designed in association with Neil Peter Jampolis (sets and costumes); Beverly Emmons (lighting); and Richard Fitzgerald (sound). The music and lyrics were by Stephen Oliver; and the musical director was Donald Johnston.

AUTHOR'S INTRODUCTION

On November 19, 1979, a group of about 50 people sat down in a large circle in a rehearsal room in Stratford-upon-Avon, to discuss the possibility of turning Charles Dickens' vast, panoramic novel *Nicholas Nickleby* into a theatrical entertainment. This group consisted of a large number of actors and actresses, two directors, an assistant director, four stage managers, and a writer. Over the following months, this line-up changed: some actors left, others joined, the team acquired two designers, an assistant designer, a composer and lyricist, a musical director, a band, a script assistant, a lighting director, lighting and sound technicians, dressers and stage-hands. During this period, the performers had experimented, improvised and completed 20 research projects into aspects of early Victorian life, the directors had overseen these exercises, had discussed, organised and undertaken rehearsals; the writer had written. By January 1980 it had become clear that early hopes of a one-evening project had to be jettisoned; if we were to tell the entire Dickens' story (as we were determined to do) then we would need two evenings: as spring approached it became clear that these would be very long evenings indeed. And by our opening night, June 5, 1980, we had two vast plays: the first lasting four hours, the second four and a half.

The opening of the play, at the Royal Shakespeare Company's London theatre, was not the end of the story. After a short run in the summer of 1980, the production was brought back into the company's repertoire on two occasions; the show was adapted for television and recorded in the summer of 1981; the stage production transferred to New York in the fall of that year. Each revival and transfer saw cast changes, the production developed, and the script was rewritten and (I hope) improved.

This is not the place for a history of the way *Nickleby* came about (there is a good one, written by Leon Rubin, called *The Nicholas Nickleby Story*). But it is important to give some impression of the process, for two reasons. The first is a matter of simple justice. Most scripts are developed and improved by the directors and performers who work on them, but *Nickleby* was perhaps unique as a collaborative venture. The original idea came from the directors, John Caird and Trevor Nunn; the style and texture of the adaptation was created by the performers; the set and the score helped to define not just how the show looked and sounded, but the basic method of story-telling as well. The script published here is thus a collective possession, in a very real sense: it was created over nearly two years by the best part of a hundred people.

The second point concerns the extent to which it has been possible to produce an acting edition in the conventional sense. While I have tried to make clear, in the notes that follow the text and in the text, how the show was and thus could be costumed, set and staged, many of these decisions resulted from the specific conditions in which we worked (and indeed from our personnel). It is open to future companies to make their own decisions, based on their own resources.

Two further things should be said by way of introduction. The first is that *Nicholas Nickleby*, Parts One and Two, tells the entire story of a huge Dickens novel. One can imagine all sorts of good reasons for doing one part but not the other, or even for doing versions of the play which contain some plots but not others. But I would nonetheless beg producers to consider attempting the whole, because one of the unique things about our adaptation was that, unlike every Dickens film and stage adaptation (and most of the television serialisations as well), we did it all, because we felt strongly that the only way to represent Dickens' achievement was to display it in its entirety.

Finally, I am aware that the notes and stage directions in this text may seem woefully inadequate to companies used to the excellent documentation provided in most acting editions. I hope they will understand that in order to present such detail in a show in which at least 39 performers play round about 123 speaking parts in 95 scenes would require a book of at least twice this size. Luckily, however, producers are able to purchase, at most good bookshops, a companion volume which contains the most comprehensive acting, costuming, staging and setting instructions, and a lot else besides. It is called *The Life and Adventures of Nicholas Nickleby*, and it was written by the English novelist Charles Dickens in the early years of the 19th century.

David Edgar

PART ONE

ACT I

SCENE 1

As the audience come in, the Company mingles with them, welcoming them to the show. Eventually, the whole company assembles on stage. Each member of the company takes at least one of the lines of opening narration:

NARRATION. There once lived in a sequestered part of the county of Devonshire, one Mr. Godfrey Nickleby, who, rather late in life, took it into his head to get married.

And in due course, when Mrs. Nickleby had presented her husband with two sons, he found himself in a situation of distinctly shortened means,

Which were only relieved when, one fine morning, there arrived a black-bordered letter, informing him that his uncle was dead and left him the bulk of his property, amounting in all to five thousand pounds.

And with a portion of this property, Mr. Godfrey Nickleby purchased a small farm near Dawlish,

And on his death some fifteen years later, he was able to leave to his eldest son three thousand pounds in cash, and to his youngest, one thousand and the farm.

The younger boy was of a timid and retiring disposition, keen only to attach himself to the quiet routine of country life.

The elder son, however, resolved to make much use of his father's inheritance.

For young Ralph Nickleby had commenced usury on

a limited scale even at school, putting out at interest a small capital of slate pencil and marbles,

And had now in adulthood resolved to live his life by the simple motto that there was nothing in the world as good as money.

And while Ralph prospered in the mercantile way in London, the young brother lived still on the farm,

And took himself a wife,

Who gave birth to a boy and a girl,

And by the time they were both nearing the age of twenty, he found his expenses much increased and his capital still more depleted.

Speculate. His wife advised him.

Think of your brother, Mr. Nickleby, and speculate.

And Mr. Nickleby did speculate,

But a mania prevailed,

A bubble burst,

Four stockbrokers took villa residences at Florence,

Four hundred nobodies were ruined,

And one of them was

Mr. Nickleby.

And Mr. Nickleby took to his bed,

Apparently resolved to keep that, at all events.

Cheer up, sir!

Said the apothecary.

You mustn't let yourself be cast down, sir.

Said the nurse.

Such things happen every day,

Remarked the lawyer,

And it is very sinful to rebel against them,

Whispered the clergyman,

And what no man with a family ought to do,

Added the neighbours.

But Mr. Nickleby shook his head,

And he motioned them all out of the room

And shortly afterwards his reason went astray,

And he babbled of the goodness of his brother and the merry times they'd had at school,

And one day he turned upon his face,

Observing that he thought that he could fall asleep.

And so, with no-one in the world to help them but Ralph Nickleby,

(MRS. NICKLEBY, KATE and NICHOLAS are emerging from the crowd.)

MRS. NICKLEBY. The widow,
KATE/NICHOLAS. And her children,
NARRATOR. Journeyed forth to—LONDON!

(And immediately, the company becomes the population of London, jostling and bustling round, past and through the NICKLEBYS, until we can see them no more, and the next scene has emerged.)

SCENE 2

The London Tavern. A public meeting. On stage, some seated, some standing, are the organisers of the meeting: SIR MATTHEW PUPKER, MR. BONNEY, a FLUNKEY, several gentlemen, and, sitting a little apart, RALPH NICK-

LEBY. *In and around the audience are representatives of the lower classes: in particular, a large number of* MUFFIN-BOYS, *who distribute muffins to the audience from the trays they carry round their necks. There are also a few policemen to keep public order, and, as we shall discover, an* IRATE GENTLEMAN *and a* FURIOUS GENTLEMAN *as well. The* FLUNKEY *bangs his staff for silence.*

FLUNKEY. My lords, ladies and gentlemen. Pray give silence for Sir Matthew Pupker, Honourable Member of the Commons of England in Parliament assembled. (*Applause. The odd cat-call. The* POLICE *finger their truncheons.*)

SIR MATTHEW. Good morning. It falls to me today to announce the opening of a public meeting to discuss the propriety or otherwise of petitioning Parliament in urgent condemnation of the appalling, deplorable, and generally heinous state of the Hot Muffin Baking and Delivery Industry. (*The* IRATE GENTLEMAN *shouts from the audience.*)

IRATE GENTLEMAN. Crumpets. (*Polite applause.*)

SIR MATTHEW. Ladies and gentlemen, in troubled times like these, when naked riot stalks the frightened streets at home, and overseas the Russian bear is pawing at the very vitals of the Empire, there could not be a greater nor a nobler task than this we face today. (*Applause. To stop it,* SIR MATTHEW *raises his hand.*) So, Mr. Bonney will now read the resolution. (BONNEY *stands, coughs, and reads.*)

BONNEY. The Resolution. That this meeting views with alarm and apprehension, the present state of the Muffin trade.

IRATE GENTLEMAN. (*Shouts.*) And crumpet trade.

BONNEY. . . . that it considers the present constitution of the Muffin Boys—

IRATE GENTLEMAN. (*Shouts.*) And crumpet boys!

SOME. Order—shh—

BONNEY. (*After a slight pause.*) . . . wholly undeserving of the confidence of the public, and that it deems the whole Muffin System—

IRATE GENTLEMAN. Crumpet! (BONNEY *turns to* SIR MATTHEW *in frustration.*)

SIR MATTHEW. Now, what— (*The* IRATE GENTLEMAN *has marched up on to the stage.*)

IRATE GENTLEMAN. Sir, I must protest.

SIR MATTHEW. I beg your pardon?

IRATE GENTLEMAN. Sir, I must protest and I must insist. I must insist and I must demand.

SIR MATTHEW. Yes? What?

IRATE GENTLEMAN. And crumpets, sir. And *crumpets*. Not just muffins. Crumpets. (*Pause.*)

SIR MATTHEW. Is that an amendment?

IRATE GENTLEMAN. It's a demand. And an amendment, too.

SIR MATTHEW. I see. Well, then. All those in favour?

ALMOST EVERYONE. Aye! (*One* FURIOUS MAN, *however, shouts.*)

FURIOUS MAN. No, no, a thousand times, no! You'll rue the day. (*And he strides out.*)

SIR MATTHEW. The ayes appear to have it. Mr. Bonney.

BONNEY. And it deems the whole Muffin and Crumpet system prejudicial to the best interests of a great mercantile community. (*Applause.*) My lords, ladies, and gentlemen: I must state that I have visited the houses of the poor, and have found them destitute of the slightest vestige of a muffin, or a crumpet, which there appears to be much reason to believe some of these persons to not taste from year's end to year's end. (*Boos and expressions of shock and horror: "It's a scandal", "This must stop", "Fancy that".*) It is this melancholy state of affairs that the company proposes to correct. (*During the following a certain amount of protest develops among those sectors of the audience who are in fact muffin and crumpet sellers themselves, and have thus far been sympathetic to the emotional description of their sad and miserable lot.*) . . . firstly, by prohibiting under dire penalties all private muffin and crumpet trading of every description; (*Applause—dies down, and we hear* MUFFINEERS.)

1ST MUFFINEER. Eh?

2ND MUFFINEER. What's he saying?

BONNEY. . . . and secondly, by ourselves providing the public generally, with muffins and crumpets of first quality at reduced prices— (*Applause—dies down, we hear* MUFFINEERS.)

1ST MUFFINEER. He must be joking.

2ND MUFFINEER. It's our livelihood!

BONNEY. . . . and it is with this object that a bill has

been introduced into Parliament; (*The* MUFFINEERS *are striding off towards the stage.*) . . . it is this bill that we have met to support;

1ST MUFFINEER. What about the muffin boys! (*Some* MUFFINEERS *have reached the stage. Others are throwing their muffins on to the stage. Some disreputable members of the audience probably join in too.*)

MUFFINEERS. So what about the Muffin Boys
So what about the Muffin Boys
So what about the—

(*The* MUFFINEERS *are roundly truncheoned by the* POLICE *for this anarchic display, and are ejected, as* BONNEY:)

BONNEY. . . . and, finally, it is the supporters of this bill who will confer undying brightness and splendour upon England, under the name of the United Metropolitan Improved Hot Muffin and Crumpet Baking and Punctual Delivery Company! Capital five millions, in five hundred thousand shares of Ten—Pounds—Each! (*Wild applause,* BONNEY *accepts hand-shakes from supporters and wipes his brow. Eventually, the applause dies.*)

SIR MATTHEW. Well, thank you, Mr. Bonney. (*Pause. Something should have happened.* SIR MATTHEW *looks to* RALPH NICKLEBY, *who has sat, impassively, throughout the proceedings.*) Mr. Nickleby?

RALPH. Seconded.

SIR MATTHEW. All those in favour?

EVERYONE. Aye!

SIR MATTHEW. Carried by an acclamation! Meeting closed. (*And suddenly,* SIR MATTHEW, MR. BONNEY, *the gentlemen, and everyone else disperse, and* RALPH *walks forward.*)

SCENE 3

RALPH NICKLEBY *is greeted by his clerk* NEWMAN NOGGS, *a sallow-faced man in rusty-brown clothes.* NOGGS *carries a letter. We suppose we are in the street, outside the meeting.*

RALPH. Noggs.
NOGGS. That's me.
RALPH. What is it?
NOGGS. It's a letter.

RALPH. Oh. The Ruddles mortgage, I suppose?

NOGGS. No. Wrong.

RALPH. What *has* come, then?

NOGGS. I have.

RALPH. (*Irritated.*) What else?

NOGGS. (*Handing over the letter.*) This. Postmark Strand, black wax, black border, woman's hand, C.N. in the corner.

RALPH. Black wax. I know the hand, too. Newman, I shouldn't be surprised if my brother was dead. (*He opens the letter and reads.*)

NOGGS. I don't think you would.

RALPH. (*Reading.*) Why not, sir?

NOGGS. You never are surprised at anything, that's all.

RALPH. (*Folding the letter.*) It's as I thought. He's dead.

NOGGS. Children alive?

RALPH. Yes, well, that's the point. They're both alive.

NOGGS. Both?

RALPH. And a widow too, and all three of 'em in London, damn 'em. (*Slight pause.* RALPH *looks at* NOGGS, *who is looking neutral. Enter* MR. BONNEY.)

NOGGS. (*Unconvincingly.*) Terrible. (*Slight pause.*)

RALPH. Go home. (BONNEY *coughs.* RALPH *turns to* BONNEY. NOGGS *does not go.*) Ah, Bonney. Put me down for 500, would you?

BONNEY. They'll nearly double in a three-month, Mr. Nickleby.

RALPH. I'm sure of it.

BONNEY. And when they have . . . You'll know just what to do with 'em. (*Slight pause. Embarrassingly confidential.*) Back quietly out, at just the right time, eh?

RALPH. Indeed. (*He notices* NOGGS *is still there.*) I told you to go home.

NOGGS. I'm going. (NOGGS *snaps his knuckles and goes out.*)

BONNEY. What a very remarkable man that clerk of yours is.

RALPH. Kept his own hounds and horses, once. But squandered everything, borrowed at interest, took to drinking . . . I'd done a little business with him, as it

happens, and he came to me to borrow more, I needed
to employ a clerk . . .

BONNEY. Yes, yes, just so.

RALPH. So, then—five hundred, Bonney. (BONNEY
goes. RALPH *waves the letter. To himself.*) What are they
to me? I've never even seen 'em. Damn 'em! (*And he
too turns to go.*)

SCENE 4

Outside and inside a house in the Strand. RALPH *walks
round the stage, as narrators describe his journey:*

NARRATORS. And so Ralph Nickleby proceeded to the
Strand . . .

And found the number of the house . . .

And stopped,

And gave a double-knock, (*Someone bangs a stick twice
on the floor.*)

And waited for an answer. (*A dirty-faced servant,* HAN-
NAH, *appears.*)

HANNAH. Yes?

RALPH. Mrs. Nickleby at home?

HANNAH. La Creevy.

RALPH. Beg you pardon?

HANNAH. Name, isn't what you said. It's Miss La
Creevy.

RALPH. (*Waving the letter.*) But— (*A female voice
from off.*)

MISS LA CREEVY. Who is it, Hannah?

HANNAH. There's a man here, wanting something.
(*Enter* MISS LA CREEVY, *a small lady of 50 in a yellow
bonnet, carrying a paintbrush.*)

MISS LA CREEVY. Who? And wanting what? (HAN-
NAH *shrugs, nods at* RALPH.) Oh, sir—

RALPH. Madam, to whom—

MISS LA CREEVY. Oh, sir, I'm Miss La Creevy, sir, I
am a painter of portraiture in miniature, sir, and if I may

presume to speak such, you have a very strongly marked countenance for such a purpose, sir, should that be your—

RALPH. Is there a widow lodging here? A Mrs. Nickleby?

MISS LA CREEVY. Oh, you're for Mrs. Nickleby?

RALPH. That's right. I am Mr. Ralph Nickleby.

MISS LA CREEVY. Oh, Hannah, what a stupid thing you are. Why, sir, yes, they have their apartments just across the hall from mine, just there, sir, and I must say what an extremely affable lady she is, though of course very low in her spirits, and the children too, most pleasant—

RALPH. Over here, you say?

MISS LA CREEEVY. That's right, sir, but may I remark, that if you should ever wish to have a miniature . . . (RALPH *turns back, looks darkly at* MISS LA CREEVY, *who retains sufficient composure to produce a small card.*) Perhaps you will have the kindness to take a card of terms. (RALPH *takes the card. With a humourless smile.*)

RALPH. Of course.

MISS LA CREEVY. Now, Hannah, go on, and announce Mr. Nickleby to Mrs. Nickleby.

RALPH. I thank you. (MISS LA CREEVY *goes out, as* NICHOLAS, KATE *and* MRS. NICKLEBY *come forward.* NICHOLAS *carries a chair, on which* MRS. NICKLEBY *sits.* HANNAH *leads* RALPH *to them.* HANNAH *tries to make a proper announcement.*)

HANNAH. Uh. Mrs. Nickleby, here's . . . Mr. Nickleby. (HANNAH *withdraws.*)

RALPH. Ah, young Nicholas, I suppose. Good morning sir. And, Kate.

MRS. NICKLEBY. That is correct, sir. These are my— (*Unable to get out the word "children",* MRS. NICKLEBY *bursts into tears.*)

RALPH. Well, ma'am, how are you? You must bear up against sorrow, ma'am, I always do. You didn't mention how he died.

MRS. NICKLEBY. The doctors could attribute it to no particular disease. We have no reason to fear that he died of a broken heart.

RALPH. Hm. What?

MRS. NICKLEBY. I beg your pardon?

RALPH. I don't understand. A broken leg or head, I know of them, but not a broken heart.

NICHOLAS. Some people, I believe, have none to break.

RALPH. What's that? How old is this boy, ma'am?

MRS. NICKLEBY. Nineteen.

RALPH. And what's he mean to do for bread?

NICHOLAS. To earn it, sir. And not look for anyone to keep my family, except myself.

RALPH. I see. Well, ma'am, the creditors have administered, you say, and you spent what little was left, coming all the way to London, to see me.

MRS. NICKLEBY. I hoped . . . It was my husband's wish, I should appeal to you—

RALPH. I don't know why it is. But whenever a man dies with no property, he always thinks he has the right to dispose of other people's. If my brother had been acquainted with the world, and then applied himself to make his way in it, then you would not now be in this— in your situation. I must say it, Miss Nickleby: my brother was a thoughtless, inconsiderate man, and no-one, I am sure, can feel that fact more keenly than you do.

MRS. NICKLEBY. Well, well. That may be true. I've often thought, if he had listened to me . . . Yes. It may well be true. (NICHOLAS *and* KATE *give an uncertain glance at each other.* RALPH *clocks this.*)

RALPH. So, what's your daughter fit for, ma'am?

MRS. NICKLEBY. Oh, Kate has been well-educated, sir.

KATE. I'm willing to try anything that will give me home and bread.

RALPH. (*Slightly affected by* KATE.) Well, well. (*To* NICHOLAS, *briskly.*) And you, sir? You're prepared to work?

NICHOLAS. Yes, certainly. (RALPH *takes a newspaper cutting from his pocket.*)

RALPH. Then read that. Caught my eye this morning. (NICHOLAS *takes the cutting and reads.*)

NICHOLAS. Education. The Master of the Academy, Dotheboys Hall, near Greta Bridge in Yorkshire, is in town, and attends at the Saracen's Head, Snow Hill.

Able assistant wanted. Annual salary five pounds. A Master of Arts would be preferred.

RALPH. Well. There.

MRS. NICKLEBY. But he's not a Master of Arts.

RALPH. That I think can be got over.

KATE. And the salary is too small, uncle, and it is so far away—

MRS. NICKLEBY. Hush, Kate, your uncle must know best.

RALPH. And I'm convinced that he will have you, if I recommend it. (*Pause.*) Ma'am, if he can find another job, in London, now, which keeps him in shoe leather . . . He can have a thousand pounds. (*Pause.*)

KATE. We must be separated, then, so soon?

NICHOLAS. Sir, if I am appointed to this post, what will become of those I leave behind?

RALPH. If you're accepted, and you take it, they will be provided for. That will be my care. (*Pause.*)

NICHOLAS. Then, uncle, I am ready to do anything you wish.

RALPH. That's good. And, come, who knows, you work well, and you'll rise to be a partner. And then, if he dies, your fortune's made.

NICHOLAS. Oh, yes? (*To his family, to cheer them up, but becoming convinced himself.*) Oh, yes, to be sure. Oh, Kate, and who knows, perhaps there will be some young nobleman or other, at the school, who takes a fancy to me, and then I'll become his travelling tutor when he leaves . . . And when we get back from the continent, his father might procure me some handsome appointment, in his household, or his business. Yes? And, who knows, he might fall in love with Kate, and marry her . . . (*To* RALPH.) Don't you think so, uncle?

RALPH. (*Unconvincingly.*) Yes, yes, of course. (KATE *goes to* RALPH.)

KATE. Uncle. We're a simple family. We were born and bred in the country, we have never been apart, and we are unacquainted with the world.

RALPH. Well, then, my dear—

KATE. It will take time for us to understand it, to apply ourselves to make our way in it, and to bear that separation which necessity now forces on us. I am sure you understand. (*Pause.*)

RALPH. Oh, yes, indeed I do. (NICHOLAS *embraces his mother and sister.*) Now, sir . . . Shall we go? (NICHOLAS *follows* RALPH *out one way, as* MRS. NICKLEBY *and* KATE *leave the other.*)

SCENE 5

The coffee house of the Saracen's Head. A table, on which WACKFORD SQUEERS *is sitting, reading a newspaper. Near him is a little trunk, on which a small boy,* BELLING, *is sitting. This scene is set up during the following narration:*

NARRATOR. And so the uncle, and his nephew, took themselves with all convenient speed towards Snow Hill, and Mr. Wackford Squeers. (*The narration is carried on by* WILLIAM, *a waiter at the Saracen's Head.* TWO MAIDS *enter, and stare at* MR. SQUEERS.)

WILLIAM. And in Snow Hill, near to the jail and Smithfield, is the Saracen's Head, and outside the Saracen's Head are two stone heads of Saracens, both fearsome and quite hideously ugly, and inside, on this January afternoon, stood Mr. Squeers, whose appearance was not much more prepossessing. (SQUEERS *lowers the newspaper. We see him as the* TWO MAIDS *describe him to each other.*)

1ST MAID. He's only got one eye.

WILLIAM. While the popular prejudice runs in favour of two.

2ND MAID. And, look, the side of his face is all wrinkled and puckered.

WILLIAM. Which gave him a highly sinister appearance, especially when he smiled.

1ST MAID. And the eye he's got's a very funny colour.

WILLIAM. Which indeed it was, a kind of greenish grey, in shape resembling the fanlight of a street-door, through which Mr. Squeers was glaring at a tiny boy, who was sitting on a tiny trunk, in front of him. (*And indeed* SQUEERS *and* BELLING *are looking at each other.* BELLING *sneezes as* WILLIAM *and the* MAIDS *withdraw.*)

SQUEERS. Hallo, sir! What's that, sir? (THE MAIDS *withdraw.*)

BELLING. Nothing, please, sir.

SQUEERS. Nothing, sir?

BELLING. Please, sir, I sneezed, sir.

SQUEERS. (*Taking the boy by the ear.*) Sneezed? You Sneezed? Well, that's not nothing, is it?

BELLING. No, sir.

SQUEERS. Wait till Yorkshire, my young gentleman. And then I'll give you something to remember. (BELLING *is crying. Reenter* WILLIAM.)

WILLIAM. Mr. Squeers, there's a gentleman who's asking for you.

SQUEERS. Show him in, William, show him in. (WILLIAM *goes out.* SQUEERS *looks at* BELLING, *who is still sniffing.* BELLING *cringes at this look, and is somewhat surprised when* SQUEERS *sits on the bench, and puts his arm round the tiny boy.*) Now, dear child, why are you weeping? All people have their trials, but what is yours? You are losing your friends, that is true, but you will have a father in me, my dear, and a mother in Mrs. Squeers. (WILLIAM *admitting* SNAWLEY, *a sleek, flat-nosed man in sombre garments, and two little* SNAWLEY BOYS.) At the delightful village of Dotheboys, near Greta Bridge in Yorkshire, where youth are boarded, clothed, booked, furnished with pocket-money, provided with all necessaries, (SNAWLEY *checks* SQUEERS' *speech against a newspaper advertisement he carries. It is the same.*) . . . instructed in all languages, living and dead, mathematics, orthography, geometry, astronomy, trigonometry, the use of the globes, algebra, single stick (if required), writing, arithmetic, fortification, and every other branch of classical literature. Terms, 20 guineas per annum, no extras, no vacations, and diet unparalleled, why good day, sir, I had no idea . . . (*And* SQUEERS *has turned to* SNAWLEY *and extended his hand.*)

SNAWLEY. Mr. Squeers?

SQUEERS. The same, sir.

SNAWLEY. My name is Snawley. I'm in the oil and colour way.

SQUEERS. Well, how do you do, sir? (*To the little* SNAWLEYS.) And how do *you* do, young sirs?

SNAWLEY. Mr. Squeers, I have been thinking of placing my two boys at your school.

SQUEERS. Sir, I do not think you could do a better thing.

SNAWLEY. At—£20 per annum?

SQUEERS. Guineas.

SNAWLEY. Pounds for two, perhaps? They're not great eaters.

SQUEERS. Then we will not be great feeders, sir. I am sure that we can reach accommodation.

SNAWLEY. And this is another boy, sir?

SQUEERS. Yes, sir, this is Belling, and his luggage that he's sitting on. Each boy requires two suits of clothes, six shirts, six pairs of stockings, two nightcaps, two pocket handkerchiefs, two pairs of shoes, two hats and a razor.

SNAWLEY. Razor? Sir, whatever for?

SQUEERS. To Shave With. (*Pause.* SNAWLEY *takes* SQUEERS *aside. The little boys look at each other.*)

SNAWLEY. Sir, up to what age . . . ?

SQUEERS. As long as payment's regularly made.

SNAWLEY. I see. (*Slight pause.*)

SQUEERS. Sir, let us understand each other. Are these boys legitimate?

SNAWLEY. They are.

SQUEERS. They are?

SNAWLEY. But I am not their father. (*Slight pause.*)

SQUEERS. Go on.

SNAWLEY. I'm the husband of their mother. (*Slight pause.*) And as it's so expensive, keeping boys . . . And as she has so little money of her own . . . (*Slight pause.*) And hearing of a school, a great distance off, where there are none of those ill-judged comings-home three times a year, that do unsettle the children so . . . (*Pause.*)

SQUEERS. And payments regular, and then, no questions asked. (*Slight pause.*)

SNAWLEY. I should . . . I should want their morals particularly attended to. (WILLIAM *brings in* RALPH *and* NICHOLAS.)

SQUEERS. Well, you've come to the right shop for morals, sir. I think we do, now, understand each other.

RALPH. Mr. Squeers.

SQUEERS. Yes? What is it?

RALPH. A matter of business, sir. My name is Ralph Nickleby. Perhaps you recollect me.

SQUEERS. Why, yes, sir . . . Did you not pay me a small account for some years . . . on behalf of parents of a boy named Dorker who . . .

RALPH. That's right. Who died, unfortunately, in Yorkshire.

SQUEERS. Yes, sir, I remember well. (SNAWLEY *looking at* SQUEERS.) And I remember too, how Mrs. Squeers nursed the boy . . . Dry toast and warm tea when he wouldn't swallow, and a candle in his bedroom on the night he died, a dictionary to lay his head upon . . .

RALPH. Yes, yes. So, shall we come to business? You have advertised for an able assistant, and here he is. (SQUEERS *looks at* NICHOLAS.) My nephew Nicholas, hot from school, with everything he learnt there fermenting in his head, and nothing fermenting in his pocket. (*Pause.*) His father lies dead, he is wholly ignorant of the world, he has no resources whatever, and he wants to make his fortune.

SQUEERS. Well . . .

NICHOLAS. I fear, sir, that you object to my youth, and my not being a Master of Arts?

SQUEERS. Well, the absence of a college degree *is* an objection . . .

RALPH. And if any caprice of temper should induce him to cast aside this golden opportunity, I shall consider myself absolved from extending any assistance to his mother and sister. Now the question is, whether, for some time to come, he won't exactly serve your purposes. (*Pause.* SQUEERS *a little gesture. He and* RALPH *withdraw a little.*)

SNAWLEY. (*To convince himself.*) A fine gentleman, sir. That Mr. Squeers, a gentleman of virtue and morality.

NICHOLAS. (*To convince himself.*) I'm sure of it. (RALPH *and* SQUEERS *back.*)

RALPH. Nicholas, you are employed.

NICHOLAS. (*Delighted.*) Oh, sir—

SQUEERS. The coach leaves eight o'clock tomorrow morning, Mr. Nickleby—and you must be here a quarter before.

NICHOLAS. I shall be. Surely.

RALPH. And, your fare is paid. (SQUEERS *takes* SNAWLEY *aside, taking money from and inserting something in a ledger.* NOGGS *enters.*)

NICHOLAS. Well, thank you, uncle. I will not forget this kindness.

RALPH. See you don't.

SQUEERS. Mr. Snawley . . . (SQUEERS, SNAWLEY, *the little* SNAWLEYS *and* BELLING *withdraw as* RALPH *and* NICHOLAS *meet* NOGGS D.)

RALPH. Noggs.

NOGGS. (*Hands* RALPH *a letter.*) Mortgage letter's come. And Mr. Bonney says—

RALPH. (*Taking the letter and opening it.*) Oh, yes. I know what Mr. Bonney says. A matter of investment. (*He opens the letter and reads.* NOGGS *is looking fixedly at* NICHOLAS. NICHOLAS *doesn't quite know what to do. After a few moments, to break the silence.*)

NICHOLAS. Um, I'm—

NOGGS. Yes, I know. (RALPH *pocketing the letter.*)

RALPH. And we're late. You'd best go home and pack, sir. Early in the morning, you heard Mr. Squeers. (*Exit* RALPH *and* NOGGS.)

SCENE 6

The Nicklebys' rooms. MRS. NICKLEBY *and* KATE, *carrying a suitcase, books and clothes, enter to* NICHOLAS *as he speaks:*

NICHOLAS. And there was so much to be done.

KATE. And so little time to do it in, (*The* NICKLEBYS *quickly packing* NICHOLAS' *suitcase.*)

MRS. NICKLEBY. So many kind words to be spoken,

KATE. And so much bitter pain to be suppressed,

NICHOLAS. That the preparations for the journey were mournful indeed.

KATE. (*Putting a book in the suitcase.*) A hundred things deemed indispensable for his comfort, Nicholas left behind,

NICHOLAS. (*Taking the book out again.*) As they might prove convertible into money if required. (*As* KATE *puts the book back into the suitcase.*)

MRS. NICKLEBY. A hundred affectionate contests on such points as these took place;

NICHOLAS. And as they grew nearer and nearer to the close of their preparations,

KATE. Kate grew busier and busier, and wept more

silently. (*During the following,* KATE *and* MRS. NICK-LEBY *leave* NICHOLAS, *alone with his suitcase.*)

NICHOLAS. And bed at last, and at six the next morning, Nicholas rose up, and wrote a few lines in pencil to say goodbye, and resolved that, come what may, he would bear whatever might be in store for him, for the sake of his mother and his sister, and giving his uncle no excuse to desert them in their need. (*And by now, the Saracen's Head has reappeared behind him.*)

SCENE 7

The Saracen's Head. SQUEERS *sitting at the table with a plate of eggs and ham. The two* SNAWLEYS *and* BEL-LING *sitting with nothing. A maid stands next to* WILLIAM, *carrying a tray, on which is a jug of water, and a plate of one piece of bread and butter.* SQUEERS *is holding up a mug of milk.* NICHOLAS *stands apart, watching.*

SQUEERS. This is two penn'orth of milk, is it, William?

WILLIAM. S'right, sir.

SQUEERS. What a rare article milk is in London, to be sure. Now fill it up with water, will you?

WILLIAM. To the top, sir?

SQUEERS. (*Starting to eat.*) That's correct.

WILLIAM. But, sir, you'll drown the milk.

SQUEERS. Well, serve it right for being so expensive. Now. Where's bread-and-butter?

WILLIAM. Here, sir. (*He puts the bread-and-butter on the table. The little boys quickly reach for it.*)

SQUEERS. Wait! (*The boys freeze. Their hands go back.* WILLIAM *goes away.* SQUEERS *divides the slice of bread into three, as* NICHOLAS *approaches.*) Good morning, Nickleby. Sit down. We're breakfasting.

NICHOLAS. Good morning, sir.

SQUEERS. Now, boys, when I say 'One', young Snawley takes a drink of milk and eats his bread. when I say 'two', the older Snawley, and then three is Belling. Clear?

BOYS. Oh, yes, sir.

SQUEERS. (*Eating.*) Right. Now, wait. Subdue your appetites, my dears, you've conquered human nature. One! (SNAWLEY JNR. *eats and drinks.*) Say 'thank you'.

SNAWLEY JNR. (*Eating.*) 'Ank 'ou. (*Pause.* SQUEERS *eats.*)

SQUEERS. Two! (SNAWLEY SNR. *eats and drinks.*) Well?

SNAWLEY SNR. Thank you, sir. (SQUEERS *finishes his food.*)

SQUEERS. And— (*He is interrupted by the blowing of a horn.*) Oh, dear Belling, there's the horn. You've missed your turn. Come, my dears, let's bustle. (*And at once there is tremendous bustle, and, during the following dialogue, one of two things occurs; if there is a mobile truck available, it is brought on, and the company build on it, out of skips, tables, chairs and luggage, a representation of an early Victorian stagecoach; or the sudden, noisy entrance of coachmen, passengers, porters, flower- and newspaper-sellers and passers-by gives the impression that the coach has arrived offstage and is nearly ready to go. Either way, everything suddenly becomes totally busy and confusing, as* SQUEERS *marshals the little boys, and* NICHOLAS *is collared by* NOGGS, *who appears out of the crowd.*)

NOGGS. Psst.

NICHOLAS. I'm sorry? Mr. Noggs!

NOGGS. (*Handing him a letter.*) Hush. Take it. Read it. No-one knows. That's all. (*He is going.* MRS. NICKLEBY *and* KATE *appear.*)

NICHOLAS. Stop!

NOGGS. No. (*Exit* NOGGS.)

NICHOLAS. But—

MRS. NICKLEBY. Nicholas!

NICHOLAS. Oh, mother, Kate—you shouldn't.

KATE. How could we just let you go . . . (SQUEERS, *dragging* BELLING, *comes to* NICHOLAS.)

SQUEERS. Now Nickleby, I think you'd better ride behind. I'm feared of Belling falling off, and there goes 20 pounds a year.

NICHOLAS. Right, I, uh—

SQUEERS. (*Dragging* BELLING *away.*) And, dear Belling, if you don't stop chattering your teeth and shaking, I'll warm you with a severe thrashing in about half a minute's time. Come Nickleby!

KATE. Oh, Nicholas, who is that man? What kind of place can it be that you're going to?

NICHOLAS. Well, I suppose—that Yorkshire folk are rather rough and uncultivated—

SQUEERS. *(Calling.)* Nickleby, God damn you! *(If the coach is onstage, it is complete, and its passengers are clambering on to it, with the* COACHMAN *sitting up front with his whip, the horn-blower beside him; or it is clear from waving passers-by and exiting passengers that its departure is imminent.)*

NICHOLAS. Goodbye, mother. To our meeting, one day soon. And goodbye, Kate.

KATE. You'll write?

NICHOLAS. Of course I will.

COACHMAN. Stage leaving! Stage leaving! Everyone for the stage, up and sit fast! *(And* NICHOLAS *climbs up on to the back of the coach, next to* BELLING; *or he runs out past the waving passers-by.* NARRATORS *speak to the audience.)*

NARRATORS. And a minute's bustle,

And a banging of the coach doors,

A swaying of the vehicle,

A cry of all right,

A few notes from the horn—

(The horn sounds. The coach departs, everyone on and off it waving. If we imagine the coach, then there is a further line of narration:)

NARRATOR. And the coach was gone, and rattling over the stones of Smithfield. *(And one way or another, everyone except* KATE *is gone.)*

SCENE 8

Miss La Creevy's house: MISS LA CREEVY *with her painting equipment in front of her on a little platform. This is set up as* KATE *speaks to the audience:*

KATE. And on the second morning after Nicholas' departure, Kate found herself sitting in a very faded chair, raised upon a very dusty throne, in Miss La Creevy's room, giving that lady a sitting for a portrait. (KATE *sits on the other chair, and poses.* MISS LA CREEVY *painting.*)

MISS LA CREEVY. Well, I think I have caught it now. And it will be the sweetest portrait I have ever done, certainly.

KATE. It will be your genius that makes it so, I'm sure.

MISS LA CREEVY. Well, my dear, you are right, in the main: though I don't allow that it's of such great importance in the present case. Ah! The difficulties of art, my dear, are very great.

KATE. I have no doubt.

MISS LA CREEVY. They are beyond anything you can form the faintest perception of. What with bringing out eyes and keeping down noses, and adding to heads, and taking away teeth altogether, you have no idea of the trouble one little miniature can be.

KATE. The remuneration can scarcely repay you.

MISS LA CREEVY. Well, it does not, and that's the truth. And then sitters are so dissatisfied and unreasonable, that nine times out of ten there's no pleasure in painting them. Sometimes they say, "Oh, how very serious you have made me look, Miss La Creevy," and at others, "La, Miss La Creevy, how very smirking!", when the very essence of a good portrait is that it must be either serious or smirking, or it's no portrait at all.

KATE. Indeed! And which, dear Miss La Creevy, which am I? (MISS LA CREEVY *beckons* KATE, *who goes to look at the portrait.*) Oh!

MISS LA CREEVY. Dear, now what's the matter?

KATE. Oh, it's just, the shade. Is my face, really, that—

MISS LA CREEVY. Oh, that's my salmon pink, my dear. Originally, I hit upon it for an officer. But it went down so well, among my patrons, that I use it now for almost everything. It is considered, in the art world, quite a novelty.

KATE. (*Returning and sitting.*) I am convinced of it.

MISS LA CREEVY. (*Continuing to paint.*) And now, my dear, when do you expect to see your uncle again?

KATE. I scarcely know. I'd thought to, before now.

MISS LA CREEVY. Hm. I suppose he has money, hasn't he?

KATE. I'm told he's very rich.

MISS LA CREEVY. Hm. You may depend on it, or he wouldn't be so surly.

KATE. Yes, he is a little rough.

MISS LA CREEVY. A little rough! A porcupine's a featherbed to him.

KATE. It's only his manner, I believe. I should be sorry to think ill of him unless I knew he deserved it.

MISS LA CREEVY. Well, that is very right and proper. But mightn't he, without feeling it himself, make you and your mama some nice little allowance . . . What would a hundred a year, for instance, be to him?

KATE. I don't know what it would be to him. But it would be unacceptable to me.

MISS LA CREEVY. He is your uncle, dear . . .

KATE. *(Stands.)* From anyone. Not him, particularly. Anyone. *(Pause.)* I'm sorry. I have moved.

MISS LA CREEVY. It doesn't matter, dear. *(HANNAH is there. Someone knocks.)* Now, who can that be? Yes, come in. *(HANNAH steps into the room.)*

HANNAH. Um . . . It's Mr.—um . . .

MISS LA CREEVY. It's who? *(Enter RALPH NICKLEBY.)*

RALPH. Your servant, ladies.

KATE. *(Standing.)* Uncle.

RALPH. Hm. Where's Mrs. Nickleby?

MISS LA CREEVY. Hannah. *(Exit HANNAH.)*

RALPH. Is it my niece's portrait, ma'am?

MISS LA CREEVY. Well, yes it is, sir, and between you and me and the post, sir, it will be a very nice portrait too, though I say it myself as shouldn't.

RALPH. Well, don't trouble yourself to show it to me, ma'am, I have no eye for likenesses. Is it nearly finished?

MISS LA CREEVY. Why, yes. Two more sittings will—

RALPH. Have them done at once, ma'am, for she'll have no time to idle over fooleries. Have you let your lodgings, ma'am?

MISS LA CREEVY. I have not put a bill up yet, sir.

RALPH. Then do so, at once. For neither of them's going to need your rooms, or if they do, can't pay for 'em.

KATE. Uh—uncle, we are moving? Where?

RALPH. I'm not yet sure where either of you will be placed.

KATE. Oh, uncle, do you mean we're to be separated?
(HANNAH *admits* MRS. NICKLEBY.)

MRS. NICKLEBY. Brother-in-law.

RALPH. Ma'am. I've found a situation for your daughter.

MRS. NICKLEBY. (*Sitting in* KATE'S *chair.*) Well: This
is good news. But I will say it is only what I would have
thought of you. (RALPH *about to say something.*) "Depend on it", I said to Kate only yesterday at breakfast,
"that after your uncle has provided in that most ready
manner for Nicholas, he will not leave us until he has
done at least the same for you!" (RALPH *about to say
something.*) Those were my very words, as near as I can
remember, Kate, my dear, why don't you thank your—

RALPH. Let me proceed, ma'am, pray.

MRS. NICKLEBY. Kate, my love, let your uncle proceed.

KATE. I am most anxious that he should, mama.

MRS. NICKLEBY. Well, if you are, you had better
allow your uncle to say what he has to say, without
interruption.

RALPH. I am very much obliged to you, ma'am. An
absence of business habits in this family apparently leads
to a great waste of words before business is arrived at at
all.

MRS. NICKLEBY. (*With a sigh.*) I fear it so, indeed.
Your poor brother—

RALPH. My poor brother, ma'am, had no idea what
business was. (*Pause.* MRS. NICKLEBY *says nothing.*) The
situation that I have made interest to procure for your
daughter, is with a milliner and dressmaker.

MRS. NICKLEBY. A milliner.

RALPH. Yes, and milliners in London, as I need not
remind you, ma'am, are persons of great wealth and
station.

MRS. NICKLEBY. Well, now, that's very true. That's
very true, Kate, for I recollect when your poor papa and
I came to town after we were married, that a young lady
brought me home a chip cottage bonnet, with white and
green trimming, and a green persian lining, in her own
carriage, which drove up to the door at a full gallop—at
least, I am not quite certain whether it was her own
carriage or a hackney chariot, but I remember very well
that the horse dropped dead as he was turning round,
and that—

RALPH. The lady's name is Madam Mantalini. She lives near Cavendish Square. If your daughter is disposed to try the situation, I'll take her there on Monday. Now, I must—

MRS. NICKLEBY. Kate, have you nothing that you wish to say? To tell your uncle?

KATE. Yes, I have. But I'd prefer to speak to him alone.

MRS. NICKLEBY. Now Kate, I'm sure—

KATE. I'll see you out then, uncle. *(She firmly gestures* RALPH *out of the room.)*

RALPH. Then—I'm your servant, ma'am. (KATE *and* RALPH *leave the room, and come downstage together.* MRS. NICKLEBY, MISS LA CREEVY *and the furniture leave during this dialogue.)* So? What d'you want to say?

KATE. I must ask one question of you, uncle. Am I to live at home?

RALPH. At home? Where's that?

KATE. I must—we must, me and my mother, have some place we can call home. It may be very humble—

RALPH. "May be!" Must be. "May be" humble!

KATE. Well, then, must be. But, my question, uncle. You must answer it. *(Pause.)*

RALPH. I'd some idea . . . providing for your mother, in a pleasant district of the country . . .

KATE. Out of London?

RALPH. Yes, I'd thought so, but if you're quite determined that you want to stay with her . . .

KATE. I am.

RALPH. Yes. I had thought you would be. *(Slight pause.)* Well, I have an empty house. It's in the East End. Till it's rented, you can live in it. I'll send my clerk on Saturday to take you there. So—is that satisfactory? (KATE *is cracking.)*

KATE. I'm very much, obliged to you, dear uncle. *(Pause.)* Very much—

RALPH. Please don't begin to cry.

KATE. It's very foolish, I know, uncle.

RALPH. Yes, it is. And most affected, too. *(To* KATE.) Let's have no more of it. (RALPH *goes out.* KATE *goes out another way).*

SCENE 9

Outside and inside Dotheboys Hall. A bare stage. Snow falls. Wind blows. SQUEERS, NICHOLAS, BELLING, *and the two* SNAWLEYS *walk D. with the luggage. They stop.*

NICHOLAS. Dotheboys Hall.

SQUEERS. Oh, sir, you needn't call it a hall up here.

NICHOLAS. Why not?

SQUEERS. Cos the fact is, it ain't a hall. (*As* SQUEERS *leads the party round to the side of the stage,* NICHOLAS *speaks to the audience.*)

NICHOLAS. A host of unpleasant misgivings, which had been crowding upon Nicholas during the whole journey, thronged into his mind. And as he considered the dreary house and dark windows, and the wild country round covered with snow, he felt a depression of heart and spirit which he had never experienced before.

SQUEERS. No, we call it a hall up in London, because it sounds better, but they don't know it by that name here. (*He bangs an imaginary door. Someone makes the sound.*) A man may call his house an island if he likes; there's no Act of Parliament against that, I believe?

NICHOLAS. No, I think not, sir.

SQUEERS. (*Banging.*) Well, then. Hey! Door! (*From the darkness,* SMIKE *appears. He is about 19, but bent over with lameness, and dressed in ragged garments which he has long since outgrown. He pulls open the huge door, and the wind howls as* SQUEERS *strides into the house.*) Smike. Where the devil have you been?

SMIKE. Please, sir, I fell asleep.

SQUEERS. You fell awhat?

SMIKE. Please, sir, I fell asleep over the fire.

SQUEERS. Fire? What fire? Where's there a fire? (*During the following,* SQUEERS, SMIKE, NICHOLAS, *and the* BOYS *with their luggage move round the stage—as if passing along corridors—as the* SQUEERS' *servant* PHIB *brings on a big chair and then a table to centre stage. This is the* SQUEERS' *parlour, and* PHIB *goes out again to bring on a tray of brandy, glasses and water, placing it on the table.*)

SMIKE. Please, sir, Missus said as I was sitting up, I might be by the fire for a warm . . .

SQUEERS. Your missus is a fool. You'd have been a

deuced deal more wakeful in the cold. *(From off, we hear the voice of* MRS. SQUEERS.*)*

MRS. SQUEERS. *(Off.)* Squeers!

SQUEERS. *(Calls.)* My love!

MRS. SQUEERS. Squeers! *(By now* SQUEERS *is in the parlour area, the* BOYS *are standing in the corridor with their luggage, and* NICHOLAS *is between them, as if in the doorway, not knowing quite what to do.)*

SQUEERS. *(To* SMIKE.*)* There's boys. The boys, to bed. *(*SMIKE *takes the* BOYS *out, leaving their luggage, as* MRS. SQUEERS *enters.)*

MRS. SQUEERS. Oh, Squeers. How is my Squeery, dearie. *(The* SQUEERSES *embrace.)*

SQUEERS. Well, well, my love. How are the cows?

MRS. SQUEERS. All right, every one of 'em.

SQUEERS. And the pigs?

MRS. SQUEERS. As well as they were when you went.

SQUEERS. Well, that's a great blessing. *(These sweet nothings over,* SQUEERS *leaves* MRS. SQUEERS *and takes letters and documents from his pocket. As an afterthought.)* The boys all as they were, I suppose? *(*MRS. SQUEERS, *taking the letters from* SQUEERS *and placing them on the table, glancing at one or two.)*

MRS. SQUEERS. Oh yes, they're well enough. But young Sprouter's had a fever.

SQUEERS. *(Taking off his greatcoat.)* No! Damn the boy, he's always at something of that sort. *(*PHIB *takes* SQUEERS' *huge coat and stands there, holding it.* SQUEERS *goes to the table, sits,* MRS. SQUEERS *pours him a brandy and tops it up with water. As:)*

MRS. SQUEERS. Never was such a boy, I do believe. Whatever he has is always catching, too. I say it's obstinacy, and nothing shall ever convince me that it isn't. I'd beat it out of him, and I told you that six months ago.

SQUEERS. So you did, my love. We'll try what can be done. *(Slight pause.* MRS. SQUEERS *nods in the direction of* NICHOLAS, *who is still standing near the door, not knowing what to do.)* Ah, Nickleby. Come, sir, come in. *(*NICHOLAS *comes a little further into the room.)* This is our new young man, my dear.

MRS. SQUEERS. *(Suspiciously.)* Oh. Is it?

SQUEERS. He can shake down here tonight, can't he?

MRS. SQUEERS. *(Looking round.)* Well, if he's not particular . . .

NICHOLAS. *(Politely.)* Oh, no, indeed.

MRS. SQUEERS. That's lucky. *(She looks at SQUEERS and laughs. SQUEERS laughs back. They laugh at each other. Meanwhile, SMIKE reappears. MRS. SQUEERS looks at PHIB, and snaps her head towards the door. PHIB goes out with the big coat. Slight pause. Then, with a wink to SQUEERS, as if to ask if NICHOLAS should be given a drink.)* Another brandy, Squeers?

SQUEERS. *(Nodding back.)* Certainly. A glassful. *(MRS. SQUEERS pours a large brandy-and-water for SQUEERS, and a smaller one for NICHOLAS. She takes the drink to NICHOLAS. SQUEERS is looking through the letters. NICHOLAS takes the drink. SMIKE stands, staring fixedly at the letters on the table. MRS. SQUEERS goes and picks up one of the boys' bags and takes it back to the table.)* Bolder's father's short.

MRS. SQUEERS. Tt tt.

SQUEERS. But Cobbey's sister's sent something. *(MRS. SQUEERS starts going through the boys' luggage, picking out the bits and pieces she fancies.)*

MRS. SQUEERS. That's good.

SQUEERS. And Graymarsh's maternal aunt has written, with no money, but two pairs of stockings and a tract.

MRS. SQUEERS. Maternal aunt.

SQUEERS. My love?

MRS. SQUEERS. More likely, in my view, that she's Graymarsh's maternal mother. *(The SQUEERSES look at each other. Then SQUEERS notices that SMIKE is very close, craning to see the letters.)*

SQUEERS. Yes? What's to do, boy?

SMIKE. Is there—

SQUEERS. What?

SMIKE. Is there . . . there's nothing heard . . . ?

SQUEERS. No, not a word. And never will be.

MRS. SQUEERS. *(The very idea.)* Tt. *(Pause. SQUEERS decides to rub it in.)*

SQUEERS. And it is a pretty sort of thing, that you should have been left here all these years and no money paid after the first six—nor no notice taken, nor no clue to who you belong to? It's a pretty sort of thing, is it not, that I should have to feed a great fellow like you, and never hope to get one penny for it, isn't it? *(SQUEERS looking at SMIKE.)*

NICHOLAS. *(Out front.)* The boy put his hand to his head, as if he was making an effort to remember something, and then, looking vacantly at his questioner, gradually broke into a smile.

SQUEERS. That's right. Now, off with you, and send the girl. *(SMIKE limps out. MRS. SQUEERS has finished sifting the boy's bag. She looks for something on the table.)*

MRS. SQUEERS. I tell you what, Squeers, I think that young chap's turning silly.

SQUEERS. *(Wiping his mouth.)* I hope not. For he's a handy fellow out of doors, and worth his meat and drink anyway. *(He stands.)* But come, I'm tired, and want to go to bed.

MRS. SQUEERS. Oh, drat the thing.

SQUEERS. What's wrong, my dear?

MRS. SQUEERS. The school spoon. I can't find it.

SQUEERS. Never mind, my love.

MRS. SQUEERS. What, never mind? It's brimstone, in the morning.

SQUEERS. Ah, I forgot. *(He helps the search.)* Yes, certainly, it is.

NICHOLAS. Uh . . . ?

SQUEERS. We purify the boys' bloods now and then, Nickleby.

MRS. SQUEERS. *(Crossly.)* Purify fiddle-sticks. Don't think, young man, that we go to the expense of flour of brimstone and molasses just to purify them; because if you think we carry on the business in that way, you'll find yourself mistaken, and so I tell you plainly. *(SQUEERS is not sure this intelligence is quite discreet. Enter PHIB, who tidies round the table, putting things back on the tray.)*

SQUEERS. My dear . . . should you . . .

MRS. SQUEERS. Nonsense. If the young man comes to be a teacher, let him understand at once that we don't want any foolery about the boys. They have the brimstone and treacle, partly because if they hadn't something or other in the way of medicine they'd always be ailing and giving a world of trouble, and partly because it spoils their appetites and comes cheaper than breakfast and dinner. So it does them good and us good at the same time, and that's fair enough, I'm sure. (SQUEERS *looking embarrassed.* MRS. SQUEERS *shoots a glance at him.*) Now, where's the spoon? (PHIB *has picked up the tray.*)

PHIB. Uh. Ma'am.

MRS. SQUEERS. What is it?

PHIB. S'round your neck. (*And indeed the spoon is round* MRS. SQUEERS' *neck. She cuffs* PHIB *lightly for telling her.*)

MRS. SQUEERS. Why did you not say *before.*

PHIB. M'sorry, ma'am. (PHIB *picks up the tray, leaving the brandy bottle, and goes out.*)

MRS. SQUEERS. (*Pleasantly.*) And so, dear Mr. Nickleby, good night. (MRS. SQUEERS *goes out. Pause.*)

SQUEERS. A most invaluable woman, Nickleby.

NICHOLAS. Indeed, sir.

SQUEERS. I do not know her equal. That woman, Nickleby, is always the same: always the same bustling, lively, active, saving creature that you see her now.

NICHOLAS. I'm sure of it.

SQUEERS. (*Warming further to his theme.*) It is my custom, when I am in London, to say that she is like a mother to those boys. But she is more, she's ten times more. She does things for those boys, Nickleby, that I don't believe half the mothers going would do for their own sons.

NICHOLAS. I'm certain of it, sir.

SQUEERS. And so, goodnight, then, Nickleby. (*He tries to make a solemn exit, undermined by spotting the brandy, which he returns to pick up.*)

NICHOLAS. Goodnight, sir. (SQUEERS *nods gravely and goes out.* NICHOLAS *stands a moment, then takes off his coat. He sits, on the floor. He notices* NOGGS' *letter in his coat pocket. He opens it and begins to read.* NOGGS' *himself appears, with a glass of brandy. He sits on the arm of* SQUEERS' *chair, and he speaks his letter as we see* NICHOLAS *read it.*)

NOGGS. My dear young man. I know the world. Your father did not, or he would not have done me a kindness when there was no hope of return. You do not, or you would not be bound on such a journey. If ever you want a shelter in London, they know where I live at the sign of the Crown, in Silver St., Golden Square. You can come at night. Once, nobody was ashamed—never mind that. It's all over. Excuse errors. I have forgotten all my old ways. My spelling may have gone with them.

NICHOLAS. *(Reads.)* Yours obediently, Newman Noggs.

NOGGS. P.S.: If you should go near Barnard Castle, there is a good ale at the King's Head. Say you know me, and I am sure they will not charge you for it. You may say Mr. Noggs there, for I was a gentleman then. I was indeed. *(NOGGS shambles out. NICHOLAS crumples to the floor. He is crying. Blackout.)*

SCENE 10

Dotheboys Hall. The school bell rings, the lights come up. The parlour chair and table have gone. SQUEERS shouts to NICHOLAS, who wakes.

SQUEERS. Past seven, Nickleby! It's morning come, and well-iced already. Now, Nickleby, come, tumble up, will you? *(SQUEERS, with his cane, strides round the stage. NICHOLAS jumps up and, pulling on his coat, follows. MRS. SQUEERS enters, followed by SMIKE, who carries a bowl of brimstone and treacle. SQUEERS and NICHOLAS arrive at one side of the stage, MRS. SQUEERS and SMIKE at the other. Then, through the darkness at the back of the stage, we see, approaching us, the boys of Dotheboys Hall. They are dressed in the ragged remains of what were once school uniforms. They move slowly, through lameness and sullenness and fear. Then they form themselves into a kind of line, and each boy goes to MRS. SQUEERS to receive a spoonful of brimstone and treacle.)* There. This is our shop, Nickleby. *(Each boy gives his number, name, age and reason for being at the school before receiving his dose. Clearly, this is an accepted ritual.)*

TOMKINS. First boy. Tomkins. Nine. A cripple.

COATES. Second boy. Coates. Thirteen. A bastard.

GRAYMARSH. Third boy. Graymarsh. Twelve. Another bastard.

JENNINGS. Fourth boy. Jennings. Thirteen. Disfigured.

MOBBS. Fifth boy. *(Pause.)* Mobbs. Uh—'leven. *(Pause.*

He doesn't know what's wrong with him. MRS. SQUEERS *hits him on the side of the head.)*

MRS. SQUEERS. Simpleton!

MOBBS. Fifth. Mobbs. Eleven. Sim-pull-ton.

BOLDER. Sixth. Bolder. Fourteen. Orphan.

PITCHER. Seventh. Pitcher. Ten.

MRS. SQUEERS. Yes! *(Pause.)*

PITCHER. I'm very. Very. Slow.

MRS. SQUEERS. Move on. Move *on.*

JACKSON. Eighth. Johnny.

MRS. SQUEERS. Johnny?

JACKSON. Jackson. Thirteen. Illegitimate.

COBBEY. Ninth. Cobbey. Fifteen. Cripple.

PETERS. Tenth. Uh—Peters. Seven. Blind.

SPROUTER. Eleventh. Sprouter. Seven. My father killed my mother.

MRS. SQUEERS. Yes?

SPROUTER. Sent away.

ROBERTS. Twelfth. Roberts. Ten. There's something wrong—my brain. *(*SQUEERS' *young son,* WACKFORD, *well-dressed and stout, pushes forward the two* SNAWLEY BOYS *and* BELLING.*)*

SNAWLEY SNR. Robert Arthur Snawley.

MRS. SQUEERS. Number!

SNAWLEY SNR. I'm eleven.

MRS. SQUEERS. *(Twisting* SNAWLEY SNR'S *ear.)* Number, is thirteen.

SNAWLEY SNR. Thirteen.

SNAWLEY JNR. Uh—fourteen-th. Snawley, H. Uh—seven.

BELLING. Fifteen. Anthony Belling. Seven years of age. A classical and modern—moral, education. *(*MRS. SQUEERS *wipes her hands on* SMIKE. SQUEERS *to* WACKFORD.*)*

SQUEERS. Thank you, young Wackford. Thank you, son. And what do you say? And what d'you say, to this? *(Pause.)*

BOYS. For what we have received, may the lord make us truly thankful.

SQUEERS. Amen.

BOYS. Amen.

SQUEERS. That's better. Now, boys, I've been to London, and have returned to my family and you, as strong and well as ever. *(Pause.* MRS. SQUEERS *gestures to a boy.)*

COATES. *(Feebly.)* Hip hip.

BOYS. *(Equally feebly.)* Hooray.

COATES. Hip. Hip.

BOYS. Hooray.

COATES. Hip hip.

BOYS. Hooray. *(*SQUEERS *takes various letters from his pockets and wanders around among the boys as he speaks.)*

SQUEERS. I have seen the parents of some boys, and they're so glad to hear how their sons are doing, that there's no prospect at all of their going home, which of course is a very pleasant thing to reflect upon for all parties. *(He continues to perambulate.)* But I have had disappointments to contend with. Bolder's father, for an instance, was two pound ten short. Where is Bolder? *(The boys around* BOLDER *kick him and he puts up his hand.* SQUEERS *goes to* BOLDER.*)* Ah, Bolder. Bolder, if your father thinks that because—*(*SQUEERS *suddenly notices warts on* BOLDER'S *hand. He grabs the boy's arm.)* What do you call this, sir?

BOLDER. Warts, sir.

SQUEERS. What, sir?

BOLDER. Warts, sir.

SQUEERS. Warts?

BOLDER. I can't help it, sir. They will come . . . It's working in the garden does it sir, at least I don't know what it is, sir, but it's not my fault . . .

SQUEERS. Bolder. You are an incorrigible young scoundrel, and as the last thrashing did you no good, we must see what another will do towards beating it out of you. *(*BOLDER *looks terrified.)* La—ter. *(He lets* BOLDER *go and walks on, reading.)* Now, let's see . . . A letter for Cobbey. Cobbey? *(*COBBEY *puts his hand up.* SQUEERS *hardly acknowledges, but walks on.)* Oh. Cobbey's grandmother is dead, and his uncle John has took to drinking, which is all the news his sister sends, except eighteenpence, which will just pay for that broken square of glass. Mobbs! *(*MOBBS, *not sure whether this will be good or bad news, nervously puts up his hand. It is clear it is not good news when* SQUEERS *walks to him and stands near.)* Now, Mobbs' step-mother took to her bed on hearing that he would not eat fat, and has been very ill ever since. She wishes to know by an early post where he expects to go to, if he quarrels with his vittles; and with what feelings he could turn up his nose at the cow's liver broth, after his good master had asked a blessing on it. She is disconsolate to find he is discontented, which is sinful and horrid, and hopes Mr. Squeers will flog him into a happier state of mind. *(Into* MOBB'S *ear.)* Which— he—will. *(Long pause to let this sink in to everyone. Then.)* Right, boys. I'd like you all to meet my new assistant, Mr. Nickleby. Good morning, Mr. Nickleby.

BOYS. Good morning, Mr. Nickleby.

NICHOLAS. Good morning.

SQUEERS. Now, this is the first class in English spelling and philosophy, Nickleby. We'll soon get up a Latin one and hand that over to you. *(*NICHOLAS *joins* SQUEERS.*)* Now, then, where's Smallpiece?

BOYS. Please, sir . . .

SQUEERS. Let any boy speak out of turn and I'll have the skin off his back! *(He points to* JENNINGS.*)*

JENNINGS. Please, sir, he's cleaning the back parlour window.

SQUEERS. So he is to be sure. We go on the practical mode of teaching, Nickleby; C-l-e-a-n, clean—

BOYS. Clean.

SQUEERS. Verb active, to make bright, to scour. W-i-n, win,—

BOYS. Win—

SQUEERS. d-e-r, der—

BOYS. der, winder—

SQUEERS. Winder, a casement. When a boy knows this out of a book, he goes and does it. It's just the same principle as the use of the globes. Where's Grinder? *(*COATES *puts his hand up.* SQUEERS *points to* COATES.*)*

COATES. Please, sir, he's weeding the garden.

SQUEERS. To be sure. So he is. B-o-t, Bot—

BOYS. Bot—

SQUEERS. T-i-n, tin—

BOYS. Tin—

SQUEERS. Bottin—

BOYS. Bottin—

SQUEERS. N-e-y, Ney—

BOYS. Ney—

SQUEERS. Bottiney—

BOYS. Bottiney—

SQUEERS. Noun substantive, a knowledge of plants. When he has learned that bottiney means a knowledge of plants, he goes and knows 'em. That's our system, Nickleby. What do you think of it?

NICHOLAS. It's a very useful one, at any rate.

SQUEERS. I believe you. Graymarsh, what's a horse?

GRAYMARSH. A beast, sir.

SQUEERS. So it is. A horse is a quadroped, and quadroped's Latin for beast, as anybody that's gone through the grammar knows, or else where's the use in having grammars at all?

NICHOLAS. Where indeed.

SQUEERS. *(To* GRAYMARSH.*)* And as you're so perfect in that, go to *my* horse, and rub him down well, or I'll rub *you* down. The rest go and draw water up till somebody tells you to leave off, for it's washing day tomorrow, and they'll want the coppers filled. *(The boys hurry out,* MOBBS *and* BOLDER *hurrying more than the others.)* Except—for Mobbs and Bolder. *(Everyone stops. Some of the boys push* MOBBS *and* BOLDER *forward, towards* SQUEERS. *Then the others go out, as* MRS. SQUEERS *and* WACKFORD *go too.* SMIKE *tries to go as well.)* Stay there, Smike. They'll need taking to their beds. *(He turns to* NICHOLAS.*)* This is the way we do it, Nickleby. *(*SQUEERS *lifts his cane. Blackout. Some of the older men of the company appear in a little light. As they speak this narration, we see* NICHOLAS *sit morosely down at the side of the stage.* SQUEERS, SMIKE, MOBBS, *and* BOLDER *have gone.)*

NARRATORS. And Nicholas sat down, so depressed and self-degraded that if death could have come upon then he would have been happy to meet it.

The cruelty of which he had been an unwilling witness,

The coarse and ruffianly behaviour of Squeers,

The filthy place,

The sights and sounds about him,

All contributed to this feeling.

And when he recollected that, being there as an assistant, he was the aider and abetter of a system which filled him with disgust and indignation,

He loathed himself.

(Blackout.)

SCENE 11

Bare stage. Outside Dotheboys Hall. Enter MRS. SQUEERS, and, from the other side, her 20-year-old daughter FANNY.

FANNY. Mama! Mama, I'm home!

MRS. SQUEERS. Fanny. *(Enter FANNY'S friend TILDA PRICE, followed by her swain JOHN BROWDIE, carrying luggage.)*

FANNY. Tilda Price brought me home, mama.

MRS. SQUEERS. Miss Price.

TILDA. *(A little bob.)* Good morning, ma'am.

JOHN. Ah, 'allo, missus. How's thissen?

FANNY. And John as well.

MRS. SQUEERS. I see.

FANNY. *(Aside to MRS. SQUEERS.)* Mama, do ask them in.

MRS. SQUEERS. Hm. Would you care for a glass of something, Miss Price? *(Slight pause.)* Mr. Browdie?

JOHN. Ay. We would that, certainly.

MRS. SQUEERS. Well, then—

JOHN. As soon as tied me 'orse. *(JOHN goes out to tie his 'orse. FANNY confidentially to MRS. SQUEERS.)*

FANNY. Engaged.

MRS. SQUEERS. Who is?

FANNY. She is.

MRS. SQUEERS. To who?

FANNY. To him.

MRS. SQUEERS. At her age? *(Pause.)* Well, I suppose, she is quite easy on the eye.

FANNY. And, after all, he's hardly what you'd call a gentleman. *(Re-enter JOHN.)*

JOHN. Right then. Let's have that glass of summat, missus, and let's have it sharpish, eh? *(He and* TILDA *go out, as:)*

FANNY. *(To* MRS. SQUEERS.*)* No. Certainly. Not what you'd call a gentleman, at all. *(*FANNY *and* MRS. SQUEERS *follow out* JOHN *and* TILDA.*)*

SCENE 12

THE BOYS *drag on a sofa to represent the Squeers' parlour.* SQUEERS *is drinking,* MRS. SQUEERS *is trying Belling's clothes on young* WACKFORD. PHIB *is in attendance.*

SQUEERS. Well, my dear, so what do you think of him?

MRS. SQUEERS. Think of who? *(*FANNY *comes in, having just said her goodbyes to* TILDA *and* JOHN. *She sits, knits, and listens, as:)*

SQUEERS. The new man.

MRS. SQUEERS. Oh. Young Knuckleboy.

SQUEERS. Young Nickleby.

MRS. SQUEERS. Well, if you want to know, Squeers, I'll tell you that I think him quite the proudest, haughtiest, turned-up nosediest—

SQUEERS. He is quite cheap, my dear. In fact, he's very cheap.

MRS. SQUEERS. I don't see why we need another man at all.

SQUEERS. Because it says in the advertisement quite clearly—

MRS. SQUEERS. Fiddlesticks it *says*. You *say*, in the advertisement, it's "Education by Mr. Wackford Squeers and his able assistants", but that don't mean you have to have 'em, does it? Sometimes, Squeers, you try my patience.

SQUEERS. Sometimes, you try mine.

MRS. SQUEERS. What's that?

SQUEERS. Well, my love, any slave-driver in the West Indies is allowed a man under him, to see his blacks don't run away, or get up a rebellion; and I want a man under me, to do the same with our blacks, till such time as little Wackford is able to take charge.

WACKFORD. Oh, am I?

MRS. SQUEERS. *(Impatiently.)* Am you what?

WACKFORD. Oh, am I to take charge of the school when I grow up father?

SQUEERS. Yes, of course you are.

WACKFORD. Oh. Oh. Oh, won't I give it to 'em. Won't I make 'em shriek and squeal and scream. *(The* SQUEERSES *look at each other. This exemplary attitude on the part of their son has brought them back together.)*

SQUEERS. Of course you will, my boy, of course you will.

FANNY. *(Unable to keep silence.)* Papa . . . *(*SQUEERS *and* MRS. SQUEERS *look at* FANNY.*)* Who is this—person? This young man?

MRS. SQUEERS. *(Impatient again.)* Oh, he's the new assistant, and your father has got some nonsense in his head he's the son of a gentleman that died the other day.

FANNY. A gentleman.

MRS. SQUEERS. Yes, but I don't believe a word of it. If he's a gentleman's son at all, he's a fondling, that's my opinion.

SQUEERS. Foundling, and he's nothing of the kind. His father was married, *to* his mother years before he was born, and she's alive now.

MRS. SQUEERS. Well, all I say—

SQUEERS. *(Stands.)* And if you do dislike him, dear, I don't know anyone shows dislike better than you do, and if there's a touch of pride about him, then I do not believe there is a woman living that can bring a person's spirit down as quick as you.

MRS. SQUEERS. Oh, is that so.

SQUEERS. My love. *(Pause.* MRS. SQUEERS *looks at* SQUEERS. *Then she laughs.* SQUEERS *laughs too.)*

MRS. SQUEERS. Come, Wackford. *(*MRS. SQUEERS, *still laughing, gestures* WACKFORD *to follow her, and goes out.* SQUEERS, *laughing too, goes out.* FANNY *and* PHIB *left.)*

FANNY. Well? So what's he like?

PHIB. He's lovely.

SCENE 13

THE BOYS *take out the sofa and some lie down, to represent the common dormitory.* SMIKE *is sitting.* NICHO-

LAS, *still sitting on the side of the stage, now stands, and goes to* SMIKE. NICHOLAS *carries a book.*

NICHOLAS. Hallo. (SMIKE *looks up, scared, and flinches a little.*) Please, don't be frightened. (NICHOLAS *crouches down near* SMIKE. *He puts down his book.*) Are you cold? (SMIKE *shakes his head.*) You're shivering. (*Pause.* NICHOLAS *stands to go. He stops when* SMIKE *speaks.*)

SMIKE. Oh, dear. (NICHOLAS *turns back.*) Oh, dear, oh, dear. My heart. Will break. It will. (*Louder, more forceful.*) It *will.* I know it *will.*

NICHOLAS. (*Embarrassed, looking round.*) Shh, shh.

SMIKE. Remember Dorker, do you?

NICHOLAS. Dorker?

SMIKE. I was with him at the end, he asked for me. Who will I ask for? Who? (*Pause.* NICHOLAS *doesn't know what* SMIKE *is talking about.*)

NICHOLAS. Who will you ask for when? (SMIKE *back into himself again.*)

SMIKE. No One. No Hope. Hope Less. (*Slight pause.*)

NICHOLAS. (*Feebly.*) There's always hope.

SMIKE. (*To himself.*) Is there? (SMIKE *turns again to* NICHOLAS. *Forcefully.*) O-U-T-C-A-S-T. A noun. Substantive. Person cast out or rejected. Abject. And foresaken. Homeless. Me. (NICHOLAS *looks at* SMIKE. *He doesn't know what to say. Pause. Then* FANNY *enters, behind* NICHOLAS. *She takes in the scene.*)

FANNY. Oh—I'm sorry. (NICHOLAS *turns.*) I was looking for my father.

NICHOLAS. He's not here.

FANNY. I see. (*Pause.*) I beg your pardon, sir. How very awkward.

NICHOLAS. Please, please don't apologise.

FANNY. I thank you, sir. Oh . . . Sir. (FANNY *curtseys, turns, turns back, turns again and goes.* NICHOLAS *to go out too, when he realises he's left his book. He looks back to* SMIKE, *who has picked up the book and is holding it to himself.* NICHOLAS *decides to leave* SMIKE *with the book.* SMIKE *is left alone, with the sleeping boys. Blackout.*)

SCENE 14

Miss La Creevy's house in the Strand. Enter KATE *and* HANNAH, *with luggage, from upstage.*

HANNAH. Is it the East End that you're going to, Miss?

KATE. That's right. Is that unusual, as a place to live?

HANNAH. *(Trying to avoid answering "yes.")* Well, uh . . . *(Enter* MRS. NICKLEBY *and* MISS LA CREEVY.*)*

MISS LA CREEVY. Well, I'm still afraid that millinery is not a healthy occupation, for your dear Kate or anyone else. For I remember getting three young milliners to sit for me, and they were all very pale and sickly.

MRS. NICKLEBY. Oh, Miss La Creevy, that's not a general rule by any means. For I recall employing one to make a scarlet cloak, at the time when scarlet cloaks were fashionable, and she had a very red face—a very red face indeed.

MISS LA CREEVY. Perhaps she drank.

MRS. NICKLEBY. Well, I don't know how that may have been, but I do know she had an extremely red face, so your argument goes for nothing. *(Pause.)* And Kate, who knows, if you work well, you might be taken into partnership with Madame Mantalini. *(Pause.)* Think. Nickleby and Mantalini. How well it would sound. And, who knows, Dr. Nickleby, the headmaster of Westminster School, living in the same street . . . *(Slight pause.)* It's not impossible, at all. *(Enter* HANNAH, *followed by* NEWMAN NOGGS.*)*

HANNAH. Uh—it's a gentleman. I think. *(*MISS LA CREEVY *looks peevishly at* HANNAH.*)*

NOGGS. Name's Noggs. From Mr. Nickleby. To Thames Street.

KATE. Yes. We'll need a coach, I fear.

NOGGS. I'll get one.

MRS. NICKLEBY. Uh, Mr. Noggs . . . did we see you on the morning when my son departed on the coach for Yorkshire?

NOGGS. Me? Oh, no.

MRS. NICKLEBY. I'm sure of it, I—

NOGGS. No. First time I've been out, three weeks. I've had the gout. You ready?

KATE. Yes. *(She turns to* MISS LA CREEVY.*)* We are sorry, very sorry, to leave you, Miss La Creevy.

MISS LA CREEVY. Oh, that's stuff. You cannot shake me off that easily. I'll see you very often, come and call, and hear how you get on. (KATE *smiles.)* And if, in all the world, there's no-one else to take an interest in your welfare, there will still be one poor, lonely heart that prays for it night and day.

NOGGS. Uh—can we go? *(And the* NICKLEBYS *leave with* MR. NOGGS, MISS LA CREEVY *and* HANNAH *waving, the former with a handkerchief pressed to her nose.)*

SCENE 15

The parlour at Dotheboys Hall. Early evening. Enter TILDA *and* FANNY, *both dressed up to the nines.* PHIB *enters, too, setting the table with tea and a plate of bread and butter.*

TILDA. Engaged!

FANNY. No, not exactly. Not exactly, as it were, engaged. But going to be, there is no question. *(They sit on the sofa.)*

TILDA. Fanny, that is *wonderful.*

FANNY. Because, you see, his very presence, coming here to live with us, beneath this roof, and under the most mysterious circumstances . . .

TILDA. Fanny, what's he said? *(Slight pause.)*

FANNY. What do you mean?

TILDA. I mean—what has he *said*? *(Pause.)*

FANNY. Don't ask me what he said, my dear. If you had only seen his look . . .

TILDA. Was it like this? *(*TILDA *gives a love-lorn look.)*

FANNY. Like that?

TILDA. John looked at me like that.

FANNY. Well, so did he. Like that, entirely, only rather more genteel.

TILDA. Well, then, that's it.

FANNY. That's what?

TILDA. He must mean something, if he looks like that. He must feel . . . something very strong.

FANNY. Oh, I'm so jealous of you, Tilda!

TILDA. Why?

FANNY. Because you are so fortunate. That your mama and papa are so readily agreeable to your engagement, indeed appear not to have thought twice about it, whereas my mother and my father are so bitterly opposed to my dear Nicholas; and will throw all kinds of obstacles in our way; and will force us to meet in secret, and deny our passion . . . Oh that my course of love were half as simple, quiet and smooth as yours! *(Pause.)*

TILDA. I cannot wait to see him.

FANNY. Oh, I'm shaking!

TILDA. Yes, I know just how you feel. *(Knock, knock.)*

FANNY. Oh, there he is! Oh, Tilda!

TILDA. Shh. Just say, come in.

FANNY. *(Almost silently.)* Come in! *(*TILDA *a glance at* PHIB, *who looks away. Nothing.)*

TILDA. Come in! *(*NICHOLAS *comes in.)*

NICHOLAS. Good evening. I understood from Mr. Squeers that—

FANNY. Oh, yes. It's all right. Father's been called away, but you won't mind that, I dare venture.

NICHOLAS. *(Out front.)* And Nicholas opened his eyes at this, but he turned the matter off very coolly—not minding particularly about anything just then—and went through the ceremony of introduction to the miller's daughter with as much grace as he could muster. *(Bowing to* TILDA.*)* Your servant, ma'am.

FANNY. We are only waiting for one more gentleman.

NICHOLAS. *(Out front.)* It was a matter of equal moment to Nicholas whether they were waiting for one gentleman or twenty; and being out of spirits, and not seeing any especial reason why he should make himself agreeable, looked out of the window and sighed. *(He looks "out of the window" and sighs.)*

TILDA. Oh, Mr. Nickleby.

NICHOLAS. *(With a start.)* I'm sorry.

TILDA. Please, don't apologise. Perhaps your langour is occasioned by my presence. But, please, don't heed me. You may behave just as you would if you two were alone.

FANNY. *(Blushing.)* Tilda! I'm ashamed of you! *(The young women giggle.)*

NICHOLAS. And here the two friends burst into a verity of giggles, glancing from time to time at Nicholas, who, in a state of unmixed astonishment, gradually fell into one of irrepressible amusement.

TILDA. Come, now, Mr. Nickleby. Will you have tea?

NICHOLAS. *(Cheerfully, going over to sit.)* Oh, certainly. I'm honoured. And delighted. *(The women look at each other.* TILDA *a little nod,* FANNY *a deep breath.)*

FANNY. Some—bread-and-butter?

NICHOLAS. Please. *(*NICHOLAS *being poured tea and helping himself to bread-and-butter when there's another knock.* TILDA *stands,* FANNY *gestures to* PHIB, *who admits* JOHN BROWDIE, *looking scrubbed and uncomfortable in a huge collar and white waistcoat.)*

TILDA. Well, John.

JOHN. Well, lass.

FANNY. I beg your pardon, Mr. Nickleby—Mr. John Browdie.

JOHN. Your servant, sir.

NICHOLAS. Yours to command, sir.

FANNY. Please, Mr. Browdie, sit down. *(*JOHN, *as he sits.)*

JOHN. Old woman gone awa, be she?

FANNY. She has.

JOHN. *(Helping himself to bread-and-butter.)* And schoolmaster as well?

FANNY. Yes, yes.

JOHN. An' just the four o' us?

FANNY. That's right. Do have some bread-and-butter. *(*JOHN, *in mid-bite, grins hugely. Then, to* NICHOLAS.)*

JOHN. Tha won't get brea-and-butter ev'ry night, eh, man? *(*NICHOLAS *a weak smile.)* In fact, I tell thee, if tha stay here long enough, tha'll end up nowt but skin and bone. *(*JOHN *laughs hugely.* NICHOLAS *annoyed by this criticism of his employer.* JOHN *elbows* FANNY.)* Just skin and bone, eh, Fanny? *(*JOHN *looks back to* NICHOLAS. *To explain.)* I tell tha, man, last teacher, 'ad 'ere, when turned sideway, couldn't tell were there! *(*NICHOLAS *suddenly to his feet.)*

NICHOLAS. Sir, I don't know whether your perceptions are quite keen enough, to enable you to understand that your remarks are highly offensive, to me and my employer, but if they are, please have the goodness to— *(*TILDA *stops* JOHN'S *response.)*

TILDA. If you say one more word, John, only half a word, I'll never speak to you again.

JOHN. Oh. Weel. I'll shut me mouth, then. Eh? (JOHN *eats bread-and-butter and slurps his tea.* FANNY, *overcome, stands and runs to the side.* TILDA *follows.* NICHOLAS *looks alarmed.*)

TILDA. Fanny, what's the matter?

FANNY. Nothing.

TILDA. There was never any danger of an altercation, was there, Mr. Nickleby?

NICHOLAS. (A step towards the women.) No, none at all. (TILDA to NICHOLAS, FANNY still sniffing.)

TILDA. Say something kind to her.

NICHOLAS. Why, what—

TILDA. Or better, why don't John and I go off next door, and leave you two together? For a little while.

NICHOLAS. Whatever for?

TILDA. Whatever for? And her dressed up so beautifully, and looking really almost handsome. I'm ashamed of you.

NICHOLAS. My dear girl, what is it to me how she is dressed, or how she looks? It's hardly my concern. (TILDA *quickly to the table.*)

TILDA. Don't call me a dear girl, or Fanny will be saying it's my fault. We will play cards. Phib, dear, please clear the table. (PHIB *clears the table,* TILDA *whispers to* FANNY, *and* JOHN *finishes the bread-and-butter, as* NICHOLAS *speaks out front.*)

NICHOLAS. And all of this was completely unintelligible to Nicholas, who had no other distinct impression, than that Miss Squeers was an ordinary-looking girl, and her friend Miss Price a pretty one, and that he had been called to join in a game of Speculation. (FANNY *and* TILDA *both standing near the chair opposite* JOHN.)

TILDA. So, who's to partner whom?

NICHOLAS. (Obviously, moving to a chair opposite an empty chair.) I'll partner you, Miss Price.

TILDA. Oh, *sir.*

NICHOLAS. (Taking this response as meaning assent.) It will be my great pleasure. (TILDA *glances at* FANNY, *and sits opposite the chair beside which* NICHOLAS *is standing.* FANNY *sits opposite* JOHN. NICHOLAS *tearing up cards for chips.*)

FANNY. *(Hysterically.)* Well, Mr. Browdie, it appears we're to be partners.

JOHN. *(Dumbfounded.)* Aye.

NICHOLAS. I'll deal?

FANNY. Oh, please, do deal. (NICHOLAS *deals five cards to each player. They look at their cards.)* Well, Mr. Browdie?

JOHN. *(Pushing two chips into the centre.)* Two on spades.

NICHOLAS. Miss Price?

TILDA. *(Three chips.)* Bid three. On hearts.

FANNY. *(Putting one chip in.)* I'll—pass.

NICHOLAS. *(Putting one chip in.)* Then hearts it is. (FANNY *a sharp intake of breath. The hand is played out in total silence. The principle is the same as whist, with each player laying a card for each trick, hearts being trumps.* TILDA *and* NICHOLAS *win.)* Well, then. We've won.

FANNY. And Tilda something that she'd not expected to win, I think.

TILDA. *(Ingenuously.)* Oh, only seven, dear. (JOHN *dealing another hand.)*

FANNY. *(To* TILDA.) How dull you are.

TILDA. Oh, no, indeed. I am in excellent spirits. I was thinking *you* seemed out of sorts.

FANNY. Oh, me? Why, no.

TILDA. Your hair's coming out of curl, dear.

FANNY. Pray, dear, don't mind me. You'd better attend to your partner.

NICHOLAS. Thank you for reminding her. She had. (JOHN *looking black.)*

TILDA. One diamond.

FANNY. Two clubs.

NICHOLAS. Two diamonds.

JOHN. Three clubs.

TILDA. Pass.

FANNY. Pass.

NICHOLAS. Pass. (JOHN *looks round.* NICHOLAS *and* TILDA *indicate they have no further bid. The hand is played, and, surprisingly,* NICHOLAS *and* TILDA *win again, on the last trick, with* NICHOLAS' *king of clubs.* NICHOLAS *pulls in the chips.* TILDA *deals again during:)*

TILDA. Well, I never had such luck. It's all you, Mr.

Nickleby, I'm sure. I should like to have you for a partner always.

NICHOLAS. Well, I wish you had.

TILDA. Though if you win at cards, of course, you'll have a bad wife, sure as sure.

NICHOLAS. Not if your wish is gratified, Miss Price. *(He picks up his cards. Aware of the silence of the others.)* We have all the talking to ourselves, it seems.

FANNY. Oh, but you do it so well, Mr. Nickleby. It would be quite an outrage to interrupt you, wouldn't it? Two hearts.

NICHOLAS. Pass. *(Pause.)*

TILDA. John, dear, your bid.

JOHN. My what?

TILDA. Your bid.

JOHN. *(Throwing down his cards.)* Well, damn me if I'm going to take this longer. *(Pause. The young women very shocked.)*

NICHOLAS. Erm . . .

JOHN. *(Stands.)* And you are coming home with me, now, Tilda, and him o'ert there can look sharp for a broken head next time he comes near me.

TILDA. Mercy on us, what is all this?

JOHN. Home! Home, now, home! *(FANNY crying.)*

TILDA. And here's Fanny in tears, now. What can be the matter?

FANNY. Oh, don't you bother, ma'am. Oh, don't you trouble to enquire.

TILDA. Well, you are monstrous polite, ma'am.

FANNY. Well, I shall not come to you to take lessons in the art, ma'am.

TILDA. And you need not take the trouble to make yourself plainer than you are, ma'am, because it's quite unnecessary.

FANNY. Oh! Oh, I can thank God that I haven't the boldness of some people!

TILDA. *(Standing.)* And I can thank God I haven't the envy of others. While wishing you a good night, ma'am, and pleasant dreams attend your sleep.

FANNY. Tilda, I hate you! *(TILDA sweeps out, followed by JOHN, with a dark look at NICHOLAS. FANNY, weeping, thumps PHIB. NICHOLAS, out front:)*

NICHOLAS. This is one consequence, thought Nicholas,

of my cursed readiness to adapt myself to any society into which chance carries me. If I had sat mute and motionless, as I might have done, this would not have happened. *(Pause. End of reportage.* NICHOLAS *flails.)* What did I do? What did I do? *(*NICHOLAS *withdraws.)*

FANNY. Oh, I swear that there is no-one in the world more miserable than I. And never has been. And never will be. *(Pause.)*

PHIB. *(Carefully.)* Well, I can't help saying, miss, if you were to kill me for it, that I never saw anyone look so vulgar as Miss Price this night.

FANNY. Oh, Phib, how you do talk. *(Pause.)*

PHIB. And I know it's very wrong of me to say so, Miss, Miss Price being a friend of yours and all, but she do dress herself out so, and go on in such a manner to get noticed: well, if people only saw themselves.

FANNY. Now, Phib, you know you mustn't talk like that.

PHIB. So vain. And so, so plain.

FANNY. And I will hear no more of this. It's true, Miss Price has faults, has many, but I wish her well. And above all, I wish her married. And I think it desirable— most desirable, from the nature of her failings—that she is married as soon as possible.

PHIB. Yes, miss. *(A knock.)*

FANNY. Who's that? Come in. *(Enter* TILDA. PHIB *exit.)*

TILDA. Well, Fanny. *(Slight pause.)* Well, Fanny, you see I have come back to see you. Although we had bad words.

FANNY. I bear no malice, Tilda, I am above it.

TILDA. Don't be cross, please, Fanny. I have come to tell you something.

FANNY. What may that be, Tilda?

TILDA. Well . . . Well, this. After we left here, John and I had the most dreadful quarrel. But after a great deal of wrangling, and saying we would never speak again, we made it up, and John has promised that first thing tomorrow morning he'll put our names down in the church, and I give you notice to get your bridesmaid's frock made now. There!

FANNY. Oh, *Tilda*. Oh, dear Tilda. *(And the two*

women burst into tears and embrace each other.) Oh, I'm
so *happy.* (TILDA *decides to strike while the iron is cool.*)

TILDA. But, now, Fanny, there's the matter of young
Mr. Nickleby.

FANNY. Oh, him. He's nothing to me.

TILDA. Oh, come, now, Fanny, that's not true.

FANNY. It is. I hate him. And I wish that he was dead.
And me as well.

TILDA. Now, dear. You know you'll think very differently in five minutes, and wouldn't it be much nicer to
take him back in favour?

FANNY. Oh, Tilda. How could you have acted so mean
and dishonourable. I wouldn't have believed it of you.

TILDA. Now, Fanny, you're talking as if I murdered
someone.

FANNY. Very near as bad.

TILDA. Oh, don't be silly. It's not my fault I've got
enough good looks to make some people civil. Persons
don't make their own faces, and it's no more my fault if
mine is a good one than it is other people's fault if theirs
is not.

FANNY. (*In horror.*) Oh, *Tilda.*

TILDA. Fanny, I don't mean—

FANNY. Now, go. Go back home at once.

TILDA. Oh, Fanny—

FANNY. Now, at once, d'you hear me?

TILDA. Very well, but—

FANNY. NOW. (FANNY *turns firmly away.* TILDA *to
the exit. She turns back.* FANNY *turns slowly to* TILDA.
TILDA *gives a little, shruggy, affectionate gesture, as if to
apologise. Pause. Then* FANNY *runs to her friend, crying.*)
Oh, I'm so *happy* for you, Tilda.

SCENE 16

THE BOYS clear the Dotheboys Hall furniture and set
two meagre, broken chairs and a threadbare carpet. The
Nicklebys' new house in Thames St. MRS. NICKLEBY,
KATE *and* NOGGS—who carries their luggage—enter during the narration.

NARRATION. And at that very moment, Kate and Mrs.
Nickleby arrived at their new home.

Around, the squalid slums of the East End of London—

And behind, a wharf that opened to the river—

And nearby, an empty kennel, and some bones of animals—

Past which they quickly walked,

And went inside.

NOGGS. *(Putting down the luggage.)* Well, here it is.
KATE. I see.
NOGGS. It's not, of course . . . There are some bits of furniture. And there's a fire made up. I'm sure, although it looks like a little gloomy, it can be made, quite . . .
KATE. Yes. *(Pause.)*
MRS. NICKLEBY. Well, well, my dear. Is it not thoughtful and considerate of your kind uncle? To provide us with . . .
NOGGS. Your uncle, yes. *(NOGGS picks up the luggage and takes it to another room in the house.)*
KATE. Oh, mama, this house is so depressing. I—one could imagine that some dreadful—that some awful thing had—
MRS. NICKLEBY. Lord, dear Kate, don't talk like that, you'll frighten me to death.
KATE. It's just a foolish fancy.
MRS. NICKLEBY. Well, Kate, I'll thank you to keep your foolish fancies to yourself, and not wake up my foolish fancies to keep them company.
KATE. Yes, I'm sorry. *(The two women look at each other. Then, quite suddenly, they embrace. NOGGS enters.)* Mr. Noggs, we need detain you no longer.
NOGGS. Is there nothing more?
KATE. No, nothing, really. Thank you.
MRS. NICKLEBY. *(Fumbling in her purse.)* Perhaps, dear, Mr. Noggs would like to drink our healths.
KATE. I think, mama, you'd hurt his feelings if you offered it. *(NOGGS bows and withdraws. The women sit.)*
NARRATION. Gloomy and black in truth the old house was—

No life was stirring there—

And everything said coldness, silence and decay.

SCENE 17

Outside Dotheboys Hall. Day. Enter NICHOLAS.

NICHOLAS. And so it happened that, the next day, during the short daily interval that was suffered to elapse between what was pleasantly called the dinner of Mr. Squeers' pupils and their return to the pursuit of useful knowledge, Nicholas was engaged in a melancholy walk, and brood, and listless saunter. *(*NICHOLAS *perambulates as* TILDA *and* FANNY *enter, arm-in-arm.)*

TILDA. And Miss Price, who had stayed the night with Miss Squeers, was at that same being taken by her best friend at least as far home as the second turning of the road.

FANNY. *(Seeing* NICHOLAS.*)* Ah! Him!

TILDA. Oh, Fanny, shall we turn back? He hasn't seen us yet.

FANNY. No, Tilda . . . It is my duty to go through with it, and so I shall. *(*NICHOLAS *walks straight past* TILDA *and* FANNY.*)*

NICHOLAS. *(As he passes.)* Good morning.

FANNY. *(Nudging* TILDA *violently.)* He's going. I shall faint.

TILDA. Oh, Mr. Nickleby, come back!

FANNY. *(Staggering slightly, and needing to be supported by* TILDA—*)* I know I shall—

TILDA. Oh, Mr. Nickleby— *(*NICHOLAS *turns back, and comes to* TILDA *and* FANNY.*)*

NICHOLAS. Um, what's the—

TILDA. Just, please, help— *(*NICHOLAS *to hold* FANNY, *when that young lady expertly twists and falls backwards into his arms. For a moment, they stand there, and then* NICHOLAS, *unable to prevent himself, falls over backwards,* FANNY *on top of him.)*

NICHOLAS. Miss Squeers . . .

FANNY. *(Coming around.)* Oh, dear, this is foolish faintness—

TILDA. It's not foolish, dear. You have no reason to feel shamed. It's others, who provoke it, who should—

NICHOLAS. Ah. I understand. (NICHOLAS *manhandles* FANNY *to a sitting position.*) You are still resolved to fix it upon me. I see. Although I told you last night it was not my fault.

TILDA. There, he says it was not his fault. Perhaps you were too jealous, or too hasty with him? He says it was not his fault. I think that is apology enough.

NICHOLAS. Um—

FANNY. All right, Tilda. You've convinced me. I forgive him. (FANNY *lies back on* NICHOLAS *again.*)

NICHOLAS. Oh, dear. This is more serious than I supposed. Allow me— (*He dislodges* FANNY, *and stands.* FANNY *stands with* TILDA.) May I speak? (*The two women look at him with eager anticipation.*) I must say— that I am very sorry—truly and sincerely so—for having been the cause of any difference among you last night. I reproach myself most bitterly for having been so unfortunate as to cause the dissention that occurred, although I did so, I assure you, most unwittingly and heedlessly. (*Pause.*)

TILDA. Well, that's not all you have to say, surely.

NICHOLAS. No, it is not, I fear there is something more. (*Slight pause.*) It is a most awkward thing to say, as the very mention of such a supposition makes one look like a puppy—but, still . . . May I ask if that lady supposes that I entertain . . . a sort of . . . (*Quickly.*) Does she think that I'm in love with her?

FANNY. Oh! (*Change of tack.*) Oh, answer for me, dear.

TILDA. Of course she does.

NICHOLAS. She does?

TILDA. Of course.

FANNY. And you may say, dear Tilda, that if Mr. Nickleby had doubted that, he may set his mind at rest. His sentiments are completely recipro—

NICHOLAS. Stop!

FANNY. Whatever for?

NICHOLAS. Pray hear me. This is the grossest and wildest delusion, the completest and most signal mistake, that ever human being laboured under or committed. I have scarcely seen the young lady half a dozen times, but if I had seen her sixty times, or sixty thousand, it would be and will be precisely the same. I have not one thought, wish, or hope, connected with her unless it be— and I say this, not to hurt her feelings, but to impress her with the real state of my own—unless it be the one object dear to my heart as life itself, of being one day able to turn my back on this accursed place, never to set foot in it again or to think of it—even think of it—except with loathing and disgust. *(Pause. Then NICHOLAS, out front.)* And with this particularly plain and straightforward declaration, Nicholas bowed slightly, and waiting to hear no more, retreated. *(NICHOLAS retreats.)*

TILDA. But oh, poor Fanny! Her anger, rage and vexation are not to be described.

FANNY. Refused! *(Fanny starts to push at TILDA, to make her go away, as punishment for encouraging her.)*

TILDA. *(Being pushed, and beginning to enjoy FANNY'S fury, and find it amusing.)* Refused by a teacher picked up by advertisement at an annual salary of five pounds payable at indefinite periods . . . *(Really taunting now.)* . . . and this too in the presence of a little chit of a miller's daughter of eighteen,

FANNY. *(Pushing and shoving.)* . . . who was going to be married, to a man who had gone down on his very knees to ask her! *(And, with a little, dismissive gesture, FANNY turns, runs to the side and weeps, while TILDA, still laughing, dances out the other way, and NICHOLAS speaks out front.)*

NICHOLAS. And it may be remarked, that Miss Squeers was of the firm opinion that she was prepossessing and beautiful, and that her father was, after all, master, and Nicholas man, and that her father had saved money and Nicholas had none, all of which seemed to her conclusive arguments why the young man should feel only too honoured by her preference, and all too grateful for her deep affection . . . *(And NICHOLAS turns and sees FANNY. She has composed herself now, but this has the effect of making her look even more crumpled. She marches to NICHOLAS, with an effort at dignity, but then breaks down.)*

FANNY. Sir . . . I pity you. *(She turns and runs back, as MRS. SQUEERS and SMIKE appear, as if from the house.)* You're right, mama.

MRS. SQUEERS. Right? What about?

FANNY. *(Crying.)* About that Knuckleboy. *(She runs out, as if into the house.)*

MRS. SQUEERS *(To NICHOLAS.)* You, sir!

NICHOLAS. Yes, ma'am?

MRS. SQUEERS. You've been wanted in the classroom for ten minutes.

NICHOLAS. Certainly. *(He goes towards MRS. SQUEERS, as if into the house.)*

MRS. SQUEERS. Not through the house, sir. Round that way. *(Pause. Then NICHOLAS turns his collar up against the cold, and goes out another way. SMIKE makes to follow him.)* Smike! *(SMIKE turns back to MRS. SQUEERS.)* In here. You haven't finished. *(She cuffs SMIKE on the head as he passes her into the house.)*

SCENE 18

The dormitory at Dotheboys Hall. Night. The BOYS enter and lie down, on the bare stage. SMIKE enters and sits, with Nicholas' book. NICHOLAS enters with a candle, to see SMIKE trying to read the book. SMIKE can't work out what to do.

SMIKE. Can't do it. With the book. Can't do it, with the book, at all.

NICHOLAS. Oh, please. Don't try. *(SMIKE crying.)* Don't. For God's sake. I cannot bear it. *(SMIKE whimpering.)* They are more hard on you, I know. But, please . . .

SMIKE. Except for you, I die.

NICHOLAS. No, no. You'll be better off, I tell you, when I'm gone. *(SMIKE picks it up after a second.)*

SMIKE. You gone?

NICHOLAS. Shh. Yes.

SMIKE. You going?

NICHOLAS. I was speaking to my thoughts.

SMIKE. *Tell* me. Will you? Will you go? *(Pause.)*

NICHOLAS. I shall be driven to it. Yes. To go away. *(Pause.)*

SMIKE. Please tell me. Is away as bad as here? *(Pause.)*

NICHOLAS. Oh, no. Oh, no, there's nothing—

SMIKE. Can I meet you there? Away?

NICHOLAS. Well, yes . . . you can, of course . . .

SMIKE Can meet you there? Away? And I will find you, in away?

NICHOLAS. You would. And, if you did, I'd try to help you. (Pause. NICHOLAS moves away with the candle and sits. He takes out a paper and a pen. He is writing a letter to KATE.) I miss you terribly, but at least I feel that if my work here prospers—I miss you terribly. (Pause.) I took a Latin class today. The boys are—they are not advanced and there is much to do. (Pause.) The country-side is— (Pause. He puts away the letter. He blows out the candle. Darkness.)

SCENE 19

The same. A bell rings offstage, and then cold, morning light. The BOYS and NICHOLAS are in the same positions, but, in the blackout, SMIKE has slipped away.

SQUEERS. (Off.) Hey! Hey, you up there? Are you going to sleep all day?

NICHOLAS. We shall be down directly, sir. (He gestures to the BOYS, who speed up.)

SQUEERS. (Off.) Well, you'd better be, or I'll be down on some of you in less—Where's Smike? (NICHOLAS goes to Smike's place, but sees he isn't there. The BOYS nearly fully up.) (Off.) I said—where's Smike? (NICHOLAS turns and calls.)

NICHOLAS. He isn't here, sir.

SQUEERS. (Off.) What? Not there? (Pause. SQUEERS enters, rushes to Smike's place. He sees Smike is absent.) What does this mean? Where have you hid him?

NICHOLAS. I have not seen him since last night.

SQUEERS. Oh, no? (Turning to the BOYS.) And you? You boys? Have any of you— (JENNINGS, who is ob-scured from SQUEERS by other boys.)

JENNINGS. Please, sir . . .

SQUEERS. Yes? What's that?

JENNINGS. Please, sir, I think he's run away.

SQUEERS. Who said that?

BOYS. Jennings, sir.

SQUEERS. And, where is Jennings?

Boys. Here, sir. *(Jennings is pushed forward by his fellows. Squeers to Jennings.)*

Squeers. So, you think he's run away, do you?

Jennings. Yes, sir. Please, sir.

Squeers. And what, sir, what reason have you to suppose that any boy would *want* to run away from this establishment? *(Squeers hits Jennings on the face.)* Eh, sir? *(Jennings says nothing. Squeers looks to Nicholas, who is looking away. Squeers to Nicholas.)* And you, Nickleby. I s'pose you think he's run away?

Nicholas. I think it's highly likely, yes.

Squeers. You do? Perhaps you *know* he's run away?

Nicholas. I do not know, sir. And I'm glad I did not, for it would then have been my duty to have warned you.

Squeers. Which, no doubt, you would have been devilish sorry to do.

Nicholas. I should indeed, sir. *(Mrs. Squeers enters.)*

Mrs. Squeers. What's going on? Where's Smike?

Squeers. He's gone.

Mrs. Squeers. *(An order, to Squeers.)* Gone? Well, then, we'll find him, stupid. We must search the roads. He hasn't any money, any food. He'll have to beg. He must be on the public road.

Squeers. *(Going towards the exit.)* That's true.

Mrs. Squeers. *(Following.)* And when we catch him, oh . . . *(Squeers turns back to the Boys. Slowly.)*

Squeers. And when we catch him, I will only stop just short of flaying him alive. So, follow your leader, boys, and take your pattern by Smike. If you dare. *(The Squeerses go out. Nicholas and the Boys follow.)*

SCENE 20

The streets of the West End of London. Early morning. During this opening narration, we set up the breakfast room of the Mantalinis: a table and two chairs on the one side, and a single chair on the other. The Narration is delivered by Kate Nickleby and four or five Milliners.

Kate. It was with a heavy heart, and many sad forebodings, that Kate Nickleby left the city when its clocks yet wanted a quarter of an hour of eight, and threaded her way, alone, amid the noise and bustle of the streets, towards the West End of London.

MILLINERS. At this early hour many sickly girls,

Whose business, like that of the poor worm, is to produce with patient toil the finery that bedecks the thoughtless and luxurious,

Traverse our streets, making towards the scene of their daily labour,

And catching, as if by stealth, in their hurried walk,

The only gasp of wholesome air and glimpse of sunlight which cheers their monotonous existence during the long train of hours that make up the working day.

The MILLINERS *dispersing, as a tall, old* FOOTMAN *enters, a little unsteadily.)*

KATE. Kate saw, in their unhealthy looks and feeble gait, but too clear an evidence that her misgivings were not wholly groundless. (KATE *goes to the* FOOTMAN, *as a male* NARRATOR *enters.)*

NARRATOR. She arrived at Madame Mantalini's at the appointed hour, and was admitted to a small, curtained room, by a tall, elderly footman. (*During the following,* MR. *and* MADAME MANTALINI *enter to the breakfast table and sit.* MADAME MANTALINI *is a handsome, well-dressed middle-aged woman. Her husband wears a morning gown, with a green waistcoat and Turkish trousers, a pink kerchief, bright slippers, black curled whiskers and a moustache. He is younger than his wife.)*

KATE. Excuse me—Mantalini? Are they Italian?

FOOTMAN. Muntle.

KATE. I beg your pardon?

FOOTMAN. Changed his name. From Mr. Muntle. To Mr. Mantalini.

KATE. Oh, I see. (*The* FOOTMAN *nods gravely and goes out.* KATE *sits on the single chair. We gather from the fact that the* MANTALINIS *do not notice her that the room is divided by an imaginary curtain. There is a bad-*

tempered silence between the MANTALINIS, *which is broken when* MR. MANTALINI *speaks.)*

MANTALINI. I tell you again, my soul, that if you will be odiously, demnibly, outrageously jealous, you will make yourself most horrid miserable.

MADAME MANTALINI. *(Pouting.)* I *am* miserable.

MANTALINI. And I tell you, my fastness, that it is a pretty bewitching little countenance you have, but if it is out of humour, it quite spoils itself, and looks very much like a hobgoblin's.

MADAME MANTALINI. It's very easy to talk.

MANTALINI. Not so easy when one is eating an egg and one is provoked into a passion by demned false accusations, my jewel, for the yolk runs down the waistcoat, and yolk of egg don't match it. 'Cept, of course, a yellow waistcoat. Which this ain't. *(Pause.* MADAME MANTALINI *breaks.)*

MADAME MANTALINI. You flirted with her all night long.

MANTALINI. No, no, my love.

MADAME MANTALINI. I watched you all the time.

MANTALINI. Oh, bless the little winking eye—was on me all the time?

MADAME MANTALINI. And I say, Mantalini, that you waltz with anyone but me again, I will take poison. I will swear it, now.

MANTALINI. Take poison?

MADAME MANTALINI. Yes.

MANTALINI. You'll take demned poison on account of Mantalini, preciousness?

MADAME MANTALINI. I will.

MANTALINI. He would could have had the hands of a dowager and two countesses—

MADAME MANTALINI. *One* countess.

MANTALINI. *(Stands and goes round to his wife's side of the table.)* But who at a morning concert saw the demndest little fascinator in the world, and married it, and fiddlesticks to every countess in the world?

MADAME MANTALINI. Oh, Mantalini.

MANTALINI. Oh, my little cherub. I'm forgiven?

MADAME MANTALINI. Well . . . Oh, well.

MANTALINI. *(Moving briskly back to his seat.)* Now, tell me, sapphire, how are we for cash? For there's a horse for sale at Scrubbs, for next to nothing, and if I can raise some discount from Ralph Nickleby, a hundred guineas buys him, mane and crest and legs and tail, all of the demdest beauty. (KATE *looks up in alarm.* MADAME MANTALINI *turns her head away.*) Then I can ride him in the park, before the very chariots of the rejected countesses. (*Moving back to his wife.*) My little—princess.

MADAME MANTALINI. Oh, my—Mantalini. (KATE *coughs loudly.* MANTALINI *stands and mimes pulling back the curtain—we hear the swish and rattle from offstage,* MANTALINI *sees* KATE.)

MANTALINI. Well. What's this?

MADAME MANTALINI. Child, who are you?

KATE. (*Standing.*) I—I am sent here, by my uncle. I am sent here for a situation.

MANTALINI. (*Coming closer to* KATE.) And, my dear, you'll have one.

MADAME MANTALINI. Mantalini. (KATE *thrusts Ralph's letter at* MADAME MANTALINI.)

KATE. There's a letter. From my uncle, Mr. Nickleby.

MADAME MANTALINI. (*Taking the letter, opening it, a little tartly.*) Oh, yes.

MANTALINI. (*Trying to look at the letter.*) Ralph Nickleby?

KATE. I'm sorry, I was—I was left here, by your footman.

MANTALINI. What a rascal is that footman, dear. To keep this sweet young creature waiting—

MADAME MANTALINI. (*Folding Ralph's letter.*) Well, dear, I must say that that's your fault.

MANTALINI. My fault, my joy?

MADAME MANTALINI. Of course. What can you expect, dearest, if you will not correct the man? (*Slight pause.*)

MANTALINI. Well, then. Indeed. He shall be horse-whipped.

MADAME MANTALINI. Well, my dear. Your uncle recommends you, and we are, connected with him, in commercial matters. Now, do you speak French?

KATE. Yes, ma'am, I do.

MANTALINI. But do you speak it like a native?

MADAME MANTALINI. (*Ignoring* MR. MANTALINI.)

Miss Nickleby, we have twenty young women constantly employed in this establishment.

MANTALINI. Some of them demned handsome, too. (MANTALINI *a knowing smirk at* KATE. MADAME MANTALINI *clocks it.*)

MADAME MANTALINI. Of whom, I am pleased to say, Mr. Mantalini knows nothing, as he is never in their room, as I will not allow it. (MANTALINI *shrugs, poutishly, and lies down on the sofa.*) Now, our hours are from nine to nine, with extra if we're busy, for which there's a little payment, and I'd think your wages would be in the region of five to seven shillings. Is that satisfactory?

KATE. Oh, yes. It's . . . Certainly.

MANTALINI. Demned satisfactory.

MADAME MANTALINI. Miss Nickleby, you will pay no attention, please, to anything that Mr. Mantalini says.

KATE. I will not, ma'am.

MADAME MANTALINI. So, then, let me take you to the workroom, now, Miss Nickleby. (MADAME MANTALINI *leads* KATE *out.* MANTALINI *goes too.*)

SCENE 21

The Mantalinis' workroom, downstage, and the showroom, upstage. The scene change is performed by MILLINERS. *In the workroom are clothesrails, tailors' dummies, hatboxes, and uncompleted dresses and hats. In the showroom are display tailors' dummies, more hatboxes, a chaise longue and a tall mirror. For the movement, the showroom is empty, and the workroom is full of working* MILLINERS, *presided over by a short, bustling, overdressed lady called* MISS KNAG. MADAME MANTALINI *and* KATE *enter. The* MILLINERS *look* KATE *up and down, whisper and giggle.*

MADAME MANTALINI. Miss Knag?

MISS KNAG. Madame Mantalini.

MADAME MANTALINI. Ah, Miss Knag, this is the young person I spoke to you about.

MISS KNAG. Oh, good morning, miss. (*To the gawping* MILLINERS.) Come on, come on, no gawping, is there no work to be done? *(The* MILLINERS *set about their tasks with bad humour.)*

MADAME MANTALINI. I think, for the present, it will be better for Miss Nickleby to come into the showroom with you—

MISS KNAG. Showroom, yes.

MADAME MANTALINI. And try things on for people.

MISS KNAG. People, yes.

MADAME MANTALINI. She'll not be much use yet in any other way,

MISS KNAG. Way, no.

MADAME MANTALINI. And her appearance will—

MISS KNAG. Suit very well with mine. *(*MISS KNAG *to* KATE.) For, yes, I see, Miss Nickleby and I are very much a pair—although I am just a little darker, and I have, I think, a slightly smaller foot. Miss Nickleby will not, I am sure, be too much offended at my saying that, as our family has always been quite celebrated for its feet—the smallness of them—ever since the family had feet at all.

MADAME MANTALINI. You'll take care, Miss Knag, that she understands her hours,

MISS KNAG. Hours,

MADAME MANTALINI. And so forth.

MISS KNAG. So forth, yes.

MADAME MANTALINI. And I'll leave her with you.

MISS KNAG. Yes, of course, dear Madame Mantalini.

MADAME MANTALINI. Good morning, ladies.

EVERYONE. Good morning, madame. *(*MADAME MANTALINI *goes out. As she leaves, she finds* MANTALINI *skulking near the doorway. She looks at him, and shakes her head, near tears, and runs off.* MANTALINI, *dramatically, follows.)*

MISS KNAG. Well, what a charming woman.

KATE. Yes. I'm sure she is.

MISS KNAG. And what a charming husband.

KATE. Is he?

MISS KNAG. You don't think so?

KATE. Well—

MISS KNAG. Oh, goodness gracious mercy—where's your taste? And such a dashing man, with such a head of hair and teeth.

KATE. Well, p'raps I'm very foolish—

MISS KNAG. *(With a conspiratorial look at the* MILLI-NERS.*)* Well, I should say you—

KATE. But as my opinion is of very little importance to him or anyone else, I think I shall keep it, just the same. *(Pause.* MISS KNAG *slightly thrown. The odd* MILLINER, *aware of this, giggles.* MISS KNAG *turns to them.)*

MISS KNAG. Well, come on, girls, where are your manners? Make Miss Nickleby welcome. Take her shawl. *(The* MILLINERS *bustle round* KATE.*)*

1st MILLINER. Your shawl, miss?

2nd MILLINER. Can I take your bonnet?

KATE. *(Giving the* MILLINER *her shawl.)* Oh, thank you.

1st MILLINER. Oh, *miss*. And all in black.

KATE. Well, yes, I—

3rd MILLINER. Don't you find it quite intol'r'ble hot? And dusty?

KATE. *(Almost in tears.)* Yes. I do. Oh, yes, I do. *(Embarrassed pause.)*

1st MILLINER. Was it a near relation, Miss?

KATE. My father.

MISS KNAG. *(Calls.)* For what relation?

2nd MILLINER. Father.

MISS KNAG. A long illness, was it?

2nd MILLINER. I don't know.

KATE. Our misfortune was very sudden. Or I might, perhaps, be able to support it better now. *(And the* MIL-LINERS *turn out front.)*

MILLINERS. And then there came a knock at Madame Mantalini's door,

And there entered a great lady,

Well, a rich one,

Who had come with her daughter for approval of some court dresses,

Long in preparation,

Upon whom Miss Nickleby was told to wait,

(MADAME MANTALINI, MISS KNAG, KATE, *a* RICH
LADY *and her* RICH DAUGHTER *are in the showroom.
The* RICH LADY *sits on the chaise, the* RICH DAUGHTER
stands trying on a coat and hat, near the mirror.)

MADAME MANTALINI. Bonjour, madame.
1st MILLINER. With Miss Knag,
MISS KNAG. Mademoiselle—
3rd MILLINER. And officered of course by—
MILLINERS. Madame Mantalini.
KATE. (*Bustling about with clothes and hats.*) Kate's
part in the pageant was humble enough—
MISS KNAG. (*Taking something from* KATE.) La, ma
chere—
KATE. Her duties being limited to holding the articles
of costume until Miss Knag was ready to try them on . . .
MISS KNAG. (*Taking something else.*) Ici . . .
KATE. And now and then tying a string,
MISS KNAG. Or fastening a hook and eye . . .
Merci . . .
KATE. And thinking that she was beneath the reach
of all arrogance and ill-humour.
MISS KNAG. (*Surveying the effect.*) Ah. Mais *oui.*
RICH LADY. (*Off-hand.*) Alors . . .
MILLINERS. But as it happened, both the rich lady and
her rich daughter were in a terrible temper,

And Miss Nickleby came in for a considerable share
of their displeasure.

(KATE *steps backwards from the* RICH DAUGHTER,
nearly stepping on the foot of the RICH LADY.)

RICH LADY. She's so awkward.
1st MILLINER. They remarked. (KATE *fumbling, trying
to tie a hat on the* RICH DAUGHTER.)
RICH DAUGHTER. Her hands are cold.
2nd MILLINER. They said. (KATE *accidentally pushes
the hat forward, so it falls over the* RICH DAUGHTER'S
face.)
RICH LADY. Can she do nothing right? (*The* RICH
DAUGHTER *takes off the hat,* MISS KNAG *takes her coat,
the* DAUGHTER *and the* RICH LADY *preparing to go, as:*)

3rd MILLINER. And they wondered how Madame Mantalini could have such girls about her—

MADAME MANTALINI. Madame, je regrette infiniment . . .

1st MILLINER. And requested they might see some other young person the next time they came . . .

RICH LADY. Cher Madame, au revoir! (The RICH LADY and her RICH DAUGHTER sweep out.)

2nd MILLINER. And so on,

3rd MILLINER. And so forth. (The MILLINERS disperse. KATE moves into the workroom area, leaving MADAME MANTALINI and MISS KNAG in the showroom.)

KATE. And so common an occurrence would hardly be worthy of mention, but for its effect on Kate, who shed many bitter tears when these people were gone, and felt, for the first time, humbled by her occupation. She had, it is true, quailed at the prospect of hard work and drudgery; but she'd felt no degradation in the thought of labour, till she found herself exposed to insolence and pride. (KATE stays.)

MISS KNAG. Well, now, Madame Mantalini. That Miss Nickleby is certainly a very creditable young person, indeed.

MADAME MANTALINI. Well, Miss Knag, beyond putting an excellent client out of humour, Miss Nickleby has not done anything very remarkable thus far that I'm aware of.

MISS KNAG. Aware of, no. But, dear Madame, you must make allowances for inexperience. And such.

MADAME MANTALINI. Well, yes, Miss Knag, of course but in my view she still remains among the awkwardest young girls I ever saw. And not, despite the opinion of her uncle, not that pretty either.

MISS KNAG. Pretty, no. But, Madame Mantalini. That is not her fault, now is it? She should not be blamed for that, and be denied our friendship, should she? (Slight pause. MADAME MANTALINI breathes deeply.)

MADAME MANTALINI. No.

MISS KNAG. No. (MADAME MANTALINI goes out. A great beam is spreading across MISS KNAG's face, as KATE takes out a letter.)

KATE. Oh, Nicholas. How happy it makes me to hear from you, in such good spirits. It consoles me so, to think that you at least are comfortable and happy. (*Exit* KATE. MISS KNAG, *quickly.*)

MISS KNAG. I love her. I quite love her. I declare I do.

SCENE 22

The Dotheboys Hall schoolroom. Bare stage. The BOYS *enter, two of them dragging a pair of steps, the thrashing-horse. They put it centre stage. The* BOYS *form two lines either side of it.* NICHOLAS *enters, and looks in horror at the thrashing-horse.* SQUEERS *enters, with a long cane.*

SQUEERS. Is every boy here? Every boy keep his place. (*Pause.*) Nickleby, to your place, sir. Coates. Jackson. (COATES *and* JACKSON *go out.* NICHOLAS *moves near the thrashing-horse.* MRS. SQUEERS, FANNY, YOUNG WACK-FORD *and* PHIB *enter, and stand to one side.* COATES *and* JACKSON *re-enter, dragging* SMIKE, *who is bound, and filthy, clearly having been caught after spending the night rough. He is brought down to the thrashing-horse.*)

SQUEERS. Untie him, sirs. (*The two boys untie* SMIKE.) Now, sir, what do you have to say for yourself? (*Pause.*) Nothing, I suppose? (*Pause.* SMIKE *glances at* NICHOLAS, *who is looking away.*) Well, then. Let's begin.

SMIKE. Oh, spare me, sir.

SQUEERS. What's that?

SMIKE. Oh, spare me, sir.

SQUEERS. Oh, that's all, is it? Well, I'll flog you within an inch of your life, but I will spare you that. (*Pause.*) Coates, Jackson. (COATES *and* JACKSON *help* SMIKE *on to a step of the thrashing-horse, so that* SMIKE'S *chin just reaches over the top.* COATES *and* JACKSON *tie ropes around* SMIKE'S *hands and the horse, to keep him in place for the flogging.*)

SMIKE. I was driven to it, sir.

SQUEERS. Driven to it? Not your fault, but mine?

MRS. SQUEERS. Hm. That's a good one. (SQUEERS *goes a little upstage turns, runs, and delivers the first blow.* SMIKE *cries out,* SQUEERS *grunts. He goes upstage again, runs, and delivers the second blow. He is back upstage again, when* NICHOLAS *takes a slight step forward.*)

NICHOLAS. Uh . . . This must stop. (SQUEERS *looks round.*)

SQUEERS. Who said that? Who said stop?

NICHOLAS. I did. I said that it must stop, and stop it will. *(Pause.)* I have tried to intercede. I have begged forgiveness for the boy. You have not listened. You have brought this on yourself.

SQUEERS. *(Dismissively, preparing for his next stroke.)* Get out, get out. (NICHOLAS *walks to stand between* SQUEERS *and* SMIKE.)

NICHOLAS. No sir. I can't.

SQUEERS. Can't? You can't? We'll see. (SQUEERS *walks to* NICHOLAS *and strikes his face.* NICHOLAS *doesn't respond.*) Now leave, sir, and let me to my work. (NICHOLAS *turns, as if to go, then suddenly turns back, grabs* SQUEERS, *pulls him round, and hits him.*) What?

NICHOLAS. You have— (SQUEERS *tries to hit* NICHOLAS, *but* NICHOLAS *seizes the cane and beats* SQUEERS *with it. During the ensuing, the following things happen:* MRS. SQUEERS, WACKFORD *and eventually* FANNY *come to* SQUEERS' *aid—somewhat ineffectually: The* BOYS *crush round to see, and eventually to obscure, the fight. And* SMIKE, *let go, slips away. There is much shouting.*)

MRS. SQUEERS. What do you think you're doing, you madman?

FANNY. Get off him! Get off him, you monster!

WACKFORD. Beastly! Beastly, man! You beast! *(And* NICHOLAS, *finished, breaks through the* BOYS *and runs out.)*

MRS. SQUEERS. After him! After him, you vermin! Move, run after him! *(The* BOYS, *who have no intention of doing anything of the sort, nonetheless disperse, revealing* SQUEERS, *sitting on the ground, holding himself.*) Oh, Squeery, Squeery. *(She helps* SQUEERS *to his feet.*) Oh, my Squeery. (MRS. SQUEERS *takes* SQUEERS *out.* WACKFORD *and* FANNY *follow.*)

SCENE 23

In the countryside. Bare stage. Darkness. NICHOLAS *running.* JOHN BROWDIE *enters with a lamp. He carries a stout staff.*

JOHN. Hey! Hey! Who's that, who's there? Hey! (JOHN's *light reveals* NICHOLAS.) Eh. It's tha. From school.

NICHOLAS. Yes, I'm afraid so.

JOHN. What's tha mean, afraid?

NICHOLAS. Well, only—

JOHN. Eh, man, what's the matter with thy face?

NICHOLAS. Oh, it's a cut. A blow. But I returned it to the giver, and with interest, too.

JOHN. Nay. Did tha?

NICHOLAS. Yes. For I have been the victim of considerable mistreatment.

JOHN. Eh?

NICHOLAS. At, from the hands of Mr. Squeers. But I have beaten him quite soundly, and am leaving here as a result.

JOHN. Tha what?

NICHOLAS. I said—I've beaten him. (*And* JOHN BROWDIE *goes into strange, silent convulsions. It is not immediately clear that he is vastly amused.*) Uh—what . . . ?

JOHN. Tha beat the schoolmaster!

NICHOLAS. Yes, I'm afraid—

JOHN. Who ever heard the like!

NICHOLAS. I'm very sorry, but I was—

JOHN. Give me tha hand.

NICHOLAS. Give you my hand?

JOHN. (*Taking* NICHOLAS' *hand and pumping it firmly.*) That's right. Give me tha hand. Tha beat the schoolmaster!

NICHOLAS. Yes, I did, and as a consequence—

JOHN. Eh, man, where is tha going?

NICHOLAS. Well, to London . . .

JOHN. Has tha owt, in way of cash?

NICHOLAS. Well, no, but as I plan to walk—

JOHN. To walk to Lunnon? Look, man, tha needs cash. At least, for food, and suchlike. (*Finds his purse.*) So, here's money.

NICHOLAS. Oh, I couldn't possibly—

JOHN. Tha couldn't possibly? Tha couldn't possibly without. So, come on, man. At least, accept a sovereign.

NICHOLAS. Well, I don't know . . .

JOHN. And, p'raps, tha'll not use all of it, and send the surplus back, eh? Oh, and take this timber. If tha's walking that far, need this too. (NICHOLAS *takes the staff. Pause.*) Now, go, be off with thee. (*Pause.*)

NICHOLAS. I cannot thank you, sir, enough. I—after what, the words we had—I cannot—

JOHN. Beat the schoolmaster. I've not heard good as that, for twenty year. (*And* JOHN *gives* NICHOLAS *a big, bear-like hug, and goes out.* NICHOLAS *follows.*)

SCENE 24

The parlour at Dotheboys Hall. Bare stage. Enter FANNY, *furious, clutching a letter she has written. To the audience:*

FANNY. To Mr. Ralph Nickleby. Golden Square. In London. Sir. My pa requests me to write to you, the doctors considering it doubtful whether he will ever recover the use of his legs, which prevents him holding a pen. We are in a state of mind beyond everything, and my pa is one mask of bruises, both blue and green . . . When your nephew, which you recommended for a teacher, had done this to my pa, and jumped upon his body, with his feet, and language I will not pollute my pen with describing, he assaulted my ma with dreadful violence, dashed her to the earth, and drove her back comb several inches into her head. A little more and it must have entered her skull. We have a medical certificate that if it had, the tortoiseshell would have affected the brain. Me and my brother were then the victims of his fury; I am screaming out loud all the time I write and so is my brother which takes off my attention rather, and I hope will excuse mistakes. The monster, having satiated his thirst for blood, ran away, taking with him a boy of desperate character that he had excited to rebellion. I remain yours, and—cetrer, Fanny Squeers. (FANNY *folds the letter. A knock at the door.*) Phib! (PHIB *enters.*) Someone at the door. P.S.: I pity his ignorance, and despise him. (PHIB *goes to the "door". BROOKER enters. He is an old man, dressed in rags, and covered in mud and snow.*)

PHIB. (*Frightened, turning to* FANNY.) Uh . . . (FANNY *looks at* BROOKER. *She looks scared, too.*)

BROOKER. (*Takes a step into the room.*) Boy. I've

come about a boy. Lived here. (FANNY *looks at* PHIB *in panic.* PHIB *runs out.* BROOKER *takes another step into the room.*) My name is Brooker. Come about a boy. (FANNY *runs out*, BROOKER *following.*)

SCENE 25

NICHOLAS *on his own in the countryside. Bare stage.*

NICHOLAS. It's morning. (NICHOLAS *starts to walk out. Something he hears makes him stop. He turns back.* SMIKE *stands there.*) Oh, Smike. Oh—Smike. (NICHOLAS *quickly to* SMIKE, *who falls to his knees.*) Why do you kneel to me?

SMIKE. To go. Go anywhere. Go everywhere. The world's end. To the churchyard grave. (*Pause.*) I can. You'll let me. Come away with you. (*Pause.*) You are my home. (NICHOLAS *stands there. He doesn't know what to do.* SMIKE *turns his face away. He's crying.* NICHOLAS *puts his hand out to* SMIKE. SMIKE *looks back. He sees the hand.* NICHOLAS *helps* SMIKE *to his feet, and the two of them go slowly out together.*)

ACT II

SCENE 1

A group of NARRATORS *on the bare stage. During the following,* NOGGS *enters and sits in his old armchair. A hard-featured, thin-faced man, wearing a dirty nightcap and carrying an unlit candle, is behind him. This man is* MR. CROWL.

NARRATION. In that quarter of London where Golden Square is situated,

There is a bygone, tumbledown old street,

Two rows of blackened, battered houses,

At the top of one of which there is a meagre garret room;

Where, on a wet and dismal winter's evening,

Newman Noggs,

The clerk to that great man of business Ralph Nickleby,

Sat studying a letter,

Written to his master,

Which had arrived that very afternoon.

NOGGS. *(Reading.)* My pa requests—one mask of bruises—language—thirst for blood. Oh, dear. And cetrer, Fanny Squeers. Oh, dear, oh, dear. *(MR. CROWL knocks.)* What's that?
CROWL. *(Unnecessarily loud.)* It's Mr. Crowl. Your neighbour. Have you got a light?
NOGGS. Oh, yes, do come in, Mr. Crowl.

(NARRATORS *withdraw as* CROWL *to* NOGGS.)

CROWL. A nasty night, Mr. Noggs.

NOGGS. Oh, does it rain outside?

CROWL. Oh, does it rain? I'm wet through.

NOGGS. (*Looking at his threadbare sleeve.*) Well, it doesn't take much to wet you and me through, does it, Mr. Crowl.

CROWL. Well, but that only makes it more vexatious, doesn't it? (*Pause.*)

NOGGS. You'll forgive me, Mr. Crowl. I must go downstairs to supper.

CROWL. To the Kenwigses?

NOGGS. That's right. It is their wedding anniversary, and Mrs. Kenwigs' uncle is expected, the collector of the water-rate, and I am invited to make up the punch and the numbers. So, you'll let me—

CROWL. Well, now, think of that.

NOGGS. Yes, what?

CROWL. I was invited too.

NOGGS. You were?

CROWL. Indeed I was, but resolved not to go, thinking you were not invited, and planning to spend the evening in your company.

NOGGS. Well, um . . . I was obliged . . .

CROWL. And now, what's there for me to do? (*Pause.* NOGGS *gestures vaguely.*) I know. I've got it. I'll still spend the evening here. And keep your fire up for you. Hm?

NOGGS. Oh . . . very well. (NOGGS *turns to go.*)

CROWL. Um, Mr. Noggs, it being such a night . . . Where do you keep your coals?

NOGGS. They're in the coal scuttle. Where coals ought to be. (NOGGS *goes out,* CROWL *pushes out the armchair.*)

CROWL. (*Out front.*) The following, having the misfortune to treat of none but common people, is necessarily of a mean and vulgar character.

SCENE 2

The Kenwigs' living room. A small, cluttered room, full of furniture and people. They are the pregnant MRS. KENWIGS, *her eldest daughter* MORLEENA, *two other* LITTLE

KENWIGSES—*both girls,* MR. *and* MRS. CUTLER, MISS
GREEN, MRS. KENWIGS' SISTER, *a young man called*
GEORGE, *a fierce-looking* STOUT LADY, *in a book-muslin
dress, and* MISS PETOWKER, *an actress.* NOGGS *sits by a
small table on which are glasses, trays and a bowl of
punch.* MRS. KENWIGS *is just greeting him.*

MRS. KENWIGS. Dear Mr. Noggs. Now, Miss Petowker, have you met my husband's old friend, George?

GEORGE. I'm most delighted.

MRS. KENWIGS. Miss Petowker's from the Theatre
Royal, Drury Lane, and later on she may recite for us.

MISS PETOWKER. Oh, Mrs. Kenwigs . . . (MRS. KEN-
WIGS *going to her* SISTER.)

GEORGE. Miss Petowker, tell me, how do you fill your
days?

SISTER. *(Referring to the* STOUT LADY.*)* My dear, who
is that woman?

MRS. KENWIGS. Oh, she's the lady from downstairs.

SISTER. What *does* she think she's wearing?

MRS. KENWIGS. Well, she wouldn't wear it here, but
for the fact our supper's cooking on her grate.

SISTER. I see. (KENWIGS *enters, briskly.*)

KENWIGS. Now, Mrs. Kenwigs, if everything's prepared, wouldn't it be best to begin with a round-game?

MRS. KENWIGS. Kenwigs, my dear, I am surprised at
you. Would you begin without my uncle?

KENWIGS. Ah. I forgot the collector.

MRS. KENWIGS. *(To* MRS. CUTLER.*)* He's so particular, that if we begin without him, I shall be out of his
will forever.

MRS. CUTLER. Oh, my dear!

MRS. KENWIGS. You have no *notion* how he is. *(To*
KENWIGS.*)* And yet, of course, as good a creature as
ever breathed.

KENWIGS. Indeed. The kindest-hearted man that ever
was.

GEORGE. It brings the very tears to his eyes, I believe,
to be forced to cut the water off when people don't pay.

MRS. KENWIGS. Now, George, if you please.

GEORGE. Oh, I'm sorry. Just my—

MRS. KENWIGS. We'll have none of that.

GEORGE. Was just my little joke.

KENWIGS. Now, George. A joke is a good thing, an excellent thing, but when a joke is made at the expense of Mrs. Kenwigs' feelings I set my face against it. And, even putting Mrs. Kenwigs out of the question—if I *could* put Mrs. Kenwigs out of the question on such an occasion as this—I myself have the honour to be connected with the collector by marriage, and I cannot allow these remarks in my . . . in my apartments. *(Pause.)*

GEORGE. Just my little joke.

KENWIGS. The subject is now closed. *(A ring.)* The bell!

MISS PETOWKER. That's him?

MRS. CUTLER. That's the collector?

STOUT LADY. Who?

MRS. KENWIGS. Yes, yes, it must be, dear Morleena, run straight down and let your uncle in and kiss him most directly when the door is open. Hurry, girl!

MORLEENA. Yes, yes, mama. *(Exit* MORLEENA.*)*

MRS. KENWIGS. And, everyone, we must appear to be engaged in light and easy conversation of a general character.

MISS GREEN. Light and easy?

MRS. KENWIGS. Yes, so as to look—

MR. CUTLER. And of a general character?

MRS. KENWIGS. Yes, yes, now Miss Petowker, tell us, if you'd be so kind—

MRS. CUTLER. So as to look— *(*MRS. KENWIGS *has turned as she sees* MR. LILLYVICK, *who has been admitted by* MORLEENA.*)*

MRS. KENWIGS. Oh, uncle, I'm so pleased to see you.

LILLYVICK. Susan.

MRS. KENWIGS. Oh, so glad.

LILLYVICK. As I, my dear, as I. And may I wish you every happiness. *(*MR. LILLYVICK *kisses* MRS. KENWIGS.*)*

MRS. CUTLER. Well, look at that.

MR. CUTLER. A tax-collector.

MISS GREEN. Kissing.

GEORGE. Actually.

MRS. KENWIGS. And so, uncle, where will you sit?

LILLYVICK. *(Sitting.)* Oh, anywheres, my dear. I'm not particular, at all.

MRS. CUTLER. You hear that?

MR. CUTLER. Anywheres.

MISS GREEN. He's not particular.

GEORGE. At all.

KENWIGS. Um, Mr. Lillyvick, some friends of mine, sir, very anxious for the honour . . .

LILLYVICK. As I am, Kenwigs, just as I am . . .

KENWIGS. Mr. and Mrs. Cutler, Mr. Lillyvick.

MR. CUTLER. I'm proud to know you, sir. As having heard of you so often. In your professional capacity.

KENWIGS. My old friend George you know, I think; of course, Mrs. Kenwigs' sister; Miss Green, who makes up Mrs. Kenwigs' dresses, Mr. Lillyvick; and Mrs. um, downstairs . . . And, Mr. Lillyvick, this here is Miss Petowker of the Theatre Royal Drury Lane, and very glad I am indeed, to make two public characters acquainted.

MISS PETOWKER. I am so pleased to meet you, sir.

LILLYVICK. Yes, yes, most privileged, I'm sure.

KENWIGS. Now, Morleena, where's your sisters, so they can kiss your uncle? (MORLEENA *pushes forward the two* LITTLE KENWIGSES, *and* MR. LILLYVICK'S *attention is reluctantly removed from* MISS PETOWKER *so he can kiss them; meanwhile* MRS. KENWIGS *is whispered to about* MR. NOGGS *by her* SISTER.)

SISTER. Why doesn't he . . . the threadbare gentleman?

MRS. KENWIGS. Oh, Mr. Noggs, he'd be embarrassed, to be taken notice of. He was a gentleman, you see, before.

LILLYVICK. And where is little Lillyvick?

MRS. KENWIGS. Oh, uncle, in safe hands, in Miss Green's bed, and sleeping like a baby . . .

LILLYVICK. Well, he is a baby.

MRS. KENWIGS. Yes, and minded by a girl, of course, MISS GREEN. Who's being paid nine pence,

MRS. KENWIGS. And thus will see to it no harm befalls your namesake, uncle.

LILLYVICK. Yes, it should be so. (*Pause.*) Well. Susan. Kenwigs. Anniversary.

KENWIGS. Eight years.

LILLYVICK. Eight years. I still recall my niece . . .

STOUT LADY. Recalls his niece?

LILLYVICK. That very afternoon, she first acknowledged to her mother a partiality for Kenwigs. "Mother," she says, "I love him."

MRS. KENWIGS. Actually, "adore him," I said, uncle.

LILLYVICK. "Love him," you said, Susan, I remember it, and instantly her mother cries out 'what?' and falls at once into convulsions.

MRS. CUTLER. What?

MISS GREEN. Convulsions?

LILLYVICK. Into strong convulsions. For, I'm sure that Kenwigs will forgive me saying so, there was a great objection to him, on the grounds that he was so beneath the family, and would disgrace it. You remember, Kenwigs?

KENWIGS. Certainly.

LILLYVICK. And I, I must confess, I shared that feeling . . . and perhaps it's natural, and perhaps it's not . . .

MRS. CUTLER. Well, I'd say—

STOUT LADY. *Quite* natural.

LILLYVICK. And after they were married, I was the first to say that Kenwigs must be taken notice of. And he *was* taken notice of, because I said so; and I'm bound to say, and proud to say, that I have always found him a most honest, well-behaved and upright sort of man. Kenwigs, shake hands.

KENWIGS. *(Doing so.)* I am proud to do it, sir.

LILLYVICK. And so am I.

KENWIGS. And a very happy life I have led with your niece, sir.

LILLYVICK. And it would have been your own fault if you hadn't, sir.

MRS. KENWIGS. *(Overcome.)* Oh, dear Morleena, kiss your uncle once again.

LILLYVICK. Oh. Well . . .

MRS. KENWIGS. And all of you, dear children, come and kiss your uncle . . .

LILLYVICK. Well, indeed, and now to see these three young lively girls . . .

MRS. KENWIGS. Oh, yes, oh yes, they are too beautiful.

LILLYVICK. Too beautiful for what, my dear?

MRS. KENWIGS. Too beautiful to live.

MISS GREEN. Oh, Mrs. Kenwigs . . . *(MRS. KENWIGS in tears.)*

MRS. KENWIGS. Oh, far, far too . . .

MRS. CUTLER. Oh, dear, Mrs. Kenwigs, please . . .

SISTER. Oh, come now, Susan, don't distress yourself.

MISS GREEN. Don't give way, dear . . .

MRS. KENWIGS. I'm sorry, but I cannot help it, it don't signify. They're just . . . they are too beautiful.

KENWIGS. Um, Mrs. Kenwigs, should, perhaps . . . While Mr. Noggs makes up the punch, Morleena do her figure dance for Mr. Lillyvick?

MISS GREEN. Oh, yes. It is a spectacle.

MRS. KENWIGS. Oh, no, my dear, it will only worry my uncle.

MISS PETOWKER. Come, I'm sure it won't, now will it, Mr. Lillyvick?

LILLYVICK. I'm sure, dear lady, it is most—

MRS. KENWIGS. (*Recovered.*) Well, then, I'll tell you what. Morleena does the steps, if uncle can persuade Miss Petowker to recite for us afterwards the Blood Drinker's Burial. (*Much applause and encouragement.*)

GEORGE. Oh, yes, indeed.

MISS GREEN. Oh that would be a treat.

STOUT LADY. Blood Drinker's what?

MISS PETOWKER. Oh, now, you know that I dislike doing anything professional at private parties.

MRS. KENWIGS. Oh, but not here? We're all so very friendly and pleasant, that you might as well be going through it in your own room; besides, the occasion . . .

MISS PETOWKER. Well . . . I can't resist that. Anything in my humble power, I shall be delighted. (*More applause.*)

KENWIGS. Come, then, everyone, form a space here . . .

MRS. KENWIGS. Morleena, dear, have you chalked your shoes?

STOUT LADY. She's going to do a poem?

MRS. CUTLER. No, a dance.

MISS PETOWKER. All ready? (MORLEENA *nods. Some musical accompaniment—from* MISS PETOWKER, *humming or otherwise; or perhaps another member of the party.* MORLEENA *does her dance—"a very beautiful figure, comprising a great deal of work for the arms," and it is received with unbounded applause. During this,* NOGGS *hands round punch.*)

GEORGE. Bravo!

MRS. CUTLER. Quite wonderful.

MISS GREEN. Oh, Mr. Kenwigs, you must be so proud . . .

MR. CUTLER. Can say with confidence, have never seen the like.

MRS. CUTLER. I wouldn't like to meet her teacher, that's all I can say.

MR. CUTLER. I say, I'd like to shake her teacher by the hand.

KENWIGS. Ah, Noggs, please, the collector first . . .

MRS. KENWIGS. *(To* LILLYVICK.*)* You see, how beautifully she . . . Oh, dear me . . .

MISS PETOWKER. You know— *(*MISS PETOWKER *gains attention.)* If I was ever, blessed . . . And if my child were, such a genius as that . . . I'd have her in the opera at once.

KENWIGS. The opera?

MISS PETOWKER. What's wrong?

MRS. KENWIGS. I think that Kenwigs thinks . . . the younger dukes and marquises . . .

LILLYVICK. Yes, very right.

MISS PETOWKER. Oh, sir, one only needs to keep one's pride. I've kept my pride, and never had a thing of that sort. Not a thing.

KENWIGS. Well, then. Perhaps we should give it serious consideration. *(*MISS PETOWKER *graciously prepares herself. She whispers to* GEORGE, *and they put out some of the lights to give a better effect.)*

STOUT LADY. What's she doing now? Another dance?

MRS. CUTLER. She's going to recite.

STOUT LADY. What, in the dark?

KENWIGS. Ladies and gentlemen. Pray silence, please, for Miss Petowker. *(Applause.* MISS PETOWKER *strikes an attitude. During this,* CROWL *enters and goes towards the party.)*

MISS PETOWKER. 'Twas in a back-street tavern that one night it did perchance,

> While the wind was howling fiercely, all the bottles were a-dance,
> The candle gutted fitful as they, fearful, drank their ale,
> When a dark-eyed stranger entered, bought a drink, and told a tale.

Oh, he was a—

*(*CROWL *knocks loudly.)* What?

MRS. KENWIGS. What's that?

KENWIGS. It sounded like a—

CROWL. It's Mr. Crowl, and Mr. Noggs is wanted.

KENWIGS. *(Admitting* CROWL.*)* Mr. Noggs?

NOGGS. Who, me?

CROWL. Two people in his room. Both very queer-looking. And covered up with rain and mud.

NOGGS. What, me? By name?

CROWL. By name. *(To* KENWIGS.*)* The one's a kind of scrawny chap, and not quite right, it seems to me; the other's straighter, darkish, twenty years or so . . . (MISS PETOWKER *shrugs at* GEORGE, *who relights candles.* NOGGS, *who has been going towards the exit, turns back.)*

NOGGS. Dark? Twenty years?

CROWL. Or so. *(Suddenly,* NOGGS *rushes back into the room, grabs a candle, and takes the cup of punch from* MR. LILLYVICK.*)* Excuse me. Please. *(*NOGGS *rushes out.)* Well, look at that—

MRS. KENWIGS. Well, suppose it should be an express sent up to say his property has all come back again, and the express accounting for the mud and—

KENWIGS. Well, it's not impossible, perhaps, in that case, we should send a little extra punch up—

LILLYVICK. Kenwigs. I'm surprised at you.

KENWIGS. Why, what's the matter, sir?

LILLYVICK. *(Standing.)* Why, making such a remark as that, sir. He has had punch already, has he not? My punch, in fact. Now, it may well be customary to allow such things here, but it's not the sort of thing I have been used to, when a gentleman is raising up a glass of punch and then another comes and collars it without a 'with your leave' or 'by your leave.' . . . This may be called good manners, but it's not by me, and now it's past my hour to go to bed, and I can find my own way home.

MRS. KENWIGS. Oh, uncle!

KENWIGS. Sir, I'm sorry, sir.

LILLYVICK. Then it should have been prevented, sir, that's all.

KENWIGS. Well, sir, I didn't . . . Just a glass of punch, to put you out of temper . . .

LILLYVICK. Out of temper? Me? Morleena, get my hat.

MISS PETOWKER. *(Bewitchingly.)* Oh, you're not going, sir . . .

LILLYVICK. I am not wanted here. My hat! *(MORLEENA, terrified, goes to find LILLYVICK'S hat.)*

MRS. KENWIGS. Oh, do not speak so, uncle, please . . .

LILLYVICK. My hat!

KENWIGS. *(Grabbing the hat from MORLEENA.)* Sir, I must grovel at your feet, and beg you, for your niece's sake, that you'll forgive me.

LILLYVICK. Hm?

KENWIGS. For, for your niece's sake. And little Lillyvick.

LILLYVICK. Well, then. *(Pause.)* Well, then. You are forgiven. *(Applause.)* But let me tell you, Kenwigs, that even if I'd gone away without another word, it would have made no difference respecting that pound or two which I shall leave among your children when I die.

MRS. KENWIGS. Morleena Kenwigs. Now, go down upon your knees, next to your father, and beg Mr. Lillyvick to love you all his life, for he is more an angel than a man, and I have always said so. *(LILLYVICK smiles benignly as MORLEENA, rather uncomfortably, kneels beside her father.)*

MORLEENA. Uh. Uncle Lillyvick. Uh . . . *(Suddenly, three high-pitched screams from another room.)*

KENWIGS. What's that?

GEORGE. Where is it?

MRS. KENWIGS. *(To MISS GREEN.)* Oh, it's your—oh, my baby! *(MRS. KENWIGS trying to run out, stopped by her SISTER.)* Oh, my blessed, blessed—

SISTER. Susan, please—

KENWIGS. Now, I will go at once and—

MRS. KENWIGS. Let me go!

KENWIGS. Come, George—

GEORGE. Of course. Where is the—?

MISS GREEN. Up the stairs, just—

MRS. KENWIGS. Oh, my own dear darling, innocent— Oh, let me go—

LILLYVICK. What: Little Lillyvick? *(KENWIGS is nearly out of the room, followed by GEORGE, when NICHOLAS bursts into the room, holding little LILLYVICK in his arms.)*

KENWIGS. Oh, sir.

LILLYVICK. What's this? Who's this?

NICHOLAS. *(Breathlessly.)* Don't be alarmed. Here is the baby. Safe and sound.

MRS. KENWIGS. *(Rushing to take the baby from NICH-OLAS.)* Oh, oh, my baby . . .

NICHOLAS. It was—a nothing. All that happened was the little girl who watched the baby fell asleep, and the candle set her hair on fire.

MISS GREEN. The wretch! *(MISS GREEN strides out.)*

NICHOLAS. I heard her cries. And ran down. And the baby was not touched. I promise you.

MISS PETOWKER. Oh, sir, without you, he would certainly have burned to death.

NICHOLAS. Well, no, I'm sure you would have heard it too, and rushed to her assistance. *(Enter MISS GREEN, pushing a little GIRL with singed hair.)*

MISS GREEN. Here is the wretch! Look, here she is. Her head all singed.

MRS. CUTLER. And costing ninepence.

MISS GREEN. Which she *won't* receive. Be off with you!

MRS. CUTLER. Yes, off, off, now! *(The poor little GIRL is pushed out, the LITTLE KENWIGSES running to catch a glimpse of her singed head before she's gone.)*

LILLYVICK. Now, sir. You have done service, and we must all drink your health.

NICHOLAS. Well, in my absence, I'm afraid, sir. I have had a very tiring journey, and would be most indifferent company. So please forgive me if I go back up to Mr. Noggs. Good night. *(NICHOLAS goes out.)*

MRS. KENWIGS. That is—the man.

SISTER. And quite delightful.

KENWIGS. Quite uncommonly. Now, don't you think so, Mr. Lillyvick?

LILLYVICK. Well, yes, he is—he seems to be a gentleman.

MISS PETOWKER. Oh, yes . . . There's something in him, looks, now what's the word?

MISS GREEN. What word?

MISS PETOWKER. You know, when lords and dukes and things go breaking knockers, and playing at coaches, and all that sort of thing?

LILLYVICK. Aristocratic.

MISS PETOWKER. Yes, that's right. That's what he is.

MISS GREEN. Indeed.

KENWIGS. Well, now, perhaps . . . There is still supper to be had . . .

STOUT LADY. Downstairs.

KENWIGS. Downstairs. *(Everyone, going out, as:)*

LILLYVICK. I shall . . . I should esteem it a great honour, Miss Petowker, soon to hear the ending of your recitation.

MISS PETOWKER. Oh, dear Mr. Lillyvick, you shall. I swear you shall. *(And* MR. LILLYVICK *takes the arm of* MISS PETOWKER, *and leads her into supper.)*

SCENE 3

Noggs' garret room. NICHOLAS *and* SMIKE, *and* NOGGS, *who has a bottle and two glasses.* NICHOLAS *sits in* NOGGS' *chair, reading Fanny Squeers' letter.*

NICHOLAS. Monster . . . boy of desperate character . . . So, has my uncle yet received this outrageous letter?

NOGGS. Yes, he has—

NICHOLAS. Then, I must go to him at once—

NOGGS. No, no, you mustn't—

NICHOLAS. Mustn't? Why?

NOGGS. Because he hasn't read it yet. And he's gone away from town. Three days.

NICHOLAS. My mother and sister do not know of this?

NOGGS. They don't.

NICHOLAS. Well, then. At once, I must go to them. Tell me, quick, where are they living? I must go there now.

NOGGS. No, no, you mustn't.

NICHOLAS. Mustn't? Why?

NOGGS. *(Handing glasses to* NICHOLAS *and* SMIKE.) Because . . . please, be advised by me. Your uncle—Do not be seen to be tampering with anyone. You do not know this man. And also—*(He pours a drink for each of them. They don't yet drink it.)*

NICHOLAS. Yes? And also?

NOGGS. You come home, after just three weeks. No money, no position. What—what will your mother—

NICHOLAS. Mr. Noggs, I tell you, that three weeks or three hours, if I had stood by—

NOGGS. I know, I know, but still, my dear young man . . . you can't, you mustn't give way to—this sort of thing will never do, you know, and if you want to get on in the world, if you take the part of everybody that's ill-treated. . . . *(Suddenly, clapping* NICHOLAS *on the arm.)* Damn it, I'm proud of you. I would have done the same myself!

NICHOLAS. Oh, Newman, Newman, thank you. But you're right, at least. . . . I must find something. Something to keep myself in shoe-leather. Before I see them. *(Cheerfully.)* Well, tomorrow, I will set about it. *(Depressed again.)* We haven't even got a place to stay.

NOGGS. Well, tonight you stay with me. Tomorrow, there's a room downstairs to let. It's hardly less a mean one than my own, but. . . .

NICHOLAS. Mr. Noggs. Your kindness. Unsurpassable. *(Pause.)* I have three friends. Three friends, in all the world. That bluff young fellow up in Yorkshire; Smike, yourself; and Mr. Noggs, our benefactor. *(Slight pause.)* And it is enough. It is enough, indeed. (NICHOLAS *drinks his drink.* SMIKE, *in imitation, drinks his. After a second, the effect hits* SMIKE. *His eyes pop. He bangs his chest.* NICHOLAS *and* NOGGS *look alarmed. Firmly,* SMIKE *puts his glass out to* MR. NOGGS *for more.)*

SCENE 4

Westminster. At once, sounds of many busy people. Set up, on one side of the stage, the office of SIR MATTHEW PUPKER, *consisting of a desk, an impressive map of the world, and* SIR MATTHEW *himself, sitting on a chair, his feet up on desk, his head covered by* The Times, *asleep. This happens during the following: a sturdy* DEPUTATION, *consisting of many firm-faced* GENTLEMEN, *enters, as* NICHOLAS *appears and speaks out front:*

NICHOLAS. And the next morning, Nicholas proceeded to the General Employment Office, in search of a position; where, much to his surprise, he was informed that the great member of Parliament, the renowned Sir Matthew Pupker, was seeking a young man of conscientiousness and character, to fill the position of his secretary, at the Palace of Westminster. *(He turns to the passing* DEPUTATION.*)* Excuse me . . . I have business with Sir Matthew Pupker—

A DELEGATE. What, you as well? Come, follow me. *(The* DEPUTATION *is at Sir Matthew's door. It knocks.)*

SIR MATTHEW. Wait! *(*SIR MATTHEW *removes* The Times *from his face, adjusts the map, as* NICHOLAS *catches up with the rest of the* DEPUTATION.*)* Come! *(The* DEPUTATION, *and* NICHOLAS, *enter the room.)* Gentlemen, I am rejoiced to see you. Please, come in. *(*SIR MATTHEW *returns to his desk as the leader of the Deputation, a* MR. PUGSTYLES, *pushes himself to the front.)* Now, gentlemen. I see by the newspapers that you are dissatisfied with my conduct as your member.

PUGSTYLES. Yes, we are.

SIR MATTHEW. Well, now, do my eyes deceive me? Or is that my old friend, Pugstyles?

PUGSTYLES. I am that man.

SIR MATTHEW. Give me your hand, my worthy friend. Pugstyles, I am so sorry you are here.

PUGSTYLES. I am sorry too, but your conduct has rendered this deputation quite imperative.

SIR MATTHEW. My conduct, Pugstyles? You speak of my conduct?

PUGSTYLES. Yes.

SIR MATTHEW. Well, then . . . *(Rhetorically.)* My conduct, gentlemen, has been, and ever will be, regulated by a sincere regard for the true interests of this great and happy country. Whenever I behold the peaceful, industrious communities of our island home, I clasp my hands, and turning my eyes to the broad expanse above my head, exclaim, "Thank heaven, that I am a Briton!" *(Long pause.)*

A DELEGATE. Gammon.

SIR MATTHEW. The meaning of that term, I must confess, is quite unknown to me. But if it means you think I'm too benign, too sanguine, too complacent, sir, you would be right. *(He goes to the map and gestures.)* For e'en as we sit here, and lightly chatter, Russia's surly armies, fixed on vile conquest, surge across her borders, threatening the very jugular . . . Sir, do you know Kabul?

THIRD DELEGATE. No, sir.

SIR MATTHEW. Or have you met the Amir of the Afghans, he whose name is perfidy?

THIRD DELEGATE. I have not, sir.

SIR MATTHEW. Or heard the hideous war-cry of the Slavic hordes, intent on rape and pillage?

THIRD DELEGATE. No, I have not heard the Slavic hordes, sir, or their hideous war-cry.

SIR MATTHEW. Well . . . well then. What is the little matter you would speak of? Fishing rights, or water-rates, or timber duty? (PUGSTYLES *puts on his spectacles and takes out a list of questions. The rest of the* DEPUTATION *also take out lists of questions, to check Pugstyles' reading.*)

PUGSTYLES. Question number one. Whether sir, you did not give a voluntary pledge, that in the event of your being returned you would immediately put down the practice of coughing and groaning in the House of Commons. And whether you did not submit to being coughed and groaned down in the very first debate of the session? *(Pause.)*

SIR MATTHEW. Go on to the next one, my dear Pugstyles.

PUGSTYLES. Have you any explanation to offer with reference to that question, sir?

SIR MATTHEW. Certainly not. (*The* DEPUTATION *looks at each other.* PUGSTYLES *breathes deeply, and continues.*)

PUGSTYLES. Question number two. Whether, sir, you did not likewise give a voluntary pledge that you would support your colleagues on every occasion; and whether you did not, the night before last, desert them and vote upon the other side, because the wife of a leader on that other side had invited Lady Pupker to an evening party? *(Pause.)*

SIR MATTHEW. Go on.

PUGSTYLES. Nothing to say on that either, sir?

SIR MATTHEW. Nothing whatever. *(Pause.)*

PUGSTYLES. So, Question number three. If, sir, you did not state upon the hustings, that it was your firm and determined intention, if elected, to vote at once for universal suffrage and triennial parliaments?

SIR MATTHEW. Oh, no!

THE DEPUTATION. Oh! Oh!

SIR MATTHEW. No, not at all. What happened was, that an illiterate voter in the crowd inquired if I would vote for universal suffering and triangular parliaments. To which I replied, in jest of course, "why, certainly." *(A groan from the* DEPUTATION.*)* So, is that all?

PUGSTYLES. No. Question four. Will you resign?

SIR MATTHEW. No.

PUGSTYLES. Sorry?

SIR MATTHEW. I said, no.

PUGSTYLES. You won't resign, under any circumstances?

SIR MATTHEW. Absolutely not.

PUGSTYLES. Then . . . Then, good morning, sir. *(The* DEPUTATION *turns to go.)*

SIR MATTHEW. Good morning to you all. *(As the* DEPUTATION *leaves.)* God bless you! Every one! *(Left alone, as he thinks,* SIR MATTHEW *notices* NICHOLAS.*)* What? Who's this?

NICHOLAS. It's me, sir.

SIR MATTHEW. Ha! A secret voter! Out, sir, out, you've heard my answer. Follow out your deputation.

NICHOLAS. I should have done so if I had belonged to it.

SIR MATTHEW. *(Tossing down the map.)* You don't? Then what the devil are you in here for?

NICHOLAS. I wish to offer myself as your secretary.

SIR MATTHEW. That's all you came for, is it?

NICHOLAS. Yes.

SIR MATTHEW. You've no connection with the papers?

NICHOLAS. No.

SIR MATTHEW. And what's your name?

NICHOLAS. My name is Nickleby. *(Slight pause.* SIR MATTHEW *eyes* NICHOLAS *beadily.)*

SIR MATTHEW. Related to Ralph Nickleby?

NICHOLAS. I am.

SIR MATTHEW. Well, then, sit down.

SIR MATTHEW. So, you want to be my secretary, do you?

NICHOLAS. Yes.

SIR MATTHEW. Well, what can you do?

NICHOLAS. Well, I suppose that I can do what usually falls to the lot of other secretaries.

SIR MATTHEW. What's that?

NICHOLAS. Well, I presume, correspondence . . .

SIR MATTHEW. Good.

NICHOLAS. The arrangement of papers and documents—

SIR MATTHEW. Very good, what else?

NICHOLAS. Well, um—the general one, of making myself as agreeable and useful as I can.

SIR MATTHEW. Well, now, that's all very well, young Mr. Nickleby, as far as it goes, but it doesn't go far enough. I should require, for example, to be crammed, sir.

NICHOLAS. Crammed?

SIR MATTHEW. Yes, crammed. My secretary would need to make himself acquainted with all domestic and all international affairs, to scan the newspapers for paragraphs of lasting or of passing interest, for revolutions, wars, disturbances in Birmingham, "the mysterious disappearance of a potboy," on which I might found a speech or question; he would be required, as well, to study all the printed tables, and to work up arguments about the dire consequences of a raise in tax, or else the terrible result of lowering it, on why we need to increase government expenditure, on the national defence, or else decrease it, to encourage thrift among the lower classes; of gold bullion, and the supply of money, all those things it's only necessary to talk fluently about, as no-one understands 'em; and that's just a hasty, basic outline of your duties, except of course for waiting in the lobby every night, and sitting in the gallery, and pointing me out to the populace, and noting that that sleeping gentleman's none other than the celebrated and renowned Sir Matthew Pupker, and for salary, I'll say at once, although it's much more than I'm used to give, it's fifteen shillings every week and find yourself. So. Any questions? *(Pause.)*

NICHOLAS. One. While I'm performing all your duties, sir, may I inquire what you'll be doing?

SIR MATTHEW. Eh?

NICHOLAS. I said, while I'm performing all your duties, sir, may I inquire what you'll be doing? *(Pause.)*

SIR MATTHEW. Out! Get out! Out, now!

NICHOLAS. *(Turns to go.)* I'm sorry to have troubled you.

SIR MATTHEW. Well, so am I. Out, upstart! Trouble-maker! *(NICHOLAS has been going, but he turns back.)*
NICHOLAS. Humbug.
SIR MATTHEW. Chartist!
NICHOLAS. Charlatan!
SIR MATTHEW. Potboy!
NICHOLAS. Politician! *(This is too much. SIR MAT-THEW goes, and NICHOLAS does too.)*

SCENE 5

The Mantalinis' workroom and showroom. In the work-room, the MILLINERS, MISS KNAG entering, and KATE. In the showroom, an OLD LORD, his YOUNG FIANCEE and MADAME MANTALINI.

MISS KNAG. Well, bless you, dear, how very clumsy you were yesterday, again.
KATE. I know, Miss Knag.
MISS KNAG. But don't you worry, I can do all that needs doing, and all you have to do is stay quiet before company and your awkwardness will not be noticed.
KATE. No, indeed.
MISS KNAG. Oh, I do take the liveliest of interests in you, dear, upon my word. It's a sister's interest, actually. It's the most singular circumstance I ever knew. *(MA-DAME MANTALINI pulls a bell pull. A bell rings.)* Ah, that's the showroom. Now, perhaps it's best dear, after yesterday, if you do not come up. *(Unlikely.)* Unless, of course, you're called for. *(MISS KNAG to the showroom.)*
1st MILLINER. Well.
2nd MILLINER. *Well.*
3rd MILLINER. Has herself took a shine to you. *(The focus shifts to the showroom, as the MILLINERS narrate.)*
MILLINERS. And it so happened that an old lord of great family,

Who was going to marry a young lady of no family in particular,

Came with the young lady to witness the ceremony of trying on two nuptial bonnets,

Which were presented to her by Miss Knag,

In a charming if not breathless state of palpitation.

(MISS KNAG *now in the showroom. The* OLD LORD *is very upper class, very lecherous, and a bit gaga. The* YOUNG FIANCEE *is not very upper class at all.*)

YOUNG FIANCEE. Well, now. How d'I look?

MADAME MANTALINI. Oh, mademoiselle, tres elegante.

MISS KNAG. Mais oui. C'est entierement exquise, n'est ce pas?

YOUNG FIANCEE. Exsqueeze?

MISS KNAG. Exquisite.

YOUNG FIANCEE. Oh, yes? Is that so? (*A slight hiatus.*)

MADAME MANTALINI. So what do you think, my lord?

YOUNG FIANCEE. Yur, do you think that I'll look fitting, darling?

OLD LORD. Fitting?

YOUNG FIANCEE. For our wedding day.

OLD LORD. Oh, yes. Oh, very fitting. For our wedding day. (*The* YOUNG FIANCEE *blushes, grins, and pokes the* OLD LORD.)

YOUNG FIANCEE. Oh, you are, really.

OLD LORD. Am I? Am I, really?

YOUNG FIANCEE. Yur, you are. (MISS KNAG *a clucking, disapproving look at* MADAME MANTALINI. *The* YOUNG FIANCEE *notices it.*) Mm? Can I help you?

MISS KNAG. Peut-etre—

YOUNG FIANCEE. Pardon?

MISS KNAG. Would madam care to try—?

YOUNG FIANCEE. Yur, why not. (*The* YOUNG FIANCEE, *trying on another bonnet.*) Oh, by the way, dear Madame Mantalini?

MADAME MANTALINI. Mademoiselle?

YOUNG FIANCEE. Tell me, where is that pretty creature we saw yesterday? The young one.

MADAME MANTALINI. Pretty . . . young . . .

MISS KNAG. (*Helpfully.*) Miss Nickleby.

YOUNG FIANCEE. That's right. 'Cos if there's one thing that I can't abide, it's being waited on by frights.

MISS KNAG. Frights, no.

MADAME MANTALINI. By—what? *(MISS KNAG has got there.)*

YOUNG FIANCEE. By frights. By old frights, in particular. Well, elderly. *(Pause.)*

MADAME MANTALINI. Mais oui. Certainement. Miss Knag, send up Miss Nickleby.

MISS KNAG. Bring up?

MADAME MANTALINI. Send up. You need not return. *(Pause. MISS KNAG goes out as the YOUNG FIANCEE looks at her new bonnet in the mirror.)*

YOUNG FIANCEE. Oh, yur. Mais oui. C'est entirement exquise. *(Focus shifts back to the workroom as MISS KNAG enters.)*

MISS KNAG. *(To KATE.)* You're wanted in the showroom.

KATE. Me?

MISS KNAG. Yes, you. You have been Asked For.

KATE. Oh, I . . . very well. *(She goes to the door. MISS KNAG rather obviously not following.)* Are you not coming?

MISS KNAG. I? Why should I come? A fright like me? *(Pause.)*

1st MILLINER. What's that?

2nd MILLINER. A fright?

MISS KNAG. Why should I come? You chit, you child, you upstart!

KATE. Please, Miss Knag, what have I done?

MISS KNAG. What have you done? She asks me, what she's done?

3rd MILLINER. *(Whispers to 2nd MILLINER.)* What has she done?

MISS KNAG. I'll tell you what I've done, my dear Miss Nickleby, what I've done is to be, for fifteen years, the ornament of this room and the upstairs. And what have you done? Nothing.

KATE. Well, I would not—

MISS KNAG. And never, fifteen years, have I been victim of the vile arts, a creature who disgraces us with her proceedings, and makes proper people blush to see her machinations.

KATE. Miss Knag, what have I—

MISS KNAG. Yes, here she is, look carefully . . . the

one who everyone is talking of, the belle, the beauty . . .
Oh, you boldfaced thing!

KATE. Miss Knag, please tell me—

MISS KNAG. I will tell you. Go! You're asked for in
the showroom. Go! (KATE *stands a moment, shrugs desperately and goes out. Pause.* MISS KNAG *throws herself into a chair. She is surrounded by* MILLINERS.) Oh, have
I worked here, fifteen years. And to be called a fright.
(*Pause.*)

1st MILLINER. Oh, no.

3rd MILLINER. Oh, absolutely not.

MISS KNAG. And have I laboured, all these years, to
be called elderly.

2nd MILLINER. What, elderly?

1st MILLINER. Well, what a thing to say.

MISS KNAG. (*Stands.*) I hate her. I detest and hate
her. Never let her speak to me again. And never let
anyone who is a friend of mine have words with her. The
slut. The hussy. Impudent and artful, hussy!

SCENE 6

Downstage, NOGGS' *garret, represented by his chair.*
NOGGS *and* SMIKE. *Upstage, the Kenwigs' room, with*
MRS. KENWIGS, MORLEENA, *the two* LITTLE KEN-
WIGSES, MR. LILLYVICK *and* MISS PETOWKER. *We will
discover that* MR. LILLYVICK *has a glass of brandy and
a jug of water. Enter* NICHOLAS.

NICHOLAS. And so, with a sad and pensive air, Nicholas retraced his steps homewards.

NOGGS. Come back?

NICHOLAS. Yes, and tired to death, and might have
stayed at home for all the good I've done.

NOGGS. Couldn't expect too much, one morning.

NICHOLAS. Well, I did. And so am disappointed. I see
little to choose between assisting a brutal pedagogue and
being a toad-eater to a mean and ignorant upstart, member or no member. Oh, Newman, show me in all this
wide waste of London, any honest means by which I
could at least defray the hire of our poor room; I would
not shrink from it, I will do anything, except that which
offends my common pride.

NOGGS. Well, then . . . I hardly know . . .

NICHOLAS. Yes? What?

NOGGS. There is a prospect I could offer. . . .

NICHOLAS. Please, dear Newman, tell me.

NOGGS. It concerns the Kenwigses, downstairs. I told them you were Mr. Johnson, thinking perhaps, your circumstances being, as it were . . .

NICHOLAS. Yes, yes.

NOGGS. And said you were a teacher, and she said, well, having talked to Mr. Kenwigs, as is only right, she said that she had long been searching for a tutor for her little ones, to teach them French as spoken by the natives, at the weekly stipend of four shillings current coin, being at the rate of a one a week per each Miss Kenwigs, with a shilling over for the baby. That's all, and I know it's beneath you, but—

NICHOLAS. Dear Newman. I accept at once. Please tell the worthy mother, now, without delay.

NOGGS. *(Delighted.)* Right, then.

(Narration into the Kenwigs' room, in which will be MR. LILLYVICK, MISS PETOWKER, MRS. KENWIGS, MORLEENA, *the* LITTLE KENWIGSES *and* NICHOLAS. NOGGS *and* SMIKE *will have gone.)*

NOGGS. And Newman hastened with joyful steps to inform Mrs. Kenwigs of his friend's acquiescence,

NICHOLAS. And soon returning, brought back word that they would be happy to see Mr. Johnson in the first floor as soon as convenient,

NOGGS. And that Mrs. Kenwigs had upon the instant sent out to secure a second-hand French grammar and dialogues,

MISS PETOWKER. Which had long been fluttering in the six-penny box at the bookstall round the corner,

MRS. KENWIGS. And that the family,

LILLYVICK. Highly excited at the prospect of this addition to their gentility,

MRS. KENWIGS. Wished the initiatory lesson to come off

MORLEENA. Immediately!

MRS. KENWIGS. Now, uncle, this is Mr. Johnson.

LILLYVICK. How d'ye do, sir?

NICHOLAS. Splendid, thank you sir.

MRS. KENWIGS. Mr. Johnson, this is Mr. Lillyvick, my uncle, The Collector Of The Water Rate.

NICHOLAS. *(Uncertain of how he is supposed to react to this intelligence.)* The Water Rate? Indeed.

MRS. KENWIGS. And this is Miss Petowker, of the Theatre Royal Drury Lane.

NICHOLAS. Oh, I am highly honoured. *(Wrong.)* To make, both of your acquaintances.

MRS. KENWIGS. Now, Mr. Johnson is engaged as a private master to the children, uncle.

LILLYVICK. Yes, Susan, so you said.

MRS. KENWIGS. But I hope, Mr. Johnson, that they don't boast about it to the other children, and that if they must say anything about it, they don't say no more than: "We've got a private master come to teach us at home, but we ain't proud, because ma says it's sinful." Do you hear, Morleena?

MORLEENA. Yes, ma.

MRS. KENWIGS. Then mind you recollect, and do as I tell you. Shall Mr. Johnson begin, then, uncle?

LILLYVICK. In a moment, Susan, in a moment. First, I'd like to ask a question. Sir, how do you think of French?

NICHOLAS. What do you mean, sir?

LILLYVICK. Do you view it as a good language, sir? A pretty language? Sensible?

NICHOLAS. A pretty language, certainly. And as it has a name for everything, and admits of elegant conversation on all topics, I assume it's sensible as well.

LILLYVICK. I see. *(Gesturing with his glass.)* So, what's the French for this, then, sir?

NICHOLAS. For brandy?

LILLYVICK. No, for water. As in, "water rate."

NICHOLAS. Oh, water, sir, is "l'eau."

LILLYVICK. I thought as much. You hear that, Miss Petowker? Water. Low. I don't think anything of that. I don't think anything of French at all.

MRS. KENWIGS. But, still, the children may—

LILLYVICK. Oh, yes. Oh, let them learn it. I have no wish to prevent them. *(Pause. MISS PETOWKER a slight smile. MRS. KENWIGS nervously.)*

MRS. KENWIGS. Well, then . . . Mr. Johnson?

NICHOLAS. Well, then . . . Lesson One. *(Enter NOGGS, breathless.)*

NOGGS. Oh—oh, Mr. Johnson, this is terrible—

LILLYVICK. What's this?

MRS. KENWIGS. Why, Mr. Noggs!

NOGGS. He's back again—he's gone off to your mother's—

NICHOLAS. What?

NOGGS. —your uncle, and I got the wrong day and I'm terribly—

LILLYVICK. *(To MISS PETOWKER.)* It's him again.

NICHOLAS. Oh, I must go there now.

NOGGS. Yes. Yes, I s'pose you must.

MRS. KENWIGS. But Mr. Johnson—

NICHOLAS. Oh—un—mes enfants . . . on doit continuer la lecon demain. Pardon. *(To LILLYVICK, taking his drink and giving it to NOGGS.)* Pardon. *(NICHOLAS rushes out.)*

SCENE 7

The Nicklebys' house in Thames St. All that is needed is one chair for MRS. NICKLEBY. MISS LA CREEVY, KATE and RALPH are also there. RALPH is folding up Fanny Squeers' letter.

KATE. No, I won't believe it. Never. It's a lie, that they've invented.

RALPH. No, my dear, you wrong the worthy man. These aren't inventions. Mr. Squeers has been assaulted, Nicholas is gone, the boy goes with him. It's all true.

KATE. It can't be true. Mama, how can you stand there, listening to this?

RALPH. She's no choice, my dear. Her son's committed conduct for which he might well hold up his head at the Old Bailey. *(Pause.)* And it would be my duty, if he came my way, to give him up to justice. As a man of honour and of business, I would have no other course. Though I would wish to spare the feelings of his mother, and his sister.

MISS LA CREEVY. Perhaps I'd better . . .

KATE. No, please, Miss La Creevy, stay.

RALPH. *(Suddenly, forcefully, waving the letter.)* Madam,

everything combines to prove the truth of this. He steals away at night, he skulks off with an outlaw boy? Assault, and riot? Is this innocent? *(Unnoticed by anyone,* NICHOLAS *stands there.)*

MRS. NICKLEBY. Well, I don't know, I'm sure.

KATE. Oh, mother!

MRS. NICKLEBY. And I never would have thought it of him, certainly.

KATE. You never *would have* thought?

MRS. NICKLEBY. Your uncle—is your uncle, dear.

NICHOLAS. But what he says is still untrue.

RALPH. Oh. You.

MRS. NICKLEBY. Oh, Nicholas! *(NICHOLAS marching towards* RALPH, KATE *getting in the way.)*

KATE. Oh, Nicholas, be calm, consider.

NICHOLAS. What?

KATE. Please, please, consider . . . and refute these accusations.

NICHOLAS. What are they? Tell me what he's said to you.

RALPH. I've said, sir, what is true. That you attacked your master, and you nearly killed him, and you ran away. *(Pause.* NICHOLAS *is calmer now.)*

NICHOLAS. I see. *(NICHOLAS speaks to* KATE *and* MRS. NICKLEBY, *not to* RALPH.*)* I interfered to save a miserable creature from the vilest cruelty. In doing so, I did inflict punishment upon the wretch who was abusing him. And if the same scene was repeated now, I'd take exactly the same part. Except, that I would strike him heavier and harder.

RALPH. Hm. The penitent.

KATE. Please, Nicholas, where is this boy?

NICHOLAS. He's with me now.

RALPH. Will you restore him?

NICHOLAS. No. Not to that man. Not ever.

MRS. NICKLEBY. Oh, I don't know what to think . . .

RALPH. Now, sir, you'll listen to a word or two?

NICHOLAS. Say what you like. I shan't take heed of it.

RALPH. Then I won't speak to you, but to your mother. She may find it worth her while to listen, because what I have to say is, that he, Nicholas, shall not have access to one penny of my money, or one crust of my bread, or one grasp of my hand that might save him from the gallows. I will not meet him, and I will not hear his name. I will not help him, nor help anyone who helps him. So, now he knows what he has brought on you, by coming back, and as I will not ask you to renounce him, I must renounce you. *(Pause.)*

MRS. NICKLEBY. Oh, I can't help it—

RALPH. What?

MRS. NICKLEBY. I know you have been good to us. But still, I—even if he has done everything you say—

KATE. You heard what he said, mother—

MRS. NICKLEBY. Still. I can't renounce my son. I really can't. *(Pause. MRS. NICKLEBY weeping.)* And all that, thinking that he'd be headmaster. . . .

RALPH. Then I'll go.

NICHOLAS. You needn't.

RALPH. Needn't I?

NICHOLAS. Because I will. *(KATE runs to NICHOLAS and embraces him.)*

KATE. Nicholas, oh Nicholas, don't say so, or you'll break my heart . . . Mama, please speak to him. Mama, don't let him go. Don't leave us here, with no-one to protect us. Please.

NICHOLAS. I can't protect you. How can I protect you?

RALPH. My dear, there is your answer.

MRS. NICKLEBY. Oh, Kate. We'll go to rack and ruin. To the workhouse, or the Refuge for the Destitute. Or Magdalen Hospital. One or the other. Or the third. *(NICHOLAS takes KATE's arms from him.)*

NICHOLAS. No, mother. I'm the one that's going.

KATE. *(Horrified.)* Where? Where, Nicholas?

NICHOLAS. Don't know. *(Pause.)* It is hard. To have done nothing, but to be proscribed, just like a criminal. And to be forced to leave the ones I love. It is quite hard to bear. But still, I must, or else . . . you're destitute.

KATE. It might be—years.

NICHOLAS. Don't know. *(NICHOLAS turns to go. KATE runs after him, embraces him.)*

KATE. Please, you won't—

NICHOLAS. I must—

KATE. You won't forget us. Everything we had. The days, the years we spent together.

NICHOLAS. *(Taking her arms from him.)* And I don't

need to entreat your sympathy. I know you won't forget
them.

MISS LA CREEVY. No.

NICHOLAS. *(To* RALPH.*)* This isn't over. You will hear
from me. *(To* KATE.*)* Oh, my darling girl. *(*NICHOLAS
goes out, leaving MRS. NICKLEBY, MISS LA CREEVY, *and*
KATE.*)*

SCENE 8

The street. Early morning. Bare stage. NICHOLAS,
SMIKE *and* NOGGS *appear during the narration, which is
delivered by members of the company who stand round,
watching the scene.* NICHOLAS *and* SMIKE *have bundles.*
NOGGS *has a can.*

NARRATORS. It was a cold, foggy morning in early
Spring . . .

And a few meagre shadows flitted to and fro in the
misty streets.

At intervals were heard the tread of slipshod feet,

And the chilly cry of the sweep as he crept shivering
to his early toil;

The sluggish darkness thickened as the day came on,

And those who had the courage to rise and peep at
the gloomy street from their curtained windows,

Crept back to bed again,

And coiled themselves up to sleep.

NICHOLAS. But Nicholas and Smike were up,

NOGGS. And Newman too, who had expended a day's
income on a can of rum and milk to prepare them for
their journey. *(*SMIKE *shoulders the bundles.)* Which way
are you going?

NICHOLAS. Kingston first.

NOGGS. And afterwards? *(Slight pause.)* Why won't you tell me?

NICHOLAS. Because I scarcely know myself.

NOGGS. I am afraid you have some deep scheme in your head.

NICHOLAS. So deep that even I can't fathom it. Don't worry, I'll write soon.

NOGGS. You won't forget?

NICHOLAS. Oh, I'm not likely to. I've not so many friends that I can grow confused about the number, and forget the very best.

NOGGS. And, despite Newman's insistence that he be allowed to walk an hour or two with them,

NICHOLAS. Nicholas and Smike eventually made their farewells and turned, and left, and turned again,

NOGGS. To see their friend still waving to them,

NICHOLAS. Till they turned the corner, and could see old Newman Noggs no more. (NOGGS *has gone.* SMIKE *and* NICHOLAS *trudging on.*)

NICHOLAS. Now, listen to me, Smike. We're bound for Portsmouth.

SMIKE. Ports—mouth.

NICHOLAS. Yes, because it is a seaport town, and I am thinking we might board some ship. I'm young and active, so are you.

SMIKE. And I am very willing.

NICHOLAS. Yes, you are. Too willing, for example, with that bundle. Let me carry it a while.

SMIKE. *(Stops.)* No. No.

NICHOLAS. *(Stops.)* Why not?

SMIKE. Because I thought of carrying it. For you. *(They walk on. Narration:)*

NARRATORS. It was by this time within an hour of noon, and although dense vapour still enclosed the city they had left,

As if to clothe its schemes of gain and profit,

In the open country it was clear and fair.

SMIKE. Hey I—

NICHOLAS. Yes, Smike?

SMIKE. The ship. On ship. I, when I was at—that place—(*He doesn't want to name Dotheboys Hall.*)

NICHOLAS. Yes?

SMIKE. I used to milk the cows and groom the horses.

NICHOLAS. Um—it is a ship, Smike. Not that many cows and horses on board ship. Well, I don't believe . . . (*SMIKE looks at NICHOLAS. He gets the joke. It's infectious. NICHOLAS laughs too. Music plays and the NARRATORS sing. As they sing, SMIKE jumps on NICHOLAS' back, and the two of them career round the stage, blissfully happy.*)

NARRATORS. (*Sing.*)*A broad fine honest sun
Lightened up the green pasture
And dimpled water with the semblance of summer,
Leaving the travellers with the freshness of spring.

The ground seemed to quicken their feet,
The sheep bells were music to their ears,
And hoping made them strong
And strength awakened hope
And they pushed onward with the courage of lions.

And so the day wore on
And so the day wore on
And so the day wore on.

(*NICHOLAS and SMIKE stop, put down the bundles, and sit.*)

NICHOLAS. Smike. Do you have a good memory?

SMIKE. I don't know. I had once, I think. But now all gone.

NICHOLAS. Why do you think you had one once?

SMIKE. Because I could remember, when I was a child.

NICHOLAS. Do you remember, when you went to Yorkshire? What the day was like. The weather, hot or cold?

SMIKE. Wet. Very wet. And afterwards. When it was raining. I could see myself. The day I came.

NICHOLAS. Did you come there alone?

SMIKE. No. No. A man—a dark and withered man, they used to say. And I think I remember, too. Remember—being frightened of him. Glad he went away. But frightened at the place he left me, too.

NICHOLAS. Now look at me. Don't turn away. Do you remember, anything or anyone or anywhere, before that house in Yorkshire? Think, Smike, think. *(Pause.)*

SMIKE. A room. *(Slight pause.)* I slept once in a room, a large and lonesome room, beneath the attic, there was a hook in the ceiling above me. I was frightened of it, covered up my head. *(Pause.)* Used to dream. Dream terribly about the room. And the people in it. Things, that changed. But that room—never changes. *(Pause.)* Till now, I have not known two days together, when I haven't been afraid. *(A* NARRATOR—*the actor who will play the* LANDLORD, *enters, as a table and a bench are brought in behind him.)*

LANDLORD. And the sun went down, and in the morning it rose up again, and they rose with it, and walked onwards, until Smike could go no further. And they found a little inn, yet twelve miles short of Portsmouth.

SCENE 9

The courtyard of a roadside inn. The LANDLORD, *sitting on the bench beside the table.* NICHOLAS *and* SMIKE *standing there, looking bedraggled and tired.*

NICHOLAS. Ah. How far to Portsmouth, sir?

LANDLORD. Twelve miles. Long miles.

NICHOLAS. A good road?

LANDLORD. No. A bad one.

NICHOLAS. We must get to Portsmouth by tonight.

LANDLORD. Well, don't let me influence you, in any way . . . But if I were you, I wouldn't go.

NICHOLAS. You wouldn't?

LANDLORD. No.

NICHOLAS. Look, I . . . Look here, it's obvious enough. We are both very humble, and we can't afford to stay the night. But if you had a little food . . . ?

LANDLORD. What would you like?

NICHOLAS. Cold meat?

LANDLORD. No, sorry.

NICHOLAS. Mutton chops.

LANDLORD. Clean out.

NICHOLAS. An egg?

LANDLORD. No, yesterday, had more than we could cope with. And tomorrow, mountains of 'em coming in.

NICHOLAS. Today?

LANDLORD. No eggs today. (*Enter* MR. VINCENT CRUMMLES *and his sons*, MASTER CRUMMLES *and* MASTER P. CRUMMLES. MR. CRUMMLES *is a theatrical manager. His sons are dressed in sailor suits, and are presently practising a stage fight with wooden swords. The fight finishes spectacularly, with the defeat of the taller* MASTER CRUMMLES *by the shorter* MASTER P. CRUMMLES. CRUMMLES *himself applauds.*)

CRUMMLES. That's capital! You'll get a double encore if you take care, boys. You'd better go and get your travelling clothes on now. (*The boys go out, one of them leaving his sword where it fell.* NICHOLAS *to the* LANDLORD.)

NICHOLAS. Well, then, we'll have to walk on hungry. Portsmouth, twelve bad miles. (NICHOLAS *and* SMIKE *turn to go.*)

CRUMMLES. Portsmouth?

NICHOLAS. Sir?

CRUMMLES. You're set for Portsmouth?

NICHOLAS. Yes, we—

CRUMMLES. So am I.

NICHOLAS. I'm pleased to hear it, sir. (CRUMMLES *comes over.*)

CRUMMLES. And may I venture, short of money for the stage?

NICHOLAS. You've guessed it, sir.

CRUMMLES. Why, then, you'll ride with me, upon my phaeton.

NICHOLAS. Um—

CRUMMLES. That's settled. Landlord, see my pony's fetched. (*The* LANDLORD *goes out.* CRUMMLES *sees the dropped sword, picks it up, and waves it.*) So, what d'you think of that, sir?

NICHOLAS. What? Oh, very good indeed. Quite— capital.

CRUMMLES. You won't see such as that too often.

NICHOLAS. No. And if they'd been, perhaps, a little better matched—

CRUMMLES. What, matched? Why sir, it's the very essence of the combat that there should be a foot or two between 'em. Otherwise, how are you to get up the sympathies of the audience in a legitimate manner?

NICHOLAS. Oh, I see. They are—you are—theatricals?

CRUMMLES. Why yes, of course. And playing Portsmouth from tonight. Yes, I am Vincent Crummles, and I am in the theatrical profession, my wife is in the theatrical profession, and my children are in the theatrical profession. I had a dog that lived and died in it from a puppy, and my chaise-pony goes on in Timour the Tartar. *(The* MASTER CRUMMLESES *re-enter with baggage. Re-enter, too, the* LANDLORD, *and a* STABLE-BOY. *During the following, they move the table, place the bench in front of it, and pile baggage on the table, so that the table is converted into the small carriage that* CRUMMLES *calls his "phaeton." The final additions are two washing tubs and a water-pump, piled on top, and two reins, running out from the front of the table, which, when* CRUMMLES *picks them up, will suggest the presence of the imaginary pony in front of the carriage.)* Ah, now it's just my baggage, and we're set to go.

NICHOLAS. This is—this is most generous.

CRUMMLES. Oh, not at all. It's my self-interest. I have an eye for talent, Mr. . . . .

NICHOLAS. Oh, uh, Johnson.

CRUMMLES. Johnson? And yours struck me immediately.

NICHOLAS. Talent for what?

CRUMMLES. Why, for the stage! There's genteel comedy, your walk and manner, juvenile tragedy, your eye, and touch-and-go farce in your laugh.

NICHOLAS. But, sir—

CRUMMLES. *(Dropping his voice.)* And as for your associate, I've never seen a better for the starving business. Only let him be quite tolerably well-dressed for the Apothecary—Romeo and Juliet—the slightest red dab on his nose, and he'll be guaranteed three rounds the moment he pops his head round the practicable door.

NICHOLAS. The practicable—

CRUMMLES. In the front grooves, O.P. Sir, can you write?

NICHOLAS. Well, I am not illiterate.

CRUMMLES. Well, that could not be better. You will

write our new piece, for a week on Monday, if you'd be so kind. Now, boys—

NICHOLAS. But, sir—I can't—I've never written anything.

CRUMMLES. What stuff! Do you speak French?

NICHOLAS. Yes, like a native. (CRUMMLES *takes a script from a bag and tosses it to* NICHOLAS.)

CRUMMLES. Then turn that into English, put your name on it, and there's the play. Oh, but for one more thing . . . I've just bought a real pump and two fine washing tubs—I got 'em cheap—and you must work them in. You know, the bills, we'll advertise 'em: "Splendid Tubs," "A Real Pump," that kind of thing, you'll probably be writing out the bills yourself, now are we set and can we go?

NICHOLAS. Sir, I must ask one more question. (CRUMMLES *turns back.*)

CRUMMLES. Ask away.

NICHOLAS. Will I be paid for this?

CRUMMLES. Will you be paid? Will you be paid? Dear sir, with your own salary, your friend's, and royalties, you'll make a pound a week!

NICHOLAS. A pound a week.

CRUMMLES. At least. Now come, sirs, come. (NICHOLAS *turns to* SMIKE *who is looking rapt.*)

NICHOLAS. Well, Smike, what times we've fallen on, who could have . . . Smike?

SMIKE. The stage! (*Everyone now on the phaeton. Music, a light change, and horse-shoe effect from off.* CRUMMLES *has picked up the reins, and everyone mimes being on a moving vehicle. The* LANDLORD *and* STABLE-BOY *have gone.*)

CRUMMLES. (*With a nod at the pony.*) He's a good pony at bottom.

NICHOLAS. I am sure of it.

CRUMMLES. And quite one of us. His mother was on the stage, of course.

NICHOLAS. She was?

CRUMMLES. Yes, yes, ate apple-pie at a circus for upwards of fourteen years, fired pistols, went to bed in a nightcap, and in short, took the low comedy entirely. (CRUMMLES, *confidentially, to* NICHOLAS.) His father was a dancer.

NICHOLAS. Oh? Distinguished?

CRUMMLES. No, not very. The fact is, that he'd been jobbed out in the days originally, and never lost his bad habits. He was cleverish in melodrama, but too broad, too broad. And when the mother died, he took the port-wine business.

NICHOLAS. Port-wine business.

CRUMMLES. Yes, you know, the drinking of the port-wine with the clown. But he was greedy, and one night he bit the bowl right off, and choked himself to death. Vulgarity—the end of him at last. (*And they have arrived. Everyone gets off the phaeton, and the boys strike the props, bench and table, as:*) Well, here we are boys, Portsmouth, for three weeks. All men have their trials, and this is ours. Come on, boys, bustle, bustle.

NICHOLAS. And Nicholas jumped out, and, giving Smike his arm, accompanied the manager up the High Street towards the theatre, feeling nervous and uncomfortable at the prospect of an introduction to a scene so new to him. (NICHOLAS *follows* CRUMMLES *out.* SMIKE *and the* MASTER CRUMMLESES *follow, too.*)

SCENE 10

The stage of the Portsmouth Theatre. It is bare, and looks very dusty and dour. Enter most of the Crummles Theatre Company. They are MR. BANE, MR. WAGSTAFF, MR. PAILEY, MR. FLUGGERS, MR. HETHERINGTON, MR. BLIGHTEY, MISS BRAVASSA, MISS BELVAWNEY, MISS GAZINGI, MRS. LENVILLE, *and, at the centre of it all,* MRS. CRUMMLES. *A moment as they survey the scene. Then* MRS. GRUDDEN, *the stage manager, pulls a clothes rail across the stage. A certain amount of animation follows:* MR. BANE *and* MR. HETHERINGTON *fetch a chair and table for* MRS. CRUMMLES, *others open luggage, practise attitudes, look round. The bustle continues throughout the scene. Enter* CRUMMLES, NICHOLAS, SMIKE *and the* MASTER CRUMMLESES.

CRUMMLES. Well, there we are. Good afternoon to one and all. And welcome to Portsmouth! (*The* PERFORMERS *look back, not very enthusiastically.* MRS. CRUMMLES *calls to her husband.*)

MRS. CRUMMLES. Vincent.

CRUMMLES. *(Going to her.)* Ah—Mrs. Crummles.

MRS. CRUMMLES. Vincent *(They embrace.* MRS. CRUMMLES *notices* NICHOLAS *and* SMIKE.*)* Who are those men, so withered and so wild in their attire? *(*CRUMMLES *whispers to* MRS. CRUMMLES.*)*

SMIKE. Is this a theatre? I thought it would be a blaze of light and finery.

NICHOLAS. Why, so it is. But not by day, Smike, not by day.

CRUMMLES. Uh, Mr. Johnson. Please, meet Mrs. Crummles. *(*NICHOLAS *and* SMIKE *come over.)*

MRS. CRUMMLES. I am so glad to see you sir, so glad. And overcome to welcome you, *(To* CRUMMLES.*)* provisionally, *(To* NICHOLAS.*)* as a promising new member of our corps. *(She looks at* SMIKE.*)* And this—yet more? An undernourished friend. You too are welcome, sir. *(*SMIKE *is brought forward to shake the hand of* MRS. CRUMMLES *as the* INFANT PHENOMENON *dances on. She is of doubtful age, though dressed in a little girl's ballet costume. She pirouettes and falls in an attitude of terror. She is followed on by* MR. FOLAIR, *a pantomimist, not in the first flush of youth, who wears buff slippers and is brandishing a walking stick.* MRS. GRUDDEN *appears with a list and tries to attract* MR. CRUMMLES' *attention as it becomes clear that* FOLAIR *and the* PHENOMENON *are practising a dance.)*

FOLAIR. And one and two and three—

CRUMMLES. What's this?

MRS. CRUMMLES. It's the Indian Savage and the Maiden.

FOLAIR. Pose and one and two and growl and threaten—

CRUMMLES. *(Explaining to* NICHOLAS.*)* Oh, yes, the little ballet interlude. Capital, capital.

FOLAIR. And attitude . . . and he loves her, and she loves him, and spin . . . *(The* PHENOMENON *executes a little spin, aided by* FOLAIR. *A trailing hand hits* FOLAIR *in the mouth.)* . . . Thank you, and climax . . . *(A complicated and uncertain climax, culminating with* FOLAIR *kneeling, and the* PHENOMENON *standing with one foot on his knee, her hand over his face.* CRUMMLES *applauds.)*

CRUMMLES. Bravo, bravo! *(*CRUMMLES *takes the* PHE-NOMENON *to introduce her to* NICHOLAS. *During the fol-*

lowing, two late-comers, MISS SNEVELLICCI *and* MISS
LEDROOK, *appear. The former is the leading young actress of the company, and knows it. She whispers to* MISS
BRAVASSA, *asking her about* NICHOLAS.) And, this, sir,
is Miss Ninetta Crummles, better known to half the nobility of England as the Infant Phenomenon.

NICHOLAS. Your daughter?

CRUMMLES. Our daughter, sir, and the idol of every
place we go into. The talent of this child is not to be
imagined. She must be seen, sir, seen—to be even faintly
appreciated. Now, kiss your mother, dear. (*The* INFANT
PHENOMENON *kisses* MRS. CRUMMLES. *Something unpleasant transfers itself from daughter to mother.*)

MRS. CRUMMLES. What has the child been eating.
Mrs. Grudden? Where are you? (MRS. CRUMMLES *drags
the* PHENOMENON *off.*)

NICHOLAS. May I ask how old she is?

CRUMMLES. You may, sir. She is ten years of age, sir.

NICHOLAS. Not more!

CRUMMLES. Not a day.

NICHOLAS. Dear me, it's quite—extraordinary! (FOLAIR *joins the conversation.* SMIKE *has wandered off, and
soon he will be collared by* MRS. GRUDDEN, *who tries
costumes on him.*)

FOLAIR. Oh, great talent, there, sir. Great talent.

NICHOLAS. Well, yes, ind—

FOLAIR. Oh, yes, she shouldn't be in the provinces,
she really shouldn't.

CRUMMLES. (*Suspiciously.*) What do you mean?

FOLAIR. I mean that she is too good for country
boards, and that she ought to be in one of the large
houses in London, or nowhere; and I tell you more, that
if it wasn't for envy and jealousy in some quarters, she
would be. Perhaps you'll introduce me here, Mr.
Crummles.

CRUMMLES. Mr. Folair. This is Mr. Johnson, who's to
write our new piece for Monday, and when he's done
that he's to study Romeo—oh, don't forget the tubs and
pumps, sir, by-the-by . . . (CRUMMLES *is presenting*
NICHOLAS *with bits of script from his pockets.*) and
Rover, too, of course, you might as well while you're
about it, and Cassio and Jeremy Diddler. You can easily

knock them off; one part helps all the others so much. Here they are, cues and all.

NICHOLAS. But—

CRUMMLES. Ah, there's Miss Belvawney. *(CRUMMLES goes off after MISS BELVAWNEY.)*

FOLAIR. Happy to know you, sir. *(He shakes NICHOLAS' hand.)* Well, did you ever see such a set-out as *that. (He tosses his head in the general direction of the PHENOMENON and pulls a face.)*

NICHOLAS. Do you mean the Infant Phenomenon?

FOLAIR. Infant humbug, sir. With half a pint of gin a morning, every day since infancy, you could look ten for life, I'd venture.

NICHOLAS. I see. You seem to take it to heart.

FOLAIR. Yes, by Jove, and well I may. Isn't it enough to make a man crusty to see that sprawler put in the best business every night, and actually keeping money out of the house? Why, I know of fifteen and sixpence that came to Southampton to see me dance the Highland Fling, and what's the consequence? I've never been put up in it since—never once—while the Infant Phenomenon has been grinning through artificial flowers at five people and a baby on the pit, and two boys in the gallery, every night. Oh, halloa, fellow, how are you? *(For some moments, NICHOLAS has been aware of MR. LENVILLE, the Tragedian, fencing towards him.)*

LENVILLE. Well, Tommy, do the honours, do the honours.

FOLAIR. Ah, yes. This is Mr. Johnson, joined us suddenly, this afternoon. Mr. Lenville, who does our first tragedy.

NICHOLAS. First tragedy?

FOLAIR. Oh, yes, the major tragic roles, and—

LENVILLE. What's he joined to play, then, Tommy?

NICHOLAS. Well, I've been asked to—

FOLAIR. *(Interrupts.)* Bits and pieces, bits and pieces. Cassio, and other things, and such.

LENVILLE. What other things?

FOLAIR. And writing a new piece as well.

LENVILLE. A new piece, eh? What's in it?

NICHOLAS. Well, the play is based on a fascinating French fable—

LENVILLE. I meant for me. Something, you know, in

the tragic and declamatory line—(*Luckily*, MR. LEN-VILLE *has said this while looking round at other activity, so* FOLAIR *can whisper to Nicholas.*)

FOLAIR. But Not Too Young.

NICHOLAS. Oh, yes. Well, sir, there is a character who turns his wife and child out of doors, and in a fit of jealousy stabs his eldest son in the library.

LENVILLE. Ah yes, that's very good.

NICHOLAS. After which, he is troubled by remorse till the last act, and then he makes up his mind to destroy himself. But just as he—or, you—are raising the pistol to your head, a clock strikes ten.

LENVILLE. I see. Yes, excellent.

NICHOLAS. You pause. You recollect to have heard a clock strike ten in your infancy. The pistol falls from your hand, you burst into tears, and become a virtuous and exemplary character for ever afterwards.

LENVILLE. Capital. Yes, sir, that will definitely serve. Ha.

FOLAIR. (*Anxiously.*) Anything for me?

NICHOLAS. (*Enjoying himself.*) Well, let me see . . . I imagine you would play the faithful and attached servant who is turned out of doors with the wife and child—

FOLAIR. Always coupled with that infernal phenomenon! (*He strides off.* SMIKE, *who has been dressed in a vaguely renaissance costume—a long grey gown and velvet hat—rushes forward to* NICHOLAS, *waving in delight, and rushes back again to* MRS. GRUDDEN. MISS SNEVELLICCI *glides over to* NICHOLAS.)

MISS SNEVELLICCI. I beg your pardon, sir. But did you ever play at Canterbury?

NICHOLAS. Uh . . . No, never.

MISS SNEVELLICCI. It's just—I recollect meeting a gentleman at Canterbury, only for a few moments, for I was leaving the company as he joined it, so like you that I felt almost certain it was the same.

NICHOLAS. Well, I do assure you that you are mistaken, for I'm certain, if we had met, I'd remember it.

MISS SNEVELLICCI. Oh, I'm sure that's very flattering of you to say so. But now, as I look at you again, I see that gentleman had not your eyes. You'll think me foolish, doubtless, that I take notice of such things.

NICHOLAS. Why, not at all. How can I feel otherwise than flattered by your notice in any way?

MISS SNEVELLICCI. Oh, Mr. Johnson. All you men are such vain creatures, aren't you? Mm? *(SNEVELLICCI has been gesturing with a hand to MISS LEDROOK, who refuses to come over, so SNEVELLICCI turns and calls.)* Led, my dear.

MISS LEDROOK. Yes, what is it?

MISS SNEVELLICCI. It's not the same.

MISS LEDROOK. The same what?

MISS SNEVELLICCI. He never was at Canterbury, come here, I want to speak to you. *(CRUMMLES appears. MISS LEDROOK doesn't move, so MISS SNEVELLICCI has to go to her, and they have a little argument, as:)*

CRUMMLES. A genius, sir, a genius. I'm thinking, that we will bring out your new piece for her bespeak.

NICHOLAS. Bewhat?

CRUMMELS. Her benefit, when her friends and patrons bespeak the play. In fact, sir, you might do us some other little assistance. There is a little—what shall I call it—a little canvassing on these occasions—

NICHOLAS. Among the friends and patrons? *(MISS SNEVELLICCI aware of this conversation.)*

CRUMMLES. Yes, just half an hour tomorrow morning, calling on the houses, drumming up support . . . You know, new author, all the way from London, book now to avoid a disappointment, all that kind of thing . . .

NICHOLAS. Now, sir, I'm afraid that I should not like to do that.

CRUMMLES. Not even with the infant?

NICHOLAS. No. *(MISS SNEVELLICCI rushes to CRUMMLES and NICHOLAS.)*

MISS SNEVELLICCI. Oh, Mr. Johnson. Sir, you surely aren't so cruel, so heartless . . . and after I have been so looking forward to it, too.

NICHOLAS. Well, I'm very sorry, but—*(MRS. CRUMMLES sails in.)*

MRS. CRUMMLES. What's this? A problem, with the canvass?

CRUMMLES. Yes, dear. Mr. Johnson seems to have objections.

MRS. CRUMMLES. What? Object? Can this be possible?

NICHOLAS. Well, it's—

MRS. CRUMMLES. This Mr. Johnson, is it, with objections? This one, plucked, as 'twere, from dark obscurity, took off the streets—the highway—and presented with a chance that half of London would donate a vital limb for? Vincent, this is inconceivable. I am convinced his sense of what is proper, nay is chivalrous, nay once again is gallant, all will sweep him to enlistment in this noble cause. (*Looking at* NICHOLAS. *Slightly coquettishly.*) Is this not so?

NICHOLAS. Well . . . It is not in my nature to resist any entreaty, unless it is to do something positively wrong. I know nobody here, and nobody knows me. So be it, then. I yield.

MRS. CRUMMLES. (*With a look at* CRUMMLES, *as if to say*, "*must I cope with everything?*") Well. There. (*And* MRS. CRUMMLES, CRUMMLES *and* MISS SNEVELLICCI *leave* NICHOLAS, *and join the company.* NICHOLAS *now sees the full* COMPANY *ranged before him.*)

MRS. GRUDDEN. Quiet. Quiet, everybody!

CRUMMLES. Ladies and gentlemen! May I introduce to you Mr. Johnson and Mr.—

NICHOLAS. (*Giving a new name to* SMIKE.) Digby.

CRUMMLES. Thank you. Mr. Johnson, you have met Mr. Folair and Mr. Lenville, Miss Snevellicci and my wife and family. This is Mr. Bane, who does the tenor lovers; (MR. BANE *waves weakly.*) Mr. Wagstaff, who's our virtuous old gentleman; (MR. WAGSTAFF *is holding a suitcase, and as he stands to nod at* NICHOLAS, *we hear the clink of many bottles inside it. This confirms the impression that his red nose and uncertain gait has already given us.*) And Mr. Fluggers, who does the cloth, and can do everything from country parsons to the Pope. (MR. FLUGGERS *looks up from his newspaper.*) Now, that is Mr. Blightey, who's irascible—

BLIGHTEY. (*Benignly.*) Hallo.

CRUMMLES. Mr. Hetherington, who swaggers, and Mr. Pailey who is country comical; (MR. PAILEY *grins.*) There's Miss Ledrook, who's our secondary romance, Miss Belvawney, who does the pages in white hose; Mrs. Lenville, who's the wife to Mr. Lenville; Miss Bravassa, Miss Gazingi, and Mrs. Grudden. Now, tomorrow morning, ten o'clock, we'll call The Mortal Struggle and then it's all the Chorus for the Raising of the Siege of Ghent.

Good evening, everyone! *(As all the* COMPANY *except for the* CRUMMLES FAMILY *itself disperse:)*

MRS. GRUDDEN. Ten o'clock, call, ten o'clock. The Mortal Struggle. Half past Siege of Ghent. All those lodgings, go to 'em. All those without, see me. Good evening, everyone. *(*MRS. CRUMMLES *leads her* FAMILY *to* NICHOLAS *and* SMIKE. NICHOLAS *a little shrug, which* MRS. CRUMMLES *interprets as a request that he should be put out of his agony.)*

MRS. CRUMMLES. Yes, sir, I think you'll do. *(*CRUMMLES *relieved. The* FAMILY *sweep out.* NICHOLAS *and* SMIKE *follow.)*

SCENE 11

The Mantalinis' showroom. The mirror, a clothes rail, clothes stands, and tailors' dummies. MISS KNAG *crossly fiddling about. Enter* KATE.

KATE. Um, Miss—

MISS KNAG. Oh, well. If it isn't that young and pretty creature, Miss Kate Nickle—

KATE. Please, Miss Knag. You're wanted in the workroom.

MISS KNAG. Workroom. Thank you. *(As she goes.)* Well, one might have thought, some people would have had the sensitivity, to seek alternative employment. Yes, one might have thought, but it's a queer world. *(*MISS KNAG *goes out. Enter* MADAME MANTALINI.*)*

MADAME MANTALINI. *(Adjusting a dress on a stand.)* Well, Miss Nickleby, and how are you?

KATE. I'm quite well, thank you, Madame Mantalini. *(*KATE *starting to help.)*

MADAME MANTALINI. Hm. I wish that I could say the same.

KATE. Why, Madame Mantalini, what's the matter?

MADAME MANTALINI. Nothing, nothing. Now, get these things in order, do. *(*MANTALINI'S *head pops into the room.)*

MANTALINI. Now, is my life-and-soul here present?

MADAME MANTALINI. No.

MANTALINI. But how can that be so, when I see it

blooming in the room before me like a little rose in a demd flowerpot? So, may its popper enter?

MADAME MANTALINI. No, he may not. For he knows he's not allowed in here. So, go along. (MANTALINI *enters the room and embraces* MADAME MANTALINI.)

MANTALINI. Oh, will it vex itself?

MADAME MANTALINI. I said that—

MANTALINI. Will it twist and crunch its little face?

MADAME MANTALINI. Oh, I can't bear you—

MANTALINI. What, can't bear me? I, whose only joy is gaining such a lovely creature, such a Venus, such a demd enchanting, and bewitching, and engrossing, capitivating little Venus?

MADAME MANTALINI. (*Breaking away.*) Mantalini, you, your debts, extravagances, they will ruin me.

MANTALINI. (*Airily.*) Oh, that. Oh, it's a nothing, money will be made, and if it don't get made, enough, old Nickleby can stump up once again, or else I'll cut his jugular from ear to—

MADAME MANTALINI. Hush. Hush, don't you see?

MANTALINI. Oh. Dear Miss Nickleby. Well, I'll be demd. (*Pause.*) Well, then, as I am commanded, and quite demnibly admonished, by my little rapture . . . I'll withdraw. (*He goes to the door. Then turns back.*) Unless . . . My little joy and bliss . . . Would care to join her slave for breakfast? (*Pause. Then, after a look to* KATE, MADAME MANTALINI *follows* MANTALINI *to the door. He holds it open for her to go through. Pause.* KATE *carries on, working alone, for a moment. Then a new head pops round the door. It belongs to* MR. SCALEY, *a rather rough-and-ready, though completely professional, gentleman.*)

SCALEY. Psst.

KATE. Oh! What?

SCALEY. (*Coming into the room.*) Please don't alarm yourself, Miss. Is this the millinery concern, proprietor one Mister Muntlehiney?

KATE. Yes, what do you want?

SCALEY. (*Calling out of the door.*) Yes, Mr. Tix, we have the right establishment. (*Enter* MR. TIX, *another professional gentleman.* KATE, *fearing that these men are thieves, backing away.*) Oh, please don't go yet, Miss. I haven't yet presented you my card. (*He hands a square, white card to* KATE.) My name is Scaley. This is Mr. Tix. Perhaps you'd be so kind as to acquaint your guv'nor with our presence. (KATE *backs to the wall and pulls the bell pull. Bell rings.*) Thank you ever so. (*Pause.* KATE *stands there, by the bell pull.* MR. TIX *is looking up at the ceiling.*)

TIX. I like the ceiling. Nice high ceiling.

SCALEY. Isn't it.

TIX. A boy could grow up here, grow up to be a man, a tall 'un too, and never bump his head on that.

SCALEY. Now, that is very true. (*Tapping a mirror.*) Good plate here, Tix.

TIX. Oh, yur. (*Fingering a dress.*) And this here article weren't put together without outlay of considerable expense, nor, neither. (*Pause as they continue looking round the room. Then* TIX, *to lighten the atmosphere, to* KATE.) And a very pretty colour. (*Enter* MADAME MANTALINI.)

MADAME MANTALINI. Kate, what's the—oh? Oh!

SCALEY. Ah. Mrs. Muntlehinney?

KATE. Madame.

SCALEY. (*He waves at* TIX.) Mr. Tix. (*He waves a document.*) This is a writ of execution, and if it's not immediately convenient to settle, we'll set to work at once, please, taking the inventory. (MADAME MANTALINI *stumbles in horror, grabs the bell, pulls it, and falls into a chair.* KATE *to her.*) Oh, dear. I do suspect, Tix, that we'd better make a brisk commencement. (TIX *has already taken out his inventory book. He stands behind a dress on a stand, to note its features, so that, to us, he appears to be wearing it.*)

TIX. Dress. One. Fetching shade of blue. (*Enter* MANTALINI.)

SCALEY. Ah. Um, monsieur? (MANTALINI *stands there a moment. He is not unused to this situation, or to men like* SCALEY *and* TIX.)

MANTALINI. So, what's the total, demn you?

TIX. Fifteen hundred, twenty-seven pound, and four and ninepence ha'penny.

MANTALINI. The ha'penny be demd.

SCALEY. By all means. And the ninepence, too. But with regard to the outstanding . . . ? (MANTALINI *shrugs, and waves his hand.* MADAME MANTALINI *is in tears.*)

SCALEY. Oh, well. I fear that Mrs. Tix and all the little Tixes'll be minus their papa a day or two.

TIX. *(Looks around.)* Or even three.

SCALEY. *(To comfort* MADAME MANTALINI.*)* Now, come on, madam, take a little consolation, for I'll warrant half of this stuff isn't been paid for, eh? *(*SCALEY *and* TIX *set about their business as* MANTALINI *goes to his wife.)*

TIX. Two cheval-glasses. One with damaged frame.

MANTALINI. Now, dear, my cup of happiness's sweetener, will you listen to me for two minutes?

MADAME MANTALINI. *(Suddenly, in great passion.)* Oh, don't you speak to me. You've ruined me, and that's enough.

TIX. Three bonnets. Styling, various.

MANTALINI. *(Recoiling, as if from a blow.)* What? Do not speak to you? All this, and I, your drudge and potboy, I am not to speak to you? *(*KATE *looking at* MANTALINI *with some cynicism, as are* MESSRS. SCALEY *and* TIX.*)*

TIX. One bust. A Roman gentleman.

MANTALINI. Oh, it's too much. Too much! *(*MANTALINI *rushes from the room.* MADAME MANTALINI *stands, quickly.)*

MADAME MANTALINI. Quick! Quick, Miss Nickleby! Make haste, for heaven's sake, he will destroy himself. *(She runs to the exit.)* I spoke unkindly to him, and he cannot bear it. Alfred, Alfred! *(She runs out. Suddenly, chase music.* MANTALINI, *who has found a pair of scissors, runs on, pursued by* MILLINERS *and* MADAME MANTALINI. *The chase goes all round the stage, and even, if possible, into the auditorium, before arriving back in the showroom.)*

MANTALINI. No, I'm going to do it. Right now. No question. Going to do it. Yes, I'm going to do it. I will do it now! *(Everyone is back in the showroom.* MISS KNAG *appears on the sidelines.* MR. SCALEY *and* MR. TIX *carry on their work calmly.)*

1st MILLINER. Eh, what's he doing?

2nd MILLINER. Got my scissors.

1st MILLINER. Lor.

MADAME MANTALINI. *(Flinging her arms round her*

husband.) Oh, Alfred, stop, I didn't mean to say it, promise you, I didn't mean to say . . .

2nd MILLINER. That's highly dangerous.

MANTALINI. I have brought ruin on the best and purest creature ever threw herself away on some demned vagabond. I'll do it! Demmit, let me go! *(He pulls himself away from her.)*

MADAME MANTALINI. Compose yourself, my angel, please, someone, disarm him! *(MANTALINI raises the scissors, to plunge them in his breast. The TWO MILLINERS, without much difficulty, grab him and disarm him.)*

2nd MILLINER. Now, come on, Mr. Mantalini—

1st MILLINER. Drop the scissors, like a nice man.

2nd MILLINER. There!

MANTALINI. No! No! You, fetch me poison!

2nd MILLINER. Poison?

MADAME MANTALINI. It was no-one's fault.

MANTALINI. *(Banging his head against an absent wall.)* Fetch me a pistol. You, ma'am, blow my brains out.

1st MILLINER. Me?

MADAME MANTALINI. It was my fault as much as yours—*(MANTALINI grabs the scissors back from the 2ND MILLINER.)*

2nd MILLINER. Hey—

MANTALINI. Rope! A rope to hang myself—*(He tries to hang himself by the bell pull. The bell rings. He looks at MADAME MANTALINI.)* What did you say?

MADAME MANTALINI. I said—that it was no-one's fault. Or, if it was, then mine as much as yours. My love. *(Pause. MANTALINI raises the hand in which he holds the scissors.)*

MANTALINI. Oh, my little pepperpot. Demnation, gravy-boat. *(He drops the scissors.)*

SCALEY. One pair, scissors . . .

MANTALINI. My—little—apfel strudel. *(MADAME MANTALINI aware for the first time of the open-mouthed MILLINERS and the faintly smiling MISS KNAG.)*

MADAME MANTALINI. Please, now, Alfred. Come. *(MADAME MANTALINI puts out her hand to MANTALINI. He walks to her, and they go out together. MISS KNAG picks up the scissors.)*

1st MILLINER. Well, hark at that.

2nd MILLINER. Well, hark at *her.*

MISS KNAG. Well, now, young ladies. After all this wild excitement, shall we return, and recommence our labours? Hm? (*The* MILLINERS *turn out front to narrate.*)

MILLINERS. And return they did, but after half an hour they were informed their services would be immediately dispensed with;

And on the next day Mr. Mantalini's name appeared among the list of bankrupts;

And on the third day, the young ladies were all re-engaged,

Except for Miss Kate Nickleby.

MISS KNAG. (*Maliciously, to* KATE.) Miss Nickleby. I think *you* needn't recommence your labours. I think that *you* Need Not Return. (*She goes out, the* MILLINERS *go out too, and finally* KATE.)

SCENE 12

Portsmouth, various locations. Bare stage. Enter NICHOLAS.

NICHOLAS. And at the hour next morning stipulated for the canvassing of Miss Snevellicci's friends and patrons, Nicholas repaired to the lodgings of that lady, which were at the house of a tailor in Smollet St. And having been admitted to her apartments by the tailor's daughter, he was told to wait. (*Enter* MISS SNEVELLICCI, *carrying a pile of sheets and towels, and, on top of them, a scrapbook. She is followed by the* INFANT PHENOMENON.)

MISS SNEVELLICCI. Oh, Mr. Johnson. Please forgive me. We're all at sixes and sevens this morning.

NICHOLAS. Oh, I'm sorry to—

MISS SNEVELLICCI. My darling Led—Miss Ledrook, from the company . . .

NICHOLAS. Oh, yes.

MISS SNEVELLICCI.—was taken so ill in the night, we had to all move rooms. I thought she would expire, there, in my arms!

NICHOLAS. Well, such a fate is almost to be envied. But—

MISS SNEVELLICCI. Oh, Mr. Johnson, what a flatterer you are. (MISS SNEVELLICCI, *moving towards the exit, artfully drops the scrapbook.*) Oh, dear, look—

NICHOLAS. *(Picking up the scrapbook.)* Allow me, please.

MISS SNEVELLICCI. Oh, thank you, sir. Forgive me for a moment. (MISS SNEVELLICCI *goes out.* NICHOLAS *reads the scrapbook.*)

NICHOLAS. "Sing, God of Love, and tell me in what dearth,

Thrice-gifted Snevellicci came on earth,

To thrill us with her smile, her tear, her eye,

Sing, God of Love, and tell me quickly why."

(MISS SNEVELLICCI *has reappeared, without the sheets and towels*.)

MISS SNEVELLICCI. Mr. Johnson!

NICHOLAS. Oh, I'm—

MISS SNEVELLICCI. Mr. Johnson, I'm surprised at you.

NICHOLAS. I'm sorry, I—

MISS SNEVELLICCI. You are a cruel creature, I'm ashamed to look you in the face.

NICHOLAS. I thought, perhaps . . . You'd dropped it here on purpose?

MISS SNEVELLICCI. Mr. Johnson. I would not have had you see it For The World. Now, shall we go? (NICHOLAS *out front, as* MISS SNEVELLICCI *and the* PHENOMENON *move to the area which will represent the home of the Curdles*.)

NICHOLAS. And go at once they did and the first house to which they bent their steps was situated in a terrace of respectable appearance, where lodged the Curdles, to whose apartments they were instantly directed. (NICHOLAS *joins the* PHENOMENON *and* MISS SNEVELLICCI.)

MISS SNEVELLICCI. Now, Mrs. Curdle is well-known to have quite the London taste in matters relating to the drama; and as to Mr. Curdle, he has written a pamphlet of sixty-four pages,

NICHOLAS. *(Out front.)* Proving that by altering the received mode of punctuation, any one of Shakespeare's plays could be made quite different, and the sense completely changed. (*Enter* MR. *and* MRS. CURDLE. MR. CURDLE *has a chair for his wife, who sits.*)

CURDLE. To be or not? To be that, is the question! Hm?

NICHOLAS. Oh, yes, indeed.

MRS. CURDLE. Dear Miss Snevellicci, and how do you do?

MISS SNEVELLICCI. Oh, I'm alarming well, dear Mrs. Curdle, and ventured to call for the purpose of asking whether you would put your name to my bespeak.

MRS. CURDLE. Oh, I really don't know what to say. . . . It's not as if, now is it, that the theatre was in high and palmy days—the drama's gone, perfectly gone.

MISS SNEVELLICCI. Well, p'raps, but surely—

CURDLE. As an exquisite embodiment of the poet's visions, and laying upon a new and magic world before the mental eye, the drama is gone, perfectly gone.

MRS. CURDLE. What man is there now living who can present before us all those changing and prismatic colours with which the character of Hamlet is invested?

CURDLE. What man indeed—upon the stage; why, Hamlet! Pooh! He's gone, perfectly gone. (*Pause.*)

MISS SNEVELLICCI. The play is new.

MRS. CURDLE. Oh, yes, what is the play?

MISS SNEVELLICCI. A new one, written by this gentleman, and in which he will make his first appearance on the stage.

CURDLE. I trust he has preserved the unities.

NICHOLAS. The piece is in French—originally—there is an abundance of incident, sprightly dialogue, well-fleshed, three-dimensional characters, two tubs, a pump—

CURDLE. All unavailing—pump and all—without the unities.

NICHOLAS. May I inquire, sir, as to what are the unities?

CURDLE. The unities, sir, are a completeness—a kind of universal dove-tailedness, and oneness, and general warmth, and harmony, and tone . . .

MISS SNEVELLICCI. And I am sure that Mr. Johnson will preserve the unities—all three of them—most closely. May I put your names . . . ?

CURDLE. (*Taking a sheet of paper from* MISS SNEVELLICCI.) Well, I suppose . . . We must accept it as our duty to the drama, even if— Four Shillings?

MISS SNEVELLICCI. Yes, that's right.

MRS. CURDLE. Four shillings for *one box*?

MISS SNEVELLICCI. Yes, that's correct.

CURDLE. Four shillings for *one play*? (MISS SNEVELLICCI *looks desperately at* NICHOLAS.)

NICHOLAS. Well. With a lot of people in it. (*Slight pause.*) And it is very long.

CURDLE. Well, it had better be.

NICHOLAS. (*Out front.*) And Miss Snevellicci took the money with many smiles and bends, and Mr. Curdle rang the bell as a signal for breaking up the conference. (*The* CURDLES *going.*)

CURDLE. Oh, what? A rogue and peasant slave, am I? (*Exit the* CURDLES.)

NICHOLAS. What odd people.

MISS SNEVELLICCI. Oh, I assure you, Mr. Johnson, they get even odder. (MISS SNEVELLICCI *and the* PHENOMENON *leaving during:*)

NICHOLAS. As indeed they did, and three hours later, with two pounds and nine shillings taken—

MISS SNEVELLICCI. (*Calls.*) And a further ten and sixpence definitely promised—

NICHOLAS. Nicholas repaired, as he had been instructed, to the lodgings of the Vincent Crummleses. (*Enter* CRUMMLES *in a dressing gown.*)

CRUMMLES. Ah, Johnson, there you are. Come in, come in. How goes it, Johnson?

NICHOLAS. Uh—the canvass?

CRUMMLES. No, the play.

NICHOLAS. It's not quite finished yet.

CRUMMLES. Thank heavens.

NICHOLAS. Oh?

CRUMMLES. I have another novelty, that must at all costs be included, in a prominent position.

NICHOLAS. Uh . . . I'm sorry, I can't guess.

CRUMMLES. What would you say to a young lady from London? Say, Miss Someone, of the Theatre Royal, Drury Lane?

NICHOLAS. Well, that would look excellently, on the bills.

CRUMMLES. Exactly. (CRUMMLES *produces a poster, unrolls it, on which is prominently displayed the name of*

MISS PETOWKER, *of the Theatre Royal, Drury Lane*.) So, what d'you think of that?

NICHOLAS. Dear me. Miss Petowker, I know that lady.

CRUMMLES. Then you are acquainted, sir, with as much talent as was ever compressed into one young person's body. The Blood Drinker, sir, the Blood Drinker will die with that girl; and she's the only sylph *I* ever saw who could stand upon one leg, and play the tambourine on her other knee, *like* a sylph.

NICHOLAS. When is she expected?

CRUMMLES. Why, today. She is an old friend of Mrs. Crummles's, who taught her, as it happens, everything she knows. And here she comes. (MRS. CRUMMLES *entering*.) You're probably aware that Mrs. Crummles was the original Blood Drinker.

NICHOLAS. I didn't know that, no.

MRS. CRUMMLES. Why, yes indeed, sir. I was obliged to give it up, however.

NICHOLAS. Oh, I'm sorry, why?

MRS. CRUMMLES. Oh, the audiences, sir. They couldn't stand it. It was too tremendous. Vincent, there's a letter here—from Miss Petowker.

CRUMMLES. Ah. (CRUMMLES *reads the letter*. NICHOLAS *feels it necessary to converse with* MRS. CRUMMLES.)

NICHOLAS. You teach, I gather, ma'am.

MRS. CRUMMLES. Oh, yes, I do. In fact, I did receive some pupils here in Portsmouth, on a previous occasion. I imparted some tuition in the art of acting to the daughter of a dealer in marine provisions. Sadly, it emerged that all the time she was coming to me she'd been totally insane.

NICHOLAS. Insane! How—most extraordinary.

MRS. CRUMMLES. Well, I thought so too, until I learnt she was of the strong opinion she was living on the moon, which sad delusion went a long way to explain the style of her performances, which were distinctly lunar. So, then, Vincent, it *is* true! (*For* MR. CRUMMLES *has finished the letter*.)

CRUMMLES. Well, so it must appear. Who would have thought it?

MRS. CRUMMLES. I would, Vincent. Any woman would. It is—demonstrably—her mission.

MISS PETOWKER. (*Off*.) Mrs. Crummles! Mr. Crummles!

MRS. CRUMMLES. Ah, and here she is. Boys, boys! (*The* MASTER CRUMMLESES *run on, and help* MISS PETOWKER *and her luggage into the room.*)

MISS PETOWKER. Oh, Mrs. Crummles, Mr. Crummles . . . Oh, why, Mr. Johnson!

MRS. CRUMMLES. You two are acquainted?

NICHOLAS. Yes, we . . .

MISS PETOWKER. Mr. *Johnson*. We met—oh, I don't recall, on two or three occasions, Lady—Thing, and Mrs. Whatsit's salon, at the opera . . . Well, Mr. Johnson, what a pleasure. (NICHOLAS *is embraced by* MISS PETOWKER. MISS PETOWKER *to* MRS. CRUMMLES.) Why, Mrs. Crummles, I had no *idea*. . . .

MRS. CRUMMELS. We are all quite delighted, Henri-etta, with The News.

MISS PETOWKER. (*Confidentially*.) Oh, but now, Mrs. Crummles, there must be no *word*, no *hint*, of anything. . . .

MRS. CRUMMLES. My lips, my dear, are glued. Now, at this instant, dinner. (MRS. CRUMMLES *has been escorting* MISS PETOWKER *into another room. She changes her mind, however, and turns back to* NICHOLAS, *who is moving towards the door.*) Mr. Johnson?

NICHOLAS. Mrs. Crummles?

MRS. CRUMMLES. We have but a shoulder of mutton with onion sauce but such as our dinner is, we beg you to partake of it.

NICHOLAS. Oh, Mrs. Crummles, I should be delighted.

MRS. CRUMMLES. (*As she escorts* MISS PETOWKER *out.*) Then let the mutton and onion sauce appear! (*Exit the two women as the* MASTER CRUMMLESES *and the* PHENOMENON *run on and drag* NICHOLAS *into dinner.*)

SCENE 13

Ralph Nickleby's office. To one side, Ralph's desk and chairs either side, in one of which RALPH *sits, working. To the other side, a high stool and ledger table, on which are account books and a bell. This is Noggs' room, and we imagine the two rooms are divided.* NOGGS *is in Ralph's part of the office.* MR. MANTALINI *is banging the bell on Noggs' desk.* NOGGS *goes out of the "door" and round into his own area.*

MANTALINI. What a demnation long time you have kept me ringing at this confounded old cracked tea-kettle of a bell, every tinkle of which is enough to throw a strong man into blue convulsions.

NOGGS. Didn't hear it more than once, myself.

MANTALINI. Then you are most demnibly and outrageously deaf. Now, where's Ralph Nickleby?

NOGGS. Might not be home. What purpose?

MANTALINI. (*Striding past* NOGGS *to Ralph's office.*) Purpose? It's to melt some dirty scraps of paper into bright and shining, clinking, trinkling demd mint sauce. (RALPH NICKLEBY *looks at* MR. MANTALINI.) Ah. Nickleby. You are at home. (RALPH *a look at* NOGGS, *who has followed.*)

NOGGS. (*Shrugs.*) He wouldn't wait. (RALPH *tosses his head at* NOGGS. NOGGS *returns to his desk.*)

MANTALINI. Well, Nickleby, you're looking well today. You look quite juvenile and jolly, demmit!

RALPH. What do you want with me?

MANTALINI. Demnation discount.

RALPH. Money's scarce.

MANTALINI. Demnd scarce, or else I wouldn't want it.

RALPH. But—as you're a friend . . . Bills of exchange?

MANTALINI. Yes, two. One for £40, and one for thirty-five.

RALPH. So, seventy-five in all. When are they due for payment?

MANTALINI. Two months one, the other four.

RALPH. Names of the guarantors? (MANTALINI *hands over the bills. The front doorbell rings again.* NOGGS *goes to answer it.*) Well, they are not cast-iron . . . But they're safe enough. I'll give you fifty for 'em.

MANTALINI. Only fifty.

RALPH. Yes.

MANTALINI. Not even, just a little more, as we are friends . . .

RALPH. But this is business, Mr. Mantalini. You'll not get a better rate. (NOGGS *admits* MADAME MANTALINI *and* MISS KNAG.) And so? Do you accept?

MANTALINI. I must.

RALPH. (*Opening a cash box.*) Well, then . . . (MA-

DAME MANTALINI, *followed by* MISS KNAG, *has strode in past* NOGGS *and into Ralph's office.*)

MADAME MANTALINI. Oh, here you are.

MANTALINI. Oh. You.

MADAME MANTALINI. Yes. Me. Forgive us, Mr. Nickleby, for this intrusion. Which is attributable to the gross and most improper misbehaviour of, of Mr. Mantalini. (MANTALINI *stands and tries to embrace* MADAME MANTALINI.)

MANTALINI. What's this you're saying, juice of pineapple?

MADAME MANTALINI. No, none of that. I won't allow it. I will not be ruined by your profligacy any more. (MANTALINI *sits*.) Mr. Nickleby, I call on you to witness what I'm going to say.

RALPH. Pray, do not ask me, madam. Settle it among yourselves.

MADAME MANTALINI. Well, settle it is what I plan to do. (*To* MANTALINI.) This morning, you appropriated, from my desk, some bills belonging to the company, without permission. Is that not the case?

MANTALINI. It is, my precious, it is true, my tulip. I'm the demdest villain ever lived.

MADAME MANTALINI. And, knowing of my debts and obligations, caused by your extravagance, you have come here to change those bills of mine to cash. Do you deny it?

MANTALINI. No, I cannot. Oh, I'll fill my pockets up with ha'pennies, and drown myself.

MADAME MANTALINI. Well then, I tell you, Mr. Nickleby, Miss Knag, once and for all, that I never will supply this man's extravagance again. (*Pause.* MANTALINI *looks up at his wife. He says nothing.*) I have been his dupe and his fool for long enough, and in future, he shall support himself if he can, and he may spend all that he pleases, and on whom he likes, but it shall not be mine.

MANTALINI. What are you saying, seraphim?

MADAME MANTALINI. I am insisting on a separation.

RALPH. Madam, you are not in earnest.

MADAME MANTALINI. Oh, I am.

RALPH. Madam, consider. A married woman has no property. The company belongs to Mr. Mantalini.

MADAME MANTALINI. Oh, no, sir. It does not. That

company is bankrupt. But, to save what little has been left, of the furnishings and stock, I was obliged to call upon another party, who had, I'm pleased to say, sufficient capital to meet outstanding bills, to re-employ the staff, and to engage me as the manager of her new company.

MISS KNAG. New company. (*Slight pause.* MANTALINI *looks at* MISS KNAG *in horror.*) Yes, it's quite true, Mr. Nickleby. It's very true indeed. And I never was more glad in all my life, that I had the strength of mind to resist all offers of marriage, however advantageous, than I am when I think of my present position as compared with your most unfortunate and most undeserved one, Madame Mantalini. (*To* RALPH.) Otherwise, where would I be today?

MANTALINI. Oh, demmit, demmit, will it not slap and pinch the envious dowager, that dares so to reflect upon its own delicious?

MADAME MANTALINI. No, of course not. For Miss Knag is now, perforce, my very greatest friend.

MANTALINI. This is a dream, a demned, demned horrid dream.

MADAME MANTALINI. You have brought it on yourself.

MANTALINI. Oh, has it come to this? Oh, have I cut my heart into a demned extraordinary number of little pieces, and given them away one after another to the same little engrossing captivator, and it's come to this?

MADAME MANTALINI. It has. You know it has. (*Slight pause.* MADAME MANTALINI *goes to* RALPH *and puts out her hand.* RALPH *hands over the Bills of Exchange.* MISS KNAG *trots over, and puts out her hand.* MADAME MANTALINI *gives the Bills to* MISS KNAG. *To* RALPH.) I did . . . A long time. I did love that creature, Mr. Nickleby. (MADAME MANTALINI *and* MISS KNAG *go out.* MANTALINI *runs, and cries after them.*)

MANTALINI. Oh, I will drown myself! (*But they have gone. Back to* RALPH.) Oh, Nickleby, how can you sit there, watching such a cruel, brazen chick-a-biddy savaging the very heart of one who—

RALPH. Come, sir, you must put away these fooleries, now.

MANTALINI. You—what?

RALPH. And live by your own wits again. (*Pause.*)

MANTALINI. But, demmit, you'll help me, won't you, Nickleby?

RALPH. No, I will not. Good day.

MANTALINI. You can't be serious.

RALPH. I seldom joke. Good day.

MANTALINI. Now, look here, Nickleby, you know, without me, you'd've not got one brass farthing out of—

RALPH. Without you, sir, my credit would not have been needed. As you well know. And now, good day to you. (*Pause.*)

MANTALINI. Well. Well, demnation—cruelty. (*He makes to go, turns back. He can't believe it.*) It's over. (MANTALINI *goes out.*)

RALPH. Hm. Love him. Love that. All love is cant and vanity. (NOGGS *has appeared. He coughs.*) Yes, what?

NOGGS. (*Presenting a card to* RALPH.) Two gentlemen. Are out the back. Their card. (*Enter* MR. SCALEY *and* MR. TIX.)

SCALEY. Well, good day, Mr. Nickleby. Here is the tally. Thirteen hundred pounds. That's plus or minus the odd bonnet, or an underskirt or two.

RALPH. I thank you.

SCALEY. And dare I venture, you'll be kindly helping out the business once again? Another loan? And in a threemonth, when the interest falls due . . .

RALPH. No, I think not, Mr. Scaley. There has been a change of ownership. The business is now in more able hands.

TIX. Oh, dear.

SCALEY. Oh, very sorry, sir.

RALPH. So, then, your task's complete. How much? (SCALEY *hands* RALPH *a bill, which* RALPH *signs and hands back to* SCALEY.)

SCALEY. It's always such a pleasure doing business with you, Mr. Nickleby.

TIX. It's such a joy.

SCENE 14

Portsmouth. In the wings of the theatre. The CRUMMLES COMPANY *runs on from their curtain call. We hear applause. They have been performing* NICHOLAS' *play for* MISS SNEVELLICCI'S *benefit. The women are mostly clus-*

tering round NICHOLAS, *the* MEN *round* MISS PETOWKER.
SMIKE *looks on.*

MISS GAZINGI. Oh, Mr. Johnson, what a triumph.

NICHOLAS. Well, I—Was it?

MISS BRAVASSA. Oh, my dear, you quite divided the
applause, despite it being for Miss Snevellicci—

NICHOLAS. Well, I'm sure I——(CRUMMLES *comes to*
NICHOLAS, *as* MRS. CRUMMLES *sweeps back on to the*
stage.)

CRUMMLES. Johnson. Sir. This has been magnificent.
Why, quite magnificent. I have not, sir, seen such a
debut since the Phenomenon herself first danced the
Fairy Porcupine. (*The* INFANT PHENOMENON *curtseys*
and does a twirl.) And everyone, well done. (*The* PHE-
NOMENON *bumps into* MISS BRAVASSA *and there is a little*
altercation. LENVILLE *and* FOLAIR *step forward.*)

LENVILLE. Hm. In my view, grossly over-rated.

FOLAIR. (*Leading him aside.*) Oh, come on, now, old
man . . .

CRUMMLES. (*Taking* NICHOLAS' *arm.*) So what did
you think of Miss Petowker, sir?

NICHOLAS. Oh, quite extraordinary. (CRUMMLES *looks*
at NICHOLAS *quizzically. During this a knock at the outer*
door and the Page-clad MISS BELVAWNEY, *out of force*
of habit, goes out to answer it.) Good, is not the word.
But what I did observe, additional to all her talents, was
that every time she spoke, or even entered, there was
quite a fearful opening and closing, in the upper boxes,
of a green umbrella.

CRUMMLES. Was there? I can't say I noticed.

NICHOLAS. Yes, it was most striking. Every time she—
(MISS SNEVELLICCI *approaches bearing vast numbers of*
flowers, followed by MISS LEDROOK, *carrying the rest.*)

MISS SNEVELLICCI. Mr. Johnson.

NICHOLAS. Oh, Miss Snevellicci.

MISS SNEVELLICCI. Mr. Johnson, I—(*But even* MISS
SNEVELLICCI *is interrupted by the entrance of* MRS.
CRUMMLES.)

MRS. CRUMMLES. So, are you *all* deaf?

CRUMMLES. Why, Mrs. Crummles, what's the matter?

MRS. CRUMMLES. What's the matter? The audience is
what's the matter, the great Portsmouth public is the

matter, they are calling for an encore from the shepherd-
esses, they're insisting Miss Petowker does another
dance, they're shrieking out for anything from Mr. Johnson, there is a concerned move to rip the cupids and the
muses from the lower boxes if Miss Snevellicci doesn't—

CRUMMLES. Then, come, let's return! Come, come, at
once!

MRS. CRUMMLES. If you'd all be so kind. (*The* COM-
PANY *running back on, as* MISS BELVAWNEY *appears.*)

MISS BELVAWNEY. Psst, Mr. Johnson.

NICHOLAS. Yes?

MISS BELVAWNEY. There's someone here to see you.

NICHOLAS. But—

MISS BELVAWNEY. He says it's very urgent.

NICHOLAS. But I—(NICHOLAS *sees that* MR. LILLY-
VICK *has come in.*) Why, in the name of wonder, Mr.
Lillyvick! (MISS BELVAWNEY *scuttles across and out.*)

LILLYVICK. (*A little bow.*) Sir, I am your servant. (*He
puts down a large, green umbrella.*)

NICHOLAS. And I yours. Why, there's the green
umbrella!

LILLYVICK. Ah, yes, that it is. What did you think of
that performance?

NICHOLAS. Your performance with the—?

LILLYVICK. What? No, I refer to Miss Petowker's.

NICHOLAS. Well, as far as I could judge, I found it
most agreeable.

LILLYVICK. Agreeable? I would say, sir, it was much
more than agreeable. I'd say, in fact, it was delicious.

NICHOLAS. Well, she is a clever girl.

LILLYVICK. She's a divinity. I have known divine actresses before now, sir; I used to collect the water rate
at the house of a divine actress, but never in all my
experience did I see a diviner creature than Miss Henri-
etta Petowker.

NICHOLAS. Well, yes—

LILLYVICK. (*Grasping* NICHOLAS' *arm.*) A bachelor's
a miserable wretch, sir.

NICHOLAS. Is he?

LILLYVICK. I have been one nigh on sixty years. I
ought to know.

NICHOLAS. That's certain.

LILLYVICK. But you know that the reason, the great

reason, against marriage, is expense. That's what has kept me off it, or else, lord! I might have married fifty women.

NICHOLAS. Fifty.

LILLYVICK. But, you see: the wondrous Miss Petowker earns a salary herself. (*Pause.* LILLYVICK *leaves* NICHOLAS' *arm. He moves a step or two away and eyes* NICHOLAS *inquiringly.*)

NICHOLAS. Uh, Mr. Lillyvick, d'you mean you're going to marry Miss Petowker?

LILLYVICK. Day after tomorrow, sir.

NICHOLAS. Well . . Mr. Lillyvick. Congratulations.

LILLYVICK. The only problem is, the family.

NICHOLAS. What family?

LILLYVICK. The Kenwigses, of course. If my niece and her husband had known a word of it before I came away, they'd have gone into fits at my feet, and never have come off 'em till I took an oath not to marry anybody, or they'd have got out a commission of lunacy, or some such dreadful thing.

NICHOLAS. Yes, they would certainly have been quite jealous.

LILLYVICK. To prevent which, we resolved to marry here, in fact, to be married from the Crummleses, old friends of Miss Petowker, and we should be most pleased if you were there for breakfast, nothing fancy, muffins, coffee, p'raps a shrimp or something for a relish. . . .

NICHOLAS. Mr. Lillyvick, I'd be delighted. And I am most happy for you both.

LILLYVICK. Most happy? Yes. Yes—I should think it *is* a pleasant life, the married one—eh?

NICHOLAS. There is no doubt about it.

LILLYVICK. Um. No doubt. Oh, yes. Yes, certainly. (*Enter* MRS. CRUMMLES.)

MRS. CRUMMLES. Ah, Mr. Johnson. *Here* you are.

NICHOLAS. Oh, Mrs. Crummles. (LILLYVICK *slips out, as:*)

MRS. CRUMMLES. Mr. Johnson, you are called for, in the lower circle. You're demanded in the gallery, which is, in fact, quite near collapse from all the stamping. Your appearance was entreated by dear Mrs. Curdle, till she had a palpitation and was rushed off horizontal in a fly . . . Without, of course, the wish in any way to interrupt your evening—would you be so kind, sir, as to come?

NICHOLAS. Of course I will. (MRS. CRUMMLES *sweeps out.* NICHOLAS *turns out front to introduce the next scene.*)

SCENE 15

Portsmouth. Miss Snevellicci's apartments, and the Crummles' lodgings. Bare stage, but as NICHOLAS *speaks,* MISS SNEVELLICCI, MISS PETOWKER *and* MISS LEDROOK *enter with a chair on one side; and* FOLAIR, LENVILLE, LILLYVICK *and the rest of the* CRUMMLES COMPANY MEN *enter the other side.*

NICHOLAS. And on the morning designated for the nuptial coupling of Mr. Lillyvick and Miss Petowker, the parties were assembling; with the bridegroom and his best man Tom Folair already at the Crummleses; and Miss Petowker being finally prepared at the apartments of Miss Snevellicci. (MISS PETOWKER *is sitting, having a sustaining glass of something.*)

MISS PETOWKER. Oh, Lillyvick! If you only knew what I am undertaking . . . Leaving all my friends, the friends of youthful days, for you!

MISS LEDROOK. Of course he knows it, love, and never will forget it.

MISS PETOWKER. Are you sure? You're sure that he'll remember?

MISS SNEVELLICCI. Oh, yes, I'm absolutely sure that he'll remember. (*Focus shifts to* LILLYVICK.)

FOLAIR. Come, sir, cheer up, it is soon done.

LILLYVICK. What is?

FOLAIR. The tying up, the fixing of one with a wife. It is quickly o'er. Just like a hanging, what?

LILLYVICK. Like hanging?

LENVILLE. Come on, now, Tommy none of that.

FOLAIR. Yes, yes, you know, to hang oneself takes but a moment—

LILLYVICK. Do you compare, sir, do you draw a parallel—(FOLAIR *miming a hanging.*) Between my matrimony and a hanging?

FOLAIR. (*Still miming.*) Yes, yes, the—

LILLYVICK. You say this in the house of Mr. not to mention Mrs. Crummles, who have brought up such a family, chock full of blessings and phenomena, you call their state a noose?

FOLAIR. Well, just a little joke—(*The* BRIDAL PARTY *has arrived.*)

MISS PETOWKER. Oh, Lillyvick.

LILLYVICK. (*Turning to* MISS PETOWKER.) My dear, d'you know what this, your actor friend—

MISS PETOWKER. Oh, Lillyvick . . . (LILLYVICK *stops, realising his Bride has arrived in her full finery on her wedding morning. He embraces* MISS PETOWKER.)

MISS PETOWKER. Oh, Lillyvick . . . You will remember, won't you? Always, always, always?

LILLYVICK. Uh, remember what, my dear? (*Enter* CRUMMLES *in 18th-century costume, clearly dressed as the Heavy Father, followed by the* INFANT PHENOMENON, *covered in artificial flowers, and* MRS. CRUMMLES, *as the Distraught Mother. Some "oohs" and "ahs" from the rest.* MRS. CRUMMLES *kisses* MISS PETOWKER, *and is overcome.*)

CRUMMLES. Come, stir, stir, stir! The second cock hath crow'd, the curfew bell has rung, 'tis—(*He looks at an enormous fob watch.*) Nine o'clock.

MISS PETOWKER. (*Dramatically.*) 'Tis nine o'clock, dear Lillyvick. Come, sir. (*A wedding anthem plays.* MR. CRUMMLES *takes the arm of the* BRIDE, *and walks upstage with a feeble gait. The* COMPANY *form into a procession, two by two: the* BRIDESMAIDS, MRS. CRUMMLES *with the* PHENOMENON, *the other* ACTRESSES; *then* LILLYVICK *and* FOLAIR, *the other* ACTORS, NICHOLAS *and* SMIKE, *and, at the rear, the drunken* MR. WAGSTAFF. MR. LILLYVICK *is having difficulty trying to imitate the dramatic gait of the* COMPANY, *and in particular of* MRS. CRUMMLES. *The* COMPANY *arrives at the back of the stage, forms up in two lines—the* BRIDE *and* GROOM *now together in the middle—and they all walk forward.*)

THE ANTHEM. How blest are they that fear the Lord.
And walk in His way
For thou shalt eat the labour of thine hands
Well, well is thee and happy shalt thou be.
Thy wife shall be

The fruitful vine on the walls of thy house
Thy children like the olive branches
Growing, growing round about thy table.
Lo, thus shall the man be blest
That feareth the Lord.
Lo, thus shall the man be blest
That feareth the Lord.

(*And there is Narration as the* BRIDE *and* GROOM *run out, the former throwing her bouquet, which is caught by* MISS SNEVELLICCI.)

NARRATORS. And Mr. Lillyvick and his bride departed to take the steamboat to Ryde, where they were to spend the next two days in profound retirement. (*The Company beginning to disperse, leaving only* NICHOLAS *and* SMIKE.)

And Mr. Crummles declared his intention of keeping the celebrations going till everything to drink was disposed of;

But Nicholas, having to play Romeo for the first time on the ensuing evening, and anxious on account of Smike—who would have to sustain the character of the apothecary—contrived to slip away. (*And only* NICHOLAS *and* SMIKE *are left.*)

SCENE 16

Portsmouth and London. Bare stage. This is a double scene, counterpointing NICHOLAS' *rehearsal of* SMIKE *as the* APOTHECARY *with* RALPH'S *dealings in London. There is an overlap between each scene, so* SMIKE *and* NICHOLAS *don't go out until the next little sequence is underway, and vice versa. First,* NICHOLAS *and* SMIKE; *and, during it,* RALPH *and* NOGGS *enter.* NICHOLAS *has a copy of* Romeo and Juliet *with him.*

NICHOLAS. (*Prompting.*) Who calls so loud?
SMIKE. Who calls so loud.
NICHOLAS. Come hither, man. I see that thou art poor.
Hold, there is forty ducats. Let me have

A dram of poison. Such soon-speeding gear
As will disperse itself through all the veins
That the life-weary taker may fall dead,
And that the trunk may be discharged of breath
As violently as hasty powder fired
Doth hurry from the fatal cannon's womb.
(*Pause. Prompting.*)
Such mortal drugs I have—
SMIKE. Such mortal drugs I have . . .
NICHOLAS. But Mantua's law—
SMIKE. But Mantua's law. . . .
Is death to any—one who utters them.
NOGGS. Are you at home?
RALPH. I'm not.
NOGGS. You're sure?
RALPH. Of course I'm sure.
NOGGS. Well, they're downstairs.
RALPH. Who are?
NOGGS. Two gentlemen.
RALPH. You didn't tell me.
NOGGS. Didn't ask. Ah, here they are. (*Enter* SIR
MATTHEW PUPKER *and* MR. BONNEY. NOGGS *remains
in the background.*)
RALPH. Sir Matthew Bonney. What can I—
BONNEY. Look, Nickleby. This matter, your invest-
ment in our company—
RALPH. Yes, yes. I have resolved to realise my capital.
BONNEY. But, Nickleby—withdrawal of a sum of that
proportion, now—nine thousand?
RALPH. Ten.
BONNEY. At this stage, when the stock's still going
up—
RALPH. Will make the price fall. Yes, I know.
BONNEY. The bubble—bursts!
RALPH. Yes, certainly. But I have need of it.
SIR MATTHEW. Now, Nickleby. . . .
RALPH. Sir Matthew?
SIR MATTHEW. Have you not considered this, this mat-
ter, who's involved? The highest level? Have you no
thought for your country?
RALPH. I have thought of it, my country, to the same
extent as you have, sir. Good day. (SIR MATTHEW *looks
at* BONNEY, *who shrugs apologetically*. SIR MATTHEW,

with a huge gesture of rage and frustration, storms out followed by BONNEY. RALPH *to* NOGGS.) My hat and stick.

NOGGS. Your hat and stick.

RALPH. Well, then? Don't stand, repeating what I've said. You're not a parrot.

NOGGS. Wish I was.

RALPH. Well, so do I. Then I could wring your neck. And then I would be done with you. (RALPH *strides out.* NOGGS *stands there for a few moments, as* SMIKE *and* NICHOLAS *re-enter.*)

NICHOLAS. Art thou so bare and full of wretchedness,
And fearest to die? Famine is in thy cheeks,
Need and oppression starveth in thy eyes,
Contempt and beggary hangs upon thy back;
The world is not thy friend, nor the world's law;
The world affords no law to make thee rich;
Then be not poor, but break it, and take this.
(*Pause. Prompting.*)
My poverty—

SMIKE. My poverty. . . .

MRS. NICKLEBY. (*Off.*) Kate. Kate, my dear.

NICHOLAS. But not my will—

KATE. (*Off.*) Mama?

SMIKE. But not my will—consents.

(SMIKE *and* NICHOLAS *go as* MRS. NICKLEBY, *with* RALPH, *enters to* KATE.)

MRS. NICKLEBY. You are to dine, with your uncle, half-past six tomorrow.

KATE. Uncle, what is this?

RALPH. I have a party of—of gentlemen, to whom I am connected in some business, at my house tomorrow and your mother's promised that you shall keep house for me. I'm not much used to parties; but such fooleries are often part of business—and I hope that you won't mind obliging me.

MRS. NICKLEBY. Mind? Mind? My dear Kate, tell—

KATE. I shall be very glad, of course—but I'm afraid you'll find me very awkward and embarrassed.

RALPH. No, oh no . . . Come when you like, and take

a hackney coach. I'll pay for it. Good night and, um, God bless you. (*Exit* RALPH.)

MRS. NICKLEBY. Well, Kate. Your uncle's taken quite a fancy to you, that is clear, and if good fortune doesn't come to you from this, I shall be most surprised. (KATE *and* MRS. NICKLEBY *go out during* SMIKE *and* NICHOLAS.)

SMIKE. My poverty and not—

NICHOLAS. My will—

SMIKE. Consents.

My poverty and not my will consents.

NICHOLAS. I pay thy poverty and not thy will.

SMIKE. My poverty and not my will consents.

NICHOLAS. Uh—no—(NICHOLAS *takes* SMIKE *out, as a* MAN *enters one side, and on the other,* RALPH *and* NOGGS. NOGGS *has a plate of muffins, which he gives to* RALPH.)

NOGGS. He's here. I got him tea. But he's not eating it. (RALPH *gestures to* NOGGS, *who goes.* RALPH *to the* MAN.)

RALPH. Sir Mulberry. (SIR MULBERRY HAWK *is an elegant, though dissipated, rake. He holds a bottle and a glass.*)

HAWK. (*Pouring a drink.*) Hm. Nickleby. Is everything arranged?

RALPH. It is. Um—have you taken tea? (SIR MULBERRY HAWK *raises his glass, in answer.*) The gull will come?

HAWK. Lord Frederick? Of course. I told him that the evening would be both—an entertainment, and of profit. Will it be?

RALPH. Oh, yes. For us, at least. And, for the first, I think . . . there will be an attraction, for his lordship, present. For the second, I am able to advance. . . . as much as he, and you, will need.

HAWK. You're sure of that?

RALPH. Oh, yes. I am prepared. (*Offering the plate.*) Look, please, Sir Mulberry, at least . . . Do have a muffin. Hm? (*Enter* SMIKE *and* NICHOLAS. *They are in costume for the performance:* NICHOLAS *as* ROMEO *and* SMIKE *in a grey gown as the* APOTHECARY.)

NICHOLAS. There is thy gold—worse poison to men's souls,

Doing more murder in this loathsome world,
Than these poor compounds that thou mayst not sell.
I sell thee poison; thou hast sold me none.
Farewell.
(RALPH *goes*. MRS. GRUDDEN, *dressed as* JULIET'S
NURSE, *marches across the stage.*)
MRS. GRUDDEN. Act Three! Act Three! Beginners,
orchestra! (NICHOLAS *and* SMIKE *smile at each other.*)
SMIKE. Who calls so loud?
NICHOLAS. Who calls so loud. (*They go out.*)

SCENE 17

*Ralph's drawing room, in London. A chaise longue,
surrounded by* MEN *in evening dress, including* SIR MUL-
BERRY HAWK, *his young friend* LORD FREDERICK VERI-
SOPHT, *and his acolytes* MR. PLUCK *and* MR. PYKE. *On
another chair sits the elderly* COLONEL CHOWSER, *near to
him stand the* HONOURABLE MR. SNOBB *and a* MAKE-
WEIGHT. *A* FLUNKEY *is in attendance.* RALPH *enters with*
KATE.

RALPH. Gentlemen. My niece, Miss Nickleby. (KATE
notices they're all men.)
VERISOPHT. Eh. What the devil.
PYKE. (*To* PLUCK.) Hm . . . Hm.
RALPH. My niece, my lord. Kate, Lord Frederick
Verisopht.
VERISOPHT. (*Coming forward.*) Well, then me ears did
not deceive me, and it's not a waxwork. How d'ye do,
Miss Nickleby. (KATE *curtseys.*)
PYKE. (*Coming forward.*) Now, don't you leave me
out, now, Nickleby.
RALPH. And this is Mr. Pyke.
PLUCK. Nor me.
RALPH. And Mr. Pluck, my dear. (KATE *curtseys
again.* SNOBB *stands.*) And the Honourable Mr. Snobb,
and (CHOWSER *getting to his feet, not without difficulty.*)
this is Colonel Chowser. (*The* MAKEWEIGHT *obviously
isn't going to be introduced, but takes advantage of the
situation to go and get another drink from the* FLUNKEY.)
CHOWSER. Pleased. So very pleased. (*A slight hiatus,
broken as* SIR MULBERRY HAWK, *in one assured move-*

ment, takes the MAKEWEIGHT'S *glass of wine,* KATE'S *arm, and everyone's attention.*)

HAWK. Miss Nickleby, forgive us. Let me sit you down.

KATE. Why, sir I—

HAWK. (*Gliding* KATE *to the chaise.*) And, as I'm left out, damn you, Nickleby, I'll do the offices myself. (KATE *sits.*) Hawk, Miss Nickleby, and at your service. (HAWK *gives* KATE *the glass of wine.*)

KATE. Why, thank you, sir.

RALPH. (*To explain to* KATE.) Sir Mulberry. (VERISOPHT *to* RALPH.)

VERISOPHT. An unexpected pleasure, Nickleby. Indeed, one might say, it'd almost warrant the addition of an extra two and a half percent.

HAWK. (*Turns to* PLUCK.) Eh, Nickleby should take the hint, and tack it on the other five-and-twenty, and give me half for the advice. (PLUCK *and* PYKE *laugh uproariously as* VERISOPHT *comes to stand on the other side of* KATE'S *chair from* HAWK.)

VERISOPHT. Well, certainly, if he'll see to it you're not monopolising dear Miss Nickleby all night, Sir Mulberry.

RALPH. (*Lightly, as he goes to the* FLUNKEY.) Well, my lord, he does have a tolerable share of everything you lay claim to.

VERISOPHT. Gad, so he has. Devil take me, sometimes, if I know who's master in me own house. But I swear . . . I'll cut him off with but a shilling, if he—

HAWK. Sir, when you're at your last shilling, I'll be cutting you. While here is poor Miss Nickleby who's doubtless bored to tears with all this talk of discount, and hoping that some gallant fellow'll make love to her. Now, ain't that so, Miss Nickleby?

KATE. No, sir, indeed. . . .

HAWK. In fact, I'll hold you, any of you, fifty pounds, that Miss Nickleby can't look me in the face, and then deny that she was hoping so. (*To* LORD FREDERICK VERISOPHT.) My Lord?

KATE. Oh, sir. . . .

VERISOPHT. Well, why not? Done! Within a minute.

HAWK. Done. Now, Mr. Snobb, you'll take the stakes, and keep the time?

SNOBB. (*Coming to them.*) Of course. (*The* GENTLE-

MEN *produce money.* KATE *standing and going to* RALPH.)

PYKE. That's fifty pounds. . . .

CHOWSER. (*Unable to get up, pulling at* PLUCK.) Hey, you, sir, pass me bet. . . .

KATE. Uncle, please. . . . please, stop them making me the subject of a bet.

RALPH. Oh, my dear . . . It's done in a moment, and there's nothing in it. . . . If the gentlemen insist—

SNOBB. One—minute! (HAWK *comes and takes* KATE'S *hand, and leads her back to the chaise.*)

HAWK. I don't insist on it. That is, I don't insist that she denies, for even if I lose, it's worth it just to see her eyes, which seem to love the carpeting so much.

VERISOPHT. That's true. It's just too bad of you, Miss Nickleby.

PYKE. Too cruel.

PLUCK. Quite horrid cruel.

SNOBB. The lady can't deny that she was hoping for a gentleman to—um—within a minute . . . (*45 second pause.*)

HAWK. How goes it, Snobb?

SNOBB. Fifteen seconds left.

VERISOPHT. Won't you, for me, Miss Nickleby, just make one effort. . . .

HAWK. Oh, not a chance, my lord. Miss Nickleby and I understand each other very well.

SNOBB. Six, five, four, three. . . . (KATE, *outraged, looks* SIR MULBERRY *straight in the eye. Pause. Then she breaks, stands, and runs to the side of the room.*)

HAWK. Capital. That's a girl of spirit, and we'll drink to her health. (HAWK *nods to the* FLUNKEY, *who passes round drinks as* HAWK *collects his winnings.*)

PYKE. Oh, yes, we will.

PLUCK. Most definitely.

PYKE. Many times.

RALPH. But, perhaps, sirs, now the sport is over, you would care to drink it over dinner.

HAWK. Well, certainly. (PYKE *and* PLUCK *dislodge* CHOWSER *from his chair.* LORD VERISOPHT *to* KATE.)

VERISOPHT. (*Offering his arm.*) Miss Nickleby. . . .

KATE. No, no. . . .

RALPH. (*Gesturing the Company out.*) I'm sure Miss

Nickleby will join us in a moment. When she has composed herself.

VERISOPHT. But, Nickleby—

RALPH. I'm sure she will be down directly. Please, please, gentlemen. (*The Company leaves.* RALPH *is the last to go and* KATE *goes to him.*)

KATE. Please, uncle, don't—

RALPH. My dear. We are connected. And I can't afford . . . What is it, after all? We all have challenges. And this is one of yours. (RALPH *goes out.* KATE *is left there. Enter a heavily edited section of Act Three, Scene Five of* Romeo *and* Juliet, CRUMMLES *as* CAPULET, MRS. CRUMMLES *as* LADY CAPULET, MISS SNEVELLICCI *as* JULIET *and* MRS. GRUDDEN *as the* NURSE. *This scene is played around* KATE.)

CAPULET. How? Will she none? Does she not give us thanks?
Is she not proud? Doth she not count her blest,
Unworthy as she is, that we have wrought
So worthy a gentleman to be her bride?
JULIET. Proud I can never be of what I hate.
CAPULET. God's bread! It makes me mad.
Day, night; hour, tide, time; work, play;
To have her matched; and having now provided
A gentleman of noble parentage,
To answer "I'll not wed. I cannot love;
I am too young, I pray you pardon me."!
Graze where you will, you shall not house with me.
Nor what is mine shall never do thee good.

(*Exit* CAPULET.)

JULIET. Is there no pity sitting in the clouds
That sees into the bottom of my grief?
Oh, sweet mother, cast me not away!
LADY CAPULET. Talk not to me, for I'll not speak a word.

(*Exit* LADY CAPULET, JULIET *and the* NURSE. *Re-enter* HAWK.)

HAWK. Yes, capital.
KATE. Oh, sir. . . .

HAWK. What a delightful studiousness. Was it real, now, or only to display the eyelashes? Why did I speak and destroy such a pretty picture?

KATE. Then please, be silent, sir. (HAWK *goes and sits next to* KATE.)

HAWK. No, don't. Upon my life, you mustn't treat me like this, dear Miss Nickleby. I'm such a slave of yours.

KATE. I wish, sir . . . You must understand, that your behaviour. . . .

HAWK. Come on, now, be more natural, Miss Nickleby, more natural, please. . . . (KATE *looks at him. Then she stands quickly.* HAWK *catches her skirt.*) A bit more natural, eh?

KATE. Oh, sir. Please. Instantly! Please let me go at once.

HAWK. Not for the world, Miss Nickleby. . . . (RALPH *has entered.*)

RALPH. What's this? (HAWK *looks round. He sees* RALPH, *lets* KATE *go, sits down and crosses his legs.* KATE *gestures vaguely.*) (*To* HAWK, *gesturing towards the door.*) Your way lies there, sir. (*Pause.* RALPH *shaking.*)

HAWK. (*Furious.*) Do you *know* me, you madman?

RALPH. Well. (*Pause.*)

KATE. (*In tears.*) Please, uncle. Let me go.

RALPH. Yes. Yes, of course. I'll take you to your carriage presently. (RALPH *takes* KATE'S *arm.*) But just one word. I didn't know it would be so; it was impossible for me to foresee it. (KATE *looking at* RALPH. RALPH *looking over her shoulder at* HAWK.) You have done no wrong. (KATE *goes out.*)

HAWK. Hm. You want the lord. Your pretty niece an "entertainment" for that drunken boy downstairs. (*He turns to* RALPH.) And if *he'd* come up here instead of me, you would have been a bit more blind, and deaf, and a deal less flourishing than you have been? (*Pause.*) Who brought him to you first? Without me, could you wind him in your net?

RALPH. That net's a large one, and it's rather full. Take care that it chokes no-one in its meshes.

HAWK. Oh—

RALPH. I tell you this. That if I brought her here, as a matter of business—

HAWK. Oh, yes, well, that's the word—

RALPH. (*Interrupts.*) Because I thought she might make some impression on the silly youth that you are leading into ruin, I knew, knowing him, that he'd respect her sex, and conduct. But I did not envisage I'd subject the girl to the licentiousness of a hand like you. And now we understand each other. Hm?

HAWK. Especially, of course, as there was nothing you could gain by it.

RALPH. Exactly so. (*Enter* LORD FREDERICK VERI SOPHT.)

VERISOPHT. So, there you are, the both of you. Now, are we not to dine? And do some business too?

RALPH. (*Deliberately.*) Of course, my lord. We'll dine. But business first. Two months to pay. At interest of twenty-five percent. Those are the terms, what sum had you in mind?

VERISOPHT. Oh, five—or ten?

HAWK. Say, ten.

RALPH. Ten thousand pounds. Now, gentlemen, I'll join you very soon. (HAWK *and* VERISOPHT *go out one way,* RALPH *another. Two* CRUMMLES STAGE-HANDS *run in with flats, which they set up as if the prompt side wing of our theatre was the audience of the Portsmouth Theatre.* NICHOLAS, *as* ROMEO, *walks on to "stage"—facing off our stage. In the Portsmouth wings, downstage in our theatre, are* MASTER CRUMMLES, *waiting to enter as* BALTHAZAR, *and* SMIKE, *waiting to go on as the* APOTHECARY. SMIKE *is concentrating very hard, mumbling through his lines.*)

ROMEO. If I may trust the flattering truth of sleep,
My dreams presage some joyful news at hand.
(*"Enter"* BALTHAZAR.)
News from Verona! How fares Juliet?
For nothing can be ill if she be well.
BALTHAZAR. Then she is well, and nothing can be ill.
Her body sleeps in Capel's monument,
And her immortal part with angels lives.
ROMEO. Is it e'en so? Then I defy you, stars!
Thou knowest my lodgings. Get me ink and paper
And hire post-horses. I'll be with you straight.
(*Exit* BALTHAZAR.)
Well, Juliet, I will lie with thee tonight.
Let's see for means. O mischief, thou art swift
To enter in the thoughts of desperate men!

In do remember an apothecary,
And hereabouts 'a dwells, which late I noted
In tatt'red weeds, and overwhelming brows,
Culling of simples. This should be the house.
What, ho! Apothecary!
(*Pause.* SMIKE *has been concentrating so hard, he's missed his cue.* NICHOLAS *repeats.*)
What, ho! Apothecary!
(SMIKE *rushes on, and bellows out.*)
APOTHECARY. Who calls so loud?
(*And* NICHOLAS *leads him away, as* RALPH *brings* KATE *downstage.*)
KATE. And as the door of her carriage was closed, a comb fell from Kate's hair, close to uncle's feet; and as he picked it up and returned it into her hand, the light from a neighbouring lamp shone upon her face. (RALPH *is lit.*)
RALPH. The lock of hair that had escaped and curled loosely over her brow, the traces of tears yet scarcely dry, the flushed cheek, the look of sorrow, all fired some dormant train of recollection in the old man's breast; and the face of his dead brother seemed present before him, with the very look it wore on some occasion of boyish grief, of which every minute circumstance flashed upon his mind, with the distinctness of a scene of yesterday. (*And* NEWMAN NOGGS *appears.*)
NOGGS. And Ralph Nickleby, who was proof against all appeals of blood and kindred—who was steeled against every tale of sorrow and distress—staggered while he looked, and reeled back into the house, as a man who had seen a spirit from a world beyond the grave. (*Darkness.*)

SCENE 18

The stage of the Portsmouth Theatre. A tatty, Crummlesian set for the last scene of Romeo and Juliet. *Downstage,* MISS SNEVELLICCI—as JULIET—*and* MR. LENVILLE—as TYBALT—*lie on couches, as if dead. Upstage, a badly painted cut-out of two arches, and behind that, a backcloth of Verona.*
A note on this scene: There is much opportunity here, in addition to the written jokes, for merriment. In the orig-

inal production, one of the best visual jokes was an increasing pile of mattocks, irons, torches and swords that were dumped, during the first half of the scene, downstage, between the two couches, and over which people had to walk. There are many other opportunities for making the point that the Crummles Company are a troupe of not-very-good actors and actresses who have to rehearse plays very quickly, and therefore do not always get everything sorted out beforehand. Enter MR. BANE *as* PARIS *and* MISS BELVAWNEY *as his* PAGE.

PARIS. Give me thy torch. Do as I bid thee, go.

PAGE. (*Aside.*) I am almost afraid to stand alone.

Here in the churchyard; yet I will adventure.

PARIS. Sweet flower, with flowers thy bridal bed I strew

Which with sweet water nightly I will dew;

(*The* PAGE *whistles.*)

The boy gives warning something doth approach.

(PARIS *retires. Enter* NICHOLAS *as* ROMEO, *and* MASTER CRUMMLES *as* BALTHAZAR, *with a mattock and a crow of iron.*)

ROMEO. Give me that mattock and the wrenching iron.

Give me the light. Therefore hence, be gone.

Live, and be prosperous, and farewell, good fellow.

BALTHAZAR. (*Aside.*) For all this same, I'll hide me hereabout.

His looks I fear, and his intents I doubt.

(BALTHAZAR *retires.* ROMEO, *opening the tomb.*)

ROMEO. Thou detestable maw, thou womb of death,

Gorged with the dearest morsel of the earth.

(PARIS *strides forward.*)

PARIS. Stop thy unhallowed toil, vile Montague!

Condemned villain, I do apprehend thee.

ROMEO. Good gentle youth, tempt not a desperate man,

By urging me to fury. O, be gone!

PARIS. I apprehend thee for a felon here.

ROMEO. Wilt thou provoke me! Then, have at thee, boy!

PARIS' PAGE. O, lord, they fight! I will go call the watch.

(PARIS *falls.*)

PARIS. Oh, I am slain! If thou be merciful,
Open the tomb, and lay me with Juliet.
(*He shuts his eyes.*)

ROMEO. In faith I will. Let me peruse thy face.
Mercutio's kinsman, noble County Paris!
(*Pulling* PARIS' *body into the tomb.*)
I'll bury thee in a triumphant grave.
A grave? Oh, no, a lanthorn, slaughtered youth,
(*Dropping* PARIS' *body and running to* JULIET.)
For here lies Juliet, and her beauty makes
This vault a feasting presence full of light.
Tybalt, liest thou there in thy bloody sheet?
Why art thou yet so fair? Shall I believe
That unsubstantial death is amorous.
For fear of that I still will stay with thee
With worms that are thy chambermaids. O, here
Will I set up my ever lasting rest.
Here's to my love! Thus with a kiss I die.

(*He drinks the poison and kisses* JULIET. *Outside the tomb, enter* MR. FLUGGERS *as* FRIAR LAWRENCE. *He carries a crow and spade.*)

FRIAR. St. Francis be my speed! How now! Who's there!

BALTHAZAR. Here's one, a friend, and one that knows you well.

FRIAR. Alack, alack, what blood is this which stains
The stony entrance of this sepulchre?

BALTHAZAR. Then what I took to be a dream is true,
And—further horror—I did hear him speak
Of some fell liquor that with venomous speed
Would him to death's black bosom swift despatch.

FRIAR. Then all is lost! Juliet still sleeps—
What unkind hour is guilty of this chance!
The watch approaches, we must fast away;
Come, come, good friend, we dare no longer stay.

(*The* FRIAR *and* BALTHAZAR *run out. In the tomb,* JULIET *wakes.*)

JULIET. What's here? A cup, closed in my true love's hand?
Poison, I see, hath been his timeless end.
Oh, churl! Drunk all, and left no friendly drop
To help me after? What, and Paris too?

(JULIET *goes to* PARIS' *body*.)

Oh, County, that would take my maidenhead:

Lie here, thy dagger rests in Juliet's bed.

(JULIET *about to stab herself with* PARIS' *dagger*. ROMEO *sits up*.)

ROMEO. Hold, hold! I live!

JULIET. What, Romeo, not dead?

ROMEO. The pothac's poison coursed throughout my veins

A dizzy drowsiness which I mistook

For that numb torpor which doth presage death,

But in an instant it has passed. What, Juliet?

JULIET. Oh, Romeo, thou starts. I am not dead

For I too drank a draught of fluid that

Had longer but the same benign effect!

(*The* WATCHMAN, *played by* MR. PAILEY, *the comic countryman, appears*.)

WATCHMAN. What's there? Who's that within! What's there! What ho!

Come, lights! Come, malting hooks! Look! Here! Look ho!

ROMEO. We are approached.

(*Enter the* PRINCE, *played by* MR. WAGSTAFF, *the drunken, virtuous old man. Falling to his knee*.)

WATCHMAN. Good morrow, noble Prince.

PRINCE. What calls our person from our morning rest?

(*He goes into the tomb. The* WATCHMAN *stands. Enter* CRUMMLES *as* CAPULET.)

CAPULET. What should it be, that is so shrieked abroad?

(*He goes into the tomb. Enter* MRS. CRUMMLES *as* LADY CAPULET, *and* JULIET'S LITTLE BROTHER, *played by* MASTER P. CRUMMLES, *and* PETER, *played by* MR. FOLAIR.)

LADY CAPULET. What fear is this which startles in our ears?

(*They go into the tomb*.)

PRINCE. Ah, Romeo!

JULIET'S BROTHER. Oh, sister!

LADY CAPULET. Paris!

PETER. Slain!

CAPULET. What strange reversal hath this morning brought,

With Romeo returned—

LADY CAPULET. He having fled,

Dead Juliet alive,

CAPULET. Quick Paris dead.

(PARIS *sits up*.)

PARIS. Not dead so much as stunned, for Romeo's blow.

Deflected from my heart, did but a moment give

The appearance and accoutrements of death.

JULIET. As with my potion!

ROMEO. And the pothac's draught!

(*Enter the irascible* MR. BLIGHTEY *as* MONTAGUE, MRS. LENVILLE *as* LADY MONTAGUE, MISS GAZINGI *as an* ATTENDANT, *and the* PHENOMENON *as* ROMEO'S LITTLE SISTER.)

MONTAGUE. What's this? The people cry of blackest death,

LADY MONTAGUE. Some others of deliverance divine,

MONTAGUE. Talk both of grief and joy's on every breath:

(*Enter* MISS LEDROOK *as* ROSALINE.)

ROSALINE. Oh Romeo!

ROMEO. Good heavens.

(*To* JULIET.) Rosaline.

(*Pause.* MR. WAGSTAFF'S *attention has wandered.* MRS. GRUDDEN'S *head appears from the prompt corner.*)

MRS. GRUDDEN. But mourning—

PRINCE. But mourning flowers now adorn a festival,

And merry peals o'ertake the tolls of funeral.

ROMEO. 'Tis true, our joy demands a cheerful bell:

Oh, Mother, Father, Sister mine as well!

(ROMEO *embraces his* LITTLE SISTER. *Pause. Someone nudges* MR. WAGSTAFF.)

PRINCE. Who's there?

(*Enter the* FRIAR, *who throws himself to the ground before the* PRINCE.)

FRIAR. Dread sovereign, in guilty flight

I did attempt to 'scape your wrathful judgement.

But conscience stayed my steps, and turned them round,

And, penitent, I here abase myself.

PRINCE. What, penitent? There is no crime, stand, see!

All those in chains of death are unbound, free.

FRIAR. What joy! Then further tidings I must tell,
For on my hurried passage, I did meet
Another whom the jaws of death let go:
See, here, Prince, is your kin, Mercutio!

(*Enter* MR. HETHERINGTON, *the swaggerer, as* MERCUTIO, *and* MISS BRAVASSA, *dressed as a man, as* BENVOLIO.)

CAPULET. Mercutio! Recover'd!
MERCUTIO. Ay, sirs, ay,
For though thought dead, and bourn for balming up
My friend Benvolio observed a breath
Of slight proportion on my countenance
And I was taken to a nearby town,
Where I was cured by surgeons of renown.
FRIAR. And further news comes with him. Speak, Benvolio!

(*Pause.* FOLAIR *gestures to* MISS BRAVASSA, *who shrugs, and points at* MR. WAGSTAFF.)

MRS. GRUDDEN. (*Appearing again.*) Yes, yes—
PRINCE. Yes, yes, Benvolio, speak.
BENVOLIO. I shall, my lord,
But 'tis a tale I fear will try thy patience,
But I swear 'tis true. My friends know, oft
In their society have I been told
In jest, I am too gentle for our revels,
And almost feminine in countenance,
With not a hair of manhood on my chin.
Oft has it been so said; and I have laughed,
And spoken gruff, and slapped my thigh, to counter it.
But now deception's o'er, and I confess
That from this same near town I once did flee,
Pursuant of a love that fate denied,
And so t'effect my passage, took myself
The form and outward clothing of that sex
To which my love but not myself belongs.

(BENVOLIO *reaches up, takes off his cap, and lets fall her long hair.*)

From nature let deceit no more disbar:
Benvolio become Benvolia!
PARIS. Ah me.
CAPULET. Ah?
LADY CAPULET. You?

BENVOLIA. Ay, sirs, 'tis he,
Who thus from fell disguise releases me.
PRINCE. So everything is done—
(*Enter* PARIS' PAGE, *followed by* BALTHAZAR *and the*
APOTHECARY.)
PAGE. What Paris? Oh!
Hath sweet concord o'ertaken—
BALTHAZAR. Romeo!
Upon the road, in flight, I did perchance
To come upon this wizened, withered man,
Who hobbling was along the way from Mantua,
And asked where he might find a desperate man
Who might have bought a deathly liquid from him.
From your description I resolved it was
That self-same wretch from whom you bought the
dram
Of poison in that self-same town. I asked
What was his purpose, and he told me straight,
The darkness, and his age, and dread infirmity,
Had caused him to prepare not poison, but
An harmless cordial, of sharp effect
But of no lasting peril.
(BALTHAZAR *notices everything else.*)
Oh. What's this?
ROMEO. Good Balthazar, all matters are resolved,
And good apothecary, thy mischance
Has proved the most enduring, happy circumstance.
PRINCE. And now at last may tocsin loudly ring?
And tabor sound? And minstrels sweetly sing?
ROMEO. Yes, yes. All's concluded. Everything is done.
(*The* COMPANY *is leaving the tomb, when* LADY CAPU-
LET *runs to the corse of* TYBALT, *and cradles it in her
arms.*)
LADY CAPULET. But what of Tybalt? Tybalt, still lies
locked
Within the dread embrace of dreader death.
CAPULET. Why, come, dear wife, a half an hour ago,
We'd thought a half-a-dozen kin were slain.
Let grievance cease, let Tybalt's bones remain.
LADY CAPULET. Yes, let it be.
(*She drops* TYBALT *back on the slab. This gesture hurts*
MR. LENVILLE'S *head.*)
Let Tybalt lie still there.

And to a merry dance let us repair.
PRINCE. A blooming peace this morning with it brings,
The sun for happiness shines forth his head,
Go hence, to have more talk of happy things,
All shall be pardoned, and none punished.
For never was a story better set
Than this of Romeo and his Juliet.

(*Blackout. The* CRUMMLES COMPANY *form up for their
curtain call, except for* MRS. CRUMMLES, *and the dou-
bles—if they are in the Company—of* SQUEERS, YOUNG
WACKFORD *and* BROOKER, *who have a quick change.
The lights come up, for the* COMPANY'S *curtain call. Then
they go down again, and* MRS. CRUMMLES *enters as* BRI-
TANNIA, *with helmet and union flag. The lights come up,
and with them, the music of the* CRUMMLES' *closing
song.*)
     MRS. CRUMMLES. England, arise:*
Join in the chorus!
It is a new-made song you should be singing.
See in the skies,
Fluttering before us,
What the bright bird of peace is bringing.
     CRUMMLES COMPANY. See upon our smiling land,
Where the wealths of nations stand,
Where Prosperity and Industry walk ever hand in
hand.
Where so many blessings crowd,
'Tis our duty to be proud:
Up and answer, English yeomen, sing it joyfully aloud!
Evermore upon our country,
God will pour his rich increase:
And victorious in war shall be made glorious in peace.
(*And now the* CRUMMLES' *closing song becomes our clos-
ing song, and the rest of our* COMPANY *enter:* KATE,
MRS. NICKLEBY, MR. *and* MRS. LILLYVICK; SQUEERS,
YOUNG WACKFORD *and one or more* DOTHEBOYS HALL
BOYS; *the* MANTALINIS; *available* KENWIGS; SIR MAT-
THEW PUPKER, HAWK, VERISOPHT *and* RALPH, *repre-
senting High Society;* MR. CROWL, NOGGS *and the ragged
beggar* BROOKER *representing the low. And in the middle,*

*See special note on copyright page.

NICHOLAS *and* SMIKE, *triumphant; as the Song moves to its climax.*)

WHOLE COMPANY. See each one do what he can
  To further God's almighty plan:
  The beneficence of heaven help the skillfulness of man.

  Every garner filled with grain,
  Every meadow blest with rain,
 Rich and fertile is the golden corn that bears and bears again.

  Where so many blessings crowd,
  Tis our duty to be proud:
  Up and answer, English yeomen, sing it joyfully aloud!

  Evermore upon our country
  God will pour his rich increase:
  And victorious in war shall be made glorious in peace.

(*And the lights fade finally on the tableau.*)

(END OF PART ONE)

PART TWO

ACT I

SCENE 1

As the audience come in, the COMPANY *mingles with them, welcoming them to the show. Eventually, the whole company assembles on stage. A* NARRATOR *steps forward, to start the re-cap of the story of Part One. During this Narration, the* COMPANY *makes small tableaux that remind us of incidents in Part One. It does not matter at all if actors or actresses who double appear, now, in the "wrong" costume.*

NARRATOR. The story so far. There once lived, in a sequestered part of the county of Devonshire,

MRS. NICKLEBY. A mother,

KATE. And a daughter,

NICHOLAS. And a son,

NARRATORS. Who, recently bereaved, were forced to journey up to London,

And to throw themselves upon the mercy of their only living relative, Ralph Nickleby.

RALPH. All three of 'em in London, damn 'em,

NOGGS. He'd growled to his clerk,

RALPH. And you, sir? You're prepared to work?

NARRATORS. He'd demanded of his nephew,

And receiving the firm answer

NICHOLAS. Yes!

NARRATORS. Ralph took Young Nicholas and found him a position in a school in Yorkshire run by

SQUEERS. Mr. Wackford Squeers.

NICHOLAS. Well, thank you, uncle. I will not forget this kindness.

NARRATOR. And arriving at the school, he met with

MRS. SQUEERS. Mrs. Squeers,

FANNY. Their daughter Fanny,

YOUNG WACKFORD. Their son young Wackford,

NARRATOR. And their poor drudge:

MRS. SQUEERS. Smike!

NARRATORS. And forty boys,

With pale and haggard faces,

Lank and bony figures,

Children with the countenances of old men,

All darkened with the scowl of sullen, dogged suffering.

SQUEERS. So—what d'you say?

BOYS. For what we have received, may the Lord make us truly thankful.

NARRATORS. Meanwhile, in London,

Nicholas' sister Kate

Was found employment by her uncle

MISS KNAG. At the millinery establishment,

MADAME MANTALINI. Of Mr. Mantalini,

MANTALINI. And his demned, engaging, captivating little Venus

MILLINER. Of a wife.

NARRATOR. She and her mother were taken from their lodgings in the Strand

MISS LA CREEVY. And from their friend and landlady, the portrait painter Miss La Creevy

NARRATOR. To a grim and meagre house nearby the Thames.

NOGGS. I'm sure, although it looks a little gloomy, that it can be made, quite—

KATE. Yes.

NARRATOR. While up in Yorkshire, Nicholas took tea with Fanny Squeers

TILDA. Her best friend Tilda Price

JOHN. And her bluff beau John Browdie

NARRATOR. And tried to make it absolutely plain to everyone that his supposed affection for Miss Squeers

NICHOLAS. Is the grossest and most wild delusion that a human being ever laboured under or committed.

NARRATOR. A statement which did not improve his status at the school—

FANNY. Oh, sir, I pity you—

NARRATOR. Any more than did his firm resolve to stop the thrashing of the poor drudge Smike—

NICHOLAS. Uh—this must stop.

NARRATOR. His beating of the schoolmaster himself—

MRS. SQUEERS. Get off him! Off him, monster!

NARRATOR. Or his and poor Smike's escape with the assistance of John Browdie.

JOHN. Eh? What? Beat the schoolmaster?

NARRATORS. To London.

Where their new friend Newman Noggs

NOGGS. Was making up the number and the punch

NARRATOR. At a party given by the Kenwigses downstairs.

KENWIGS. That's Mr.—

MRS. KENWIGS. Mrs.—

MR. LILLYVICK. And the latter's uncle, Mr. Lillyvick, the collector of the water-rate—

NARRATOR. And the latter's uncle's fancy—

MISS PETOWKER. Miss Petowker of the Theatre Royal, Drury Lane.

NICHOLAS. Three friends.

NARRATOR. Said Nicholas,

NICHOLAS. Three friends, in all the world. That bluff young fellow up in Yorkshire, Smike, yourself; and Mr. Noggs our benefactor. And it is enough. It is indeed.

KATE. I won't believe it,

NARRATOR. Kate cried to her uncle, who had heard of everything from Fanny Squeers.

NICHOLAS. It is untrue,

NARRATOR. Insisted Nicholas.

MRS. NICKLEBY. I don't know what to think,

NARRATOR. Said Mrs. Nickleby.

RALPH. Then I'll renounce you all—

NARRATORS. Announced their uncle.

And Nicholas was forced to leave his family once again . . .

NICHOLAS. Or else . . . you're destitute.

NARRATOR. And he and Smike then journeyed south to Portsmouth, with the thought, perhaps, of going on board ship, and little knowing what in fact did lie in store for them.

CRUMMLES. Yes, I am Vincent Crummles, and I am in the theatrical profession, my wife is in the theatrical profession, and my children are in the theatrical profession.

NICHOLAS. What?

CRUMMLES. (*Handing scripts to* NICHOLAS): And you can study Romeo, and Rover too, of course, you might as well, while you're about it, Cassio . . .

NARRATORS. And also an array of histrionic talent

That has never been assembled in one place

And on one stage before!

OTHER NARRATORS. Or since.

SMIKE. The stage!

MRS. GRUDDEN. Stand by! (*We are now beginning to transform into the next scene.*)

KATE. And Kate,

NARRATOR. In London,

MISS KNAG. Lost her situation with the millinery establishment.

NARRATORS. While Nicholas,

In Portsmouth,

MISS SNEVELLICCI. Found *his* increasingly congenial.

KATE. And Kate was invited by her uncle to a private party

RALPH. For some gentlemen with whom he was connected in a business matter.

NICHOLAS. While Nicholas was witness to the secret nuptials of Mr. Lillyvick and Miss Petowker,

MISS PETOWKER. Lately—of the Theatre Royal, Drury Lane. (NICHOLAS *and* SMIKE *slip out.*)

NARRATOR. And at her uncle's, poor Kate was subjected to attentions that were neither honourable nor welcome—

VERISOPHT. How d'ye do, Miss Nickleby.

HAWK. Oh, come on, now, be more natural, Miss Nickleby, more natural, please . . .

NARRATORS. While, back in Portsmouth,

Nicholas and Smike

Went on from strength to strength,

And it seemed

For at least that moment

That their troubles and misfortunes were at last behind them.

(SMIKE *enters in his Apothecary costume, with* NICHOLAS, *carrying his Romeo costume.*)

SMIKE. (*Raptly.*) Who calls so loud?

NICHOLAS. Who calls so loud. (*And we are in the next scene.*)

SCENE 2

Portsmouth Theatre. Backstage. A couple of skips, a flat or two. It is immediately after the Crummles' triumphant performance of Romeo and Juliet. MRS. GRUDDEN *drags a clothes rail across the stage. The rest of the* COMPANY *are going around, packing their costumes and props, preparing to go.*

MRS. GRUDDEN. All called at ten. Theatre now closing. Have you no homes to go to? (SMIKE *happily lopes off to give his costume to* MRS. GRUDDEN. LENVILLE, *who is clearly in some passion, is haranguing a doubtful-looking* FOLAIR, *as* MISS SNEVELLICCI *glides over to* NICHOLAS.)

MISS SNEVELLICCI. Well, Mr. Johnson.

NICHOLAS. Ah. Miss Snevellicci.

MISS SNEVELLICCI. Mr. Johnson, I have asked some members of the company to come to supper, Sunday.

My father, and my dear mama, are to visit me in Portsmouth, and I am sure will be dying to behold you.

NICHOLAS. Well, I'm sure I—

MISS SNEVELLICCI. And the Lillyvicks have now returned from honeymoon, and are so keen to see you once again.

NICHOLAS. Dear Miss Snevellicci, I can require no possible inducement, beyond your invitation.

MISS SNEVELLICCI. Oh, Mr. Johnson. How you—how you talk. (*The* MISSES BRAVASSA *and* GAZINGI *cross the stage, as* MISS SNEVELLICCI *graciously withdraws and* FOLAIR, *leaving* LENVILLE, *drifts over to* NICHOLAS.)

MISS BRAVASSA. So I said to Mr. Crummles, that it's him or me—

MISS GAZINGI. Well, I said, if he does that trip again, once more, I'll kill him.

FOLAIR. Well, Johnson. Yet another great performance.

NICHOLAS. (*Thinking he was referring to* MISS SNEVELLICCI.) Was it? (*Realising he isn't.*) Oh. You think so?

FOLAIR. Yes. Oh, yes. And Mr. Digby. After all the pains you took, with his rehearsal. (SMIKE, U., *is having a whale of a time, in conversation with* MR. BLIGHTEY *and* MISS LEDROOK.)

NICHOLAS. Well, he deserves all the help and kindness I can give him.

FOLAIR. He is a little—odd, though, isn't he?

NICHOLAS. He is, God help him.

FOLAIR. And devilish close. Nobody can get anything out of him.

NICHOLAS. What *should* they get?

FOLAIR. Zooks, Johnson! I'm only talking of natural curiosity. Of who you are, and who he is, and if indeed your name is really Mr. Johnson, and if Digby's Digby, and if not—

NICHOLAS. Whose—natural curiosity?

FOLAIR. Oh, Johnson, it's just jealousy, you know, theatricals, I tell them, after all, what if you had, escaped from gaol or something of that sort, or—(LENVILLE *is now standing watching* FOLAIR *and* NICHOLAS, *surrounded by other men.*)

LENVILLE. Well, Tommy, have you told him?

FOLAIR. Oh. (*Slight pause.*)

NICHOLAS. Um—told me what?

FOLAIR. (*Whispering.*) Oh, it's just that, since you joined, you see, old Lenville never gets the rounds he used to, and you get a couple every scene . . .

LENVILLE. Well, Tommy?

FOLAIR. (*Still whispering.*) And then the final insult, Tybalt, after all . . .

NICHOLAS. Go on.

FOLAIR. Go on. (*Breathes deeply.*) Now, Mr. Johnson, I'm to tell you, Mr. Lenville's ire will not be brooked.

NICHOLAS. That's Mr. Lenville's what?

FOLAIR. He naturally presents his compliments, via me, and informs you that it's his intention—(*To* LENVILLE.) Now? (MR. LENVILLE *nods.*) Intention, now, to pull your nose in front of all the company.

NICHOLAS. To pull my nose?

FOLAIR. That's right.

NICHOLAS. Folair, I've half a mind to pull your nose for saying so.

FOLAIR. (*Whispering.*) Now, come on, Johnson— (LENVILLE *strides forward.*)

LENVILLE. Right. (*He takes a step or two towards* NICHOLAS, *and then strikes a pose.*) Object of my scorn and hatred. I hold you in the most rank contempt. (LENVILLE *adjusts his cuff, walks over, and is promptly knocked down by* NICHOLAS, MRS. LENVILLE *utters a scream and runs to the prone* MR. LENVILLE, *and falls on him.*)

MRS. LENVILLE. Lenville! Dear, my Lenville.

LENVILLE. (*Raising his head.*) Do you see this, monster? Do you see this?

NICHOLAS. (*Walking over.*) What? Oh, yes. Well, now, why don't you apologise for all this nonsense, and we'll say no more about it.

LENVILLE. Never!

MRS. LENVILLE. Yes, yes, for my sake, Lenville, please, unless you'd see your wife a blasted corpse, dead at your feet!

LENVILLE. This is affecting. Yes, the ties of nature. The weak husband, and the father that is yet to be . . . relents.

NICHOLAS. Well, then, very good. And p'raps, sir, you'll be very careful, to what lengths your envy carries you another time, before you've ascertained your rival's temper. (*And* NICHOLAS *picks up Lenville's cane and breaks it across his knee, dusts his hands, and walks ove. to the exit, where he bumps into the entrance of* CRUMMLES, MRS. CRUMMLES, *and the* INFANT PHENOMENON.)

MRS. CRUMMLES. Mr. Johnson. Pray, pray, what is going on?

NICHOLAS. Oh, Mrs. Crummles. Well—

MRS. CRUMMLES. It is past midnight. (MRS. GRUDDEN *crossing.*)

MRS. GRUDDEN. Everybody out!

MRS. CRUMMLES. (*To everyone.*) We have performances to give. Upon the morrow. We must be prepared. Have slept. And rested. Run through our lines. Mused on our dance steps. And rehearsed our songs. Resolved to act a little better. Sobered up. (*Varied mumblings.*)

BLIGHTEY. Yes, well . . .

MISS BRAVASSA. Certainly. . . .

MRS. CRUMMLES. (*Sweeping all before her.*) So, now, stand not upon the order of your going. Go. Be off. Be absent. Now. Begone. (*The* COMPANY *disappear, except for* CRUMMLES, SMIKE *and* NICHOLAS.)

CRUMMLES. Ah, Johnson. What a woman.

NICHOLAS. Yes. I'm sorry, Mr. Crummles—

CRUMMLES. No. No, no. (*Pause.*) Sometimes, I think, the strain, the running of a company . . . Sometimes, I think, we're not immortal, Johnson. Even Mrs. Crummles. Sometimes I think, to settle down, a plot of land, we might bequeath to those who follow us . . . (*Pause.*) But, then. We're strolling players, Johnson. Outcasts. Rogues and vagabonds. That is our lot. We carry on. (MRS. CRUMMLES *reappears.*)

MRS. CRUMMLES. Well, Vincent?

CRUMMLES. (*More cheerfully.*) Yes. We carry on. (CRUMMLES *goes out with* MRS. CRUMMLES.)

SMIKE. Outcast.

NICHOLAS. No, Smike. Not any more. (*Slight pause.*) Oh, Smike. I wish that this was over.

SMIKE. What's the matter?

NICHOLAS. Smike, I'm worried. And I've written to our dear friend Newman Noggs. To ask him of my mother and my sister.

SMIKE. Worried. Why?

NICHOLAS. Because . . . Because I have an enemy. He's rich and powerful, and he's done me many wrongs.

SMIKE. What is his name?

NICHOLAS. He is my uncle. His name's Ralph Nickleby.

SMIKE. I'll learn that name by heart. Ralph Nickleby. (SMIKE *notices Lenville's stick and picks it up*.) You beat my enemy.

NICHOLAS. Oh, Smike. The time that we've spent dallying here. (MISS SNEVELLICCI *and* MISS LEDROOK, *in their street clothes, stand there*.)

MISS SNEVELLICCI. Oh, Mr. Johnson.

NICHOLAS. Ah, Miss Snevellicci. (*Slight pause*.) Might I have the privilege . . . escort you home? (MISS SNEVELLICCI *puts out her arm*.)

MISS SNEVELLICCI. With the very greatest pleasure, Mr. Johnson. (NICHOLAS *takes* MISS SNEVELLICCI's *arm and leads her out*. SMIKE—*imitation*—*takes the arm of* MISS LEDROOK *and leads her out too*.)

SCENE 3

Regent St., London. A sofa, on which SIR MULBERRY HAWK *and* LORD FREDERICK VERISOPHT *are asleep. Debris around them.* MR. PLUCK *and* MR. PYKE *explain.*

PYKE. The place:

PLUCK. A handsome suite of private apartments in Regent Street. The time:

PYKE. Three o'clock in the afternoon to the dull and plodding—

PLUCK. The first hour of the morning to the gay and spirited. The persons: one: Lord Frederick Verisopht.

PYKE. And, two: his friend, the gay Sir Mulberry Hawk. (*The two men note the debris.*)

PLUCK. Two billiard balls, all mud and dirt.

PYKE. A champagne bottle, with a soiled glove twisted round the neck,

PLUCK. To allow it to be grasped more firmly in its capacity as an offensive weapon. A broken cane—

PYKE. An empty purse—

PLUCK. A handful of silver, mingled with fragments of half-smoked cigars,

PYKE. All hinting at the nature of last night's gentlemanly frolics. (*Pause. Then* LORD VERISOPHT *wakes*.)

VERISOPHT. What's that?

HAWK. (*Waking.*) What's what?

VERISOPHT. What's that you said?

HAWK. I didn't.

VERISOPHT. Yes, you did. Last night. You said something. About, eight hours ago. (*Slight pause.*) And then I fell asleep.

HAWK. Perhaps . . . I do recall. Uh—Nickleby.

VERISOPHT. The moneylender or the niece?

HAWK. The niece, of course.

VERISOPHT. Ah, yes. The niece. (VERISOPHT *sits up. Shortly.*) You promised me you'd find her out.

HAWK. I did. But thinking of it. You should find her out yourself.

VERISOPHT. Who, me? Why. How?

HAWK. (*Sits up.*) Just ask her uncle. Say to Nickleby, you must know where she lives, or else you'll cease to be his customer. That's if you're that concerned.

VERISOPHT. Oh, I am, that concerned. Upon my soul, Hawk, she's a perfect beauty, a—a picture. 'Pon my soul, she is.

HAWK. Well, if you think so—

VERISOPHT. You thought so. You were thick enough with her that night at Nickleby's.

HAWK. Oh, just enough for once. But hardly worth the trouble to be agreeable again. (*Pause. He stands.*) So. Shall we go?

VERISOPHT. (*Stands.*) Let's go. (*As they turn to go, the two men notice* MR. PLUCK *and* MR. PYKE.)

PLUCK. Good morning.

PYKE. Good morning.

HAWK. Good morning, Pyke.

VERISOPHT. Good morning, Mr. Pluck. (VERISOPHT *and* HAWK *walk out uneasily.*)

PYKE. And so Sir Mulberry accompanied his pupil, young Lord Verisopht,

PLUCK. to old Ralph Nickleby's at Golden Square.

SCENE 4

A drawing room in Sloane St. A chaise longue, a small table with a bell, and two chairs, are set up during the Narration. Enter KATE *and* MRS. NICKLEBY.

KATE. As, meanwhile, Miss Kate Nickleby herself,
MRS. NICKLEBY. And her mother Mrs. Nickleby,
NARRATORS. Set off from their mean lodgings in the
East End for Cadogan Place, off Sloane St.

Cadogan Place:

With the air and semblances of loftiest rank,

But the realities of middle station;

Cadogan Place: the one great bond that joins two great
extremes;

The link between the aristocratic pavements of Belgravia
And the barbarism of Chelsea.

Upon this doubtful ground lived Mrs. Julia Wititterly,

Whose advertisement for a companion had been read
that day by Mrs. Nickleby,
MRS. NICKLEBY. In a newspaper of the very first re-
spectability. (*And now* MRS. WITITTERLY *herself, a delicate woman in her late 30s, is reclining on the chaise
longue,* MRS. NICKLEBY *and* KATE *are sitting on the
chairs, and the page,* ALPHONSE, *is standing in attendance.* ALPHONSE *wears his wig and livery untidily. He
doesn't much like being called* ALPHONSE, *either.*)
MRS. WITITTERLY. Now leave the room, Alphonse.
ALPHONSE. Or right. (ALPHONSE *goes.*)
KATE. I have ventured to call, ma'am, from having
seen your advertisement.
MRS. WITITTERLY. Yes . . . One of my people put it
in the paper. (*Pause.*)
KATE. If you've already—
MRS. WITITTERLY. Oh, dear, no. I am not so easily
suited. Dear me, no. Well, I really don't know what to
say. How is your temper?
KATE. Well, I hope it's good.
MRS. WITITTERLY. You have a respectable reference
for everything?
KATE. I have. (*As she places a card on Mrs. Wititterly's*

table, MRS. WITITTERLY *glowers at her through her eye-glasses.*) Mr. Ralph Nickleby. My uncle.

MRS. WITITTERLY. (*Ringing her little bell.*) I like, I do like your appearance. (*Enter* ALPHONSE.) Alphonse, request your master to come here.

ALPHONSE. Please. (*A look from* MRS. WITITTERLY. ALPHONSE *goes.*)

MRS. WITITTERLY. Now, you have never actually been a companion before? (MRS. NICKLEBY *can stay silent no longer.*)

MRS. NICKLEBY. No, not to any stranger, ma'am, but she has been a companion to me for some years. I am her mother, ma'am.

MRS. WITITTERLY. Oh, yes. I apprehend you.

MRS. NICKLEBY. I assure you, ma'am, that I very little thought at one time that it would be necessary for my daughter to go out into the world at all, for her poor dear papa was an independent gentleman, and would have been so now if he had listened to my entreaties—

KATE. Please, mama.

MRS. NICKLEBY. My dear Kate, if you will allow me, I shall take the liberty—(*She is interrupted by the entry of* MR. WITITTERLY, *who is 38.*)

MR. WITITTERLY. (*To* MRS. WITITTERLY.) Yes? My love?

MRS. WITITTERLY. (*With a vague gesture.*) Companion. And her mother.

MR. WITITTERLY. Oh, yes. Yes, this is a most important matter. For Mrs. Wititterly is of a very excitable nature, very delicate, very fragile: one could describe, a hothouse plant; one could say, an exotic.

MRS. WITITTERLY. Oh, now, Henry, dear.

MR. WITITTERLY. You are, my love, you know you are. One breath and—(*He blows, as if a feather.*) Phoo, you're gone. (MRS. WITITTERLY *sighs.*) Your soul is too large for your body. Your intellect wears you out, and all the doctors say so. "My dear doctor", said I to Sir Tumley Snuffim in this very room, "dear doctor, what's my wife's complaint? Please tell me, I can bear it." "My dear fellow", he replied, "be proud of her, that woman. Her complaint is soul."

MRS. WITITTERLY. You make out worse than I am, now, Henry.

MR. WITITTERLY. I do not, Julia, do not: think, my dear, the night you danced with the baronet's nephew at the election ball at Exeter. It was tremendous!

MRS. WITITTERLY. (*To* KATE.) Yes, I always suffer for these triumphs afterwards.

MR. WITITTERLY. My wife is sought after by glittering crowds and brilliant circles. She's excited by the opera, the drama, the fine arts.

MRS. WITITTERLY. Henry, hush—

MR. WITITTERLY. I'll say no more. I merely mention it to demonstrate that you are not an ordinary person, and that there is a constant friction going on between your mind and body, that you must be soothed and tended, and that you must have a companion, in whom there is gentleness, great sweetness, an excess of sympathy, and of course, complete repose.

MRS. WITITTERLY. I am decided, Henry, that Miss Nickleby would be quite suitable. Now, I'm growing weary. Please . . .

MR. WITITTERLY. Yes, of course. (*To* KATE.) So, can you start tomorrow?

KATE. Yes, that would be most convenient.

MR. WITITTERLY. Then that is settled.

MRS. WITITTERLY. And in the evening you will join us to the opera.

MR. WITITTERLY. And Alphonse will appear to show you out. (MR. WITITTERLY *leads out* MRS. WITITTERLY.)

MRS. NICKLEBY. They are distinguished people, certainly.

KATE. You think so?

MRS. NICKLEBY. She is pale, however, and looks much exhausted. I do hope she isn't . . . wearing herself out.

KATE. What do you mean?

MRS. NICKLEBY. Oh, just . . . if suddenly the gentleman became a widower, and, after some appropriate elapse of time, decided to remarry, and, of course, with you engaged here—

KATE. (*Getting it.*) Oh, mama! You are impossible. (ALPHONSE *enters to show the ladies out.*)

ALPHONSE. This way.

SCENE 5

Ralph's office. On one side, a desk, with chairs either side. On the other side, a high stool in front of a high clerk's desk, on which are ledgers and a bell. RALPH sits at his desk, a watch to his ear. NOGGS is on his high stool.

NARRATOR. And at the very moment that they left Cadogan Place, in Golden Square, Kate's uncle Ralph sat in his office, being stared at through the little grubby window by his clerk, (RALPH *rings a little handbell on his desk.*) Who heard the bell, and went to answer it. (NOGGS *goes round into Ralph's office.*)

RALPH. How now?

NOGGS. (*Turns to go.*) I thought you rang. I'm sorry.

RALPH. Stop. I did ring.

NOGGS. Yes. What for?

RALPH. I called to say my watch had stopped.

NOGGS. I'm sorry.

RALPH. And to know the time.

NOGGS. It's half past three. Perhaps it isn't wound.

RALPH. It is.

NOGGS. Or overwound, then.

RALPH. That can't be.

NOGGS. Must be. It's stopped.

RALPH. Well, then. Perhaps it is. (HAWK, VERISOPHT, PLUCK *and* PYKE *appear in Noggs' office. Hawk rings the bell.*) That is the bell.

NOGGS. It is.

RALPH. Then answer it. (NOGGS *goes out and is passed by* HAWK, VERISOPHT, PLUCK *and* PYKE. *There is some acidity between* RALPH *and* HAWK.)

RALPH. Gentlemen. Good afternoon.

HAWK. Is it?

RALPH. Ah. A late night. But, I trust, a pleasurable one.

VERISOPHT. (*Joking.*) Well, an expensive one, at any rate. I'm fearful, Nickleby, I shall be drawing on your generosity again. (*A look from* HAWK *to* RALPH.)

RALPH. Oh, if . . .

VERISOPHT. And now, concerned with that, I'd like a word with you.

RALPH. Um . . . Certainly. (HAWK, PYKE and PLUCK *withdraw a little.*) What is it, then, my lord?

VERISOPHT. Your niece, sir.

RALPH. So, what of her?

VERISOPHT. She's a devilish pretty girl. You can't deny it.

RALPH. I believe she is considered so.

VERISOPHT. Look, Nickleby, I want another peek at her. And you must tell me where she lives. (*Slight pause.*)

RALPH. My lord—

VERISOPHT. Now, come on, Nickleby—

RALPH. My lord, she is a virtuous, country girl. She has been well brought up. It's true, she's poor, and unprotected—

VERISOPHT. Nickleby, I only want to look at her. (*Slight pause. Raising his voice.*) Nickleby, you know you're making a small fortune out of me, and 'pon my soul—

RALPH. (*Interrupting, in case* HAWK *hears.*) My lord, if I *did* tell you—

VERISOPHT. Yes?

RALPH. (*With a nod towards* HAWK.) You would, you'd have to keep it to yourself.

VERISOPHT. Oh, yes, of course I wouldn't—(*Enter* NOGGS.)

NOGGS. Erm—

RALPH. (*Sharply.*) What is it?

NOGGS. Mrs. Nickleby. (HAWK *gestures to* VERISOPHT. *They withdraw a little—as do* PYKE *and* PLUCK— *so* MRS. NICKLEBY *sails in.*)

MRS. NICKLEBY. Dear brother-in-law, I'm sorry to intrude, but I was sure you'd want to be the first to know that Kate is situated as companion with a Mrs. Julia Wititterly—(*Pause.* RALPH *stops her with a gesture.* MRS. NICKLEBY *notices the gentlemen.*) Oh, I'm so sorry—

HAWK. Mrs. Nickleby! (NOGGS *goes out.*)

RALPH. Uh, sister-in-law, these gentlemen were leaving—

HAWK. Leaving? Nonsense. So, this is Mrs. Nickleby, the mother of Miss Nickleby? But no. It can't be. No. This lady is too young.

MRS. NICKLEBY. I think, dear brother-in-law, you can tell the gentleman, that Kate Nickleby's my daughter.

HAWK. (*To* VERISOPHT.) Daughter, my lord, did you hear that? Daughter!

MRS. NICKLEBY. Lord?

HAWK. Now, Nickleby, at once, please, you must introduce us.

RALPH. Mrs. Nickleby: Lord Frederick Verisopht. Sir Mulberry Hawk. And, uh, Mr. Pluck and Mr. Pyke.

VERISOPHT. Upon my soul, this is a most delightful thing. Uh—how d'e do?

HAWK. I'm deeply charmed, dear lady.

PYKE. As am I.

PLUCK. And not to mention me.

MRS. NICKLEBY. (*Confused.*) Well, I don't—I'm quite overcome. (*Pause.* HAWK *nods at* VERISOPHT.)

VERISOPHT. And, how's your daughter, Mrs. Nickleby?

MRS. NICKLEBY. Oh, she's quite well, I am obliged to you, my lord . . . Quite well. She *wasn't* well for some days after she dined here, and I can't help thinking, that she caught cold in that hackney coach coming home. Hackney coaches, my lord, are such nasty things. I once caught a severe cold, my lord, from riding in one. I think it was in eighteen hundred and seventeen, and I was sure I'd never get rid of it, and I was only cured at last by a remedy that I don't know if you've happened to hear of, my lord. (SIR MULBERRY HAWK *nods to* PYKE *and* PLUCK, *who glide, as if on oiled rails, to either side of* MRS. NICKLEBY.) You heat a gallon of water as hot as you can possibly bear it, with a pound of salt and six pen'orth of the finest bran, and sit in it for twenty minutes every night, well, not all in it, obviously, but just your feet, and I tell you I used it on the first day after Christmas Day and by the end of April it had gone, the cold I mean, and I had had it since September. Now isn't that a miracle, my lord? (*Pause.* VERISOPHT *doesn't know quite how to react.* MRS. NICKLEBY *becomes aware of the presence of* MR. PLUCK *and* MR. PYKE.)

PYKE. What an affecting calamity.

PLUCK. It sounds quite—perfect horrid.

PYKE. But worth the pain of hearing, Pluck, to know that Mrs. Nickleby recovered.

PLUCK. That's the circumstance which gives it such a thrilling interest, there's no doubt, Pyke.

MRS. NICKLEBY. Oh, do you think so?

RALPH. Gentlemen . . .

HAWK. So. Your daughter has secured an attractive situation, ma'am?

MRS. NICKLEBY. That's right, Sir Mulberry, as from tomorrow, when her first task is to escort her new employers to the opera. (HAWK *flashes a look at* PLUCK *and* PYKE. MRS. NICKELBY *misinterprets*.) And I knew you'd be so pleased, dear brother-in-law, I walked straight here to tell you so. (*Another look from* HAWK.)

PYKE. But surely you don't intend walking home, Mrs. Nickleby?

MRS. NICKLEBY. Oh, no, Mr. Pyke, I intend to go back in an omnibus.

PLUCK. Well, isn't that a strange coincidence.

MRS. NICKLEBY. It is?

PYKE. Seeing as how the omnibus lies quite directly on our route, Pluck, isn't that the case?

PLUCK. It is indeed, and as we were just going—

PYKE. At this very instant.

PLUCK. We can escort dear Mrs. Nickleby.

MRS. NICKLEBY. (*Overcome.*) Well—I would be most grateful.

PLUCK. (*Ushering* MRS. NICKLEBY *out*.) Not half so grateful, Mrs. Nickleby, as we. (MRS. NICKLEBY *goes out with* PYKE *and* PLUCK. *A silence between* RALPH *and* HAWK *and* VERISOPHT. *The latter two bow and go out.* RALPH *alone*.)

RALPH. Sometimes—I wish I had not done this. (*Slight pause*.)

But still—she must take her chance.

SCENE 6

A London street. Bare stage. Enter MRS. NICKLEBY, PLUCK *and* PYKE.

MRS. NICKLEBY. Well, Mr. Pyke, and Mr. Pluck, I must express my gratitude, a seventh time.

PYKE. Oh, please don't, Mrs. Nickleby. A friend of Sir Mulberry Hawk, a friend of ours. Is that not so, Pluck?

PLUCK. Pyke, it's automatic. And, particularly, someone whom Sir Mulberry holds in such esteem.

MRS. NICKLEBY. Oh, surely not—

PLUCK. Now, Pyke, is Sir Mulberry's esteem of Mrs. Nickleby the highest?

PYKE. I should say the very highest, Pluck.

PLUCK. She cannot be in ignorance, of the immense impression that her daughter has—

PYKE. Pluck! Pluck, beware. (MRS. NICKLEBY'S *eyes popping. Pause.*)

PLUCK. Pyke's right. I should not have mentioned it. Thanks, Pyke.

PYKE. Pluck, not at all.

MRS. NICKLEBY. I'm sure that—

PLUCK. Mrs. Nickleby should take no heed of what I said. It was imprudent, rash. And injudicious.

PYKE. *Very* injudicious.

MRS. NICKLEBY. Now, you mustn't—

PLUCK. But, to see such sweetness and such beauty on the one hand, and such ardour and devotion on the other—pardon me, I didn't mean to speak of it again. Please change the subject, Pyke.

PYKE. Consider it, Pluck, changed.

PLUCK. But to think that we may actually see your daughter, at the opera, tomorrow evening!

MRS. NICKLEBY. What's that?

PLUCK. Oh, you didn't know?

PYKE. Of course she didn't, Pluck, how could she? It is just, dear Mrs. Nickleby, as luck would have it, we— that is, Sir Mulberry, Lord Verisopht, myself and Pluck, are going to the opera tomorrow!

MRS. NICKLEBY. You are!

PYKE. We are. (*Pause. Elaborately,* PLUCK *and* PYKE *snap their fingers, as if to indicate that they have here simultaneously realised the most obvious thing in the world.*)

PLUCK. Pyke, are you thinking what I'm thinking?

PYKE. Pluck, I believe our minds must be as one. Mrs. Nickleby.

MRS. NICKLEBY. Yes?

PYKE. Would you care to join us, in our box, at the opera tomorrow?

PLUCK. When we are sure you would be more than welcome.

MRS. NICKLEBY. But—

PLUCK. There's not a but in it, dear Mrs. Nickleby, we'll send a carriage round, at twenty before seven.

PYKE. And, see, here is the omnibus. (*Enter the* OMNI-BUS. *It is formed by Performers, jogging in pairs, each pair holding a pair of chairs behind and in front of them. In front jogs a* COACHMAN *with a whip. The* OMNIBUS *stops, the Chairs are put down. The coachman sits on the back of a chair, his feet on its seat.* MRS. NICKLEBY *sits on one of the back chairs. The Performers left without chairs become standing* PASSENGERS. *They mime being on a moving vehicle.* PLUCK *and* PYKE *disappear. The* PASSENGERS *narrate.*)

PASSENGER. And Mrs. Nickleby leant back in the furthest corner of the conveyance, and, closing her eyes, resigned herself to a host of most pleasing meditations.

MRS. NICKLEBY. Oh, Lady Hawk!

PASSENGER. She thought,

MRS. NICKLEBY. On Tuesday last, at St. George's Hanover Square! By the most Reverend the Bishop of Llandaff! To Catherine, the only daughter of the late Nicholas Nickleby, Esquire, of Devonshire!

PASSENGERS. And then her thoughts flew back, to old meditations, and the times she'd said that Kate would marry better with no fortune than some other girls with thousands,

And as she pictured, with all the brightness of a mother's fancy, all the grace and beauty of the girl who'd struggled cheerfully with her new life of hardship,

Her heart grew too full, and tears began to trickle down her face.

(*Fade on* MRS. NICKLEBY.)

SCENE 7

A London Opera House. Downstage are two boxes, represented by four chairs on either side of the stage. They face downstage. We imagine a corridor behind them. Behind that is the actual stage of the opera house, on which a genuine, complete, three-minute Opera is presented, in Italian. It tells the story of two lovers, the father of the female one of whom objects strongly to their secret love. Downstage of this, the following things happen in dumb-show: A box-keeper leads on MR. PLUCK *and* MR. PYKE, *who in turn are escorting* MRS. NICKLEBY. *Much solicitation of the latter by the two gentlemen. They are led into the first box, when the box-keeper realises from the tickets he has made a mistake, and leads them out again. As* PLUCK *leads* MRS. NICKLEBY *into the second box,* MR. PYKE *clearly threatens the poor box-keeper with great violence for his error;* PLUCK *seats* MRS. NICKLEBY *in the second box with great charm and ceremony.* PYKE *joins them.*

The box-keeper, having gone out, re-enters with SIR MULBERRY HAWK *and* LORD FREDERICK VERISOPHT, *both dressed up to the nines, but a little unsteady. The box-keeper, fearful of meeting up with* PYKE *again, points the two men to the second box.* HAWK *and* VERISOPHT *enter, greet* PLUCK, PYKE, *and, with much bowing and kissing of hands,* MRS. NICKLEBY. MRS. NICKLEBY *looks round, as if expecting someone else, but as no-one else is there, allows herself to be settled.*

The box-keeper enters again, this time with KATE NICKLEBY, JULIA WITITTERLY *and* HENRY WITITTERLY. *They are shown into the first box. Conversation about who should take which chair is overheard by* SIR MULBERRY HAWK, *who lays his finger on his lips—*MRS. NICKLEBY *is speaking—and summons* VERISOPHT *to the front of the box.* MRS. NICKLEBY *recognises her daughter's voice, stands, and greets her.*

MRS. NICKLEBY *indicates the other gentlemen in her box to* KATE, *who is clearly not best pleased.* MRS. NICKLEBY *gestures that she is coming round, and she—followed by the entire population of the second box, ups, goes into the corridor—during which* KATE *is explaining who these people are to the* WITITTERLIES, *the male half of which rushes eagerly to welcome all these lords and baronets.* KATE *stands there as* MRS. NICKLEBY, HAWK, VERISOPHT, PYKE *and* PLUCK—*the latter two only just— enter the box.*

MRS. NICKLEBY *gestures towards* KATE *to recognise* SIR MULBERRY. KATE *turns away but* SIR MULBERRY HAWK *comes forward with extended hand, and she is forced to shake it.* MRS. NICKLEBY *then gestures* KATE—

with some impatience, to recognise the others—VERI-
SOPHT, PLUCK *and* PYKE—*and then* MRS. NICKLEBY, *un-
able to understand* KATE'S *reticence, waves at her to
indicate that she should introduce the party to the* WITIT-
TERLIES. KATE *introduces* VERISOPHT, PLUCK, PYKE *and*
HAWK *to* MR. *and* MRS. WITITTERLY.

At the end of this ceremony, PLUCK *suggests to* HAWK
*that they should, perhaps, adjourn, as this box is very full.
"With so much skill were the preliminaries adjusted, that
Kate, despite all she could do or say to the contrary, had
no alternative but to be led away by Sir Mulberry Hawk."*
KATE *and* HAWK *are joined in the second box by* PLUCK,
who occupies MRS. NICKLEBY *in conversation. Remaining in the first box are* VERISOPHT, *the* WITITTERLIES
and PYKE. *The young lord is being fawned upon by* JULIA
WITITTERLY. MRS. NICKLEBY *is studiously avoiding in-
terfering with the conversation between* HAWK *and her
daughter.*

Finally, HAWK'S *attentions become intolerable, and*
KATE *stands, and makes to run into the corridor. At this
point, everyone turns their chairs upstage, to face the
opera, and so the corridor that* KATE *runs into is downstage of the chairs.* HAWK *follows and tries to kiss her.*
KATE *pushes him away.* VERISOPHT *emerges, with* PYKE,
from the WITITTERLIES' *box.* KATE *runs back into the*
WITITTERLIES' *box, and* HAWK *and* PYKE *escort* VERI-
SOPHT *back into their box, so we are now back where we
started, as the Opera finishes, and everyone except* KATE
stands and applauds the PERFORMERS. *Flowers are
thrown as the chairs are whisked away.*

SCENE 8

Ralph's office. RALPH *at his desk.* NOGGS *admits* KATE
to her uncle.

RALPH. Well, well, my dear. What now? (RALPH *a
sharp gesture.* NOGGS *withdraws, but we see he waits outside the room and listens.* KATE *too upset to say anything.*) Sit down, sit down. And tell me what's the
matter. (KATE *sits.* RALPH *sits near her. "He was rather
taken aback by the sudden firmness with which Kate
looked up and answered him."*)

KATE. Uncle, I've been wronged. My feelings have been hurt, insulted, wounded, and by men who are your friends.

RALPH. What friends? I have no friends, girl.

KATE. By the men I saw here, then. And have been persecuting me. And if they're not your friends, and you know what they are—more shame on you for bringing me among them.

RALPH. There's something of your brother in you, I can see.

KATE. I hope there is. I should be proud to know it. I will not bear these insults any longer.

RALPH. Insults? What d'you mean?

KATE. What do I mean? You ask me that? Remember, uncle, what took place in this house. (*Pause. She stands, goes to* RALPH, *puts her hand on his shoulder.*) I'm sorry, I don't mean to shout, be angry, violent. But you don't know what I have suffered. Oh, of course, you cannot tell what being a young woman feels like—how could I expect it?—but still, when I tell you that my heart is breaking, I am wretched, all I can ask is that you believe me. (RALPH *looking away.*) Uncle. I have had no counsellor, no-one to help or to protect me. Mother thinks they're honourable men, distinguished, and that, sad delusion, is the only thing she has to make her happy, and how could I undeceive her? You're the only person left. My only friend at hand. Almost my only friend at all. I need your help.

RALPH. Help? How can I help you, girl?

KATE. By telling them to stop. To leave me be. (RALPH *looks up at* KATE. *Pause.*) So will you tell them, uncle? (*Pause.*)

RALPH. No. They are my friends, in business. I cannot afford for them to be my enemies. Please understand. (*He turns to her. A slight smile.*) Some girls would be quite proud, to have such gallants at their feet. (*Pause.*) And even if, they are . . . it won't last long. Oh, soon enough, they'll find another entertainment. (*Pause.*) Surely, it is not too much to bear, just for a time?

KATE. Just for a time? I am to be wretched and degraded, and debased? Just for a time? (*Pause.*) Oh, uncle. You've been selling me. (*She turns and runs out.* RALPH *motionless. Outside,* KATE *stops, and breaks.*

NOGGS *steps towards her, puts his arm round her. She i.
too far gone to resist.)*

NOGGS. Oh, yes. Oh, yes. You're right to cry. But
even righter, not to give way, back in there. Oh that was
even righter. Now, cry, cry. I shall see you soon—and
so will someone else.

KATE. Must—go. Bless you.

NOGGS. You too. Yes, yes, of course, must go. (NOGGS
takes her towards the door.) Oh, you were right, in there,
right not to let him see you cry. (KATE *goes out.* NOGGS
*returns to his desk. A determined look on his face. "New-
man Noggs stood at a little distance from the door, with
his face towards it. And, with the sleeves of his coat turned
back at the wrists, was occupied in bestowing the most
vigorous, scientific, and straight-forward blows upon the
empty air. At first sight, this would have appeared merely a
wise precaution for a man of sedentary habits, with the view
of opening the chest and strengthening the muscles of the
arms. But the intense eagerness and joy depicted in the face
of Newman Noggs, which was suffused with perspiration:
The surprising energy with which he directed a constant suc-
cession of blows towards a particular panel about five feet
eight from the ground, and still worked away in the most
untiring and unpersevering manner, would have sufficiently
explained to the attentive observer, that his imagination was
threshing, to within an inch of his life, his body's most active
employer, Mr. Ralph Nickleby." NOGGS recovers from his
exertion. He goes to his desk. He finds a sheet of paper. He
looks round, to doublecheck he is alone. He begins to write
a letter.)*

NOGGS. My dear young man. (*He crosses out.*) Dear
Nicholas.

SCENE 9

*Portsmouth. Miss Snevellicci's apartments. The com-
pany is gathering for the party. It is simplest to describe
how they end up when* MR. SNEVELLICCI *calls for silence.
There are tables of various heights and sizes, all covered
with white cloths, jugs of wine, and glasses, arranged in
a rectangular shape, with one side—the audience's side—
of the rectangle missing. There is thus a long, central section, and two shorter sections coming downstage. Eventu-*

ally, the set-up will be that MR. SNEVELLICCI *is dead centre, with* MRS. SNEVELLICCI *on one side, and* MR. *and* MRS. CRUMMLES *on the other. The rest of the* COMPANY *fan out from there, with, as a general rule, the* WOMEN *on stage left and the* MEN *on stage right. The exceptions to that rule are* NICHOLAS, *who will sit next to* MISS SNEVELLICCI, MRS. GRUDDEN, *who sits at the downstage end of the Stage Right table,* MR. LILLYVICK, *who sits near, but not next to, his wife, the erstwhile* MISS PETOWKER, *and* SMIKE, *who hovers around pouring drinks and being helpful.*

At this point, however, not everyone is here: those not here appear in the next few moments. Downstage of the tables are, in three groups: NICHOLAS, SMIKE *and* FOLAIR; MR. *and* MRS. SNEVELLICCI *and* MISS SNEVELLICCI; *and* MR. *and* MRS. LILLYVICK. MR. SNEVELLICCI *is red-faced, bombastic, irritable and on the way to being drunk.*

FOLAIR. Well, there he is.

NICHOLAS. That's Mr. Snevellicci?

FOLAIR. Yes, it is.

NICHOLAS. And he—he is theatrical as well?

FOLAIR. Oh, certainly. Been in the business since he first played the ten-year-old imps in the Christmas pantomime. He can sing a little, dance a little, fence a bit, and act, but not too much . . . And since he's took to so much rum and water, tends to play the military visitors and speechless noblemen, you know . . . Ah, dear Mr. Snevellicci. (*For* MR. SNEVELLICCI *has come over to* FOLAIR, *with* MISS SNEVELLICCI.)

MISS SNEVELLICCI. Ah, mamma, papa, please do meet Mr. Johnson.

MR. SNEVELLICCI. Oh, a privilege, a privilege.

MRS. SNEVELLICCI. Indeed.

NICHOLAS. The pleasure's mine.

MR. SNEVELLICCI. And have to say, dear boy, that haven't seen a hit like that since my great, dear friend Mr. Glavormelly played the Coburg.

FOLAIR. (*Drifting off.*) Glavormelly. (*The rest of the Company still arriving.*)

MR. SNEVELLICCI. Ever see him, sir?

NICHOLAS. No, I'm afraid I never did.

MR. SNEVELLICCI. What, never saw old Glavormelly? Not seen acting, then, dear boy. If he had lived—

NICHOLAS. He's dead?

MR. SNEVELLICCI. Oh, yes, completely. Pushing up the daisies now, the bourne from which no traveller, et-cetera, and least can hope the poor old boot's appreci-ated there. Ah, there he is. Old bricks and mortar. Go and do my stuff. Excuse us, sir. (*And indeed, the* CRUM-MLES *family have entered, with last of the Performers, and* MRS. GRUDDEN. *As* MR. SNEVELLICCI *goes over to greet him,* MRS. SNEVELLICCI *takes the opportunity for a little word.*)

MRS. SNEVELLICCI. My daughter speaks quite strongly of you, sir.

NICHOLAS. Oh, does she?

MRS. SNEVELLICCI. Yes, she does. Quite, quite un-common strong.

NICHOLAS. Well, I assure you—

MRS. SNEVELLICCI. Yes, I know. (MRS. SNEVELLICCI *looks at* NICHOLAS, *and gives a little wink and a smile, and goes off to join her husband.* NICHOLAS *turns to see* MR. LILLYVICK, *whose wife is engaged in animated chat-ter with the other women.*)

NICHOLAS. Well, Mr. Lillyvick. And how are you?

LILLYVICK. Quite well, sir. There is nothing like the married state, depend on it.

NICHOLAS. Indeed!

LILLYVICK. How do you think she looks, sir? Mrs. Lillyvick, tonight?

NICHOLAS. She looks as handsome as she ever did. You are a lucky man.

LILLYVICK. You're right there, sir, you're right. I often think, I couldn't have done better if I'd been a young man, could I? You could not have done much better, could you? (*Jabbing* NICHOLAS *with his elbow.*) Eh?

NICHOLAS. Oh, no, I—(*He is interrupted by* MR. SNEVELLICCI, *who has finished greeting the* Crummleses, *has had another drink, and feels it's time to get this jambo-ree on the road.*)

MR. SNEVELLICCI. Right then! Silence! Class to order. (*The stragglers sit, including* NICHOLAS, *whose closeness to* MISS SNEVELLICCI *is noticed by the others.*) Ladies! Gen-tlemen. All welcome. In particular, the first. (*The ladies blush, the gentlemen applaud.*) And so, raise glasses. To the ladies. May God bless 'em. All of 'em. Unspliced and spliced, and those who are now in the former state, and who knows, very shortly, in the latter. (*This is so obvious a reference to* MISS SNEVELLICCI *and* NICHOLAS *that the actress reacts.*)

MISS SNEVELLICCI. Oh, papa!

MR. SNEVELLICCI. But then, who knows? I don't. Does anyone?

MISS SNEVELLICCI. Papa! (*And* MISS SNEVELLICCI *turns and runs, but is caught up with by the ladies, who cluster round her, covering her confusion.*)

MR. SNEVELLICCI. What's this? (MISS LEDROOK *runs from the cluster to* MR. SNEVELLICCI.)

MISS LEDROOK. Oh, don't take any notice of it, sir. Say, that she exerts herself too much.

MR. SNEVELLICCI. She whats?

MRS. LILLYVICK. (*Approaching.*) She's only weak, and nervous. She has been so since this morning.

MR. SNEVELLICCI. Weak?

MRS. SNEVELLICCI. They mean—don't make a fuss of it, my dear.

MR. SNEVELLICCI. A fuss? What do you mean? (MISS SNEVELLICCI, *recovered, comes over from the dispersing cluster.*) What? I'm to be instructed? Given marching orders? Told what I may do and say?

MISS SNEVELLICCI. Oh, pa, please don't—

MR. SNEVELLICCI. Don't what?

MISS SNEVELLICCI. Talk in that manner.

MR. SNEVELLICCI. Manner? Talk in any manner that I please. (MISS SNEVELLICCI *and* MRS. SNEVELLICCI *look at each other.*) I'm not ashamed. The name is Snevellicci. Found in Broad Court, Bow Street, when in town. If out, inquire at the stage door. Look, dammit, had me portrait in cigar shops round the corner. Mentioned in the papers. Tell you what, if I found any chap was tampering, affections of me daughter, wouldn't talk. I would astonish him. In silence. That's my way. That is—my manner. (*He downs his drink.*) Hmph. What was I saying?

MRS. CRUMMLES. You were toasting everyone.

MR. SNEVELLICCI. (*Remembering.*) Oh, yes. The ladies. All of 'em. I love 'em, every one. (*All the* MEN, *for the sake of getting it over with, raise their glasses.* MR. LILLYVICK *has been growing agitated for some little time.*)

THE MEN. The la—

LILLYVICK. Not all of them, sir, surely?

MR. SNEVELLICCI. Oh, yes. Every one.

THE MEN. The la—

LILLYVICK. But that includes the married ladies, sir.

MR. SNEVELLICCI. Oh course! The memsahibs, certainly.

THE MEN. The—

MR. LILLYVICK. What, including Mrs. Lillyvick?

MR. SNEVELLICCI. (*Impatiently.*) Why, yes, of course, including Mrs. Lillyvick. If I may say so, Mrs. L. especially. (*And* MR. SNEVELLICCI *winks at* MRS. LILLYVICK. *Then he blows her a kiss*) Eh, what? (MRS. LILLYVICK *blushes.* MR. LILLYVICK *strikes* MR. SNEVELLICCI *on the nose.*) Hey, what this? Fisticuffs? (*The Company reacts as* MR. SNEVELLICCI *tries to hit* MR. LILLYVICK.) You strike me, sir?

LILLYVICK. I do. (NICHOLAS, SMIKE, *one or two other actors rush in to separate them.*)

MISS BRAVASSA. What's this?

MISS GAZINGI. What's happening?

MRS. LILLYVICK. Oh, lor.

LILLYVICK. (*Still struggling.*) You see that, sir? Here's purity and elegance combined, whose feelings have been violated—

MRS. LILLYVICK. Lord, what nonsense, Lillyvick. He ain't said nothing to me. (*Pause. The men let* LILLYVICK *go. He turns to* MRS. LILLYVICK.)

LILLYVICK. Said, Henrietta? It was how he looked—

MRS. LILLYVICK. Well, d'you suppose that nobody is ever going to *look* at me again? A pretty thing, it would be, to be married, if that was the law!

LILLYVICK. You didn't mind it?

MRS. LILLYVICK. Mind it? What I minded was . . . You know, you ought to go down on your knees, I tell you, Lillyvick, and beg for everybody's pardon, that you ought.

LILLYVICK. Pardon, my dear?

MRS. LILLYVICK. Yes, and mine first. Do you suppose I ain't the best judge of what's proper and what's improper. (*Pause.*)

MISS BRAVASSA. Well, to be sure.

MISS LEDROOK. We'd notice.

MISS GAZINGI. If there'd been anything that needed to be taken notice of.

MR. SNEVELLICCI. Hm. Absolutely right. Spot on. There. So now that's settled—charge your glasses, one and all. (*And* MR. SNEVELLICCI *goes round the ladies, starting with* MRS. LILLYVICK, *giving them kisses.* LILLYVICK, *broken, stumbles to the side.*)

MRS. GRUDDEN. (*Hiccups.*) Beg pardon. (*We realise that* MRS. GRUDDEN *is slightly inebriated. She reaches into her reticule for a handkerchief and finds a letter.*) Oh. Mr. Johnson.

NICHOLAS. Yes?

MRS. GRUDDEN. There's a letter for you. Sorry, it completely slipped my mind. (MRS. GRUDDEN *a little giggle.* NICHOLAS *a quizzical look, takes the letter. Increasingly worried look.* MR. SNEVELLICCI *has finished kissing all the ladies.*)

MR. SNEVELLICCI. So—a toast.

MRS. GRUDDEN. Toast.

MR. SNEVELLICCI. To—to the brightest male star in your way blue yonder—Mr. Johnson.

EVERYONE. Mr. Johnson.

FOLAIR. Speech! Speech!

MRS. GRUDDEN. Speech. (*Applause.* NICHOLAS *steps forward.*)

NICHOLAS. My dear friends, I am very sorry.

CRUMMLES. Sorry?

NICHOLAS. That I must—in a nutshell, I must leave your company. (*Pause.*)

MISS SNEVELLICCI. What? Leave?

MRS. GRUDDEN. Oh, hoity-toity.

FOLAIR. Stuff.

NICHOLAS. There are some—circumstances, that call me away.

CRUMMLES. But to return, sir, surely?

NICHOLAS. No.

CRUMMLES. (*Quietly.*) Not even if, your salary was—

NICHOLAS. No. (*Pause. Everyone looks at* MRS. CRUMMLES, *who has been building up to her reaction.*)

MRS. CRUMMLES. This is Astounding.

NICHOLAS. I am sorry that I could not have prepared you for it, Mrs. Crummles.

MRS. CRUMMLES. So am I. (*Pause.*)

CRUMMLES. Well, then. . . . Well then. . . . We will announce it. Monday. Positively last appearance. Posters, first thing in the morning.

NICHOLAS. Sir, I'm—

MRS. CRUMMLES. Yes, of course. And then, on Tuesday, reengagement for just one night more, and then on Wednesday, Thursday, yielding to the wishes of our numerous and influential patrons—

NICHOLAS. Ma'am, I must be off tonight.

MRS. CRUMMLES. Tonight?

NICHOLAS. Immediately. At once.

MRS. CRUMMLES. No positively last appearance?

NICHOLAS. No.

MRS. CRUMMLES. Not one night more, by popular demand?

NICHOLAS. No, sorry.

MRS. CRUMMLES. There's nothing we can do or say, to move you from this awesome pass? There's nothing I can do or say, to melt your stern, unyielding heart?

NICHOLAS. There isn't, I'm afraid.

MRS. CRUMMLES. Then—there's no more to say. (*She turns. Turns back.*) Except—farewell.

CRUMMLES. Farewell, my noble, lion-hearted boy! (CRUMMLES *embraces* NICHOLAS. *The* PHENOMENON *bursts into tears. Others dab their eyes with handkerchiefs.*)

MR. HETHERINGTON. Farewell.

MISS BELVAWNEY. Farewell.

MR. BANE. Farewell.

CRUMMLES. If nothing can detain you with us. . . .

MISS SNEVELLICCI. Nothing?

CRUMMLES. Then—

MRS. CRUMMLES. (*Embracing* NICHOLAS.) Farewell. (*The Great Embrace is still occurring when* MRS. GRUDDEN *makes an announcement.*)

MRS. GRUDDEN. I shall. Now sing. A song. (*Consternation.*) I shall require. A player at the pianofort. (*More consternation.*) To sing it.

MRS. CRUMMLES. Mrs. Grudden, what is going on?

MRS. GRUDDEN. I am. (*To the musicians.*) Thank you. (NICHOLAS *collars* SMIKE.)

NICHOLAS. Come, Smike, let's go—

SMIKE. (*Fascinated.*) But—look—(MRS. GRUDDEN *is getting her note. She begins to sing an extraordinarily sen-*

timental ballad. During it, various members of the Company come to NICHOLAS *and shake his hand.* LENVILLE'S *shake is reconciliatory, but he is clearly delighted. The penultimate shaker is* MISS SNEVELLICCI. *As they finish shaking, the Company members join* MRS. GRUDDEN'S *song, or burst into tears, or something.*)

MRS. GRUDDEN & COMPANY—SONG.*
O stay but for an hour;
If any power I have in pleading,
No way but only this to yield a kiss
And feel my death succeeding,
O how can I be strong
As you would have me be
Though duty calls I long to keep you here with me,
But no, go, and hold this memory

Farewell, my dear, farewell,
For ever let us part:
But don't, I pray you, tell the news to my aching heart.
Be kind, my dear, be kind: Though hope at last be
gone,
And even my love be blind,
O let it go hoping on.

(*During the next verse as the attention has completely transferred,* NICHOLAS *taps* SMIKE'S *arm, and nods regretfully, and* SMIKE *realises they have to go.* NICHOLAS *is nearly out when he is confronted by* MR. LILLYVICK.)

LILLYVICK. Sir. I can—I can see nothing.
NICHOLAS. What?
LILLYVICK. I can see nothing, more, in Mrs. Lillyvick. Of Miss Petowker. (*Pause.*)
NICHOLAS. I'm—so sorry. (NICHOLAS *and* SMIKE *leave. The song reaches a tumultuous climax.*)
MRS. GRUDDEN & COMPANY.
Farewell, my dear, farewell.*
For ever we must part
But don't, I pray you, tell the news to my aching heart.
Be kind, my dear, be kind:
Though hope at last be gone,
And even my love be blind,

O let it go hoping on.
Farewell, my dear, farewell,
For ever we must part:
But don't, I pray you, tell the news to my aching heart.
Be kind, my dear, be kind:
Though hope at last be gone,
And even my love be blind,
O let it go hoping on.

(*And, miraculously, the chairs and tables, and the Company of Mr. Vincent Crummles, have all disappeared.*)

SCENE 10

The Wititterlies'. The chaise-longue, and one chair. Enter KATE *and* MRS. WITITTERLY.

MRS. WITITTERLY. Now, child, you must tell me how you came to know Lord Frederick, and all those other charming gentlemen.

KATE. Oh, I met them at my uncle's.

MRS. WITITTERLY. I was so glad—if surprised—at the opportunity which that respectable person, your dear mother, gave us of being known to them.

KATE. Yes, I, too, was surprised.

MRS. WITITTERLY. Though, of course, we have been nearly introduced a dozen times. (*A bell.*) Ah, that will be them now. Alphonse! (ALPHONSE *goes out.* KATE *agitated.*) I naturally told them they could call. Miss Nickleby . . . You cannot think of going.

KATE. You are very good. But—

MRS. WITITTERLY. Please, please don't upset me, make me speak so loud, Miss Nickleby, I beg—(*Enter* ALPHONSE.)

ALPHONSE. Uh, Mr. Hawk, Lord Mulberry Pyke, Sir Frederick Pluck, and Mr. Verisopht. Or something. (*Enter the above-named.*)

MRS. WITITTERLY. Gentlemen, I am delighted, I am sure. Please, gentlemen, my lord, sit down. (*As they do so:*)

HAWK. And how are you today, Mrs. Wititterly?

MRS. WITITTERLY. Well, I must own, Sir Mulberry, that I am still quite torn to pieces.

HAWK. (*With a look at* KATE.) Mm?

MRS. WITITTERLY. (*To* VERISOPHT.) I am always ill after drama, my lord, and after the opera I scarcely exist for several days.

VERISOPHT. Yes . . . I'm the same. (MR. WITITTERLY *bursts in.*)

MR. WITITTERLY. (*To* LORD FREDERICK VERISOPHT.) My lord, I am delighted, honoured, proud. I am indeed, most proud. (*To* MRS. WITITTERLY.) My soul, you'll suffer for this thrill tomorrow.

VERISOPHT. Suffer?

HAWK. Pray, whatever for?

MR. WITITTERLY. Oh, the reaction, sir, this violent strain upon the nervous system, what ensues? A sinking, a depression, lowness, lassitude, debility. My lord, if Sir Tumley Snuffim were to see that frail creature at this moment, he'd not give a—(*With a toss of snuff.*) this, for her continued life! (MRS. WITITTERLY *sighs.*)

PYKE. It's obvious that Mrs. Witsisterly's a martyr.

MR. WITITTERLY. Oh, she is.

PLUCK. Perhaps, in fact . . . the other room, in order to escape the draught . . . ?

MRS. WITITTERLY. (*Less faintly.*) What draught . . . ? (PYKE *and* PLUCK *leading* MRS. WITITTERLY *to the "other room."*)

PYKE. A constitution like a flower, just the slightest puff of wind, it's clear—

MRS. WITITTERLY. (*Vaguely.*) Sir Mulberry, my lord . . .

(HAWK *gestures to* VERISOPHT *that they must follow.* VERISOPHT *stands, annoyed, and follows* MRS. WITITTERLY, *her husband,* PLUCK *and* PYKE. KATE *is trying to follow too, when* HAWK *turns, and stands in her way. This during:*)

MR. WITITTERLY. You're right, sir, you're so right. If anybody will produce to me a greater martyr than my wife . . . (*And, as* MRS. WITITTERLY *is fussed round,* KATE *is in the first room alone with* SIR MULBERRY HAWK.)

HAWK. Don't hurry, now, don't hurry—(KATE *tries to pass,* HAWK *prevents her.*) Now, then, stay—

KATE. You'd better not detain me, sir.

HAWK. Why not? Oh, my dear creature, why d'you keep up this show of anger with me, eh?

KATE. Show? Show? How dare you, to presume to speak to me, sir—to address me—

HAWK. You look pretty in a passion, dear Miss Nickleby.

KATE. I hold you, I must tell you, in the bitterest detestation and contempt. If you find looks of disgust, aversion, if you find such looks attractive—let me go, sir, let me join—

HAWK. Oh, I will let you join, Miss Nickleby, I promise you. (KATE, *speechless, looks at* SIR MULBERRY HAWK.) And I will see you very often, we're invited here, whenever and however we—desire. (KATE *makes another attempt to get past* HAWK, *who tries, roughly, to embrace her. Meanwhile, both* MRS. WITITTERLY *and* LORD VERISOPHT *have realised the device that has been used on them.* MRS. WITITTERLY *is insisting to her husband on going back into the first room.* KATE *pulls herself back from* HAWK. *He decides to leave it there.*) I will be joining you, Miss Nickleby. (KATE *turns to go. Then, she decides to turn back, to speak to* HAWK. *During this,* MRS. WITITTERLY *appears in between the two rooms, followed by* VERISOPHT, PLUCK, PYKE *and* MR. WITITTERLY.) Now, my lord. We should not outstay our welcome.

VERISOPHT. No. (*Pause.*) We shouldn't.

HAWK. We hope, Mrs. Wititterly, to find you soon in better health. Don't we?

PLUCK. Certainly we do.

PYKE. Indubitably. (*Enter* ALPHONSE.)

MR. WITITTERLY. My lord, Sir Mulberry, I trust that you will—

HAWK. Oh, yes. Very soon. (MR. WITITTERLY, *who doesn't understand the atmosphere, fusses round as* VERISOPHT, HAWK, PYKE *and* PLUCK *depart. Then* MR. WITITTERLY *moves towards his wife, who has not moved. She dismisses him with a gesture.* MR. WITITTERLY *goes out.* MRS. WITITTERLY *takes a step towards* KATE.)

MRS. WITITTERLY. Miss Nickleby, I wish to speak to you. I'm sorry, but you leave me no alternative. (KATE *says nothing.*) Your—this behaviour is so very far from pleasing me . . . I'm very anxious that you should do well, Miss Nickleby, but you will not, if you go on as, as you do. (KATE *turns away.* MRS. WITITTERLY *stri-*

dently.) And you needn't think that looking at me in that way, Miss Nickleby, will stop me saying what I'm going to say, which I regard as a religious duty. You will not look at me, in that, that manner. I am not Sir Mulberry, no, nor Lord Frederick Verisopht, Miss Nickleby; nor am I Mr. Pluck, nor Mr. Pyke. If such things had been done when *I* was a young girl—I don't suppose it would have been believed.

KATE. I don't—

MRS. WITITTERLY. Please, I will not be answered! I will not, Miss Nickleby. D'you hear?

KATE. I hear you, ma'am.

MRS. WITITTERLY. And I must tell you, once, for all, I must insist upon your altering your forward manner with those gentlemen, who visit at this house. It's not becoming. It's improper. It's—unchaste.

KATE. Oh. Is not this too cruel, too hard to bear? It's not enough, that I should suffer as I do, from contact with these people, but I am exposed to this unjust and most unfounded charge!

MRS. WITITTERLY. You'll have the goodness to recall, Miss Nickleby, that when you use such terms as "unjust" and "unfounded," you are implying in effect, that I am stating that which is untrue.

KATE. I do. I say that. It is vilely, grossly, willfully untrue. Oh, is it possible! That someone of my own sex can sit by, and not have seen the misery those libertines have caused me! Is it possible that you can't see the disrespect, contempt they hold for both of us? And can I not expect from you, another woman, and so much my senior, a little—female aid and sympathy? I can't believe it.

MRS. WITITTERLY. What? Disrespect? Contempt? What, senior? (MR. WITITTERLY *and* ALPHONSE *run into the room.*)

MR. WITITTERLY. What's the matter? Heavens, Julia! Look up, my life, look up!

MRS. WITITTERLY. Sir Tumley! Get Sir Tumley!

MR. WITITTERLY. (*To* ALPHONSE.) Run, run quickly— fetch Sir Tumley. Go! (ALPHONSE *scuttles out. To* KATE.) I knew it, knew, Miss Nickleby. All that society, it's been too much for her. This is, this is all soul, you know, soul, every bit of it. Come, help, to get her to her room. (KATE *to the aid of* MR. WITITTERLY. MRS. WITITTERLY *looks up at* KATE.)

MRS. WITITTERLY. Please, take your hands off me. (MR. WITITTERLY *looks surprised and confused. He picks up his wife and carries her out.* KATE *left alone. Enter* SIR MULBERRY HAWK. KATE *sees him. He picks up a cane that he has left behind.*)

HAWK. Oh, poor Miss Nickleby. Where can you look, now, for protection.

SCENE 11

The streets of London. Bare stage. NARRATORS *burst on to the stage. Amidst them are* SMIKE *and* NICHOLAS.

NICHOLAS. London at last! (NARRATORS *tell us and show us of the Great City.*)

NARRATORS. And there they were in the noisy, bustling crowded streets of London,

Now displaying long double-rows of brightly-burning lamps, and illuminated besides with the brilliant flood that streamed from the windows of the shops.

Streams of people apparently without end poured on and on, jostling each other in the crowd, and hurrying forward, scarcely seeming to notice the riches that surrounded them on every side;

Emporia of splendid dresses, the materials brought from every corner of the world;

Vessels of burnished gold and silver, wrought into every exquisite form of vase, and dish, and goblet;

Screws and irons for the crooked, clothes for the newly-born, drugs for the sick, coffins for the dead, and churchyards for the buried—

Pale and pinched-up faces hovered about the windows where was tempting food,

Hungry eyes wandered over the profusion guarded by one thin sheet of brittle glass—

Life and death went hand in hand—

Wealth and poverty stood side by side—

Repletion and starvation laid them down together—

But, still—

It was—

London! (*The music changes. More urgent, darker. The streets more threatening than gaudy, as* NICHOLAS *and* SMIKE *rush through them, to knock on a door.* CROWL *appears above.*)

NICHOLAS. Oh, Mr. Crowl. Is Newman here?

CROWL. Oh, no. But you're expected. Laid out food and drink as well.

NICHOLAS. D'you know when he'll be home?

CROWL. A troublesome affair of business keeps him. Not be home, he says, till twelve o'clock.

NICHOLAS. Then, sir, look after this young man for me? And see he's fed and rested?

CROWL. Of, of course I will. Make sure he's fed, and warmed. (*Music again, and* NICHOLAS *runs round through the ever-darkening streets, as if to another front door. He knocks.* HANNAH—*Miss La Creevy's Maid—appears above.*)

NICHOLAS. Oh, Hannah. Is your mistress in?

HANNAH. Who? Miss La Creevy?

NICHOLAS. Yes, of course.

HANNAH. Oh, no. She's out.

NICHOLAS. Where out?

HANNAH. Out at the theatre.

NICHOLAS. Which? And when will she return?

HANNAH. Dunno. (*And* NICHOLAS *runs off again, through the streets till finally he comes to another "door" and beats on it.*)

NICHOLAS. (*Banging on the door.*) Hey, mother! Mother! Kate! Kate, are you there? (*He leans against the door, exhausted.*) What *is* this? Where *are* they? *All* of them!

NARRATORS. And then Nicholas suddenly recalled, from Newman's letter, that his sister's new employers lived in Chelsea,

And with the firm resolve to leave no stone unturned,
    he set his course to Sloane Street,

And such was his state, confused and tired and
    desperate,

He hardly saw, outside the fashionable coffee-house,
    the cabriolet that juddered to a halt before him.

SCENE 12

*Inside and outside a fashionable coffee-house. During
the following, the coffee-house is set up: three tables, two
with customers dining, being served by two* WAITERS *and
a* SERVING-GIRL, *whom we shall call* WALTER, WILBUR
and WANDA. *But, for the moment, our attention is on*
NICHOLAS, *downstage, as* HAWK, VERISOPHT, PLUCK
and PYKE *enter, on their way to the coffee-house. We
imagine that the door to the coffee-house is behind* NICHO-
LAS, *and the entering* REVELLERS *need to pass round him
to get to it.*

HAWK. Now, gentlemen, another pint or two of wine?
VERISOPHT. Why not? Another toast?
PLUCK. Oh, yes.
PYKE. Indeed. (PYKE *is already in the coffee-house,*
PLUCK *following.* VERISOPHT *needs to be kept upright by*
HAWK.)
PLUCK. Hey, waiter, magnum!
HAWK. To whom, my lord?
VERISOPHT. Who else? The lady we've been drinking
to all evening. That damned, enchanting little . . .
HAWK. (*Promptly.*) Kate.
VERISOPHT. Kate Nickleby. (HAWK *and* VERISOPHT
enter the coffee-house. NICHOLAS *follows.*)
HAWK. Hey, waiter! Magnum!
PLUCK. Where is that girl? Girl with the magnums? Is

there no service here? (WANDA *hurries in with the bottles
on a tray.* WALTER *hurries up with a corkscrew.* HAWK,
who is sitting on the edge of the empty table with LORD
VERISOPHT, *grabs the screw.*)

HAWK. I'll do it myself, dammit. Doubtless you'll take
half-an-hour, and break the cork. (*To* WANDA.) You—
glasses! (WALTER *bows obsequiously, and nods to*
WANDA, *who hurries out, having her bottom pinched by*
HAWK *on the way.* NICHOLAS *has entered. The place is
rather richer than he is used to patronising, and he is
aware that he is dusty and travel-stained.*)

PYKE. (*To a terrified* CUSTOMER.) Excuse me, sir, but
could I— (*Taking glasses from the table.*) Thank you ever
so.

HAWK. (*Opening the magnum and spilling its contents.*)
The thing is, my dear lord, about this little Nickleby, is
that she is, in fact, quite similar to that old crow, her
uncle. (HAWK *pours wine into the glasses which* PYKE
and PLUCK *have liberated from the other* CUSTOMERS.)

VERISOPHT. Damned sight prettier. (WANDA *enters
with the glasses. The party raise their glasses to her. She
looks to* WALTER, *who nods at her, and she goes out,
having her bottom pinched by* MR. PLUCK. *One of the
other customers gestures to* WALTER, *and they whisper
about the intrusion.*)

HAWK. Indeed. But, nonetheless, in essence, quite the
same. You need something from her in the way of—
interest, she holds back, to be more sought after—as he
does; and when she/he relents, at last, the bargain's doubly hard, but the advance is more than doubly welcome.

PLUCK. The advance.

PYKE. Let's have some oysters, dammit! (WALTER *has
gone to* NICHOLAS.)

WALTER. Yes, can I help you?

NICHOLAS. No. (*And* NICHOLAS *marches over to* SIR
MULBERRY HAWK. HAWK *looks up at* NICHOLAS.) Sir,
may I have a word with you?

HAWK. With me?

NICHOLAS. That's what I said. (*The rest of the coffee-
house becoming aware of what's going on.*)

HAWK. Well. A mysterious intruder.

NICHOLAS. Will you step apart with me, or d'you
refuse?

HAWK. Sir, name your business, and then go away. (WANDA *coming in with a tray of food.* NICHOLAS *takes a card from his pocket and throws it on the table.*)

NICHOLAS. There, sir. My business you will guess. (WANDA *stops in her tracks, turns to go,* WALTER *gestures to her, and she puts down the tray as far as possible from the hostilities, and goes out.*) Now, sir. Your name, and your address.

HAWK. Sir, I will give you neither. (*The customer who has paid his bill gets up and leaves.*)

NICHOLAS. Then—if there's—one gentleman, among this party, he will tell me who you are, and where you live. (NICHOLAS *is talking too loudly.*) I am the brother of the lady who has been the subject of this conversation. I demand—some satisfaction. (PLUCK *and* PYKE *a step towards* NICHOLAS.)

HAWK. Oh, no, let the fellow talk. I've nothing serious to say to a boy of his station, and his pretty sister shall save him a broken head, at least.

NICHOLAS. I'll follow you. All night, if need be. I will know you.

HAWK. (*Laughs.*) Hm. (HAWK *pours another drink. Another customer gestures to* WILBUR, *who goes and takes his money.* NICHOLAS *to* WALTER.)

NICHOLAS. Do you know this person's name?

WALTER. This gentleman? No, sir, I don't, sir.

HAWK. (*To* WALTER.) Do you know *this* person's name?

WALTER. I don't know anyone.

HAWK. (*Tossing* NICHOLAS'S *card to* WALTER.) Then you will find his name, there, sir. And when you've mastered it, then you can burn it.

WALTER. Burn it. Right. (WALTER *picks up the card and withdraws.* WALTER, WILBUR *and* WANDA *now in a little huddle by the kitchen door.*)

HAWK. (*To* NICHOLAS.) You are an errand boy, for all I know. And now, be off with you. (HAWK *turns to his friends.*)

NICHOLAS. I am the son of a country gentleman. Your equal in birth and education, and your superior, I trust, in everything besides. (HAWK *laughs.*) (*Blurted.*) Miss Nickleby's my sister, sir! I will not leave. (*The last customer hurries out.*)

HAWK. Well, then, we'll go.

NICHOLAS. I'll follow you.

HAWK. Well, then, we'll stay. (*Long pause.*)

VERISOPHT. I think, perhaps, I will go. It's very late.

HAWK. Oh, is it? Very well, my lord.

PLUCK. Perhaps my lord would like a travelling companion.

PYKE. Or two.

HAWK. Then all of you—do go. (*Slight pause.* VERISOPHT *goes to* WALTER, *and signs the instantly proffered bill.*)

VERISOPHT. Good night, then. (VERISOPHT, PLUCK *and* PYKE *go out.* HAWK *picks up the magnum, goes to another table. He sits and drinks.* NICHOLAS *is watching* HAWK *like a hawk. A very long pause. A clock chimes.* WALTER, WILBUR, *and* WANDA *look at the clock and at each other. Another long pause.* HAWK *finishes his wine.*)

HAWK. Waiter—my cane. (*He stands.* WILBUR *brings* HAWK'S *cane.* HAWK *takes it, and throws some coins on the table.*)

NICHOLAS. So, will you make yourself known to me, sir? (*Pause.*)

HAWK. No. (HAWK *goes,* NICHOLAS *follows.* WALTER, WILBUR *and* WANDA *walk forward and deliver their lines out front, as the chairs and tables of the coffee-room disappear, and the cabriolet is set up in the darkness.*)

WILBUR. And there was a private cabriolet in waiting,

WANDA. And the groom opened the apron,

WALTER. And jumped out to the horse's head,

WILBUR. Who was a thoroughbred,

WANDA. And consequently Very Highly Strung. (*Now we can see the cabriolet. It is a small, private carriage, represented by a chair, carried by four actors and pointing upstage, on which* HAWK *sits with his whip. Upstage of that are more actors, covered with a long black cloth, to represent the* HORSE, *as, in a moment, it rears and bolts. This effect relies on careful lighting, so that we hardly see the other actors, but only* HAWK, NICHOLAS *and the head of the* HORSE.)

WALTER. And the young man walked up to the older gentleman,

WILBUR. And grasped his arm, and spoke: (NICHO-

LAS, *held up by actors, as if on the footboard of the carriage.*)

NICHOLAS. So, will you make yourself known to me?

HAWK. No, damn you. (*To his* COACHMAN.) Barton!

NICHOLAS. I'll hang on to the footboard.

HAWK. You will be horsewhipped if you do. Barton, let go her head.

NICHOLAS. (*Clinging on to* HAWK.) You shall not—shall not go—I swear—till you have told me—

HAWK. Now! Leave go! (*The "*HORSE*" plunges and rears.*) Will you let go?

NICHOLAS. Will you tell me who you are?

HAWK. No!

NICHOLAS. No! (HAWK *strikes* NICHOLAS *with his whip.* NICHOLAS *grabs the whip and strikes* HAWK. *The "*HORSE*" is rearing wildly. Screams of passers-by.* NICHOLAS *strikes* HAWK *again. The* HORSE *bolts: in other words, the horse actors rush upstage, outside of the light, followed by the actors carrying* HAWK. NICHOLAS *reels away. A huge crash and darkness.*)

SCENE 13

Noggs' garret and the Nicklebys' house in Thames Street. Bare stage. Early morning. NOGGS *and* SMIKE *enter one side,* NICHOLAS *the other. He is bleeding.*

NICHOLAS. Don't be alarmed. There's no harm done, beyond what a basin of water will repair.

NOGGS. No harm! What have you been doing?

NICHOLAS. I know everything. I have heard a part, and guessed the rest. But now we must go and see them. You see, I am collected. Now, good friend.

NOGGS. Your clothes are torn. You're walking lame. Please, let me see to you.

NICHOLAS. No. No. I must go to them. (*Pause.* NOGGS *nods to* SMIKE, *who is looking upset by* NICHOLAS' *appearance. To* SMIKE.) Smike, we're going to my home.

SMIKE. We—home? Your home?

NICHOLAS. Our home. (*And* NICHOLAS *takes* SMIKE'S *hand, leading him, to* KATE. NOGGS *goes out. We are now in the Nicklebys' house in Thames Street.*)

NICHOLAS. So Kate, this is my faithful friend and fellow-

KATE. (*Going to* SMIKE.) Dear Smike. I've been so looking forward, after all my brother's told me. And to thank you, for the comfort you have been to him.

SMIKE. I'm—very pleased to meet you. Uh—he's my only friend. I would lay down my life, to help him. (*Enter* MRS. NICKLEBY, *and* MISS LA CREEVY, *with luggage.*)

MRS. NICKLEBY. Well, Lord bless my life. To think that Sir Mulberry Hawk should be such an abandoned wretch; when I was congratulating myself every day on his being an admirer of our dear Kate's. . . .

MISS LA CREEVY. Now, come, dear Mrs. Nickleby, please try to cheer up, do.

MRS. NICKLEBY. Oh, I dare say, dear Miss La Creevy, that it's very easy to instruct someone to cheer up, but if you had had as many reasons to cheer down as I have—and, oh mercy, think of Mr. Pyke and Mr. Pluck, two of the perfectest true gentlemen that ever lived. . . .

KATE. But come now, mother, there's a coach outside, to take us to the Strand. To Miss La Creevy's.

MISS LA CREEVY. Everything is ready, and a hearty welcome too. Now let me go with you downstairs. (MISS LA CREEVY *and* MRS. NICKLEBY *turn to go and see* SMIKE.)

MRS. NICKLEBY. Oh, uh—uh, Nicholas—

NICHOLAS. Oh, mother, Miss La Creevy. This is Smike. My friend—who came with me from Yorkshire. You remember?

MRS. NICKLEBY. Smike.

NICHOLAS. That's right.

SMIKE. I'm very—

MRS. NICKLEBY. Oh, dear . . .

KATE. Uh, mother—

MRS. NICKLEBY. Oh, it's so like Pyke. I shall be better presently. (*She makes to go. Then turns back, trying hard to be a good hostess.*) I don't suppose, that, while in Yorkshire, Mr. Smike, you might have taken dinner with the Grimbles, of Grimble Hall?

SMIKE. The Grimbles.

MRS. NICKLEBY. A most proud man, Sir—Sir Hadley

Grimble—with six quite lovely daughters, and the finest park in the North Riding.

NICHOLAS. Oh, mother. D'you suppose that this—unfortunate poor outcast would receive an invitation to the finest house in the North Riding?

MRS. NICKLEBY. Finest park, dear. The house was not, I think . . .

MISS LA CREEVY. Now, please come, Mrs. Nickleby. (MRS. NICKLEBY *a last look, and then she goes out.* MISS LA CREEVY *realizes that brother and sister wish to talk to each other, so:*)

MISS LA CREEVY. And, Mr. Smike? (*She takes* SMIKE'S *hand.*)

SMIKE. New home. (MISS LA CREEVY *takes* SMIKE *out.* NICHOLAS *and* KATE *left together.*)

NICHOLAS. I'd thought, to run away would help you. Thought, if I stayed here, you'd be without protection. (*Pause.* KATE *runs and embraces* NICHOLAS.)

KATE. Oh, I've been so unhappy.

NICHOLAS. Oh, my darling girl.

KATE. Don't leave me any more. You promise me?

NICHOLAS. Of course. I'll never leave you. (*Slight pause.*) Tell me—tell me that I acted for the best.

KATE. Why should I tell you what we know so well? (*They part to go out.* NICHOLAS *stops her.*)

NICHOLAS. I will write to him. I will tell him we renounce him, and will not be beholden to him any more. (*Pause.*)

KATE. We are just beholden to each other. (SMIKE *enters to pick up the last of the luggage.*)

SMIKE. I'm very pleased to meet you, Kate. Kate Nickleby. (KATE *and* NICHOLAS, *smiling, lead* SMIKE *out.*)

SCENE 14

The apartments of Sir Mulberry Hawk. VERISOPHT *tending to the broken form of* SIR MULBERRY, *who lies on a couch, "with a shattered limb, a body severely bruised, a face disfigured with half-healed scars, and pallid from the exhaustion of recent pain and fever." Enter* PLUCK *and* PYKE, *with newspapers.*

HAWK. Well, then?

PLUCK. It is—it's noised abroad in all directions.

PYKE. Every club and gaming room has rung with it.

PLUCK. There's even been a song composed, we hear, and printed too—

PYKE. With most—unfunny lyrics, wouldn't you agree, Pluck?

PLUCK. Yes, Pyke, in the very worst of taste.

HAWK. When I am off this cursed bed—I will have such revenge as never man had yet. By God, I will. He's—this damned accident—has marked me for a week or two, but I'll put such a mark on him that he will carry to his grave. I'll slit his nose and ears—I'll flog him—maim him—(VERISOPHT, *nervously*.)

VERISOPHT. Yes, you might. Might try. But if you did—I should try to prevent you.

HAWK. What?

VERISOPHT. I have—been thinking. (*Slight pause*.) And—It is my view, in fact—that you—you should have told him who you were. And given him your card. For as it is—you did wrong. I did too. Because I didn't interfere. What happened afterwards was more your fault than his, and it should not, shall not, be cruelly visited upon him. It shall not, indeed.

HAWK. You pale, green boy, you parsonage, what's this?

VERISOPHT. I do believe, too, on my honour, that the sister is as virtuous and modest a young lady as she is a handsome one: and, of the brother, I say that he acted as a brother should. And I wish, with all my heart and soul, that any one of us came out of this—thing, half as well as he does. (*Exit* LORD FREDERICK VERISOPHT.)

HAWK. Well, Well, there's a thing. Well, there's a turnaround. (*He turns, and screams at* PLUCK *and* PYKE, *who have been notably silent and unsupportive over the last few moments*.) Don't you agree?

PYKE. Don't you agree that there's a turnaround, then, Pluck?

PLUCK. Pyke, don't you think that there's a—thing? (HAWK *looks at his lieutenants. They look at each other. They go out*.)

SCENE 15

The street. Bare stage. Enter NICHOLAS.

NICHOLAS. And the next morning, Nicholas went once more to the General Agency Office, in search of a position. (NICHOLAS *goes downstage, and mimes looking in the window of an employment exchange. He is joined by* POOR PEOPLE, *who narrate the following sequence.*) The office looked just the same as when he had left it last, NARRATORS. And indeed, with one or two exceptions, there seemed to be the very same placards in the window that he has seen before. (*They are joined, looking at the placards, by a short, elderly* GENTLEMAN, *dressed in a somewhat untidy, old-fashioned, comfortable style.*)

There were the same unimpeachable masters and mistresses in want of virtuous servants,

And the same virtuous servants in want of unimpeachable masters and mistresses.

And the same magnificent estates for the investment of capital,

And the same enormous quantities of capital to be invested in estates,

And, in short, the same opportunities of all sorts for people who wanted to make their fortunes. (*The* POOR PEOPLE *disperse. The old* GENTLEMAN, *who is smiling, and even chuckling a little at the placards, is still there. His name is* MR. CHARLES CHEERYBLE.)

LAST NARRATOR. And a most extraordinary proof it was of the national prosperity, that people had not been found to avail themselves of such advantages long ago. (NICHOLAS *and* MR. CHARLES *looking at the cards, and, occasionally, when they think the other isn't, at each other. This pantomime carries on for a few moments, when* MR. CHARLES *turns to go, and* NICHOLAS *catches his eye, and stammers out, in embarrassment.*)

NICHOLAS. Oh, I'm sorry, I—

MR. CHARLES. (*Who is Welsh.*) Oh, no offence. Oh,

no offence, at all. (*They both smile.* NICHOLAS *waves at the cards.*)

NICHOLAS. A great many opportunities here, sir.

MR. CHARLES. A great many people, willing and anxious to be employed, have thought so very often, I dare say. (*Pause. They both smile again.*)

NICHOLAS. Yes, I, um—

MR. CHARLES. Yes you um what, young sir?

NICHOLAS. (*At a rush.*) I merely hoped, or, thought, I mean to say—you had some object in consulting these advertisements?

MR. CHARLES. You mean, you thought that I was seeking a position? Eh? Hm? Eh?

NICHOLAS. Un—no.

MR. CHARLES. A very natural thought. Whatever. A highly comprehensible opinion. And, in fact, you'll split your sides at this, young sir, I thought the same of you.

NICHOLAS. Well sir, if you had, you'd not be too far from the truth.

MR. CHARLES. Eh? What? Dear me. No, no. A well-behaved young gentleman, reduced to such necessities. Can such things be?

NICHOLAS. (*Turning to go.*) I'm sorry, but they are, in my case; you'll forgive me.

MR. CHARLES. Stay. What do you mean, forgive you? What in heaven's name should I forgive you for? (NICHOLAS *turns back.*)

NICHOLAS. Oh, merely that your face and manner—both so unlike any I have seen—tempted me into an avowal, which to any other stranger in this wilderness of London, I should not have dreamt of making. (*Slight pause.*)

MR. CHARLES. Now, that's very good. That is most aptly put. Yes, yes, a wilderness. As it was once to me.

NICHOLAS. It was?

MR. CHARLES. (*Sticking out a foot.*) Bare feet.

NICHOLAS. I beg your pardon?

MR. CHARLES. Came here. They did. Bare and naked. I remember to this day. So what brings you to London?

NICHOLAS. Well, my father—

MR. CHARLES. Died? And left a widowed mother?

NICHOLAS. Yes.

MR. CHARLES. And little brothers, sisters?

NICHOLAS. Sister. One.

MR. CHARLES. And you a scholar too, I dare say?

NICHOLAS. Well, I have been tolerably educated—

MR. CHARLES. (*Looking at his watch.*) Oh, a great thing, education. I have often wished that I'd had more of it myself. So, shall we go?

NICHOLAS. Go?

MR. CHARLES. Yes.

NICHOLAS. Go now?

MR. CHARLES. That's right.

NICHOLAS. Go where?

MR. CHARLES. Why, dear young man, go to the omnibus. And while we're travelling, you can be telling me the story of your life. (*He is striking out.* NICHOLAS *stops.* MR. CHARLES *turns back.*)

NICHOLAS. Please, sir. I must ask one question.

MR. CHARLES. Ask away.

NICHOLAS. Who are you, sir?

MR. CHARLES. My name's Charles Cheeryble.

NICHOLAS. Charles Cheeryble.

MR. CHARLES. That's right. Now, please, sir, not another word.

SCENE 16

Ralph's office. RALPH *sits at his desk, alone.*

RALPH. I am not a man—the world knows—to be moved by a pretty face. I look and work beneath the surface, and I see the grinning skull beneath. (*Pause.*) And yet . . . And yet, I almost like the girl. If she had been less proud, less squeamishly brought up . . . And if the mother died . . . Who knows. This house might be her home. (*He stands.*) It is a splendid house. The rooms are costly. Glorious. But yet—a little still. And rather cold. (*Pause.*) A young girl's voice. Her laughter. And, when she's not there, a hundred little tokens of her presence. To remind . . . (RALPH *sits.*) But still. The world knows. That I know it. And myself. (*Enter* NOGGS.) Yes? What?

NOGGS. You in?

RALPH. To whom?

NOGGS. To him.

RALPH. Who's him?

NOGGS. He is. (NOGGS *turns to go. Turns back, correcting himself.*) They are. (*He turns to go. Turns back.*) And there's a letter come for you. Marked urgent.

RALPH. Give it here. And then get out. (NOGGS *gives* RALPH *the letter.*)

NOGGS. See? Urgent. (NOGGS *potters out. He is given an odd look by the entering* SQUEERS *and* YOUNG WACKFORD.)

RALPH. Well, this is a surprise. I should know your face, Mr. Squeers.

SQUEERS. Ah, and you'd know it better, sir, if it hadn't been for all I've been a-going through.

RALPH. Ah, yes, sir, I trust you are now fully recovered from my nephew's scoundrelly attack?

SQUEERS. Well, if I am, it's only just, sir. I was one blessed bruise, sir, right from here to there. Vinegar and brown paper, sir, from morning to night. As I lay there, all of a heap in the kitchen, you might have thought I was a large brown paper parcel, chock full of nothing but groans. Did I groan loud, Wackford, or did I groan soft?

WACKFORD. Loud. (RALPH *a quizzical look at the boy.*)

SQUEERS. My son, sir, little Wackford. I've brought him up, on purpose, to show the parents and guardians. I've put him in the advertisement this time, too: Look at a boy—himself a pupil. So, what do you think, sir?

RALPH. Think of what?

SQUEERS. Of him, sir, for a specimen of our feeding? Ain't he fit to burst right out of his clothes, and start the seams, and make the very buttons fly off with his fatness? (*Poking and pinching* WACKFORD.) Ooh, here's flesh, here's firmness, and here's solidness. Why, you can hardly get enough of him between your finger and your thumb to pinch him anywheres.

WACKFORD. Ow!

SQUEERS. Oh, well, been a long time since he had his breakfast. Ooh, but look, sir, at those tears. There's oiliness!

RALPH. He certainly looks fit and well.

SQUEERS. In fact . . . D'you have such a thing as twopence, Mr. Nickleby?

RALPH. I—think I have. (RALPH *produces "after much rummaging in an old drawer, a penny, a half-penny, and two farthings."*)

SQUEERS. I thankee. (*He gives the money to* WACKFORD. RALPH *looking at the letter* NOGGS *brought him.*) Now, you go and buy a tart—and mind you buy a rich one. What d'you say?

WACKFORD. Yes, thank you, father. (WACKFORD *goes out.*)

SQUEERS. Pastry makes his flesh gleam a good deal, and parents think that that's a healthy sign. (*Turning back to* RALPH.) So, Mr. Nickleby. (RALPH *still immersed in the letter.*) Um—Mr. Nickleby? (RALPH *looks up, darkly. Something in the letter has made him angry.*)

RALPH. Sit down. Attend to me. (SQUEERS *sits.*) I am not to suppose, that you are dolt enough to have forgotten or forgiven very readily the violence that was committed on you?

SQUEERS. Never.

RALPH. Or to lose the chance to pay it back, with interest.

SQUEERS. Try me.

RALPH. And maybe, it was some such object brought you here?

SQUEERS. Well . . . I had thought, perhaps, some compensation—

RALPH. Who's the boy? The boy that he took with him?

SQUEERS. Name of Smike.

RALPH. And is he old, young, healthy, sickly, tractable, rebellious?

SQUEERS. Well, wasn't young. Young for a boy, that is.

RALPH. That is, he's not a boy.

SQUEERS. I think, 'bout twenty. But—a little wanting, here, (*Taps forehead.*) like, nobody at home.

RALPH. How did he come to you?

SQUEERS. Oh, fourteen years ago, a strange man brought him to my place, and left him there. The money came some six or seven years. But then it stopped. I kept him, out of—

RALPH. Charity?

SQUEERS. That is the word. Though he's been useful, in the recent years,

RALPH. Yes, yes. Now, Mr. Squeers, we'll talk of this again, when I've had time to think about it. So, where are you staying?

SQUEERS. (*Presenting a card.*) With a Mr. Snawley, Somers Town. I've got two lads of his, and he's that pleased with how they're being treated, that—

RALPH. (*Stands.*) We are alone, sir. There's no need to advertise to me. (*A thought.*) This Snawley got two boys, you say, with you?

SQUEERS. That's right. Remarried, wife's two sons, you know.

RALPH. I do. (NOGGS *brings in* WACKFORD, *stuffing his face with a tart.* SQUEERS *stands.*)

SQUEERS. Ah, Wackford. He's a fine boy, ain't he, Mr.—

NOGGS. Very.

SQUEERS. Pretty swelled out, eh? The fatness, twenty boys.

NOGGS. Oh, yes, he has. The fatness—twenty, thirty even. More. He's got it all. Ha! Ha! Oh, Lord.

SQUEERS. (*To* RALPH.) Is this man drunk? Or mad? (RALPH *shrugs.* NOGGS *cracking his knuckles.*) We'll speak then, Mr. Nickleby. (SQUEERS *and* WACKFORD *go out.*)

NOGGS. God help the others.

RALPH. What? Get out.

NOGGS. Get out. (NOGGS *goes out.* RALPH *alone, furious, with the letter.*)

RALPH. Yes. Yes. To wound him through his own affections. Yes. To strike him, through this boy.

SCENE 17

The offices of the Brothers Cheeryble. In fact, Ralph's office, with its desk and Noggs' high desk and stool, remains downstage—it will become Mr. Charles' office later. Upstage, in a mirror-effect, is another high desk and stool, on the opposite side from Noggs', and another desk with two chairs, on the opposite side to Ralph's. This upstage area represents the counting-house of the Cheerybles; their old, round, white-haired clerk TIM LINKINWATER *sits at*

*the high desk working: above him hangs a birdcage with
a blackbird inside. At the desk sits, facing upstage,* MR.
NED CHEERYBLE, *and, upstage of him, a beautiful, if
distressed,* YOUNG WOMAN. CHARLES CHEERYBLE *enters
Tim's section of the office, with his new friend* NICHOLAS
NICKLEBY.

MR. CHARLES. Ah, Tim, you knave, God bless you.
Is my brother in.

TIM. Yes, he is, sir, but someone's with him.

MR. CHARLES. Then we will not disturb him for the
moment. Tim. This young man is called Mr. Nicholas
Nickleby.

NICHOLAS. I'm pleased to meet you, sir.

TIM. And you. Hm, sir.

MR. CHARLES. And, this, dear Nicholas, is Mr. Tim
Linkinwater, possibly the most ferocious lion in the general region of Threadneedle St. Am I not right, Tim Linkinwater? Hm? (TIM *shrugs and allows himself a little
smile.*)

MR. CHARLES. (*To* NICHOLAS.) Note, sir, at first, the
order. Paper pens, inks, ruler, sealing wax, Tim's hat,
Tim's glove, Tim's other coat, Tim's blackbird and Tim
himself; and you shift any one of them, without a by-
your-leave or even with it, and you do so at your peril.
Isn't that correct? (MR. NED CHEERYBLE *opens his door.
To let his visitor out.* MR. NED *looks exactly the same as
his brother* MR. CHARLES. NICHOLAS *double-takes.*)

MR. NED. Ah, dear Brother Charles. And how are
you?

MR. CHARLES. I am in quite outrageous health, dear
brother Ned. And how are you?

MR. NED. I am in precisely the same condition,
Brother Charles.

MR. CHARLES. Now, Brother—(MR. NED *puts his
finger to his lips. The beautiful* YOUNG WOMAN *comes
out of the office.*)

MR. CHARLES. My dear Miss Madeline. Has Brother
Ned explained to you our view—has he expressed our
most sincere entreaty?

YOUNG WOMAN. Yes, he has. But my opinion is, and
must remain, the same. Your generosity, your kindness,
is quite unsurpassable. But still—I cannot do what you

would have me do. I cannot . . . For reasons that I know you understand.

MR. CHARLES. Of course . . . Of course, we understand. (MR. NED *guides the* YOUNG WOMAN *to the door. She goes out.* NICHOLAS *following her with his eyes.* MR. NED *turns back to his brother.*) Now, Brother Ned, are you busy, or can you spare time for a word or two with me?

MR. NED. Brother Charles, my dear fellow, don't ask me such a question. (MR. CHARLES *notices that* NICHOLAS *is still looking after the* YOUNG LADY.)

MR. CHARLES. Um—Mr. Nickleby—

NICHOLAS. I'm sorry.

MR. CHARLES. P'raps you'd grant us the inestimable privilege of entering my room.

NICHOLAS. Of course. (*They go into* MR. CHARLES' *office, which is Ralph's office.*)

MR. CHARLES. Now, Brother Ned, here is a young friend of mine we must assist. You will wish, of course, to have his statements, made to me, repeated, and then—

MR. NED. Brother Charles, it is enough that you say he should be assisted. When you say that, no more statements are required. It would be churlish to demand them. Assisted he shall be. What are his needs, and what does he require? Where is Tim Linkinwater? (MR. NED *is striding back towards the working* TIM LINKINWATER.)

MR. CHARLES. Stop, dear brother, stop. Before we—um, involve Tim Linkinwater—who, as I have said, dear sir, is quite a veritable tiger—I've a plan to put to you.

MR. NED. Then put it, Brother Charles.

MR. CHARLES. I shall, dear Brother Ned. Now, Tim is getting old, and Tim has been a faithful servant, and I don't think pensioning his mother and his sister and the buying of a little tomb when his poor brother died, was a sufficient recompense for all his services.

MR. NED. Sufficient! It was miserly.

MR. CHARLES. Exactly, so if we could somehow lighten old Tim's duties—

MR. NED. (*To* NICHOLAS.) Parsimonious.

MR. CHARLES. Prevail on him to go into the country now and then, and sleep in the fresh air—

MR. NED. Cheeseparing.

MR. CHARLES. And then come in, an hour later in the morning—

MR. NED. Niggardly.

MR. CHARLES. Then who knows, he'd grow young again in time.

MR. NED. He would indeed. I'll go and tell him so. (MR. NED *strides Upstage and confers with* TIM LINKINWATER *as* MR. CHARLES *talks to* NICHOLAS.)

MR. CHARLES. If Brother Ned, whom I hold dearer than I hold myself, has but a fault, it is an eagerness, enthusiasm, quickness of response, that sometimes edges close to the impulsive. Now, sir, what I had in mind was taking you on as clerk, assistant to Tim Linkinwater, at a salary of one hundred and twenty pounds a year, which pennypinching churliness will without a doubt provoke you to depart my presence at an instant. So, good morning, sir.

NICHOLAS. Oh, sir.

MR. CHARLES. What's this? Not gone?

NICHOLAS. Sir, I do not know how I can begin to thank you. (TIM *and* MR. NED *enter* CHARLES' *room.*)

MR. CHARLES. Start by keeping quiet. Now, Tim Linkinwater, do you understand that we intend to take this gentleman into the Counting-Room?

TIM. Hm. Yes. I do.

MR. CHARLES. Subject, of course, to your inspection and investigation and interrogation.

TIM. Hm. So I should think.

MR. CHARLES. And what is your opinion of this course of action?

TIM. Hm. Not coming in an hour later in the morning, that's for sure. Not going to sleep out in the fresh air, or be packed off to the country. Hm! A pretty thing to make a man do, at my time of life. The country. Phoo.

MR. CHARLES. What's this?

MR. NED. Phoo?

MR. CHARLES. Damn your obstinacy, Tim.

MR. NED. What do you mean, sir?

TIM. It is three and thirty, next May, since I first kept the books of the Brothers Cheeryble. There ain't—I've said it again and again—such a square as this in all the world. There's not such a spring in England as the pump under the archway. There's not such a view in England as the view out of my window. I have slept in that room for three and thirty years, and if it isn't inconvenient, and doesn't interfere with the business, I shall request leave to die there.

MR. CHARLES. Damn you, Tim Linkinwater.

MR. NED. How dare you talk of dying? Do you hear that, Brother Charles?

TIM. That's all I've got to say. It's not the first time, Brother Edwin, Brother Charles you've talked of super-annuating me; but I'd appreciate it if it was the last. (TIM LINKINWATER *goes back to his desk. Pause.*)

MR. CHARLES. He must be done something with, dear Brother Ned.

MR. NED. That's true, dear Charles;

MR. CHARLES. We must disregard his old scruples.

MR. NED. They cannot be tolerated. He must be made a partner, Brother Charles.

MR. CHARLES. And if he won't submit to it peaceably:

MR. NED. We must have recourse to violence.

MR. CHARLES. Quite right. Quite right, dear brother. If he won't listen to reason, we must do it against his will, and show him that we are determined to exert our full authority. We'll quarrel with him, Brother Ned.

MR. NED. We'll quarrel with him now. (MR. NED *is striding out, as* MR. CHARLES *is giving a look to* NICHO-LAS, *as if to say: "Impulsive!"* MR. NED *bumps into the re-entering* TIM LINKINWATER.) Now, then, Tim Linkin-water, curse you—

TIM. I've been thinking.

MR. CHARLES. Yes?

TIM. That if the young man measures up—

MR. NED. He will, of course he will—

TIM. Then it's all right. As long—

MR. CHARLES. Yes, what's—as long?

TIM. As there's No Country.

MR. NED. (*Pumping* TIM'S *hand.*) Well, then, Tim Linkinwater, devil take you sir, God bless you.

MR. CHARLES (*To* NICHOLAS.) Sir, you are approved. (MR. CHARLES *takes* TIM *back into the counting-room as* MR. NED *takes* NICHOLAS' *arm.*)

MR. NED. Now would it be beyond the bounds of the conceivable, for you to suffer the intolerable inconve-nience of starting work on Monday? (*Pause.*)

NICHOLAS. Sir, sir, I—Yes. (MR. NED *goes after his brother*, NICHOLAS *turns out front*.) And Nicholas' heart was so full up with gratitude, that he could hardly speak, and he felt, more than at any time since he had come to London, truly happy.

NARRATOR. But his heart was even fuller, with a matter he could not reveal, still less show thanks for to his benefactors. For, since he had seen her, he had found it hard to think of anything except the dark-eyed lady who had walked so sadly through the counting-room.

NICHOLAS. I would, he thought, I would . . . I'd know her in ten thousand.

SCENE 18

Ralph's office. NICHOLAS *remains there, as* RALPH *strides into what is now his own office again.* NICHOLAS *is quoting from the letter* RALPH *is reading.*

RALPH. So, this is it. He's loose again.

NICHOLAS. Your brother's widow and her orphan children spurn the shelter of your roof, and shun you with disgust and loathing.

RALPH. So, I'm to be defied, am I? And held up in the worst and most repulsive colours?

NICHOLAS. We, your kindred, now renounce you, and your riches—

RALPH. And, of course, she will be taught to hate me, and to feel there is infection in my touch and taint in my companionship . . .

NICHOLAS. Let them corrupt and rot you, we'll be free of their infection—

RALPH. And always. Always. When my brother was like him, the first comparisons were made; he, open, liberal, gallant; and I cold and cunning, with no spirit but the thirst for gain:

NICHOLAS. I know you.

RALPH. Well, let it be so. If he, if they both, affect to despise the power of money, I must show them what it is. (RALPH *goes out, as* NICHOLAS, *rapt:*)

NICHOLAS. I would, he thought, I would: I'd know her in ten thousand . . .

SCENE 19

The streets of the city of London. Just after dark. SMIKE *is wandering round. There are sellers of everything, and buyers of it too: There are* STREET-HANDS, *and* BALLAD-EERS, *and* BUSKERS. SMIKE *is entranced.*

("He had been gazing for a long time through a Jeweller's window, wishing he could take some of the beautiful trinkets home as a present, and imagining what delight they would afford if he could, when the clocks struck three quarters past eight. Roused by the sound, he hurried on at a very quick pace, and was crossing the corner of a bye-street when he was violently brought to, with a jerk so sudden that he was obliged to cling to a lamppost to save himself from falling.") SMIKE *has been collared by* MR. SQUEERS *and* YOUNG WACKFORD.

WACKFORD. Oh father, father—

SQUEERS. Well. Well, here's a go! Here's a quite delicious go. (*Onlookers are looking on.* MR. SNAWLEY, *who has been with the* SQUEERSES, *but has become detached in the hubbub, hurries up.*)

SNAWLEY. What's happening? Who's this?

SQUEERS. This is the boy I told you of, dear Snawley, one that ran away. Hey, Wackford, fetch a hackney coach!

WACKFORD. A coach! (WACKFORD *runs out.*)

A LABOURER. Hey. What's this lad been a-doing of?

SQUEERS. What doing of? Why, everything! Like running off, and joining in bloodthirsty attacks upon his master—oh, there's nothing he ain't done. Oh, what a most delicious go! (*Hitting* SMIKE.)

SMIKE. I must—

SQUEERS. Yes, sir? What must you?

SMIKE. Must go home.

SQUEERS. Oh, will. You'll go home very soon. A week, locked up, our lodgings, Eh Snawley, and then to that delightful village, Dotheboys, in Yorkshire. That's your home.

SMIKE. Go home. (*Re-enter* WACKFORD.)

WACKFORD. I've found a coach! I've found one, father!

SQUEERS. Right. (*He is dragging* SMIKE *out when* SNAWLEY *speaks.*)

SNAWLEY. Hard-heartedness and evil-doing never prosper, sir.

SQUEERS. That's true. That's very true.

SMIKE. Home!

SQUEERS. What a go! What a delicious go! (SMIKE *is dragged out by* SQUEERS. SNAWLEY *and* WACKFORD *follow.*)

SCENE 20

The garden of the Nicklebys' new home at Miss La Creevy's. A pair of flats represent a wall. There is a bench. Enter KATE *and* MRS. NICKLEBY. *It's afternoon.*

MRS. NICKLEBY. No, Kate, before your dear papa, and I, and even after, for a while, we met at least, I was besieged by suitors. Quite besieged, and it was certainly a matter of some comment and occasionally a little jealousy.

KATE. Well, I am convinced of it, mama.

MRS. NICKLEBY. It must have been, suitors I mean— at least a dozen.

KATE. Oh, mother, surely not!

MRS. NICKLEBY. Well, yes, indeed, my dear, and that is not including your papa, or the young gentleman who used to go to the same dancing school and would send round gold watches to our house in gilt-edged paper—all returned, of course—and who, unfortunately, was sent out to Botany Bay, in a convict ship, and then escaped into a bush and started killing sheep—I don't know how they got there—and was going to be hung, until he accidentally choked himself, and so they pardoned him. No, there was Lukin—(*A bunch of radishes flies over the wall.* KATE *astounded.*) Mogley—(*A cabbage.*) Tipslark—(*A turnip.*) Cabbery—(*A bunch of carrots.*) Young Smifser—

KATE. Uh—mama—

MRS. NICKLEBY. Good heavens. What can all these be?

KATE. They're vegetables, ma'am.

MRS. NICKLEBY. Well, so they are indeed. They must be from the gentleman.

KATE. What gentleman?

MRS. NICKLEBY. The one next door. It appears to be his custom, to communicate his feelings in this—charmingly eccentric way.

KATE. So this intrusion has occurred before?

MRS. NICKLEBY. Oh yes, why, certainly. The cucumbers we ate at dinner yesterday—

A VOICE. A-hem!

KATE. That's him?

MRS. NICKLEBY. Yes, yes, it must be, but I wouldn't say intrusion, dear, in fact, you will recall the cucumbers were excellent and I am seriously considering pickling the rest for winter, and—

THE VOICE. A-hem!

KATE. Mama, he's—

MRS. NICKLEBY. Now, don't be alarmed, my dear. It's not intended to scare anyone; we must give everyone their due—

KATE. What do you mean, mama? (*The* GENTLEMAN NEXT DOOR *has climbed up a ladder behind the wall and appears above it. He is quite old, and wears a nightcap. He looks—and is—crazy.*)

KATE. Now, mother. We are going to stand up and very calmly walk back to the house.

MRS. NICKLEBY. Oh, Kate, you're such a coward. (*To the* GENTLEMAN.) Sir, what do you want? How dare you look into this garden?

THE GENTLEMAN. Queen of my soul. This goblet—sip. (*He empties a basket of more vegetables into the garden.*)

MRS. NICKLEBY. Nonsense, sir.

THE GENTLEMAN. Won't you sip the goblet? Oh, do sip the goblet.

MRS. NICKLEBY. Go away, sir!

THE GENTLEMAN. Go away? Go quite away?

MRS. NICKLEBY. Yes, certainly.

THE GENTLEMAN. Go now?

MRS. NICKLEBY. Exactly now!

THE GENTLEMAN. Without the chance of asking you one question?

MRS. NICKLEBY. Well—

KATE. Mama!

MRS. NICKLEBY. One must be civil, dear.

THE GENTLEMAN. The question is—are you a princess?

MRS. NICKLEBY. Sir, you mock me.

THE GENTLEMAN. No, but really.

MRS. NICKLEBY. I am not, sir. Obviously.

THE GENTLEMAN. Then are you a relation to the Archbishop of Canterbury? Or the Pope of Rome? Or the Speaker of the House of Commons? Forgive if I err, but I was told you were the niece to the Commissioner of Paving, which would account for your relationship to all three.

MRS. NICKLEBY. Whoever has spread such reports has taken a great liberty, and one which I am sure my son, were he aware of it, would not allow one instant. The idea! Niece to the Commissioner of Paving.

THE GENTLEMAN. Beautiful madame—

KATE. Now, mother. Come away.

MRS. NICKLEBY. Be quiet, dear.

THE GENTLEMAN. I am no youth, ma'am, but I venture to presume that we are fitted for each other.

MRS. NICKLEBY. Oh, dear, Kate—

THE GENTLEMAN. I have estates, ma'am—jewels, lighthouses, fishponds, and a whalery of my own in the North Sea, and several oyster-beds of great profit in the Pacific Ocean. But I've enemies about me, ma'am—the Messrs. Gog and Magog—who would poison me and steal my property. But if you bless me with your hand and heart, we'll have the Lord Chancellor call out the military, and so clear the house before the service is performed. Then, bliss and rapture! Bliss and rapture! Love, be mine, be mine! (*Pause.*)

MRS. NICKLEBY. (*To* KATE.) I don't know what to say.

KATE. Surely, mama, you need only say one word.

MRS. NICKLEBY. Sir, just one word. While I acknowledge that your peroration—if only to a small extent—is quite agreeable—

KATE. Mama, inside.

MRS. NICKLEBY. I have made up my mind to stay a widow, and devote myself to my two children. It's a painful thing, of course, rejecting a proposal—but—

KATE. Now!

MRS. NICKLEBY. As I'm, somewhat rudely, summoned, sir, good day. (*The* GENTLEMAN *slumps suddenly, as if the ladder had been pulled. He looks down.*)

KEEPER. Oi!

THE GENTLEMAN. Oh. You. (*The voice of the* GENTLEMAN'S KEEPER.)

KEEPER. That's right.

THE GENTLEMAN. How's the Emporor of Tartary?

KEEPER. Oh, much the same as usual.

THE GENTLEMAN. In that case. Perhaps I'd best descend.

KEEPER. Well, yes. Perhaps you had. (*The* GENTLEMAN *descends. His* KEEPER *then appears.*)

KEEPER. Ah. Beg your pardon, ladies. Has this gentleman been making love to either of you?

KATE. Yes.

KEEPER. Oh, dear. He always will, you know. There's nothing will prevent him making love.

KATE. Out of His Mind?

KEEPER. Way out.

KATE. A long time?

KEEPER. Very long.

KATE. And there's no hope for him?

KEEPER. No, none at all. And don't deserve to be. I tell you, he's a great deal pleasanter without his wits than with 'em. (*Pause.*) Well. So sorry you've been trouble, ladies. Afternoon. (*And he climbs down the ladder out of view.*)

KATE. (*Firmly.*) Out of his mind. (MRS. NICKLEBY *picking up all the vegetables except one cucumber.*)

MRS. NICKLEBY. Oh, Kate! You don't think—you don't believe the gentleman is mad?

KATE. Of course I do. You heard—

MRS. NICKLEBY. Oh, yes, I heard. Oh, yes, dear, I heard everything. (MRS. NICKLEBY *sails into the house.*)

KATE. Mama! (KATE, *in frustration, picks up the cucumber and throws it back over the wall.* NICHOLAS *stands there.*)

NICHOLAS. Kate, what are you doing?

KATE. Oh, Nicholas—

NICHOLAS. Kate, do you know where Smike is?

KATE. Why, isn't he—I thought he'd gone to meet you.

NICHOLAS. No. Well, at all events . . . *Kate*. (NICHOLAS *suddenly panics, and runs into the house.* KATE *follows. The rumble of thunder.*)

SCENE 21

Outside the Saracen's Head. Bare stage. Enter TILDA *and* JOHN BROWDIE. JOHN *is carrying an immense amount of luggage, which he puts down.*

JOHN. So did tha see that, Tilda? See that Post-Office? Ecod, if that's a Post-Office, I'd like to see the house of the Lord Mayor of Lunnon. Wouldn't tha?

TILDA. I would indeed, John.

JOHN. (*Shouts off.*) Come on, Fanny! Raise thissen! We're here! (*And* FANNY SQUEERS *shuffles on. She looks as if it's been a very long journey.*) Eee, lass, tha looks like summat that's been dragged from Yorkshire, 'stead of coming on a big clean coach. Ee, don't tha think so, Tilda?

FANNY. Tilda. How you have been kicking me throughout this blessed night.

TILDA. Well, I like that! When you had nearly the whole coach to yourself. (*Enter* WILLIAM *the waiter.*)

FANNY. No, don't deny it, Tilda, for it's true, although of course you won't have noticed it, as being fast asleep, but I've not closed my eyes a single wink, and so I think I am to be believed.

WILLIAM. Good morning, ladies. Sir. Welcome to the Saracen's Head.

JOHN. Eh. I were right. I said that it were Sarah, Sarah Summat.

FANNY. What.

JOHN. Sarah-Son's head. I told 'ee, Fanny.

FANNY. (*Clocking* WILLIAM.) Tilda, dear, please stop him, we'll be taken for I don't know what.

JOHN. Oh, let 'em take us how they find us. I'm a married man. Here be the wedding party: bride and bridesmaid, and the groom, and we've not come to Lunnon for another purpose but to 'joy oursens, now have we? (FANNY *looks at* JOHN. JOHN *elbows* FANNY.) Have we, Fanny. Eh?

FANNY. (*To* WILLIAM.) I wonder, sir, if you could tell me if my father's in.

WILLIAM. Your father? Who may that be, Miss?

FANNY. (*Impatiently*.) It's Mr. Wackford Squeers. He should be stopping—staying—in this here establishment.

WILLIAM. Oh, him. Oh, he's not stopping here, Miss. Stopping somewhere else, entirely, with some friends of his, to save on the expense, I would imagine. But he comes in every day. I'll go and tell him he's been asked for. (*Enter* SQUEERS.)

SQUEERS. Eh. Fanny. Mr. Browdie. Tilda Price. Well, who'd have thought of this? (*Exit* WILLIAM.)

TILDA. It's Tilda Browdie now, sir. John and I are wed.

JOHN. And come down for our honeymoon.

SQUEERS. Well, Fanny, here's a thing. It's your turn to be married now. You must make haste.

FANNY. Oh, I am in no hurry, dear papa.

TILDA. No, Fanny?

FANNY. No, dear Tilda. I can wait.

TILDA. So can the young men, it appears.

FANNY. Oh, *Tilda*.

SQUEERS. Eh. Eh, Fanny. Who do you suppose we laid our hands on yesterday?

FANNY. Oh, pa! Not Mr. Nick—

SQUEERS. No. But just about next door.

FANNY. You can't mean, Smike?

SQUEERS. I can. I do. I've got him hard and fast.

JOHN. What's that? You got that poor, damned scoundrel? Where?

SQUEERS. Why, at the top back room, my lodging. Him on the one side and a great key the other.

JOHN. (*Greatly amused*): At tha lodging! Got him at the lodging! Eh, I'm damned, but I must shake tha hand for that. (*He pumps* SQUEERS' *hand.*) Eh. Got him at tha lodging. (*He punches* SQUEERS *merrily on the chest.*)

SQUEERS. Yes. That's right. My lodging. Thankee— and please don't do that again.

FANNY. Where are your lodgings, father?

SQUEERS. Oh, a place called Somers Town. It's quite a way but you must come to tea and meet the Snawleys, Fanny.

JOHN. 'Course we will. We'd come if it were 20 mile. Eh. Tilda? (TILDA, *a shruggy smile.*)

SQUEERS. Uh—

JOHN. (*Picking up the baggage.*) We can go and see the sights, tomorrow, can't we?

TILDA. Uh, John—

JOHN. Oh, certainly. We'll be there. Now. Where is that fellow? (*He turns back. He is still amused.*) Be there. At the lodging. Come on, Tilda! (*He takes the bags out.* FANNY *and* SQUEERS *look at* TILDA.)

TILDA. (*Nervously.*) I think—perhaps he's sickening for something. I have seen him—just the same. When he's been sickening. (*She goes out.*)

SQUEERS. I think he's lost his wits.

FANNY. Poor Tilda. (SQUEERS *looks at his daughter. Thunder rumbles again, and they run indoors.*)

SCENE 22

A park. Bare stage. Thunder. RALPH *runs on, his collar up against the rain. He stops centre stage, looks up. We imagine he's under a tree. A beggar passes. The beggar turns back, looks at* RALPH. *Then he speaks. It's* BROOKER.

BROOKER. Oh, you. At last. (*Pause.*)

RALPH. What's that?

BROOKER. At last, I've found you.

RALPH. What do you want?

BROOKER. What do I want? You see me. I'm a miserable and wretched outcast, nearly sixty years of age, and destitute and helpless, wanting even one dry crust of bread. So, what'd you think I want?

RALPH. I'm sixty, and neither destitute nor helpless. Work, sir, work. Don't beg for bread, but earn it. (RALPH *makes to go.*)

BROOKER. Do you not know me? (RALPH *turns back.*)

RALPH. No. Why, should I?

BROOKER. Do you not remember, 30 years ago, a man you threw in jail for owing you some paltry sum of money?

RALPH. Well, I've had many debtors in my time, and have arrested many, too.

BROOKER. But the one who you released—and took into your service? As a clerk, who wasn't overnice, and knew a little of the trade you drove? (*Pause.*)

RALPH. Oh, yes. Perhaps I do remember.

BROOKER. And how I served you always faithfully?

RALPH. Well, yes. You had your wages and you did your work. You owed me money, and you owe it still. Now, tell me what you want.

BROOKER. I've been looking for you, now, two days.

RALPH. Well, now you've found me. What d'you want?

BROOKER. I want to pay you back.

RALPH. Oh, yes? What with?

BROOKER. With interest. With something—that will interest you.

RALPH. Yes? What?

BROOKER. I know, there's something that I know. I took advantage of my place, with you. There's something that I did, to get at you. And you would, you'd give half of what you own to know it.

RALPH. Would I, now.

BROOKER. (*Forcefully.*) I've been a convict now, for seven years. For some small trickery that lay outside the law, a nothing to the trickery you money-makers do within it. I have now returned, the broken creature that you see before you. (*Slight pause.*) I haven't come to beg. I've come to sell. My expectations are not monstrous, but I have to live. (*Pause.*)

RALPH. Well, Mr.—I don't know the name to call you.

BROOKER. By my old one. I don't care.

RALPH. Then hear this, Mr. Brooker. You have claimed you have a hold on me. My answer is: you keep it, or publish it, for *I* won't care.

BROOKER. That wouldn't serve me.

RALPH. Sir, I know the world, the world knows me. Whatever sin of mine you've gleaned, the world knows it already. You could tell it nothing that would shock it about me. I am reviled and threatened every day.

BROOKER. You're proud of that.

RALPH. Indifferent. For all the rank contempt in which I'm held, things roll on just the same, and I grow richer by them. So, now, go.

BROOKER. I won't.

RALPH. Then I will.

BROOKER. Then I tell you—you will hear from me again.

RALPH. Then I tell *you*, that if I do, and you so much as notice me by one small begging gesture, you shall see the inside of a jail once more, and contemplate your hold on me in there! That is my answer to your trash. So, take it! (RALPH *strides off.*)

BROOKER. Oh, you'll hear from me again. (*"The man remained upon the same spot with his eyes fixed upon the retreating figure until it was lost to his view, and then drawing his arms about his chest, as if the damp and lack of food struck coldly to him, lingered with slouching steps by the wayside, and begged of those who passed along".*)

SCENE 23

The top back room of the Snawleys' house in Somers Town. SMIKE is there, locked up. A rattle of keys, and JOHN BROWDIE enters. SMIKE shrinks in terror. JOHN grabs SMIKE, and puts his hand over SMIKE'S mouth. Note: this scene is peculiarly effective if a trapdoor is available, and the "door" is the trap.

JOHN. My name is Browdie. I'm from Yorkshire. I'm a friend of your friend, lad who beat the schoolmaster. Don't say a word. (*Pause.* SMIKE *nods.* JOHN *lets him go and takes a screwdriver from his pocket.*) I've snuck up, making out I'm poorly. When you gone, I'm going to prise the lock off, make it look as how you did it.

SMIKE. Go where?

JOHN. Where? Go away. Go home. (SMIKE *looking confused.*) Escape. Do you understand?

SMIKE. Yes, yes. I understand. (SMIKE *is beginning to go. Then he suddenly grabs* JOHN.) He brought me back, before. He'll do again. I know he will.

JOHN. He won't. Now, come on, quickly, off with 'ee. (SMIKE *can't move.*) Oh, th'art a broken-down old chap. I shouldn't shout at thee. Go down the stair, go quiet past the door t'where they are's tight shut, I swear they'll never hear thee. (SMIKE *releases* JOHN.)

SMIKE. Now?

JOHN. Yes, now. One more thing. Just tell young master, when tha sees him, as I'm spliced to Tilda now, and staying at the Saracen's. Tha can remember that?

SMIKE. Yes, yes. Spliced to Tilda.

JOHN. Now, go, go. (SMIKE *a look at* JOHN, *then he goes.* JOHN *with his screwdriver, goes to prise off the lock. But something is preventing him holding it steady. He is shaking, as if in a strong convulsion. It gradually becomes apparent that* JOHN BROWDIE *is even more vastly amused than he has ever been vastly amused before.*)

SCENE 24

The roads to and from the country. Enter SMIKE, *desperately running on the spot.*

NARRATOR. And without pausing for a moment to reflect upon the course he was taking, he fled away with surprising swiftness, borne upon such wings as only fear can wear. (SMIKE *is in a spot running. Behind him, through the darkness, we see, as a fantasy, a nightmare vision of Dotheboys Hall:* MRS. SQUEERS, *ringing her bell,* MR. SQUEERS *with his cane,* WACKFORD *laughing,* FANNY, *the* BOYS. *We hear lines too, echoed and distorted: "And a pretty thing it is". "O.U.T.C.A.S.T.". "Foresaken". "Homeless". "In here, you haven't finished". "I'll flog you within an inch of your life". And gradually, the noises coalesce, and become the swishes of a cane, growing louder and louder.* SMIKE *puts his hands to his ears. The sounds grow even louder: they're inside his head. Finally, the nightmare fades,* SMIKE *stops, takes his hands from his ears, and there is silence. An owl hoots. Silence.*)

NARRATORS. And it was not until the darkness and quiet of a country road recalled him to the world outside himself,

And the starry sky above him warned him of the rapid flight of time,

That, covered with dust and panting for breath, he stopped to listen and look about him.

All was still and silent.

A glare of light in the distance, casting a warm glow upon the sky, marked where the huge city lay.

It was late now.

He turned back, and taking the open road, made again for London. (SMIKE *turns and walks. Passers-by cross the stage, and continue the Narration.*)

NARRATORS. And by the time he re-entered it at the western extremity, the greater part of the shops were closed. Of the throngs of people who had been tempted abroad after the heat of the day, but few remained. (*Suddenly, out of the passers-by leaps* NEWMAN NOGGS, *who grabs* SMIKE. SMIKE *nearly jumps out of his skin.*)

NOGGS. Dear fellow; oh, dear fellow.

SMIKE. Uh—uh—

NOGGS. Smike, it's only me.

SMIKE. Oh, Mr. Noggs—

NOGGS. Where have you been? They've been half mad about you.

SMIKE. Who have?

NOGGS. (*Obviously.*) Mr. Nicholas. His mother. And Miss Nickleby. And I must take you home at once.

SMIKE. Yes. Yes. (NOGGS *is striding off.* SMIKE *not.* NOGGS *turns back, looks, questioningly.*) Miss Nickleby.

NOGGS. That's right.

SMIKE. Miss Nickleby . . . Half mad about me too? (*Pause.* NOGGS *a little nod, goes and takes* SMIKE'S *arm. They go out together.*)

ACT II

SCENE 1

The coffee-room of the Saracen's Head. NICHOLAS sits at a table with a white cloth. Two other chairs. Enter JOHN BROWDIE, TILDA and WILLIAM the waiter.

JOHN. A gentleman? What gentleman? (*Sees NICHOLAS.*) Eh! Schoolmaster's assistant.

NICHOLAS. Mr. Browdie.

JOHN. (*To WILLIAM.*) Well, din't stand there—gentleman has come to see us. Fetch some food, some pies, some cuts of beef, a tongue or two, a fowl, some ale. Come on, sir, bustle.

TILDA. John, we have just had dinner—and, p'raps, Mr. Nickleby as well—?

JOHN. What? Call that dinner? Come now, bustle, bustle.

WILLIAM. Yes, sir, certainly. (*WILLIAM goes out.*)

JOHN. Well, then.

NICHOLAS. Sir, I have come here with three purposes. The first is to express my heartfelt thanks to you, releasing that poor lad, at such a risk—

JOHN. Oh, weren't no risk.

NICHOLAS. Well, I am sure that's not the case, but still. The second, naturally, is to express my most sincere congratulations on your recent nuptials.

JOHN. Oh, ay.

NICHOLAS. And trusting that I'll be allowed to take the usual license, Mr. Browdie.

JOHN. Oh, ay—take whatever—dinner's coming soon.

NICHOLAS. I thank you. Mrs. Browdie. (*NICHOLAS kisses TILDA.*)

TILDA. Mr. Nickleby!

JOHN. Oh, I see. Do, do make thaself at home.

NICHOLAS. I shall, of course—on one condition.

JOHN. Ay, what's that?

NICHOLAS. That when you have occasion for one, you'll make me a godfather.

TILDA. Oh, Mr. Nickleby.

JOHN. (*Hugely tickled.*) What's that? A godfather? Oh, ay. Oh, don't say another word. Tha'll not beat that. A godfather. Eh, Tilda, hast tha ever heard the like? Wha's going on? (*And indeed, during the last few moments, we have become aware of a disturbance.*)

TILDA. I don't know, John. (*Enter a gaggle of people, including an* ANGRY FELLOW *with a bleeding nose and torn collar,* WILLIAM, *a* YOUNG MAN, *rolling up his sleeves, and a number of* CUSTOMERS *and* WAITRESSES.)

ANGRY FELLOW. (*To* WILLIAM.) Police! I want the police. (*Pointing to the* YOUNG MAN.) I want that man arrested.

1st CUSTOMER. Right, so he should be.

1st WAITRESS. What a thing to do!

WILLIAM. Now, sir, please, if we could just keep calm about this—

ANGRY FELLOW. Calm? He asks me to be calm!

2nd CUSTOMER. (*To* 1st WAITRESS.) He asks him to be calm.

ANGRY FELLOW. The police, sir! Now!

JOHN. What's going on here, then?

ANGRY FELLOW. I'll tell you, sir, what's going on, that if a fellow sitting quietly with a drink, conversing with his friends, is liable to be assaulted by a perfect stranger—

2nd WAITRESS. Well, it's certainly a scandal.

ANGRY FELLOW. Sitting, quietly, doing nothing but conversing—

1st CUSTOMER. Nothing else.

ANGRY FELLOW. And then to have some great young lout come up to him, and tear his collar, punch him on the nose—

NICHOLAS. Could one inquire—what is the explanation of the gentleman concerned?

ANGRY FELLOW. Well—do you hear that! "Gentleman". "An explanation". Hmph!

2nd CUSTOMER. "Could one inquire".

1st WAITRESS. "The gentleman concerned". (*The* YOUNG MAN *steps forward. He is Welsh.*)

YOUNG MAN. One could inquire, sir, and I would be pleased to give an explanation. I have just returned, sir, from a journey of some distance, and was sitting in the coach-house with a pint of wine, when I could not but overhear that person, choosing to express himself in very disrespectful and familiar terms, of a young lady. I informed him, with considerable civility, that I was sure he was mistaken in his vile conjectures, which were of a most offensive nature, and demanded he withdraw them unconditionally. This he refused to do, and so I took his collar and I punched him on the nose. (*Pause.*)

NICHOLAS. I see. Well—that does sound, it seems you did have cause, sir, certainly—you know the lady, I presume?

YOUNG MAN. Oh, no, I never heard of her.

NICHOLAS. But, um—

YOUNG MAN. But it would be a pretty state of things, if names of ladies could be bandied round the town, without a let or hindrance, merely for the want of some acquaintance of the bandied person being present to defend their honour. Wouldn't it?

1st WAITRESS. Well, now—

2nd WAITRESS. That certainly sounds reasonable.

1st CUSTOMER. If not, I mean, uh—

1st WAITRESS. Where would be the end of it?

YOUNG MAN. My view entirely. (*To the* ANGRY FELLOW.) Now, sir, I'd suggest we both allow our tempers to cool down. I can be contacted at this address. (*He hands the* ANGRY FELLOW *a card.*) If you should wish to bring a charge. But now, I'd seriously advocate, that everyone proceeds about their business with no more ado.

1st CUSTOMER. Right, then.

2nd WAITRESS. Yes, back to business.

1st CUSTOMER. What an excellent idea. (*They have all gone, except for the* ANGRY FELLOW.)

YOUNG MAN. Good evening, sir. (*The* ANGRY FELLOW *goes out. To* NICHOLAS.) Well, I must thank you for your intervention, sir, and ask to know where I may find you to express my formal gratitude. Here is my card. Good evening, sir. (NICHOLAS *gives the* YOUNG MAN *his card, as he accepts the Young Man's.*)

NICHOLAS. Good heavens. You're a Cheeryble.

FRANK CHEERYBLE. (*For it is he.*) That's right, sir.

TILDA. (*To* JOHN.) What's a Cheeryble?

NICHOLAS. But surely not—that Cheeryble, who's nephew to the other Cheerybles, who has been for the last four years establishing an agency in Lancashire, and is expected back tomorrow?

FRANK. Yes, I am that Cheeryble, indeed, sir. And may I presume to ask if you are that same Mr. Nickleby whom I have learnt was recently employed by my two uncles, and of whom I've heard, by letter and by wire, the most complete and constant good report?

NICHOLAS. Well, of the good report, I cannot speak. But I am Mr. Nickleby.

FRANK. Well, there's a thing.

NICHOLAS. Yes, isn't it.

FRANK. You, Mr. Nickleby. Do call me Frank.

NICHOLAS. You, Mr. Cheeryble. Please call me Nicholas.

JOHN. (*To* TILDA.) D'you s'pose the dinner'll have come?

NICHOLAS. (*Suddenly.*) Oh, Mr. Browdie. I said I had come with a threefold purpose, and I did not complete my mission. Would you and Mrs. Browdie do us the great honour of calling on us at our house tomorrow night. And if you would forgive me making one addition to the party, I would hope that Mr. Cheeryble might join us too.

FRANK. I would be most delighted.

TILDA. So would we.

NICHOLAS. Right, then. That's settled. (*Enter* WILLIAM.)

WILLIAM. (*To* JOHN.) Sir, I have laid out what you ordered in your room. I would point out, though, that I didn't realise your party was—of only four. There is enough for twice or thrice that number, sir.

JOHN. In that case. It'll do.

SCENE 2

The Kenwigs' front room. Chairs, tables, a clothes-horse with towels hanging. Downstage, kettles and tea-pots. At least three MARRIED LADIES, MRS. CUTLER, MISS GREEN, *and* MORLEENA, *who is nursing* LITTLE LILLYVICK, *the baby.* MR. KENWIGS *himself is standing looking nervous, for* MRS. KENWIGS, *offstage, is having another baby. The* NARRATORS *fill us in as the scene is set up:*

NARRATORS. And after a substantial supper with the Browdies,

Nicholas walked on to Golden Square,

And to the house of Newman Noggs,

Not knowing that downstairs from his old friend,

There had been an addition to the family of the Kenwigs,

An event which half the neighborhood had come to witness and to celebrate.

(*Enter a* NURSE *from* MRS. KENWIGS' *room of confinement. All the* LADIES *eagerly move towards her. The* NURSE *looks quickly round to select the most suitable people for the tasks in hand. Behind her enters* DR. LUMBEY, *the doctor, whose task is completed, and is rolling down his sleeves.*)

NURSE. Morleena. Fetch your ma a cup of something hot. And—Madam, will you fetch more salts. (KENWIGS *stepping forward.*) No, not yet, Mr. Kenwigs! (*The* NURSE *goes back into the other room.* MORLEENA *puts* LITTLE LILLYVICK *in his crib, goes to the hob, pours a hot drink, and takes it in.* DR. LUMBEY *talks to* KENWIGS *and goes to pick up the abandoned* LITTLE LILLYVICK.)

DR. LUMBEY. It's a fine boy, Mr. Kenwigs, there's no doubt about it.

KENWIGS. Oh, Dr. Lumbey, do you think so?

DR. LUMBEY. Now this is—

KENWIGS. Little Lillyvick (*Enter the* NURSE.)

NURSE. Please, madam, put more water on to boil. And—(*To* MISS GREEN.) Miss, please run down to the corner shop and get a bottle of sal volatile. In a few moments, Mr. Kenwigs! (MISS GREEN *goes out to the shop.*)

KENWIGS. (*To* DR. LUMBEY.) Morleena was a fine child as well.

DR. LUMBEY. Oh, they all were, sir. (*To the Baby*.)
Goo goo goo goo.

KENWIGS. She'll be a treasure to the man she marries.
Did you ever see her dance?

DR. LUMBEY. No, I haven't had that privilege. (*To
the Baby*.) Gob gob gob gob.

KENWIGS. Not to speak of course, about her expectations.

2nd MARRIED LADY. What expectations?

MRS. CUTLER. Mm.

KENWIGS. Well, ma'am; it's not perhaps for me to say.
It's not for me to boast of any family with which I have
the honour to be linked—but shall we say, my children
might come into a small matter of a hundred pounds-a-
piece. Perhaps. P'raps more; but certainly that much.

1st MARRIED LADY. A very pretty little fortune.

KENWIGS. I will make mention of no names, but many
of my friends have met a relative of Mrs. Kenwigs in this
very room, as would give dignity to any company, that's
all.

MRS. CUTLER. I've met him. In this very room.

KENWIGS. And it's naturally most gratifying—(*Enter
the* NURSE.)

NURSE. Morleena, dear, the kettle.

KENWIGS. To my feelings as a father—

NURSE. (*To* KENWIGS.) You—stay there! (NURSE *goes
out.* MORLEENA *goes and fills a teapot from the kettle*.)

KENWIGS. To see a man like Mrs. Kenwigs' uncle, Mr.
Lillyvick, a man like that a-kissing and a-taking notice of
my—(*Enter* MISS GREEN.)

MISS GREEN. Well, now, Mr. Kenwigs, look who I
found, coming up the stairs.

KENWIGS. (*Irritated*.) Who is it? (*Enter* NICHOLAS. *He
is slightly breathless*.) Why, Mr. Johnson! What a privilege.

NICHOLAS. I fear, sir, that in fact my purpose was to
Mr. Noggs and must be, very soon, but having heard
about your circumstance—

KENWIGS. Ah, yes. My circumstance. And, as I was
saying, it is naturally very gratifying to my feelings as a
husband and a father, to consider how dear Mr. Lillyvick, how he will feel when he is made acquainted with
this—happy circumstance.

NICHOLAS. Uh—Mr. Lillyvick.

KENWIGS. That's right. (*To* 1st MARRIED LADY.) The Collector of the Water-Rate.

NICHOLAS. I wonder—if you've heard from him at all.

KENWIGS. No, not for several weeks. Oh a week or two. (*To* 2nd MARRIED LADY). And Mrs. Kenwigs' uncle.

NICHOLAS. Or had a message.

KENWIGS. Why? Is there a cause for one?

NICHOLAS. Well. . . .

KENWIGS. Well what? (*Pause.*)

NICHOLAS. Sir, you remember Miss Petowker?

KENWIGS. Yes, of course I do.

NICHOLAS. He's married her. (*Long pause.*)

KENWIGS. He's married Miss Petowker.

NICHOLAS. Yes, that's right. In Portsmouth.

KENWIGS. Portsmouth. Mr. Lillyvick has married Miss Petowker.

NICHOLAS. That's correct. (*Pause.* MORLEENA *drops the kettle.*)

KENWIGS. My children! My defrauded, swindled infants!

1st MARRIED LADY. What's this? (MORLEENA *goes rigid and starts screaming.*)

NICHOLAS. Um—

KENWIGS. Villain! Cur! And traitor!

2nd MARRIED LADY. Hmph! (*Enter the* NURSE *and the* 3rd MARRIED LADY.)

NURSE. What's all this? What's going on? What is this noise?

KENWIGS. Be silent, woman!

NURSE. You be silent, sir. Have you no feelings for your baby?

KENWIGS. No!

EVERYONE. Oh! Oh!

NURSE. Then, shame on you. Unnatural monster!

KENWIGS. Let him die! He has no expectations, and no property to come into. We want no babies here— take 'em away! Take all of them—off to the Foundling! (MORLEENA *screaming.* DR. LUMBEY *trying to attend to* MORLEENA.)

MRS. CUTLER. Mr. Kenwigs!

KENWIGS. Oh, the attention. The attention that I've shown that man. The oysters he has eaten, and the pints of ale he's drunk, here in this house—

MRS. CUTLER. Now, Mr. Kenwigs, naturally, it's most upsetting—

KENWIGS. The presents that I've given him. The pipes, the snuff-boxes, a pair of india-rubber galoshes, costing six-and-sixpence—and then, for this—for this—Be quiet, Morleena! (MORLEENA *stops screaming*.)

MORLEENA. Sorry, Pa.

NURSE. Oh, drat that stupid man! (*The* NURSE *goes out*.)

KENWIGS. That man! His wild and careless passion— it has ruined us. (*He goes out, dramatically*.)

NICHOLAS. Uh, I appear to be . . . the bearer of bad tidings. Please—excuse me. (NICHOLAS *goes out*.)

1st MARRIED LADY. *Well.*

MRS. CUTLER. What a performance.

2nd MARRIED LADY. What a vulgar man.

DR. LUMBEY. Goo goo. Goo goo.

SCENE 3

NOGGS *pottering round his garret*. NICHOLAS *bursts in*.

NICHOLAS. Newman, I've come to thank you.

NOGGS. What?

NICHOLAS. For finding him, and bringing him to us.

NOGGS. Oh, don't, please don't.

NICHOLAS. And Newman, and to tell you something. Something I've been bursting with for days and cannot tell another living soul.

NOGGS. What's that?

NICHOLAS. It is—it is—oh, Newman, if you'd only seen her!

NOGGS. Seen her? Who?

NICHOLAS. Her lips, her eyes, her hair—

NOGGS. Uh—it's a lady?

NICHOLAS. Yes, of course, it is a lady. And, oh, what a lady. And—I had to tell you. (*Pause*.) There. (*Pause*.)

NOGGS. Uh—tell me all about her.

NICHOLAS. I know nothing of her.

NOGGS. Nothing?

NICHOLAS. No. Except her first name. Which is Madeline. But now, I must—oh, if you saw her, Newman! (*He runs out.*)

NOGGS. If. (*Slight pause.*) Oh, Nick. (*Pause.*) In Love. With lips and eyes and hair. With Madeline.

SCENE 4

The Cheerybles' offices, upstage, and Ralph's house, downstage. For the Cheerybles, all we need is Mr. Ned's desk and three chairs; for Ralph's house, Noggs' desk, his high stool, and a low stool as well. Narration, as NOGGS *enters and sits at his desk.*

NARRATORS. The next morning, in his little office

And on the top of his little stool,

Newman Noggs heard the chime of a neighbouring church clock,

Looked up,

And clicked his tongue,

And soliloquised.

NOGGS. Three quarters past! My dinner is at two. And him not back. And told to wait. Three quarters of an hour. (*Pause.*) It's done on purpose. Just like him. (*Pause.*) I don't believe he has an appetite. Except for pounds, shillings and pence. I should like to have him made to swallow one of every English coin. (*Pause.* NOGGS *relishes the idea.*) The penny. (*He laughs.*) Ha— two shillings. (*He laughs.*) And—the crown!

NARRATORS. His humour being in some degrees restored, Newman brought forth a little bottle,

Shook it,

Opened it,

And drank,

And restored it even more. (MR. CHARLES, MR. NED
and NICHOLAS *assembling. Narration cont.*)

While at the same time,

At the offices of the Brothers Cheeryble,

Nicholas was asked by Mr. Charles and Mr. Ned

If they could beg the quite immeasurable delight

Of having one quick word with them

In the privacy of their room.

NICHOLAS. Well, yes. Of course. Indeed. (NICHOLAS,
MR. CHARLES *and* MR. NED *sit at the table.*)
NARRATOR. While Newman, having put away his bottle, heard the door, and voices—(*The* NARRATORS
withdraw.)
NOGGS. Well, that's it. There's someone with him. It'll
be—"Stop till this gentleman has gone." Well, I won't
do it, and that's flat. (NOGGS *hides and* RALPH *enters
with* ARTHUR GRIDE, *an old, wizened miser.*)
RALPH. Noggs! Where are you, Noggs? (*To* GRIDE.)
He must have gone to dinner. Hm. (GRIDE *shrugs and
grins.* NOGGS *a look out of his closet. He sees the two
men aren't going.*) Well, we'll use his room. It's cool and
in the shade. (*Another look from* NOGGS. *He realises he's
stuck.* GRIDE *shrugs and grins.*) So, sit down, Mr. Gride,
and tell me what's your business. (GRIDE *sits on the low
stool,* RALPH *on the high one.* GRIDE *laughs.*) Hm.
What's this?
GRIDE. Oh, you're bold and deep one, Mr. Nickleby.
(*Transfer focus to* CHEERYBLES.)
MR. CHARLES. Now, sir, we would like to employ you,
on a confidential and delicate mission.
MR. NED. The object of the mission is a—um, young
lady.
MR. CHARLES. Nay, a very beautiful young lady,
whom I think you caught sight of in these very offices
the first day you came here.

NICHOLAS. Ah, yes, I do remember, certainly. (*Transfer to* RALPH *and* GRIDE.)

RALPH. So, then?

GRIDE. I'm going to be married.

RALPH. Hm. Some old hag with a fortune?

GRIDE. No, a pretty, dainty and bewitching little creature, of not yet nineteen. Do you remember Walter Bray?

RALPH. Oh, yes, indeed. The man about town, for whom the town became beyond his means. He owes me money. As I recall, nine hundred and ten pounds, four and—something.

GRIDE. Yes. And he owes me money too. A little more. And he is dying. And he has a daughter. (*Transfer to* CHEERYBLES.)

MR. CHARLES. The lady's father, sir, was married to a friend of ours. He was a wastrel and a profligate.

MR. NED. His wife died, oh, about a year ago. He was committed to the King's Bench Prison.

NICHOLAS. So—she is destitute.

MR. CHARLES. She is.

NICHOLAS. Can such a—is this possible?

MR. NED. Well, yes, Mr. Nickleby, I'm afraid it is. (*Transfer to* RALPH *and* GRIDE.)

RALPH. So what you plan is this. You offer to release Bray from his debts, perhaps you give him an allowance, so he can live out his dying days in reasonable comfort, and, in exchange, you have his dainty daughter for your wife.

GRIDE. That's right.

RALPH. And as I'm the other creditor, you come here to ask me what I would accept.

GRIDE. Just so. I'd thought, nine shillings in the pound. . . .

RALPH. Gride, tell me the whole story.

GRIDE. What? (*Pause.*) Oh, well . . . (*Transfer to* CHEERYBLES.)

MR. NED. And so, good brother Charles and I considered, and debated, and resolved, that we must undertake a harmless subterfuge.

MR. CHARLES. That someone, feigning to be dealing in small ornaments and drawings and the like, should go to her and purchase what she makes for cash.

NICHOLAS. Uh—someone?

MR. NED. So, then, there being no time like the present, can you go there now?

NICHOLAS. (*Going quickly to the door.*) Yes, yes. At once, without delay. (*He runs out. Transfer to* RALPH'S.)

GRIDE. Oh. Well. Supposing I was in possession of a deed, concerning some small property to which this pretty lady was entitled, of which nobody knows anything, except for me, and which her husband would lay claim to, would that, p'raps, account for—

RALPH. For the whole proceeding. Yes. You have the deed about you?

GRIDE. Oh, very well. If I'm to have my bride. (*He hands over the deed.* RALPH *reads it.*) My dainty bride. (RALPH *reads.*) Her eyelashes, and lips, and hair the fingers itch to play with . . .

RALPH. I've little eyes for beauty, I'm afraid. But if you choose to think you're buying her for love, then I can't stop you.

GRIDE. Buying her.

RALPH. Oh, Mr. Gride, you have your dainty creature, Bray has his debts paid off, and I *my* debt, the full amount, and my share of your inheritance. (GRIDE *looks up in alarm.*) And so we're all content. Now, shall we go? (GRIDE *and* RALPH *go.* NOGGS *emerges.*)

NOGGS. I think . . . I think I've lost my appetite. (*Transfer to* CHEERYBLES. NICHOLAS *bursts back in.*)

NICHOLAS. Oh—Mr. Charles.

MR. CHARLES. What, back so soon?

NICHOLAS. You haven't told me where she lives. Or who she is. Or anything.

MR. NED. Oh, please forgive us. (*Handing over a slip of paper and an envelope.*) Here is the address; the money; and the order. The young lady's name is Madeline. Her father's name is Walter Bray. (*As the scene disperses.*)

NICHOLAS. And Nicholas, repressing every feeling that he should perhaps have stated his emotions with regard to the young lady, turned and left the chambers of the Brothers Cheeryble, and set a sprightly pace for the King's Bench Prison, and the meager debtors' houses that surround it.

SCENE 5

Near the King's Bench prison. Bare stage, but full of beggars, criminals, the poor and the mad. For the first time, we are seeing London's super-poor, the lowest of the low. As NICHOLAS walks through them, he is grabbed and begged. Into the middle come MADELINE, pushing her father WALTER BRAY in his wheelchair. The beggars and criminals withdraw, but their presence remains with us for this and the next scene.

BRAY. Madeline, what's this? Who told a stranger that we could be seen? Who is it?

MADELINE. I believe—

BRAY. Oh, yes, you always do, believe. What is it?

NICHOLAS. Sir, I've called with a commission. For a pair of handscreens, and some painted velvet for an ottoman. I have a sum here, as deposit, of five pounds. (*He hands the envelope to* MADELINE.)

BRAY. Hm. See it's right then, Madeline.

MADELINE. I'm sure it's absolutely right, papa.

BRAY. You're sure? How can you be. "I'm sure". (MADELINE *takes a five pound note out of the envelope*.)

MADELINE. Well, I was right to be, papa.

BRAY. Now, go and get a newspaper, some apples, and two bottles of that port I had last week, and—and—I can't remember half of what I want. Well, you can always go out twice. And you can go too, sir, as soon as you've had your receipt.

NICHOLAS. It is no matter, sir.

BRAY. No matter? What d'you mean, sir? Do you think you bring your paltry money as a gift? It's business, sir, return for value given. Damn you, sir, d'you know that you are talking to a gentleman, who at one time could buy up fifty of such men as you, and all you have?

NICHOLAS. I merely meant that as I shall have many dealings with this lady, I'll not trouble her with forms.

BRAY. Well, we will have all the forms we need. My daughter, sir, requires no charity, and will not be the object of your pity. Business, sir! Now, Madeline, receipt! (MADELINE *writing a receipt*.)

NICHOLAS. (*To* MADELINE.) When shall—when shall I call again?

BRAY. When you're requested, sir, and not before.

MADELINE. Oh, not for three or four weeks, sir. It is not necessary, I can do without.

BRAY. What? Not for three or four weeks, Madeline?

MADELINE. Then, sooner—sooner, if you please.

NICHOLAS. A week?

MADELINE. (*Giving* NICHOLAS *the receipt.*) Yes, then, a week. Here's your receipt, sir.

NICHOLAS. Thank you. In a week's time, then. Good-bye. (*He goes out.* MADELINE, *after a moment, following.*)

BRAY. Where are you going, my dear?

MADELINE. Oh, he's left his—

BRAY. What?

MADELINE. I—I'll be a moment, father—

BRAY. (*Unable to move without assistance.*) What has he left? (MADELINE *catches up with* NICHOLAS.)

MADELINE. Oh, sir, I don't know if I'm doing right, but pray—don't mention to your masters what has happened here this morning. He has suffered much. Today he's very bad. I beg you, sir.

NICHOLAS. You only have to hint a wish, and I would risk my life to gratify it. (MADELINE *turns away.*) Oh, I speak the truth. I can't disguise my heart from you. I'd—I would die to serve you. What else can I say?

MADELINE. Say nothing. (*She goes out.*)

NICHOLAS. A week. How can I stand a week.

SCENE 6

The same, a little later. BRAY *has been joined by* RALPH *and* ARTHUR GRIDE. NICHOLAS *and* MADELINE *have gone.*

RALPH. It must be in a week, sir. And we must know in five days. (*Pause.*) Now, sir, it's Mr. Arthur Gride. An offer any father would be proud of! Think what a haul it is. (BRAY *looks at* GRIDE.) Come, sir. Mr. Gride has money but no youth. Miss Madeline has youth and beauty but no money. Tit for tat. A deal of heaven's making. Hm?

GRIDE. Matches are made in heaven, so they say.

RALPH. So, what do you reply? (*Pause.*)

BRAY. It's not for me to say. It's for my daughter.

RALPH. Yes, of course. But you have still the power to advise.

BRAY. Hm. Hm. Advise. I tell you, Nickleby, there were times when my will carried against everyone: her mother's family and friends, whole pack of 'em. With power and wealth on their side, and just my will on mine.

RALPH. Well, there we are. Your wish is her command, I'm sure. But if it isn't . . . (BRAY *looks miserably at* GRIDE. RALPH *nods to* GRIDE, *who withdraws a little.*)

BRAY. What? If I can't convince her?

RALPH. Well, shall we say . . . I see two pictures. One of Walter Bray, the fashionable fellow, as he once was, shining in society, in free air, and under brighter skies, who knows, in France, but certainly in luxury. Another lease of life. (*Moving closer.*) Or else, another picture. In a churchyard, with a gravestone and a date. Perhaps two years, perhaps a little less, not more. Now, is it really not for you to say? It's really for your daughter to decide? (*Pause.*) You'll have cheated nature, Mr. Bray. (*Pause.*)

BRAY. But, Nickleby. Is this not cruel?

RALPH. Cruel? If he were younger, yes. But think, how long is it before your daughter is a widow?

BRAY. Yes, but still—

RALPH. By this, she is made rich. And you'll be young, and bright, and blazing once again.

BRAY. Yes, yes. (*Pause.*) You're right. It is for her, as well as me. (RALPH *gestures* GRIDE *back.*)

RALPH. Exactly. And she'll live to thank you. (*Sound of* MADELINE *returning.*)

BRAY. Hush. It's her. (*Enter* MADELINE *with apples, two bottles of port, and a newspaper.*) Ah, Madeline. Here are two gentlemen.

MADELINE. I see them, father.

BRAY. (*Trying to make a joke.*) Huh. She used to say, Gride, that the very sight of you would make me worse. Well, p'raps she'll change her mind on that point; girls can change their minds, you know—you look so tired, my dear.

MADELINE. I'm not, indeed.

BRAY. Oh, yes, you are, you do too much.

MADELINE. I wish I could do more.

BRAY. I know. But still you overtax yourself, this wretched life, my love, it's more than you can bear, I'm sure of it. . . . (*Pause*.) It's more than I can bear. (*Slight pause*. MADELINE *goes and kisses her father*.)

RALPH. Five days, then, Mr. Bray.

BRAY. Yes, very well. Five days. (RALPH *turns to go*. GRIDE *trying to take* MADELINE'S *hand to kiss it*.)

GRIDE. And if the lady. . . . if the lady condescends. . . . (MADELINE *shrinks from* GRIDE. GRIDE *looks to* RALPH *who gestures him to go*. RALPH *and* GRIDE *leave* BRAY *and* MADELINE. GRIDE *a feeble grin to* RALPH *before scuttling off*.)

RALPH. Oh Lord, how do people dupe themselves. (NOGGS *is there. The* BRAYS *have gone*.) They're here?

NOGGS. They've been here half an hour.

RALPH. Two men? One Mr. Squeers?

NOGGS. That's right. In your room now.

RALPH. Good. Get a coach.

NOGGS. A coach. Whatever for?

RALPH. To ride in. To the Strand. (RALPH *goes Upstage. We can see him greet* SNAWLEY *and* SQUEERS. NOGGS *gesturing vaguely*.)

NOGGS. A coach. The Strand. Coach! The Strand! The Nicklebys. Oh, I should follow—but he'd see me. (*He waves, agitatedly. We see* BROOKER *groping along*.) Coach! On, the Strand, there's mischief in it. There must be! (*He spots* BROOKER.) Are you a coach?

BROOKER. No.

NOGGS. (*Searching in his pocket*.) Uh—

BROOKER. Are you the clerk of Mr. Nickleby?

NOGGS. Oh—no. Mean—yes.

BROOKER. Get him his coach. And see him off in it. And then, I want a word with you.

NOGGS. Coach!

SCENE 7

The Nicklebys' rooms in the Strand. A party. MRS. NICKLEBY, KATE, SMIKE, MISS LA CREEVY, JOHN *and* TILDA BROWDIE, FRANK CHEERYBLE *and* TIM LINKINWATER. *A rug on the floor. Narration as the scene is set up*.

NARRATORS. And meanwhile, at the Strand,

At Miss La Creevy's.

The evening party was well under way,

And it was universally agreed by all the guests

That they could not remember when they had had such a time,

And, in particular, John and Tilda Browdie wished it to be known by one and all that they

JOHN. Would not have missed it for the world. (*The* NARRATORS *withdraw.*)

MISS LA CREEVY. Well, thank you *so* much, Mr. Browdie, as it happens, I can't think—

MRS. NICKLEBY. Well, yes, indeed, it's very good of you, dear Mrs. Browdie too, because of course you come to see us in a very plain and homely manner. As I said to Kate—

MISS LA CREEVY. I just can't think of when I've had a better—

MRS. NICKLEBY. As I said "Kate, dearest, you will only make the Browdies feel uncomfortable, if we indulge in great display, and how very inconsiderate that would be". But that is not to say—

MISS LA CREEVY. Of when I've had a better time myself.

MRS. NICKLEBY. To say, of course, that we have no experience of high society, Kate, d'you recall those parties at Peltiroguses? They used to live about a mile from us, not straight you understand, but turning sharp left by the turnpike at the point the Plymouth mail ran over someone's donkey, Kate, you do recall those parties at the Peltiroguses?

KATE. (*Very firmly.*) Mama, I entertain of them the most distinct and vivid memory. (*Slight pause.*) But also, I recall that earlier this evening Mr. Browdie promised us that he would sing a song, and I am sure we are all most impatient that he should redeem his promise, and I'm certain that it will afford you much more pleasure and amusement than it's possible to think of.

MISS LA CREEVY. Oh, now, what a treat.

MRS. NICKLEBY. Sing a song?

KATE. That's right, mama. Now, Mr. Browdie?

JOHN. Oh, well, uh—

TIM. Oh, yes.

MISS LA CREEVY. Oh, Mr. Browdie, please—

JOHN. Well, um— (*To* TILDA.) Sam Tansey's Fancy?

TILDA. No, John.

JOHN. Ballad of John Barleycorn?

TILDA. I think that's better.

JOHN. Right. (*He stands, clears his throat.*) Aye, right. (*He sings:*)

There came three men from out the west

Their victory to try—(*A very loud knocking.*)

TILDA. What's that?

NICHOLAS. Must be some mistake. There's no-one who would come here at this hour.

MRS. NICKLEBY. Perhaps it's—some—

KATE. I'll answer it. (NICHOLAS *going to stop* KATE, *for fear that it's some malefactor, but* KATE *has got there, and* RALPH NICKLEBY *walks in.*) Oh, uncle.

MRS. NICKLEBY. Brother-in-law. Why, what on earth—

RALPH. Now, stay, before the boy speaks, you will hear me, ma'am.

NICHOLAS. You won't, mama. Don't hear him. I will not have it. I do not know that man.

JOHN. (*Restraining* NICHOLAS.) Come now, come now.

NICHOLAS. I cannot bear his presence, it's an insult to my sister, and I will not—

KATE. Oh, please, Nicholas—

NICHOLAS. This is my house, am I a child? Oh, this will drive me mad!

FRANK. Who is this man?

MISS LA CREEVY. It's Nicholas' uncle. Calls himself Ralph Nickleby.

SMIKE. Ralph Nickleby. (*Pause.*)

RALPH. Ah. So this is the boy. (*He goes and speaks outside.*) Please come in, gentlemen. And Miss.

SMIKE. Ralph Nickleby! (*Enter* SQUEERS, SNAWLEY *and* FANNY.)

JOHN. Eh, school master!

TILDA. Oh, Fanny!

SMIKE. (*Clinging to* MISS LA CREEVY.) Huh. The enemies.

NICHOLAS. Am I to stand here and allow this? To allow my house to be invaded by these people?

RALPH. It will not last long, sir. I have come here on a simple mission, to restore a child to his parent—

NICHOLAS. What!

RALPH. —his son, sir, kidnapped and waylaid by you, with the base design of robbing him some day of any little wretched pittance which he might inherit.

SQUEERS. Oh, I bet you didn't think of this, eh? Got a father, has he?

RALPH. And as a proof, this is the father. Mr. Snawley, there's your son. (*Pause.*)

KATE. Oh, no.

SNAWLEY. Oh, yes. Yes, there he is. My son! My flesh and blood!

JOHN. Not that much flesh.

SNAWLEY. Come to me, boy. (*Pause.* SMIKE *rigid with terror.*)

MISS LA CREEVY. Stay here.

RALPH. Then it is clear we must have further proof. You had a son by your first marriage, Mr. Snawley?

SNAWLEY. Yes, I did, and there he stands.

RALPH. You and your wife were separated, and then you heard after a year or two, the boy had died.

SNAWLEY. Yes, I did. And now, the joy of—

RALPH. Whereas, in fact, you have discovered that your son's death was an invention by your former wife, to wound you, and in fact the boy had lived but was of an imperfect mind, and she had sent him to the school of Mr. Squeers. Is that not so?

SNAWLEY. You talk like a good book, sir, that's got nothing inside it but the truth.

NICHOLAS. I am expected to believe this fantasy? (RALPH *producing documents from a case.*)

RALPH. Certificates of marriage, birth, the letters of the wife, and other documents. Perhaps you'd like to read them, sir.

NICHOLAS. Frank, Tim, please help me look at these. (FRANK, TIM *and* NICHOLAS *put documents on the table and read them.* RALPH *sits.*)

SQUEERS. Well, sir, it seems you're reunited with your child. Oh, what a blessed moment!

SNAWLEY. Sir, I knew the very moment when you

brought him to my house. I felt—at once—a tingling, a burning, and a palpitation.

SQUEERS. That's parental instinct, sir.

SNAWLEY. That's what it was, no doubt about it. My heart yearned.

SQUEERS. It only shows what nature is, sir. She's a rum one, nature.

SNAWLEY. She's a holy thing. (TIM, NICHOLAS *and* FRANK *have finished*.)

FRANK. I'm afraid there's little doubt about it. Everything's in order.

TIM. It's a shame to say it, but it's so.

KATE. Oh, Nicholas, this can't be true. (NICHOLAS *shrugs.* RALPH *goes to the table and collects the documents*.)

KATE. (*Quickly, to* SNAWLEY.) Sir, if you are the father of this boy, then look, sir, at the wreck he has become, and tell us if you plan to send him back to that vile den my brother took him from.

SQUEERS. Vile den! You hear that, Mr. Nickleby?

RALPH. Now, there's a carriage waiting. Everything is proved. Let's take young Master Snawley and begone. (*Pause.*)

NICHOLAS. There is—the documents speak clearly. If our pleas won't move this man, there's nothing to be done.

SNAWLEY. They won't indeed. Hmph! Have a father to abandon his own child? (SNAWLEY *goes and takes* SMIKE'S *arm.*) Come, son. The coach is waiting. (MISS LA CREEVY *looks away as* SMIKE *walks halfway towards* SNAWLEY. *He stops.*)

SMIKE. O.U.T.C.A.S.T. A noun. Substantive. (SNAWLEY *looks bemused. He turns to* SQUEERS *who shrugs and smiles, as if to imply that* SMIKE *is delirious.* NICHOLAS *turns away.*)

SMIKE. Cast. Out. Home. Less. No! (*He runs back to* MISS LA CREEVY.) I won't. Won't go away again.

KATE. You hear that? Smike has chosen for himself.

SNAWLEY. Oh, this is cruel. Do parents bring children into the world for this?

JOHN. (*Nods to* SQUEERS.) Do they bring 'em into the world for *that*?

SQUEERS. Now, come on, blockhead, clear the way, and let him take his boy.

RALPH. Yes, sir, you have all blustered long enough.

JOHN. What, blockhead! Bluster? Well, I tell 'ee—I've released this poor chap from your clutches once—and I'll not stand by and see 'im going back to 'em again.

FANNY. Oh, Father, it was him! It was him let Smike go!

JOHN. Ay, 'twere, Fanny, and I tell 'ee—Get tha hands off me! (*For* SQUEERS *has been trying to get past* JOHN *and at* SMIKE. JOHN *elbows* SQUEERS *in the chest.*) I've had enough of this. The lot of you, get out, and leave the poor chap be. (*And he starts pushing* SQUEERS *and* SNAWLEY *to the door.*)

SQUEERS. I tell you, sir—

JOHN. I'm telling you! Out! Out!

FANNY. Oh, Tilda! Stop him!

TILDA. Stop him what?

FANNY. He's beating up my father. Stop him!

TILDA. How?

SNAWLEY. I want my son! Ungrateful boy!

SQUEERS. Oh, he always was sir—he never loved me, never loved our Wackford, who is next door to a cherubim—

JOHN. Out, now, out!

SQUEERS. I warn you, sir—(*But* JOHN *has got* SQUEERS *and* SNAWLEY *out.*)

JOHN. Well, done for two of 'em—(*To* RALPH.) You'd best get to your carriage, too, sir. And you, Fanny.

FANNY. Tilda.

SQUEERS. Eh, Fanny, s'got me hat! (TILDA *shrugs.*)

FANNY. Tilda, I renounce you. I—I throw you off, for ever, I—I wouldn't have a child named Tilda—not to save it from its grave.

JOHN. Come on, now, Fanny—

FANNY. Don't you meddle with my Christian name. Don't you—

SQUEERS. Eh, me hat, or else he'll steal it!

FANNY. (*To* TILDA.) Viper! False friend! Vixen! Artful—vulgar—myrmidon!

TILDA. Oh, don't be silly, Fanny.

NICHOLAS. Yes, Miss Squeers, your father's gone—

SQUEERS. Not going. Not without me hat, I'm not.

FANNY. Oh, don't you speak to me. (FANNY *runs out.* SQUEERS *runs back in, grabs his hat.*)

SQUEERS. I'll have you, Knuckleboy! (*And* JOHN *ejects him once again.*)

RALPH. Well, sir. If reason and good feeling fail you, it will have to be the law. (*Slight pause.*) But one thing can be said. I take it your romance about this boy has been destroyed. No, unknown, lost descendant of a man of high degree; but the weak, imbecilic son of some poor tradesman.

NICHOLAS. Sir. Now. Leave this house!

RALPH. I know you, sir. At least, do not delude yourself. I know your nature. Ma'am, goodnight. (RALPH *goes out. Pause.*)

TIM. Well, what a business.

MRS. NICKLEBY. I don't know—he's right of course, we should be reasonable. If only it was possible to settle it in a friendly manner—say, if Mr. Snawley would agree to furnish something certain for Smike's board and lodging. . . . wouldn't it be very satisfactory and pleasant for all parties?

KATE. No, mama. It wouldn't. You don't understand. (*Slight pause.*)

MRS. NICKLEBY. No, well—perhaps I don't. Perhaps I do—from time to time—find things a little hard to understand. (*Pause. A hiatus. Then* SMIKE *runs to* KATE *and embraces her. Pause.* MISS LA CREEVY *goes to* SMIKE.)

MISS LA CREEVY. Now, Mr. Smike, it's very late, and with all that excitement—shouldn't you be off to bed? (*She takes* SMIKE'S *hand and leads him towards the door.* SMIKE *turns back, to* JOHN BROWDIE.)

SMIKE. I am so grateful. Everything went black. I couldn't see. (*He turns and goes out with* MISS LA CREEVY.)

JOHN. Well, now, don't this call for a celebration? Come on, gentlemen. . . . (*The* MEN *pouring drinks for everyone.*)

NICHOLAS. Well, yes, indeed. Frank.

FRANK. Now, Mrs. Browdie—(*The rug begins to move. Note: This effect relies on a trap door. In the book, this incident involves an intrusion down the chimney.*)

TILDA. What's that?

FRANK. What's what? (*The rug is beginning to stand up.*)

TILDA. Oh, just, I thought I—oh, I did!

TIM. It's—under—

KATE. Oh, it's—from the cellar—

MRS. NICKLEBY. From the— (*The rug stands up. Under it is the* GENTLEMAN FROM NEXT DOOR.) Oh, good heavens!

FRANK. What's this?

TIM. An intruder!

MRS. NICKLEBY. Oh, it's him!

NICHOLAS. Mama, you know this person?

THE GENTLEMAN. (*Revealing himself.*) Oh maid! Oh maid, I thee entwine! (*He presents* MRS. NICKLEBY *with a cucumber.*)

KATE. Oh, it's the man—the madman from next door!

MRS. NICKLEBY. Now, Kate, I won't have that.

KATE. You won't?

MRS. NICKLEBY. No, not at all. And I'm surprised at you. This is a most unfortunate and persecuted gentleman, in my view, to be aided rather than abused.

THE GENTLEMAN. That's excellent. So, bring the bottled lightning, one clean tumbler, and a corkscrew. Fetch the thunder sandwiches. (*No-one fetches the thunder sandwiches. Enter* MISS LA CREEVY.)

MISS LA CREEVY. What's going on?

KATE. Oh, Miss La Creevy, it's—

THE GENTLEMAN. Ah, she is come!

MRS. NICKLEBY. What's this?

THE GENTLEMAN. She's come! Take all three graces, all nine muses, melt 'em down with fourteen of the biscuit-bakers daughters of Oxford Street and make a woman half as lovely. Phoo! I defy you! (*"After uttering this rhapsody, the old gentleman subsided into an ecstatic contemplation of* MISS LA CREEVY'S *charms". He takes the cucumber from* MRS. NICKLEBY *and gives it to* MISS LA CREEVY.)

FRANK. He seems to, um . . . have changed his mind.

MRS. NICKLEBY. Oh, nonsense. He's mistaken me, that's all. It's often so. I am mistaken, frequently, for Kate. Now, sir—

THE GENTLEMAN. (*To* MRS. NICKLEBY.) Avaunt ye, cat.

MRS. NICKLEBY. I beg your pardon? (*The* MEN *move in to eject the* GENTLEMAN.)

JOHN. Right now, that's enough.

THE GENTLEMAN. Cat! Puss! (MRS. NICKLEBY *faints quite away*.)

THE GENTLEMAN. Tit! Kit! Grimalkin!

FRANK. Or we may use force upon you.

THE GENTLEMAN. Tabby! Brindle! Whoosh! (*As he departs, to* MISS LA CREEVY.) Miss Milky Way—I am your puppet and your slave. (*The* GENTLEMAN *and the* MEN *have gone*.)

MISS LA CREEVY. Well.

MRS. NICKLEBY. (*Reviving*.) Kate. Is he gone?

KATE. He is, mama.

MRS. NICKLEBY. Oh, Kate, how dreadful.

KATE. Is it that.

MRS. NICKLEBY. I do believe the gentleman has lost his mind.

KATE. You do?

MRS. NICKLEBY. And I am the unhappy cause.

KATE. You are?

MRS. NICKLEBY. Of course. You saw him, just the other day, you see what he is now. You've heard the dreadful nonsense he has talked this evening, oh, can anybody doubt that he has gone quite mad and it is my refusal of him that has made him so. (*Exit* MRS. NICKLEBY. *The* MEN *returning*.)

KATE. And with this, Mrs. Nickleby turned tail, and, apologising to her guests, went off to bed.

NICHOLAS. And soon the gentlemen came back, the old man having been returned to his custodian.

TILDA. And John and Tilda, having to depart tomorrow morning, took their leave, with many thanks, and invitations to the company, if ever in North Yorkshire, to drop by.

ALL. North Yorkshire. (*Exit* JOHN *and* TILDA.)

NICHOLAS. And although it was past midnight, Frank and Tim remained a moment more.

TIM. Dear Miss La Creevy, please assure me you've recovered from your terrible ordeal.

MISS LA CREEVY. Oh, yes. Certainly, dear Mr. Linkinwater.

FRANK. Dear Miss Nickleby, I trust that all these violent altercations have not too disturbed your constitution.

KATE. No, I assure you, Mr. Cheeryble. (*And as the lights fade, we see* SMIKE, *behind them, looking fixedly at* KATE *and* FRANK CHEERYBLE.)

SCENE 8

The house of Arthur Gride. Bare stage. GRIDE *enters, dragging an old, battered, metal trunk, which is all the set we will need. He is singing "the fag end of some forgotten song."*

GRIDE. Tarantarantoo
Throw the old shoe
And may the wedding be lucky . . .

(*He opens the trunk, and takes out a bottle-green jacket.*)

Young, loving and fair . . .
Oh, what happiness there . . .

(*He looks at the jacket.*) The bottle green? Now, that's a famous suit, for when I bought it at the pawnbroker, there was a tarnished shilling in the waistcoat pocket. So, it's a lucky suit . . . I'll marry in the bottle green. (*He calls.*) Peg! (*Pause.*) Peg! Peg! Peg Sliderskew! (*"This call, loudly repeated twice or thrice, brought into the apartment a short, thin, sweasen, blear-eyed old woman, palsy-stricken and hideously ugly." It is Gride's deaf housekeeper,* PEG SLIDERSKEW. *She is Scottish.*)

PEG. What's that?

GRIDE. Ah, there you are, Peg. I've decided. I'll—

PEG. Wha's that you calling?

GRIDE. Yes, of course, I wanted—

PEG. Or was't just the clock? It must ha' been one or the other—nothing else stirs in *this* house, that's for—

GRIDE. (*Tapping his chest.*) Me, Peg, me.

PEG. Oh, you. What do you want?

GRIDE. I want, Peg, to be married in the bottle green.

PEG. Huh? (*Slight pause.*) What's this, dress up to be married? Why, what's wrong with what you usually wear?

GRIDE. But look my best, Peg, look my best.

PEG. What for? I tell ye, master, she's as handsome as you say, she won't look much at you, whatever you're decked up in: bottle-green, sky-blue or tartan-plaid, won't make a fig of difference.

GRIDE. Now, Peg, I've told you, I've decided—

PEG. Och, I know—

GRIDE. And after, there'll be only she and me, and you, and we can live, the three of us, as cheap as you and I have always done . . .

PEG. Oh, is that so?

GRIDE. So take up the loose stitches in the bottle-green, Peg, best black silk, and put new buttons on the coat, you'll do this for me, Peg? My wedding day? (*Pause.*)

PEG. Och, aye. I'll do't. (*She takes the coat. The bell rings.* PEG *laughs*). Och, who'd have thought.

GRIDE. The bell, Peg.

PEG. That old Arthur Gride—(*Bell rings.*)

GRIDE. The bell. Peg.

PEG. (*Still laughing.*) Falling for a wee—

GRIDE. The bell! (*Slight pause.*)

PEG. You what?

GRIDE. Go to it!

PEG. Go to what? What's wrong, me stopping here?

GRIDE. (*Gesturing a ringing bell.*) It Is The Bell. (*Slight pause.*)

PEG. Och. Aye. Well—I'll go answer it. (PEG *goes out.*)

GRIDE. Hm. Half a witch that woman, I believe. But very frugal, very deaf, her living costs me next to nothing. Oh, she'll do, she'll do. (*Calls.*) Who is it, Peg? (PEG *leads in* NOGGS.)

PEG. It's him.

GRIDE. Ah, Mr. Noggs, my good friend, so what news d'you bring for me? (*Exit* PEG.)

NOGGS. (*Handing over a letter.*) No news. A letter. Mr. Nickleby. The bearer waits.

GRIDE. (*Opening it eagerly.*) A letter? Then it's news. (*Quickly reading.*) Oh, yes, and good news, too. The very best there could be.

NOGGS. The bearer waits.

GRIDE. And will not wait much longer—a verbal answer. Tell him: "Yes."

NOGGS. Just "Yes"?

GRIDE. That's right. He'll understand.

NOGGS. (*Turning to go.*) I'm sure he will. (NOGGS *going.*)

GRIDE. Oh—Mr. Noggs?

NOGGS. Got the answer. "Yes."

GRIDE. I wondered—

NOGGS. Yes?

GRIDE. If you would like to join me in a little drop. To celebrate. (*Pause.*)

NOGGS. Oh, well . . .

GRIDE. I know you're partial, Mr. Noggs.

NOGGS. Oh. Very well. (GRIDE *opens the trunk to find a bottle and two small glasses. The hand which holds the letter is on the top of the trunk so* NOGGS *can read it.*)

NOGGS. Poor girl. Poor girl. (GRIDE *has got the bottle and glasses, and suddenly shuts the trunk.* NOGGS, *to cover, stares "at the wall with an intensity so remarkable that* ARTHUR *was quite alarmed."*)

GRIDE. Oh. Do you see anything in particular, Mr. Noggs?

NOGGS. Only a cobweb.

GRIDE. Oh. Is that all?

NOGGS. No. There's a fly in it.

GRIDE. There's a good many cobwebs here.

NOGGS. So there are in our place. And flies too. (*"Newman appeared to derive great entertainment from this repartee, and to the great discomposure of Arthur Gride's nerves, produced a series of sharp cracks from his finger-joints, resembling the noise of a distant discharge of small artillery." Then:*) Sorry. (*He looks balefully at the bottle.* GRIDE's *grin reappears.*)

GRIDE. I tell you, you have never tasted anything like this, I swear. Called eau d'or. It means "golden water". Water—turned to gold. I tell you, it's a sin to drink it. (GRIDE *looks at* NOGGS, *who looks balefully at him.*) Still. (*He pours two small measures.* NOGGS *picks up his glass.*) Oh, wait a minute, Mr. Noggs. Don't drink it yet. I've had this bottle twenty years. And when I take a little taste, and that's not often, I do like to look at it. And think about it. For a moment. Tease myself. (*Pause.*)

NOGGS. Uh—

GRIDE. Yes?

NOGGS. Uh—bearer waits.

GRIDE. Well, then. We'll drink it. Drink a toast. We'll drink it—to a lady.

NOGGS. To the ladies?

GRIDE. No—a lady. Little Madeline. (*Slight pause.*)

NOGGS. What's that?

GRIDE. What's that? Oh, Mr. Noggs, that is the prettiest, and daintiest, and—

NOGGS. Madeline?

GRIDE. That's right. With eyelashes, and—

NOGGS. (*Suddenly.*) Bearer waits. You hea—, her health. To Little Madeline. (*He knocks the drink back in one.*) I pray it can't be—But I fear it is. Good night. (*He runs out, bumping into* PEG *as she comes in.*)

PEG. So. Who's that lunatic?

GRIDE. He's Nickleby's.

PEG. He's who's?

GRIDE. Oh, doesn't matter. (GRIDE *gestures with* NOGGS' *glass, to indicate* NOGGS *is a tippler.*)

PEG. Oh. I see.

GRIDE. Peg. Peg. It's Wednesday. Two days time.

PEG. What is?

GRIDE. My wedding day. (*Pause.*)

PEG. It's time for bed. (PEG *shuffles off.*)

GRIDE. Huh. There's a change come over you, Mrs. Peg. I don't know what it means. But if it lasts, shan't be together long. You're turning crazy, Mrs. Peg, and if you do, I'll turn you out. All's one to me. (*He comes across a document in the trunk.*) Oh, here it is. Oh, here it is, my little beauty. "To Madeline." "To come of age or marry." Oh, my darling, dainty little deed. (*He kisses the document and puts it away. Locking up.*)

Young, loving and fair,
Oh, what happiness there.
The wedding is sure to be happy.

(GRIDE *goes out. We are aware that, in the gloom,* PEG *stands there. She has, if not overheard, at least overseen,* GRIDE *with the document. She potters forward.*)

PEG. Huh—huh. A wedding, eh? A precious wedding. Huh. (*Pause.*) Wants someone better than this old Peg, eh? Take care of him. (*Pause.*) And wha's he said? So many times. Keep me content wi' short food, little wages and no fire? "My will, Peg, Peg, I've nobody, but you. Just think—my will." (*Pause.*) And now it's a new mistress, is it? Baby-faced young chit. (*Pause.*) She won't come in my way. Says you. Well, no she won't. I tell you, Arthur, boy. She won't. But you—you don't know why. (*Pause.*) You're stuck to me, old Arthur Gride. You'll never throw out old Peg Slider. (*Slight pause.*) 'Cos she's stuck to you. (*Fade.*)

SCENE 9

A street. Bare stage. Enter NICHOLAS, *followed by* NOGGS.

NICHOLAS. Tomorrow!

NOGGS. Yes—I didn't—never told me what her second name was—

NICHOLAS. But—*tomorrow*—

NOGGS. Had no way to know, you see; now, we must think—

NICHOLAS. I will go straight to Bray's. I'll see this man. And if there's one—small feeling of humanity, still lingering—

NOGGS. I doubt it.

NICHOLAS. Then what am I to do? You are my best friend, Newman, and I must confess I don't know what to do.

NOGGS. The greater need, then, for a cool head, reason and consideration. Thought.

NICHOLAS. There's only one thing. I can go to her. And try to reason with her, and point out the horrors she is hastening to.

NOGGS. Yes, yes, that's right! You see? That's bravely spoken.

NICHOLAS. Entreat her, even now, at least to pause. To pause! (NICHOLAS *runs out.*)

NOGGS. He is a violent man. He has a violent streak. But still—I like him for it. There is cause enough. (NOGGS *potters out.*)

SCENE 10

The King's Bench prison area. BEGGARS, CRIMINALS, *etc. around again.* MADELINE *wheels in* BRAY. NICHOLAS *arrives.*

NICHOLAS. Sir. Miss Madeline.

BRAY. Well, sir, what do you want?

NICHOLAS. I, um—I have come to—

BRAY. Hm. I s'pose you think you can burst in on us without a with-your-leave, because without the—paltry sums you bring, we'd starve?

NICHOLAS. My business, sir, is with the lady—

BRAY. With the daughter of a gentleman! Your business, sir! We didn't look to see your face again till Thursday, at the earliest.

NICHOLAS. (*With a piece of paper.*) Yes, but . . . My employers would appreciate, Miss Madeline, if you could undertake—

BRAY. Oh, I see, you have brought more orders, sir? (BRAY *takes the paper from* NICHOLAS.)

NICHOLAS. That's not the term I would prefer to use. Commissions, yes.

BRAY. Well, you can tell your master that they won't be undertaken; you can tell him that my daughter—Miss Madeline Bray—condescends no longer, that we don't need his money, and that this is my acknowledgment of your "orders", sir! (*He tears the paper.*) So, unless you've any further "orders," sir . . .

NICHOLAS. No, I have none. Except . . .

BRAY. Yes, what?

NICHOLAS. I do have fears. And I must state them: fears, that you are consigning the young lady to something worse, worse even than to work herself to death. Those are my fears, sir. (BRAY *furious, hitting the side of his chair.*)

MADELINE. For heaven's sake, sir, please remember that he's ill—

BRAY. I am not ill! Out, out! I will not see his face a moment longer. Take me out of here! Please. (*Slight pause.*) Please, Madeline. (MADELINE *wheels* BRAY *out. She returns to* NICHOLAS.)

MADELINE. If you are charged with some commission to me, please don't press it now. The day after tomorrow—come here then.

NICHOLAS. It will be too late, then, for what I have to say, and you will not be here. Please listen to me.

MADELINE. No, I can't, I won't.

NICHOLAS. You will. You must. I must beseech you,

contemplate again this fearful course to which you've been impelled.

MADELINE. What's this? What course?

NICHOLAS. This marriage. Yours. Fixed for tomorrow, by two men who have never faltered in a bad intent, and who have wound a web around you, and betrayed you, and bought you for gold.

MADELINE. I will not hear this.

NICHOLAS. But you must, you must. I know you don't know half of what this evil man has done—Think of the mockery of pledging yourself to this man, at the altar—solemn words, against which nature must rebel—and, think, too, of the days and days with him that stretch before you . . . Oh, believe me, that the most degraded poverty is better than the misery you'd undergo as wife to such a man as this. Believe me, Madeline. (MADELINE *looks at* NICHOLAS.)

MADELINE. Believe me, sir. This evil, if it is an evil, is of my own seeking. I'm impelled by nobody, but follow this course of my own free will. It is my choice.

NICHOLAS. How *can* you say this?

MADELINE. Because it is true. (*Slight pause.*) I can't disguise—although perhaps I ought to—that I've undergone great pain of mind, since you were last here. No, I do not love this gentleman. He knows that, and still offers me his hand. Please don't think of me I can feign a love that I don't feel. Do not report this of me, for I couldn't bear it. He's content to have me, as I am. And I am happy for that. And I will grow happier.

NICHOLAS. You're crying with your happiness. Oh, just just one week, postpone this marriage, for a few days, even just a day—

MADELINE. Before you came here, my father was talking of the new life that he would lead, the freedom that will come tomorrow. And he smiled—a smile I haven't seen for—he was smiling, laughing at the thought of open air, and freshness, and his eyes grew bright, his face lit up—I'll not defer it for an hour.

NICHOLAS. These are—just tricks to urge you on—

MADELINE. It is no trick, my father's dying, sir. By doing this, I can release him not just from this place, but from the jaws of death itself. How *can* you tell me to act otherwise? (*Pause.*)

BRAY. (*Off.*) Hey! Madeline!

NICHOLAS. There's nothing I can say that will convince you.

MADELINE. Nothing.

NICHOLAS. Even if I—knew a plot, that you might, be entitled to a fortune that would do all that this marriage can accomplish? More?

BRAY. (*Off.*) Where are you Madeline?

MADELINE. He's calling. What you say's a childish fantasy.

NICHOLAS. If I could prove to you the things I know—

MADELINE. It would mean nothing. I am happy in the prospect of what I'll achieve so easily.

BRAY. (*Off.*) Come, Madeline!

MADELINE. Now, I must go to him.

NICHOLAS. We'll never meet again?

MADELINE. No. No. Of course not. (*She goes, turns back.*) Sir, the time may come when to remember this interview might drive me mad. (*Slight pause.*) Please tell them I looked happy.

BRAY. (*Off.*) Madeline! (*Exit* MADELINE. NICHOLAS goes out.*)

SCENE 11

A gambling house. At once, lights, music. Smoke, laughter. Downstage, are two tables, either side, with chairs. Upstage, a crowd of people, concealing a CROU-PIER, *upstage of them. He has a football rattle, with which to give the impression of a roulette wheel. At one of the tables sits* VERISOPHT, PLUCK, PYKE, *and a* CAPTAIN ADAMS, *with* LADIES OF LEISURE *and bottles of wine. The crowd round the "table" upstage includes* MEN OF PLEASURE *and* LADIES OF LEISURE, *and, in particular, a rival of* SIR MULBERRY HAWK *called* HANDSAW, *and a couple of his young male friends. As the scene assembles:*

CROUPIER. The wheel of fortune, gentlemen. Place your bets on red or black, or odd or even, on a number. Double with a colour, gentlemen, and much, much more, if the wheel points to your number. How do you do, sir, can I take your bet. Bets till the wheel spins, gentlemen—and then it's just waiting till we see who's won. All bets in now. The wheel's about to spin. Your bets please, gentlemen! (*But the* CROUPIER *stops, as he, and shortly everyone else, has noticed the entrance of* SIR MULBERRY HAWK, *attended by* MR. WESTWOOD. HAWK *gives his cape to an attendant. The* PROPRIETOR *goes over to him.*)

PROPRIETOR. Why, Sir Mulberry. Good evening. This is—a great pleasure. Please, sir, let me escort you to a table. (VERISOPHT *looks at* HAWK, *but* HAWK *goes to the empty table, with* WESTWOOD, *and sits. We see* HAWK *still has a slight limp.* VERISOPHT *whispers to the waitress, who takes a bottle to* HAWK. *The* PROPRIETOR *nods to the* CROUPIER.)

CROUPIER. Last bets, gentlemen. And let the wheel of fortune spin! (*Noise back in, as the wheel is spun, and the bettors watch and shout eagerly.*) Number 27! Red! Red 27, gentlemen! (*The* CROUPIER *pays out as* HANDSAW *comes over to him. He has a couple of young men in tow.*)

HANDSAW. Well, Hawk, and how are you, sir? (VERISOPHT *stands and goes over to* HAWK'S *table as:*)

HAWK. Well, I am very well.

HANDSAW. Still limping, I observe.

HAWK. But very nearly mended, I assure you.

HANDSAW. Yes, but still a little, ah, my Lord, a little pulled down, rather, still, out of condition, eh?

VERISOPHT. I'd say, still in very good condition. I'd say, nothing much the matter. Actually.

HANDSAW. Upon my soul, I'm glad to hear it. And to see, of course, your good friend back, so soon, into society. It's bold, it's game: To withdraw just long enough for people to get curious, but not for men to have forgotten that, unpleasant—tell me, Hawk, I've never understood why you didn't give the lie to all those damned reports they printed in the papers . . . looked there every day—

HAWK. Look in the papers, then, tomorrow, or the next day.

CROUPIER. Place bets. Place your bets, gentlemen!

HANDSAW. Oh. What will I find there?

HAWK. Something that will interest you, I'm sure.

HANDSAW. What's that? (HAWK *gestures towards the*

"wheel." HANDSAW *bows and he and his acolytes leave* HAWK *and* VERISOPHT.)

VERISOPHT. Good evening, Hawk.

HAWK. My Lord. (*He waves his glass.*) My thanks to you.

VERISOPHT. What should he look for in the papers?

HAWK. Oh . . . well, it won't be a murder. But, still, something near. If whipcord cuts and bludgeons bruise.

VERISOPHT. Bruise who?

HAWK. Who do you think?

CROUPIER. Last bets! Last bets please, gentlemen! (HAWK *stands, to go and place a bet.* VERISOPHT *stops him.*)

VERISOPHT. I'd hoped—that after all this time, you would have reconsidered.

HAWK. Well, sir, I have not. So, there is your answer.

VERISOPHT. Then I hope you will remember what I said. That if you were to take this course, I would try to prevent you.

HAWK. I'd mind your business, if I was you, and leave me to mind mine.

VERISOPHT. It *is* my business. I shall make it so. It's mine already. I'm more compromised by all this than I ought to be. (HAWK *turns to go, but turns back to* VERISOPHT.)

HAWK. My Lord, I will be straight with you. I am dependent on you, as you know. But, if that's so, then your dependence upon me is ten times greater. Do not interfere with me in this proceeding, I warn you; or else you'll force me to destroy you. And I will.

CROUPIER. Come on, now, gentlemen. Last bets. Last bets before the spinning of the wheel. (HAWK *turns and quickly goes to join the crowd round the wheel and places a bet.*) Ah, Sir Mulberry. Most privileged. A bet, sir? Thank you. And let the wheel of fortune spin—(VERISOPHT *pauses, then goes to his table. His party bobbing to their feet, when* VERISOPHT, *on a sudden impulse, turns, strides over to* HAWK, *and, as the wheel is spun, grabs his shoulder and pulls him round.*)

HAWK. What? What's this?

VERISOPHT. I will not have it, Hawk. I cannot have it.

HAWK. Let me go, boy.

VERISOPHT. No. (HAWK *tries to push* VERISOPHT

away. VERISOPHT *hits* HAWK *across the face. Everyone's attention suddenly focused.* WESTWOOD *stands. The wheel clatters to a stop unheeded.*)

HAWK. He struck me. (*Pause.*) Do you hear? He struck me! Have I not a friend here? Westwood! (WEST-WOOD *to* HAWK.)

WESTWOOD. I hear, sir. Come away, now, for tonight.

HAWK. No, I will not, by God. A dozen men here saw the blow.

WESTWOOD. Tomorrow will be ample time.

HAWK. No it will not. Tonight—at once—here.

VERISOPHT. (*Turning to* ADAMS, *who has joined the group round the wheel.*) Captain Adams. I say, let this quarrel be adjusted now. (WESTWOOD *whispering to* HAWK.)

ADAMS. My lord, an hour or so, at least.

VERISOPHT. Then, very well. An hour. (*He walks aside.*)

HAWK. (*Shouts, at the Company.*) No more. (HAWK *marches out.* WESTWOOD *to* ADAMS. ADAMS *nods, to say, "In a moment." He goes to* VERISOPHT.)

WESTWOOD. Captain Adams.

ADAMS. You will not—

VERISOPHT. Only if he will retract. The things he said. (ADAMS *shrugs.*)

ADAMS. He is a splendid shot, my lord.

VERISOPHT. So I have heard. (*Slight pause.* VERI-SOPHT *laughs.* ADAMS *looks at him oddly.*) Oh, so I've heard. Are you a married man, dear Captain?

ADAMS. No, I'm not.

VERISOPHT. (*Still laughing.*) Well, nor am I. Oh, nor am I. (*He stops laughing.*) I'll see you in an hour, then. (VERISOPHT *goes out. The* PROPRIETOR *nods to the* CROUPIER.)

CROUPIER. Uh—place your bets. Your bets, please, gentlemen. (ADAMS *to* WESTWOOD. *They talk. The* PRO-PRIETOR *whispers to the* CROUPIER. *The* CROUPIER, *with more enthusiasm.*) Sir Mulberry, this side! Lord Freder-ick, the other—place your bets now, gentlemen! (*And* PLUCK *and* PYKE *move in to place their bets. And the wheel and the* GENTLEMEN *disappear. And* VERISOPHT *is there alone.*)

VERISOPHT. It was daybreak. And as they walked

towards the place agreed, he saw the trees, and the
fields, and gardens, and they all looked very beautiful,
as if he'd never noticed them before. And young Lord
Verisopht felt little fear; but more a sense of something
like regret, that it should come to this.

SCENE 12

Dawn. By the river. Bare stage. Enter ADAMS *to*
VERISOPHT.

ADAMS. So here we are, my lord. My lord, you're
shivering.

VERISOPHT. I'm cold.

ADAMS. It does strike cool, to come out of hot rooms.
Do you want my cloak?

VERISOPHT. No, no. (HAWK, WESTWOOD, *the* GEN-
TLEMAN *acting as* UMPIRE, *a* SURGEON, *one or two other*
GENTLEMEN, *come in. Among the group, too, at the*
back, unnoticed, are MR. PLUCK *and* MR. PYKE.) Well,
here they are. (*He laughs.*)

ADAMS. My lord?

VERISOPHT. It's nothing. (ADAMS *goes to* WESTWOOD
and they talk. VERISOPHT *jumpy, laughing to himself,*
light-headed. ADAMS *returns to him.*)

ADAMS. My lord. They're ready.

VERISOPHT. Ready. (*As the* UMPIRE *opens the box of*
pistols, VERISOPHT *comes over to him and* HAWK.)

VERISOPHT. Uh—Hawk.

HAWK. (*Gruffly.*) My lord?

VERISOPHT. Hawk, just one word.

HAWK. Yes? What? Speak, quickly.

VERISOPHT. I—you know, I owe Ralph Nickleby
£10,000. (*Pause. Everyone looking edgy.*)

HAWK. I know. (*Pause.*)

VERISOPHT. I am not married.

HAWK. That is true. Can we begin? (*Slight pause.*)

VERISOPHT. And being in that state, my debts die with
me. (*Pause.*)

HAWK. What?

VERISOPHT. I don't mean . . . We must settle this, of
course. But, just to let you know. (*Slight pause. He looks*
at the pistols.) The terms. My father's will. I die unmar-

ried—and I die a pauper. And my creditors live, paupers, too. (*A slight laugh. He takes a pistol from the case. Pause.*)

HAWK. What's this?

VERISOPHT. So. Either way, Hawk, I'll destroy you. Won't I. (VERISOPHT *laughs.*) Won't I. Eh? (*Pause.* HAWK *takes a pistol from the case.* VERISOPHT *turns his back to* HAWK. HAWK *turns his back on* VERISOPHT.)

HAWK. (*To the* UMPIRE.) Begin.

UMPIRE. Yes. Yes. Sir Mulberry. My lord. Proceed. One, two, three, four, five, six, seven, eight, nine, ten. (HAWK *and* VERISOPHT *take ten paces. They turn and fire.* VERISOPHT *falls. The* SURGEON *to* VERISOPHT. *He finds that* VERISOPHT *is dead. He nods. Quickly:* ADAMS *takes* VERISOPHT'S *pistol, and* WESTWOOD *gives it to* HAWK, *who shakes his head and pockets his pistol; the* UMPIRE *and the other* GENTLEMEN *depart. Only, still at a distance,* PLUCK *and* PYKE *are left.*)

WESTWOOD. Now, Hawk, there's not a moment to be lost. We must leave here immediately—for Brighton, and then France. (*Pause.* HAWK *impassive.*) Come, Hawk. This is a dreadful business, and delay will make it worse.

HAWK. An hour. Meet you at the stage-coach: in an hour. (*Striding out.*)

WESTWOOD. But—but, Hawk—

HAWK. An hour! (*Exit* HAWK. WESTWOOD *looks at* ADAMS, *shrugs and goes out.* ADAMS *nods to* PLUCK *and* PYKE. *They come forward.*)

PLUCK. Well. Is this a bad business, Pyke?

PYKE. Is this a dreadful business, Pluck?

ADAMS. You both know what to do. (ADAMS *goes out.* PYKE *and* PLUCK *take* VERISOPHT'S *watch, rings and all valuables. Then they pick him up by the arms and drag his body out.*)

SCENE 13

London. Dawn. NICHOLAS *enters, on a bare stage.* KATE *stands to the side. During the following, we hear the hiss of gas lights, and a* LAMPMAN *slowly crosses the stage with a long pole. He mimes shutting off the gas at the top of an imaginary street lamp. Then, slowly, the stage fills with the* POOR OF LONDON *at dawn: maids scrubbing doorsteps, blind men begging, street-sweepers sweeping, prostitutes soliciting, and pimps watching. There are mothers and fathers with babies and children, too. Gradually, the naturalistic evocation of a London morning turns into a Chorus: the POOR move forward into a phalanx around NICHOLAS, eventually surrounding and obscuring him.*

NICHOLAS. And at the same daybreak, Nicholas arose,
KATE. And softly left the house,
NICHOLAS. And wandered into London. And as he paced the streets and listlessly looked round on the gradually increasing bustle of the day, everything appeared to yield him some new occasion for despondency. Last night, the sacrifice of a young, affectionate and beautiful creature to such a wretch had seemed a thing too monstrous to succeed. But, now, when he thought how regularly things went on:
POOR PEOPLE. From day to day

In the same unvarying way

How crafty avarice grew rich, and manly honest hearts were poor and sad

How few they were who tenanted the stately homes,

And how many those who lay in foul and rancid tenements,

Or even

Lived

And died

Father

And son,

Mother,

And child,

HALF. Race upon race,

ALL. And generation upon generation, without a home to shelter them

PROSTITUTE. How in seeking, not a luxurious and splendid life, but the bare means of a most wretched and inadequate subsistence,

ALL. Subsistence.

PROSTITUTE. There were women and children in that one town, divided into classes,

PIMP. And reared from infancy to drive most criminal and dreadful trades—

YOUTHS AND CHILDREN. How ignorance was punished and never taught—

PROSTITUTES AND THIEVES. How jail-door gaped and gallows loomed for thousands.

ALL. How many died in soul, and had no chance of life—

NICHOLAS. How many who could scarcely go astray, turned haughtily from those who could scarce do otherwise,

ONE THIRD. How much injustice,

TWO THIRDS. Misery,

ALL. And wrong there was, (NICHOLAS *now surrounded and is obscured as*:)

NICHOLAS. And yet how the world rolled out from year to year, alike careless and indifferent, and no man seeking to remedy or redress it:—when he thought of all this, and selected from the mass the one slight case on which his thoughts were bent, he felt indeed that there was little ground for hope, and little cause or reason why it should not form an atom in the huge aggregate of distress and sorrow, and add one small and unimportant unit to the great amount. (*The* POOR *look at us. And then they split and melt away. And* NICHOLAS *is left alone.* NOGGS *appears*.)

NICHOLAS. Oh, Newman. Legal right, the power of money, everything is on their side. And I can't save her.

NOGGS. Don't say that. (NICHOLAS *looks at* NOGGS.) Oh, don't say it, Nick. Never lose hope, never leave off it, it don't answer. *I* know that. If nothing else, I have learnt that. (*Pause*.) Don't leave a stone unturned. At least you know you've done the most you could. Or else—how could you bear to live with it? (*Pause.* NICHOLAS *looks at* NOGGS. NICHOLAS *goes out.*) Hope. Always hope. (NOGGS *goes out, too.*)

SCENE 14

Ralph's house. A room, set up for a wedding ceremony. All that is needed are two chairs, on one of which sits MADELINE, *and* BRAY'S *wheelchair behind.* BRAY *looks very ill; he is dressed up in uncomfortable finery. A* MINISTER *stands waiting.* GRIDE *enters, and is met by* RALPH.

RALPH. Well, good day, Mr. Gride. Congratulations, on your wedding morning.

GRIDE. Nickleby. Is everything prepared?

RALPH. It is. Your bride waits to receive you, sir.

GRIDE. And, how is she?

BRAY. Bray says that she accepts it. She is calm. She may be safely trusted, now. It won't be long.

GRIDE. What won't be?

RALPH. (*With a nod at* BRAY.) Paying his annuity. You have the devil's luck in bargains, Gride. (*He turns to go to the ceremony.*)

GRIDE. Uh, Nickleby—

RALPH. Yes? What? (GRIDE *takes two crushed carnations from his pocket.*) What's this?

GRIDE. To wear. Your buttonhole. It is a wedding day. (*Slight pause.* RALPH *shrugs. The two men put on their buttonholes. Then they go to the* MINISTER. RALPH *nods at the* MINISTER. GRIDE *sits next to* MADELINE. *The* MINISTER *begins the service.*)

MINISTER. Dearly beloved, we are gathered together here in the sight of God and in the face of this congregation to join together this man and this woman in Holy Matrimony, which is an honourable estate, instituted of God in the time of man's innocency, signifying unto us the mystical union that is between Christ and his church which holy estate Christ adorned and beautified—(RALPH *gestures to the* MINISTER *to hurry it along. The* MINISTER *turns the page.*) I require and charge you both, as ye will answer at the dreadful day of judgment, when the secrets of all hearts shall be disclosed, that if either of you know any impediment, why ye may not be lawfully joined to-

gether in matrimony, yet do now confess it. (NICHOLAS'
voice, from off.)

NICHOLAS. Won't you? Won't you confess it, Madeline?

GRIDE. What's this? What, Nickleby?

BRAY. It's him—him, Madeline—

MADELINE. Oh—sir—(NICHOLAS and KATE are in the
room, RALPH to them.)

RALPH. I don't believe it.

GRIDE. Who is this man? This girl? Why have they
come here?

NICHOLAS. We know everything. We've come to stop
this marriage. And we won't go till we have.

RALPH. Gride. This is my niece. And this, her brother.
I'm ashamed to say, my brother's son.

NICHOLAS. Oh, you're ashamed—

KATE. Nicholas—

RALPH. Now, you, my dear, retire. We can use force
on him, and will if need be, but I would not hurt you if
it could be helped. (Slight pause.) Retire!

KATE. I won't, and you misjudge me if you think I
will. You may use force on me—and it would be most
like you if you did; but I will not go till we've done what
we have come to do.

NICHOLAS. Well said.

RALPH. Oh, yes. I see. This fellow here—he brings
with him, you note, his sister, as protection. I shouldn't
be surprised, in fact, Gride, if he doesn't have a mind to
marry Madeline himself.

GRIDE. What's that?

RALPH. Well, why d'you think he's here? Philanthropy?

NICHOLAS. I tell you, both of you, that there has been
no word of love, no contract, no engagement—

RALPH. Certainly, there's no engagement. This young
lady is engaged already. And about to be a bride.

GRIDE. My bride!

NICHOLAS. And we demand to speak with her.

GRIDE. And how we'll laugh together, she and me, at
how this little boy was jilted—

NICHOLAS. Will you let me speak with her?

GRIDE. And I wonder, is there anything of mine he'd
like besides? He wants my bride, perhaps he'd like his
debts paid, and his house refurnished, and a few bank-
notes for shaving paper, if he shaves at all? (NICHOLAS

tries to push past Gride. Kate *is between* Ralph *and* Nicholas, *and* Ralph, *to get to* Nicholas, *clasps her arm.* Nicholas *turns and takes* Ralph's *collar, when they are all interrupted by the entrance of* Sir Mulberry Hawk.)

Hawk. Well, look at this. A family reunion. (Ralph *pulls himself free from* Nicholas.) And—a wedding, too? Well, I'm sorry, Nickleby, to interrupt, but I have urgent news about an opposite affair.

Ralph. What's that?

Hawk. A funeral.

Ralph. Whose funeral?

Hawk. Lord Frederick Verisopht's. (Kate *a step forward. Pause.* Hawk *takes out his pistol.*) He struck me—as a consequence of something I had said—concerned with a young lady. And her brother. So . . . I had my answer. (*There is something strange about the face of* Walter Bray, Madeline *wheels her father a little further apart, and looks at him, and loosens his collar. The* Minister, *seeing that no-one is noticing him, slips out.*)

Ralph. But—

Hawk. Oh, yes. You know. For you know everything. Unmarried. And his bills, and mine on his account, all guaranteed by you, all over town. What would you say? Ten thousand pounds? (Ralph *looking blank.*) You do—you understand?

Ralph. I understand.

Nicholas. (*Laughs.*) Oh, yes. At last you understand. (Hawk *quickly to* Nicholas, *with the pistol.*)

Hawk. I tell you. That this should have been for you. (Madeline *has left* Bray. *She looks at* Hawk, *bemused.*) I'm sorry, ma'am. To frighten you. (*He is going.*)

Madeline. He's dead. (*It almost sounds like a question.* Hawk *doesn't understand.*)

Hawk. Oh, yes. He's dead. Indeed. (Hawk *goes out. The penny drops for* Ralph, Gride, Kate *and* Nicholas, *as they see* Bray, *slumped in his chair.*)

Madeline. He looked at me. And whispered that he couldn't bear to see—And shut his eyes. And wouldn't open them again.

Ralph. What's this you say? (Ralph *and* Gride *rush to the body of* Bray. Kate *to* Madeline.)

KATE. Oh, I'm so sorry. (GRIDE *trying to get to* MADELINE.)

GRIDE. Oh, Madeline. My pretty little Madeline.

NICHOLAS. Oh, no. Her obligation to you's ended, now.

RALPH. This man—she's still his wife-to-be. And he shall have her.

GRIDE. Oh, she still shall be my wife, my dainty—now—with no-one, she will need me, won't she—precious—

MADELINE. No. Of course not. You said you would save him. And you've killed him.

GRIDE. What is this? What, me, my chick?

MADELINE. Yes, Indeed. That's what he meant. He couldn't bear to see me married to you. (*Suddenly, furiously, to* GRIDE.) How *can* you think that I could bear it, now?

NICHOLAS. Kate, downstairs. (KATE *taking* MADELINE'S *arm*.)

RALPH. You will not take her, girl.

KATE. Uncle, I will.

RALPH. You have no right to do this—

KATE. I have more right to do this, uncle, much more right, than you had to allow what happened to me here. (*She makes to lead* MADELINE *out*. MADELINE *to* NICHOLAS.)

MADELINE. Please, sir—I want him taken from here. (NICHOLAS *nods*. KATE *takes* MADELINE *out*. NICHOLAS *to the wheelchair*.)

RALPH. Just one word.

NICHOLAS. Not even one. Your bills are now waste paper. Your debts will not be paid—save this—the one great debt of nature. (*He takes out the body of* WALTER BRAY. *Long pause*.)

GRIDE. It's not my fault.

RALPH. Who said it was?

GRIDE. You look as if you thought I was to blame.

RALPH. I don't. I blame him. Bray.

GRIDE. What for?

RALPH. For not—not living an hour longer. (*Pause*.) Now, go Gride. (*To himself*.) Ten thousand pounds. (GRIDE *turns to go. He is suddenly aware of something in the movement. He pats his coat, outside a pocket. He feels inside the pocket. Nothing there. He feels in the other pockets. He rips his coat off, searching desperately for something.*) What are you doing, Gride?

GRIDE. Lost something.

RALPH. Something? What.

GRIDE. It's gone.

RALPH. What is?

GRIDE. The deed. She's taken it.

RALPH. Who has?

GRIDE. Peg Sliderskew. Old, mad and deaf Peg Slider. She has robbed me of the deed! (*He waves his coat.*) I had it in my pocket. And it's gone!

RALPH. Now, come, Gride, first go home—

GRIDE. Oh, Nickleby. I shouldn't have it. It's not mine. Someone will read it for her. And she'll take it to the police. And then—and then—I'm done for.

RALPH. Gride. At least go home, and see you didn't drop it somewhere. See it isn't locked up where you left it.

GRIDE. I tell you Nickleby. I know it's gone. And I tell you something else. You said you'd help me to be married. And it's been prevented, by your flesh and blood. I tell you, if I go down with this business, then you're going too. (*Pause.*)

RALPH. All right, Gride. Yes. Now, tell me all about it. And we'll try and get it back. (*And they go out together.*)

SCENE 15

The Nicklebys' Garden. Bare stage, with dappled light. SMIKE is tending pot plants in a tray downstage, helped by KATE who wears gardening gloves. Enter NICHOLAS.

NICHOLAS. How's Madeline?

KATE. She's sleeping.

NICHOLAS. But is she—

KATE. She's exhausted, nothing more. (*Enter MRS. NICKLEBY.*)

MRS. NICKLEBY. Well, now, Nicholas, perhaps you can explain all this to me.

NICHOLAS. Mother, I thought we'd—

MRS. NICKLEBY. Well, you did, indeed, at length, but still I can't see why, in the name of wonder, Nicholas

should go about the world forbidding people's banns?
(NICHOLAS *flapping with frustration*.)

KATE. I don't think, mother, you quite understand.

MRS. NICKLEBY. Not understand? I have been married myself, Kate, and have seen other people married, frequently, and as to this Miss Magdalen marrying a man that's older than herself, I would remind you of Jane Dibabs, who—

NICHOLAS. Jane Dibabs!

MRS. NICKLEBY. Yes, that's right, who used to live in that attractive little cottage past the lunatic asylum, and she married someone twenty or so years above her, and who was so honourable and excellent, that she was blissfully content about the whole arrangement, and remains so to this day. (*Pause*. KATE, *very patiently*.)

KATE. Mama, the husband in this case is greatly older; he is not her own choice; his character is quite the opposite of that which you've described; mama, don't you see a broad distinction between the two cases?

MRS. NICKLEBY. Well, I daresay, I'm very stupid, Kate—

KATE. Mama! (KATE *runs to* SMIKE, *and helps him with the garden, to cover her anger and frustration*.)

MRS. NICKLEBY. Well, I don't know what that's about, I'm sure. (NICHOLAS *about to join his sister when enter* HANNAH.)

MRS. NICKLEBY. Yes, Hannah, dear?

HANNAH. There are three gentlemen without.

MRS. NICKLEBY. Now, Hannah, dear, what gentlemen?

HANNAH. Uh . . . (*Enter* MR. NED CHEERYBLE, MR. CHARLES CHEERYBLE *and* FRANK CHEERYBLE. HANNAH *goes out*.)

FRANK. Mrs. Nickleby.

MR. CHARLES. Oh, my dear young man, my dear young man. Miss Madeline is safe?

NICHOLAS. Yes, she is safe. (KATE *comes to the* CHEERYBLES, *followed by* SMIKE.)

MR. NED. And you, sir, we have had the scantiest of reports, have sustained no injury?

NICHOLAS. I am completely well.

FRANK. And your dear sister, sir, we hear that she too was involved in this heroic enterprise—(FRANK *has moved to* KATE.)

KATE. And have survived my humble part in it, sir, I assure you.

MR. NED. May we inquire—if it is possible to see the lady? (KATE *smiles and goes out, followed by* MRS. NICKLEBY. MR. CHARLES *to* NICHOLAS.)

MR. CHARLES. We cannot express, sir, our full admiration of your actions on this day. We will, sir, at the earliest opportunity, relieve you of the burden of her upkeep. (*Slight pause.*)

NICHOLAS. Well . . . (*Re-enter* KATE.)

KATE. Miss Bray's awake—and would be most delighted to speak with you, gentlemen.

FRANK. (*Taking* KATE'S *arm.*) Now, Kate, please tell me everything . . . I wish for every detail . . . (*The* BROTHERS, *followed by* FRANK *and* KATE, *go out.* NICHOLAS *looks at* FRANK *and* KATE *together. He stands a moment, and then goes into the garden.* SMIKE *is sitting clutching his knees, looking miserable.*)

NICHOLAS. Well, Smike. And how are you today? (SMIKE *doesn't reply.*) How are you feeling? (SMIKE *doesn't reply.*) Smike, please answer me. (SMIKE *looks at* NICHOLAS.) Smike, what's the matter.

SMIKE. It's my heart. It is so very full. I cannot tell you why. You cannot tell how full it is.

NICHOLAS. Come on, now, Smike. It's growing chilly. Stand up, and let's go in. (*Pause.*)

SMIKE. I can't. I feel so ill. (NICHOLAS *looks at* SMIKE. *Suddenly, he calls.*)

NICHOLAS. Frank! Kate! (FRANK *and* KATE *appear to help* NICHOLAS *with* SMIKE.)

SCENE 16

The same. As KATE *and* FRANK *arrive, five* NARRATORS, *dressed in dark costumes, emerge from the darkness at the back of the stage. They walk forward together, obscuring* SMIKE. BROOKER *enters behind them, and stands, staring at* SMIKE, *who is now dressed for travelling, surrounded by luggage.*

NARRATORS. There is a dread disease which so prepares its victim, as it were for death

In which the struggle between soul and body is so gradual, quiet and solemn,

That day by day

And grain by grain

The mortal part wastes and withers, and the spirit part grows light and sanguine with its lightening load,

A disease which medicine never cured, wealth warded off, or poverty could boast exemption from—which sometimes moves in giant's strides, and sometimes at a tardy, sluggish pace, but slow or quick

Is ever sure and certain.

(*The* NARRATORS *disappear.* SMIKE *looks at* BROOKER.)
    BROOKER. I know you. Do you know me?
    SMIKE. I—know you. (BROOKER *hears something and scuttles away.* KATE *and* NICHOLAS, *dressed for travelling, enter, with* MRS. NICKLEBY, MISS LA CREEVY *and* HANNAH.)
    NICHOLAS. Come, Smike. It's all right. Time to go.
    SMIKE. To Devon. (SMIKE *looks at* MISS LA CREEVY *and* MRS. NICKLEBY.)
    MISS LA CREEVY. Oh, Mr. Smike. To your return.
    MRS. NICKLEBY. Yes. Yes, dear Mr. Smike. Please. Soon. (NICHOLAS *and* KATE *help* SMIKE *to his feet. They leave with him, the other Women waving.*)

ACT III

SCENE 1

Upstage, the Kenwigs' front room. MR. *and* MRS. KEN-
WIGS *eating a meal at the table. The crying of the new
baby.* MR. LILLYVICK *appears downstage. He looks nervous. From offstage, we hear him knocking.*

MRS. KENWIGS. Morleena! Morleena!

MORLEENA. (*Off.*) Yes, Ma!

MRS. KENWIGS. Door, Morleena!

MORLEENA. (*Off.*) What, Ma?

MRS. KENWIGS. Door! (MORLEENA *runs on as baby
cries.*) Shh, Shh. Hush, baby. (MORLEENA *sees* MR.
LILLYVICK.)

MORLEENA. Uh?

LILLYVICK. Morleena.

MORLEENA. Oh, it's—Uncle Lillyvick!

LILLYVICK. It is. It is. (*Pause.*) Morleena, tell me—
did your mother have the child?

MORLEENA. Oh, yes. She did. A boy. That's him.

LILLYVICK. And was it—she said—that she hoped that
he would look like me.

MORLEENA. Oh, yes. He does. I s'pose. At least.

LILLYVICK. I would like someone, looked like me.
(*Pause.*)

MORLEENA. Oh, Uncle. Heard about your wedding,
Uncle. Made Ma cry. And Pa got very low as well. And
I was ill, too. But I'm better now. Oh, Uncle. (*Pause.*)

LILLYVICK. Would you—give your uncle—just one
kiss, Morleena? (*Pause.*)

MORLEENA. Yes. I would. But not Aunt Lillyvick. I
won't kiss her. She is no aunt of mine.

MRS. KENWIGS. Who is it at the door, Morleena?

LILLYVICK. Take me to them. Take me up, Morleena.
(MORLEENA *takes* LILLYVICK *to the* KENWIGS *as:*)

MRS. KENWIGS. Morleena!

KENWIGS. Now, don't shout, dear.

MRS. KENWIGS. Suppertime, Morleena!

KENWIGS. Please, don't shout, dear.

MRS. KENWIGS. Oh, I do declare.

KENWIGS. Yes, what do you declare, dear?

MRS. KENWIGS. (*Pouring herself a drink.*) That there's nobody, in all the world, as tired as I am. Nobody. That's all.

MORLEENA. Uh—ma—

KENWIGS. Oh, Mr. Lillyvick.

LILLYVICK. Kenwigs, shake hands.

KENWIGS. (*Standing.*) Oh, sir, the time has been when I was proud to shake hands with the kind of man that now surveys me. Oh, the time has been, sir, when a visit from that man's excited in my and my family's bosoms feelings both uplifting and awakening. But now I look at him, and ask, where is his human nature. (*Pause.*)

LILLYVICK. Susan Kenwigs, will you speak to me?

KENWIGS. She is not equal to it, sir. What with the nursing of her child, and the reflecting on your cruel behaviour, four pints of malt liquor, daily, has proved insufficient to sustain her. (MR. KENWIGS *looks away*.) Oh, I remember thinking, all the time it was expected, if the child's a boy, what will its uncle say. Will it be Pompey, he will ask to be called; or Alexander, or Diogenes; and when I look at him, a precious, helpless, cut-off child . . . Was it the money that we cared for, Susan?

MRS. KENWIGS. No, it was not. I scorn it.

KENWIGS. Then what was it, Susan?

MRS. KENWIGS. It was seeing your back turned upon us, Uncle. It was feelings—mine have been quite lancerated.

KENWIGS. Poor Morleena's pined, the infant has been rendered most uncomfortable and fractious—

MRS. KENWIGS. I forgive all that, and with you, Uncle, we can never quarrel. But I won't receive her, Uncle. Never ask me. For I will not. No, I won't, I won't. I won't—(KENWIGS *ministering to his wife when* LILLYVICK *intervenes.*)

LILLYVICK. You will not need to. Susan. Kenwigs. For a week ago last Thursday, she eloped.

KENWIGS. Eloped?

LILLYVICK. That's right. With three sovereigns of mine, eight silver teaspoons, and the proprietor of a travelling circus. (*Slight pause.*) With moustaches. And a bottle nose. (*Slight pause.*) 'Twas in this room—this very room—I first set sight on Miss Petowker. It is in this room I cast her off for ever. (*Pause.*)

KENWIGS. Oh, Mr. Lillyvick. What suffering have you endured.

MRS. KENWIGS. Oh, Uncle. You'll forgive our harshness, please.

KENWIGS. And furthermore, the fact that we have nurtured in our bosoms that—that—

MRS. KENWIGS. Viper.

KENWIGS. Yes, and—

MRS. KENWIGS. Adder.

KENWIGS. Absolutely, and that—

MRS. KENWIGS. Serpent, snake and crocodile.

KENWIGS. Indeed. And all we pray now is that you, dear Mr. Lillyvick, won't give way to unprevailing grief, but seek for consolation in the bosom of this family, whose arms and hearts are ever open to you. (*Bursting into tears.*)

MORLEENA. Yes. (*She runs and puts her arms round* MR. LILLYVICK.) Yes, yes.

KENWIGS. Morleena, leave your uncle be. (MORLEENA *leaves* LILLYVICK.)

LILLYVICK. I gave her everything she asked for. Humoured her in every whim. Those teaspoons, for but one example. (*Slight pause.*) I feel I'll never knock a double-knock again, upon my rounds. I can't see how I'll manage it. (*Slight pause.*) But still. Important matters. Kenwigs. Susan. First thing in the morning, I shall settle on your children all these moneys I once planned to leave them in my will. Don't argue, don't protest—that's my decision.

KENWIGS. Mr. Lillyvick!

MRS. KENWIGS. Morleena—quickly, kiss your uncle, beg his blessing, fall down on your knees.

LILLYVICK. Yes, yes. Let her approach.

KENWIGS. This is a happening on which the Gods themselves look down!

SCENE 2

Ralph's house. Bare stage. Enter RALPH.

RALPH. Ten. Thousand. Pounds. How many years of scrimping, scraping, calculating. For ten thousand pounds. And what I would have done with it. How many proud dames would have fawned and smiled. How many spend-thrift nobles would have cringed and begged. How many smooth-tongued speeches, courteous looks, and pleading letters. And how many mean and paltry lies would have been told, not by the money-lender, but by his debtors . . . All your thoughtless, generous, liberal, dashing, folk, who wouldn't be so mean as to save a sixpence for the world! (*Pause.*) Ten—thousand—pounds. (*Pause.* NOGGS *and* SQUEERS *appearing.*) But now. I'm firm. I must be. Come what may. (NOGGS *coughs.* RALPH *turns.*)

RALPH. Ah, Mr. Squeers.

SQUEERS. You sent a letter.

RALPH. Yes, indeed.

SQUEERS. First, let me say—

RALPH. First, let *me* say, Noggs.

NOGGS. Yes? What?

RALPH. Go to your dinner.

NOGGS. But it isn't time.

RALPH. Your time is mine, and I say it is.

NOGGS. You change it every day. It isn't fair.

RALPH. Begone. (NOGGS *withdraws.*) Now. What?

SQUEERS. I'm worried about Snawley.

RALPH. Why? Where is the risk?

SQUEERS. You know the risk as well as I do.

RALPH. No, I don't. There is no risk. The certificates are genuine, he *has* been married twice, his former wife *is* dead, and the only lie is Snawley's, and he'll stick to it, why should he not? He tells the truth, and he's in gaol for perjury. So where's *your* risk in this conspiracy!

SQUEERS. I say, don't call it that—just as a favour, don't.

RALPH. But now, attend to me. The purpose of the fabrication of this tale was to cause hurt and pain to someone who half-cudgelled you to death. Now, is that so?

SQUEERS. It is.

RALPH. And are your bruises at his hands forgotten and forgiven?

SQUEERS. They are not.

RALPH. So. There's an opportunity to hurt him once again. There is a deed—a will. If it is found by him, then it will make a girl he wants to marry very rich. If it is found by us, and then destroyed, then all his expectations crumble.

SQUEERS. Well. Go on.

RALPH. Together, we are going to find the person with the will. You're going to take it from this person, and I'm going to give you fifty pounds in gold. (SQUEERS *scratches his ear.*) A hundred pounds.

SQUEER. Well, in that case . . . I suppose, as you're a friend . . .

RALPH. Attend to me. (SQUEERS *is led out by* RALPH. *In the shadows,* NOGGS *follows.*)

SCENE 3

Devon. Bare stage, dappled light. KATE, NICHOLAS *and* SMIKE *enter.*

NARRATOR. Dividing the distance into two days' journey, in order that their charge might sustain the less exhaustion and fatigue from travelling so far, Nicholas and Kate found themselves at the end of the second day back in the village where they had grown up together.

NICHOLAS. Look, there's our garden, Smike. That's where we used to play, and run, and hide.

SMIKE. You used to hide?

NICHOLAS. Yes, Smike, you know, the game.

KATE. And Nicholas would climb that tree: that big one, over there, to look at young birds in their nests— and he'd shout down, look Kate, how high I've climbed.

NICHOLAS. And you'd be frightened, and you'd tell me to come down.

KATE. And you, you wouldn't come down. But climb even higher, waving all the time.

SMIKE. You climbed up there.

NICHOLAS. And that's the house, Smike, where we used to live, that was Kate's room, behind that tiny window.

KATE. I remember still, the way the sun would stream in, every morning.

SMIKE. Every morning? Winter too?

KATE. I think . . . I can't remember.

NICHOLAS. I suspect that it was always summer here. (SMIKE *has been looking at "the tree".*)

SMIKE. Is it the same. As when. It is the same. (KATE *and* NICHOLAS *look at each other.*)

NICHOLAS. Things look a little different, Smike. The tree looks smaller. And the garden has become a little overgrown. But still—it is the same. (SMIKE *goes towards the tree.*)

SMIKE. You climbed up there. (KATE, NICHOLAS *and* SMIKE *move round the stage.*)

NARRATOR. And from the house they walked on to the churchyard, where their father lay, and where Kate and her brother used to run and loiter in the days before they knew what death was, let alone its meaning.

NICHOLAS. Once, Smike, Kate was lost, and we searched for an hour, and we couldn't find her, and at last we found her here, beneath that weeping willow, fast asleep. And so our father, who was very fond of her, picked up her sleeping body in his arms, and said that when he died he wanted to be buried here, where his dear, little child had lain her head. Do you remember, Kate?

KATE. I've heard it told so often, I don't know.

SMIKE. You lay down here?

KATE. (*Smiling.*) Yes. So they say. (KATE *wanders a little away.* SMIKE *takes* NICHOLAS' *hand.*)

SMIKE. Please promise me.

NICHOLAS. What promise? If I can, you know I will.

SMIKE. Please, if I can, may I be buried near—as near as possible—to underneath that tree?

NICHOLAS. Of course. Yes, yes, you will. (KATE *turns back from her wander. She puts out her arms and spins round.*)

NARRATORS. And in a fortnight, Smike became too ill to move about. And he would lie upon an old couch, near the open doors that led into a little orchard.

(*Two actors set a couch upstage.*) And Nicholas and Kate would sit with him and talk for hours and hours together.

Till the sun went down, and Smike would fall asleep.

(SMIKE *on the couch. It's sunset.* KATE *and* NICHOLAS *leave* SMIKE *and walk downstage. During the scene, it grows darker, and we can no longer see* SMIKE *through the dusk.*)

KATE. Nicholas.

NICHOLAS. Yes, what?

KATE. What is it?

NICHOLAS. I was thinking about those we left behind.

KATE. One person, in particular? (*Pause.* NICHOLAS *turns to* KATE.)

NICHOLAS. It is, I suppose . . . I love her, Kate.

KATE. I know. Your feelings are as obvious to me, as mine must be to you. (*Pause.*)

NICHOLAS. Oh, Kate. Oh, both of us. Has he—

KATE. He has proposed.

NICHOLAS. What did you say?

KATE. I said—that it was very painful for me, very difficult. But, still. I had to tell him, no.

NICHOLAS. And why?

KATE. Because—you know why.

NICHOLAS. Tell, me, Kate.

KATE. Because—of all the kindness of the brothers, to you, and to all of us. Because—Frank's rich, and we are poor, and it would look as if, we'd taken gross advantage of . . .

NICHOLAS. There's my brave Kate. (*Pause.*) You've no idea, how much your strength in making your, this sacrifice, will help me making mine.

KATE. But Nicholas, it's not the same.

NICHOLAS. It is the same. For Madeline is bound to our two benefactors with ties just as strong—and she too has a fortune. (*Pause.*)

KATE. So—we shall stay together.

NICHOLAS. Yes. And when we're staid old folk, we will look back, on these times, and wonder that these things could move us so. And, even, who knows, we might thank the trials which bound us to each other, and which turned our lives into a current of such peace and calm. (*Pause.*) We'll always be the same.

KATE. Oh, Nicholas. I cannot tell you how, how happy I am, that I've acted as you would have had me.

NICHOLAS. And you don't, at all, regret . . .

KATE. I don't regret. At least. Perhaps . . . No, no. I don't regret. (*Slight pause.*) And, yes, I hope and pray we'll never change. (SMIKE *stands there.*)

SMIKE. Who calls? Who calls so loud? (NICHOLAS *and* KATE *look at* SMIKE. KATE *to go towards* SMIKE, *but* NICHOLAS *stops her with a touch.* SMIKE, *insistent.*) Who calls so loud? (NICHOLAS *a step towards* SMIKE.)

NICHOLAS. Come hither, man. I see that thou art poor. Hold, there is forty ducats. Let me have—

SMIKE. Such mortal drugs I have, but Mantua's law is—is—

NICHOLAS. Oh, Smike—

SMIKE. Is death to any he that utters them. (*Promising.*) Art thou so bare—?

NICHOLAS. Art thou so bare and full of wretchedness, And fearest to die? Famine is in thy cheeks, Need and oppression starveth in thy eyes. Contempt and—

SMIKE. No. No, I don't fear to die. My will consents. (NICHOLAS *turns to embrace* SMIKE, *who throws his arms round* NICHOLAS' *neck to stop himself collapsing.*) You know, I think, that if I could rise up again, completely well, I wouldn't want to, now. (SMIKE *looking over* NICHOLAS' *shoulder at* KATE.) For nothing—can be ill, if she be well.

NICHOLAS. Then all is well, and nothing can be ill. (*Pause.*) Her body sleeps in Capel's monument. (*Pause.*) But her immortal part with angels lives. (NICHOLAS *lifts* SMIKE *up into his arms.*)

SMIKE. Is it. E'en so. I see a garden. Trees and happy children's faces. And her body sleeps. Light on the faces. Living with the angels. Dreamt my lady came and found me dead. Such happy dreams. (*He pulls himself up to whisper in* NICHOLAS' *ear. Then, out loud, to* KATE:) I'm going home. Who calls. Who calls so loud? (SMIKE *is still.* NICHOLAS *realises he is dead. He turns to* KATE. *He is crying.*)

NICHOLAS. He said—I think you know. (*Pause.* KATE *can say nothing.*) And then he said he was in Eden.

SCENE 4

Lambeth. Two adjacent attic rooms, represented simply by the people in them. On one side, SQUEERS *sits, on a wooden box, with a candle, drinking. On the other side— presently in darkness—* PEG SLIDERSKEW *sits, surrounded by rubbish.*

NARRATORS. It was a dark, wet, gloomy night in autumn—

An obscure street in Lambeth, muddy, dirty and deserted—

A mean and miserable house—

A bare and wretched attic chamber—

And a grotesque, one-eyed man.

SQUEERS. Well. Here's a pretty go. Uncommon pretty. Here have I been—what is it—six weeks—a following up this blessed old dowager—and the Academy run regular to seed the while. Hm. It's the worst of getting in with an audacious chap like Nickleby. You never know when he's got done with you. You go in for a penny, find that you're in for a pound. (*Slight pause. He grins.*) A hundred pounds. (*He takes another drink.*) I never saw a file like that Old Nickleby. To see how sly and cunning he grubbed on, day after day, a-worming and a-plodding and a-tracing and a-turning, and a-twining of himself about, until he found out where this precious Mrs. Peg was hid, and cleared the ground for me to work upon— creeping and crawling, gliding—out of everybody's depth, he is. (*Slight pause.*) Well. So. (*He looks at a letter.*) The pigs is well. The cows is well. The boys is bobbish. Young Mobbs has been a-winking, has he? Well, I'll wink him when I'm back. And Cobbey would persist in sniffing while he was a-eating of his dinner, saying that the beef was so strong as it made him. Well, then, Cobbey, see if we can't make you sniff a little without beef. Oh, and Pitcher was took with another fever—so he would be— and fetched by friends, he died the moment he got home.

Of course he did, to aggravate us. An't another chap in all the school but that boy would arrange to die exactly at the quarter's end. If that's not spite or malice, then I do not know what is. (*He puts the letter away. Standing.*) Well, so. It's pretty nigh to time, to wait on the old woman. Pretty sure, that if I'm to succeed at all, I shall succeed tonight. So one quick glass to wish myself success, and put myself in spirits. (*He pours the drink and raises it.*) Mrs. Squeers. Young Wackford. Fanny. Here's your health. (SQUEERS *drinks. Then he turns and goes out of his room and into the other room.*) Well, my Slider!

PEG. Huh? That you?

SQUEERS. It is. It's me. And me's first person singular, the nominative case, agreeing with the verb "its," governed by "Squeers" understood. And if it isn't, you don't know any better.

PEG. Wha? What's that?

SQUEERS. (*Coming over to her.*) This. Is a bottle, Peg. You see?

PEG. O' course I see.

SQUEERS. And this here is a glass. And see, I fill the glass, and I say "Your health, Slider" and I empty it— (*He does so.*) I fill it once again, and hand the glass to you.

PEG. (*Takes the glass and drinks.*) Your health.

SQUEERS. That's right, that's right. You understand that, anyways. Now, Peg, how's the rheumatics? (SQUEERS *filling* PEG'S *glass.*)

PEG. Ooh, they're better. Ooh, much better, thank'ee, sir. (*She drinks.*)

SQUEERS. You look a great deal better, Peg, than when I first came here.

PEG. Och, well . . . you frightened me.

SQUEERS. I did?

PEG. Och, aye. You knew me name. And where I'd ganged from, and the reason why I'se hiding here. (*Slight pause.*) Nae wonder. I was frightened. Eh? (SQUEERS *pouring* PEG *another drink.*)

SQUEERS. Oh, well, Peg, yes, I understand. But see, there's nothing of that kind takes place that I don't know about. See, I'm a sort of lawyer, Peg, of first rate standing, and of understanding, too; I'm the intimate and confidential friend of nearly everyone as has got themselves into a difficulty by being a bit nimble with their fingers. See, I'm a—what's the matter, Peg? (*For* PEG *has been chuckling for a few moments, and is now cackling.*)

PEG. So he weren't married after all.

SQUEERS. No, Peg. He wasn't. No.

PEG. And some wee lover came and carried off the bride, eh? From beneath his very nose.

SQUEERS. That's right, Peg, yes. (PEG *becoming very affectionate with* SQUEERS.)

PEG. So. Tell it me again? Will ye? Tell it me again, beginning at the beginning, now, as if you'd never told me. Tell it again, and then, who knows, I might show you the paper, you'se so keen to see. (*Pause.*)

SQUEERS. Oh, might you, Slider?

PEG. Och, I might. But only if you tell me how the old goat lost his dainty bride. (*Pause.* PEG *caressing* SQUEERS.) Go on.

SQUEERS. Well, certainly, I will. But after you've shown me the paper, Peg. (*He pours her another drink.*) And then, we'll drink the health of Arthur Gride. (PEG *cackles with pleasure, and stands, and potters off into the gloom.*)

PEG. Och, aye, then. But only if you tell me the tale. If you promise. Will you?

SQUEERS. Of course I will, Peg, course I will. (PEG *comes back with the deed.*)

PEG. Then here you'se are. Right! (SQUEERS *eagerly opens the deed.*) He said it was his beauty. Well, he's lost his beauty, now. Lost both of 'em. (SQUEERS *reading.*)

PEG. So, then. What's it say?

SQUEERS. "To Madeline". "To come of age or marry". "The said Madeline . . ." That's it. This is the go! (SQUEERS *stands, to go out.*)

PEG. Uh? Where you'se going?

SQUEERS. (*Too quietly for* PEG *to hear.*) Out. I've finished with you, Peg.

PEG. Wha's tha' you're saying? I can't hear.

SQUEERS. (*Shouts.*) I'm going, Mrs. Sliderskew! (PEG *bobbling across the room after him.*)

PEG. But wha' about the tale! And toasting Arthur Gride! You canna just get up an' leave me! Hey!

(SQUEERS *gets to the "door", and finds two* OFFICERS, FRANK CHEERYBLE *and* NEWMAN NOGGS.)

SQUEERS. What's this?

NOGGS. That's him.

OFFICER. You're Mr. Squeers?

PEG. (*Stumbling to the door.*) Hey!

NOGGS. And that's her.

SQUEERS. What's this? What's going on?

OFFICER. I have a warrant, issued on advice from these two gentlemen. (*Slight pause. Neighbours, including a* YOUNG WOMAN, *appear.*)

PEG. The polis?

SQUEERS. Yes, Peg, yes.

NOGGS. That's right.

PEG. Hey—it's the lunatic!

SQUEERS. Huh—so it is. (*The* OFFICER *grabbing at* PEG, *who waves the bottle wildly.*)

PEG. Hey! Get your hands off me! (*The attention of the officers on* PEG, *as* SQUEERS *makes a run for it.* FRANK *notices.*)

FRANK. Hey, stop! Stop that man! (*Many neighbours now watching, as* FRANK *and an officer chase* SQUEERS *round the stage, and, if possible, round the audience as well. Finally,* SQUEERS *finds a little hiding place and his pursuers rush past him. Everyone is thus shouting and pointing in an opposite direction when* MR. SQUEERS *appears, takes off his hat, brushes it, and attempts to sneak off unnoticed.* NEWMAN NOGGS, *however, has spotted him, and brings a metal tray down firmly on his head.* SQUEERS *collapses.*)

NOGGS. Hey, not so much of the lunatic! Not so much, Mr. Squeers and Mrs. Sliderskew! Eh! Eh?

FRANK. (*Putting his hand on* NOGGS' *arm.*) Now, Mr. Noggs, we must go home, and tell my uncles what has happened. (*The* OFFICERS *take out* SQUEERS *and* SLIDERSKEW. NOGGS *and* FRANK, *with the deed, follow.*)

SCENE 5

Ralph's room; and his run round London. A large number of NARRATORS *form a semi-circle round* RALPH NICKLEBY, *who stands in what we imagine to be his dining room.*

NARRATOR. And on the next day, half-way through the morning, Ralph Nickleby sat alone, in the solitary room where he was accustomed to take his meals.

RALPH. What is this, that hangs over me, and I can't shake it off? I'm never ill, I've never moped, and pined—but what can any man do without rest? (*Slight pause. The sound of a bell.*) Night after night goes by, I have no rest. I sleep, and I'm disturbed by constant dreams. I wake. I'm haunted by this heavy shadow of—I don't know what. (*Slight pause. The sound of a bell.*) One night's unbroken rest, and I should be a man again. (RALPH *suddenly aware that the bell has been ringing.*) Noggs! Noggs! (*Silence. He picks up his watch.*) What? Noon? Where is he? Noggs! (*No answer. The bell.* RALPH *turns and goes to the "wall" of people, two of whom step aside to form a door. A* MESSENGER *stands there.*) Yes? Who are you?

MESSENGER. Is this the residence of Mr. Nickleby?

RALPH. I am that man.

MESSENGER. A letter, sir. (*He takes the letter.*)

RALPH. Thank you. (RALPH *turns back downstage, and the wall closes behind him. He reads the letter.*) What is this? "It's most urgent", "Matters come to light". "We will explain it". "Dreadful news". What are the old fools mad? Or is this, from its wildness, just another waking nightmare? Sent to haunt me? (*The wall splits up and becomes the bustling streets of London.*)

NARRATORS. And like a haunted man, without his hat or coat, Ralph stumbled through the door, into the street.

At first he drifted aimlessly, a sleepwalker, but then his pace grew brisker, and he almost ran . . .

The streets and people swirled around him, and the sounds of London merged into a single roar, as Ralph sped on, he scarcely could tell why, towards a house in Somers Town.

(*The actors have formed into three lines, facing* RALPH, *their arms straight up in the air, like the gables and rooves of houses.* RALPH *bangs on the floor.*)

RALPH. Door! Door! Where are you, Snawley? Door!

(SNAWLEY'S WIFE *pokes her hand between two of the actors, as opening a door a little way. She looks terrified.*)

MRS. SNAWLEY. Who—oh—

RALPH. I wish to see your husband, ma'am.

MRS. SNAWLEY. He's not in. Gone away.

RALPH. Do you know who I am?

MRS. SNAWLEY. Oh, yes, I know, but still, he's gone away.

RALPH. Tell him I saw him, through the window-blind above. Tell him that I must speak to him, most urgently.

MRS. SNAWLEY. There's nothing that he wants to say to you. Except that, wasn't him that forged the letter. You or schoolmaster did that, so don't you try to lay it at this door.

RALPH. He sets me at defiance, does he?

MRS. SNAWLEY. Yes, he does. And so, sir, so do I. (*And she withdraws, and the "door" closes behind her. The wall of actors breaks up again and swirls around* RALPH.)

NARRATORS. And so Ralph turned again, and hurried back,

Through different streets across the city,

To another house,

Whose windows were closed shut,

Whose blinds were drawn,

All silent, melancholy and deserted. (*And the three-line wall has formed again, but, this time, with the hands of each of the back two lines placed over the eyes of the line in front.* RALPH *knocking.*)

RALPH. Gride! Gride! (GRIDE *stands on a chair behind the lines, as if at an upper window.*)

GRIDE. What? Who's that?

RALPH. Gride, let me in.

GRIDE. Hush. Hush, no. Go away.

RALPH. Come down!

GRIDE. I won't. Don't speak to me, don't knock . . . Don't call attention to the house—Just go away.

RALPH. I'll knock, I'll shout, I'll sweat, till I have all

your neighbours up in arms, if you don't tell me what
you mean by lurking there!

GRIDE. I mean—I mean—it isn't safe. Please, please,
don't talk to me. Just go away. (GRIDE *disappears behind
suddenly raised hands, as if he had slammed his shutters
closed*.)

RALPH. How is this? They all fall from me and shun
me like the plague! How have they changed! These men
who used to lick the dust from my feet. I *will* know what
it is, I must, at any cost. (*The wall breaks again, and
swirls, and reforms as a long single line of backs, from
upstage centre to downstage left*.)

NARRATORS. And so Ralph set off once again,

And crossed the river,

And determined now to hazard everything, came to the
meagre house in Lambeth where his tried auxiliary the
schoolmaster had lately lodged. (RALPH *runs downstage
along the line. A* YOUNG WOMAN—*clearly a Prostitute—
appears at the end of the line*.)

YOUNG WOMAN. Hallo. What can I do for you?

RALPH. (*Breathless*.) Old woman. Old, and wizened.
Deaf. Top floor.

YOUNG WOMAN. You what?

RALPH. And a man. Short, stunted. With a leer. One
eye.

YOUNG WOMAN. Oh, yur. I know them people. What
d'you want?

RALPH. I want to know where they are now.

YOUNG WOMAN. They're gone.

RALPH. Gone where?

YOUNG WOMAN. Gone with the constables. The
Police-Office, I think.

RALPH. Where is the police office?

YOUNG WOMAN. (*With a shrug*.) Now, that—I know.
(RALPH *takes the* YOUNG WOMAN'S *arm and hurries her
back upstage along the line. The line breaks, obscuring
the set-up of the next scene, and then forming a new semi-
circle upstage*.)

SCENE 6

The Lambeth Police Office. WACKFORD SQUEERS *is revealed, sitting on a bench, with a bandaged head. He is drunk.*

NARRATORS. And in the Lambeth Police-Office there was a kind of waiting room, and Ralph was shown to it, and told to wait:

And shortly afterwards an officer admitted him to Mr. Wackford Squeers. (*The semicircle breaks, as a door for* RALPH *to come to* SQUEERS.)

SQUEERS. Hm. I say, young feller, you have been and done it now.

RALPH. You have been drinking.

SQUEERS. Hm. Well, not *your* health, I can assure you, my old codger.

RALPH. Why did you not send to me? (SQUEERS *sits. Not answering the question.*)

SQUEERS. With me locked up here hard and fast, and you all loose and comfortable.

RALPH. It's only for a few days. They will give you bail. They cannot hurt you, man.

SQUEERS. Well. S'pose that's right. If I explain it all. (*Slight pause.*) "Prisoner," he says, the powdered head, "you have been found in company with this old woman; as you were apprehended in possession of this document. In absence of a satisfactory account, I shall detain you." (*Slight pause.*) Well, then, what I say now is, that I *can* give a satisfactory account. I can hand in my card, and say, "I am the Wackford Squeers as is therein named, sir. Whatever's wrong's no fault of mine. I'm merely an employee of a friend—my friend Ralph Nickleby, of Golden Square."

RALPH. What documents?

SQUEERS. *The* document. The Madeline Whatsit document. The will.

RALPH. Whose will? How dated? Benefitting whom? To what extent?

SQUEERS. I can't remember. In her favour, all I know. (*Pause.*)

RALPH. I tell you once again. That they can't hurt you. We'll devise a story for you; if you need a thousand pounds security, you'll have it. All you have to do is keep your wits about you, and keep back the truth.

SQUEERS. Oh, that's it, is it? That's what I'm to do? Well, I tell 'ee, Mr. Nickleby. That what I do, or say, is up to me, what serves me most, and if I find it serves me to reveal your part in this, then reveal it's what I'll do. (*Slight pause.*) My moral influence with them lads, is tottering to its basis. (*Slight pause.*) The images of Mrs. Squeers, my daughter Fanny, and my son, all short of victuals, is perpetually before my eyes. All other thoughts just melts away and just vanishes in front of 'em. (*Slight pause.*) In short, the only number in arithmetic I knows of as a husband and a father, now, is Number One. In this most fatal go. (RALPH *looks at the wall. A door forms, and a* POLICE OFFICER *stands there. But* SQUEERS *hasn't finished.*) A-double-L. All. Everything. A cobbler's weapon. U-P, up, an adjective, not down. S-Q-U-double-E-R-S. Squeers, noun substantive. (*Pause.*) In sum total. It's All Up With Squeers. (*And the wall closes round in front of* SQUEERS *and* RALPH *appears in front of it again.*)

RALPH. So. This fellow turns on me as well. They are all struck with fear, while, yesterday, was all civility, compliance. But they shall not move me. I won't budge an inch. (*The wall dispersing.*)

NARRATORS. And so, then, finally, with a reluctant, grudging step, Ralph Nickleby set course towards the City.

He had not eaten or drunk anything all day, he felt sick and exhausted, and his every sense was numb, except for one of weariness and desolation. (*The wall has gone. The next scene is revealed.*)

SCENE 7

The Cheerybles' house. One chair, beside a small table with a lamp on it. RALPH *approaches* MR. CHARLES, MR. NED *and* TIM LINKINWATER.

RALPH. So—which is Mr. Charles?
MR. CHARLES. I am.
RALPH. You sent me this, this morning, asking me—

demanding that I come here to your house at half past seven o'clock. Well, it is only shortly after. I am here. (*Slight pause.*) As no-one bids me to a seat, I'll take one for I am fatigued with walking. (RALPH *sits.*) And now, if you please, gentlemen, I wish to know, I demand to know, I have the right to know—what you have to say to me which justifies the tone you have employed. (*Waving the letter.*)

MR. CHARLES. Very well, sir. Brother Ned. (MR. NED *goes out and returns with* NEWMAN NOGGS.)

RALPH. Oh—this—this is a good beginning. Oh, yes, you are candid, honest, open-hearted and fair-dealing men! To tamper with a fellow such as this, who'd sell his soul for a drink, whose every word's a lie—oh, this is a beginning!

NOGGS. I will speak.

RALPH. Oh, yes, I'm sure you'll—

NOGGS. I *will* speak. And ask, who made me "a fellow such as this"? (*Slight pause.*) If I would sell my soul for a drink, why wasn't I a thief, a swindler, a robber of pence from the trays of blindmen's dogs, rather than your drudge and packhorse? If my every word was indeed a lie, why was I not a pet and favourite of yours! A liar! When did I ever fawn and cringe to you? (*Slight pause.*) I served you faithfully. You were talking just now about tampering. Who tampered with the Yorkshire schoolmaster? Who tampered with a jealous father, urging him to sell his daughter to old Arthur Gride, and tampered with Gride too, and did so in a little office *with a closet in the room*? (RALPH *a sharp gesture.*) Aha! You mind me now! And what first set the drudge to listening at doors, and watching close and following? The master's cruel treatment of his flesh and blood, his vile designs upon a young girl, which made the miserable and drunken hack stay on in service, in the hope of doing her some good, when he might have otherwise relieved his feelings by pummelling his master soundly, and then going to the Devil. I'm here now because these gentlemen thought it best. When I sought them out—as I did, there's no tampering with me—I told them that I wanted to help to find you out, to track you down, to finish what I had begun, to help the right; and that when I'd done it I would burst into your room, and face you man to man, and—like a man.

And now I've done it. Now I've had my say. Let anybody say theirs. I've done. (*Pause.*) At last. (*Pause. A general gesture.*) So—fire away!

RALPH. Hm. (*Pause. A little wave.*) Go on, go on.

MR. CHARLES. It is, sir, simply told. (*He waves to* MR. NED.)

MR. NED. We knew about the deed, and how Gride had acquired it, and we heard, from neighbours, of the great to-do Gride made when it was gone.

MR. CHARLES. Our dear friend Mr. Noggs acquainted us with Squeers' visit to you, and as you and he pursued Peg Sliderskew, we in our turn followed you, and then the schoolmaster, and found the house in Lambeth, and procured a warrant to arrest them for possession of a stolen document.

MR. NED. Which then was done. The woman, and the schoolmaster, and most of all, the deed, are now in police possession.

MR. CHARLES. Now, sir, you've heard it. How far are you implicated on this matter, you best know. But we would not—would not see an old man like you disgraced or punished.

RALPH. Sir, you have not the man to deal with that you think you have. (*Pause.*)

MR. NED. What's this?

RALPH. Oh, merely, that I have not heard a word of proof of any of these wild allegations; that I spit on your fair words and your false dealings; and that there is law, still, to be had, and I will call you to account. Take care, sir, you have said enough already. I'd advise you, say no more.

MR. CHARLES. Then we've not said enough. (*He looks at* MR. NED.)

MR. NED. No, no, indeed.

MR. CHARLES. Sir, what would you say if we said that this man Snawley had confessed?

RALPH. Snawley? Then I'd reply that Snawley is a frightened coward, and that this "confession" was most likely forced from him.

MR. CHARLES. And if we told you that the boy was dead? (*Pause.*)

RALPH. You mean—the simpleton—

MR. NED. Is dead, indeed. (*Pause.* RALPH *laughs.*)

RALPH. Oh, gentlemen, then I forgive you everything. For this news, I am in your debt, and bound to you for life.

NOGGS. Oh, you. Oh, how can—it's unnatural.

MR. CHARLES. It is. (*He nods to* MR. NED *who goes out*.)

RALPH. What's this? Another? Have you dredged my nephew up, to add to all these lies? (*Re-enter* MR. NED *with* BROOKER.) What? Him? D'you know, this is a felon, a convicted criminal?

MR. NED. You asked, sir, for our proof that broken boy was not the son of Snawley.

RALPH. Yes. I did. Well—

MR. NED. Our proof is not concerned with papers, or confessions. It is that we know the poor boy was another's son.

RALPH. Another's? Whose?

BROOKER. Yours. (*Pause.* RALPH *presses the palms of his hands against his temples*.)

RALPH. What? (*Pause.*)

BROOKER. Do you remember? About, oh, what, a quarter of a century ago? A family in Leicestershire? A father and a daughter? A father that you'd wound into your net, you'd cheated, like you cheated me? But a daughter who had grown attached to you, because, of, he was young, then, charming in his way, and she could not believe he was not their family's benefactor? And who fell in love with you, Ralph Nickleby. And married you. (*Pause.*) But, of course, it had to be a secret, from the father. He was rich. And if he'd known, the daughter would have lost a great inheritance. And that would never do. Oh, would it. So, a secret wedding. And a little secret son. Put out to nurse. A long way off. So not to interfere. (*Pause.*) And then, as time went on, began to see her less and less. Stayed up in London, making money. And your wife, a young girl, alone, in a dull old country house. And eventually, she couldn't bear it any more. Could she? (*Pause.*) And so she ran off? Didn't she? (*Pause.*) And you ordered me to fetch the boy, to keep him from her—didn't you? (*Pause.*) And you had used me ill. And cruelly. The boy was hidden in an attic, and neglect had made him sickly, and the doctor said that he must have a change of air or else he'd

die. You went away. Six weeks. When you returned, I
told you that the child was dead. (*Pause.*) And you—I
think—realised—you missed him. When he'd gone. You
missed someone who thought well of you. He brightened
up your house, and made a little laughter in your halls.
And you missed him. Didn't you? (*Pause.*)

MR. CHARLES. So the boy was not, then, dead.

BROOKER. Sirs, I offer no excuses for myself. You
could say, I was harshly treated and driven from my real
nature. But, I'm guilty. (*Slight pause.*) Yes, I stole the
boy. And took him to a Yorkshire school. And paid his
fees, for six years. And then went away. (*Pause.*) But
then . . . came back. And went to look for him. I
couldn't find him, there, he'd gone. So—came to London. And confronted him. No use. But then, a month,
six weeks ago, I saw the boy. He was sitting in a garden.
Knew his face. And he, I think, knew mine. (*To* RALPH.)
The school was run by your friend, Mr. Wackford
Squeers. I gave the boy a name. Do I need to tell you?

RALPH. Smike. (*Pause. Throughout* BROOKER'S *speech,
it has been growing steadily darker. Now the only source
of light is the lamp on a table near* RALPH.)

MR. NED. Unhappy man. Unhappy man.

MR. CHARLES. But doubly, trebly, ten times more unhappy must *you* be, Ralph Nickleby. (*Pause. Then, like
a reptile's tongue,* RALPH'S *hand shoots out towards the
lamp. It crashes and there is darkness.*)

SCENE 8

In the darkness, the wall forms again. Lights, and
RALPH *is running along it, parallel to the front of the
stage.*

NARRATORS. Creeping from the house, and slinking
like a thief . . .

Groping like a blind man . . .

Ralph Nickleby went from the city, and took the road to
his own home.

(The wall is forming into a cloud, hands stretching out towards Ralph.)

And there was one black, gloomy mass that seemed to follow him,

Not hurrying in the wild chase with the others,

But lingering, sullenly, behind, and following him.

(The wall reforms. At the back, a line of people, at crazy angles, like bent and broken iron railings; in front, a pile of bodies, forming hideous shapes.)

He passed a poor, mean burial ground,

A rank, unwholesome spot, where the very grass and weeds appeared to tell that they had sprung from paupers' bodies, and Ralph peered in through the iron railings . . .

(And the railings become a group of drunks, careering round in front of the bodies, one actor playing a pipe.)

And then there came towards him, full of shouts and singing, a group of fellows full of drink, in high good humour.

And a member of their company, a little, weazen, humpbacked man, began to dance . . .

(And indeed a little man does dance, to the music of the pipe, and RALPH joins in the clapping, until he is swallowed up and disappears. And suddenly, everything stops, and the NARRATORS stand there, still.)

And Ralph came home.

He could hardly make up his mind to turn the key and open up the door.

And when he had—

And closed it, with a crash behind him—

He felt as if he had shut out the world.

(*The* NARRATORS *dispersing now. One* NARRATOR *appears, with a single chair*.)

There was no light. How dreary, cold and still it was.

He groped his way towards the stairs, and climbed, up to the very top—

To the front garret—

Which was now a lumber room.

(*If there is a trap,* RALPH *appears through it. If not, he enters. The last* NARRATOR *places the chair carefully.*)

LAST NARRATOR. Here Ralph remained. (*The* NARRATOR *goes.* RALPH *stands there. We see he is holding a piece of rope.*)
RALPH. I know this room. This room was where he slept. I was his father. But he didn't die here. And he didn't die with me. He died—elsewhere. (*Pause.*) But if he hadn't . . . If he'd grown up here. Might we have been— a comfort to each other. And might I—have been a different man. A man more like my nephew. Or my brother. Nicholas. (*He begins to tie the rope into a noose.*) But now. To be held up in the most repulsive colours. And to know that he was taught to hate my very name. "Ralph Nickleby". (*Pause.*) "To wound him, through his own affections. Oh, to strike him through this boy . . ." (*Pause.*) "All love is cant and vanity". (*A knocking on the door downstairs.*)
RALPH. What's that? (*We hear* TIM'S *voice.*)
TIM. (*Off.*) Is that—Ralph Nickleby?
RALPH. What do you want with him?
TIM. (*Off.*) I'm from the Brothers. They want to meet with you tomorrow.
RALPH. Yes, yes. Tell them, they can come tomorrow.
TIM. (*Off.*) At what hour?
RALPH. At any hour! What time they like. (*Pause.*)

All times will be alike to me. (RALPH *looks up*.) That hook. Big, black one, in the ceiling. Never noticed it before. (*Slight pause*.) Perhaps he noticed it. Perhaps it frightened him. (*Slight pause*.) It frightens me. (*Slight pause*.) But it would hold me. (*He looks round the room where his son had slept*.) Outcast. A noun. Cast out. And homeless. (*Long pause*.) Me. (RALPH *quickly puts the noose round his neck and raises it above him. A dummy on a rope falls from the flies, down through the trap. The light just catches* RALPH, *swaying, as if from the rope. Darkness. A moment. Then light.* RALPH *has gone. The rope has fallen through the trap.* MR. CHARLES, MR. NED *and* TIM LINKINWATER *stand there*.)

MR. CHARLES. And in the morning, they went round, and knocked, and knocked again.

MR. NED. And eventually, they broke a window, and went in, and searched the house.

TIM. And they found the body of Ralph Nickleby, and cut it down. (*Blackout*.)

SCENE 9

The Cheerybles' house. Just two chairs represent it.

NARRATORS. And some weeks passed, and the first shock of these happenings subsided.

Madeline was living in the house of friends of the Mr. Cheerybles;

Young Frank was absent;

And Nicholas and Kate were trying, in good earnest, to stifle their regrets, and to live for each other and their mother.

And there came one evening,

Per favour of Mr. Linkinwater,

An invitation from the Brothers Cheeryble for dinner on the next day but one,

An invitation comprehending not just Nicholas, his mother and his sister

But their great friend Miss La Creevy, too—

Who much to the astonishment of Mrs. Nickleby,

Was most particularly mentioned. (*And the* NICKLEBYS *and* MISS LA CREEVY *are greeted by* MR. CHARLES, MR. NED *and* TIM LINKINWATER.)

MR. CHARLES. Now, we took the liberty, dear friends, of naming one hour before dinner, as we had a little business to discuss, which would occupy the interval. I wonder, Tim, if you would be so kind as to escort dear Mrs. Nickleby and Miss La Creevy too—to show them something of the house, perhaps, and p'raps to tell them something too.

TIM. It would be my great pleasure. Ma'am. And Ma'am. (*Pause.* MRS. NICKLEBY, KATE *and* NICHOLAS *in their different ways, looking bemused.*)

MRS. NICKLEBY. Well, certainly, I—

MR. NED. (*His finger to his lips.*) Not another word. (*And, with as much grace as she can muster, Mrs. Nickleby allows herself to be escorted out by* TIM, MISS LA CREEVY *following, a little smile on her face.*)

MR. CHARLES. Now, Kate, my dear. Tell me. Have you seen Madeline since your return to London?

KATE. No, sir. And I have not heard from her.

MR. CHARLES. Not heard from her? What do you think of that, Brother Ned? Is that not sad?

MR. NED. Oh, very, Brother Charles. Yes, very sad. The whole thing's so upsetting, that you will forgive me if, for just a moment, I withdraw myself into another room. (*Much winking between the* BROTHERS: MR. NED *withdraws.*)

MR. CHARLES. Poor Brother Ned, as I've remarked to you before, sir, often, always such a prey to his emotions. Now. We were engaged, I think, upon the topic of Miss Madeline, who, as you know, becomes entitled, on her marriage, to a certain sum of money.

NICHOLAS. Yes, we know that, sir.

MR. CHARLES. In fact, a sum amounting to twelve thousand pounds, from the will of Madeline's maternal grandmother. One could say, quite a dowry. Hm? (*Pause.*)

NICHOLAS. You did receive our letter, sir?

MR. CHARLES. Yes, yes, we did. You both explained your feelings—yours for Miss Madeline, and Kate's for nephew Frank. You had resolved, despite those feelings, to reject all thought of love and matrimony—and to live, instead, just for each other.

NICHOLAS. Yes, sir. That is our resolve.

MR. CHARLES. A noble sentiment. But still, perhaps, a selfish one.

NICHOLAS. What, selfish? Why?

MR. CHARLES. Because of other people's feelings. For an instance, those of Brother Ned and I.

NICHOLAS. I'm sorry. I don't understand. (MR. NED *has appeared. Behind him, unseen by* NICHOLAS *and* KATE, *are* FRANK *and* MADELINE.)

MR. NED. You don't? You don't see why *we* are offended? To have it thought that we were such mean judges of two persons' characters. To think that we'd consider for a moment that your love for Madeline, or Kate's for Frank, had anything to do with money? Come, how could you think so!

KATE. We—we did not think so, sir.

MR. CHARLES. And worse than that. Much worse. To think that you yourselves would be corrupted and debased, by marrying the people whom you've set your hearts upon?

NICHOLAS. Sirs, I had thought we'd made it plain. We have—my sister and I have—learnt nothing in our journeyings so strongly as we've learned what happens to the kindest, and the noblest and the gentlest people, when their souls are tainted by the touch of money.

KATE. We have seen our father, and our uncle, sirs, the one who was most dear to us, the other, one who should have been, destroyed; one in the want of money; and the other by the having it, and loving it too much.

FRANK. Oh, Kate. Oh, Nicholas. How can you be so blind? They stand in front of you!

MR. NED. Now, Frank—

FRANK. No, no, you cannot say it, Uncle Ned, you cannot say it, Uncle Charles; but I can: that you see before you, Nicholas and Kate, two men who walked barefoot to London, penniless and hungry, and who have made their fortune, and have they been tainted or debased? Have they been made ignoble, or ungentle, or unkind? You see them, Nicholas.

KATE. Frank. Back.

MR. NED. Yes, yes, returned most unexpectedly, without so much as a presentiment.

MR. CHARLES. As is his wont.

MR. NED. And with him, someone else whose feelings we might take into account. (NICHOLAS *sees* MADELINE.)

NICHOLAS. Oh, Madeline. You've heard, all this?

MADELINE. Yes, yes. I've heard.

NICHOLAS. And you—they've told you, everything, I—

MADELINE. Yes they have. (NICHOLAS *is completely thrown*.)

NICHOLAS. This is—I told you, sirs, in confidence, my feelings for Miss Madeline, I . . . I have no idea, of course, if they, if she—what feelings she has entertained, I— do you understand?

MADELINE. I understand what I have understood since we first met. And I understand that, since then, you have changed.

NICHOLAS. Oh, no—

MADELINE. And that you cannot see me any more, but only my inheritance. (*Pause.* MADELINE *takes* NICHOLAS' *hands*.) Oh, Nicholas. That someone who has been through what you've been through, who has striven as you've striven, who has learnt what you have learnt, could think that it is right to sacrifice our happiness for such a superstition, to believe that there are any barriers between us that we can't surmount.

NICHOLAS. Our happiness.

MADELINE. Oh, Nicholas. How could you ever think that I felt otherwise? (*Pause.* NICHOLAS *turns to* KATE.)

NICHOLAS. We're over-ruled. (KATE *to* FRANK.)

KATE. So it would seem.

MR. CHARLES. And so it is.

MR. NED. And so it is. (*We hear* MRS. NICKLEBY *approaching*.)

MRS. NICKLEBY. Oh, Mr. Linkinwater, this is too extraordinary.

MR. NED. Quick, quick, everyone away . . . and talk among yourselves, if you've got anything to talk about . . .

MR. CHARLES. Yes, hurry, all out, everyone—(NICHOLAS, MADELINE, KATE *and* FRANK *go apart as:*)

MRS. NICKLEBY. (*Approaching.*) Now, of course it's very pleasant, if it is true, but I assure you, if it isn't, it's a most cruel . . . Mr. Cheeryble. (*And* MRS. NICKLEBY, MISS LA CREEVY *and* TIM *are now back in the room.*)

MR. NED. Yes, Mrs. Nickleby?

MRS. NICKLEBY. Can this be true?

MR. CHARLES. Not only can, but is. (*Slight pause.*)

TIM. Hm. Didn't keep 'em in suspense as long as said you would. Impatient, what I call it.

MR. CHARLES. What, d'you hear that, Brother Ned, from Tim, who has been wearying us from morning until night—

MR. NED. It's true, Charles, it's all true, the man's a wild young fellow, he must sow his wild oats, and then perhaps he'll come in time to be a respectable and normal member of society—(*The* BROTHERS *taking the arms of* MRS. NICKLEBY.)

MR. CHARLES. I'm sure that Mrs. Nickleby agrees, dear brother—(*The* BROTHERS *leading* MRS. NICKLEBY *out.*)

MRS. NICKLEBY. (*With a desperate look back at* TIM *and* MISS LA CREEVY.) Well, I . . . I mean, if I am asked my view . . . Uh—oh—(*And they are gone.* TIM *and* MISS LA CREEVY *left alone.* MISS LA CREEVY *sitting.* TIM *moves the other chair closer, and sits.*)

TIM. Well, isn't it a pleasant thing. To people like us, to see young folks we are so fond of brought together.

MISS LA CREEVY. Yes, it is. Indeed.

TIM. Although—although it makes one feel, oneself, quite solitary. Almost cast away. I don't know, if you feel . . .

MISS LA CREEVY. Well, certainly, that's true, I mean, it's true, that I don't know.

TIM. It's . . . almost something that would make one think of getting wed oneself. Now isn't it?

MISS LA CREEVY. Oh, nonsense, Mr. Linkinwater.

TIM. Now, is it? Is it nonsense? Really? (*Pause.* MISS LA CREEVY *holding her breath.*)

Miss La Creevy. Now, Mr. Linkinwater, you are mocking me.

Tim. No, no, I'm not.

Miss La Creevy. Why think—how we'd make people laugh.

Tim. Well, let 'em. We'll laugh back.

Miss La Creevy. And, think, as well: what would the brothers say?

Tim. Why, Miss La Creevy, bless your soul! You don't suppose I'd think of such a thing without their knowing it? Why, they left us here on purpose!

Miss La Creevy. Oh, I can never look them in the face again.

Tim. Now, come. Let's be a comfortable couple. We shall live in this old house; we'll sit and talk, or sit and sit, quite calm and perfectly contented. Oh, let's be a comfortable couple, let's, my dear.

Miss La Creevy. Oh, Mr. Linkinwater, since you put it in that—most affecting fashion—yes. (*They kiss. Then they look up to see, behind them.* Frank, Kate, Madeline, Nicholas, Mr. Charles, Mr. Ned *and* Mrs. Nickleby.)

Mrs. Nickleby. Oh, Miss La Creevy! (Tim *stands up*.)

Tim. There is not, I swear, another woman like her in the whole of London, I just *know* there ain't.

Mrs. Nickleby. And—Mr. Linkinwater! (*A knock at the outside door.* Mr. Ned *slips out, as:*)

Mr. Charles. Mrs. Nickleby, I wonder, might I be granted the incalculable pleasure of escorting you to dinner?

Mrs. Nickleby. (*Vaguely.*) Yes, of course . . .

Mr. Charles. And, everyone, and everyone . . . (*And* Mr. Charles *and* Mrs. Nickleby, Kate *and* Frank, Tim *and* Miss La Creevy, *go into dinner, followed by* Nicholas *and* Madeline, *the last. As they are going, re-enter* Mr. Ned, *followed by* Newman Noggs.)

Mr. Ned. Uh, Mr. Nickleby. Forgive me. (Mr. Ned *takes* Madeline's *arm.*)

Nicholas. Yes, of course, I—

Noggs. Nick. (Nicholas *to* Noggs, *as* Mr. Ned *takes* Madeline *out.* Noggs *is "genteelly dressed in black".*)

NICHOLAS. *Oh, Newman. Newman.*

NOGGS. Yes, it's your own Newman. Nick, my dear boy, I give you—everything. All health, all happiness, and every blessing. I can't bear it, it's too much—it makes a child of me!

NICHOLAS. Where have you been? How often have I asked for you, and been told that I should hear before long!

NOGGS. I know, I know. They wanted all the happiness to come together. I've been helping 'em. I—I—look at me, Nick, look at me!

NICHOLAS. (*"In a tone of gentle reproach".*) You'd never let *me* buy you such a suit. I offered to.

NOGGS. I didn't mind, then. Couldn't have the heart to put on clothes like these. They'd have reminded me of old times, made me miserable. But now—I am another man, Nick—Oh, my dear boy, I can't speak, please don't do anything—you don't know what I feel today; you can't, and never will.

NICHOLAS. I can. I think I do. But, come, let's go to dinner. (*And as* NICHOLAS *takes* NOGGS' *arm,* MR. NED, MR. CHARLES *and* KATE *re-appear.*)

MR. NED. And never was there such a dinner since the world began.

MR. CHARLES. And at the end of all the toasts and speeches, Nicholas took Kate apart—

NICHOLAS. And whispered to her that, in all his happiness, there was still one dark cloud, and that his joy could never be complete until it was dispelled. (*The scene breaking.*)

KATE. And so the two of them set forth, the next afternoon, to book Nicholas a place on the coach for Greta Bridge in Yorkshire.

NARRATORS. And on their way back to the Strand, as luck would have it, they passed by a little theatre,

On which was displayed a boldly-printed bill,

Announcing that tonight would be the positively last appearance of the celebrated company of Mr. Vincent Crummles, and his wife and family.

SCENE 10

The stage door of a theatre. Enter CRUMMLES, *dressed as a Bandit, to* NICHOLAS *and* KATE.

CRUMMLES. My dear young man! My dear young man!

NICHOLAS. Oh, Mr. Crummles. This is—a most happy chance. May I introduce my sister?

CRUMMLES. (*Pumping* KATE'S *hand.*) It's a pleasure. It's a double pleasure, meeting you, Miss Johnson. (KATE *a look to* NICHOLAS, *who shrugs.*) I'm delighted, sir, I'm quite delighted, with this chance to say goodbye.

NICHOLAS. Goodbye? Why, are you going? Where?

CRUMMLES. Oh, haven't you seen it, in the papers?

NICHOLAS. No.

CRUMMLES. Well, that's a wonder. It was there, in the varieties. Ah, look (*Producing a cutting.*) I have it here.

NICHOLAS. (*Reads.*) "The talented Vincent Crummles, long favourably known to fame as a country manager and actor of no ordinary pretensions, is about to cross the Atlantic"—!—"on a histrionic expedition. Crummles is to be accompanied, we hear, by his wife and gifted family. Crummles is quite certain to succeed." (*Handing the cutting back.*) America!

CRUMMLES. That's right, sir.

NICHOLAS. With—with all the company?

CRUMMLES. Well—no. In fact, sir, I must own our numbers have been much depleted since we saw you last. Finances, sir, the main cause—always, sir, finance. But there have been departures, too: old Fluggers joined the church, by reasons of his years of practising; and Tom Folair defected to a company that mounts spectaculars hard-by the bridge at Waterloo: attracted by the glitter, sir, and promises of quick and easy fame. Well, he'll find out, of course . . . and even, this may well upset you rather more, Miss Snevellicci left us—

NICHOLAS. Oh?

KATE. Miss Snevellicci.

CRUMMLES. Yes, to marry the good-looking young wax chandler who supplied the candles to the Portsmouth theatre . . . but apparently, deliriously happy.

KATE. Ah.

CRUMMLES. So, we thought . . . We have a fair start—

The Americans are much devoted to grand gesture and the melodrama, and I've heard, on quite the best authority, that they'll pay anything . . . and then, who knows, we might buy that little plot of land, support ourselves in our old age . . .

NICHOLAS. I think, as always, you have acted wisely, sir.

CRUMMLES. But, see—it is herself approaching! (MRS. CRUMMLES *sailing over, with the* MASTER CRUMMLESES *and the* INFANT PHENOMENON, *all in costume.*)

MRS. CRUMMLES. Mr. Johnson! What an unexpected joy! And—Mrs. Johnson?

KATE. Miss.

MRS. CRUMMLES. Sir, here are two you know. And another. (NICHOLAS *is kissed by the* PHENOMENON. *He shakes hands with the* MASTER CRUMMLESES.)

NICHOLAS. I'm very pleased to see you once again. I'm very pleased—to see—see everyone.

MRS. CRUMMLES. So are you coming—to tonight's performance? It is positively, quite unalterably, the last.

NICHOLAS. I know. But sadly, I regret—

MRS. CRUMMLES. Regret? That's all that I remember of you, Mr. Johnson. All the time, regretting.

NICHOLAS. I have, unfortunately, to be up at dawn, for a journey of my own. And in fact—have such preparations to complete . . .

MRS. CRUMMLES. And if not regretting, then farewelling, Mr. Johnson. (*Pause. Something in* NICHOLAS'S *tone has deflated the bombast.*)

NICHOLAS. Yes, I am afraid . . . (*A smile.*) Yes, yes. (*He shakes* CRUMMLES'S *hand.*)

CRUMMLES. We are a happy little company, Johnson. You and I never had a word. I shall be very glad tomorrow morning to remember that I saw you once again, but now I almost wish you hadn't come. (*Slight pause.*)

KATE. (*Out front.*): And Mr. Johnson submitted to another hug with even better grace than before, if that were possible; and waving his hat as cheerfully as he could, took farewell of the Vincent Crummleses. (*The* CRUMMLESES *go out.*)

SCENE 11

The journey to Yorkshire; Dotheboys Hall. The NAR-RATORS, as the stage grows darker and darker:

NARRATORS. And the next morning, Nicholas began his journey. It was now cold, winter weather,

And sometimes, he would recognise some place which he had passed on his journey up to Yorkshire, or on the long walk back,

And as night fell, it began to snow, and everything became as he remembered it, and it was easy to believe that everything which had since happened had been but a dream, and that he and Smike were plodding wearily along the road to London, the world before them. (*Very early morning gloom. We can hardly see. A scrape, a scuffle—someone running, others running after. Some of the boys are chasing* YOUNG WACKFORD. *It is a slow, stumbling, dark kind of chase.*)

JACKSON. Hey, Wackford, Wackford—

COATES. Where's your pa then, Wackford?

BOLDER. Where's he be? (*Slight pause.*)

WACKFORD. Dunno. (*A violent scuffle as the* BOYS *follow* WACKFORD'S *voice. Three or four boys find* WACKFORD *and pinion him against a wall.*)

JACKSON. Dunno? Come on, now, Wackford. Summat's happened. We know that.

SNAWLEY SNR. We heard your mam cry, through the parlour window.

JACKSON. Heard your sister, screaming in the night.

JENNINGS. Tell us what happened, Wackford.

BOLDER. Or we'll. . . .

JACKSON. There's no telling what we'll do.

WACKFORD. My ma—

JACKSON. Yuh? What?

WACKFORD. My ma said—

SNAWLEY SNR. Yuh?

WACKFORD. Pa's gonna be transported to Australia. And some old lady with him. And one man he worked for's going to jail. And another one's gone and hanged hisself. What else d'you want to know? (*Slight pause.*)

JACKSON. Right, then. (*The heavy noise of footfall. The* BOYS *quickly push* WACKFORD *away. All the* BOYS *now on stage. Enter* MRS. SQUEERS, FANNY, PHIB *and a small* BOY *who has become the* NEW SMIKE, *carrying the brimstone-and-treacle bowl.* MRS. SQUEERS *carries the spoon.*)

MRS. SQUEERS. What's going on? Where's Wackford? (WACKFORD *hurries to his Mother, looking nervously at the* BOYS.) It's brimstone-and-treacle morning! Every boy on line. Quick! Quick! What are you thinking of? First boy! (*The* BOYS *get into line.*)

TOMKINS. First boy. Tomkins. Twelve. A cripple.

COBBEY. Second boy. Cobbey. Thirteen. Another cripple.

PETERS. Third boy. Peters. Seven. Blind.

GRAYMARSH. Fourth boy—(*And he is interrupted by* JACKSON, *who pushes himself forward, through the line, and past* JENNINGS.)

JACKSON. Jackson.

MRS. SQUEERS. What's this?

JACKSON. (*Grabbing the spoon.*) Johnny Jackson. (BOLDER, *pushing his way through the line.*)

MRS. SQUEERS. Boy!

BOLDER. Fifth boy. Bolder. (*He grabs the bowl from the* NEW SMIKE.)

MRS. SQUEERS. Right, then, Bolder—(*She lifts the cane. It is grabbed by* COATES.)

COATES. Sixth. Coates. Eat.

MRS. SQUEERS. Have you gone mad?

JACKSON. Said—eat. (JACKSON, COATES *and* BOLDER *push* MRS. SQUEERS *to her knees, helped by the others.* JACKSON *forces the spoon into* MRS. SQUEERS' *mouth.*)

JACKSON. Eat.

MRS. SQUEERS. You—little—(*But she is forced to eat the brimstone.*)

BOLDER. There. What now?

JACKSON. It's the end of term. It's break-up. So let's break up. Break it all up. Break it all up—now. (*And a few* BOYS *start to chant. And the chant grows louder. And, as it grows, the bigger* BOYS, *followed by the smaller* BOYS, *start to rush about, smashing everything they can see, pulling at* MRS. SQUEERS *and* FANNY, *and dipping* WACKFORD'S *head in the brimstone bowl.*)

BOYS. Break—up. Break—up. Break—up. Break—up. (*And in the general melee,* MRS. SQUEERS *manages to escape, pulling* WACKFORD *after her, but* FANNY *and* PHIB *are pinioned, pinched and prodded by groups of* BOYS, *while the others continue to smash up Dotheboys Hall. The chant louder and faster.*)

BOYS. BREAK—UP BREAK—UP BREAK—UP BREAK—UP BREAK—UP (*And as the chant and the smashing-up build on, until they can grow no faster and louder, and* JOHN BROWDIE, TILDA *and* NICHOLAS *burst in.*)

JOHN. Stop! Stop! Hey, all of 'ee—ye lads—stop! STOP! (*And everything stops.*) What's happening? What's going on here, eh? (*Pause. A little voice.*)

SNAWLEY SNR. Please sir. Squeers is in prison, sir, and going to be transported, sir, and—

COBBEY. And we're breaking out.

BOYS. Break-up—break-up.

JOHN. Well, I'll not stop ye. But—don't hurt the women, eh? Where's Mrs.?

GRAYMARSH. Run away, sir.

JOHN. Little fat one?

TOMKINS. Gone with her.

JOHN. And Fanny? (FANNY *and* PHIB *are allowed to come to* JOHN.) Right, then. So—that's it. (*Pause.*)

BELLING. Can we—go now, sir?

NICHOLAS. (*Suddenly.*) Yes. Yes, go. Go, run away. As far as possible. Don't hurt them, don't hurt anyone, but still—yes, break it all up, then go. Go! Go! (*And cheering, the* BOYS *run out, some confidently, some tearfully, some fast, some slowly, reluctantly, taking everything with them.*)

FANNY. Well, Mr. Browdie. And your friend as well. Excited all our boys to run away. But we will pay you out for it, even if our pa's unfortunate, and trod down by his enemies, we'll pay you out, I promise, you, and him, and Tilda!

JOHN. No, tha won't. I tell thee, Fanny, that I'm glad the old man's been caught out at last, but you'll have enough to suffer from without me crowing. More than that, tha'll need a friend or two to help thee get away, and here we are, and ready to lend thee a hand. So, are tha coming? (FANNY *turns away, arms folded.*)

TILDA. Come on, Fanny, please. (FANNY *turns back. She's crying.* TILDA *takes her arm, and she,* FANNY *and* PHIB *go out.* JOHN *and* NICHOLAS *left there for a moment.*)

JOHN. Well, then. Bloodshed. Riot. Eh? (*Pause.*)

NICHOLAS. Thank God—at least—it's over. (*And as they go,* NARRATORS:)

NARRATORS. And for some days afterwards, the neighbouring countryside was over-run with boys.

And some were found crying under hedges, frightened by the solitude; (*We see a* BOY *wandering on from some hiding place. He holds the brimstone bowl and spoon.*)

One was discovered sleeping in a yard nearby the building; (*We realise the* BOY *is the* NEW SMIKE.)

And another wandered twenty miles, lost courage, and lay down in the snow, and slept. (*And the* BOY *sits, at the very front of the stage.*)

And in the course of time the Hall and its last breaking up began to be forgotten by the neighbors,

Or only spoken of as among things that had been. (*And the stage is empty now, except for the* NEW SMIKE, *sitting alone at the front of the stage.*)

SCENE 12

Devon at Christmas. The NEW SMIKE, *in the loneliness and silence, begins to sing what he can remember of a Christmas carol.*

THE NEW SMIKE. God—rest ye, merry gentlemen— Let—uh—uh—you, dis-play (*Pause.*) For uh-uh-uh, our uh-uh-uh, Was born on, Christmas Day—(*Pause.*) To la-la-la from Satan's power When—uh, uh gone astray— (*Pause.*) Oh, oh, uh, uh of comfort and joy—(*Slight pause.*) Comfort and joy . . . (*Pause.*) Oh, oh, tidings of comfort and joy. (*And the* NEW SMIKE *is still. And then, very faintly, we can hear the tune of the carol, being hummed. And more voices join, and we are in Devon, at Christmas. And the Families enter, to form a pleasant, almost photographic tableau:* NICHOLAS, KATE, MRS. NICKLEBY, MADELINE, MR. CHARLES, MR. NED, FRANK, TIM, MISS LA CREEVY *and* NEWMAN NOGGS. *And during their final narration, the carol grows behind them.*)

MADELINE. And when her term of mourning had expired, Madeline gave her hand and fortune to Nicholas.

KATE. And on the same day and at the same time, Kate became Mrs. Frank Cheeryble.

MR. CHARLES. And it had been expected that Tim Linkinwater and Miss La Creevy would have made a third couple on the occasion,

MISS LA CREEVY. But they declined,

TIM. And two or three weeks afterward went out together one morning before breakfast,

MR. NED. And,

KATE. Coming back with merry faces,

MR. CHARLES. Were found to have been quietly married that day.

NICHOLAS. And the money which Nicholas acquired in right of his wife he invested in the firm of the Cheeryble Brothers, in which Frank had become a partner.

FRANK. And before many years elapsed, the business began to be carried on in the names of "Cheeryble and Nickleby".

MRS. NICKLEBY. So that Mrs. Nickleby's prophetic anticipations were to be realised at last.

TIM. The twin brothers retired.

FRANK. Who needs to be told that they were happy?

KATE. They were surrounded by happiness of their own creation, and lived but to increase it.

NICHOLAS. The first act of Nicholas, when he became a rich and prosperous merchant, was to buy his father's old farm;

MADELINE. And soon, he and his wife were blessed with a group of lovely children.

FRANK. And within a stone's throw was another such retreat, enlivened by children's voices, too,

KATE. And here lived Kate, with many new cares and occupations,

NICHOLAS. But still, the same true loving creature and the same gentle sister, as in her girlish days.

MRS. NICKLEBY. And Mrs. Nickleby lived sometimes with her daughter and sometimes with her son,

MADELINE. And spent much time relating her experience,

MRS. NICKLEBY. Especially on the matter of the management and bringing up of children,

KATE. With much importance and solemnity.

MR. CHARLES. And there was one grey-haired,

MR. NED. Quiet,

MR. CHARLES. Harmless gentleman,

NOGGS. Who lived in a little cottage hard by Nicholas' house, and in his absence, attended to the supervision of affairs.

MADELINE. His chief delight and pleasure was the children,

NOGGS. With whom he became a child himself, and master of the revels. The little people could do nothing without dear, old Newman Noggs.

KATE. And, as time went on, the house in which young Nicholas and Kate had spent their childhood was enlarged and altered, to accommodate the growing family.

NICHOLAS. But no old rooms were ever pulled down,

KATE. No old tree was rooted up,

NICHOLAS. Nothing with which there was the least association of old, bygone times and childhood days was ever cut down,

KATE. Or removed,

NICHOLAS. Or even—changed. (*And all the Company are singing now, and* JOHN *and* TILDA *run in to join the Families, who are shaking each others' hands, and talking and moving from person to person, and embracing: the happiest of Christmases.*)

COMPANY. Now to the Lord Sing Praises
All you within this place,
Like we true loving brethren,
Each other to embrace. (*And* NICHOLAS *a little apart, looks downstage, as if out of a window, and sees the* BOY, *sitting outside in the snow.*)

For the merry time of Christmas
Is drawing on apace—(*And, unnoticed,* NICHOLAS *slips away, and trudges over to the still* BOY.)

And it's tidings of comfort and joy,
Comfort and joy,
And it's tidings of comfort and joy. (NICHOLAS *has reached the* BOY. *He touches him. The* BOY *does not move.* KATE *and* MADELINE *notice that* NICHOLAS *has gone.*)

God bless the ruler of this house
And send him long to reign. (NICHOLAS *turns back to the house. He sees his wife and his sister appear. They look at him. Upstage of them, the party is going on.*)

And many a merry Christmas.
May live to see again . . . (NICHOLAS *takes a step back towards the house. But he can't leave the* BOY. *A despairing look at* KATE *and* MADELINE.)

Among our friends and kindred
Let's sing with mickle main . . . (*And, as the carol builds up to its climax, with descants and the organ coming in,* NICHOLAS *turns back to the* BOY *and picks him up in his arms, looking at his wife and sister.*)

Oh, it's tidings of comfort and joy,
Comfort and Joy—(*And then he turns to us, and stands there, holding the boy in his arms.*)

Oh, it's tidings of comfort and joy,
Comfort and joy,
Comfort and joy. (*Darkness.*)

THE END

CASTING NOTES

One of the central concepts of *Nicholas Nickleby* was that the acting company were in collective possession of an entire story, which they were then to tell to an audience. True, certain actors would tell more of the story than some others; but everybody knew it, how it started and how it ended, and the company as a whole was, in one sense, the single character of the play. Everybody took part in the narration (it is important, for example, that in the two narration sequences that open the plays, everybody should have at least one line) and actors not playing a named part would, when not changing or preparing for an entrance, sit or stand round, on the set, watching their story unfold.

For this reason, there are no "extras" in *Nicholas Nickleby*. All the available performers should take part in the collective, narrative sequences; and it is no matter if, for example, Fanny Squeers turns up as a Milliner at the Mantalinis, or Ralph Nickleby as a blind beggar in the London street scenes of Part Two. Indeed, in the Dotheboys Hall sections, it is vital that the Boys are played by adult performers, who reappear in other guises in the rest of the play (in the original production, Mr. Snawley sent his wretched children off to Dotheboys Hall in Act One Scene Six, and reappeared playing the Boy Tomkins in Scene Ten). Because of the sexual breakdown of the original company, actors put on skirts and bonnets to supplement the Milliners in Part One and the guests at Mrs. Kenwigs' confinement in Part Two; and actresses appeared as some of the Boys at Mr. Squeers' loathsome Academy. And, in some scenes where large numbers of specific types of people were felt to be useful, everybody available was roped in: every free actor played a member of Mr. Pugstyles' deputation in Part One, and every actor not in the Crummles Theatre Company attend Ralph's dinner party at the end of Act Two; in Part Two, almost the entire company entered the Saracen's Head coffee room in Act Two Scene One; and the majority were involved as walls, doors, railings, bodies and revellers in the long sequence leading up to Ralph's suicide.

The specific casting, too, will depend on what talents

are available. To give an idea of the breadth of our company, there is the example of Mr. Folair, the pantomimist, who in the original run of the play was doubled with Young Wackford Squeers; in the New York revival, he was played by the actor whose other main part was the down-and-out Brooker. The opera singers were chosen because they could sing (one of them also played Ralph Nickleby); the Infant Phenomenon started off doubling with Tilda Price, and ended up being played by the actress who also performed Morleena Kenwigs, Snawley Minor and Miss La Creevy's maid Hannah. There is no need for the Fanny Squeers actress also to play Miss Snevellicci and Peg Sliderskew (though it is a wonderful triple for an actress), not even for every performer to have at least two speaking parts (although it is preferable, and we managed it with everyone except the actor playing Nicholas himself). The cast lists given here are thus merely two of many possible combinations.

ALL THE WORLD'S A STAGE

(0451)

☐ **FOUR PLAYS BY TENNESSEE WILLIAMS: SUMMER AND SMOKE, ORPHEUS DESCENDING, SUDDENLY LAST SUMMER and PERIOD OF ADJUSTMENT.** Love, hate, comedy, tragedy, joy, sorrow, passion, violence—all come alive in these four magnificent plays. (525124—$5.95)

☐ **THREE BY TENNESSEE WILLIAMS: SWEET BIRD OF YOUTH, THE ROSE TATTOO and THE NIGHT OF THE IGUANA,** three of the Pulitzer prize-winning author's most brilliant plays. (521498—$5.95)

☐ **CHEKHOV: THE MAJOR PLAYS by Anton Chekhov.** New translation by Ann Dunnigan. Foreword by Robert Brustein. (522702—$3.95)

☐ **IBSEN: FOUR MAJOR PLAYS, Volume I, by Henrik Ibsen.** *The Master Builder, A Doll's House, Hedda Gabler,* and *The Wild Duck.* New translation with Foreword by Rolf Fjelde. (524063—$3.95)

☐ **ISBEN: FOUR MAJOR PLAYS, Volume II, by Henrik Ibsen.** *Ghosts, An Enemy of the People, The Lady from the Sea,* and *John Gabriel Borkman.* New translation by Rolf Fjelde. (525159—$3.50)

Prices slightly higher in Canada.

Buy them at your local bookstore or use this convenient coupon for ordering.

NEW AMERICAN LIBRARY
P.O. Box 999, Bergenfield, New Jersey 07621

Please send me the books I have checked above.
I am enclosing $_____ (please add $2.00 to cover postage and handling). Send check or money order (no cash or C.O.D.'s) or charge by Mastercard or VISA (with a $15.00 minimum). Prices and numbers are subject to change without notice.

Card #_____ Exp. Date _____
Signature_____
Name_____
Address_____
City _____ State _____ Zip Code _____

For faster service when ordering by credit card call **1-800-253-6476**

Allow a minimum of 4-6 weeks for delivery. This offer is subject to change without notice.

There's an epidemic with 27 million victims. And no visible symptoms.

It's an epidemic of people who can't read.

Believe it or not, 27 million Americans are functionally illiterate, about one adult in five.

The solution to this problem is you... when you join the fight against illiteracy. So call the Coalition for Literacy at toll-free **1-800-228-8813** and volunteer.

Volunteer Against Illiteracy. The only degree you need is a degree of caring.